Jalopy

Wes Verde

ISBN (Print): 978-1-7363986-0-9

ISBN (E-reader): 978-1-7363986-1-6

https://wesverde.com/

Cover art by Angela Fernot

Do what you can, where you are, with what you have.

Theodore Roosevelt

We shall not cease from exploration, and the end of all our exploring will be to arrive where we started, and know the place for the first time.

T.S. Elliot

Chapter 1

Etta

A rooster crowed somewhere outside. Not especially loud, but it pierced the darkness with more intensity than it had a right to. A young woman stirred. Pulled from sleep's comforting embrace, her eyes fluttered open only reluctantly. Etta Wozniak clutched her thin blanket and remained in bed for another minute. It did not feel like morning. Besides, she had just seen her sister and that could only have been a dream. Perhaps the rooster was another. Those hopes were dashed when the bastard crowed again. More than once, she had suggested – in jest – to include him in the bi-annual cull. A rooster who crowed at night must be defective, so she reasoned.

It was early, even by farmer standards, but as Etta came around, blinking away the mental cobwebs, she knew there was nothing to be done but to get started on the day. For two years she had risen before the sun without fail. It was not that she particularly wanted to be up at such an ungodly hour. There was simply too much to do.

Shivering and rubbing her eyes, Etta confronted the morning chill first with one foot, then the other. As typical of late April, the afternoons teased at the forthcoming warmth of summer, but the mornings remained firmly in winter's thrall. Sleeping fully clothed was a necessity when the temperature dropped below freezing. Even so, she could not tolerate anything touching her feet during the night. Those first few seconds before she could pull them into a pair of thick, warm socks was perhaps the worst part of her morning ritual. Feeling around the icy darkness, Etta slipped on her work apron and an extra jacket before her teeth could start to chatter.

In the kitchen, she was not entirely surprised to find the wood-burning stove had gone cold. Springtime was a chilly, but manageable season, and so the choice between a warm morning or an uninterrupted night was often a tossup. On this morning, both Etta and her father, Jakob, had decided in favor of sleep.

Things like feeding the fire had not been such a burden when there were more people living in the Wozniaks' home. Many hands made light work, but these days it was only Etta and her Papa.

The rooster crowed again and Etta shook her head, grumbling.

What on Earth does that chicken see?

The kitchen was dark, but it was a familiar space and she knew it well. The only clock in the house ticked loudly somewhere in the blackness. She gave the box of matches a habitual rattle, and frowned at the hollow sound it made. There were probably more fingers on her hands than there were matches within. Unsure how that had escaped her notice, Etta resolved to pick up more on the next trip to town.

Lighting the kerosene lamp, she squinted against the warm, golden light. It was 1928, and the house had been fitted with electric lights some ten years earlier. While far more convenient, they were also more expensive than burning oil. Once, the Wozniaks had been relatively well off and could afford to turn the lights on without a second thought. Those days, sadly, were long past.

Now able to see, her chores could begin.

Breathing into cupped hands did little to fight the numbness in her fingertips. A fleeting relief, it would serve to give her enough time to clean the stove and start on the fire. Had she discovered one or two hot coals hidden among the powdery, gray ashes that would have made things just a little easier. But no. At least Papa had made kindling the night before. By and large, Etta did things for herself but using the hatchet was one chore she would gladly leave to her father. Sharp metal swinging so close to her hands caused her a tremble that had nothing to do with the cold.

As the growing fire started to chase the ice from her bones she pulled a thick, woolen cap over her blonde head. Snug and warm, it had once belonged to her oldest brother Edward, and was knitted by their mother, Lena. Wearing it helped Etta to remember them, and warmed both body and soul.

Movement in the darkness caught her attention. Etta looked over to find a pair of large, green eyes staring back at her. A black and orange tortoiseshell cat approached the firelight, stopping just beyond arms' length but close enough to be warmed. The cat regarded Etta with apparent indifference, yet cried loudly as she dropped onto her haunches. Making no move, Etta, responded with a sigh.

"Morning, Howler," she said flippantly.

Little family that she had left, and this damn cat was one of them. She had been named by Etta's younger, sister, Irene, and out of respect to her, Etta could not bring herself to cast the animal out. As if such a thing were possible. Every morning, Etta let Howler outside, but could seldom recall letting her back in at the end of the day. Yet, without fail, she would simply reappear.

"I'll let you out when I'm damn well ready," Etta muttered.

Howler cried in response.

"Don't push me, cat."

Warm at last, a growing personal urgency could no longer be ignored. She resolved herself to going outside. If the first few seconds of exposing her feet to the frigid air was the worst part of her morning, leaving the relative warmth of the house to use the necessary was a close second. After years of this routine, the morning hours hardly bothered her anymore. But walking to the outhouse, no matter the temperature or season never got any easier. At least it was not snowing.

She opened the door and nearly tripped over Howler as the cat ran between her feet to escape. The glow of the lantern revealed a fog that had settled on the farm overnight. It was above freezing, but not by much and the air was heavy with moisture. Etta trudged on. With luck, the sun would burn off the mist when it eventually put in an appearance.

On the other hand, none of her family had been particularly blessed with luck.

In the first piece of good news, the stove was hot by the time she returned inside. Coffee was one of the few luxuries that even Papa would not do without. In the past month, Etta had skipped more than a handful of meals, but not one cup of coffee. The noise from grinding the beans was loud in the dark, but Papa never complained.

Fishing a chipped mug out of the cabinet, she was careful not to make too much noise. The door had worked itself loose sometime over the past year, and the motion of opening it produced all manner of bumps and squeaks as it shifted in place. It was just one of many things around the farm that suffered from neglect.

The table wobbled and moved as she leaned on it. With quick hands she managed to save the steaming contents of the mug before they sloshed out. One of the rare times she would be sitting today, Etta spared a few minutes to savor the piping hot cup. A splash of milk would have been nice, but none had been delivered this morning. It came as little surprise. At least the drink was hot, and banished some of the worse mental cobwebs.

A creak and thump called her attention to the ceiling. A moment later, Papa descended the stairs.

"*Dzien dobry*," he said through a yawn while rubbing his eyes. Jakob Wozniak tended to revert to Polish when half-awake or in times of stress. Both Etta's parents had come from a village outside of Warsaw before she was born. While her mother, Lena, was fluent in English prior to immigrating, Jakob was a slower learner. For years, the family spoke a mixture of English and Polish in the house. When Etta was still a child, she remembered it being a huge source of pride when Papa finally went a full week without leaning on his native tongue.

"And good morning to you," Etta returned in English. She placed a gentle emphasis on "good" and "morning", so as not to embarrass him.

She waited until Papa had poured his own cup of coffee before she said, "The water pump is leaking." It was often the case and worse in the spring. For every one part of water that made it to the bucket, two parts typically splashed the ground at her feet. Even so, it was worse than in years past. Her wet foot could attest to that.

Jakob grunted in response. While Etta had come to embrace the early morning hours, like her mother once had, Papa and the rest of the family only accepted them grudgingly. As such, she knew that she would get little from him for the next few minutes. Still, she pressed on. "Also, there was no milk delivery today."

"I know," he replied, to her surprise. "The tax bill is due this month, and I had to stop the milk delivery again." Sneaking a quick sip from his coffee, he moved the coat that had been haphazardly draped over his chair. He might have simply chosen a different seat, but old habits are hard to break. Besides, the others were taken, despite being empty.

Jakob continued, "Also, try to leave the lights off if you don't need them." Only after he said it did he notice that the electric lights were, in fact, already off. Regarding the kerosene lamp hanging from the ceiling, he nodded with approval.

Etta frowned. "How long must we go without milk this time? Or bread for that matter?" Some heat edged into her voice.

Papa peered over the top of his cup. His half-lidded eyes grew more alert at her tone and intent expression. He smiled weakly and raised a placating hand.

"We will have bread, of course. We can get milk again in a few weeks." He sighed. "You know, it never used to be like this. Then, one day, a man comes to the door and asks for money. 'What for?' I say. 'For your civic duties,' he says." Papa shook his head. "The Russians made levies as well, in the old country."

Etta made no response, having heard this all before. Jakob fell quiet.

"Are you going to lose the house, Papa?"

Etta bit her lip. That had been a mistake.

"No," he said quickly and with assurance. He looked around the room bathed in the golden light from the lamp. "This is a good house. I will make sure that we keep it."

This is an empty house, thought Etta. *Full of ghosts and memories.* She said nothing, but breathed a quiet sigh of relief. Her slip had gone unnoticed.

They finished their coffee in silence, as they usually did. Mama had always been the talkative one. Etta and her father had something of a complicated relationship. Instead of pulling them together, their mutual losses only caused the both of them to withdraw.

Every so often, one or the other would attempt a foray into conversation, but by and large, they hardly spoke. That is, about anything besides the farm and what work needed to be done. Even so, he was her father, and she could not shake the feeling of guilt that came with the knowledge that she would soon leave him.

What will he do when I'm gone?

The rest of the morning chores went as they usually did. By the time she made her way to the chickens, they were positively ravenous, and descended on the feed in their usual frenzy. Etta spared them little attention. Instead, she looked to the horizon. The sun had made some progress. Nearly peeking over the distant hills, it was light enough to extinguish the lantern. The clouds above were the color of hot coals and tinged with bright pink. Despite the long day ahead of her, she stopped to look.

The Wozniak's home was perched at the top of a hill, looking across a shallow valley. At twenty years old, Etta had seen this view in every season and manner of weather since she was old enough to remember. It never ceased to be beautiful.

The valley below was home to a few other farms. Nothing was growing in the lower fields just yet, but the spring planting was underway. A distant tractor tilled lines in the soil, chewing up the winter packed earth in anticipation of a new season. Following close behind, a black and white dog ran back and forth, chasing rabbits and mice as they darted from the ground. A similar scene was, no doubt, occurring throughout town at this very moment. Except around the lake of course.

Past the fields, the railway snaked along the opposite side of the valley. This had been the source of the town's growth, bringing out-of-towners to nearby Bott's Lake, a popular vacation spot. The trains would come all the way from New York City, some thirty miles away. Bringing both money and visitors, it was regarded as a blessing to some, a curse for others, and, in Etta's case, a means of escape.

Giving the changing colors one last look she carried on. As she had suspected, the coop yielded fewer eggs than would have been ideal. So few birds could only do so much. When the flock and her family were both larger, the farm was quite prosperous. Besides chickens, they had grown enough potatoes and cabbage to make a tidy profit. With no one left to do the work, those fields had long since gone to weed. Now, the little bit of money earned from selling meat and eggs was barely enough to cover the cost of chicken feed.

Etta frowned at the disappointing collection. Still, it was better than nothing. Picking out an even dozen, she set them aside to hard boil. For most of the next hour, she mucked the pen and loaded the remaining eggs into crates so she could bring them into town. By then, the sun was fully above the horizon, and cast long shadows amidst the golden yellow light.

The morning was late, and Etta grew anxious. Walking to town would take some time and she would have to hurry if there was any hope of selling even this modest take.

A sudden flash of optimism cut through her earlier disappointment. There was an alternative to walking, after all. It was a long shot, but perhaps Papa was feeling generous and this would be her lucky day.

Besides, it had been nearly four years ago.

With an egg crate in each hand, Etta found Jakob among the pieces of the disassembled well pump. He glanced up at her approach, casually at first, but did a double take when he noticed the egg crates.

"Only two? Are the birds eating enough?"

"More like a crate and a half," Etta replied. "And I think it's the cool nights. They like it warmer."

"We can only do so much for that. I will cut more firewood when I am finished here."

Etta nodded, but lingered as she considered her words carefully. Her optimism faltered, and she suspected that she already knew what the answer would be. Still, she had to try.

"May I take the truck?"

Papa stopped working. His mouth made a thin line as he turned to face her. This conversation was always delicate for both of them.

"I would prefer that you did not," he said and quickly returned to the pump.

"It's only to town," Etta insisted.

"Then, please take the wagon," Jakob replied, looking over his shoulder. "As you said, it is not even two full crates."

She was about to say more, but it was clear the matter was closed. Etta suppressed a sigh. While Papa had long maintained that it was out of concern for her safety, she was certain that it was a form of punishment. Though, she could not be sure, as they had not spoken of the event since it happened.

It was an accident, and it was four years ago, she thought bitterly. *You can't hold it against me forever.*

As she hoped, the clammy, pre-dawn chill was soon chased away. Turning her face into the new sun, she was able to remove her hat at last. About halfway to town, she removed her extra coat as well. All the while, her thoughts wandered. Driving would have been best, but at least it was a good day for a walk. Any time she could spend in fresh air, away from the ever-present miasma of chicken musk was to be savored.

Her mood steadily improved with each step, and her disappointment over the truck mostly faded. Now, she had an excuse to disappear from home for a few hours. Etta valued her independence. Better still, it would give her a chance to make a particular visit that had evaded her for most of the winter.

First things first. She had to offload the eggs. At the Royal Scarlet grocery store, Dominic gave her a reasonable price for the lot, and without any haggling. It helped that she was the first seller to arrive, but it had been a near thing. A truck pulled up just as Etta was leaving.

In the back were at least twenty crates. From the cab, David and Bradley Heckel waved as she walked by. Despite being direct competitors, the farmers of the town, for the most part, saw themselves as a community. At least, compared to the lakeside Townies. And even those shiftless, pampered, blue noses were better than the visiting out-of-towners.

"Beat us again, Etta?" called the father, David. "And on foot, no less."

"You'll have to get up a little earlier, I suppose," she replied with a grin.

David chuckled as he stepped down from the cab. Here was a man who had no doubts about where his next meal was coming from. Etta hoped that it was not obvious just how desperately she had needed to arrive before he did. Coming around from the far side, Bradley gave a shy wave. Too late, she turned away, pretending not to have seen. With a groan, she heard footsteps approaching and braced herself.

"Morning Etta. Nice day, isn't it?"

"It's fine," she replied without looking at him.

He matched her stride for several more paces without saying anything. Hopefully, she would not have to resort to shooing him away.

"Are you busy this week?"

"I usually am," she replied.

"Oh... Well – um – I was thinking…"

Interrupting the half-formed thought, David called his son back over to the truck.

"Better get going then," Etta urged.

"Yeah… see you around."

"Goodbye, Bradley."

Shoulders sagging, he slowed and eventually turned back to his father. Etta let out a sigh and carried on before he could say anything more.

You kiss a guy a few times, and he carries a torch for two years.

Their brief fling after Etta's mother had passed away was something she would prefer not to think about. At the time, he had caught her interest with his straw colored hair and tall build, but it was fleeting. Her mind had been all out of sorts, and she was thankful that she came to her senses before any mistakes with long-term consequences had occurred.

As she walked, she grabbed the black denim bag that rarely left her shoulder and gave her money purse a reassuring squeeze. It was heavier than when she had set out, but not by much. Just over three-dozen eggs earned them a dollar and a half. An important date was fast approaching and she would need to buy something for it. Maybe she could sneak a dime out of her earnings for the visit, but her finances weighed on her mind more than usual today. It was not their first time with an overdue tax bill. And it was certainly not the first time Papa had to put a hold on milk delivery. Even so, such decisions were never made lightly.

Etta took the shorter route back home through the summer cottages. Normally, she would avoid this area since it was popular with out-of-towners. However, the visiting season had not yet started, and few enough of them were around. Unfamiliar faces made her uncomfortable. It was even worse when she was in her work clothes and pulling the chicken cart. The combination often earned her a few disgusted looks and upturned noses.

I'm only pulling them, she would think. *You're eating them.*

Instead of snooty visitors today, the cottage neighborhood was only occupied by working men. Nearly all of them she recognized by face, if not by name. Approaching a blue cottage, two boys about her age were busy sawing and hammering. The taller of the pair looked up, squinting into the early sun. Brushing sawdust from the front of his overalls, he favored her with a warm smile.

“Mornin' Etta,” he called. “How's my favorite cousin?”

“Hi, Robert. Just making the rounds,” she replied.

Immediately, her chest felt lighter. A dour mood could not long withstand Robert McCormick’s contagious smile. Whatever concerns she had carried from the farm were lifted for the moment. Standing in Robert’s shadow was his younger brother, Daniel who acknowledged Etta with a friendly but shy nod.

Favorite or not, Etta was in fact, their only cousin. Their mother, Alicja had been Lena’s sister and aside from Papa, the three of them were the only relations left. While there was no dispute that Etta had lost more family than they did, they had the unique misfortune of being orphans. Though, if that fact bothered Robert, his ever-present grin never let on to it.

By contrast, his brother Daniel was a quiet type. So much so that those who did not know him assumed he was slow in the head. Even Etta could never be sure what he was thinking behind his perpetual, sullen brooding. Of course, one would first have to notice him in order to wonder about his thoughts. Robert had a habit of attracting attention, and his brother tended to disappear into the background.

They were so vastly different in both appearance and temperament that they often speculated they might only be half brothers.

"You're not at the station today?" Etta asked.

Robert shook his head. "Not on weekends. In fact, I switched onto the evening duty all next week so I can work on cottage upkeep during the day."

Etta frowned. As someone accustomed to long workdays that was excessive even to her. "Hope we don't have any fires next week," she said. "You'll be too exhausted to hold the hose."

"Actually, we had a call last night. Barn fire over on the Chester side of town. Took us until dawn to put it out."

"And when were you planning to sleep?"

Robert shrugged, grinning. Behind him, Daniel at last made a foray into the conversation.

"You got any hard-boiled eggs today?" he asked.

Etta nodded. "Just half a dozen. The ladies are still too cold."

"That's fine," replied Robert. "It's only the two of us that eats them. Still a dime each?"

"Family discount. Four bits for the lot."

They made the exchange, and Etta felt better still with the coins added to the purse. The dime she planned to sneak did not seem so much now.

Daniel nodded thanks before wordlessly returning to his work.

As Etta started to move away, Robert called to her.

"Hey. You – ah – seeing Helen later?"

"We'll probably all walk to church tomorrow. Why?"

Robert grinned again. "Just – um – tell her I say, 'Hello.'"

Etta narrowed her eyes, bemused. "I think you say more than 'hello', and probably see more of her than I do."

"You can say that again," he grinned.

Etta blushed at the innuendo, but laughed all the same.

With the eggs sold, and not yet midday, Papa would not miss her for a couple hours. Especially if the well pump gave him trouble. Etta deposited the empty wagon near her mailbox, out of sight from the house, and continued walking. A few minutes later, she passed the Saunders' farm. This was the home of her best friend, and Robert's sweetheart, Helen. She and Etta had been together since before either of them could remember.

It was common for her to stop in for an impromptu visit, but Helen was likely at her job, such as it was. The two girls had vastly different notions about what constituted work. Even with Helen away, Etta would often pay a visit to Mildred, who was reliable as sunrise for motherly comfort. Such was their closeness that Etta would often refer to her as Aunt Mildred.

From the road, Etta spotted her and her husband, Peter on the far end of the family's twelve-acre farm. Their brown dog, Max, sniffed around the freshly turned ground looking for whatever it is dogs look for. Mildred was a stoutly woman, broad in the shoulder, and short in stature. Her naturally thick and curly hair was chestnut colored like her daughter's, but with more streaks of gray every year. It refused to lay flat against her head, despite all attempts to control it, and served to enhance her presence, making her seem taller than she actually was.

The couple had not noticed Etta as they stood shoulder-to-shoulder, a large sheet of paper held between them. Before them was a square of recently broken ground in what was usually the potato field. Peter was maybe the hardest-working man Etta knew; always building things when he was not busy with the crops. The Saunders' house had nearly doubled in size by his hand over the years. While Peter had built it, Mildred made it a home.

Helen, of course, had her own opinion of her parents, but to Etta, they were worth aspiring to. She waved as she passed the property, though neither of them saw. Just as well. They were busy at the moment, and also content. Perhaps Etta would visit later in the day. This morning, she had other plans.

Casting a furtive, but unnecessary glance over her shoulder, Etta stepped onto a footpath where the road ended and the forest began. The entrance of which was almost completely hidden from casual view. Her steps were confident and without hesitation. Etta hitched up her skirts with one hand as the trail quickly inclined to a steep grade and thorny bushes pulled at her clothing.

At last, she approached what appeared to be a wall of boulders. Traversing a nearly hidden path, Etta soon emerged into a clearing. Before her, the valley spread out in a nearly unobstructed view. On one side could be seen several farms including her own. On the other was the railway and the two main roads that connected Bott's Lake to the rest of the world.

Her town featured a number of scenic vantage points, which were popular with the out-of-towners. A few of the better ones, unfortunately, were downright lousy with them. Thankfully, many remained known only to locals. In the case of this particular one, it was a secret that only Etta was aware of. That was well, because, in her opinion, it was the best.

Etta smiled broadly as soon as she saw it. The one feature that made it entirely unique.

Right where I left you, she thought. Not that there was a chance it would suddenly move. Since she had stumbled upon it the previous summer, she feared that others would discover it as well. And then, there was a good chance she would lose it. Having lived here all her life, it amazed her that the town still had secrets to be discovered. Eyes fixed on the wondrous thing, Etta smiled dreamily as she approached.

It was a car.

An older, touring model, it was designed on the premise that it was a carriage without a horse rather than an automobile. It had no windows. The roof was more of a canopy than a proper enclosure. Driving in inclement weather would not be pleasant.

Sitting outdoors, it fell victim to rain, snow, and general exposure. All of which took their toll, especially on the upholstery. The leather of the seats was cracked and faded. Etta had once draped an old blanket across the front in an attempt to preserve it. This helped to an extent, but the winter had been a rough one, and one blanket could do only so much.

Walking in a large circle, Etta ran her hand along the exterior of the old jalopy with affection. While the seats were weathering poorly, the outside was better off. Even so, it suffered from a few errant scratches, rusty dents, and the canvas roof had torn along part of a seam. At a glance, one might be hard pressed to understand why it had been abandoned here on this lonely hilltop. A closer look would reveal that the automobile was resting at an odd angle.

One of the wheels and the connecting linkages were bent and broken, apparently smashed on the rock where it ultimately came to rest. How the former owner had managed to get to this location in the first place was another question altogether. Had Etta not found it, there was a good chance it would have simply rusted away, alone, never to be appreciated again.

Appreciate it, she certainly did. It had quickly become her favorite place, and a jealously guarded secret; not even Helen knew. Etta counted her blessings that no one else had discovered it. Then, it would just become another spot for the local kids to go and drink, or do other things. Etta could not allow that.

This was *her* car.

She opened the door, and sat down behind the steering wheel, pushing the damp blanket aside. The seat had, of course, seen better days, but still did its job. Gripping the steering wheel, she considered where she should go today. Maybe Boston? No. Too far. Besides, she wanted music, and New York City was the only place for that. The steering wheel was locked in place, so instead, she played with the mirrors and the knobs on the dashboard.

The pantomime only lasted for a few minutes. Perhaps it was just a bit childish, but no one was around to see. Her thoughts soon transitioned to more practical matters. She opened a box attached to the underside of the console and withdrew a folded-up piece of paper. A map. With great care, she opened it. It had survived so long, protected where it was, that it would be a shame to ruin it now through carelessness.

Discovered on one of her first visits, the map was large enough to fill the entire front seat of the jalopy, and showed the entire northern half of New Jersey. If the car was her heart's desire, this was its soul. Her eyes immediately found a small dot, indicating the location of Bott's Lake, and her eyes traced a path leading to a much larger dot, marked by the words "New York City."

That's where we're going.

Papa's most recent denial to let her drive the real truck was still fresh in her mind. She sighed. Since she was first introduced to cars and what they could do, Etta had been hooked. The prospect of not being limited by her own two feet teased her with possibilities. On the other hand, it had been her over-enthusiasm for driving that had resulted in tragedy. Etta's good mood briefly faltered.

It was years ago, she thought for the second time today.

Papa would never let her drive as long as she lived here. That was the cold truth. While it was not the only reason she intended to leave, it was a major one. Looking at the map, and far away from the distractions of her daily grind, she once more considered the dot marked "New York City."

As she had come to treasure her independence, it made sense that a car would provide the incentive for her to finally leave home. This was it, she had decided. Her last summer here. When she first came across the jalopy, it was like a sign, and through the awful winter it was never far from her thoughts. Seeing the big city on a map, just inches away, cemented her decision.

Little by little, she put money aside from what she earned selling eggs and doing odd jobs around town. It was intended to get her started wherever she ended up, and buy a one-way train ticket to get there. The jalopy, unfortunately, would have to remain behind. Despite any games she might play when no one else was watching, she never had any real hope that it would run again.

Her little nest egg had taken a long while to accumulate. To Etta it was a huge sum, and represented months of skipped meals, and extra miles walked in order to sell a few more hard-boiled eggs. In the back of her mind, she doubted whether it was enough for anything at all. She tended to dismiss these nagging feelings.

This would be her last summer on the farm, and that was that.

The bigger problem was how to tell Papa. Simply walking away one day without warning was not something Etta was prepared to do. True, they had not been as close lately, especially since Mama died, but he was still her father and the farm was a lot of work.

Every so often, she asked about hiring extra hands. After all, the place had been profitable when her brothers and sisters were alive to work it. Perhaps with help, Papa could return it to some of its former prominence. Etta frowned with the thought. Papa denied such requests without exception. Every time he did, her reluctance to leave him diminished.

Leaning back, she let her thoughts wander. There would be plenty of work waiting for her when she returned home, and there was no sense in rushing back.

It was not long before she spotted a lone vehicle driving among the farms. Cars, on this side of town were unusual, and she frowned, not recognizing it. It was not often that they received visitors, but neither was it unheard of for the occasional out-of-towner to get lost and ask for directions.

Other times, it was someone bringing bad news, like when Mama died. That had been a police car, though, and this was not. Her frown deepened as the strange visitor turned up the drive to her house.

Leaning forward in the jalopy, Etta squinted for a better look. While she could see the house and the car, any details beyond that were too small to make out. A man walked to her front door then returned to the car again. If he had come to speak with Papa, he had not waited nearly long enough, or even knocked for that matter. Watching him leave, Etta found her nerves strangely unsettled. Distracted, she sighed with the realization that her borrowed time had come to an end.

Until next time, she thought, placing an affectionate hand on the door as she stepped to the ground.

The walk back to the house did not take long, and her thoughts were never far from the mysterious visitor. Going all the way down to the bottom of the valley and back uphill again, she was breathing heavily by the time she was back on her road. Remembering to grab the cart, she started up the driveway.

Papa was standing on the front porch, reading a piece of paper when she reached him. With his back toward her, she grew nervous when he did not turn at the sound of her approach. He remained starting intently at what was in his hand. Concerned, she moved next to him.

"Are you having trouble with a word?" Etta asked, but she could immediately tell that it was not the case.

Papa read English better than he spoke it. Confirming this, he shook his head without taking his eyes off the paper. Still curious, but with increasing trepidation, Etta did the same. It took her a full minute to read it twice.

"What's a 'lien'?" she asked.

"I think it's what they call it when the town takes your home," he said, voice heavy with emotion.

Etta's stomach was tied in a sudden knot. True, she fully intended to leave, but losing her family's home to the town was another matter. Papa's shaken tone was just as upsetting.

"I thought you said we weren't going to lose the house," she said.

Papa sighed. "And we are not... according to this, we have until the end of September to pay what is owed."

Etta swallowed, thinking about her hoarded purse. "How much are we short by?"

"A great deal," Papa responded. "More than what two people can make by selling eggs around town."

Etta started to fidget, preparing herself to offer up what meager amount she had socked away. Thankfully, Papa spoke first.

"We have time," he said abruptly. "We will let the flock grow and I will start to sell some of our eggs in Morristown. David Heckel has told me they go for a better price there."

Etta had been there once before and could also remember its place on the map. She frowned at what her father was suggesting.

"That's almost an hour's drive," Etta replied.

"It is," he agreed. "But it will mean more money. Just a few times each week."

"The new hens won't start laying until the end of summer," Etta replied, shaking her head. "Maybe even later."

"We can sell the pullets," he replied. "A young hen will get a good price."

Etta remained skeptical. Selling off new hens before they could start producing was risky, and spoke of desperation. They could easily find themselves without any egg-laying birds at all. Papa noticed her disquiet, and tried to appear confident.

"It is all we can do," he said evenly. "Now, I must finish with the water pump."

As Papa walked away, Etta's guilt intensified. After all, she had every intention of leaving him to work a farm by himself. Only now she knew that it was a failing one.

Chapter 2
Art

As the locomotive pulled away from the station platform, its steam whistle cut through the still air. Dressed in a fine, new suit, a young man watched it depart. Oblivious to much else, he stood utterly enamored with the mechanical linkages and pistons that made up the side of the engine.

Such was his infatuation, that it took several seconds before one of his hands shot to the top of his head and felt only an unruly mop of dark hair. With a start, he began frantically looking around his feet, hoping that he had simply dropped it after he disembarked from the train. It took a moment for him to admit that he had, in fact, left his hat on the seat. As he came up empty-handed, and watched, helplessly as the train disappeared around the first bend in the track, he considered what he would say to his father.

Arturo Adams sighed loudly as he accepted the inevitable verbal lashing that would come. He rebuked himself. Had he not been so distracted, he might have noticed that his hair was uncovered, and saved himself some trouble. The hat had been part of the new suit he was wearing and a graduation gift. However, Art – as he preferred to be called – knew the "gift" of the suit came with certain strings attached.

It marked the end of his college career, which itself had been a point of contention. His father, George, had never been to college himself, and regarded it as a needless diversion that only delayed Art's eventual involvement in the family business. Art had managed to frame it in the context of a "business investment," which had still not entirely convinced him. In the end, it was his mother who realized just how important it was to her son and intervened on his behalf. Only then, did his father have a change of heart.

George was a businessman first and always, and would not part with a thin dime if there were no profit in it. Thus, the suit itself was another kind of business investment: Art's professional appearance. He would now start to pull his weight, and he was going to look the part. Except, he had just left a piece of it sitting in a train car. He ran his fingers over his uncovered hair, trying in vain to coax it into some semblance of order. As usual, it had a mind of its own, and resisted Art's will.

At least I didn't lose my glasses...

Relative quiet returned to the train station as the last car rumbled out of sight. Deciding there was nothing else he could do for it, he looked around trying to get his bearings. The train station was adjacent to a small, yet busy town center. Though, "busy" was something of a relative term.

Previously, he lived in Philadelphia for four years, where he was accustomed to a near constant background din. By contrast, it was so quiet here that it was almost unsettling. Only for a moment. It was not long before Art found it much to his liking. Better still, once the soot and smoke from the coal-burning locomotive had dissipated, the air smelled clean. There were none of the oily, sour, or astringent aromas that had been ever-present for nearly four years.

Aside from the words "Netcong Station" on the platform railing, there was nothing else in the way of signs or a map to direct him. Arbitrarily, he followed the single, main street – literally named "Main Street," as it curved downhill. The small downtown area was home to shops and restaurants and sat beside a large lake. Briefly, he thought that might be *the* lake, but the name of the town was wrong. According to the directions from his father, the address of the cottage was in Bott's Lake, allegedly a "short walk" from the Netcong station.

Allowing himself another moment to admire the rolling, green hills he fished out the letter from his father, which he had somehow managed not to lose. As expected, it contained the address of the rented cottage, but nothing about getting to the town itself.

It took thirty minutes of looking around before he relented, and – with great reluctance – decided to ask for directions. Usually, he preferred to get by on his own and avoided unfamiliar people whenever possible. Art found a man about his own age in front of a local shop. He looked busy, or so Art told himself.

Hesitant to intrude, Art realized that he did not have any other choice. With no small effort, and taking care not to stare at his feet, he cleared his throat. Even so, he had to repeat himself more loudly when the man did not respond the first time.

"Excuse me."

The man turned from his task, and had to stand up straight in order to look Art in the eye.

"Oh, hey there. Help you?"

Thankfully, he was friendly enough, but Art still had to fight down a tremor in his leg. That was one thing to be said for a large city – it was much easier to remain ignored.

"Can you please point me in the direction of Bott's Lake?" Art was afraid he had mumbled the first part, but managed to sufficiently get his meaning across.

"Bott's Lake? Sure." the other man replied. "You visiting?"

"Ah... yeah." The tremor threatened to intensify. This was leading to small talk, and Art was not good at that sort of thing.

"If you're in town for a while, I'd recommend a couple places around here for dinner. The Lake is well and good for the view, but they can't beat Netcong for food."

Art sensed that he was expected to say something, but nothing was coming to mind. He had no knack for gab, and just wanted directions. Friendly though he was, the man eventually relented and pointed back the way Art had come.

"Turn right at the train station here and it's about two miles down Route Six. This is my last delivery for the day. If you want, I can give you a lift."

A genuine smile remained on the man's face, but Art blurted out a quick "no thank you" and hastily retreated. In general, it took some time for him to warm up to anyone. He had only made about three or four friends at school, and none were particularly close friends. That was not to say he was a recluse. Indeed, he could most certainly appreciate people... after a fashion. And despite his shyness, he had managed to catch the attention of two different women. Though, in all fairness, neither of those encounters had ended favorably.

Art followed Route Six for most of an hour before passing a sign that read "Bott's Lake." He might have made better time, but stopped to enjoy the view more than once. The landscape consisted of green farmland and distant hills. And quiet. The lack of incessant noise was especially pleasing. Eventually, the farms and open space gave way to small houses.

Cottages lined both sides of a new road. Looking around, Art suspected that not half of them were over a year old. Here and there were patches of dirt that had not yet had a chance to sprout grass. Like everywhere else, the street was quiet, with a few young families out for a walk.

Continuing, he passed a number of other small bungalows in various stages of construction. The otherwise still air was punctuated by the sounds of hammering and sawing. He paused again to watch some workers raise a wall into place, an act that held his interest nearly as well as the train had. Art simply loved to watch a thing take shape.

Leaving the neighborhood, he got his first proper view of the lake. It was large, though perhaps not huge by most standards; the far shore was maybe a mile away if he was being generous. Still, it was more than enough to accommodate the three sailboats now cruising. A breeze carried over the lake, smelling of piney resin and the crispness of clean water.

Not for the first time, Art wondered why his parents had decided on this place. The lake, while beautiful, and a pleasant surprise for him, was hardly the kind of venue that would appeal to his brothers or their wives. As far as Art knew, they were all of them content with their city lives. Though, he supposed it had been a few years since he had seen any of them. Perhaps they were craving a change of scenery. Yes, he realized, it had been years. Sighing, he wondered about what it would mean to share a roof with his three brothers again.

Then, there was of course, the other matter. The one which Art's mother had surprised him with just last month. That had been a letter as well, but not one he kept in his jacket pocket. That one he had discarded in frustration shortly after reading. Rolling his eyes, he pushed the thought from his mind, content to ignore it for a while yet. That particular topic was the last thing he wanted to think about. For now, he simply wanted to enjoy where he was.

Following the road and with the lake off his right shoulder, Art passed through a cluster of lakeside attractions. The buildings were of varying shape and function and collectively labeled "The Oasis." It gave the impression of a boardwalk in the style of Atlantic City or Coney Island. Albeit, on a smaller scale. Art passed without interest. It was a far cry from the rustic greenery he had admired up to this point, and more suited to his brothers' taste than his own. He had tolerated crowds during his time at school, but certainly would not actively seek them out.

After some wandering, Art arrived at a place that matched his father's directions and several young children chased each other around the tree-lined street. It took him a moment to recognize his oldest niece, Allyson, and her little brother, Georgie. They barely noticed, or perhaps did not recognize him. After all, she was only a toddler the last time he had seen her, and Georgie a baby.

Art tentatively raised a hand in greeting, but the children were so engrossed in whatever game they had invented that they passed by without noticing him. Allyson stopped to grab the hand of an even younger child who must have been Ruth, the newest addition to the family. Despite the children's apparently random orbits, they had not strayed far from the rented houses.

The clan had grown so large that two houses were required to comfortably fit everyone. The cottages themselves were a similar cape cod style, though the green one was larger than the blue one. Both featured covered porches that faced the street, and an identical, single dormer rising out of each roof. Identical white fences bordered each property.

Two Model T's and a Buick sedan were parked on the street out front, with several pieces of luggage still tied to the roof of one of the Fords. Even from the street, Art could hear his father's deep baritone emanating from somewhere inside the green house. Though he could not make out the words of the conversation, the laugh that followed was clear as day.

At least he's in a good mood, thought Art. With any luck, his missing hat would fall beneath notice.

Standing on the road, he was about to approach the house when the front door opened. Out came Thomas, looking tired but with a lingering grin on his face. That was something. Of his three brothers, Art probably got along best with Thomas. That was not to say that they *got along* exactly; rather, there was comparatively little animosity between them.

Art raised his hand in greeting as his brother approached. The tallest of the family, Thomas gave Art an uncritical glance and politely nodded.

"Afternoon, sir." Without even breaking stride, he walked past and continued to one of the Fords. Art slowly lowered his hand, but said nothing, disbelief plain on his face. At first, he thought perhaps Thomas was playing some kind of prank on him, but his brother was not the type. While he was the only one, aside from Art, who wore glasses, the lack of recognition was unlikely the fault of his eyes.

He really doesn't know me, does he?

Several seconds passed before Thomas noticed that someone was standing behind him and turned around. Brow furrowed, he looked at Art, evidently with his eyes open this time. It still took the span of two breaths before understanding appeared on his face.

"Oh," was all he said.

"Afternoon, sir," Art replied in a deadpan tone.

"Hey, Little Brother," Thomas said, shaking his head and smiling. "Don't mind me, I'm miles away." He approached Art and pulled him into an affectionate embrace. "Been a long day in the car with the family."

"Not at all," Art replied, clapping him on the back. "I was in the first car behind the locomotive and my ears are still ringing. Did you just get here?"

"About an hour ago." Thomas nodded toward the house. "Father and Junior already opened some of the Ballantine bottles from back home."

Art rolled his eyes, not entirely surprised. "Ma let him drive all the way from Queens with a case of beer in the car?"

"Actually, it was Junior. Had Allyson and Georgie sitting on the case."

They both laughed. Art was about to respond when he jumped at the sound of a car horn. It startled him more than he would have liked to admit, but in all fairness it was only a few feet behind his head. The laughter that followed was as much of a positive identification of the driver as if Art had seen his face.

"Hello, Ralph," said Thomas, who looked as though he could be laughing as well, but was decent enough to suppress the urge.

Art turned to face his next older brother, the second youngest of the brood, but said nothing in the way of greeting. Instead, his eyes remained narrowed, and his mouth a flat line. Ralph, naturally, was unimpressed.

"Oh, is that you, Arty?" he asked with a toothy grin. "I didn't see you there."

Ralph's eyes were hidden behind the round, tinted lenses of his sunglasses, but Art was fairly certain that they would betray the insincerity of his words. Shutting off the car, the dashing bastard hopped to the ground and gave the door a casual swing, confident that it would latch closed without his watching.

Giving an unnecessary pat to his cleanly parted hair, which had somehow remained tidy and neat despite driving in a car with no top, Ralph stomped towards Thomas in a few proud steps. The two of them grappled in a pantomime of wrestling before embracing in a genuine hug.

"Good to see you Old Sport," said Ralph, at last removing his tinted glasses.

"Yes, it's been too long. Are you fresh from the city?"

"Well, I'm recently from the home of this lovely young thing I met yesterday evening. Though I wouldn't say fresh. I'm afraid she left me a little worse for wear, if you follow me."

Thomas clapped his brother on the shoulder letting out a full-bellied laugh. "Good on you! Come and have a beer, I want to hear all about it."

With Thomas' luggage apparently forgotten for the moment, the two of them started towards the house as a new voice called out to them.

"Have a look at this tall drink of water!" It was a baritone, similar to their father's, but without the timbre and grizzled years behind it. The three of them looked up to see Junior descending the stairs, which visibly sagged under his ample weight.

Still grinning wide, Ralph called back, "Keep the water, what's a fella gotta do to get a bottle o' suds?"

He strode towards Junior, meeting him halfway. Ralph made a lazy, insincere grab for the bottle, which his brother pulled out of reach. The two of them made a show of fighting for it before embracing in a bear hug. Such was their size that it was not an inappropriate expression. While Art might be the smallest among them, the Adams men were, as a rule, large people. Junior and Ralph were easily the largest; broad in shoulder and neck, and taller than most.

Art was similar in physique, though to a lesser extent. Like Thomas, he followed more after the Italian side of the family. After another moment of boisterous reunion – and somewhat to Art's dismay – Junior's gaze settled on him at last. It had been a number of years since all of them were together, and the difference in height was not as pronounced as it once was. While Art stood just over six feet tall, he was still obliged to look up in order to meet the eyes of his oldest brother. The intensity of Junior's gaze caused Art to look away involuntarily. Old habits were hard to shake.

"And I see our little sister is here too," Junior said, eliciting a snicker from Ralph and an eye roll from Thomas.

Art said nothing, but made a conscious effort to keep his chin up and avoid the urge to look at the ground. Hard-earned lessons from years ago were coming back to him; don't show weakness.

Junior took a swig of beer and pressed on. "Been a few years, hasn't it? Will your future husband be joining us this summer?"

Ralph cackled. Junior held the beer bottle up to his lips, but paused to laugh at his own juvenile humor.

Forcing himself to look at his brother, Art considered the beer bottle and Junior's grinning face. If the man wanted a verbal spar, Art could throw it right back at him. He thought up a quip about long, hard objects, and his brother's apparent preference for them. The words were on his tongue, but ultimately, he backed down and averted his eyes. His suitcase suddenly felt heavy in his hands. Too late, he realized this display of weakness would only encourage Junior. Thankfully, Thomas came to the rescue first.

"Now, now boys," he interjected. His tone was disarming. "You forget, our little brother here is getting ready to tie the knot... with a woman," he quickly added.

Glancing at Thomas, Junior scoffed and turned back towards the house, pulling Ralph with him.

As they turned, Ralph tussled Art's hair saying, "Don't worry. I'm sure Mother picked you one with most of her teeth."

This elicited another hoot of a laugh from Junior. "Hell, I wouldn't let Mother pick my *shoes*, let alone my wife," he replied to Ralph.

The pair of them carried on as they made for the green house, leaving Art and Thomas standing by the roadside. Thomas gave a sympathetic nod to Art, who merely shuffled his feet in response. They both stood for a moment, not speaking, before Thomas remembered that he was supposed to be unpacking the car.

"Good to be home, eh?" Thomas asked, tongue firmly in cheek.

Preferring to stay outside for at least a few more minutes, Art helped pull down the remaining luggage from the car's roof. Even from the road, he could hear Ralph's warm and boisterous reception. Art and Thomas spent some time catching up. The children were getting older now. Little Maud was finally able to run around now and spent a lot of time chasing Ruth. Out of all his brothers, Art thought Thomas was the only one worth trying to emulate. He had a good life, a good family…

And he's not a complete jackass.

With a bag in each hand, Thomas nodded towards the green house.

"I'll... be there in a minute," Art said. The so-called welcome from his other brothers left him in no rush to go inside.

"At least Ma will be happy to see you," Thomas replied. With that, he started towards the front door, leaving Art to consider his options. At this point, he had not ruled out the possibility of simply turning around and making his way back to the train. If he hurried, he might even get to New York by nightfall and was confident that he could get into his parents' house. Though, truth be told, he did not want to be there either. Maybe if it was their old house.

In a burst of pure fantasy, he wondered if he could summon up the courage to finally seek out the Grants in Brooklyn as he once intended. The idea was discarded even as it formed. That ship had sailed months ago, and even if it had not, Art could not fool himself. He did not have the nerve for it when it might have made a difference, and he certainly did not have it now.

Sighing, he ultimately dismissed any notion of escape, and resolved himself to an evening with his family.

As expected, everyone was fawning over Ralph, and Art's entrance went unnoticed. For this, he was actually quite thankful. While Ralph was busy regaling everyone with the stories of an eligible bachelor living in a vibrant city, Art sneaked into the kitchen where it was clear that his mother had been preparing for their arrival. The stove had a pot on every burner, and the smell of oregano, garlic, and rosemary permeated everything. Oddly, there were no table or chairs.

Even expecting a large crowd for dinner, Art thought his mother had managed to overdo it. After a quick glance, he had to wonder if there was a butcher in town who was suddenly missing their entire inventory. Perhaps even two of them. His stomach rumbled in anticipation, and it suddenly occurred to him that he had spent all day in transit and skipped lunch. His mother would take it amiss if he started dinner early, but even so he found some bread, a wheel of cheese, and a salami.

Cutting off a portion of each, he could not help but hear Ralph's prattling carry in from the next room. Though most of the conversation was lost in a murmur, his brother had a tendency to project his voice, so his was the only one Art could clearly make out.

"Oh, yes. But we don't call them 'speakeasies.' The ones I've been to refer to themselves as clubs. No, of course I'm not. Yes, Mother. Respectful. Always, respectful."

Though he could not see him, Art heard the smug grin on his brother's face. To Art's bafflement, most people found it endearing. The rest of the anecdote was lost to him, but whatever story Ralph had been telling was followed by boisterous laughter. Honestly, it was bad enough that the bastard was good-looking, having inherited their mother's handsome, Mediterranean features and their father's husky physique, but did he have to be charming too?

Rolling his eyes, Art opened the back door and let himself out. Just beyond was a small wooden deck raised a few steps above the rest of the back garden. Sighing, he kicked the door closed behind him, muting Ralph's voice beyond the point of comprehension. The area behind the house was a small, fenced-in lot, where two large tables had been set up end to end, and another, smaller one beside them.

That explains the kitchen, he thought. Dinner was going to be quite an event. Perhaps his mother had made an appropriate amount of food after all.

Art took a bite from his improvised sandwich and admired his surroundings. There were other fenced-in gardens, and cottages in every direction. Here and there, a large pine tree would pop up. In the distance, he could just make out the glittering surface of the lake beyond a large, stone house. At the blue cottage next door, his nieces and nephews ran in and out of view, continuing whatever game they had been playing when Art first arrived. Though, now he also spotted Thomas' wife, Claudine, chasing after them.

Several cottage yards hosted families enjoying the afternoon air, but they were spread out far enough that he only heard birdsong. Leaning against the deck railing, he finally relaxed. The view and a little bit of food did wonders for his mood, and he was glad that he not absconded back to Queens.

The door behind him burst open. Before he could even turn around, he was lambasted by his mother's mezzo-soprano voice. Though higher than his father's, hers commanded similar attention.

"What's this, with the sneaking? You sneak into the house, you don't even say 'hello'? Then, you sneak back out?" An edge of her old accent crept into her words, as it sometimes did when she was especially worked up.

For a moment, he thought she might be serious, but no. If she had actually reverted to Italian, that would have been cause for grave concern. She soon pulled him into a tight hug, giving lie to the ruse.

"Hi, Ma," he replied around a mouthful of sandwich. Luciana Adams was short in stature and slim in build, and Art was obliged to bend down to return her hug. She would try to obscure this fact by keeping her hair tall, but in truth, it fooled no one. Her grip was strong – the product of a lifetime of corralling three strong-willed boys... and Art. After parting, she began to fuss over the dust on his clothes and the state of his hair.

"Have you been spending too much time in the library? You can't find a comb? And what's this you're eating? Did you see all the food I'm making? Don't you dare fill up on bread..." She left the actual threat unspoken, and instead, made a show of slapping the back of her one hand into the palm of the other on. Despite her diminutive appearance, the gesture carried real weight, though it had been years since she had actually followed through with it.

Her accent was fading, but Art knew it could flare up again on a moment's notice. She would only speak that way around the house. While it was not quite a secret, she tended to keep mum about her heritage, and went by "Lucy" in certain circles. It was a habit she had acquired from their time spent in New England, where there were fewer Italians than in New York.

"Yeah, well, it's been a long day," Art replied, almost sheepishly. "And I've got plenty more room for dinner."

She nodded, but gave him a strong poke in the ribs anyway. "I'll say you do. What, have you been fasting for Lent? Or do they just not feed you at school?"

She hemmed and hawed over his appearance for another minute. Having been through this many times, Art let her do it. He had come to understand that the fussing was an itch that she needed to scratch, and it would be done sooner or later. Best to let her have her say.

"When did you and Dad get here?" he asked, deliberately changing the subject.

"Oh, let's see... ten? Maybe half past?" she replied, thoughtfully.

His brow furrowed. "Of *this* morning?" he asked incredulously. "And you've already cooked enough for twenty people?"

"Well, we have to feed twenty people, don't we?" she replied.

Following his mother back inside, Art was still not eager to socialize with his brothers or father, despite his improving mood.

"Can I help?"

Some time later, Art had laid down a tablecloth on each of the big tables in the back garden and then started on the plates and utensils. Due to the number of place settings, he soon cleared out the kitchen in the green house, and was obliged to go to the blue one for more.

As both cottages were a similar layout, Art found the kitchen quickly. Luciana had clearly been busy. Like at the green house, there was a pot of food in every available space. As he opened the drawer to gather more cutlery, he heard a pair of voices in the next room. They remained oblivious to his intrusion.

"-more oregano. And the garlic too. I want to tell her, 'I know how to make sauce, thank you.' You know?"

"Oh, absolutely," replied the second voice. "I cut up some raw vegetables for little Ruth to chew on, and Luciana just dumps them into the steamer."

Art had met his sisters-in-law on just two occasions, but it was clear who they were. Certainly, he did not know either of them well enough to want to get into a conversation. Thus, he collected forks and spoons as quietly as possible, careful not to interrupt. Thankfully, they were too wrapped up commiserating over their shared mother-in-law to notice him. Art gently placed the dinnerware into a kerchief-lined basket and was almost out the door when he stopped at the sound of his name.

"-better than Art. Did you hear about this?"

"Oh yes. Junior told me. I know their mother is domineering, but that's just too much."

Art shifted his weight so he could lean closer without moving. Of course, he should have known better than to listen to gossip about himself, but curiosity got the better of him, as usual.

"I just can't imagine. An arranged marriage? In this day and age? Typical wop thing to do."

Now that's uncalled for. In spite of his shyness, Art was about to say something to Martha, but Claudine continued.

"From what Thomas said, it was the only way that boy was ever going to find a wife. Terribly shy, their younger brother... bit of a wimp, so he says."

Art was stunned, and the rebuke died on his tongue. While unflattering comments about himself were nothing new, he would never expect Thomas of all people to participate. Worse yet was being reminded of his engagement with a bride he had yet to meet. His shoulders sagged as he turned back to the door.

They're wrong, he thought. *I was going to get married, and I met Sarah Grant all on my own, thank you very much.*

Or rather, they would have been married, if things had gone differently. Letting out a dejected breath, Art left the pair of them to their gossip and pushed all other thoughts from his mind.

Home again. Just the way he remembered it.

Chapter 3

Etta

The days tended to run together, with little to distinguish one from the next. While the usual routine served to mark the passage of time, the odd calamity could be relied upon to add variety. After all, sometimes it rained or even snowed. Maybe there were fewer eggs than normal – or none at all. Maybe a fox got under the fence, and took out a score of birds.

The way Etta saw it "different" often meant "trouble." The routine imposed order to chaos, and was comforting even if it was exhausting, tedious, or a reminder of something painful.

A sign dangled behind the glass front door of the Royal Scarlet grocery store. It read "Closed," but she let herself in all the same. Dominic was restocking the shelves and putting everything into neat, presentable rows before opening. Like a well-maintained machine, he floated among them, making infinitesimal adjustments here and there with no wasted motions.

He did not look up as Etta let the door slowly shut behind her, and she waited politely for almost a minute before it was clear that he had not seen her. This was often a delicate process, and she made a point to clear her throat before speaking. Gently.

"Good morning Dominic," greeted Etta, taking care to pitch her voice low and soft.

A jittery sort, he startled at the sound of his name despite her best attempt to avoid doing so. Etta cringed as he nearly dropped a can of tomatoes from the top rung of the stocking ladder. She fought the urge to continue, even though she was in something of a hurry today. It would not do to rush Dominic. Turning toward Etta, he regarded her through a pair of spectacles balanced precariously at the end of his nose.

"My goodness Etta, you scared me. Is it seven already?"

"Sorry about that, and no. I'm early."

Returning the can to the shelf with one final adjustment, he pulled a watch from his front pocket and shook his head. "While I'm running late... The day is getting away from me."

I know the feeling, she thought.

"You've got eggs for me?" he asked.

"Fresh laid this morning." Etta suggested a price that was higher than the previous day. Right away, she could tell he was going to haggle with her, and just so. Lately, she had been selling to him almost exclusively since his price was fair and he always took the lot. The notice from the taxman was fresh in her mind, and she needed every penny that she could get her hands on. Hence, the reason she was hauling the eggs directly to the store, and not to a distributor as her family used to do.

Eventually, Dominic agreed, not without some hemming and hawing, to a price just slightly higher than what he preferred. Even so, it was a small enough sum that he had enough cash on hand to pay it. Etta had once suggested to simply keep track of their transactions on paper, since she was going to do some shopping anyway. At least a few of these coins would be handed back to him in a matter of minutes.

Dominic would have none of it though, as he preferred to open and close each exchange as it occurred. It was mildly annoying, but Etta did not argue.

"Bring the cart around back and I'll open the stock room door for you," he said.

Etta nodded as she dropped the money into her black denim bag. It was more of the jingling kind than the folding kind, and not much compared to what they owed the town. Still, it was more than usual, and fair.

That was another reason she liked selling to Dominic. She knew he was not one for either favoritism or charity. Ironically, if he had agreed to her initial asking price for the eggs, Etta would have suspected him of taking pity on her, and she would not tolerate that.

Leaving Dominic to arrange the eggs on the display shelf, Etta made a brisk transit of the shop, picking up a few sundry necessities. She might have offered to help unload the crates, but there were only two. Besides, Dominic seemed happier to do it alone. He was very particular, which easily made the task take twice as long. Besides that, Etta's back was sore from pulling the cart all the way from the house, and she did not relish the prospect of bending over the display case for as long as it would take to fill it.

For several reasons, she missed the days when they could afford to have someone else haul the day's take. They once produced enough eggs to afford the middleman. Of course, Etta's family had been larger at the time, and they could better manage a profitable flock. As their family dwindled, so did the number of birds.

For years, no one had gone hungry, or even thought twice about "luxuries" like milk and bread. It was the veritable halcyon days of the Wozniak family farm. A time when no one considered the electrical bill before turning on the lights. Though none of them had realized it at the time, the winter of 1920 was to be the end of that era. Her brother Edward never saw the following spring. Jakob and Lena had been utterly devastated, of course, but even missing their oldest son, the family had carried on. None of them could suspect that the worst was still to come.

Etta gave a final glance at her shopping list, confirming that she had gathered everything. Then, remembering what day it was, and why she had chosen to go shopping in the first place, she went to pick up one more thing. She hesitated. Her purse was light, despite the payment she had just received and the taxman's visit continued to prey on her mind.

I should be hoarding like a greedy miser.

Holding the Moon Pie above the counter, she debated whether to return it to the shelf. She had another moment to consider as Dominic slowly walked around behind the register. In the end, she set it down for him to ring up.

It's not for me. And that was that.

There was comfort in Etta's routine. Even when it was a reminder of something unpleasant. Today was the twenty-third of May. And that was never a good day. In fact, the whole month cast a certain shadow in her mind, despite the warmer weather. She made a point to visit the cemetery on birthdays and certain holidays – Easter had been the most recent occasion – but the anniversary of someone's death was of particular importance. By cruel happenstance, both Lena and Irene had been lost in different years, but on the same day. Today.

Upon seeing the church steeple, it was only a matter of minutes before the headstones came into view. While the Wozniaks were Polish-Catholic, all the farmers in town attended mass at the Methodist church. Under the prior stewardship of Pastor Tom, a man who was consistently elderly for all the years Etta had known him, it was as much a social gathering as a place of worship. Kindly and relaxed, he was generally well liked by all who met him.

Until Tom's unfortunate passing the previous year, Etta never had to think twice about denominational particulars. His replacement, Pastor James, was his opposite in just about every way. So much so, that one or two families had stopped coming to the Sunday service entirely.

Shortly after passing the wrought iron gates of the cemetery, she reached her destination. The overcast sky and headstones made for an ominous sight. It was somewhat offset by the blossoming trees that surrounded the church grounds.

New life among former lives, she mused.

Tucked away in a corner, further from the church itself, but nearer to a blossoming dogwood lay a cluster of headstones. Flat against the ground, they tended to accumulate random debris. Even obstructed, Etta could read the name engraved on the large, center stone. "Wozniak." Below it were five smaller ones, obscured to varying degrees by sticks and fallen tree buds. In a morbid bit of foresight, the location of the first grave had been tucked into this corner with room for the others.

At the time, the family could only afford the less expensive headstones set into the ground. Their intention had been to replace them with proper ones someday. No one would have expected the plot to fill up as quickly as it did. Indeed, digging a new grave had almost become a semi-annual event. The family lay in the order in which they were lost, with an ominous gap next to Etta's mother, Lena.

Bending down to clear off the headstones, Etta silently read each one in turn. Even though she knew the arrangement by heart, it was only proper. Starting from the left was Edward, the first of them lost at barely seventeen years old. He always loved the outdoors. It was with him that Etta had explored nearly all the forest trails around town. The life of a farmer would have suited him well. Rain or shine. Summer or winter. The weather was a minor detail, so long as he could be among nature.

Thus, it was not surprising when he took an interest in ice fishing. While it was a matter of some concern, Papa kept a close eye on him that first season which passed without incident. It was the following year that Edward started going out on his own. And then came the day he went through the ice. Passerbies had seen what happened and rushed to pull him out, but they had not been fast enough.

Next to Edward's headstone were John and Florence, who had come into the world together, and indeed, left it together. Both were far too young. For them, it had been pneumonia, barely two years after Edward died. They were born small, and in their early years were often sick. 1922 had been a particularly cold and wet winter that laid low the entire family for several weeks. While the others had gotten through with no lingering effects, the twins' recovery was troubled. Lena and Jakob had spared no expense for them, but by the time they realized how serious things were, there was nothing to be done. After they had all been spared by the Influenza of '18, it was a cruel twist that the twins would succumb to something so ordinary.

Then was the stone marked "Irene." Etta swallowed back a lump in her throat. Staring, she lingered on this one for a while, and also suppressed a shudder.

"Good morning, Little Sister," she said softly, pulling one of the items from her bag. "The Royal Scarlet has some new flavors now, but this was always your favorite." She set the Moon Pie next to Irene's headstone, and then turned quiet, her thoughts troubling.

Born in 1913, Irene had been a surprise. At five years old, Etta was just old enough to help care for the new baby, and it was a responsibility she took well to despite being a child herself. At the time, their farm included both crops and a much larger flock of chickens, and demanded a great deal of attention. With her parents and older siblings so occupied, Etta was most often watching Irene, playing with her and sometimes feeding her. As a result, she always felt a particular affection for her younger sister even as they grew older.

Finally, on the right end was her mother Lena, for whom Etta also lingered but for a different reason.

"Papa's worried," she began. "The tax man came by yesterday." Etta paused a moment, thinking. "I guess you wouldn't have been around for the last time this happened. He was worried then too, but this time is different somehow. I can't quite say why." Biting her lip, Etta continued. "He could really use your help right now, Mama. He misses you."

Silent for a long moment, she stared at her mother's headstone and composed her thoughts. A number of things had been left unspoken between the two of them. Much of it was unpleasant and none of it seemed right to bring up now. In the end, Etta said nothing more to Lena.

Returning her attention to Irene, she said, "Today is the anniversary. Four years... God, has it really been that long? I can't say it enough, but I'm sorry for what happened. I hope you don't hate me." Her voice cracked at the end and she let herself cry.

Etta sat until her eyes had dried, feeling spent. With a deep breath and a heavy sigh, she stood up and gave each headstone one last look.

"I love you all. Until next time."

She made a point never to say "goodbye" to the ones she loved. It was too... *final*.

When she first began these visits, Etta felt just the smallest bit foolish, apparently speaking to the ground. She did not know why she continued to do it, but eventually, the feeling subsided. It was cathartic, in a way, to go somewhere and have a good cry.

A gap in the clouds revealed the sun, teasing her with warmth. It quickly disappeared again as she passed through the cemetery gates. With it, the chill returned and she wrapped her arms across her chest. Springtime was a constant battle between winter and summer. And today was emblematic of it. As she walked, the temperature rose and fell several more times with the clouds and sun fighting for the heavens. Ultimately, the sun won out. As the day brightened, so did Etta's spirits.

With out-of-towners arriving every day, her shortcut through the lake cottages would take her past more strangers. The long way would avoid them, but as it was she would have little enough time to visit Helen. It would be foolish to walk more than she had to. With a deep sigh, she resolved herself to going among the strangers.

It was becoming late enough in the morning for the first of them to be walking the road. For the most part, she could avoid unwanted interactions with a polite distance. A few of the bolder young men might attempt conversation, but a firm rebuff was usually enough to dissuade them. This was her hometown, and she was secure here.

The otherwise quiet morning was interrupted by the sound of hammering and sawing as she passed a row of bungalows much like the one her cousins had been working on. Up until a few seasons ago, this area was reserved for camping, but a few regular visitors had decided to start building small houses. After that, the idea had caught on and more sprouted every year.

She sold all but four of the hard boiled eggs to the builders. Working men were dependably hungry. Robert was not out today, but Etta remembered his cryptic reference to Helen. She picked up her pace. Not just for the odd comment, but she always jumped at the chance to see her old friend.

The prospect of sitting down for a decent lunch was also enticing. Her stomach rumbled loudly to remind her that she had eaten nothing today except for a large mug of coffee and a stale crust of bread. With about four miles of walking already behind her, she found herself more ravenous than usual. Before leaving the neighborhood, she briefly considered selling the last four eggs.

The specter of the tax bill served as constant reminder that she needed to earn money. But no, those eggs were for Helen. Like with the Moon Pie for Irene, Etta might not be able to justify such an expense for herself, but a gift for a loved one was another matter.

Etta could only stare, scarcely believing what she was seeing.

Not the Becketts, she thought. *They've been here forever*. The truck in front of the house was already laden to capacity, but Edgar Beckett somehow found room for a small end table. As he tied it down with a length of rope, his wife, Bridget, spotted Etta and began to approach. Leaving her wagon on the road, Etta went to meet her.

The Becketts were a slightly older couple, who had lived a few doors down from Etta her whole life. They managed a modestly sized, but consistently producing barley farm and were a staple of the community. Having no children of their own, they were known amongst Etta's friends as an easy way to earn some spending money in exchange for a few extra chores. There was not a family in the area that had not eaten bread provided by their crop. Probably a couple of beers too ever since Edgar had learned how to malt grain.

They met halfway between the house and the road, and Bridget greeted Etta with a hug. Tears were streaking the older woman's cheeks as she composed herself.

"Mrs. Beckett," Etta began. "I had no idea..." It was all she could think to say.

Wiping her face, she released Etta and took a step back. "Oh, you call me Bridget, dear. You're not a child anymore." She took one final steadying breath before continuing. "Edgar and I kept it to ourselves. We didn't want anyone to make a fuss."

"You should have said something. We would have-" Etta stopped before she said, "Helped out," knowing that like everyone else around here, the Becketts would have stubbornly refused any charity even if it was offered. Instead she merely asked, "What happened?"

Bridget shrugged. "It's the new taxes. My parents owned this land for years before they left it to me, and in all that time, we've never paid a cent. Then all of a sudden, I've got to pay for it? Just for being here?" She shook her head. Etta looked over at the truck as Edgar continued to fuss with the ropes.

Bridget made a slow spin, looking to the empty field, the farmhouse, and then the distant hills.

"My father built this house. I was born here. Grew up here. I met my Edgar at the old schoolhouse, and then this was our home. My whole life, I've never been more than ten miles from it." She trailed off, and Etta was not sure if the older woman was speaking to her, or merely thinking out loud. Bridget's lip quivered as she took a shuddering breath.

"I think I'm ready to leave."

"Doesn't seem like you feel that way," Etta replied.

"You go down to the lake don't you? Are there a lot of out-of-towners this year?"

Etta nodded, not sure where this new thread was going.

"Never used to be that way." Bridget looked away at something unseen. "They built the first beach in aught four. It wasn't so bad at first. There might be a few visitors every summer. But then someone had the idea to build that highway and they started coming in droves. And they don't live here. They don't care about the town. Loud. Disrespectful. Even dangerous..."

Bridget cleared her throat, as she looked Etta in the eye. "I suppose you would know all about that." Suddenly, she looked uncomfortable for a different reason.

Etta furrowed her brow for a heartbeat before understanding came over her. The visit to Lena's grave was still fresh in her mind. Bridget caught herself, and quickly moved past the delicate subject.

"Do you know what I've been thinking these last few years? This place has changed so much; maybe it isn't for me anymore. It's just that... I've never known anything else. I'm not yet sixty. Maybe I should get out and see more of the world. I won't pretend that I'm not scared. On the other hand, I still have some of my best years ahead of me."

Bridget's eyes were red, and wet with fresh tears. And yet, she was smiling.

"Where will you go?" Etta asked after a moment.

"My sister and her family own a dairy out in Pennsylvania. Only a few hours from here. I've never worked with cows before…" Bridget frowned and sighed. "One way or another, it will all be fine. Maybe Edgar and I will stay there. Maybe we'll move on and try something new entirely. Truth is, I don't know where we'll end up. And that scares me. But maybe I'm a little bit excited too. Whatever happens, we'll do it together."

Edgar was finished with packing and waited beside the truck. It was time to go. Bridget looked at Etta, fresh tears on her face, but still smiling. Saying goodbye, she told Etta to take care of herself and not to work too hard. With a final wave, she stepped into the truck with her husband before starting down the dirt road. The entirety of their worldly possessions bounced along as they approached the bend, and finally turned out of sight.

It took Etta the better part of an hour to finally reach the canal. She might have made better time, but her thoughts turned heavy after watching the Becketts leave their home for the last time. It served as a reminder that the Wozniaks were at risk of a similar fate. While she had every intention of being somewhere else by this time the following year, there was a world of difference between leaving home and being forced from one's home.

After passing Mr. Shaw's farm, and reaching the forest trail, her thoughts gradually moved on to less troubling topics and her mood improved. On the other hand, without the distraction of dark thoughts, she was reminded once more of how hungry she was.

Taking the most direct path, which led past the swimming pond, she stepped gingerly over a number of half-buried rocks and exposed tree roots. Around her, the forest took on a greenish haze as the tree buds were just on the verge of blossoming. Eventually, she left the forest behind and descended a large hill.

Below her was the canal. On first glance, it looked much like any other river, but was unnaturally straight. Also unlike a river, it featured a steel and timber lock to step the water down from the upper level to the lower one.

Somewhere off to her right, she recognized the hilltop where the jalopy sat, though the car itself was out of sight. Just knowing it was there, waiting for Etta to visit again, was a comforting thought. While she was tempted to try and make such a visit before returning home, Etta did not want to rush her time with Helen. She had been neglecting her best friend for a few weeks now, and they needed to catch up. After the morning she had had, Etta could use some cheering up.

The midday sun had chased away what remained of the chill. It held the promise of a particularly warm day if Etta was a judge of such things. She made her way to a dilapidated structure on the opposite bank of the canal. Wisely, Helen Saunders sat on the bench outside of it. Humble as her surroundings were, she sat with all the haughtiness of a queen at court. Casually, Helen waved as Etta crossed the canal lock on a small footbridge.

Years ago, Etta had actually seen the lock in operation, but it rarely had cause for use these days. Automobiles and trains were such vastly superior modes of conveyance that hardly anyone bothered with canals anymore. Still, the lock was here, and someone needed to mind it, just in case. That was Helen's job in theory. In practice, it was to keep the bench from floating away.

More like a sister than a friend, Etta loved Helen, but often mused, perhaps not kindly, that tending an unused canal lock was a good fit for her. Despite living on a busy farm, Helen somehow managed to dodge even the suggestion of work whenever it tried to find her. In this, Etta was mildly envious, since she had little confidence that she would be able to pull a similar trick. Not that she would try, of course. Etta was a busybody and Helen was not.

On the other hand, she had a wide circle of friends, and somehow managed to keep up with all of them. To Etta, this was exhausting for a different reason, and had to concede that Helen had the mind for it. It helped that sitting idly by the canal all day meant that everyone knew where to find her. Indeed, it was noteworthy that Helen was unaccompanied this morning.

Even so, Mildred remained unimpressed by her daughter's status as Queen Bee. The Saunders' farm was just as busy as the Wozniaks' had once been, if not more so. Helen's laziness was a common subject of tension between them, and Etta had witnessed more than a few fights because of it. All else aside, she was a good friend, and right now, that's exactly what Etta needed.

"Good morning, Chicken Farmer," greeted Helen.

Etta smiled with the first crack to her somber mood.

"And to you, Madame Spinster," she replied.

The bench rested against the outside of the lock house. To call it a house was more than a little disingenuous. In truth, it was a barely-stable amalgamation of four walls and most of a roof that was intended to serve as shelter for the lock tender on foul weather days. More likely, it would serve as a coffin, since a strong wind was likely to bring it down. Etta sat down in the vacant place next to her friend.

"Another busy day on the canal?" she asked.

Helen shrugged, but grinned. "Maybe this'll be the summer the boats come back." She looked up at the sky, now entirely clear of anything resembling clouds. "There are worse ways to pass the time." Then, suddenly remembering something, "Oh, Mom said to ask about her dish if I saw you."

"What, from the other night? Is she missing its company or something?"

"My cousins are visiting this week and she's planning a big supper."

Etta pursed her lips in thought. "Which cousins? Have I met them before?" She did not have her friend's gift for names and faces. While she knew most everyone on the farming side of town, Helen had friends everywhere. Between her and Robert, they might have been acquainted with the entire town.

Helen smirked conspiratorially. "They're all *girls* if that's what you mean."

Etta's eyes narrowed, mildly affronted. Then, she could not help but laugh. "That's not what I meant. You think just because you have a little romance with *my* cousin that I want to hitch one of yours? God, maybe the Townies are right about us." This elicited another round of laughter.

"I might be able to find one on my father's side," Helen teased. "That is, unless you'd rather resume your fling with Bradley Heckel."

"How dare you!" Her smile gave away the insincerity of the rebuke. "Actually, I saw him the other day. Big cow eyes and all." She trailed off, wrinkling her nose.

Helen continued, "You and your father are both welcome to join for dinner, of course. My mother – for some reason – is very concerned that you're not eating enough."

Etta cleared her throat nervously.

I can't imagine why...

The dish Helen referred to had been leftovers intended for a light lunch the following day. Etta had successfully stretched it out to breakfast and lunch for two people.

Instead, she replied, "That's kind of her, but completely unnecessary."

Etta detested lying, but she was even more reluctant to reveal just how poorly she and Papa were getting by. "Speaking of food," Helen continued, "I'm starving. What have you brought me?"

It was a common question, as Etta typically brought something to share. While she was happy to do it, it had recently occurred to her that Helen almost exclusively asked but never offered. Still, Etta reasoned that Mildred was generous enough for all the Saunders put together.

"How would you like a hard boiled egg?" Etta asked, uncovering the basket on her lap. Her tone pitched with faux excitement.

Helen frowned. "Ugh... not much at all, thank you. I don't know why you like them so much."

Etta shrugged her shoulders, face deceptively impassive.

Because they're all I can afford.

She fished around the bottom of the basket, and retrieved a pair of tins. "Would salt and pepper help?"

"Barely," Helen replied with clear disdain, but still reached out for it.

"Here, we can split the cola too."

Helen brightened at that. "Well, there's something. What's the special occasion?"

In fact, Dominic had gifted Etta the bottle with compliments... and firmly denied that it was charity. Supposedly, the torn label prevented him from selling it. Although, she found the matter a bit suspicious.

Despite her complaints, Helen finished her egg and requested another before Etta had gotten halfway through hers. She looked sideways at Helen as she handed it over, brows furrowed.

"Hmf. Maybe I should have brought an even dozen. What are you, on your monthly?"

Helen tensed at that. An odd reaction. She had never been a blue nosed prude, especially with Etta. A lewd comment such as this would normally be met in kind, or at least with an unladylike snort.

"I have news," Helen began, apparently changing the subject. She paused, taking another sip from the bottle.

Etta continued chewing, but listened intently, suspecting this to be a fresh piece of gossip.

After a pause, Helen said, "Robert and I are getting married."

Etta finished chewing, and stared at her friend in surprise. Then, she brightened, saying, "Oh, that's wonderful!"

Seeing Etta look for a ring, Helen shrugged.

"It's not official yet. We only decided a couple days ago. He's good for it."

Etta nodded. It was just the sort of impulsive thing she would expect from Robert, but good news all the same.

"Can't say I'm entirely surprised. You two have been inseparable for a while."

"That's a word for it," Helen muttered, looking away.

"When's the date?" asked Etta.

Helen pursed her lips, hesitating. "The seventh of July."

Etta blinked and turned to face her.

"Of this year? That's not even two months away."

"Yes, well... the sooner the better really."

It was quick. If Etta did not know her friend the way she did, she might have missed it. As Helen's smile waned, she glanced downward before turning her eyes to the distant tree line. Realization dawned on Etta, as she recalled Robert's knowing smile from the other day, its full meaning becoming clear. Turning to face Helen directly, Etta was barely touching her seat. Gone was the playful, gently mocking tone from earlier. Now, her voice was gravely serious.

"Oh, Helen... how far along are you?" Her own eyes dropped to Helen's belly.

"Two months? Maybe three. I think. I'm not quite showing yet, but it won't be long. Even by July I think it may start to become obvious."

"Who else knows?" Etta asked, her half-eaten egg forgotten for the moment.

"My brothers. My sister. Mom. Not my father yet, but soon."

"And Robert?"

"Of course!" Helen brightened. "He actually said he was thinking about asking me even before..." she left the rest unspoken. "He's so excited. I had to remind him not to tell the whole fire company."

"That's like him. It's obvious that he's smitten with you."

What she meant was, *My cousin was never known for his restraint*, but she did not say it out loud.

"I'm happy for you and Robert. I really am." Etta paused, gathering her thoughts, and did some quick math. "You're going to need a place to live. And the baby is going to be born in winter, so you'll need warm clothes. I think I can find the midwife who delivered my sister-"

Helen interrupted Etta, putting a hand on her arm, and let out a full-throated laugh. Her first since delivering the news.

"You really do worry too much. *I'm* the one with a kid on the way. There's plenty of time for all that."

Etta let out a frustrated sigh. Yet again, the two girls failed to see eye to eye. It was something that happened more frequently than it once did, but Etta would usually shrug off these disagreements as fleeting things of no consequence. After all, Helen was a lifelong friend with whom she had shared thousands of secrets, private jokes, and giggles suppressed in the middle of the night while everyone else was asleep.

Still, an unkind question nagged at the back of Etta's mind. At first, it actually startled her that she would even think in these terms, but as the question persisted, she found that she did not have an answer to it. At least, not a satisfactory one.

Who is going to take care of this baby?

"Besides," Helen continued, disrupting Etta's thoughts. "We've got a wedding to plan. And I want you to be my maid of honor."

Etta dismissed her remaining doubts for the moment. Helen was right; this was a happy occasion. Practical matters could be dealt with later.

For the next hour, they talked about who would be in the bridal party, what the dress should look like, and the precise nature of their familial relationship. "Cousin-in-law" was the term that stuck. As the mood became more relaxed, their laughter grew louder. At one point, an especially bold rabbit poked its nose out from under a bush, only to dash off with one of their outbursts.

Chapter 4
Art

From behind the door, he heard the muffled voices of Thomas' wife Claudine and their daughter Maud. Most of the words were unclear, but enough bits and pieces carried through that he understood the gist of it.

"...know it's not like the one at home... have to go or not? No... too early... back to bed..."

And so it continued for several interminable minutes. The other cottage had a bathroom, but the risk of running into Junior was too great. Just as Art began to seriously consider sneaking out back and relieve himself behind the house, the door opened.

Claudine pulled up short, surprised to find Art standing there. Her daughter looked up defiantly, resuming whatever debate they had been having.

"But Uncle Art is awake," Maud insisted.

"No. Mommy is going back to bed, and so are you," replied Claudine.

Art said nothing, as he waited patiently for them to clear the doorway.

As they passed, Claudine said, "Art, could you ask your mother to keep it down? No one is going to get up for breakfast anytime soon. I don't know who she thinks she's cooking for."

You clearly don't know my father, Art thought.

Instead of arguing the point, he simply nodded. Anything to get them out of the bathroom. Apparently satisfied, Claudine urged Maud back to bed, and Art wasted no time in dashing inside.

A few minutes later, Art was feeling much improved, and made for the kitchen. At this hour, he would not be able to fall back asleep, and did not desire to spend any more time in the room he shared with Ralph than necessary. Besides, an enticing aroma wafted out from the kitchen: bacon, eggs, and something sweet. Probably flapjacks. His stomach rumbled despite the large dinner they had had the night before.

"Morning," Art said as he entered the kitchen. His mother turned and smiled at him while she flipped the bacon. As with the previous three mornings, she cooked while still wearing her night robe, but had somehow found the time to fix her hair.

"Good morning," she replied. "You're making a habit of getting up before your father."

Art shrugged. "Yeah. I can't sleep after the sun comes up."

He noted the usual assembly line that was his mother's system. Back at school, the kitchens had to feed an entire dormitory of young men. By Art's reckoning, his mother put them to shame.

"I thought I heard Claudine and Maud," Luciana asked. "Are they awake?"

Art recalled his sister-in-law's curt demand for quiet but decided not to mention it.

"They... went back to bed," he said instead.

Luciana scoffed. "No wonder Thomas is getting so thin. That woman never cooks. I told him, that flapper is not wife material. But does he listen?"

Silently cringing, Art looked over his shoulder to make sure they were still alone. Even if everyone in the house were able to hear his mother, maybe they would be unable to discern her exact words. The animosity among the family certainly needed no new fuel. In fact, last night's dinner had been the first one without someone angrily storming away from the table.

It turned out that the whispered griping Art had overheard between Martha and Claudine was a frequent occurrence. He walked in on at least three other such conversations, either between the sisters-in-law themselves or between them and one of his brothers. Sometimes it was about how his parents were letting the children eat too much, or that his mother was too bossy with demanding help. For the most part, he stayed out of it. It was not that he entirely disagreed with what they were saying, but for Art, that was just how things were.

"There won't be any of that for you," his mother continued. "Gertrude Kennedy did a proper job of raising Dorothy. A good Catholic girl."

Art cringed again, willing his mother to go back to complaining about her daughters-in-law. This was not a conversation he was ready to have. For three days, he had managed to dodge the topic of his upcoming engagement. This, he supposed, was one positive outcome of the simmering and on-going hostilities within the house; no one could spare any attention for him. When he was younger, anonymity had bothered him. These days, he saw a distinct benefit in remaining unnoticed.

"You'll see when you meet her in a few weeks. She's a bookish one. I think the two of you will get along. Oh, it will be so good to see Gertrude again. We really hit it off at the women's club last year." Luciana's smile faded for a moment. "You know, it was hard for us to make friends after that business with the Grants."

Art grimaced. *Please don't talk about Sarah.*

Waiting for a break in his mother's line of thought, he managed to excuse himself on the pretense of going to collect the milk from the front porch. Leaving the kitchen, he wondered how she was able to tolerate the heat for more than a few minutes. Outside, the milk delivery was there as expected, but he made no move to pick it up. Instead, he simply stared at the changing colors in the sky.

The sunrise, and the silence, was truly golden, and he stood there, basking in the quiet serenity. Green trees in every direction, peaceful, and simply wonderful. After spending the majority of his recent life in one city or another, he had grown accustomed to a constant dull roar. It was like a splinter that had been in his finger for so long he had grown accustomed to the discomfort. The sudden lack of it was a relief he had not even known he was craving.

In many ways, it reminded him of their old place in New England. His childhood home was rural, like here. Likely, he was the only Adams who remembered it with any fondness. At the time, their means had been quite limited. As a child, Art's toys were whatever could be salvaged from Father's repair shop and his playmates were his brothers, who picked on him more often than not.

In hindsight, they could rightly have been described as poor. While that had not particularly bothered him, everyone else was happier once Father changed jobs. Mother's mood especially improved when they moved to their first big town. Art found it ironic that after so many years of building a business and moving to increasingly larger cities, his parents chose to vacation at a place so similar to the one they had left. And for an entire summer no less.

Several doors down, the milk truck started up with a grinding rumble, and continued on its rounds. The driver gave a casual wave to another truck as it passed, apparently the one delivering blocks of ice. Art gave a parting look to the sun, which had just crested the horizon.

The dairy provisions for both houses came to this door, and it was almost enough that he had to make two trips. With a little balancing, he managed it in one. Two full gallons for the children, which would probably be finished by midday, and a whole quart of cream for the morning coffee. The latter sounded particularly good.

The quiet peace endured until he returned to the kitchen to find his father sitting at the table. At first, George did not look up, his attention split between the steaming cup of coffee and the ledger in which he was scribbling. It was just as Art had always remembered.

George had not even waited for Art to return with the cream, preferring to drink his coffee black. It was a habit he had picked up in the days when he worked in an unheated repair shop and adding milk made his coffee too cold. For the second time that morning, Art was reminded of the New England house, and the hours spent with his father and brothers in their old business.

Of course, they had to quit as soon as I got good at something.

Taking a sip, the cup looked dainty in George's hands. If the Adams brothers were large men, here sat the reason why. A bricklayer in his younger days, the man's bulky frame dwarfed the chair in which he sat. With his bushy mustache and reading spectacles, he had all the appearance of a gorilla that had been taught the basics of civilization. As he continued working on the ledger, the pen looked comically small, as did the coffee mug.

With George's attention so occupied, Art briefly considered backing out of the room without a word. Perhaps he could remain unnoticed until at least one of the grandchildren came downstairs. His father tended to be in a better mood around them. Recent days had served as a harsh reminder of the perils of having the man's undivided attention.

"Oh, thank you, Arturo," said his mother, surprising both him and his father.

Art and George met eyes, and his father acknowledged him with a single nod. With a quiet sigh, Art continued into the kitchen, and deposited the milk in the icebox. All the while, he waited with mounting dread for the inevitable.

At some point, his father would run out of notes to take, and lay out the plans for the day. Such had become the usual routine for life at the cottage. The room was silent for a full minute while Art poured his coffee. With a nearly invisible tremble, he added a splash of the cream he had just brought inside. Reluctantly and with care, he sat down as though he might remain unnoticed by the man sitting across from him.

"Good morning, Mr. College," George said, at a volume that could be described as booming. If he had not woken everyone in the house, at a bare minimum, he had surely disturbed those on the first floor. Art was startled, nearly to the point of spilling his drink. Recovering, he briefly wondered if that was deliberate. After all, George had waited until he sat down, but not long enough for him to take his first sip.

But no. That was something Ralph would do, not their father. Where his sons were clear about their intentional ruffling of Art's feathers, George only did so incidentally. He was simply a loud man. For as long as Art could remember, his father alternated between silence or projecting across a busy dinner table. He had been spoiled by his time at school, where people spoke at a sensible volume. If the constant din of a city was an annoying but manageable splinter, his father's baritone was a brick to the face.

"Good morning," Art replied in a clear voice that sounded nearly mute by comparison. To him, it was still too loud considering the hour. Experience had taught Art that responding too quietly would only earn him a rebuke and a command to repeat himself. Too loud, and he would wake up everyone in the house and earn some dirty looks. He grew anxious as the ceiling creaked and bumped. The rest of the house was beginning to stir. Feeling partly responsible, Art cringed.

"You and I are going to try to pick up some new clients around the Oasis today," George said without preamble. "Then, I need to find a phone to check up with the home office."

Art grunted into his mug, hoping it evaded his father's notice, but otherwise remained silent. When he made no verbal reply, George looked at him with expectation.

"Yes, sir," Art replied. Foolishly, he had been entertaining plans to explore the town. With the little bit of time he was able to sneak away from the family, he had discovered some forest trails. This was a vacation after all and he meant to treat it as such. Unfortunately, his father, a businessman first, foremost, and always, had no intention of "wasting" the summer in such a way.

George nodded, apparently satisfied, and took a pull from his own coffee cup. Art's thoughts remained foggy as he was still waking up. He did not quite realize he was speaking until the words had already left his mouth.

"Um... how long do you think?" Immediately, he clammed up, realizing his folly but the damage had been done.

Two eyes glared from the top of the small cup. The intensity of the gaze chased any lingering cobwebs from Art's head and he braced for a verbal assault. Instead, his father responded with maddening calm.

"How long do I think, what?"

Art gulped, recognizing the trap, though it had been some time since it had last come up. This was a game his father liked to play, getting Art to answer his own question, or perhaps dig himself a little deeper. He glanced at his mother, who was still busy at the stove. It was a rare occasion when she would bail him out of these situations, but he was ever the optimist. When it was clear that she did not intend to become involved, Art cleared his throat and replied.

"What I mean is, how long will we be working today?" He hoped, desperately, that the rephrasing might smooth matters, but it was not meant to be.

George sighed as if this were a repair he had made several times already, which simply refused to stick. He set the pencil down, giving Art his undivided attention.

"How long do *you* think it should take?"

"Yesterday we visited five businesses and it took us most of the day."

"There you go, then," replied George as he reached for the *napoletana* to refill his coffee cup.

Art remained silent as he mentally girded himself for another day working with his father. That meant a lot of new faces, and a lot of bothering people with sales talk. Perhaps he could escape for an hour or so before dinner. His thoughts were interrupted as his father, fresh coffee in hand, continued speaking.

"Unless, of course, you have something else to do?"

Normally, he would not press his luck. Maybe it was his imagination, but something about his father's tone and the directness of the question made him think there was a chance of salvaging the day.

"Well actually, there were a couple of forest trails around town I'd like to- I mean..." Art trailed off, realizing just how poorly he had read the situation. For how little he spoke, Art's mouth had an uncanny knack for getting him into trouble.

"Do you see the pile of food over here?" George pointed to the stove.

Art nodded, suspecting where this was going, but unable to jump off the train now that it was rolling.

“What happens if your mother takes a day off?”

At last, Art wisely remained silent. There was no mistaking his father's tone now.

“You like to eat, don't you? You like to have clothes on your back? You like this house?”

George was getting riled up, which was remarkable, considering the early hour. Art avoided eye contact, or anything else that might so much as hint at defiance. This was a familiar storm, and he knew there was naught to do but settle in for the duration.

“I knew this would happen when you went off to college. You spend all your time in books, and you forget about the real world. If your mother doesn't work, our home falls apart. If I don't work, we don't have food to put on the table. You don't-”

To Art's surprise, his father dropped off mid-sentence, and looked at the entrance to the kitchen. Art was genuinely confused by the abrupt way his father's stern lecture evaporated. Who could derail a rant like that? He dared not move to look, but it turned out that he did not have to.

As quickly as his father's scowl disappeared, a wide grin replaced it. Setting down his cup, he bent low and spread his arms wide. Maud ran into him, clutching a stuffed bear and still wearing a nightgown that was a size too large. Art barely recognized the man that embraced her, and scooped her off the floor in a hug.

“Good morning, my little cherub.”

“'Morning, Grandpa,” she said, rubbing her eyes as he sat her on his knee. “I'm hungry.”

“Nonna is hard at work. Did you say 'good morning' to Nonna?”

Maud did so, and Luciana finally set down the spatula long enough to give her granddaughter a warm embrace.

“Do you like eggies?” she asked.

Maud shook her head, still rubbing her eyes.

Mother put on an exaggerated frown. “No? What about bacon?”

Maud considered this for a moment, and nodded.

“That's more like it,” Luciana replied. “Everyone likes bacon.”

Maud turned back to Grandpa, whom Art suspected was an entirely different man from his father, despite the similarity of their outward appearance.

“Grandpa, are you working today?”

He nodded seriously, but kindly.

“Yes, sweetie. Everyone is working today,” he held a single finger. “But only for a short while.”

Art frowned. A casual observer coming in at this very moment would never suspect the barely-contained tirade that had been delivered mere seconds ago on this same topic. As if to dispel any notions that Art was imagining things, George the grandfather momentarily vanished, and George the father returned. Ostensibly speaking to Maud, it was clear that his words were intended for his youngest son.

"That's assuming everyone puts in a solid effort, and that all further bellyaching is over with."

George held his attention until Art nodded and quickly dropped his eyes back to his mug. Maud looked back and forth between the two men, sensing the unease, but not sure what to make of it.

Finally, her eyes settled on George's coffee. "I want that."

While Maud had been the first grandchild to come down to breakfast, the rest of the family followed in short order, including Martha and Junior's family from next door. As a rule, his brothers and sisters in-law appeared haggard and annoyed, and there were a few subdued grumblings about why all the milk was delivered to only one cottage.

Through poorly hushed murmurings, Art had gleaned that their domestic status quos were being disrupted. At home, Martha and Claudine would expect the children to sleep for at least another hour, but in a new house, with the grandparents downstairs, this was simply not possible.

The small kitchen reached capacity, and Luciana promptly chased everyone outside. George likewise, conscripted his sons to set up the backyard with tables and chairs, and also to carry out the trays of bacon, eggs, and flapjacks. All of which somehow became lighter during transit.

It was the typical chaotic affair to which the combined families had become accustomed. Animated discussions ensued, which included a few rebukes from Claudine and Martha about how much their husbands were eating. Thankfully a hot meal and more hot coffee quelled some of the more overt hostility.

With about half the food already eaten, Ralph finally joined the rest of the family. While he could not hear exactly what was said, Art noticed a muttered exchange between him and Junior. He suspected that it had something to do with Ralph's exploits the previous night. No doubt, the dapper prick had discovered another club that served alcohol. The pair of them shared a knowing, but restrained laugh a moment later.

Art had to concede that Ralph's manners were improving. Last night was the first time since their arrival that he had not woken Art upon his late return to their shared bedroom.

Breakfast was unhurried. Almost leisurely. Art's parents sat with Allyson and little Ruth between them, grinning and relaxed for a change. Once again, Art noted the positive effect that the grandchildren had on George's mood and was glad for it. A short reprieve was better than none.

George was positively giddy as they left the house. "There's about half a dozen stores that sell ice cream and they're using block ice! This should be easy as pie."

The family business was electric refrigeration. While not quite a new product, their specialty was fitting them to odd-shaped spaces in buildings that were never intended to accommodate them.

In some ways, Art actually enjoyed the work. Each customer required a tailor-made solution, which involved numbers and things to figure out – Art's bread and butter. Unfortunately, the engineers at the home office did much of that work and the Adamses' main focus was on management and the sale rather than the operation.

This, Art was less enthusiastic about. It typically meant a great deal of interaction with potential clients, most of whom had no interest in what they were selling.

Such had been their experience the previous day, which featured no small number of rejections. Thus, Art did not share his father's excitement regarding the ice cream stores. Sensing what was expected, he quickly forced a smile to his face. George rightly suspected that his son's enthusiasm was not genuine, but let it go. He was still in a good mood upon reaching the Oasis beach resort.

Their first call of the day met with a business owner who was both firm and clear on his lack of interest. For Art, that would have been sufficient reason to leave and he even started to do so, but George persisted. Art only grew more uncomfortable at their continued imposition, and the parlor owner grew more annoyed until George finally relented. That had been their first bust of the day, but not the last.

Their next few calls met with polite, yet firm, negative responses and one door that was literally slammed in their faces. With each failure, George's good humor chipped away a little more. Art generally remained silent during these calls, for which George increasingly assigned some of the blame. At least he could not be accused of "bellyaching."

Coming up empty-handed at the Oasis, they reached the end of George's list earlier than expected. Instead of calling it quits, George resorted to the backup list and led them further away. It was a long walk from the cottage, and the sun was in Art's eyes for most of it. Not for the first time, he wished he had not forgotten his hat in the train car.

Eventually, they reached a small hotel on the south end of the lake. Having only about ten rooms, it was located on a small but steep hill. A long, stone walkway rose up from Route Six to the front entrance. Ivy covered much of the foundation, giving testament to the age of the establishment.

As they climbed to the top of the steps, they arrived at a wide porch. A number of guests sat on rocking chairs, enjoying a picturesque scene of the lake and surrounding hills. On a clear day, such as this one was, the view went for miles.

Father and son passed beneath a wooden sign over the front entrance that read, "The Warren Inn." Just inside, Art and his father found the concierge, such as it was. George frowned at the single, unoccupied chair behind the small table and wondered, none too quietly, about where the owner was. A few moments later, a stoutly built woman with mostly gray hair strode through the room carrying a fully laden food tray.

"Be right with you," she said without breaking stride. Art and his father milled around for several minutes in the tiny lobby.

With nothing to show for the morning George ground his teeth and sighed. His mood had turned poor and Art attempted to remain inconspicuous. It did not work.

"Do you know what you're going to say?" George asked.

Art cleared his throat. "Yes. I think so." He proceeded to give a description of the refrigeration cycle, but trailed off as his father shook his head.

"No, none of that. Like I told you: think 'features' not 'operation.' She's a customer, not an engineer."

As they awaited the owner's return, George quizzed Art on their script, determined not to let him hide in silence again. What is the basic refrigeration unit? What are the credit options? Brute memorization had never been his strong trait, which made the marketing aspects difficult for him. After about twenty minutes of this, he actually sighed with relief when the hotel owner finally returned.

She greeted them with a professional, welcoming smile.

“Good morning, gentlemen. Are you checking in?”

George responded in kind with his own business face: courteous, competent, with just a dash of personable warmth. It was a patented blend that Art had seen countless times before. He hated it. Knowing what George was like in private, the Sale Smile, as he thought of it, struck him as entirely dishonest.

George started, “Good morning to you, Missus...?”

“Warren, like on the sign out front. You can call me Maggie.”

“How about that? My mother's name was Maggie.”

Art suppressed a groan.

Grandma's name was Margaret and you damn well know it.

“To answer your question, no, we are not checking in but your establishment is without equal. I mean, that view alone!” He made a show of being impressed before getting down to business. “My name is George Adams, of Adams Refrigeration and Service, and this is my son Arthur.”

Turning, George raised his eyebrows, reminding Art to put his own Sale Smile on. He had no skill at pretending and at first maintained a comfortable, neutral expression. For the sake of peace, he ultimately complied with the demand. Satisfied, George rolled on with his pitch. The man liked to talk, and Art had to concede that he was good at it. His enthusiasm was contagious.

To Art’s surprise, Maggie was genuinely receptive and particularly intrigued by the “time saver” angle. Apparently confident of the sale, George decided it was time for Art to practice.

“My son will tell you about a product of immense benefit that we offer which will keep your items cold, and requires no daily maintenance.”

Maggie looked at Art expectantly. In spite of his disdain for the sales pitch, he could not deny that it was working. He resisted the impulse to shake his head in disbelief.

Several seconds of passed before Art remembered that it was his turn to talk. Opening his mouth, he also realized that he had completely forgotten his script. Feeling the weight of his father's displeasure increase with every passing second, he improvised.

“Well,” he began. “In a nutshell, the refrigeration unit takes electricity to run a motor and pumps the refrigerant through a series of pipes-”

George surreptitiously but none too gently kicked Art in the foot. The Sale Smile remained firmly in place, but George's eyes bored into Art with fire while Maggie's began to wander.

Art cleared his throat and started again, recalling his father's last piece of advice.

"It features a lot of benefits over a traditional icebox." He paused for a moment, unable to recall the rest. Then, he remembered some of the chores that used to fall on him before his family could afford to buy their own product. "You probably have to scrub out the walls of the ice box once a week or so or else it starts to smell, right?"

This served to recapture Maggie's attention, and she nodded.

"I usually put it off to once a month, but yes. It's a big icebox, and I have to empty it first."

"A refrigeration unit can fix that too. Ice blocks make the air very moist which is great for mold growth-"

George interrupted, "Arthur, which particular unit would you recommend?"

This was a loaded question, the answer for which had been discussed beforehand. Of course, George wanted to make a show of it and so Art obliged.

"Probably the mid size unit since it would be easier to bring up all those steps. We'd have to get the exact dimensions of her cellar, but-"

George cut him off again, moving on to cost and financing. He carried on as if the sale was a foregone conclusion. From the way Maggie was responding, it probably was.

All in all, Art thought they were doing well, and actually relaxed. In fact, he nearly started to enjoy the process. Having established himself as the one with the technical answers, Maggie turned to him with a few practical questions, which he answered honestly and candidly.

They spoke for a few more minutes, and ultimately shook hands on the sale. George got Maggie's signature on a few preliminary documents and promised to have the home office write up a full proposal for her approval and signature. As they left, Art could not help but feel a certain satisfaction, thinking that he was beginning to see the appeal of this whole thing.

Upon returning outdoors, George dropped Sale Smile as quickly as he would remove an extra coat. Art recoiled, not expecting the transition, and utterly lost as to what he had done wrong. After all, they had made the sale.

George led the way back down the stone steps, and Art hesitated. By the time they reached the main road, George's usual scowl was on full display.

Art was in for it. At least things were back to normal.

“Arthur,” George began in a tone that utterly radiated annoyance. “Why on Earth would you tell a potential client that her electricity bill 'may potentially triple' if she buys the thing we're selling?” His father stood mere inches away as he spoke to Art, causing him to lean away as far as he could without moving his feet. He was genuinely confused.

“Well... she said it seemed too good to be true, and asked if there were any drawbacks. I thought I should be honest.”

George sighed. “There's *lying*, and there's less-than-the-whole-truth. Yes, of course there are drawbacks, but you don't want to scare 'em off. Next time, say something like, 'there are some modest operating costs you may consider.' Keep it vague.”

“But she still bought one.”

“Yes! After I smoothed things over.” He spoke the first through clenched teeth. “I expect she could barely hear you with the way you were mumbling to your feet. I've said this before, and here it is again: if you don’t *show* some damn confidence, they're not going to *have* any confidence in you or what your selling.”

George pulled off his hat and fanned himself. The sun was fully out now, and things were getting warm. George perked up, as though a sudden thought had just occurred to him. He pulled the watch out of his pocket and thumbed it open in a single, smooth motion.

“It's just about time for me to call the home office.” He was quiet for a moment, thinking. Finally, he let out a sigh, and calmed down at last. “All things considered, we did make a sale... finally. Let's call it early today.”

Art brightened at that. For as long as he could remember, his father had only quit early maybe three or four times. Ever. His thoughts immediately turned to possibilities for the afternoon. Then, his father continued.

“Why don't you spend another hour or two scouting around for potential customers, then head back to the cottage for supper. Make a list, and tomorrow we'll start on it.”

George looked at the top of Art’s head, and squinted suspiciously. Art tensed.

“Also, if you’re not going to wear your hat, at least get a haircut.”

"Yes, sir," he responded evenly, then looked away and suppressed a sigh.

"Hey," his father said.

Instinctively, he braced, expecting an addendum to the earlier rebuke. To his surprise, George clapped him on the shoulder.

"You did alright. Still room for improvement." With a final nod, his father turned and started up the road alone.

That was unexpected.

His thoughts soon returned to the afternoon before him. While not quite off the hook, at least he would be left unsupervised for some time. Art turned, and started walking in the opposite direction before his father could have a last-minute change of heart. Only some time later did it occur to him that "scouting around for potential customers" could mean almost anything. And if he returned home empty-handed, well, then the prospects just did not pan out.

This was a part of town Art had not yet been to. Directly across the lake he saw the Oasis, which helped to get his bearings. Keeping the lake on his right, he passed a few restaurants and other establishments. A rectangular, white building, called CasinO advertised live entertainment, and Art wondered why they bothered to capitalize the "O".

He continued to walk and made a mental note of a few places that might fit his father's criteria.

Satisfied that he had complied with the strictest letter of the request, Art turned onto a side street at random. The tree cover grew thicker here, shading him from the warm, midday sun. A cottage popped up here and there, but beyond the trees lining the road, it was mostly quiet farmland. Once again, he appreciated the lack of city noises and basked in the sounds of nature.

It was nowhere near as developed as the other side of the lake. Here, there were more fields and fewer cottages. Another twenty minutes of wandering took him uphill. The lake and the merrymakers enjoying the day soon disappeared as Art crested the hill. Starting down the opposite side, his surroundings soon transitioned to farmland interrupted by the occasional copse of trees.

As he took in the view the sudden whine of an electric motor was conspicuous. It was distant, and despite the otherwise still air, he could not immediately determine which direction it had come from. The whine was followed by a harsh, stone-on-metal sound, which Art immediately recognized as a grinder. The noise stopped a moment later without him discovering the direction of its source.

Just as he was about to continue, the silence was once again broken. This time, by the sporadic pounding of a hammer on metal. He looked around again and finally determined where it was coming from. Curious, he began walking.

Eventually, he arrived at a stone building and the source of the racket. It was about a hundred feet off the road, and two stories tall. Old-looking too. If Art was to guess, maybe late 1800's or even earlier. Too sturdy for an old barn or warehouse. Maybe a mill? A river ran alongside it, and what remained of a large water wheel was frozen in place and overgrown with weeds.

Standing in the street, Art noticed a hand-painted sign that read, "Robbins Repair and Service." The paint was chipped and faded, but still legible.

A set of large barn doors stood open on the front face of the building, revealing an amber colored shower of sparks from within the darkness. It persisted for several seconds before being replaced, once again, by the rhythmic thud of hammering metal. Art took a step onto the crushed stone driveway leading from the street. Strange machines of varying shapes and sizes littered the grassy field alongside the drive. Some were obvious in their function. A tractor here. A plow there. Others were completely alien to him, and he could not guess at their intended purpose or function detached from context.

Slowly, he made his way up the driveway, inspecting each one. Some were fabricated entirely from metal, while others incorporated timbers either as details or key structural components. The ones that really captured his interest featured exposed serpentine belts directed around multiple pulleys.

An ancient torture machine might have served as inspiration for one especially nasty-looking device. A leather conveyor belt fed into a drum studded with giant spikes. Nearly all of them had a patch or part of a different color, to indicate where they had been fixed over the years.

Still others were rusted beyond recognition, or weeds had grown around and through them. Several of the machines looked as though they had not moved in decades.

Absorbed as he was with this menagerie of wood and metal, he barely noticed the voice calling out to him. Art looked up, not entirely sure he had heard someone until he met eyes with a man standing in front of the open doors. He was short in stature, dressed in a leather apron and sleeves. A pair of round goggles rested on top of his head, which was bald, except for the sides. What little hair he did have was gray and wild, much like his mustache. The man looked up at Art expectantly.

"Beg your pardon?" Art said after a moment, when it became clear that the man was waiting for him to say something.

Looking mildly annoyed, the man lifted his chin and spoke more loudly. "I said, 'Are you dropping off or picking up?'"

"Ah..." Art was unsure how to respond. "Neither."

The gray-haired man frowned. "Are you here with the town? I'm all paid up as of last month."

Art shook his head.

"You taking the census or something?"

"No."

"Then, may I ask what's your purpose here?"

"I... well... I heard the noise, and just sort of started walking."

"So, are you nosing around, or are you selling something?"

"I suppose, technically, I'm a salesman."

The man waved him off. "Sorry. Whatever you're selling, I'm not interested." He had already turned to go back into the barn before he reached the last word.

"Wait," Art called as he followed the older man inside.

Returning to the piece he had been working on, the man stuffed a pair of cotton wads into his ears and pulled the goggles back down over his eyes.

"Do you-" Art's question was cut off by the din of the grinder switching back on. As the shower of sparks resumed, he was obliged to cover his ears. Standing there, his eyes gradually adjusted to the dim light of the workshop and he looked around.

While the driveway was lined with mostly complete machines, the inside was absolutely littered with various individual components, random tools, and half-finished assemblies. Beneath the clutter were half a dozen worktables and only a handful of clear areas between them. Art must have gotten too close at one point, because the grinding noise abruptly halted, and the gray-haired man spoke again. In fact, it was more of a shout.

"Don't fool with any of that!"

Art immediately dropped his hands, responding to the man's tone more than anything else. It carried a certain gravitas despite his short stature. Startled, Art could do nothing but stare as the man let out an exasperated sigh.

"Look, either you're here to sell something, which I've already said I don't want, or you want me to fix something, which I don't see. Other than that, I'm six week's behind on my work log and I can't have you poking around in here."

When Art made no response, the man shook his head and reached under the nearest workbench. Pulling out a long metal bar, he held one end while letting the other end drop onto a pile of junk with a loud crash. That got Art's attention. Letting the implied cudgel do most the talking, the man stared.

"Get. Out."

Art finally snapped out of his stupor and beat a hasty retreat down the packed, gravel driveway to the main road. It was not until he was some distance away that he realized that he did not know where he was. Sighing, he resigned himself to a long wander as he looked for something – anything – familiar. It gave him time to think.

The place had been a veritable trove of mechanisms and devices. He probably could have spent days there just exploring all the metal parts. Gears. Chains. Wheels. Machines of all sorts had always tickled Art's brain in a way that making sales could never hope to compete with. It was the main reason why he remembered his time in the family's New England repair shop so fondly. School had come close, but it was a poor substitute.

Here he saw a chance at getting his hands on real machines again. There was simply no way around it; he had to go back. But how? His father, of course, would never approve. After all, wrench turning was now a thing that was beneath Adams men. There was also the issue of the gray-haired gatekeeper. All these thoughts swirled around his head for the next few hours until he eventually found his way back to the cottage.

With his mind occupied, he kept to himself for the evening as he worked through the puzzle now before him.

Chapter 5
Etta

It was only the second time Etta had been inside a restaurant. The first was a decade ago, and represented a substantial expense for the Wozniaks, even relatively well off as they were. Tonight, she was working. Helen's older brother, Mark, mentioned that the CasinO restaurant was looking to bring on more staff with the season now underway. One of the busier establishments in town, it boasted live entertainment, and was easily spotted by a sign lined with electric light bulbs. For reasons that Etta could not begin to guess, the “O” was capitalized and displayed prominently.

Mark had worked here for years, recently making his way up to the senior wait staff. He said that the pay for bussers was modest, but tips were generally good from the out-of-towners. It was preferable to hauling eggs into town every day, and so she had accepted his offer to put her in touch with the owner and maître d', Mr. Mustache.

“Table six spilled a drink. Clean it up. Now.”

He had leaned in close, and Etta likewise turned her ear to hear him over the band. It was, however, unnecessary. He had been repeating the same orders to her and the rest of the staff throughout the evening: get the next course out. Keep the water glasses filled. Let them know we have wine, but only if they don't look like an out-of-town cop. Someone made a mess. Tend to it.

At first, she had taken the urgency of his tone at face value. The place was bustling, and things needed to be done quickly. So she complied. After an hour or so of running around, Etta had come to the conclusion that the urgency was perhaps unwarranted. She further suspected that Mr. Mustache was used to dealing with less responsive staff, and had fallen into a habit of speaking as if everything was an emergency.

His name, of course, was not "Mr. Mustache" and Etta was not usually one for pettiness, but something about the man just rubbed her the wrong way. As one accustomed to hard work, Etta found his commanding manner chafing. She consoled herself that the pay would be higher than what she could usually earn. Eventually, she gave less heed to his tone, and the rest of the evening went much more smoothly.

As she relaxed, Etta started to notice little things. One of the busboys was definitely pocketing silverware. One of the waitresses was making big eyes at the younger cook. And the bushy Kaiser bill mustache sported by the owner twitched in a distracting way as he spoke.

Little that she knew of fashion, the Kaiser bill had gone out of style nearly a decade ago. And the way it twitched – for some reason – reminded her of a mouse. The first time she saw it, Etta literally bit her tongue to suppress the sudden impulse to laugh. Thankfully, his habit of speaking quickly and moving on meant that she did not have to restrain herself for long.

After he walked away, Etta quickly glanced over her shoulder before allowing herself to smile. Walking towards table six and trying to get the giggles out of her system, she adjusted her necktie.

It was the first time she had ever worn one, and she had been fussing with the silly thing all evening. The tie and the white shirt were both borrowed from her father in order to comply with the staff dress code. As far as issues go, it was minor.

The occupants of table six were on the dance floor as she mopped up the spilled drink. The music had certainly been a perk. Except for the church ensemble, she could not remember the last time she had heard an actual band up close. CasinO had long been known for its entertainment, and on several occasions, she and Irene had sneaked away to listen from across the lake. On good nights, they could almost hear entire songs. Up close, it was an incredible experience even if she was working.

Throughout the evening, she stole glances at the band. One member in particular. The trumpet player was a young man with blonde, slicked back hair, and handsome as anything. They made eye contact once, but Etta was so nervous that she quickly turned away. After a while, she worked up the courage to look again and this time, she not only found him staring back at her, but he actually winked.

As Etta's brains threatened to leak out her ears, Mr. Mustache sharply admonished her to get back to work.

Though she kept her eyes down, for all intents and purposes focused on the task before her, Etta's ears were all about the music. Some songs she recognized, but many were entirely new to her. For someone without a working radio, to hear a new song was really quite the novelty. If her usual routine was comfortable, this was an area in which she was happy to try something different.

The food was another side benefit. After her first few tables, she noticed that more than a few people hardly touched their plates. As one accustomed to skipping a meal three or more times a week and unable to disregard even a morsel, this was shocking. Discretely, she pocketed as many dinner rolls would fit beneath her apron. It would be nice to have bread in the morning instead of making bread in the morning for a change.

Mark Saunders caught her attention as he walked by in his wait staff costume. Etta had come to think of everyone's attire as a costume instead of a uniform. It was in stark contrast to the second-hand work clothes he typically wore around the farm.

Throughout the evening, he had offered some guidance on the restaurant and how things were done. It was immensely helpful, allowing her to avoid a couple of faux pas. Most of it was easy enough to follow – avoid grabbing the plates while people are seated, and such. She firmly disagreed with him on his insistence that Mr. Mustache was not really an awful sort, and just took some getting-used-to. Other than that, the evening was going smoothly enough, and she hoped this job would work out. Compared to her typical day, it was a much easier way to earn a living.

“The band is about to take a break,” Mark said. “After you clear table six, can you bring out their main course as quick as you can?”

Etta hesitated. “I haven't carried the full plates before.”

Mark looked desperate. “I've got to move tables four and five and we're running behind. Can you help me?”

The dirty plates were one thing; heavy, but just tossed into a bin she could haul away without undue struggle. She had seen the wait staff carry the large serving trays all evening, and immediately doubted her balance. Never one to avoid doing her part, she agreed despite her reservations. Mark thanked her and moved away.

The band finished playing as she piled the dirty salad plates into the bin. As the crowd applauded, the bandleader informed them that they would resume after dinner. Etta cursed as the occupants of table six returned. She planned on having another two minutes at least. Hastily, she piled the remaining dishes into the bin and made for the kitchen.

At least three or four waiters yelled for her to clear out of the way as they came through with dinner plates. Reflexively, Etta pressed herself against the nearest wall to make a path. Despite seeing this sort of hustle and bustle all evening, she could not help but feel slightly chagrined when none of them said "excuse me," or "thank you."

Setting the bin of dirty dishes next to two others just like it, Etta heard the dishwashers at the sink sigh despondently. She silently mouthed the word "sorry," and went to get the food for table six. Mark scooped up a tray in one fluid motion and expertly balanced it between his outstretched hand and shoulder. It looked effortless. Of course, Mark's arms were longer than Etta's.

Meeting her eyes, he motioned to the remaining tray and headed out of the kitchen, leaving Etta alone to deal with it. With some trepidation, she approached, but had no idea how to lift it. If it were a bag of chicken feed, she could hug it and flip it over her shoulder, but that would not work here. As she stood with indecision, Mr. Mustache poked his head into the kitchen.

"Table six! Where are you?" he called from the door.

Etta's head snapped around, but he had already disappeared. Returning her attention to the food tray, she hesitated again.

"Get under it," said another voice.

She looked up to find one of the cooks standing there.

"Pardon?" she replied.

He looked familiar, but his name escaped her. A Townie for sure. Maybe she recognized him from church. His expression was harried, yet patient. Pointing at the tray, he motioned with his hands.

"Squat down, and slide it off the counter onto your shoulder."

She nodded, but he disappeared back amongst the ovens and shelves of pots and pans before she could ask any follow-up questions. Realizing that this was the last tray of food, and Mr. Mustache was growing impatient, she decided to simply act. Even anticipating the weight of the tray, it was heavier than she thought it would be. At first, she tried to copy what Mark had done with one hand, and nearly lost it.

"Two hands!" the cook yelled from somewhere unseen.

She caught it just as it started to wobble, and let out a sigh of relief as it stabilized. Once standing upright, she began a cautious, deliberate march toward the door. Upon reaching it, she hesitated and debated which hand to release. This being her first night, Etta had forgotten that the door could swing both ways to avoid this exact issue.

Before she could rediscover this for herself, the door opened before her. Standing beyond was a familiar, blonde man holding a trumpet in his free hand.

"Coming out?" he asked.

For half a second she felt her grip on the tray slip, but recovered just in time. It was her musician. The one who had winked at her. He was taller up close, and she not previously realized what a striking shade of blue his eyes were. Etta did not move, having temporarily forgotten what she had been about to do. The trumpet player watched her, an easy grin on his face, and remained holding the door.

When she made no move, he raised an eyebrow questioningly. While Etta was searching for something to say, the door to the main hall burst open with Mr. Mustache behind it.

"Table six!" The comical appearance of his twitching facial hair was somewhat offset by the now beet-red color of his face. The musician regarded the intrusion with cool detachment, as if a child was trying to get a word in edge-wise with the adults. With a smirk, he adjusted the strap of the trumpet case where it rested on his shoulder. Temporarily distracted, Etta wondered why the trumpet was not in its case, but then he looked back to her.

"Well. Better get going then."

He winked at her, and she suddenly had a rising urge to tell Mr. Mustache to deliver the tray himself. Instead, her feet carried her towards the main room of their own accord. After several steps, she glanced back to see the musician had remained, watching her go. Her wayward thoughts snapped back into focus as the glower of Mr. Mustache grew closer, and the handsome blonde man grew more distant.

The entrance to the main room was a double set of barn style doors, but Mr. Mustache was only holding one of them open. Approaching, she soon realized that the tray was not going to fit through the open side. She hesitated under the weight of his displeasure, distracted by it. Likewise, he was too busy scowling to notice that he was blocking her way.

At this point, a few things might have happened differently. Etta might have realized that she could back into the opposite door in order to push it open, same as with the kitchen. Or she could have asked Mr. Mustache to move. Likewise, had he not been focused on Etta, he might have noticed the other busboy walking up behind him.

As Etta was carefully and slowly turning sideways, thinking she could angle the tray just enough to clear the open side of the door, the opposite one burst open.

To her credit, she managed to keep both hands on the tray, but it did nothing to prevent the contents from clattering to the floor. Chicken, beef, and fish all splattered and mixed with shattered porcelain and ringing utensils. With a final flourish, Etta lost the tray itself when the busboy collided with her. It landed on the whole mess, and rolled once or twice before coming to a stop.

After it was over, she and the busboy just stared. The silence that followed, especially with the band taking a break, was near tangible. All the guests momentarily forgot about their conversations and meals, to look at the commotion. With a mix of pity, a little good-natured mockery, and no small amount of alcohol, they erupted in applause.

For her part, Etta's thoughts were partially split between utter embarrassment and dread at the inevitable verbal thrashing. However, all of it paled against her unbridled and agonizing remorse over wasted food. In one small grace, the blonde musician was no longer standing in the hallway. Perhaps he had not seen. But Helen's brother certainly did.

The look on Mark’s face was a clear indication that her dread of Mr. Mustache was not misplaced, despite any insistence that the man “wasn't a bad sort.” On top of it all, she cringed as she became aware of sauce in her hair.

Etta and the busboy spent some time cleaning up the mess. As the rest of the wait and bus staff continued to work, passing through the area, nearly all of them took the opportunity to give comment. For the most part, it was just friendly teasing, but in Etta's opinion some of it was simply mean. The word “rube” had been uttered at one point so at least one person recognized her as a farmer.

Townies...

After finishing, Etta returned to the kitchen with the tray of broken plates and mangled food and sauce in her hair. The dishwashers gave her a scathing look as she handed the mess over, but ultimately said nothing. The cook, however, gave her a sympathetic smile as he set a final plate down on the new serving tray.

“I wondered if that was you,” he said.

She frowned in response.

"Don't fret over it. We usually lose a couple of plates every week. We just met quota a little earlier than usual."

That actually did make her feel slightly better. "Mr. Mustache didn't see it that way," she said.

The cook tilted his head slightly, squinting his eyes.

Oh no, she thought, *Did I just said 'Mr. Mustache' out loud?*

The cook let out a hearty chuckle. "'Mr. Mustache.'" he repeated. "That's good. I'll have to remember that one."

He frowned at the new tray, and then held up a finger, asking her to wait. Searching the kitchen, he found what he was looking for above the stove but could not reach it. Curious, Etta watched him grab a large cutting board from somewhere out of sight and set it on top of the hot cook top. Using it to boost himself up without getting burned, he quickly retrieved a pair of salt and pepper shakers from the high shelf and set them on the tray.

"Good luck with this one," he continued. "I think we're all out of the beef, so take care. Try to spread your grip a little more and mind the door." He gave her a final nod and retrieved the cutting board.

The rest of the evening went well enough, all things considered. The occupants of table six gave her a final round of friendly teasing as she delivered their food. They were in good spirits about the whole thing, despite the delay.

Somewhat to her relief, she was relegated to filling up water glasses, and clearing dirty plates after that. She even managed to avoid any more altercations with Mr. Mustache, whose ire was focused more on the busboy who had collided with her. Even better, the band had started up again and the blonde trumpet player was with them.

Etta continued to watch the stage as much as she could without attracting the notice of Mr. Mustache. To her disappointment, she failed to make eye contact with the trumpet player again. After several songs, she started to wonder if she had actually seen him wink earlier. Then, with more embarrassment, she wondered if he had seen the incident with the food tray.

Eventually, the evening was over. The band thanked the crowd for a delightful evening, and began to pack up. The guests cleared out, still loud and boisterous. Then, the real work began.

It took the better part of an hour to clear off the tables and move the chairs off the floor. Then the floor itself had to be swept. Etta shook her head, amazed at the mess, which did nothing to improve her opinion of out-of-towners. At one point, she found a woman's abandoned shoe.

Who loses one shoe?

The busboy that caused the accident eventually approached her to apologize. That was something at least. Then, Mr. Mustache confronted the two of them, ordering them over to help wash dishes. The boy started to protest, but let the matter drop.

The two dishwashers almost gleefully handed over their aprons and left them with about five bins' worth of plates, cups, and utensils. With naught to do but get it done, Etta and the busboy set about their task. Mark came over while they still had two full bins to go, looking exhausted. Likely, he had just received an earful from Mr. Mustache regarding the new busgirl he had vouched for.

"I'll wait outside for when you're done," he said.

Etta looked at the remaining dishes and felt doubly guilty at the idea of making him wait.

"No. Go on home. No sense in you staying too."

"You sure?" he asked. He was trying to be polite and not appear too eager to leave, but he clearly wanted to take her up on the offer.

Etta nodded. After Mark thanked her and promised to see her tomorrow, he left.

It ended up being closer to an hour by the time they were finished, and they went to find Mr. Mustache to receive their payment for the evening. They found him in a small office upstairs, where he was still dressed in his dinner jacket, complete with the shirt buttoned up to his throat. Apparently, the man simply did not relax. He let them stand in the doorway for several seconds as he scribbled in a ledger.

"May I presume that you did not break any more plates while cleaning them?" he asked almost conversationally, and finally raised his eyes.

Etta and the busboy nodded, ignoring the none-too-subtle insult. Mr. Mustache regarded them both before turning around, and reached for something near to the floor. Sneaking a peak, Etta saw there was a safe with the door sitting ajar.

Retrieving a stack of greenbacks, Mr. Mustache counted out two smaller stacks for each of them.

"That's principal, plus your share of the gratuity."

Etta suppressed a groan. It was less than what Mark had originally estimated. Still, she reckoned it was more that what she would get from a few days of selling eggs. Then, to her dismay, Mr. Mustache reached out and plucked a dollar from each pile, and returned them to his stack.

He continued, "That's the cost of a table's worth of plates and glasses."

Then he pulled yet another two bills from each pile making Etta's shoulders actually slump.

"And that's the cost of the food that was on them." He squared the edges of each stack of bills and waved with his hand to indicate that he was done.

The busboy quickly grabbed for his stack and shoved it into his pocket before Mr. Mustache could trim it further. Etta made no move to take hers and looked at the maître d' expectantly. After a moment of returning her stare, Mr. Mustache sighed.

"I suppose you feel that you're being treated unfairly?"

"Not at all. I'm just waiting for you to add the payment for washing five bins' worth of dishes."

Mr. Mustache blinked, and then furrowed his eyebrows. Etta stood, unflinching. The busboy looked back and forth between them with uncertainty. After a moment, the maître d' scoffed but nodded to himself and added another dollar to her payment. The busboy leaned forward, clearly hoping for the same, but Mr. Mustache stopped him with a glare.

After squaring the stack of bills, he returned them to the safe. Turning back around, he folded his arms across his chest, making it clear that there was no more room for negotiation. Sighing, Etta finally picked up her money. She might have pressed the matter, but it was already going to be a long walk home, and dawn was only getting closer. Even so, she reckoned that she had still come out ahead. In a month, it might even be enough for the tax payment, but it would be a near thing. Before they could turn to leave, Mr. Mustache spoke.

"You can come back tomorrow," he said, nodding to the busboy. Then, to Etta, "Your services are no longer required. Good night."

Outside, the air was dry and chilly, and felt doubly so after leaving the hot kitchen. Upon clearing the door, the busboy immediately turned and walked straight away from Etta without a word. As if he might become tainted by her presence if he lingered for too long. She supposed that she could not blame him, though it underscored her predicament. Briefly, Etta thought about Mark and hoped that he would not catch any grief on her account. Mr. Mustache gave her every impression of being the vindictive type.

Now knowing what the job actually paid, Etta decided that it was not such a huge loss. If her employment continued, haggling over her payment seemed likely to be a common occurrence. To Etta, that would have been more exhausting than the work itself. Although, the music was certainly nice.

The music and that blonde trumpet player. That really was a shame. Briefly, she had thought about introducing herself the next time she was working. Maybe without smashing a tray of dishes mere seconds later.

As she turned toward Route Six to begin her long walk home, a voice caught her attention.

"Hello there." It was a man's voice, and immediately sounded familiar, but she could not place it. There had been many voices that evening. Stopping, she looked around. The restaurant's lights cast a limited aura, and blinded her to what was beyond. Instinctively, she pulled her coat tighter.

The owner of the voice stepped into the light, his blonde hair shining. Etta immediately felt her guard dissolve.

"Oh," was all she could manage to say.

His trumpet case was slung over his shoulder again, but presumably containing the instrument this time. With his hands in his pockets, he stood at ease despite the evening chill.

"I was afraid I might have missed you," he said. "Maybe you had gone out another door or something." He looked at her expectantly, and it took her several seconds to think of a response.

"No. I – ah – was just getting paid," she explained. "But I had to wash dishes first."

"Right. Didn't break any more, I hope." He grinned and winked again.

At first, her stomach fluttered, but soon gave way to a fresh wave of embarrassment.

"You saw that?"

"Oh, doll," he replied, apologetically. "The whole joint saw that." He shrugged. "Don't think nothin' of it. One time, I saw a waiter spill soup onto four different guests. You'll do better next time."

"Actually, I won't," she replied.

He cocked his head in question.

"I've been informed that 'my services are no longer required.'"

"Wow. You actually got sacked over that?"

"I think it had more to do with my demanding payment for washing the dishes." She shrugged. "Probably should have kept quiet about it."

"What? That's outrageous!"

His response was more energetic than Etta felt was warranted, and she took a step back. His sudden shift from lighthearted and charming to angry caught her by surprise.

"Damn worker exploitation is what that is." He was silent as he frowned. Then, perhaps seeing her response, he made an effort to relax and softened his tone. "You want me to talk with him? I don't mean to boast, but I have an uncle that's connected in this town. I can make life very unpleasant for this bourgeois asshole."

"Um... no thank you," Etta said. His sudden change in tone had been strange, and she was not accustomed to men swearing in front of her. She continued, "This job wasn't a good fit for me anyhow. Though, I did enjoy the music."

The trumpet player's mood brightened at the inferred compliment, and he resumed his air of easy confidence.

"Always nice to meet a fan of the craft. I've been touring with Rick for about two years now. You ever hear us play before?"

She shook her head. "No. Well, not up close anyway. Usually, the only music I hear is at church-"

He nodded as if he was listening, but carried on before she had actually finished speaking. "We're mostly booked in Jersey this summer, but we got a couple gigs in New York and Philly too."

This caught her interest, despite the interruption.

"Do you spend much time in the city?" asked Etta.

The blonde boy grinned. "A decent amount," he replied smoothly. "So, what's your name, Gorgeous?"

Still wearing her father's shirt stained with dried food, she hardly felt gorgeous. However, the compliment was well received, despite being just a little more direct than she would prefer.

"I'm Etta. And you?"

"Walter Hoffman," he said, extending his hand. "Good to meet you." As they shook, he brought up his other hand, clasping hers between both of his.

His hands were soft and completely absent of calluses, which was unlike most of the men she knew. Walter held hers for just a shade longer than propriety would normally call for. Despite Etta's typical aversion to public displays of affection, she might have let the moment continue.

Standing just outside the cone of light surrounding the restaurant, they were largely concealed by the darkness of night. Besides that, there was hardly anyone around to be concealed from. Still, something about Walter was making her uncomfortable, though she could not exactly put her finger on what it was. As she gently but firmly withdrew her hand, Walter's mouth flattened to a line, though his easy smile soon returned.

"You got a husband, Etta?"

She blinked at the directness of the question. "I beg your pardon?"

"A husband. You know, a *Mister* Plate-Breaker." He winked again over the latter part.

"I... no. Why do you ask?"

He shrugged with blatant faux innocence. "Just making conversation." He frowned at something behind her. "Who's this then?"

Etta saw their shadows suddenly cast across the side of the building. Turning around, she was temporarily blinded by the headlights of the truck. It stopped about twenty feet away, with its side facing them. Etta recognized it before her father stuck his head out the window.

"Hi, Papa," she said, suddenly feeling both surprised and extremely self-conscious of the boy standing behind her.

"Are you ready to go home, Etta?" He spoke evenly, not acknowledging that anything was amiss. Still, she could not imagine that he would leave the matter alone.

"Um... yes," she replied. As she took a step toward the truck, she fought the urge to turn around and say goodnight. There was a grasping-at-straws, naive hope that if she did not look at Walter, her father would somehow fail to notice him.

"I'll be here the next two nights," he whispered, just loud enough for her alone to hear.

Etta nodded without looking back.

After she climbed in the truck, Jakob pulled back onto Route Six heading home. Neither of them spoke for a full minute. The whole time, she tried to think up what to say about Walter, expecting her father to ask about him. Even though it was a brief and entirely innocent interaction, she was concerned about how it appeared.

"How was your first night as a waitress?" Papa finally asked.

"It was fine," she replied simply, not bothering to correct him that her role had been a buser not a waitress. Similarly, she refrained from explaining that it was also her last night. "I'm afraid I got a few kinds of sauce on your white shirt," she continued.

"A few kinds?" he chuckled. "Maybe we can scrape it off for supper."

She smiled at his dry humor, relaxing just a bit. A thought occurred to her. "How did you know to come and pick me up?"

"Helen's brother stopped by on his way home. Mentioned you were up to your elbows in dirty dishes and might be late." He paused. When he spoke again his tone was serious. "I didn't like the thought of you walking along Route Six late at night."

He left the full reason unspoken, but Etta knew all too well. This section of road had taken not one, but two members of their family.

Even now, years later, it was difficult for Jakob to talk about the accidents, at least with Etta. After all, she had been responsible for the first, and the second could arguably be put on her as well. Papa looked out the window and crossed himself as they passed an otherwise unremarkable section of roadway along the lake's southern shore.

Etta looked out the window as well, but did not move. This was one of the many ways that she and her father differed. While Jakob held reverence for the actual location where Lena had been struck by the car, for Etta it was just a place on the road. Everyone's final resting place was what Etta kept sacred.

Likewise, Jakob had never visited the cemetery. Not once, as far as Etta knew. For her first couple of visits, she had invited him to accompany her, thinking it would help them to grieve together. He had declined and eventually she simply stopped asking. Etta tried not to hold it against him. She supposed he had his reasons, but they spoke about it so seldom that she could not say what they were.

Papa soon crossed himself for a second time, and the truck slowed down just enough for Etta to notice. She did not look, but knew exactly where they were.

This was where Irene had died.

When she walked past these spots just a few hours earlier, Etta had not given them a second thought, but Papa's reaction was impossible to ignore. Perhaps that was the reason she kept her mourning in the cemetery. How crippling it would be to grant such significance to a place that one passed every day. Papa released a heavy sigh and an agonizing pang of guilt settled upon Etta.

Looking out the opposite window, away from the place that Papa regarded with misty eyes, Etta tried not to think about the day of the crash. Over the years, she had devoted much thought to how it might have gone differently. Mostly things she herself could have done.

While the jalopy on the hilltop was her most recent infatuation for an automobile, her first love had been the family's Studebaker. Papa had started giving her driving lessons after she turned sixteen; the autumn before the accident. She loved it. During the winter and following spring, she looked for any excuse to get back behind the wheel.

Papa almost always granted permission, but had been adamant that she was never to drive without him. In hindsight, his caution was understandable, as they had already lost three children by 1924. Etta had not shared this concern, wanting only to feel the wind pull her hair again.

Irene had recently turned eleven, and she wanted to spend her birthday money on some sweets at the shop in town. Thinking they could make the trip quickly enough to return undiscovered, Etta had been the one to suggest taking the car. After half a year, she reasoned that she had enough experience. In fact, Papa had already hinted at the possibility of letting her drive by herself. Soon. But not quite yet. Feeling brazen on this particular day, and with no one around to tell her "no" Etta simply disregarded the standing rule.

One moment, Etta and her sister had been driving down this particular stretch of Route Six, and the next thing she knew she was laying on the ground with several people fussing over her. Many of the details remained fuzzy to her. However, the image of Irene lying on the nearby ground, draped in a sheet would remain etched into her mind's eye for as long as she lived.

According to Papa, their car had been struck by an out-of-towner driving in the opposite direction. The man had been admiring the lake, and failed to notice that Route Six turned away at that particular spot. The same spot where Etta and Irene happened to be.

It was, by all accounts, a tragic accident.

Curiously, Papa never addressed the fact that Etta had taken the car without permission. Left unspoken was that if she had not, Irene might still be alive. As a lesser concern, maybe Papa would not have stopped her lessons, and denied any future requests to borrow their other vehicle.

Minutes passed and neither of them spoke. After they pulled off the main road and started making their way through the cottages back towards the farm, Etta remembered something less troubling.

"I almost forgot," she said, digging through her apron pockets. "Compliments of the kitchen."

He thanked her as she handed over one of the dinner rolls she had pilfered. Etta felt no need to elaborate that they had come off someone else's plate.

"Well now, this is something. You should line your pockets with handkerchiefs next time in case they want to gift you some steak."

They both chewed in silence, and she realized just how long it had been since her last meal. Papa never mentioned anything about Walter. Maybe he had simply not seen him, but that was unlikely. Even little as they spoke, it was odd that he apparently let the matter go unremarked. In the end, Etta was exhausted after a long day and was simply thankful to avoid this particular conversation.

That night, she fell asleep thinking about a life in the city, filled with music.

Chapter 6
Art

The last few days had been overcast. Despite being well into June, an unexpected and unwanted chill had returned. No one was swimming, and even the boaters were fewer than they had been the week before. A setback for most, the unseasonable weather happened to work in Art's favor. Had it been sunny and hot, he would have been sweating buckets by the time he reached where he was going. This morning, his plan required an extra set of clothes.

Getting out of the house had been a challenge. Art was reluctant to simply disappear without an explanation, and not just because he was sure to get an earful upon his eventual return. He had devoted much of the previous evening and this morning coming up with a plausible excuse. Expecting that his father would try to take him on another sales run, Art was surprised to find that it was not George who intended to fill his day.

Luciana had scheduled him to go to a local tailor to get measured for his wedding suit, wanting to have it finished before Dorothy arrived in town. Up until now, the mothers had handled most of the wedding details between themselves; an arrangement that suited all concerned. Dorothy was busy with her studies, and Art was ignoring the matter with determination. This was one instance, however, that required his direct involvement.

The original plan had been for Art and his mother to go to the tailor together. Luciana, naturally, wanted to ensure the material and cut held up to her standards. However, Art was well aware that a suit fitting in the morning would be followed by three or four other errands that would consume the better part of the day. This particular wrinkle was unexpected, and might have torpedoed his plans, but he caught a break.

Little Georgie had a bathroom accident, which required a change of clothes. To Martha's dismay, Luciana had decided to intervene. In a stroke of inspiration, Art casually mentioned that he would only have his measurements taken today, and his mother would still have a chance to make adjustments when he returned for the fitting. To his surprise, she agreed, but made him promise not to let the tailor sell him on anything too garish or loud. He was to look modest and gentlemanly. After agreeing, he bolted out the door before she could change her mind.

Once out of sight of the house, he took a quick glance around and removed the extra layer of clothes. Underneath was a set of work coveralls that he had purchased from a second-hand store. Even with the chilly air, the second set of clothes had been causing him to sweat. Rolling up the now discarded articles into a small bag, he continued walking.

Finding his way took some time, and it was nearly an hour later by the time he reached the old mill. The sound of grinding and hammering greeted him as he headed up the drive. The gray-haired man was working again. Art suddenly stopped, feet rooted to the ground in a sudden pang of doubt. It was not too late to turn around. This plan was stupid. There was no way he could pull it off. With growing uncertainty, he shifted his weight, intending to walk straight back to the cottage.

Then, he considered what he would do once he returned. He would have to explain to his mother that he had not gone to his fitting, and of course she would insist on going back out with him. Then, the rest of the day would no longer be his own. Reminded of his reasons for leaving in the first place, he turned back to the mill.

This can be done, he told himself. *Just do what Ralph would do*.

While there was no love lost between Art and his older brother, there was no denying that for some reason, people liked the jackass. Steeling himself, Art adjusted the bundle under his arm and marched toward the open barn door.

The older man had his aviator goggles pulled down, and was grinding at a part with singular focus. While he was half-facing Art, the edges of his vision were blocked off and he had not yet seen the interloper. Dismissing one last, nagging doubt, Art walked around the worktable to make himself known. After a few more seconds of grinding, the man looked up and was startled to see someone standing there. With some effort, Art remained still.

The gray man's expression quickly changed to annoyed. Art cringed, thinking that this was not a good start.

“You again,” said the man as he removed the cotton from his ears. Sliding the goggles onto his forehead, he sighed. “What do you want, now, kid?”

Art stared blankly, his shoulders threatening to slump under the implied rebuke. Then, taking a deep breath, he straightened up and put on his best smile.

“Good morning, sir. What I want is a job, if you'll have me. And my name's Art Adams, not 'kid.'”

The man let out a single, bemused laugh. Then, after a moment's pause, half his mouth turned up in a grin.

“Yeah? Just like that, huh?” He looked Art up and down. “You're certainly dressed for the part. What happened to your suit?”

“That wasn’t really appropriate for metalwork. I've actually spent some time in a shop, and know my way around tools.” Art made a show of looking around the shop. “I believe you said that you were 'six weeks behind.' Is that right?” George, rather than Ralph had inspired that last line, but in the moment Art thought it appropriate.

“That's a fact.” The man smoothed his mustache, in thought. “What’s your experience?”

“About four years' doing tool and die work, and more than that at my family's repair shop.” The latter was true enough, referring to the time when the family business was Adams Repair and they fixed the appliances instead of selling them.

The former was an exaggeration. While at school, Art took a few night shifts each month at a local fabrication shop for extra spending money. It had mostly consisted of breaking the sharp edges off finished parts and counting them. Probably not real work as the other man had asked, but Art decided to omit that detail.

“If you care to check my references, we can send a telegram to Dickey Randall in Philadelphia. He can vouch for me.”

This got a genuine chuckle from the older man.

“'References',” he repeated with a smile. “No. No need for that.”

He stared at Art, who made every effort to keep his back straight and head up.

“Alright,” the man said at last. “You can start off with finishing this part. Consider it your interview. If you still have all your fingers when you're done, you can stick around.” The man winked, and extended his hand.

Art suppressed the urge to sigh with relief. “Thank you, sir.”

The older man scoffed. “Name's Gregory Robbins. Not 'sir.'”

Art did, in fact, keep all of his fingers, even though they ached something awful by the time he was finished. Gregory had set him to work grinding a small pile of scythe-like, metal teeth into shape for something called a ripper plow. The machine, built to dig lines in packed soil in preparation for planting, had been run into a buried rock, snapping a bunch of its teeth and damaging the frame to which they were mounted.

After straightening the frame, they needed a piece of scrap to brace it. Gregory happened to have one, but it was buried within the pile of past and discarded projects. The process of digging it out was both time consuming and physically demanding.

Metal, it turned out, is quite heavy.

They spoke little as they worked, aside from occasional instructions from Gregory. Eventually, they located the piece, and Art was impressed. Judging from the amount of clutter, it might have been there for months, if not years, yet the older man had remembered both that he had it as well as its precise location. A similar process occurred throughout the day.

As different tools were necessary for different tasks, Gregory would ask Art to get it. When he inevitably came up empty-handed, Gregory would go to seemingly a random drawer without hesitation, pluck out the requested tool, and return to work. Art could not help but marvel at the mental prowess necessary to keep track of so many different things, which Gregory cryptically referred to as his "system."

Gradually, Art began to make sense of the workshop's state of organized chaos. To his credit, he never had to be shown the same location twice, and this fact was not lost on Gregory.

"I actually had a 'prentice once before," the older man said during their short break for lunch. He had left Art alone for a few minutes working a rusted nut loose, and returned holding a few hard-boiled eggs. "He quit after one day, and complained about my system the whole time. Hope you like eggs, by the way. I grabbed a couple extra from the girl that comes by."

Setting down the work piece, Art realized that he was quite hungry, despite his large breakfast.

"It's not so bad once you get the lay of the land," Art replied after taking a few bites. "But in all fairness, I would never expect to find assorted springs in the drawer right next to wrenches."

Gregory chuckled.

“That's actually a carryover from when the shop was smaller. I just put stuff wherever it would fit. Of course, the machines were still driven by water wheel back then.” He sighed. “Oh, I'm sure there are better ways to organize the place. But this is just what I know.” Gregory shook his head, and changed the subject. “As for the plow, the bracing pieces look about right. Now we need to attach them. Normally, I might cold rivet them, but I've been looking for an excuse to use this other thing.”

Gregory directed Art back to the corner of the workshop that had become the repository for random, incomplete assemblies and other junk. Taking the better part of an hour to move things around, they finally reached an item about the size of a small icebox. Art pulled away the dirty old sheet that had been covering it to reveal a pair of large, cylindrical tanks and a coil of hose draped around them.

“Gas welder,” Gregory explained. “I used to work at the Navy Storage Depot a couple towns over, back when I was in the service. After the war effort started winding down, they sold a bunch of the old equipment. Been a while since I've gotten to use it.”

“Should we practice on some scrap first?”

Gregory narrowed his eyes and pursed his lips as if he just tasted something bitter.

“Might be some benefit to that,” he muttered.

Art sensed that there was an element of pride at work here. The very suggestion that Gregory might be out of practice with one of his own tools chafed him. The likelihood that it was true only made matters worse.

“Could you *teach* me how it works?” Art ventured. He actually was genuinely curious. There was something primal and intriguing about using fire to bond metal. He had seen welders at the Philadelphia shop a handful of times, but never did it himself.

It also provided Gregory with a balm to his injured pride. Still, the older man made a show of thinking it over.

“Probably I could bang this out in an hour, but I reckon it couldn't hurt for you to know how to do it too.”

It was more of a refresher for Gregory, who – as it turned out – probably could have jumped right into the real thing. With only limited practice, his beads were neat, and tight, like a row of stacked dimes. Art's progress was more gradual, and his work was ugly. Sloppy and wide, like a dripping candle. Still, he succeeded in producing one bead that survived a heavy strike from Gregory's hammer.

They had only been able to find one pair of welding glasses, so Gregory was obliged to look away while Art was working and vice versa. Once or twice, Art attempted to watch, eager to learn and curious to see how he might improve, but Gregory chased him off.

"Keep that up, and you'll be blind before you're thirty."

A real stickler for safety, Gregory actually smacked Art in the chest for emphasis upon his second warning. He did not require a third.

The sun was low over the horizon by the time they finished. Even if he left now, it would be near dark by the time Art arrived back at the cottage. Still, he and Gregory took a few moments to stand back with their arms crossed and admire the finished plow.

"Still need to grind the welds smooth, and give it a coat of paint, but I reckon that'll do us," Gregory said.

Art nodded, feeling a certain satisfaction at the process. It had been a while since he had seen something tangible take shape, knowing he had done it with his own hands. There was simply no substitute for it. After they finished savoring a job well done, Gregory turned to him.

"I'll probably come out after supper once it's cooled down and finish up, but you can go on home." He offered his hand. "Nice working with you. Come back tomorrow if you like."

"I'd be happy to," Art replied as they shook hands.

Gregory suddenly frowned.

"I just realized we never discussed your payment. A man should get compensated for what he produces."

They spent the next few minutes in discussion. It was a challenge for both of them since Gregory had not employed anyone in years and Art had no sense of how much to ask for. They finally agreed on an amount that was fair to both, and hashed out a provisional schedule. Gregory had a daughter and granddaughter who lived out of town, and he closed the shop a few days each week to visit them.

Working days were to start early. Art agreed to arrive shortly after dawn with some hesitation. It occurred to him that disappearing before breakfast a few times each week might raise questions with his parents. On the one hand, his father might be pleased that he was earning. More likely, he would decry this kind of work as "low" and not fit for an Adams man.

Over the following week, he spent a total of four days helping Gregory. After the owner of the plow returned for it, they started on the next project. It was one of the machines Art had briefly admired upon his first visit. Looking at it again, he attempted to work out the function of the mess of pulleys, belts, gears and linkages that made up the structure. Amused by Art's apparent infatuation, Gregory let him ponder it before speaking.

"Figure it out yet?" he asked.

Art frowned, shaking his head, but his eyes remained on the machine before him.

"I mean, the engine drives the large belt and this wheel here," he pointed.

"Uh huh..."

"This here, looks like it might be a reciprocating mechanism, but missing a couple parts." Then, finally he looked over and said, "I think I know how it works, I just can't figure out what it *does*."

Gregory chuckled.

"No, I don't suppose you would've seen one of these working before. It's a hay baler." He pointed at a wide, ribbed belt near, what Art had been thinking of as the back end of the apparatus. "Loose hay goes in there." Then, he walked around to the front and pointed to a long chute. "Cubes of hay come out here."

Art looked for another long moment, considering this new information, and eventually nodded to himself. The final piece of the puzzle helped bring it all together.

"But what presses the hay into bales?" Art asked.

"That's where we come in. You were right. A piece is missing. Normally a big piston packs it in from the top of the chute here," he pointed. "But it was making an odd noise, and Mitch Grayson decided to take it apart to see what was causing it. Can't say I wouldn't have done the same, but then he misplaced the piston."

Art looked between Gregory and the machine. Based on where the part was supposed to go, he tried to guess at its approximate size.

"That couldn't have been a small part to lose."

Gregory chuckled again. "It's not. If you knew the man, you'd understand."

"Where do we get a new one?" Art asked.

Greg made a show of looking around the shop.

"There's quarter inch plate over there. If we need more, I've got a friend in Dover, owes me a favor. And we have more than enough round stock for the pins. Just need to turn 'em on the lathe. All said and done, I'd guess this will keep us busy for the next three to four weeks."

"You know what it looks like?" Art asked, furrowing his brow.

"More or less," Gregory replied without particular inflection or apparent concern. "We'll have to match it to fit the baler."

"How are we going to replace something without knowing what it looks like?" Art asked.

Gregory shrugged as if this were trivial. "We know where it has to go and what it has to do. Isn't that enough?"

"I suppose, but that seems really hard."

"It will certainly be a challenge," Gregory replied. He grinned, and after a moment so did Art.

"When do we start?"

Chapter 7
Etta

The day after her first and only evening as a busgirl, Etta returned to her usual routine. All the while, her thoughts were never far from CasinO and the promise of meeting Walter again. As her morning route took her along the lake's northern shore, her eyes kept drifting across the water, to catch a glimpse of the boxy, white building.

Briefly, she considered taking a detour from her rounds, in the hope that she might run into him. Eventually, this idea was dismissed since it would add a couple hours to her walk, which she could not afford. Besides, she was in her work clothes. While certainly comfortable, they were not right for meeting with a boy.

The invitation was plain enough, though short on details. He said that he would be around for the next two nights and so she planned to get there after the show would be over. The lateness of the hour was unfortunate, but meeting a well-traveled musician was a rare thing. The cost of a few hours of sleep was a fair trade.

Etta had every intention to return to CasinO that first evening, but never made it.

Visiting with Helen at the canal, she found her friend shaping a wreath from wild grapevine. It was not altogether unusual for Helen to fashion little baskets or decorations to pass the time, and she had a deft hand for it. This particular item was somewhat more elaborate than usual, with several small planting pots woven in. Without giving it too much thought, Etta complimented her on it.

"You like it?" Helen replied. "It's a birthday present for Mom. She said she wanted something for the front door. This one's taking longer to make than usual."

"Right. I better get her something myself. Which day is she again?"

Helen was confused by the question. "Well... today of course. You're coming to dinner, aren't you?"

Etta had, in fact, completely forgotten. Usually, she was much better about dates and major events but between everything else on her mind, and getting less sleep than usual, she must have lost track. Biting her lip, she was embarrassed and panicked in equal measure. Realizing what had happened, Helen pointed to a patch of mixed wildflowers across the foot bridge.

"Grab some of those, will you? Mom likes the pink ones."

That evening at dinner, Helen had presented the wreath to her mother as a joint gift.

"Etta too," Helen said when her mother hugged her. "She picked out the flowers."

Mildred pulled Etta into a similar, affectionate embrace and said, "You girls always know what I like."

Etta hugged back, but even as she did so felt a pang of guilt. Not that Mildred was the type to hold a grudge over something like a birthday, but it still bothered her that she had forgotten. Especially for one of the most important people in her life.

Relieved, she found Helen's eyes and mouthed the word, "Thanks."

The next day was Etta's last chance to meet Walter. The delay turned out to be fortunate since she only just realized that her wardrobe was limited, and there were a few practical issues that she needed to figure out. To the first matter, she had a dress that was "too fun" for church that should do nicely.

As for the second, she would need an excuse to get out of the house. Her father might be somewhat aloof, but she was confident that he would ask a question or two if she walked out of the house wearing a dress and lipstick. It occurred to her that she never *told* him about her sudden termination of employment.

This would, of course, be dishonest, and lying was not something she was comfortable with, especially with Papa. In the end, she simply told him that she was going to CasinO, and left the house wearing the same white shirt and black pants she had two nights earlier. Perhaps it was lying by way of omission, but for Etta, it was an acceptable compromise.

After all, it was *mostly* the truth.

Even so, she had not been prepared when he directly asked how she was getting home. She hesitated before blurting out a lie about going around the far side of the lake. It was a longer walk, but kept her off of Route Six. It had worked, and Papa made no protest as she slipped out the door.

Only after she left did it occur to her that the theatrics were unnecessary. Papa had recently started going to bed before sunset in order to wake up early enough to drive to Morristown. She might have just waited for him to fall asleep before she sneaked out and avoided the whole issue. Somehow, the *sneaking* aspect pushed it beyond the level of dishonesty that she was willing to accept. Far better, she thought, to at least let Jakob know she was leaving the house, if not the exact reason why.

Even so, she was struck by another pang of guilt as she left. As if her mother's disapproval was able to transcend Heaven and Earth to weigh on her conscience. The general unease faded as she put more steps between the house and herself, and turned her mind to the evening ahead. Meeting someone from out of town was a rarity for her, despite the large number of seasonal visitors.

Granted, this was due to the fact that she actively avoided the majority of them. Naturally, she could make an exception for a handsome young man. Especially a musician. The anticipation put a certain spring in her step and vastly improved her mood. Most of her thoughts circled around what Walter had mentioned about his travels. She wondered about New York City and wanted to hear more about it. Maybe he had been to other places that she had not even heard of before. The life of a traveling performer was unencumbered by the things that kept her so rooted.

Morristown was the furthest from home Etta had ever been, and that was the exception rather than the rule. The family had once made a day of it, attending a parade for the men returning from the Great War. It was so long ago, that the entire Wozniak family had packed, shoulder-to-shoulder, into the truck to make the journey. In a typical year, Etta might expect the occasional foray into nearby Hackettstown for chicken feed, but only when the store in town was out of stock. Other than that, she rarely went farther than she could walk in a day.

Despite her pantomime with the jalopy and pouring over the map, her aspirations were tempered by a persistent, nagging doubt. Whenever her dreams would get away from her, uncertainty would flare up, and drag her back down to Earth. Back to her routine of chores, chickens, and church.

It troubled her to consider those she would leave behind. Not least of all was Jakob, who would be alone to tend the chickens and everything else. Etta told herself that this would simply force him to hire the help she was always asking about. Still, it was hard to shake the notion that she was letting her side down, and she was never one to make others carry her load.

Shaking her head, she dispelled these troubling thoughts. Etta was getting ahead of herself. After all, this would only be her second meeting with Walter.

Even at night, in this quiet part of town, she was unwilling to strip down to her undergarments to change. In a moment of inspiration, she remembered the Beckett's now empty house. It provided the perfect solution, both as a place to change in privacy and to stash her working clothes. Still, she remained fearful of being caught in the act of letting herself inside, and decided to use the back door.

At first, she thought it was locked, but it turned out that it was merely stuck in the jamb. The Becketts, like most every other farmer, never locked their doors. It took several tries and she nearly gave up, but at last it made way for her. Inside, Etta still harbored an irrational fear that at any moment, someone would emerge and demand to know her business. In part, to quell this notion, but also out of simple curiosity she explored the rooms. While she had walked past this house for years, she had never actually been inside it.

The older couple left a few odd pieces of furniture, which apparently had not fit on the truck. This included a bed, a chest of drawers, and even a full-length mirror. She wrinkled her nose at a pervasive musty smell. The place could use an airing out, but it was not altogether unpleasant. In fact, for the most part the house was cleaner than her own.

Changing out of her shirt and pants she hesitated before placing them in the left over chest of drawers. Somehow it felt like an intrusion. While she had already invited herself inside, this was a step beyond. Shaking her head, she dismissed the feeling. No one would have a care, except for perhaps Town Hall. And it would probably take them months to come around to this out-of-the-way property. Slipping the dress down over her head, she smoothed out some of the creases from when it was stuffed into her bag.

It was one of her favorites and she rarely had a chance to wear it. Little blue flowers on a pale green field. While it had sleeves, they were short, and she could slide them over to leave the top of her shoulders exposed. The hem was also much higher than she could usually get away with. The dress had started off as a far more modest article, which she had retrieved from the church donation bin, and adjusted by her own hand. It was from a time when she had considerably more leisure hours than she did these days.

Looking in the mirror, she pulled out the tie in her hair and combed it out with her hands. Seeing her reflection, it occurred to her that this was the first time she had seen all of herself in years. She only owned a small mirror, which sufficed for basic primping on special occasions, but nothing full length.

The sun was setting on the far side of the house, making the room dark, and the house had never been wired for electricity. To make better use of the fading light, Etta turned the mirror towards the only window. As her eyes adjusted, she was able to make out additional details. The shape of her hair and her squared shoulders were immediately familiar.

It was like she was looking at her mother.

It was twilight by the time she arrived at CasinO. The air was brisk for early summer yet still pleasant. Passing the open windows of the restaurant, Etta could hear the band clearly. They would be playing for a while longer, but she had known this would be the case. But had she waited until dark, supposedly going to work, it would have raised questions.

Etta continued past the restaurant and made her way to a pair of floating docks that jutted into the lake like long fingers. It was near enough that she could hear the music, but far enough that she could sit undisturbed.

At the end of one dock, Etta slipped off her shoes and sat down. With a pleasant groan, she soaked her feet to cool them off as well as wash off the dust from the road. As it was early summer, the water still retained most of winter's chill and felt wonderful. While she was used to walking for most of the day, it was usually in her work boots, which fit and caressed her feet perfectly.

Tonight, she had covered most of the three miles from her house to CasinO in a pair of dressy flat shoes, and felt every step of it. Going barefoot for most of the last mile had helped, but only just. Hence her dusty feet.

The band played on as she gently swirled and made little waves with her foot. It was a rare treat that she could simply sit and listen to music without doing another task at the same time. The surface was glassy and still. On the far bank, a few electric lights marked the Oasis beach resort and the cottages beyond. It was the first time in a long while that she had simply sat and admired the beauty of it. Her hometown certainly had its moments.

Eventually, the music stopped for good. The bandleader was likely thanking everyone for a wonderful evening and was met with applause. A few moments later, the first of the revelers began to exit the building. Laughing and carrying on, some made their way to the handful of cars parked outside, but mostly they started walking down the road to the nearby hotels.

After the guests had long since departed, the kitchen staff, waiters, bussers, and even the band eventually did likewise. Etta watched from her seat at the end of the dock, but had not seen Walter's blonde hair among them.

At the sound of a door opening, she looked over with some excitement, thinking that he had finally shown up, but quickly sank back down when she realized that it was only Mr. Mustache. He had not seen her, which was just as well. She saw little benefit for the two of them to meet again. Apparently thinking he was alone, he unbuttoned the top of his shirt and lit a cigarette before letting out a long, smoky sigh.

Etta was mildly surprised to discover that he was, in fact, capable of loosening up. As he finished his smoke and returned inside, it was quiet again, and she debated what to do.

Had she missed Walter? Was he waiting for her on the other side of the restaurant? They had not made any specific plans to meet up, having been interrupted by her father. Was he even expecting her? How long would he wait?

Considering the dock, Etta was suddenly worried that it was too remote and concealed from CasinO. Briefly, she thought of going up to the building to meet him, but hesitated. She did not want to appear too eager. As she remained sitting in place, wracked with indecision, her thoughts were interrupted by the sound of footsteps.

So, he found me after all. I was worried over nothing, Etta thought without looking up. Then, an unfamiliar voice spoke.

"Hey there, girly."

Her head snapped around, eyes wide. It was not Walter.

Standing at the entrance to the dock and silhouetted by the exterior lights of the restaurant stood an unfamiliar man. He swayed back and forth, shifting his weight from one foot to the other. The restaurant only offered alcohol discretely, but this man had clearly discovered it. Such was the struggle to keep his balance, that when he raised his hand in a lazy wave, he nearly teetered over.

Etta remained still. When she made no response, the man continued.

"Nishe night isn't it?" he said.

As he took an unsteady step onto the dock, Etta instinctively pulled back, but quickly realized she had nowhere to go.

"Y'know, I don't think I saw you inside. Pretty thing like you, I sure woulda noticed."

The man was drunk, and that made things unpredictable.

Etta doubted that he would be shy with his hands if given the chance. Worse, he was much larger than her and effectively blocked the one exit from the dock. Both facts were unsettling. All of a sudden, she was acutely aware of her exposed shoulders and the hemline of her dress, which no longer felt "fun."

He took a wobbly step onto the floating dock, causing it to start rocking. If he came too close, Etta wondered if she could scramble across the tied up boats to the opposite dock to get away. Glancing back at the water, she was fully prepared to swim away if it came to it, despite the cold. It became difficult to remain still as her heart started thumping in her chest. Thankfully, the wobbly dock, combined with his wobbly legs, served to keep him away for the moment.

"So, what's your name?"

"Hey! Yeah, sorry I'm late," interjected a new voice. "Marty couldn't find the case for his snare drum."

This one she recognized, and nearly sighed with relief. Walter stood facing the drunken man, who remained with both hands on the entrance to the dock. From the restaurant's outdoor lights, Etta could just make out Walter's face. His smile was brittle and insincere. As if it were a facade he kept in place only with effort.

The drunken man took his time turning around, annoyed at the interruption, and still holding both sides of the dock railing. Whether it was to steady himself, or to intentionally block Walter was hard to determine. However, there was no mistaking his tone.

"Help you?" he asked with clear disdain.

Walter appeared calm, though Etta suspected that it was forced.

"Why yes. This young lady and I have a date tonight. So, if you wouldn't mind..."

Hearing Walter call it a "date" gave Etta a pleasant, fluttery sensation, but the tense standoff quickly pulled her back to the here and now. Her heart resumed its attempts to hammer its way out of her chest.

“Well,” replied the drunk. “This young lady and I were having a little chat, so if *you* wouldn't mind.”

Walter's smile remained, but his eyes narrowed as he gave a mirthless laugh.

“Matter of fact, I do.”

A soft thunk was heard, as Walter set his trumpet case down on the ground. Sighing, the drunk took his hands off the railing and turned to face Walter. He stood a full head taller than the blonde musician. Broader too, but much of that was soft and around his waist. The difference in size was striking. He stood defiantly, with his hands on his hips, steadier than before, but not by much. Growing up around boys, Etta knew a fight coming when she saw one. Sure enough, the drunk made the first move.

“That so?” he asked, and roughly shoved Walter in the chest.

Walter staggered back a single step, shaking his head. “Don't do that,” he said. His voice was low. Dangerous.

The drunk scoffed. “Or what? You gonna-”

Etta blinked, it had happened so fast. The drunk had reached out to push again. This time, Walter rolled with it, and the drunk's own imbalance made him stumble forward. As he staggered, the musician punched him once in the gut and then again in the face. The larger man groaned, and fell to the ground holding his nose. Walter stood back.

“Ergh! You sonuvabitch. That hurt!”

Etta could see blood, and realized there was a good chance the man's nose was broken.

“You should leave,” Walter said, in the same, dangerous voice.

When the man made no move, Walter kicked him violently in his side.

“Agh! Yeah, fine. I'm goin'.”

Slowly, the man rose to his feet, somehow steadier than before. Even as he walked away, Etta's hands were shaking. At some point during the altercation, she had risen to her feet, as though preparing to run. Walter watched the man leave until he was confident that the fight was truly over.

Then, turning back to Etta, his smile returned, apparently genuine this time. Shrugging his shoulders, he seemed completely unconcerned by the preceding events. Etta still did not relax. While the drunk had made her nervous, he had done nothing to warrant a broken nose. The apparent ease with which Walter brought him down left her wary of him.

“Should we try this again?” He picked up his trumpet case, and walked down the dock.

Etta took an involuntary step back as he got close, and felt the back of her heel roll partway over the edge. Had the dock post not been there, she might have gone right into the lake.

Her expression remained neutral, but she watched him carefully. Walter saw she was tense and stopped a few feet away, setting his trumpet case down.

"Hey," he said softly, raising his hands in a calming gesture. "I'm sorry you had to see that. Guys like that only understand one thing, and sometimes you gotta put them in their place."

Etta did not move or speak, and remained uneasy.

"Are you okay?" he asked, his voice softening.

Taking a deep breath, Etta fought down the compelling urge to run.

"Yes," she replied simply. "How's your hand?"

Of the fights she had seen, the more common injuries were broken fingers or at least a sprained wrist. Especially from someone who did not know how to throw a punch. Walter grinned, wiggling his fingers in a pantomime of pressing the valves on a trumpet to demonstrate their lack of injury.

"I believe I'll be able to play tomorrow night," he replied nonchalantly. Pausing, he looked her over, as if seeing her for the first time. "Look at you," he said approvingly.

"Thanks," she replied. Etta continued to calm down, but it was a slow process. A nagging voice in her head kept urging her to go home. She dismissed it, reasoning that it had been the first fight she had seen in a while, but the danger had passed.

"I hope you weren't waiting too long," he said. "Marty really did lose his snare case. Normally, for a weeknight show like this, we'd have been done earlier."

"No, it's fine," she replied. "I was just admiring the view." Etta nodded over her shoulder, at the nightscape.

Walter followed her gaze. "Yeah," he said, standing next to her. "Really dead around here midweek, isn't it?"

She frowned at him, slightly put off by the brusqueness of the comment. In fairness, the town was quiet and she did plan to leave, but it was still her home and she felt a certain pride for it.

Walter chuckled, raising his hands. "I mean no offense, lady. It's a swell place." He paused, looking her in the eyes. "Especially, the local birds." He winked and grinned. "I actually grew up a few towns over from here."

"Really? You're a local boy, then?"

Walter nodded. "That's right. Left about four years ago when I joined the band. I never meant to come back, but you gotta go where the gigs are, y'know?"

"It *is* quiet," she said, referring to his earlier remark. "Especially compared to a place like New York. I'll bet you have all kinds of stories from there."

"I might at that," he replied, looking thoughtfully off into space. The light caught his hair, making it shine gold.

She kept thinking about how handsome he was. Without preamble, he grabbed her by the hand. By reflex, she almost pulled free, but soon it was clear that he was only sitting down and inviting her to join him.

His smile was beguiling, but his grip was firm. So firm that she was not fully confident that she could have withdrawn her hand if she tried.

"Come sit with me," Walter continued, "And I'll tell you all about it."

She did so, but made sure to keep him at arm's length, under the pretext that she merely wanted to lean against the opposite wooden post. He released her hand, and the nagging voice returned, more insistent than before. This time, a deliberate effort was needed to dismiss it.

I'm just jittery. This is my first date in a while and I'm overreacting. And he is a handsome devil.

But... he hit that guy really hard.

Walter did not notice her disquiet and carried on.

"Now, I've only been there a few times, mind you, but we're going back for a gig next month. Let me tell you, the scuttlebutt doesn't do it justice. Small towns like this fold up after sundown, but New York keeps going all night. One time, we were playing this club, and – no foolin' – we didn't stop until the sun came back up."

"You must have been exhausted the next morning."

"After a night like that, I don't think anyone wakes up before noon."

Simply amazed, Etta listened in awe, wondering at a lifestyle where one did not have to wake up before sunrise. Thus, while she noticed that he was inching closer to her side of the dock as he spoke, she made no effort to stop him.

"The band is the heart of the party," he continued. "Without us, it's just a bunch of fogies with nothing to do. And Rick says I've got the voice for bandleader. I've played Master of Ceremonies once or twice already, but might be I take over for him after this season ends."

Having moved near enough that they were almost touching, Walter leaned in closer still, bringing his voice low. "That'd be something, wouldn't it? Mr. Life-of-the-Party." Placing his hand on the pillar behind her, he pressed his face closer.

A strong, oily odor assailed her, causing Etta to wrinkle her nose. So strong, that for a second, she barely noticed Walter's rather blatant attempt for a kiss. The smell was nearly overpowering. Familiar too, though she could not quite place it. There was little time to ponder it, as Walter boldly drew closer.

It was odd. Perhaps as recently as twenty minutes ago, she had thought – even hoped – that the night might end with a kiss. Now that one was upon her, she found it off-putting. The harsh, oily odor did not help matters.

What is that smell?

"That would be something," she agreed, placing her hand on Walter's chest, and halting him barely an inch from her face. "And where does Mrs. Life-of-the-Party fit into all this?"

He frowned at her, clearly not expecting to be interrupted. On top of that, the implications of the question caught him off-guard.

"*Missus*? Aren't we moving a little fast?"

"I don't know. Are we?" Etta replied, increasing the pressure of her hand on Walter's chest to underscore her meaning. He glanced down, then back at her face.

"Why, I'm just being friendly," he replied, undeterred and dropped his hand onto her shoulder.

"Why don't we just talk for a minute," Etta replied. "Y'know, *friendly*."

Her hand remained on Walter's chest until he ultimately shrugged, and backed off. The hand on her shoulder remained, but at least he did not attempt another kiss. Looking both annoyed and confused, Walter was clearly accustomed to a different outcome than this.

Frowning, he finally replied, "So. What would you like to talk about?" Though, it was clear from his tone that he did not particularly care.

Etta opened her mouth to respond, but was distracted by raised voices. They were muffled, coming from somewhere nearby, but out of sight. While she was unable to make out the words, Etta understood the urgent tone quite clearly. Someone was worked up over something and calling out in alarm. It was enough to grab her attention and she rose up for a better view. She remained oblivious to Walter's attempts to keep her seated.

"Whoa, hey. Where are you going?" he asked as Etta stood.

"Do you not hear that?" She barely noticed that he retained a firm grip on her hand.

At first, she was merely confused when she saw the police car parked in front of CasinO. Then, she saw the owner of the agitated voice and recognized Mr. Mustache. He waved his arms as he spoke and paced frantically. The officer slowly stepped out of his car while motioning for him to calm down.

During Etta's few interactions with Mr. Mustache, he had never been the nervous type. Energetic, yes. Impatient, sure. But she had always associated that with the general chaos of the restaurant. This was something else entirely. Where before, he had been busy yet comfortable, now he was anxious and genuinely worried.

"Why is there a police officer here?" she asked. It was more thinking out loud than intended as an actual question.

"Get down!" Walter hissed, pulling on her arm.

She immediately dropped out of sight, more out of reflex than anything else. A lifetime spent around dangerous farm equipment had given her cause to respond quickly when someone spoke with such urgency. It was not until afterward that she took exception to his tone and noticed his grip on her. Walter attempted to smooth things over with another smile and an entreating gesture.

"I mean-" he let out a single, nervous laugh. "Let me explain."

Before, he was bold to the point of being fresh. Now, he was almost bashful, making every appearance of trying to conceal something. Etta grew suspicious.

"Wait. Do you know something about this?" she asked, leaning away.

His grip had not loosened, despite any softening of his demeanor. Exuding a false calmness, he motioned for her to sit down, and tugged gently but firmly on her arm. At first, she tried pulling back, but he was deceptively strong, despite his slight build. Looking back, Mr. Mustache and the police officer had disappeared from view.

In spite of her growing unease, Etta agreed to sit back down, and Walter nearly breathed a sigh of relief. Once it was clear that she did not intend to run, he finally released his grip and relaxed in earnest.

"Now," he started. "I had meant for this to be a surprise for later," he paused dramatically as he reached into his coat. "But since we're *talking...*" As Walter withdrew his hand, he waved a small wad of cash. At a quick glance, it looked to be an amount similar to what Etta had made the other night. Walter pressed it into her hand and grinned.

"What's this?" she asked suspiciously.

"Back payment, plus interest. Courtesy of management."

On closer examination, it was even more than she had made the other night. Much more. Her eyes went wide as she realized that it was not just single dollar bills either. This likely represented months of selling eggs, and very well might cover her family's tax obligations all by itself. As the initial shock wore off, she was reminded of the police car parked nearby, and the connection was obvious.

"You stole this," she accused.

Walter shrugged, still grinning. "He stole from you. This is only fair."

She was about to respond with something to the effect of "this is different," but instead, was distracted by the sheer amount of money in her hand. It was no trivial sum. Any resolve she had had to shove the money back towards Walter with a firm rebuke was quickly diminishing. On the other hand, neither was she prepared to accept the ill-gotten payment.

As she debated what to do, the muffled voices returned as Mr. Mustache and the officer walked past an open window. It was a large amount to someone like her, but she remembered the sight of the open safe from the previous night. The contents were substantially more than what she was holding, and the comparatively trivial withdrawal should not have been missed. At least not this soon. A thought occurred to her.

"He's very worked up over such a small amount," she said pointedly.

Walter's eyes flicked to his trumpet case and back, but he said nothing. Etta continued to stare, unflinching. Finally, he scoffed and looked away.

"You know, this was the ninth time we played here and not once has that bastard given us a tip. Every other club throws in just a little something extra. Doesn't have to be much y'know. Just enough to let us know they appreciated the show. Not this guy. Always the agreed-to amount, and not a thin dime more.

"Sometimes, I might help myself to a small *gratuity*. The safe here is never locked, even when it's closed. But that prick was getting mouthier than usual tonight. Might be I got a little carried away." Apparently pleased with himself, Walter cracked a smile.

Thievery was not something that was treated with leniency in Etta's family, or any of the farmers for that matter. In a community where everyone left their doors unlocked at night, trust in one's neighbors was paramount.

Etta thought about the cook that had been nice to her and the rest of the workers, despite their rude remarks. She thought about the Saunders, and what portion of the money in that safe might go to Mark and help pay for their next meal or the mortgage.

"What about the other workers?" she demanded. "They get paid from that same safe."

Walter rolled his eyes and waved his hand in blatant dismissal.

"Listen, you just don't understand how money works. A prick like that, he can afford it." He looked off into the distance, clearly annoyed. Letting out a sigh, he absentmindedly scratched the top of his head with one finger, careful not to disturb its slicked-back finish. It was for the first time that she thought that it looked more greasy than oiled.

Vaseline. The off-putting, oily smell from before that she could not place. Walter's hair was slicked back with it.

Most men would use Pomade to achieve the look, but petroleum jelly would work as a cheap substitute. The shine that she had been admiring somehow was diminished with the realization. Looking at him more closely now, she noticed other things: the threadbare patches of his suit, which fit him poorly. The leather on his trumpet case was gouged and wrapped together with an old belt which might have been the only thing holding it together.

This was a man who was barely getting by. For a moment, she felt pity for him. But then the agitated voice of Mr. Mustache returned. He was back in front of CasinO with the policeman. The latter was getting back into his car and shrugging apologetically. The former was even more worked up than before, nearly shouting now.

"How... do nothing... robbed! What... going to do?"

Etta's heart started to beat faster, but for a different reason than before. Mr. Mustache was a jerk, and she might have even liked to see him laid low by some other misfortune, but not like this. She started to get up again.

A firm grip on her arm halted her abruptly. Unlike before, Walter did not let her even stand up.

"And where are you going?" he asked. A hint of anger started to color his voice.

"I'm going to give him his money back," she replied.

Walter's grip did not release and his smile flattened into a thin line. It reminded Etta of the way he had regarded the drunk moments earlier. His eyes betrayed dangerous intent, and his grip tightened.

“No,” he practically growled. “See, if you give him your cut back, then he's going to want to know where the rest of it is.”

“I didn't say 'my cut,' I said 'his money.'”

With her remaining free hand, she reached towards the trumpet case. Walter lunged, pushing her away. As she was unbalanced from bending over, they both fell to the deck. Etta let out an “oof” as he fell on top of her. It all happened so quickly, she did not even have time to brace herself before falling. The next thing she knew, he grabbed her wrists as she lay prone beneath him.

The roughness of the wood scraped against the bare skin on her arms and legs, and her head ached from where it bounced off the wood. These things she would notice later, but what most concerned her at the moment was that Walter was holding her down. Pinning her arms to her body, he pressed down with his full weight. Instinctively, she thrashed her legs, as it was all she could do.

“Get off me!” She tried to scream it, but it came out as a wheeze.

Walter was not a large man, but he was heavy enough that she could not draw a full breath.

“Let's not do anything foolish,” he said through clenched teeth.

Etta tried to twist away but only succeeded in rolling onto her back. To keep her from getting away, Walter pressed down with more of his weight, bringing his face close to hers. Panic started to well up inside her as she realized she was both trapped, and felt a growing urgency to draw a full breath.

“No one is returning anything,” he continued. “The cops don’t know who took that money, but if some bitch walks in and tells them who stole it, that'll be pretty hard to ignore.”

Etta continued to struggle, but she could not get out from beneath him.

“Besides,” he continued. “You think you can just hand him a pile of cash and he’s going to believe that you had nothing to do with it?”

Etta stopped and considered the money still clutched in her hand. She had not thought of that. When she stopped resisting, Walter's grip loosened by the smallest degree and she was able to draw most of a full breath. Still, he held her arms against her chest, his grip firm.

“That's better,” he said.

Etta's breathing was ragged as a feeling of dread mixed with panic. In the back of her mind, she was dimly aware that she had lost a shoe during the altercation and her foot rested against something hard and metallic. A belt buckle.

The hem of her dress had hitched up her thighs and the sleeve of her shoulder had pulled lower, making her uncomfortable for a different reason.

"Walter," she said with effort. "Get off me."

He shifted his weight, as if he might comply, but otherwise remained holding her at the wrists. Etta could breathe again, but now she noticed that Walter's hands were resting against her chest in a way that she did not care for. Walter made a similar realization, and leaned his smiling face closer.

"No. I don't think I will," he said.

Etta kicked out, and a splash followed a second later. Walter immediately looked toward the sound, and saw the trumpet case bobbing in the water. At first, he tried to reach out while keeping his grip on Etta, but quickly decided that he could not do both.

Abandoning Etta, he reached out for the trumpet case while hanging off the edge of the dock. It had floated beyond arm's reach. He searched the nearest boat for an oar or something to retrieve it, but came up empty handed.

Etta took the opportunity to scramble backwards, putting distance between them. Walter rounded on her, all pretense of charm completely gone. He took two steps before she pointed at the water behind him, drawing his attention. Turning around, there was just enough time to see the top of the trumpet case disappear into the inky blackness of the lake. Without bothering to remove his jacket or shoes, Walter jumped into the water with a splash, apparently not realizing that it was over his head.

Disappearing, his head popped up a second later as his arms splashed around, trying to find the case. As he came up empty-handed, his desperation and the splashing intensified.

"You bitch!" he growled. "I'll kill you! You hear me!?"

In fact, Etta did not hear him. She had already crossed CasinO parking lot, and started up Route Six. It was not until the sounds of splashing and cursing had completely faded that she realized she had lost her other shoe.

Chapter 8
Art

"Not bad. Ugly as hell, but that's what paint is for." Coming from Gregory, this was high praise. As he inspected Art's most recent work, he nodded thoughtfully before continuing. "But-" he lifted a hammer. "How does it hold up?"

Art winced as his mentor proceeded to strike the work piece with more ferocity than he thought the shorter man to be capable of. After two blows, Gregory was satisfied of the weld's strength and nodded.

A distinct relief came over Art, and he realized that he had been anxious. Though he was not without experience, his previous efforts were never assessed with such scrutiny. This work was coming from Gregory's shop, after all, and the man had standards.

Or, as he had put it, "I'm not staking my reputation on your work without first checking that you didn't half-ass it." Of course, he had said it with a wink, taking off most of the sting. Art was only just starting to become accustomed to *friendly* ribbing.

Obtaining Gregory's final approval added an element of stress, but also provided a certain motivation. His gray eyebrows scrunched up in concentration as he leaned closer to the part he had just "inspected" with the hammer.

"Looks like you welded these tabs about four inches apart?" Gregory asked.

"That's right. Just like we sketched it."

"Mm hmm," the older man replied as he brought over the mating piece.

Art let out a frustrated sigh and slumped his shoulders as Gregory was unsuccessful in his attempt to fit it between the tabs.

"So, what happened here?" he asked, raising an eyebrow.

Gregory's tone was reminiscent of how several of his old professors would speak when Art got a problem wrong. It was equal parts scold and encouragement. The former, because he had gotten it wrong, and the latter because he had the ability to get it right. The purpose of the exercise was to guide him toward the latter. A similar thing had happened three or four times this week, and Art knew there was no alternative but to think through his error. For this particular issue, he already suspected his mistake.

"Did the part shrink?" Art asked.

Gregory slowly nodded. "You positioned the second tab while the first was still hot, didn't you?"

"Yeah," Art replied. "Then when it cooled down, they moved closer."

"Right. And also, did you test the fit before you completed the weld?"

Art winced at this. The thought had actually occurred to him at the time. He had been so focused on making the weld itself, since it was a new skill for him that he had forgotten about the bigger picture.

"I did not," he replied quietly.

Gregory grunted. "If you had only tacked it and checked the fit, you would have seen that it was tight. Would have been less work to correct." He shrugged. "It's fixable, but I'd guess you have another hour and a half in order to make it right. Maybe two."

Art looked at his feet, frustrated. Gregory clapped him on the shoulder.

"C'mon. Don't mope. Like I said, it's good work. You just aren't done is all."

It was not the first, nor the last mistake Art would be forced to correct. The period of self-pity and looking at his feet grew shorter each time. When it happened next, which it inevitably did, he began thinking through solutions much more quickly. Gregory's input gradually became less review and more collaboration. As his mistakes became fewer, his confidence grew, and he started to offer ideas more readily.

"It's a bit too wobbly for my liking," Gregory said as he frowned at the work piece, which they had affectionately started referring to as "the Anchor," since it was heavy and they had thought about tossing it into the lake more than once. "My best guess is probably one season of hard use before this seam gives out."

Art had been thinking in textbook terms of "load cycles" instead of "farming seasons" but they were otherwise in agreement on this point.

"There's room for a couple of ribs here. We could weld them on in an hour," Art replied, pointing. Gregory frowned, unconvinced.

"It's already heavier than I like."

"We could add some holes to save weight. Here and here." He drew several circles using a grease pen to show what he was thinking.

Gregory frowned.

"You're gonna make it flimsy again," he protested.

Art shook his head and pulled out a piece of paper.

"Not if you just do it to the one side. Here, look." Confidently, Art made a quick sketch of the part and added a few arrows to illustrate the different forces. It was a class exercise that he had drawn countless times at school. "See. The holes will be outside the main load path," he said finally.

Gregory squinted at his drawing, and eventually grunted something that might have been concurrence.

"Okay then. Get to work."

Art spent over an hour cutting out the extra pieces he would need and then prepared the Anchor. It was finally starting to look like something. Progress had been slow, since this was not the only machine they were working on.

Gregory had a habit of accepting just about every task that was put to him. In some ways, this was admirable, but too often resulted in biting off more than he could chew.

This was the reason that the shop was cluttered with half a dozen or more partially completed projects, and why a row of machines stood sentry along the driveway. At first, Art thought these were the equivalent of a trophy wall for Gregory, but soon realized that it was simply the result of there being no room anywhere else.

Thus, the smaller jobs took priority in order to clear shop space. Gregory reasoned that Mr. Grayson had done without the hay baler for over a year, while some of the other jobs were more pressing. It was early summer and there was a certain urgency for most farmers to have their equipment returned.

In this way, Art met several people from around town. Thankfully, none of them had he met previously during sales runs with his father. At first he had been his usual, shy self, but Gregory did not let him hide for long. This method of coaxing Art out of his shell and into the conversation proved considerably more effective than George's preferred method of slapping him in the chest until he started talking.

His improving confidence suffered a considerable setback when they were visited by the owner of some machine that needed a bearing replaced. It was not due to the man himself, but rather his daughter, an especially attractive young woman. This time, Art pretended not to hear Gregory's usual invitation to join the conversation, deciding instead to remain behind the weld mask.

Gregory had seen quite clearly, what was going on, but thankfully did not press the matter until they were alone again.

"They won't bite, you know."

For the most part, Art was glad for any advice his mentor cared to offer. It was usually spot-on, but in this instance he remained skeptical.

Gregory continued to visit his daughter a few days each week, which brought their progress to a temporary standstill. When Art suggested that he could work by himself, Gregory flat-out rejected the idea with no room for argument.

"You're just not ready yet."

At first, he took it as a rebuke, but quickly recognized the wisdom in it. Being forced out of the shop turned out to be beneficial for other reasons. For the most part, being ignored by his family meant that disappearing for most of the day did not raise too many questions, except of course from his mother. George left Art alone so long as he did his part for the family business. Thankfully, he was content with how many new customers they had picked up, and they made no more sale calls for the time being.

Instead, Art helped his father draft work orders and plan out tasks for the crew that would actually install the equipment. In addition, and at George's insistence, he also listened to the weekly report from the home office.

Art could only imagine the odd sight they made; two grown men, sitting with their heads pressed together as they listened to the phone between them. Since there was none at the cottage, George had worked out a deal to borrow one at a local business. Art was indescribably thankful that it was located in a private room.

The only thing that made the work with his father tolerable was knowing that he would soon return to Gregory's shop and get his hands dirty. He thought of the deskwork as a kind of penance that had to be paid. A day spent doing something he hated for a day spent doing something he loved.

There were a few near misses.

His mother had gone to the tailor and asked about the suit that Art had supposedly been fitted for. In the excitement of his first day at the shop, he had forgotten about it entirely. Scrambling for an excuse, Art spun some story about his measurements being taken by an older seamstress, who must have misplaced them.

While not comfortable with lying to his mother, he knew that anything he told her would eventually reach his father, who would surely forbid any more time with Gregory. An Adams man performing blue-collar work was not something George would tolerate.

Luciana had insisted on the two of them going to the tailor the next day to ensure that no further "mishaps" occurred. Art held his breath as his mother made insinuations, but did not explicitly accuse the shop owner of losing the measurements.

The owner looked confused, but ultimately did not challenge his mother on this point. For which Art was very thankful. Any lingering sense of guilt soon fled as his mother fretted and fussed over every detail. He silently endured her pokes and prods, and comments about how he was not eating enough.

"Something proper for a groom, but casual enough that he can still wear it for special occasions. And make sure you leave enough room around his waist. A married man should grow about two belt sizes in the first year."

Ma...

Art was able to maintain a delicate balance of work in the shop, and family obligations for about two full weeks before he hit a snag.

Lifting his mask, the bead glowed orange as Art inspected the Anchor. Just a tack this time, in case the new rib needed to be adjusted, which it did. After giving it a few gentle taps with the hammer, he checked the angle, and nodded, satisfied.

He was at it for a few minutes, when someone entered the shop. At first, Art paid little attention, as Gregory typically greeted all new arrivals. Naturally, they wanted to speak with the man whose name was on the sign. The newcomer spoke loudly, and Art heard his voice clearly. When he did, and recognized it his chest suddenly went tight. Sure enough, it was Ralph.

The second-youngest Adams looked even taller standing next to Gregory, who managed to appear in control of the conversation despite being significantly shorter. For a moment, Art had to commend his mentor. Still, he snapped his mask closed when Ralph happened to look over at him. Resolving to stay out of it, he turned back to his work, hoping to remain unnoticed. He barely had a chance to relight the flame on the torch before he received a tap on the shoulder.

Slowly, he shut off the gas and turned around, lifting the mask just high enough to see Gregory.

"Art, we got a customer. Car trouble. Go with him to take a look. I'll be out in a minute." Without another word, Gregory walked away.

Briefly, Art considered slipping away until Ralph left on his own, and make up some excuse to Gregory later. Unfortunately, Ralph had already seen him, and was waiting by the front door with his hands on his hips.

Resigned, Art took off the mask and turned to face his brother. Ralph squinted at him, unsure he recognized Art in this unusual context. As Art marched toward his older brother, Ralph's expression was a mix of confusion, but mostly amusement. Now sure it was his younger brother, he recovered and delivered some of his usual barbs.

"Well, well. Have a look at you."

Art simply glared, not rising to the usual bait.

Undeterred, Ralph pressed on. "So, this is where you've been sneaking off to every day? Thomas thought you might have found yourself a side girl, but I knew that couldn't be it."

He whistled in a parody of being impressed as he looked around the shop.

"Boy, this place is something. I've been to most every club in this town, but can't say I've had the pleasure of visiting a factory. Though, I'm not properly attired." He reached out to tug on Art's leather welding sleeves as he said the last.

Art pushed his hand away before Ralph could touch it. It was so quick that it was almost a slap, which surprised both of them. Ralph raised an eyebrow before recovering and Art continued to fume in silence.

"Does Father know about your shiny new blue collar?"

Art bit his tongue, actually feeling more annoyed than flustered. There was plenty of work today, and this was an unnecessary distraction more than anything else.

"Something wrong with your car?" Art replied tersely, hoping to cut through the usual nonsense.

Ralph looked as though he was going to press things further, but realized that he did, in fact need something. Instead, his smile faded a few shades, and he nodded toward the open door.

The Model T was parked in the middle of the driveway as the brothers approached. Art immediately noticed a distinct lean to one side.

“I hit a rather large bump on this lousy, country road and-”

“Busted the axle on the right side,” Art interrupted. He squatted next to the damaged side for a better look as his older brother composed himself.

“Yes... I noticed that as well,” Ralph replied, struggling to hold back some scathing remark. He cleared his throat, unable to restrain himself for long. “So, can you and your new husband fix it or not?”

Art bristled at the prodding. No one could quite get under his skin the way his brother could.

Though he was becoming less sensitive to prods against himself, the disrespect to Gregory was what he took exception with. Sensing that he was getting somewhere, Ralph's unease dissipated and his usual smug grin returned. Art slouched. His brother was ready to press on, but stopped when Gregory joined them.

“How's it look?” he asked Art.

They looked up in unison. Art's shoulders were still hunched over, while Ralph had puffed out his chest. The latter began to answer.

“I seem to have a-”

“Art,” Gregory said with emphasis, silencing Ralph with a glare.

To both their surprise, Ralph shut right up.

“How does it look?” Gregory repeated, making it clear that he expected an answer from Art and no one else.

He composed himself, and after a deep, steadying breath, Art stood up to face Gregory.

“The wheel spindle is barely holding on,” he began. “Frankly, I'm amazed he was able to drive it here.” He glanced at Ralph, making it almost sound like an accusation. “No way around it. It will have to be replaced.”

Gregory nodded. “What needs to be done?” he asked. Then added, “Specifically.”

Art looked at the car, thinking. For a moment, he ignored his brother and wholly focused on the job. It was a shame too, because Ralph's look of utter bewilderment was something he should have savored. After thinking it over, Art rattled off a list of parts and the tasks needed to replace them.

Gregory nodded in concurrence. Ralph was largely at a loss, and uncomfortable at being excluded from the discussion. He straightened as Art and Gregory finally turned toward him.

"Bottom line," Gregory started, "We can fix it, but you're looking at two weeks."

"No. Unacceptable. I need this car back by tomorrow. Two days at the latest."

Art immediately tried to think of how they would be able to pull that off, but Gregory scoffed.

"Well, that's just not gonna happen."

Ralph glared at him, but Gregory was unmoved. Sensing this, he turned to his brother to try a different angle. Heading him off, the older man called his attention back.

"Don't look at him. He gave you an assessment. I decide when and *if* we actually do it."

Ralph was positively fuming. "Outrageous. I'm going somewhere else."

Gregory shrugged, unconcerned. "You are, of course, welcome to do so. But if what Art said is accurate – and I believe it is – you've got maybe a couple more miles before that wheel fails pretty spectacularly. Then, your two-week job goes to four. At least. The next closest shop that I know of is at least ten miles from here. And don't you dare ask to use my phone to call a tow truck."

Still seething, Ralph considered his options, and ultimately nodded.

"Okay then," Gregory acknowledged. "Leave it here and we'll take care of it. If we get done sooner, I reckon Art can let you know."

Without another word, Gregory turned and marched back to the shop. The brothers stood in silence, both trying to come to terms with this new development. Neither was quite comfortable with it. Ralph eventually spoke first, but quickly checked that Gregory was far enough not to hear.

"Two weeks," he repeated. "And not a day longer. Or I tell Father about how you're slumming it with the grease monkeys."

Art returned his gaze, unblinking.

"Fine. Then, I tell him how you can't take care of your things."

Ralph frowned, clearly not expecting that. He opened his mouth, as if to say something, but Art cut him off.

"Maybe we should keep this simple. You're just a customer, and I'm just providing a service."

Still bristling, Ralph eventually nodded. For the first time, Art thought that his brother did not seem as tall as he usually did. Turning on his heel to head back to the shop, he called one last thing over his shoulder.

"By the way. It's about two miles walking back to the cottage from here. Takes me nearly an hour... but then I know the way." Before Ralph could lower himself to asking for directions, Art returned inside.

Chapter 9
Etta

Coffee, Etta thought, shaking her head. *How do they always spill it on the white sheets?*

Having never stayed away from home herself, she could not comprehend the apparent disregard many hotel guests had for the linens. It was her first day as a laundress, and thus far some of the easiest work she had ever done. She considered herself lucky to have stumbled across it.

The due date for the tax bill was still approaching, and with it, the danger of losing the farm. Keeping her eyes open for potential jobs, Etta found she had to expand what she was willing to consider. After her disastrous evening as a bus girl, most opportunities vanished, at least among the restaurants in town.

Mr. Mustache, it turned out, was as loud as he was vindictive, and had told whoever would listen about "this mouthy Polack girl" who tried to coerce him into paying her more. Amazingly, and to her misfortune, that story got around more than the fact that he was robbed.

During her usual rounds, she had noticed a "Help Wanted" sign for the Hatakawana Inn. The sign had been posted for so long that it had since become part of the scenery, much like the hotel itself. For the longest time, she had assumed its presence was merely the result of the owner failing to remove it. After all, how could a position remain open for nearly a year?

On a whim, she had left her wagon on the side of the road and walked up to the hotel, work clothes and all. The Hatakawana sat on the top of a small hill, looking across the lake. It was a prime location. Close enough for people to walk to both the Oasis on the north side of the lake, and the restaurants on the south side.

It was rare that Etta discovered something new in her hometown, but this was just such an occasion. She never had cause to visit a hotel before, much less one within walking distance of her home. Only at the top of the hill did she see the small restaurant next door, as well as the recently broken ground in the adjacent lot. Construction vehicles and material littered the cleared area.

Making her way to the lobby, a man passed her on his way out. He wore a suit, and inclined his head with a polite "Good morning." Without thinking, Etta returned the greeting before recognizing him. By then, he had already left the building, and was not around to see her look of utter disdain. The town's chief tax officer had been busy lately, and she had seen his face more than a few times on her daily rounds.

At least he's pestering the Townies for a change.

Suppressing the urge to spit on the ground, she resumed looking for the hotel's owner. After finding him behind what served as the reception desk, he quickly shoved something into a drawer and out of sight, but not before Etta caught a glimpse of the bottle. The kind that took the edge off of one's nerves.

Thinking of her own family's troubles with town hall, she did not have high hopes for finding work here. After all, if he could not cover his own tax bill, how could he afford to pay her?

As it turned out, Etta's fears were unfounded. The owner, Heber Wells, was most certainly looking for help, and took her on immediately. At first, she could not believe her good luck, and breathed a sigh of relief. They had neglected to discuss compensation, and Etta had not thought to bring it up. The closest Heber had come was a casual mention that payment was doled out at the end of each week. Fortunately for her, that was today.

Her duties consisted of replacing the linens in each room while the guests were out, and washing the used ones. The soiled sheets were carried down to the basement where four Maytags sat in a row. They were similar to the machine at Etta's home, except that these were operational. At first, Etta thought this job would be easy, as she was accustomed to doing all her laundry by hand. There was already a pile of sheets in the basement, evidence of the fact that the hotel had done without a dedicated laundress for some time.

Etta gradually worked through the pile after a short delay. The detergent took a few minutes to find since the box of Oxydol was missing its label. She had to peer inside before recognizing the white powder.

Amazingly, she actually idled around the basement for several minutes during the wash cycle for lack of things to do.

The basement had become a repository of random boxes, and oddments. Supplies of one sort or another were haphazardly stored on rows of shelves. Wooden boards and other debris were scattered on the floor. After some cursory exploration, she discovered the only way in or out of the space, was the long, narrow flight of stairs she had originally descended. Looking at it, she had to wonder how they managed to get the washing machines down here in the first place.

The only other door led to the linens room.

After rinsing the first load, she ran a wet sheet through the ringer, and frowned upon seeing a coffee stain. The machine had done little for it, and she was immediately concerned that it would reflect poorly on her.

Her reputation was already tarnished thanks to Mr. Mustache, and she did not want her new employer to think her lazy. Thus, she found a washtub and scrubbed the sheets by hand. It struck her as odd that the Oxydol bubbled and hissed when she added it to the water, more than it did at home. Warmer too. Etta figured that she was just used to doing her laundry outdoors and put it from her mind. Satisfied that the sheets would hold up to scrutiny, she resumed pulling them from the washer, and was disheartened to discover that the issue of stains was pervasive.

Despite her longstanding relationship with coffee, a fervent and enduring hatred for its stains was soon born. One sheet in three had to be washed by hand, and Etta resolved herself to a long day.

After finally working through the pile on the floor, she ran them through the drying machines, and her hands were pink from all the scrubbing. Going up to collect more, she noted that Heber had neglected to provide her with a basket or any other means of bringing the sheets down to the basement. Not wanting to appear fussy or needy, lest she jeopardize this new job, she resolved to simply carry the bundles by hand.

Unfortunately, she was also in something of a rush, and the first trip nearly killed her.

The stairs to the basement were long, steep and had no railing. As she began to descend, a corner from one of the sheets had worked its way loose, and found its way beneath her foot. When she tried to take a step, her legs were tangled and for a gut-wrenching moment, she was falling forward through space. By the grace of God, she landed safely, several steps below, with little more than her pride bruised.

The only thing that had saved her was the same bundle of sheets, which cushioned her fall. Even so, her nose took a beating and was tender for most of an hour. If not for the sheets, Etta feared that she might have lost most of her front teeth or worse.

The only other people to enter the basement that morning were the kitchen staff. The hotel's dry pantry lay beyond the linens room. However, these visits were sporadic enough that had she met with an accident, she might have gone undiscovered for some time. After her nerves settled, she made two more trips without incident. Gradually, her fear of the stairs progressed into hatred, and nearly rivaled her ire for coffee stains.

Despite all that, Etta decided it was still preferable to mucking the chicken coop, or walking miles around town, or carrying heavy food trays. The day progressed quietly, save for the *wump-wump-wump* of the machines, and the occasional member of the kitchen staff passing through.

One happy surprise was lunch. Heber provided a light meal to all staff from the hotel's own kitchen. It was simple fare: cheese, bread and fruit. Etta would have been content with anything besides a hard-boiled egg, but it had been ages since she enjoyed fresh fruit. She eagerly piled it onto the plate as she heard a familiar voice.

"Don't go dropping that one," the cook teased, grinning.

Even though he was dressed in the same white apron and standing behind a counter, it took Etta a moment to recognize him from CasinO.

"Oh," she said with sudden recognition. "Good to see you again."

"And you. What's Heber got you doing here?"

"Laundry," she replied.

The cook nodded. "Can't break sheets, now can you?" he winked.

"No, I suppose not," she replied, cracking a smile.

At the sound of a small bell, the cook held up a finger, asking her to wait. He went to the far side of the kitchen to retrieve something from the dumbwaiter. After unloading the contents and closing the door again, he returned to Etta.

"Did Mr. Mustache give you the sack too?" she asked.

"I love that name, by the way. Been sharing it with the rest of the kitchen. Quietly of course. But no, I'm still working nights over there. He cut back on the day staff and the rest of us haven't been paid all week."

The cook cast a furtive glance to either side before leaning towards Etta, and lowering his tone. "Rumor is, he got robbed. Someone cleaned out the safe is what I heard."

"Really?" Etta replied evenly.

The cook raised an eyebrow at her lack of reaction.

"I hadn't heard anything about that," she quickly added.

It was not, strictly speaking, a lie. However, she did not feel compelled to add that the likely thief had also attacked her on the night in question.

It was not something she cared to revisit. Especially not after her experience with the police on the day after the incident. Despite Mr. Mustache's less-than-cordial behavior, she did not want his employees to suffer for Walter's actions.

After the robbery, she had gone to the police to let them know the identity of the CasinO thief. The officer who took her statement was familiar, and it was not until the end of the interview that she recognized him as the one who had spoken with Mr. Mustache that night. Likewise, it was only after she accused Walter Hoffman that she looked at the officer's uniform and recognized the same last name.

Suddenly, Walter's words came back to her, "My uncle is connected."

Officer Hoffman did not betray any hint of recognition. Instead, he asked coolly, "Did you *see* the money you claim this musician had taken?"

That stopped her. She thought of offering up her "cut" as evidence, but remembered what Walter had said about no one believing that she had nothing to do with the theft. And what if the rest of it never turned up? Then the only person in possession of the stolen cash would be her.

"Well... it must have been in his trumpet case."

"Mm hmm. You know, a young man recently made a complaint about a woman throwing his instrument into the lake. Seems like a clear case of destruction of property to me. That wouldn't be related, would it?"

Etta gulped. After taking a steadying breath, she replied, "Not as I'm aware."

"Mm hmm. I tell you what. I'm going to file this. If we have any more questions... I know where to find you."

The last part made the hair on her neck stand on end. Growing up, she had never been in any kind of trouble, and even the mere suggestion of being on the wrong side of the law was unsettling. Since Walter's band left town, she had seen neither hide nor hair of him. Her days were full enough without this distraction, and she decided not to pursue it further.

Even so, it stuck in her craw that he was getting away with a crime, while she nearly got in trouble for doing the right thing.

In the hotel kitchen, Heber suddenly walked in, looking considerably less anxious than he had when she first met him. He gave everyone an extra ten minutes of break time and a small token of appreciation. He nodded to the cook who pulled out several desserts. This was met with a quiet round of cheers as he turned on his heel and promptly left the room.

While she thought it was a kind gesture, and dessert was tempting, Etta had not even eaten her lunch yet. Besides, there was a clock on the kitchen wall, and it was later than she had realized. There were still evening chores to finish at home after she was done here. If she hurried, she might get done before dark, and make it to the Saunders' house for supper. Retreating from the counter, Etta quickly ate lunch by herself before returning to the basement.

She was still chewing as she left the kitchen, and headed upstairs for the last of the sheets. That was well because her hands were starting to itch from prolonged contact with the laundry detergent. Arms full with the final bundle, Etta slowly opened the door and made her way down the stairs to the basement. Recalling her experience from that morning, she resolved to be cautious, no matter how late she had to work.

Thus, she moved slowly and placed each step deliberately. This had the unintended effect of rendering her nearly silent. It was for this reason that she was able to hear the voices.

Her ears picked up a muffled conversation somewhere nearby, but out of sight. Holding the laundry, Etta remained still and listened. While she could not make out the words of the speakers, and there were at least two, their tone was furtive and conspiratorial. Added to that was the fact that, whoever they were, they were speaking behind a closed door, in the basement, far from prying ears.

Prying ears such as hers.

Etta froze. While curious, she did not want to give the appearance of eavesdropping. More than that, she had the impression that whoever was down here would not take kindly to her intrusion. The hairs on her neck stood on end for the second time that week.

As she considered retreating back up the stairs, the doorknob to the linens room started to turn. Without thinking, she dropped the sheets on top of the larger pile, and ducked behind the washing machines. They were just large enough to conceal her but only if she lay prone. The door opened, and three men emerged.

"-accident. Twelve o'clock, no one will be down here. Can you do it?"

Etta recognized the first voice as Heber's. His tone was agitated and tense again. Unlike how he had sounded in the kitchen, just minutes before.

"You got nothing to worry about, friend. Me and my brother are nothing, if not discrete." The second voice was familiar as well, but she could not place it without seeing his face.

The three men passed her and started up the stairs. Daring to peak, she only got a look at the back of one before they moved out of sight. She caught a glimpse of sandy colored hair that was long for a man. Etta remained hidden until Heber and the others had long since left. Whatever shady business he had in a dark basement was nothing she wanted to intrude upon.

It was an open secret that most establishments served alcohol, despite the Prohibition. Drinks were not openly advertised, of course, but everyone knew where to get one. Still, a certain level of discretion was required on the part of legitimate businesses. Perhaps a clandestine meeting in the basement was excessive, but Etta assumed that was what she had just witnessed.

Why they could not simply have had their discussion in Heber's office with the door closed struck her as odd, but perhaps he was accustomed to impromptu visits from Town Hall. The chief tax officer whom she passed upon her arrival came to mind. Considering her own experience with the police, Etta supposed she could not fault him for being extra cautious. On the other hand, it did not explain Heber's use of the word "accident."

The rest of the workday proceeded without incident. Only drudgery. Eventually, all the sheets were clean without a trace of coffee to be found.

Once everything was back in the basement linen closet, the same room Heber and his mystery guests had occupied, Etta's hands were pink and raw. In fact, they were closer to red than pink, and increasingly itchy. She had considered asking for a pair of gloves, but decided it would be best to avoid Heber, lest she accidentally reveal what she had seen.

When she went to his office to collect her payment, he was completely at ease. To look at him now, Etta would never guess that anything was amiss. For all she knew, it was. Maybe the visit from the taxman had only put Heber temporarily out of sorts and the two men she had witnessed were not engaged in the kind of skullduggery she had assumed. Regardless, she did not dwell on these thoughts for long, as the discomfort in her hands steadily intensified.

The itching grew worse. Concerned that fidgeting with them would make her appear impatient, she did her best to ignore it. Heber counted the day's pay with excruciating slowness, meticulously setting down each dollar. All the while, the itching progressed into a mild burn. At this point, Etta became concerned.

Increasingly desperate to leave, Etta almost snatched the money off the table when it appeared that Heber was finished counting. However, just to be thorough, he immediately began to recount it. Etta remained still, resisting the urge to soothe her hands.

The burning became painful, and even spread past her wrists. By the time Heber pushed the money towards her, Etta was ready to bolt out the door. Oblivious to her discomfort, he regarded her with a courteous, professional smile, and thanked her for her hard work.

Etta's hands were on fire as she reached for the money, and with the first contact, nearly cried out from the pain. Pride being a funny thing, she did not want Heber to know how much it hurt. With great care, she scooped the money into her bag, wincing every time her hands touched something.

"Oddly enough," he started. "I've had some difficulty keeping this position filled. I'd be happy to bring you on six days a week if you're interested."

Etta merely nodded to Heber, not trusting herself to speak. Whatever was wrong with her hands simply was not letting up, and now she was downright worried. Clenching her teeth, she managed to hold her composure as she walked out of the office, proceeded down the hallway, and left through the main entrance. Only once she finally reached the path leading to Route Six and was some distance away from the hotel did she allow herself to scream.

Plunging her hands into the cold lake provided her with respite from the pain, but she knew she had to get home. Reluctantly, she withdrew them, and the burning soon returned with a vengeance. Her walk home was no longer than it had always been, but it felt like an eternity. The whole while, she experimented with different hand positions in an increasingly desperate bid for relief.

Eventually, she discovered that the pain abated somewhat if she held her hands open, flat at her sides with her fingers splayed. It made for an odd sight as she walked down the road, but thankfully there were few enough people around to see it. About halfway back to the house, it occurred to her that she had left the wagon sitting behind the bushes by the hotel. That she did not once consider going back to retrieve it said much about her current state of agony.

When she finally did arrive back at the farm, she strode directly to the chicken pen, and thrust her hands inside the water trough. Etta remained there for a full ten minutes before daring to withdraw them. While not as cold as the lake, it still served to reduce the pain to a mild burn.

With some dread, she inspected her hands. Visually, they only appeared redder than usual. Washing clothes by hand would often leave them pink, and sometimes dry, but this was something else entirely. For the first time, she wondered about the box of white powder and the missing label.

As the cold dissipated, the pain returned. Etta rummaged through the medicine cabinet, looking for something, anything, that might help. It had been a while since she had reason to use it, and could not remember what was in supply. Being as gentle with her hands as possible, eventually she came across a near empty bottle of camphor oil which was so old, she remembered her mother using it to treat burns for her older brother John. Etta only hoped it retained its potency.

She poured the remaining contents into her cupped hand, wincing at the initial sting. After a moment, it subsided and the skin beneath actually felt cooler. Careful not to spill, she rubbed the oil all over her hands. A moment later, they finally stopped burning, and she flopped down into a kitchen chair still wary about touching anything.

In the conspicuous absence of pain, exhaustion caught up with her and she closed her eyes for what was intended to be a moment. When she opened them again, it was full twilight.

Hours had passed.

Cursing to herself, she remembered her chores. On top of that, the camphor oil had worn off and her hands were growing uncomfortable again. Flexing her fingers was especially painful, which would make the evening work a challenge. However, if she neglected to feed the chickens and collect the evening eggs, she was sure to have a mess to deal with in the morning.

Around the same time, the truck rolled up the driveway, and Jakob walked into the kitchen, looking haggard. Briefly, she thought about asking him for help finishing up, but if he knew how much pain she was in, she feared he might force her to rest. While the two of them existed in different worlds most of the time, Papa would certainly involve himself if he sensed she was at risk of harm.

Despite the drudgery of her typical day, it occurred to her that the little bit of freedom she found in leaving the farm for a few hours was not something she was willing to sacrifice. Besides, she would not have to endure for long; he had just returned home and would be going to bed soon. The drive to Morristown meant that Jakob's day started even earlier than Etta's, which was saying something.

Dining separately was not a rare occurrence these days, and it was simple enough to avoid Papa. When their paths did cross, Etta had responded to his greetings through gritted teeth. This, no doubt, came off as curt, perhaps bordering on rude, but it had the effect that Jakob left her alone. She scolded herself, as Papa did not deserve that sort of treatment. Frankly, she had more pressing concerns.

She needed a way to work without constantly fighting the urge to cry out in pain. Finding a pair of leather gloves and a tub of Vaseline, Etta scooped a handful of the jelly into each glove and placed her hands inside. It helped tremendously, although the smell reminded her of Walter. Even so, it was not a perfect solution. Gripping something still shot pain through her hands, and she was obliged to hold the feed scoop daintily, between two fingers. After a fashion, it sufficed to get her through the evening.

It was fully dark by the time she finished and later than usual. Returning inside, she found herself with a dilemma.

Although fully prepared to sleep in the clothes she was wearing, she would not sleep in her boots. However, the gloves prevented her from removing them. Tenderly, she uncovered just one hand, wincing as she carefully unlaced each boot. Eventually, she managed to get them to where she could wiggle out using only her feet, then immediately returned the glove to her exposed hand. With an audible sigh of relief, Etta promptly flopped onto her bed, utterly spent.

Sleep found her, perhaps, a minute later. Before it did, one of the last thoughts to go through her mind was the resolute, implacable determination that she would never set foot in the Hatakawana Inn again.

Chapter 10
Art

"So where are they?" demanded Junior as the car bounced over another pothole. Thomas leaned forward in the front passenger seat, eyes scanning for a road sign, or landmark of any kind, but found none. Despite the full moon, the surrounding farmland remained hidden beyond the range of the Buick's headlights. From the back seat, Ralph let out a curse as the car lurched and he banged his head.

George's question had been addressed to him.

"The guy just said they were out in the woods behind the Kovaks' farm," Ralph said, rubbing the side of his head. "That's down this road."

"Yeah, well, which one is the Kovaks' farm? Do you see a name written anywhere?" Junior shot back.

They had been driving down these back roads for about thirty minutes. Art, while somewhat familiar with the route between the cottage and the repair shop, had never been to this part of town before, and one farm looked much the same as another. The dark of night did not help matters.

It had been waning twilight when the evening began, and was full dark by the time they reached the farming side of town. The single dirt road leading away from the lake also featured more than a few bumps and divots, which only exacerbated the challenge of navigation.

"Did he give you any other landmarks?" asked Thomas, who was far more composed than their oldest brother. Having remained mostly silent during this impromptu expedition, his even temper was a welcomed contrast to Junior.

Even so, Art glared at the back of Thomas' seat. He still felt salty after learning that Thomas had referred to him as "a wimp" to his wife. From Junior or Ralph, he would have expected such a thing, but Thomas had always given the impression of being above that. Even then, Art was prepared to let the matter go, but it was Thomas' role in bringing Art along for this misadventure that made him keen to hold a grudge.

Earlier that evening, the four brothers were chasing the various nieces and nephews around the cottage after dinner. Ralph had approached Junior and Thomas, and told them about his discovery of moonshiners in town. This got the attention of both brothers, who had been looking for an excuse to get away from their respective families for a few hours.

There had been some excited discussion as the three of them debated about whose car to take, and what excuse to make. Art had been standing a short distance away in a kind of social limbo. While not quite participating in the conversation, neither was he on his own. At first, they gave no indication that he would be invited to join their excursion, which honestly suited him just fine.

Then Thomas spoke. Recent comments to his wife notwithstanding, Thomas was usually the one to look out for Art. Growing up, he ensured that their youngest brother was included in their games. And so, he had been the one to suggest the idea of a “Pre-Stag Party.”

“The soon-to-be bridegroom needs a final evening to sow his wild oats before the big day,” he said, looking toward Art.

Junior and Ralph followed his gaze, almost surprised to find their youngest brother standing there.

“The wedding isn't for six months,” protested Ralph.

“Right. Hence, it's a *pre*-stag party.”

No one was particularly sold on the idea – Art included – but when challenged by their wives and parents as to why they were going to disappear for the evening, that was the excuse used. Art still did not want to go, but without him, his brothers lost their rationale. Junior was especially eager to leave, and Art was persuaded to oblige.

“Little Sister, you get in the car or I will *put* you in the car.”

As they continued bouncing around the back roads, searching for the elusive moonshiners, Art was beginning to regret that he had not challenged it more. He doubly cursed himself with the realization that he need only have stayed with his brothers until they were out of sight of the cottage. He might have attempted to ditch while they were nearer to the lake and there was a chance of finding his way home. Now, he was just as lost as the rest of them.

Squinting into the dark with futility, Ralph said, “We’re supposed to turn when we pass a fence with one beam missing.”

Junior scoffed. “Do you see how many fences there are?” He shook his head. “I think you were duped by some hick having fun at your expense.” Junior was particularly agitated. Had he been more clearheaded, he would have noticed that all the fences they had passed thus far had been well maintained.

When Art noticed a section missing a single beam, it was plainly obvious. Having no particular inclination to go drinking with his brothers, Art’s hope was that they would take him back home after they had gotten what they wanted.

“Single beam missing. Right there,” he said, almost too quietly to be heard.

Junior stopped quickly, causing everyone to slide forward in their seats. After a moment of reversing back to the landmark, they turned off the narrow lane. If the main road, such as it was, had been merely unpaved, this new route was downright rough. The Buick rattled and bounced over every inch of their slow transit.

In the back, Ralph and Art had to brace themselves to stop from being tossed. The trees pressed in close, scratching along both sides of the car as they entered a forest.

At last, it felt like they were making progress, and the tension from a few moments ago started to abate. Despite everything, even Art began to feel a certain excitement. At last, they emerged into a clearing where a single structure came into view, perhaps a hundred yards distant. Gold orange light shone through the windows.

As they drew closer, Art saw the building in a series of quick glimpses as the Buick’s headlights flashed across it. It did not look like much. In fact, the house, such as it was, might have consisted of a single room. Another, even smaller, structure, sat behind it, and was built of the same round timbers as the main building. For all appearances, it might have been a log cabin on some frontier. The only concession to modernity was the dark shape of a truck sitting off to one side. Art then noticed a lone figure on the front porch, silhouetted against the yellow light.

“You think this is it?” asked Thomas.

Junior brought the car up closer to the house, painting the cabin’s front side with light. In doing so, Art could see the lone figure more clearly. He was a younger man but darkness and his floppy hat concealed most other details. The lights reflected off something shiny in the man's lap, but it was only a glance. The porch quickly returned to darkness, and Art was unsure of what he had actually seen.

"Yeah, this is it," Ralph said, with what was probably more confidence than he felt. They all squinted at the house.

The silhouetted man on the porch had not moved.

"He said their name was Brandelson," Ralph continued. "Also, there's a password to get in. So they know you're not a lawman." He fell silent.

"And do you know what it is?" asked Junior, his impatience returning.

"Yeah," replied Ralph. "Lemme think... it's 'Jerry sent me.' Or 'John sent me.' It's definitely a 'J' name."

"Oh, for crying out loud," muttered Thomas, whose frustration was directed at the absurdity of the situation.

Junior's, by contrast, was focused entirely on Ralph.

"Which. Is. It?" Junior bit off each word.

Ralph's eyes darted back and forth as he struggled to remember.

"It's 'Jerry'. Definitely 'Jerry,'" he blurted out.

Art suspected he was less than sure, but Junior nodded, apparently satisfied.

"Alright, wait here." He turned to leave.

Thomas put a hand on his arm saying, "You're not really going alone into a strange house with a couple of moonshiners you never met before?"

Junior waved him off. As the largest of the four brothers, he was probably the best suited for an altercation, should one arise.

"I've made sales with Jersey City bootleggers and spent time in the bad parts of Brooklyn. You think of a couple of backwater yokels scare me?"

"All the same, I'll come with you," Thomas insisted.

Junior sighed. "Fine, you old woman. Come on."

Ralph opened his door at the same time as Junior and Thomas. "I'm coming too," he said quickly.

This time, Junior did not even bother to reply. They started towards the house when Thomas paused and looked back at Art, now alone in the car. They met eyes and Thomas shrugged his shoulders as if to ask, "You staying?"

Art sighed, but ultimately followed. While he was no stranger to being ridiculed by his brothers, there was no sense in gifting them new ammunition by hiding behind like a coward. There was little doubt that he would hear about it for the rest of the summer if he were the only one to refuse adventure's call.

Thomas met him at the front of the car, and they followed behind Ralph and Junior. The oldest brother had already reached the porch steps.

Once again, Art caught the glint of something in the yellow light as the man lifted it to his lips. It was a glass mason jar filled with a clear liquid. The light caught the man's long, sandy-haired as he took a swig.

I suppose I admire someone who stands by their own product, thought Art. He shook his head. A moment ago, he could have sworn that the shiny glint looked different. As if it were metal instead of glass.

"Help you?" the young man asked after finishing his drink.

"I sure hope so," replied Junior, pitching his voice as if he were making a sale. "Might you be Mr. Brandelson?"

"I might be... you can drop the 'Mister' though."

"My brothers and I heard you were a businessman of just the sort we're looking for."

Junior shifted from surly to suave with such efficiency that Art couldn't help but shake his head.

What a cad.

The sandy-haired man, unmoved by Junior's words, cocked his head to one side, inviting him to elaborate.

Then, remembering something, Junior said, "Right. We have a mutual friend. Ah... Jerry sent me."

He finally stopped talking, but the man made no response. After a moment passed with no reply, Junior began to shift his weight. While Art was just as nervous, he appreciated the sight of his brother made uncomfortable for a change. At last, the sandy-haired man stood up and chuckled.

"I haven't heard that one in a while. You boys wanna buy some hooch or what?"

Art and his brothers breathed a collective sigh of relief.

The moonshiner beckoned them up the stairs, his demeanor more friendly than it had been. "Let me guess, you get that from Philip down at CasinO?" he asked.

Ralph nodded. The man shook his head.

"He works for us sometimes. Got this idea into his head that we should have a special password or phrase like we're some kind o' damned speakeasy. I told him to go right ahead. Been so long since he sent anyone our way, I forgot all about it."

"So... there's no password?" Ralph asked.

"What for?" replied the man.

"Well, how do you know we're not cops or something?"

This coaxed another chuckle from the man. "You sayin' you are?" he asked pointedly, putting Ralph at a loss for words.

"No. I ah…"

"Relax, fella, I'm only pulling yer leg. Firstly, I know every cop in this town. Some of my best customers in fact. Thirsty buggers, every one of 'em. 'Specially my unc-"

"Timothy!" came a shout from inside the house. "You aimin' to wag your jaw all night or bring 'em in?"

Timothy looked annoyed and appeared ready to say something in response, but held back. He contented himself with a silent sneer and an eye roll. Then, returning his attention to Junior, he opened the door without a word and casually waved them inside.

Junior, whom had remarkably kept silent, walked in first followed closely by Ralph. Timothy remained holding the door open, and raised an eyebrow at Thomas and Art, still at the base of the steps. They exchanged a quick glance, then followed.

Coming from the night outside, the relative brightness of the house was jarring. Two kerosene lamps hung from the ceiling above the four brothers as they waited on their hosts.

As Art had suspected, the cabin was little more than a shack. A single room was divided into the main lower level and a loft, which was only accessible by ladder. It smelled of soot and the potent musk of three bachelors living and working in a small space. Another, astringent aroma was present as well. Art recognized it as something he knew, but could not immediately identify.

It was cramped with all the Adams brothers inside, especially for Art who was pressed up against the pot-bellied stove. What little space remained was occupied by a large table on which rested a barrel and several dozen mason jars in various stages of being filled. One man tended the jars and was of an age with Timothy, but with much darker hair. Despite the difference in general appearance, their faces were of similar shape. Art would not have been surprised to learn they were brothers or at least relations of some kind.

A third man fiddled with a small valve on the side of the barrel. Clearly older, Art decided that he was the owner of the voice that had interrupted Timothy a moment earlier. The man's back remained turned to Art and the others as he worked.

They waited silently, unsure of how to proceed. After a moment, Junior regained some of his usual confidence, and attempted to initiate the conversation.

"Good evening, sir. I-"

"Hold there, fella," the man cut him off and motioned for him to remain where he was. "Name's Mickey and I'll be with you in a minute."

Everyone else remained silent. Mickey soon finished whatever he was doing with the barrel and handed a length of hose to the dark haired brother.

"Should be working now, Jeff. Fill 'em to half an inch from the lid. Not no higher."

"Yes, sir." As Jeff began filling the jars using the tool, the astringent odor present in the room intensified.

Ethanol, Art realized. *Of course*.

It had been a few years since he had smelled alcohol of such potency. Despite their uncertain situation with possibly unscrupulous actors, Art nodded to himself in satisfaction. He liked answering his own questions.

The place absolutely reeked of it. It made sense that a shiner shack would smell the part, but he still marveled that the air in the cabin was saturated enough for him to actually smell it. Art found his eyes drawn to the lanterns hanging overhead, now keenly aware of an open flame so close to a vaporized combustible.

"Have you considered switching to electric?" Art asked, without thinking about it.

Every eye in the room suddenly turned on him.

"Beg your pardon?" asked Mickey.

Art wilted under the intense gaze, and suddenly wished to be invisible again. Working for Gregory, he had grown accustomed to candidly offering his technical opinion without a second thought. Unfortunately, that was a vastly different environment to the one he now found himself in. When it was clear that the older man was not going to move on without a response, Art swallowed and worked up a reply.

"What I mean is... you've got ethanol in the air... and lanterns. Electric light would be less likely to start a fire."

Mickey stared at Art. "Would it now?" His tone was neutral, but there was no mistaking his annoyed expression.

Timothy and Jeff exhibited a distinct unease at this prolonged silence. This, in turn, caused Art's own discomfort to intensify. The man was clearly expecting another answer, so Art nodded.

"Yes, sir." Another moment passed.

"I'll be sure to keep that in mind," the man replied.

Both Ralph and Junior glared at Art. Even Thomas looked at him with a wide-eyed expression and shook his head in bafflement.

Mickey turned back to Junior, and thankfully continued, taking attention off the youngest Adams. Art held his tongue for the rest of the exchange, listening as Junior unsuccessfully attempted to haggle with the senior moonshiner. The bargaining got heated as Junior felt that Mickey's asking price was too high. While things never escalated to anything physical, Junior implied there would be trouble if Mickey did not budge on the cost.

Glancing at Timothy, Art thought about how far this place was from anywhere, and whether the car would even be found if it so happened they never left. To his relief, Junior backed down and they soon left with two jars of corn liquor at an exorbitant price.

Junior shoved both jars toward Thomas as they piled back into the car. Art breathed a sigh of relief as the Buick started rolling. No one spoke as they doubled back on the same dirt road they had come in on. Junior was breathing heavy and grumbled as he took the road much faster than he had on their approach. As such, the ride was even bumpier.

"Bunch of hillbilly savages," he said through gritted teeth as they wound their way down the path. "Damn extortion." He waved a finger at the three others. "And don't think you're going to get out of paying an equal share. I was willing to make it my treat for five, but twenty? Absolutely not."

Art suppressed a grin. It was rare to see his domineering older brother get bested for a change. Though Thomas was facing away from him, Art could tell from his slumped shoulders and body language that he was rolling his eyes.

"Hey Junior," interrupted Thomas, the only one of them who could get away with such defiance.

"What!?" he snapped.

"Have a drink."

Art had never been truly drunk before. Once in a while, of course, he might have a single glass of beer or wine – maybe even two. Even rarer for hard liquor, and never to excess. He was not against it, per se. He just never quite saw the appeal.

Thus far, the experience had been a mixed bag. After his first sip, which he nearly choked on, he wasn't sure he wanted any more. He might have spit it out, but was genuinely concerned that Junior would toss him from the car, while moving, if he wasted a single drop.

Apparently, it was not just his lack of experience that made the drink harsh. Both Thomas and Ralph expressed some dissatisfaction with the quality of product.

"Damn, Junior. You sure paid a lot for Turpentine." Ralph chuckled.

"The hell I did," Junior shot back. "I told you, you're all in for an equal share." He was still salty about the whole experience, but the fact that he let the comment slide was proof he was loosening up.

On the second round, Art attempted to pass to Ralph without taking a sip. His brother pushed it back at him.

"Just drink it, you woman."

Art sighed. It did not occur to him until several rounds later that he could simply put the jar to his lips and pretend to drink to avoid argument. The next sip didn't burn quite as much. As he continued to loosen up, he found he almost did not notice it. Almost.

They continued driving for some time.

"Where are you going?" asked Thomas, squinting down the road.

"Couldn't say. Not back home for sure. Martha's been driving me to madness lately. Spends money like it's going out of style. Do the children really need new clothes every time the season changes?" He glanced at Art and Ralph over his shoulder. "Take note, both of you. Hold out for as long as you can."

"Oh, it's not all bad," countered Thomas. "Family life has a lot of benefits, which I rather appreciate."

"Not me," said Ralph after another swig. "How could you ever settle for just one woman?"

Junior chuckled in a provocative manner.

"Listen to Dapper Dan back there. Bet you got 'em lining up back home, don't you?"

Grinning widely, Ralph passed the moonshine. "It's not often that I find myself lonely," he replied.

Thomas shook his head. "Come on, now. Don't you want to bring a nice girl home to meet Mother?"

"Oh, I bring nice girls home all the time. They just leave after."

Junior laughed raucously and slapped the steering wheel for good measure. "Attaboy!" he nearly shouted.

Thomas just shook his head after taking another pull of the moonshine, and passed back to Art. "Maybe you just need to meet the right one. You'd be surprised. When I met Claudine, I just knew."

Junior groaned. “Tom, I love you, but you're a damn sap sometimes,” he grumbled, to which Ralph chortled.

Undeterred, Thomas pressed on. “Serious though. All I'm saying is you might consider finding a girl who stimulates your mind and not just your trousers.”

“Yeah,” scoffed Ralph with a grin. “Then I can be as happy as Junior here.”

“Watch it,” growled Junior, making it clear that teasing was a one-way street with him.

Ralph's grin quickly vanished.

Relaxing again, Junior carried on. “And how about Mr. College back there?”

Art was struck by a fleeting panic. It was usually best for his oldest brother to be unaware of his existence, good mood or no. Besides, he didn't have much to contribute to the current conversation.

“U Penn is co-ed, right?” Junior asked. “All those young lovelies must be something... even if they are all wearing *pants* now.”

Art remained silent, content to let Junior construct his own mental picture. He took another drink – more as something to keep occupied rather than anything else. The car lurched as Junior made a sharp correction, causing Art to take a larger swallow than he had intended. The burn from the moonshine went up into his nose, and he had to suppress a cough.

“Hey Art,” Junior continued. “You gotten laid yet or what?”

Still trying to recover, Art was seized by a coughing fit.

“Good grief, Junior,” scolded Thomas.

“No way,” Ralph chimed in, answering for his brother. He took the jar from Art's loose grip. “There’s *eggs* been laid more than him.”

Art made no reply as he tried to get his coughing spell under control to no avail.

“I'm sure he's broken a respectable number of hearts,” Thomas offered. “Haven't you?”

It was actually something of a sore subject for Art. Indelicate as he had put it, Ralph was correct. Art recovered, but remained silent. He would not dare reveal any details of his romantic misadventures to his brothers. Not even Thomas.

With no women in the engineering department, and finding himself there for most of his waking hours, it was a rare occasion that he would even meet one. Rarer still for things to become romantic.

Of his two encounters in college, both were rather spectacular failures. The first was Rebecca Allen, a sorority girl two years his senior. She was something of a known flirt, and what one of his friends euphemistically referred to as “a sure thing.”

As it happened, Art caught her eye, and true to her reputation they retired to her room one evening. The word “flirt” turned out to be a profound understatement. Their little tryst held much promise, but things took an embarrassing turn when she asked Art to wear a prophylactic.

He had never seen, let alone worn one before, but dared not admit this fact to his more experienced companion. In hindsight, perhaps he should have. In the time it took for him to work out its operation, the mood had passed, and they parted ways, unfulfilled. Needless to say, the entire sorority learned about this in short order, and word quickly spread. The mockery that followed ensured that he made no other attempts for a long time.

Art kept a low profile, focusing instead on his studies and the occasional shift at the tool and die shop. That suited him just fine for a while. Three full semesters passed before he met someone again. This time, things were much more serious. Just after the winter recess of his third year, he met an undergraduate named Sarah Grant.

They met in the library on an otherwise unremarkable evening. Art happened to be walking by, and she was struggling to reach a book on a high shelf. Normally, he might have continued on his way without another word, but something about Sarah made him pause. In an act of uncharacteristic bravery, he said some off-hand comment about the subject matter in question. To his surprise, Sarah responded, and after that they really hit it off.

As a student, she was bright, and the first woman from her family to go to college. Outspoken and kind, she really pulled Art out of his shell. Their courtship lasted for the rest of the semester, and they saw much of each other. However, they were obliged to keep things quiet fort the sake of her parents who, despite having a daughter in college, were very much traditionalists in all other regards. Their plan was to make introductions after graduation, when delicate sensibilities would, hopefully, not matter as much.

That was their plan, and it might have worked out. However, like many new romances, they were eager for things to become physical. One night, while Art's roommate was out of town, she sneaked into the men's dormitory. This night was the culmination of several weeks of unsuccessful attempts to arrange some time alone. And when the night finally came... Art found himself embarrassed for a second time.

One might say the evening was over before it started, and Art counted himself lucky that the full details of his over-enthusiasm were not known to anyone who would gossip about it. At the time, they thought they would simply try again another night.

Unfortunately, they never got the chance.

Sarah had been observed leaving the men's dormitory that evening, and word eventually made its way back to her parents. Furious, they pulled her out of school, and cut off all contact with Art. Phone calls went unanswered. Letters were summarily returned to sender without being opened. Since he did, in fact, have their address, he considered doing something that could not be ignored and show up in person.

He made it as far as buying a train ticket, but never boarded. At the last minute, doubt kept his feet rooted to the station platform. Art and Sarah had only known each other a few months after all. Maybe she did not feel as strongly for him as he thought she did. After all, she had not replied to a single letter.

That was what he told himself, even though he did not really believe it. When he considered what he would say to Sarah's parents, he realized that it would be fight, and he lost his nerve. Art eventually returned to school for his final year, but Sarah did not. The two of them never spoke again.

Reflecting on it now, already in a sour mood with even darker thoughts limbered by the moonshine, Art considered that perhaps Thomas was right. He was a wimp.

The car struck another pothole. This one so deep that it was practically a ditch. By this time, Junior was already three sheets to the wind, but took another swig of hooch. He held up a finger, while drinking, to indicate a thought was forming amid his sodden wits. It occurred to Art that this would account for both hands, neither of which were currently steering. He was equal parts impressed and horrified. Thomas reached a similar conclusion and shot his own hand to grip the steering wheel before Junior shooed him away.

"Y'know," he said after his long pull. "That was a bum deal. Country bumpkin completely took me for a ride." He passed the drink to Thomas before turning his full attention back to the road. "I've got a mind to go back and tell him what's what. For that price, I should have gotten three jars of hooch. Maybe even four."

Art had been hoping that his brother would let the matter drop, but the drinking had sufficiently boosted his confidence, and diminished his common sense to the point where he was itching for a fight. Thankfully, Thomas mirrored Art's feelings on the matter and quickly passed the glass without taking a sip.

"Brother mine," he started, voice pitched carefully. "Let's leave the country bumpkin alone. We still have a whole 'nother jar here."

Art winced. That was the wrong thing to say. Direct and open contradiction to Junior was almost never successful. Thomas only realized his mistake too late.

"What I mean is, perhaps we should try again tomorrow. And make another night of it. My treat."

But Junior was already slowing down, looking for a place to turn on the narrow, dirt road. He shot Thomas a look that Art recognized too well, and the second oldest realized that further debate was over.

"That backwater rusticate is going to get a piece of my mind and then some, let me tell you."

While Thomas looked defeated, and prepared to settle in for the inevitable, Ralph actually chuckled, before snatching the drink from Art's loose grip. Growing impatient, Junior soon found a place to turn around, and the car banked sharply, once again tossing the occupants.

After shifting into reverse to complete the turn, the car shuddered with the sound of crunching metal and snapping wood. It took Art a moment to realize they had hit something. Junior shifted again and the car lurched forward, presumably back in the direction of the Brandelsons. Art caught a glimpse of the thing they had broken, before it disappeared into the night behind them. Thankfully, it was only a mailbox.

Junior resumed speaking, oblivious to the damage. "Where was that damned road to the hooch mongers?"

"It was by the broken fence," offered Ralph, apparently energized by the prospect of a fight. He and Junior were very much cut from the same cloth in that regard.

Thankfully, everyone had forgotten that Art had been the one to spot the broken fence initially. When they passed the landmark some time later, it went without remark. Art watched it sail past his window but wisely kept his mouth shut this time. He breathed a little easier as they continued navigating the back roads and put more distance between themselves, and what would surely have been an unfortunate confrontation for all involved.

As time went on, his relief soured and he was ready to go home. They had been driving for nearly twice as long as it had taken them to get here in the first place, and his stomach and bladder were competing for which one could cause the most discomfort. Finally realizing the trick of only pretending to drink, he imbibed nothing more, but the damage was done. His head was spinning independent of the motion of the car and the queasy feeling in his gut intensified.

Junior grew more frustrated as it became evident that they would not find the Brandelsons again. Thomas had since given up trying to talk him down, now hoping that Junior would burn out on his own. Art held a similar hope, now confident that Timothy had in fact been holding a gun.

In his drunken, angry state, Junior suddenly pulled the car off the road, and started bouncing through a field.

Startled, Thomas finally rediscovered his voice. "Where are you going?"

"This is a shortcut, I think. The house was in a field."

"I imagine there's more than one field around here," replied Thomas.

Thankfully, he was correct, and Junior was mistaken. Several minutes later, the car lurched to a stop, aimed towards a wall of trees. With nowhere left to go, Junior engaged the brake and opened his door.

"I'm taking a piss," he declared, stepping out into the night.

Ralph again followed after his brother while Thomas and Art breathed a silent sigh of relief. After exchanging a look, they realized they too had to make a deposit and exited.

Junior and Ralph approached the tree line, with the car's headlights casting their shadows across the edge of the forest.

"Watch out," Ralph said, pointing to a leafy vine snaked around the tree. "Poison ivy here. It'll make your dingus itch so much, you'll scratch it off."

This made Junior cackle, and Art hoped that it was the beginning of a positive mood change.

"This, from the man with no wife," Junior replied.

"Exactly," Ralph shot back. "I've got a chance of using mine again."

Junior guffawed this time, which was loud in the dark, and continued the banter. Even Thomas laughed as he lined up next to his brothers. Art had been about to stand next to him, but at the last second, decided to relocate a short distance away.

After spending well over an hour with Junior and Ralph, he was in need of a short reprieve before they all crammed back into the car.

Though just a bit wobbly on his feet he staggered over to a tree, confident that he could identify poison ivy from a safe distance.

While out of sight, Art could hear his brothers, but paid little mind to their words. It was their abrupt shift in tone combined with a new voice that gave him cause for alarm. Art peaked around the tree, now paying full attention. His wits remained slower than usual, and he struggled to see much beyond the glare of the Buick's headlights.

Junior made a rude hand gesture, but otherwise continued to relieve himself. Thomas and Ralph, like Art, strained their eyes to see past the lights.

It was the gunshot that caught their attention.

A clump of dirt and grass burst up from the ground, not ten steps from Junior's feet.

"I said, 'git off my land!'" The stranger was still hidden, but his wishes were clear.

Art tucked himself away, quick as he was able. Perhaps too quickly. He gasped as he caught himself with the zipper. Making a second, and far more careful attempt, he kept the tree between himself and the others.

It would not be until hours later that he would regret his hesitation. Naturally, his first impulse was to stay away from the sound of gunfire, but there was also a reasonable chance that Junior would talk himself out of the situation.

Per the latter, Junior was attempting to do exactly that, but the armed landowner was having none of it. His only reply was another shot. This one landed even closer to Art, causing him to duck, and rooted his feet to the spot. More than likely, Art had simply not been seen, and the farmer was firing in what he thought to be a safe direction. However, Art was not confident enough to take that chance.

With alarm, he heard the sound of doors slamming and the car started rolling back across the field. Stunned, he watched the lights dance away into the dark. It was some time later before Art realized they had left without him. Tentatively, he began to move away from the tree to give chase, but stopped upon hearing the landowner. By the time he finished sending a steady stream of profanity into the night, the lights from the car were gone.

"Damned out-of-towners," he grumbled.

Eyes adjusting to the moonlight, Art watched the man turn away. He started towards a house in the distance that none of them had noticed before. The man cursed the trespassers until his voice, too, faded into the night.

It was not until after several minutes of silence that Art finally permitted his feet to move. Even then, he kept one hand on the tree, ready to duck behind it again.

All the excitement had a temporary sobering effect, which chased the sogginess from his head. With the danger now passed, the effects of the alcohol came back in full force. And with it, the realization that it was dark, and no one was coming back for him.

It took him close to half of an hour just to find his way back to the main road. By one saving grace, the moon was close to full tonight and high in the sky. The clouds had also seen fit to leave it unobstructed. The Buick's tire marks left an unmistakable trail in some kind of leafy crop, which he was able to follow.

Once Art reached the packed dirt of the main roadway, he was forced to try and remember what route they had taken to get here. Mostly sure that the car had turned right to get onto the field, he turned left to exit, and hoped that his sodden wits were not playing games with his sense of direction.

Still quite inebriated, the simple act of walking was no minor task and worse yet, he had no idea where he was. Briefly, he considered stopping at one of the farmhouses to ask for directions, but did not see any lights on. The sound of barking dogs finally discouraged him from approaching and Art resolved to figure it out on his own. This particular stretch of road had no turns to speak of, and he was reasonably sure he was going the right way. Still, it was a long walk, and through sheer force of will he set one foot in front of another.

With the moon near full, he looked around and saw no significant landmarks of any kind. The ground was clear for as far as he could see in all directions. Nothing was familiar. As a side benefit of all the walking, his head started to clear. But just as the queasy, dizzy feeling began to subside he felt the increasingly strong pull of sleep.

It was difficult to say how long he plodded before he stumbled. After nearly falling on his face, he noticed a large hill rose up from the roadway on his right. Thinking that he might be able to determine a general direction or distance from the vantage point, he climbed while taking great care where he placed his feet.

Reaching the top, Art walked through a few rows of trees, and climbed over a low rock wall before reaching a clearing. It appeared to be another farm, with a chicken coop and barn some distance away from a small house. Thankfully, no dogs barked. Wary of meeting any more farmers, he made his way around the barn.

As luck would have it, he could see lights in the distance. While he could not be sure, Art guessed it was the Oasis or maybe one of the other lakeside attractions. His sigh of relief quickly morphed into a groan as he realized the lights were still a long way off. The pull of sleep grew stronger.

Art took a moment to consider his options as his eyelids drooped of their own accord. He did not have another mile of walking in him.

To make matters worse, the moon had become obscured by a continuous blanket of clouds. The diminished light would make the remainder of his trek that much harder. Art sighed again, this time in resignation, as he realized that he would not be sleeping in a bed tonight.

Just a couple hours until the sun comes up, he thought.

Unable to find a comfortable position on the ground, Art looked for a way into the barn. Touching one hand against the wall, he walked around two sides before he came across a large pair of sliding doors. Pushing against one, it gave way with minimal resistance. A distant, logical part of his brain commended whoever maintained it.

Once inside, he closed the door again, hoping to remain undiscovered by any more farmers. In the pitch dark, his hands came across a bunched-up, canvas tarpaulin. Wrapping himself, he barely had enough time to pull off his glasses before promptly falling asleep.

Chapter 11
Etta

The night following Etta's day as a laundress had been a rough one. Sleep came fitfully, and the pain of her burning hands had interrupted what little there was. The sky was still black when she eventually gave up on trying to keep her eyes closed. Awake even earlier than usual, Etta lay in bed, waiting for the sky outside her window to change color.

Outside, she heard Papa loading up the truck with the eggs she had collected the previous evening. Briefly, she considered getting out of bed to see him off, but remembered the gloves she was still wearing and the questions they would raise.

If Papa knew what kind of pain she was in, he would undoubtedly make a fuss, and probably stay home. If that happened, they would both lose a day of earnings, and she would lose her relative freedom. Unwilling to take the risk, Etta remained where she was and waitied for Papa to leave.

Hoping for just a bit more rest before her own day started, Etta closed her eyes. Jakob soon finished, and she expected that he would drive away. Instead, he quietly made his way back into the house.

Her bedroom door opened just a crack. Curious, she remained still, feigning sleep.

"Be seeing you," he whispered in Polish. It was soft and he did not pass the threshold of the door, but she heard the words clearly. Once again, she thought about rolling over to say goodbye, but hesitated. Papa left before she could reconsider.

Etta did not fall back asleep, but remained in bed with her troubled thoughts. Mostly, she thought about her father, and their limited interactions since Mama had died. In doing so, something occurred to her that had eluded her up until now.

Jakob was not just worried about losing the farm. He was also lonely.

Unable to strike a match, Etta had to wait until the sun was high enough to see. Thankfully, Papa had made enough coffee for both of them. The pot was lukewarm by the time she got to it, but the drink worked its magic. Her experiments with trying to remove the Vaseline-filled gloves all ended poorly. After that, she resolved to leave them on for the rest of the day at least. While it kept the pain manageable, it made a challenge of even the simplest task. She was able to grip the muck rake well enough, though it was painful. After some practice, she could collect eggs. However, using the necessary was a particular and intimate challenge. There was no alternative but to temporarily remove the gloves and bear the discomfort.

Without the full use of her hands, her normally busy day was even more difficult. Worse still, she realized that they were out of chicken feed and she would first have to retrieve the cart from where she had left it by the Hatakawana Inn. That cost her nearly two full hours of precious time. Thankfully, she was able to pull the wagon from the crook of her elbow rather than her hands. Otherwise, it would have remained where it was.

Besides the physical discomfort, her gloves must have made for an odd sight and Etta was terribly self-conscious of them while she was in town. She had gone to Dominic's, knowing he would ask the fewest questions.

It bothered her that she needed his help placing the chicken feed and a few other groceries in her cart and counting the money out of her bag. While Dominic inquired about whether she was alright, he was good enough not to press the matter. Still, hauling the laden cart back home was such an ordeal that she did not even bother attempting to hard-boil any eggs for the construction workers. Not that she could start a fire anyway.

Upon returning home, Etta started to feel lightheaded. It occurred to her that she had not eaten anything since the light lunch at the Hatakawana on the previous day. While she had skipped meals before, usually she could compensate by drinking more water. Since squeezing the handle to pump the well was incredibly painful, she went thirsty also.

Things grew so desperate that several chores were put off entirely, and she reflected on just how much she depended on her hands. At that point, she almost walked down the street to ask for help from the

Saunders. Almost. Ultimately, Etta decided that she would manage on her own. Papa might have stayed home to take care of Etta, but if Aunt Mildred became involved, her independence would certainly be forfeit.

It was a decision she would come to regret.

Her first stumble occurred shortly thereafter and turned into a harrowing experience. Feeding the chickens was something she had done countless times, and rarely thought twice about. Indeed, she was accustomed to seeing the ladies go into a frenzy when she poured the food into the trough. Feeling dizzy and suffering from even less sleep than usual, Etta's foot snagged on an exposed root. The contents of the bucket spilled all over her as she fell to the ground. When the birds went into their frenzy, it was not the trough they fell upon.

It was Etta.

What followed was pecking and scratching from all sides. Such was the intensity, that for several seconds, Etta could do nothing but react. She put her hands up to protect her face against the frantic pecking of a dozen beaks. Even through the gloves, it was painful as well as terrifying.

The onslaught only ended when she managed to kick them away long enough to find her feet and stumble out of the pen. Heart racing, and downright shaken, she crawled to the barn, and rested her back against a rain barrel.

It was a while before she calmed down enough to be able to cry.

With a grimace, Etta realized that the chickens also needed to be watered. Even if she was not willing to suffer the discomfort of pumping water for herself, she could not rightly deny the birds, even if she was still rather wary of them.

Setting herself to the task, she sighed with resignation, and grabbed the handle. Had she been thinking more clearly, Etta might have contrived some way of manipulating it other than with her hands. As it was, she was moving automatically, and simply did the same as she had always done.

Clenching her jaw, Etta pushed down as fresh pain shot through her hands. Each stroke was like plunging her hands into fire. After only two cycles, she was crying. By the fourth, she could take no more.

Sucking air through her teeth, she took a few steps before she realized she was in trouble. The dizzy, lightheaded feeling from earlier returned worse than ever, and spider webs started to creep in the edge of her vision.

Etta staggered. Then her legs gave out.

The last thing she was aware of was being on the ground, looking sideways at the house. Then, she blacked out entirely.

Some time passed where Etta slipped in and out of consciousness. It was impossible to say for how long. At some point, she was rolled onto her back and she realized she was looking up at a face. Oddly enough, she recognized Papa almost immediately, but his words made no sense.

Eventually, she worked out that he was asking what had happened, but it was still some time before she could say anything besides, "I don't know."

Trying to lift her up, Jakob reached for one of her hands.

Instinctively, Etta pulled back and screamed, "No!"

Even with her thoughts all muddled, that much she remembered. More confused than ever, Jakob nonetheless complied. Instead, he lifted her by her shoulders into a seated position and his fingers gently parted her hair as he looked at her scalp.

"Where did you bump your head?" he asked.

"I didn't," she replied as her wits finally started to return. She was about to push him away, but stopped, remembering she could not touch anything without pain. "Could I have some water, please?"

Jakob nodded and quickly disappeared into the house for a cup. She did not argue, but would have settled for the bucket just then.

Papa did not ask again about what happened, but it turned out that he did not have to. After downing the contents of the glass, which he was obliged to hold to her lips, she immediately requested another.

As he filled it again from the well, the story poured out of her in short order. Laundry at the hotel. Her itching and soon painful hands. Her agonizing walk home. Somehow, she managed to avoid saying anything about the secret meeting she had witnessed. Jakob listened intently and silently.

"And you didn't touch anything else? Just the laundry soap?"

"No."

"Are you sure that's what the powder was?"

About to nod, Etta stopped herself. "There wasn't a label or anything, but it was with the laundry supplies."

His eyes narrowed as he considered her words. Holding the water glass up to Etta's lips again, his expression turned both thoughtful and suspicious. After about three glasses' worth, she felt somewhat recovered.

Papa asked, "What did Mildred say about the powder?"

"I... didn't talk to her."

He was taken aback. "You were like this all day, and you didn't ask for help?"

"It wasn't that bad before," she lied. "It just hit me all of a sudden." Etta did not want to explain the truth.

With a shudder, she realized that if Papa had not looked in the back yard, he would have probably assumed she was at the Saunders. In that case, she might have remained outside all night.

The exertion of speaking left her feeling tired again, but she recognized it as the more mundane variety. She was ready to sleep, not about to faint.

Papa led her to bed, and she was too tired to even protest that she had more chores to finish. After getting her boots and work apron off, she rolled to one side and fell fast asleep.

This night was far more peaceful than the one before it. Sleep was only interrupted once when she rolled onto a hand. It was so restful, that for the first time in nearly two years, the sun had started the day without her. After waking, Etta briefly wondered if it had been just one night or two.

The full light of day put her into a near panic. Until she could get a look at the clock in the other room, there was no telling just how much time she had lost. Not only did she have to complete today's chores, but also the ones she had skipped yesterday.

Intending to hurry and make up for lost time, Etta pushed back her blanket but stopped upon seeing her hands.

She stared with mild horror.

The gloves had been replaced with bandages. Her fingers and thumbs were now wrapped together in a club on each arm. She simply could not work like this.

Getting up from bed, she looked for something to cut them off. The floor was cold against her bare feet as she made for the kitchen. To her surprise, a whole plate of eggs and sausage was waiting on the table. At first, she thought maybe Papa had prepared his own breakfast and neglected to put the dishes away. It was then that she noticed the food was untouched and must have been left for her.

She groaned. It was embarrassing to be unable to care for herself. On the other hand, it was more food on one plate than she had eaten in the previous week. Hunger soon overruled pride. After fumbling with using a fork, she eventually worked out a system to scoop the food into her mouth by clamping the utensil between the clubs at the end of her arms.

It was not graceful, but it worked. The food was cold now, but to her it was a banquet for a queen and she tore into it as fast as her clumsy method would allow. As Etta found the bottom of her plate, the kitchen door opened.

Mildred Saunders stood beyond and wiped her shoes on the landing before letting herself inside. She smiled in greeting, but it was underscored by distinct concern. As she approached the kitchen table, her attention was focused squarely on Etta, who remained more or less oblivious to the scrutiny.

"Morning, Aunt Mildred," she greeted, holding up one of her bandage mittens to wave.

After eating her first meal in possibly two days, Etta was feeling on top of the world and had temporarily forgotten about them. She lowered her hand sheepishly and Mildred frowned.

"You and I need to have a talk," she said, dropping her bags on the table. "But first, how are those?" She motioned to Etta's hands.

"Much better," Etta said. She was about to undo the bandage to prove it, but quickly remembered that with both hands covered, she was unable to do so. Undeterred, she fumbled with them, trying to find a loose end of bandage to work on.

"Don't you dare take those off," Mildred commanded. Even without raising her voice, her tone conveyed an imperative that would not be ignored.

Etta was startled as she considered the implications of Mildred's words. The elation from a full meal began to subside as she remembered all the chores she was surely behind on. Recovering, she resumed searching the table for a knife or something to cut the bandages off, protesting the entire time.

"Honestly, they're feeling just fine now. I really think that I can-OW!"

An involuntary yelp escaped Etta's mouth as Mildred squeezed her bandaged hand, just enough to make her point. Etta's eyes went narrow in anger for a brief second before quickly transitioning to shock.

Now that she was paying attention, she recognized Mildred's expression for what it was. Normally something reserved for Helen or her siblings when they were being especially difficult, Etta had never once thought she would be on the receiving end of it. Her shoulders slumped in tacit compliance, and Mildred took a breath.

"That's better. Now, first things first: you are not to do any work around the farm today. Helen is going to collect your eggs, and Mark is going to sell them for you. The money is still yours. Michael will clean the chicken coop and change their straw. I will take care of your laundry and cooking. Your bandages will be changed and we'll put more ointment on your hands before dinner."

"For how long?" Etta asked, even though she suspected the answer.

"For however long it takes," Mildred replied sharply. Then, more softly, "You're young, so you'll heal quickly. But I'd guess no less than a week. Maybe more."

Etta grimaced.

The older woman shook her head. "And honestly, that's lucky. Lye is dangerous."

Forgetting about her chores for the moment, Etta's eyes went wide. "Is that what Heber gave me?"

Mildred nodded seriously, looking Etta directly in the eye. "He bought the boxes with the label torn off because they were cheaper. I'm not sure he realized that's what it was."

Etta thought about what Heber said as she was getting paid. "Having trouble keeping this position filled." She shuddered, thinking about how things might have gone differently.

"Your father gave him a proper tongue lashing," Mildred continued. "And I have a few choice words for *him* once he comes back."

Etta was genuinely confused by the last. "Why?" she asked.

"For being away when you needed him. For not providing for you. How many jobs do you need to take on? You were a waitress only last week."

Busgirl, Etta thought, but wisely decided against correcting Mildred.

"And then a laundress? All this on top of working a farm that should properly be run by three or four people." Mildred shook her head. "You and your father can't keep going on like this. I don't know how, but the two of you need to sort yourselves out."

Etta wanted to protest, but was unable to come up with anything close to a plausible rebuttal. Mildred was right, of course. She had been pushing herself too hard, but she dared not reveal the reasons. Etta eventually sighed and nodded. Mildred relaxed at that, having made her point.

"Now then," Mildred continued. "Why on Earth didn't you come to me immediately?" The harshness was gone from her voice. In contrast to her earlier tirade, now she almost sounded hurt.

Etta only shrugged, not meeting her eyes and not trusting herself to answer.

"Your mother was like a sister to me. If it had been me who was lost, and not Lena – God keep her – I know she would have looked after my girls. You don't have to go it alone, you know."

Mildred bit her lip, and Etta knew she meant every word.

In the back of her mind, she wondered how Mildred would react when she finally left town. Certainly, she would do her best to convince Etta to stay, and at that particular moment, she doubted her resolve to see it through.

"The bandages are not to come off until we change them tonight," Mildred repeated.

Etta nodded with resignation. It was pointless to argue. Suddenly, it occurred to her, that she had consumed a lot of water before going to bed, and upon waking had gone directly to the kitchen.

"Um… with that bandages," Etta started. "How will I use the necessary?"

Mildred straightened. "I've raised four children, and cared for three elderly parents. I can tend to one willful young woman."

Etta groaned inwardly. *One final indignity.*

It was an unusual problem for her: how to fill the day without the usual work to keep her busy. At first, she thought she might read, but turning the pages without fingers became more hassle than it was worth. The day was getting hot and she thought about going for a swim, but the bandages could not get wet, and she was averse to being seen in public with them.

With nothing to occupy her attention, she found herself pacing the yard between the barn and the house waiting for Helen to show up. Her friend was late, which was not unusual, except that now she used her unborn child as the reason.

"It's sure getting difficult to walk around with this belly."

It had been the first thing Helen said. Not, "How are your hands?" Not, "I'm sorry for what happened to you." Not even "Hello." In truth, Helen had the barest perceptible bump. Even then, Etta suspected much of that was due to the extra food her mother had been pushing on her.

Taken by itself, Etta might have let it pass unremarked. Water under the bridge, and all that. However, this morning, her nerves were already frayed. Annoyed at her inability to perform the slightest task by herself, Etta's patience was thin, and Helen's contrived hardships were not helping.

Etta's temper grew shorter still as the two of them proceeded to collect the morning eggs. Feeling out of sorts without at least something to do, Etta hooked the basket over her elbow while Helen pulled eggs from the coop. What should have taken fifteen minutes at most was taking twice as long, and the complaints were unceasing.

"Ugh. It stinks in here. I can't believe you do this every day. Mark collects the eggs at our house, and I'm happy to let him do it. I'm already exhausted, and I have to go mind the canal lock for the whole afternoon."

For a while, Etta remained quiet, enduring Helen's nonsense while grinding her teeth in silence.

At last, she reached her breaking point. "Just stop already!"

Helen froze just as she lifted another egg, and looked at her friend in surprise. Etta had raised her voice to Helen only a handful of times in her life. For a moment, Helen thought perhaps she had simply committed some faux pas known only to chicken farmers until Etta continued.

"*You* have a mother. *You* have a family. You think you have it so tough just because you're going to have a *child?* Maybe then you'll actually have to *do* something for a change!"

Helen could only stare in shock as Etta unleashed her venom.

It turned out, only to be the beginning.

Once started, she was unable to stop, bringing up grievances that had lain dormant for years. It continued for nearly a full minute, until she noticed there were tears in Helen's eyes.

Etta's shoulders slumped, spent from the exertion. Beneath the bandages, her injured hands pulsed with her beating heart.

"I... I'm sorry."

Before she could finish, Helen stormed off, dropping the last egg on the ground as she did so.

"Wait!" Etta called.

Helen did not stop or even turn around, and soon disappeared from view. Etta was alone once again.

Some time passed and Papa still had not returned home. Unwilling to stew any longer, Etta started walking. At first, she intended to go over to the canal house and make amends with Helen. It had not been their first fight – far from it – but Etta was feeling guilty for the anger behind her words.

That most of what she said had been true only made matters worse.

All else aside, it was no way to treat a lifelong friend, and it would not do to leave things as they were. She hesitated upon reaching the forest trail, and at the last moment, took the path leading away from the canal. The wounds were still too fresh. Knowing Helen, she would carry this grudge for a while.

Instead, Etta continued and let her thoughts wander. She was already in the woods, and followed random trails for a while. The simple act of walking and looking up through the trees did much to improve her mood. It was June now. The buds had grown into leaves and the days were growing longer and warmer.

Without particularly thinking about where she was going, she found herself on the trail leading up to the jalopy.

Reaching the car did much to help settle her troubled thoughts, and sitting in it nearly put her at ease. It was an especially good view today. Sunny and clear. Etta spent probably close to an hour sitting in the old car, reflecting on recent weeks and thinking about the future.

Her attempts to earn a little extra money had been frustrating and painful in multiple ways. She wondered if perhaps Helen had the right idea to simply not try so hard. It was quickly dismissed. Helen had the option of slacking off. She had all the Saunders and now the McCormicks to support her. Etta had only herself and Papa. Or did she? Etta recalled Mildred's words from that morning, but they were easier to ignore now that she was not bearing down on her.

Etta rested her mitts on top of the jalopy's steering wheel and thought about the city. Her dreams of leaving town were stronger in the car, as they often were. Sitting up here, with nothing but her own thoughts for company, the other concerns in her life were less important. Her eyes went to the box that contained the map. Remembering her bandages, she did not even bother attempting to retrieve it.

Mildred had succeeded only temporarily in shaking Etta from her plans. Alone and in this place, her resolve hardened once more.

Perhaps it would be easiest if Etta simply disappeared one day, before anyone could talk her out of it. The thought troubled her and soon she dismissed the idea. Etta prided herself on her honesty. At least one person should know. One in particular.

As expected, Helen was still holding a grudge. When Etta sat down on the bench, her friend remained silent and continued working on the basket in her lap. Using rushes from the side of the river today, the work was not up to her usual standards. Distracted as she was, her heart was simply not in it.

It took some time, but eventually Helen warmed up to the point where she was ready to retaliate. “You can be a real bitch when you’re hungry.”

Ouch.

“Actually, I don’t even have that excuse today,” Etta replied sullenly.

Helen looked sideways at her, still working on the basket. “You hurt my feelings before... I’m not *dumb*.”

Etta bit her lip. “I’m sorry. That was uncalled for... and it’s not like *I* finished high school either.”

Helen sighed. “How’re your hands?”

“They hurt. The ointment helps though.”

Helen turned her head, and frowned as she looked at Etta’s bandages. As if she were only seeing them for the first time. “That’s rough,” she said with sympathy. “I know I’d be pretty frustrated if I couldn’t work on my baskets for a whole week.” Helen composed her thoughts. “You know, I’m not lazy either. I’m just not as much of a busybody as my mother is... or you for that matter.”

“I’m not a busybody,” Etta protested, though it sounded insincere even to her own ears.

“Oh, come on now,” Helen replied.

“Alright, fine. But it’s not because I want to be. There’s just a lot that needs to be done.”

“Mom has offered to help with that, you know. If you’d let her. People can do that without it being *charity*.”

Etta did not answer right away. She started to prepare a rebuttal, but eventually decided that this was as good a time as any for a confession.

With reluctance, she said, “Can you keep a secret?”

This got Helen’s attention, and she nodded.

“I’m leaving town this fall.”

Stunned to silence, it took a moment for Helen to respond. “What? For how long?”

“I’m not sure,” Etta shrugged. “A while.”

"And where are you going?"

"I haven't decided that either."

"Just you? What about your dad?" The basket lay forgotten in Helen's lap.

"Papa's staying here. That's why I've been taking all the extra jobs lately. I need to save money."

"Wow..." Helen said. It was quiet enough that she might have said it to herself. "My mom's going to have a fit when she finds out."

"That's why it has to be a secret. You have to promise me you won't tell her."

Helen nodded. "Okay."

"No. Promise." Etta was emphatic. While it might have been excessive, a part of her did not trust Helen to keep mum about such a big piece of news.

"I promise, I won't tell her," Helen said seriously. Then, after a moment she added, "But you probably should."

Etta sighed, knowing it to be the truth, but loathe to admit it. "She'll just talk me out of it."

"Maybe, but she can be reasonable. You just better promise to write."

Since deciding to leave, Etta had wondered how Helen would take the news. Thus far, her reaction was not quite what she expected.

"Of course I'll write. And I'll come back to visit. I don't mean to disappear entirely."

"Well, I do," Helen replied, grinning. "Once Robert and I are married, I don't plan to leave the house any more than I have to. It'll be just heavenly to have my own place to relax."

Etta considered pointing out that Helen would likely have to take on all of the daily tasks currently done by her mother. Instead, she remained quiet, not wanting to accuse her of laziness twice in one day. Etta was simply thankful that she was taking the news so well.

"I'll miss you, Chicken Farmer." Helen said at last.

"You too, Madame Spinster."

Helen smiled wanly. "Looks like we have to make this summer count."

Etta stayed with the Saunders for dinner, per Mildred's insistence, and her bandages were changed. The ointment helped tremendously. While Etta offered to pay for it, Mildred stated that it was out of the question and the matter was settled. Etta hoped both that it did not cost too much, and also that her sigh of relief was not obvious.

Papa was home by the time she returned. Concern was plain on his face. She could only imagine his shock at discovering her the previous day.

"How is that?" he asked, indicating the fresh bandages on her hands.

Etta shrugged with what appeared to be indifference, but in truth, she felt contented.

"Better than yesterday." It occurred to her that this was a late hour for Jakob if he was planning to leave for Morristown before dawn.

This was the first time they had spoken all day and she felt guilty with the realization that he had likely stayed up to wait for her.

"I stopped by the Van Dycks' today," he said. "Paul said he would gladly let you work as many hours as you wanted."

Etta wrinkled her nose.

"The butchers? I'd rather not. Once was enough."

"Why?" His eyes narrowed suddenly. "Did something happen?"

"No, I just... didn't like it. I spent the whole day in one room, up to my elbows in offal."

Papa shrugged.

"As you like. But they are older men, and cautious. They will not ask you to do anything dangerous."

Etta thought about protesting, but stopped when she remembered the state of her hands. She fussed with them for a moment without looking. The bandages were thick, and served as a reminder of her current limitations.

As for working at the butcher, the idea of letting knives anywhere near her hands was unsettling. Just the thought caused her heart to beat faster.

Jakob continued. "But you will not be doing any work for some time, so please think about it. There is a good chance that very soon you will not need to work at all."

Etta looked at him.

"Why not?"

"When I spoke with Heber about your injury today, he was very anxious for the matter to go away."

Papa pulled a wad of greenbacks out of his pocket, with the apparent intent of handing it to Etta. Having forgotten that she was unable to accept it in her state, he sheepishly placed it on the table.

"Without any asking, he offered to pay what you would have earned for the next week. With interest."

Etta was stunned. A whole week's worth of earnings – a vast sum. Then, thinking about her hands and what had been the true cost, she found it inadequate.

"Is that enough to pay for the taxes?" she asked.

Papa shook his head.

"Not even close."

"Then, how will I not have to work?"

"Mildred told Peter that I have been selling our eggs in Morristown. He and I worked out a deal for me to sell some of his vegetables as well. Also... the other farmers said I could get a better price if I go further east."

From his expression, she suspected that he was withholding something unpleasant.

"How much further?"

"The best deal, they tell me, is in Newark."

It took Etta a second to picture it on the jalopy's map. Actually, she knew it quite well due to its close proximity to New York City. She frowned with the realization.

"Oh, Papa, that's too far," she protested.

"It will be a long drive," he agreed. Though he was smiling, Papa had a tired look in his eyes. "Do not worry," he said as he put a comforting hand on her shoulder. "But you must promise me, no more dangerous jobs." He had grown serious. "It is not worth it. Promise me."

He stared at Etta with uncharacteristic intensity until she nodded.

The days became progressively easier. Etta found some lesser chores that could be accomplished with her limited dexterity, like carrying firewood. Helen no longer complained during the egg collection, and Etta was more tolerant. Once again, they were joking and bantering, like their usual selves. The discussion often came back to the realization that this might be their last summer together, and how they should make the most of it.

After the bandages finally came off a week later, Etta's hands remained sensitive. The pain was manageable with ointment, which she had insisted on paying Mildred back for. Not with money, of course, since Mildred would not hear of it, but in favors. Ironically, Etta ended up doing the Saunders laundry for all of the following week. By then, she was almost back to normal.

To maximize their profit from Papa's commute to Newark, he intended to take all of their eggs with him. This would have left none for Etta to hard boil and sell on her own, but she managed to set aside half a dozen each day. It was not much, but every contribution to her savings would help.

Delivering the eggs to Newark also shook up their usual routine in other ways. Papa had to get up even earlier to reach the market for dawn, which meant he and Etta were waking up practically in the middle of the night to load up the truck.

This time, it was Etta who asked Papa to please be careful. He promised that he would, but was unsure if he would be returning home that night.

“Please do not wait up for me,” he said.

After he left, Etta had no reason to remain awake and actually returned to bed for another two hours until daybreak.

When she awoke, she had to remind herself that even though it was later than usual, there was no need to rush. For two years, she had gotten up before dawn, and habits are difficult to break. Just a week ago, she had grown restless with the lack of something to keep busy. Indeed, the temporary loss of her hands had driven her stir crazy. It was only after the experience forced her to take a step back and accept a more reasonable workload that she realized the stumble had been inevitable.

Howler, on the other hand, had not been consulted on the change in routine, and cried at Etta from the foot of the bed. Etta rubbed her eyes as she shooed the cat away. Undeterred, Howler resumed her protest from beyond kicking range.

“...let you out when I'm damn well ready,” Etta grumbled.

The extra sleep had been nice, but even so, she was ready to start the day. The reduced intensity of this new routine was something that she appreciated. After all, it was the nearest thing to a vacation she had ever had.

In her newfound idle time, Etta’s thoughts drifted more towards her eventual flight from Bott's Lake. Perhaps she no longer needed to take extra jobs to help settle the tax bill, but she would still need money to leave town. Thus, Etta’s thoughts turned to what Papa had said about the

Van Dycks. She grimaced. Working for the butchers was not her preference.

For now, she would accept the comparatively lighter workload of "only" tending the farm and filch some eggs from the daily collection to boil and sell. The daily walk to town was nice, and even a modest contribution would be vital when she left town.

Unhurried, she dressed and made her way to the kitchen to rekindle the fire and make a fresh pot of coffee. Most of her usual chores remained, but at least she could take her time in getting to them. Outside, the ladies were making more noise than usual. While somewhat odd, it was not entirely out of the norm. Squinting though the window, Etta could not see anything wrong. Were they hungrier than usual? Granted, they were always hungry, but they were especially ravenous in the warmer weather when they produced more eggs.

Howler waited impatiently next to the back door, regarding Etta with her usual scowl. Etta let the cat slip outside, glad to be rid of her for the moment.

How is it that I always let her out, but never back in?

Rubbing the sleep from her eyes, she noted that the sun was already peaking over the horizon. Winding the big clock confirmed that the hour was later than normal, but not by much.

Her stomach rumbled as she set the percolator on the piping hot stove. One benefit of the otherwise lousy week in bandages was that Mildred had insisted on making her breakfast and dinner every day. Where before, hunger was something to which she was accustomed, now she knew what she was missing. While she would still join the Saunders for dinner, she would be hungry for most the day if she did not keep busy.

Rather than sit around and wait for the coffee pot to work its magic, she went to check for any new eggs she could grab for hard-boiling. Maybe even sneak a few for breakfast. Outside, Etta wondered why she still felt tired. By this point, she was usually hitting her stride. Thinking on it, she remembered that the night had been interrupted even before she and Papa loaded the truck. Had she heard gunshots? It could have been Mr. Kovaks chasing off another bear. Bears and foxes were always a matter of concern when it came to chickens.

The ladies perked up as Etta walked past. More than a few clucked their displeasure at her tardiness, and a couple others were already pecking at each other.

"Hey! Don't be fresh."

She frowned as she regarded the flimsy posts and chicken wire fencing. It served to keep the chickens in the pen, but if there was a bear, this would not even slow it down.

Another bird started pecking, and Etta sighed. “Alright, fine. Breakfast is coming.”

Since the birds were already getting ornery Etta would feed them before having her coffee. The longer she waited, the worse they would get. The interior of the barn was much brighter than she was accustomed to. This was another benefit of her late start. On a typical morning, she had to feel her way around in the dark. Thus, she barely looked at her surroundings and trusted her feet to know where to go.

It was for this reason that she almost failed to notice the tarp was out of sorts. While stuffed into its usual corner of the barn, it was not quite where she left it, and not just because Howler was sitting on top of it. That was also odd. At this time of day, the cat would usually be hunting for mice, not sitting inside the barn. Looking more closely, Etta noticed something else. A pair of shoes was sticking out from beneath the tarp.

Her first thought was that Papa had left his boots in the barn, but immediately realized that they were not boots, but dress shoes.

Shoes that were on someone’s feet.

Etta nearly dropped the feedbag. Fumbling, she hastily set it on the ground, careful not to spill it. The feet were not moving, and the sleeper's face and body were buried deep within the canvas. The tarp rose and fell with the man's breathing. Yes, she decided, looking at the shoes. It must be a man. But was it one she knew?

Howler, sitting on top of the bundle, rose and fell with it, but maintained her scowl. As if to annoyed by this disturbance, but also too stubborn to move elsewhere. Etta's mind went through a list of possibilities. Was it Mr. Grayson? He had gone missing again. Did he wander in here? She hoped above all else that it was not either of the Brandelsons.

On the chance that it was someone familiar, she reached for the broom instead of the pitchfork.

As she approached the sleeping intruder, she looked more closely at his shoes – the only thing visible. Though modest and showing scuffmarks from many miles of walking, they were most certainly not something a farmer would wear. Etta narrowed her eyes.

An out-of-towner then.

Etta poked at the feet with the broom. The man did not stir and she escalated to swatting him with some force. This time, he groaned and started shifting beneath the canvas. The outburst caused Howler to leap away and her usual scowl deepened. Leaving the barn, she cried over her shoulder to express the severity of her displeasure.

When the intruder resettled, Etta swatted the top of the canvas where his head might have been. Not as hard as she could have, but close to it.

"Yeah. Okay. I'm going." Though his voice was muffled, it was clear the man was only just coming to his senses.

Gaze narrowed, Etta watched with impatience as the intruder found his feet, and began to extricate himself from his makeshift bedroll. She rested the broom on the ground, but was ready to take it up again if the man needed any further encouragement. As he rose to his full height, she briefly considered going back for the pitchfork.

Chapter 12
Art

To say Art's head was throbbing was omitting half of what ailed him. He had never been hung over before, and was not previously aware that it was a full-body experience. Besides his head, he was almost incapacitated with nausea. When the tarp covering his face was struck by something unseen, it had been like a stick of dynamite going off between his ears. The gut rot he had consumed the previous night threatened to make a return appearance. Was it still night? It was very dark.

"This isn't a boarding house, sir," came a voice from outside his protective cocoon.

So much for avoiding angry farmers, he thought.

Slow as molasses, and muttering entreaties against further thrashing, he extricated himself from the tarp. The sound of something hard striking the wooden floor of the barn, served to speed him along. Each movement drove deeper whatever nail had no doubt been inserted into his head.

Am I going to die? he wondered.

Perhaps it was just wishful thinking. Sorry as he was, he still preferred to avoid another strike to his head or body, and pushed to continue his glacial movement.

"A little faster, if you please," insisted the voice.

Finally getting his feet under himself, Art pushed off the remainder of the tarp and stood up. The effects he had been enduring a moment earlier were almost tame compared to what transpired once he was standing. The combination of sunlight directly in his eyes and the blood rushing from his head served a fresh dose of misery. As he fought down the rising bile in his throat, it occurred to him that everything was fuzzy. Touching his face, he grumbled with the realization that his glasses were missing.

Turning around, he bent over to feel around for them.

"Hey! No more sleeping!" called the girl with the broom as she swatted him again. At least this time it was on his back rather than his head.

"I'm not," he mumbled, moving his hands along the ground. Bending over caused his head to throb and every second was agony. Thankfully, his hostess delivered no further encouragement. He sighed with relief when his fingers touched the familiar shape of his spectacles. Returning them to his face, at least things were clear again.

Standing up, he faced the owner of the voice, whom he could now see. Her glare and the displeasure it conveyed were enough to temporarily distract him from his otherwise miserable state. That she stood several inches shorter than him did nothing to diminish the effect.

With an outstretched arm, she rested the wooden end of the broom on the floor like a spear. As she inclined her head all Art could do was dumbly stare back. At the moment, most of his faculties were wholly focused on the arduous task of remaining on his feet.

"Have a restful evening, did we?" she asked, eyes narrowed to angry slits.

"Actually, no," Art managed in reply, not trusting himself to a response consisting of more than two words.

The girl's eyes narrowed further in response. "Are you... are you drunk?"

"Um..." He thought about it, and decided there was nothing remaining of the pleasant looseness from the previous evening. "Not anymore. I think."

Four words. Things were improving. Though, even that small exertion cast a fresh wave of nausea over him. Looking at the broom the girl was holding, Art was suddenly grateful that she had only used the straw end. With her free hand, she pointed to the open barn door.

"I'll thank you to leave," she said with open contempt.

Grimacing, Art held up his hands warding against further thrashing and forced himself to shuffle out. His body protested every step. A quiet belch left an unpleasant burning sensation in his throat and chest.

Why would someone do this more than once?

As he had done the night before, he trudged along, putting one foot in front of the other. By the time he reached the dirt drive leading to the road, the throbbing in his head had at least subsided, even if the reflux in his throat and general nausea remained. His head cleared just enough to realize that he did not know where he was going.

Turning around, he looked for the girl. As it turned out, she had been following him with the broom resting on her shoulder. Angrily, she gripped it again with both hands, as if looking for any reason to use it. This time, Art remained several feet away, just out of striking range.

"Excuse me, ma'am." He paused to collect himself, experimenting with a full sentence this time, and above all trying to sound polite. "How do I get back to the lake?"

Her nostrils flared with each breath, clearly growing more aggravated with his continued presence.

"Same way you came in, I expect," she snapped.

That's not going to work.

"I um... didn't walk here," he replied.

The girl let out an exasperated sigh then, holding the broom at her side, continued marching towards the road as Art had originally been doing.

"So, not only are you a shiftless drunk, but you also have no sense of direction. I'm not sure how you manage, sir." She took the lead, motioning with her free hand. "I have more to do than God ever intended for one woman, but I'll see you to the road if it means you'll leave."

"Thanks," he mumbled.

They walked in silence. The path leading to the road was little more than two parallel tire ruts carved into the hill. The young woman walked in one while Art followed at a respectful distance in the other. Holding the broom down at her side, she set a vigorous pace, underscoring her desire to be rid of this unwelcome guest. He dared not fall behind. Frankly, he was eager to be gone.

At first, any small disturbance threatened to bring up the contents of Art's stomach. In a small mercy, his misery gradually diminished, and he soon recovered enough to feel guilty over intruding on this young woman's life.

Oddly, the walk helped. About halfway down the driveway, his queasiness had subsided just enough for him to appreciate the wonderful view in front of him. Rolling hills and farmland as far as he could see. It was even better than what he had seen during his walk from the train station. He nearly stopped once or twice, entranced as he was, but a sharp look from his hostess returned his attention to the here and now.

As they neared the roadway, the young woman stopped short and cocked her head at something unseen to Art. Whatever it was caused her to ball up her fists. Confused, he walked up next to her, on his own path, and tried to determine what she was looking at. With sudden realization, he shut his eyes and groaned.

It turned out he had been here before. Whatever improvements he had earned by the short walk quickly faded once he saw the mailbox.

“Oh, damn it to hell,” the girl said, echoing his own thoughts. Angry, but also confused, she stomped over to it. Or rather, what remained.

At the end of the double rut path, where it met the road, a wooden post stuck out of the dirt, jagged and splintery where it had snapped. Next to it, laid the other half of the post and the partially flattened mailbox. The door was in remarkably good shape, save for the fact that it was broken at one hinge. Opening his eyes, Art quickly dropped them to his feet in utter embarrassment. What must have been a whirlwind of thoughts for her coalesced into a single question.

“How...?”

At first, the lady farmer was too distracted by the scene in front of her to notice Art, but as he was positively oozing with guilt, it did not take her long to grow suspicious. Shoulders slumped and hands in his pockets, Art chewed on his lower lip.

Looking between him and the broken mailbox, her steely gaze eventually settled on him.

“How did you get out here?” she demanded.

“I was um… out with my brothers,” he replied, now trying to work out which direction led to the cottage on his own.

She took a step closer, hands still balled into fists and shaking with anger. “So,” she began. “Do you always vandalize property when you drink or was this a special occasion?”

While he had made great progress in his recovery, Art's thoughts were still sluggish and by reflex he answered the question, not realizing it was probably rhetorical.

“Special occasion, I suppose.”

Her face flashed red. The color was especially remarkable in contrast to her blonde hair.

“You're damn lucky no one was hurt!” she yelled.

Fresh misery coursed through Art's guts as she rattled his ears, but it was nothing compared to the accompanying embarrassment. Briefly, he considered explaining that it had been his brother's doing, but decided that it probably would not help matters. Finished yelling at him, her face returned to its usual color.

"This road will bring you back to the lake, and your inebriate brothers." She began stomping back toward the house. "Have a nice day."

Art had been about to ask which direction she meant, but held his tongue. More than anything, he was relieved for the confrontation to be over. Eager to leave, he picked a direction at random.

Walking quickly, Art still was not sure how far from town he was, but at least it was progress. The morning was well underway, and he was sure his family would be worried about him. In fact, they were probably out looking for him right now.

Once again, the act of walking helped to clear his head and a thought occurred to him. For the hour he had been stumbling around in the dark, before finally arriving at the barn, there had been no sign of his brothers. In fact, he had seen no one during the entirety of his nighttime trek. Not even a distant pair of headlights.

They didn't even look for me, did they?

That farmer was shooting at us. Maybe they were just scared.

...but they left me behind.

He resumed walking.

Ma will be worried about me. I have to get home so she knows I'm alright. My brothers will catch Hell once she realizes they didn't come home with me.

Thinking on that, Art could not come up with a compelling reason to spare his brothers. Dammit, they should catch a little Hell from their mother. Frankly, he decided, they deserved it, and not just for this latest grievance.

The more he thought about it, the less he wanted to rush home at all. In all likelihood, his father would bring him along for a sales run and Art doubted he could handle that in his current state. All sense of urgency left him quite suddenly and he stopped walking.

The cottage could wait.

A light breeze picked up just then and the brisk air was refreshing. The sun was well above the horizon and the day was warming up in a pleasant way. He caught the musky scent of blossoming trees and grass. It had become more familiar since his arrival in town, but even so, it was a literal breath of fresh air. Likewise, the lack of sound was more conspicuous out here. While the neighborhood around the lakeside cottage was merely quiet, it was downright silent in the farmland. He found it to his liking.

Slowly turning in place, he took in the view, and frowned as his eyes settled on the broken mailbox. It still lay on the ground, a hundred or so paces away. The guilty feeling returned as he considered the mess caused by his brothers.

Granted, the young woman had not exactly been polite to him, but given the circumstances, her reaction was understandable. Certainly, she had not deserved for her property to be vandalized. Someone would have to clean up Junior's mess. If not her, then her father or husband, who probably had no time to spare either.

Once again, Art considered going back to the cottage, but now for the purpose of giving Junior a piece of his mind. Dammit, he was going to come out here and fix this mess. Giving it a second thought, Art scoffed at this ridiculous mental picture.

Yeah, that'll be the day.

Not twelve hours ago, he had been unable to prevent Junior from forcing him into a car. The thought of hauling him back on his ear was laughable.

Without particularly thinking about it, Art returned to the smashed up mailbox, assessing what would have to be done. This was a familiar process, and gave him something to focus on other than his aching head and body.

Art estimated about an hour's worth of work lay before him. Maybe two in his current condition. The ragged edges of the post had to be cut square. The metal of the box would need to be pounded back into shape. Mentally, he listed the various steps that would be required and the tools he would need from Gregory's shop.

Tools...

That brought him up short. He did not know how to get to the workshop from here, and even if he did, getting permission to abscond with some of Gregory's prized tools was unlikely. Besides, Art was still feeling quite embarrassed about this whole misadventure, and the fewer people who knew about it, the better.

Picking a flat rock up off the ground, he frowned at the partially flattened mailbox, and eventually shrugged his shoulders.

It's a start...

Chapter 13
Etta

The broom crashing into the wall of the barn was enough to finally chase Howler away. Etta was fuming. Not only was she getting an inexcusably late start to the day, but now she had a mailbox to fix as well. After a moment of staring at her father's tools, she shook her head. A stranger to this part of the barn, the unfamiliarity compounded her already sour mood. The closest she had ever come to carpentry was sawing through stale bread.

Even if she did have any skill with wood, she had little enough time in the day as it was. There were still chores that needed to be done, and tending to the chickens was not least among them. Though wary of pushing herself too hard, she also wanted to sell some hard-boiled eggs to pad her leaving-town fund. All told, this broken mailbox was a disruption to her routine that she could have done without.

Returning to the feedbag and portioning out the morning ration, she thought about who might owe her a favor. Robert and Daniel would help, but they had night duty at the station this week and were probably sleeping just now. Bradley Heckel next came to mind. No doubt, he would fix the mailbox without hesitation as he still harbored some romantic feelings for her. Of course, then she would have to endure a few hours of his bumbling attempts for her affection.

In the middle of retying the grain bag, her eye caught movement down near the road. Looking up, she saw the damned out-of-towner again.

What is he still doing here?

In her distraction, she accidentally spilled a handful of chicken feed. Cursing, she set the bag down more carefully and started down the tire rut. From a distance, he appeared to be resting, and she prepared to shoo him off again. Drawing closer, more details came into focus, and she realized that he was not resting, but kneeling. Furthermore, he was doing something to the mailbox.

Abruptly, she decided that she did not particularly care why he was still here; she just wanted him gone. Etta opened her mouth to tell him so, but seeing her, the boy spoke first.

"Do you have a saw?"

The question caught her entirely by surprise and halted her in mid-stride.

"A saw?" she repeated.

"Yeah, you know... ah, flat with a serrated edge. Usually has a wooden handle."

Oh, you're funny aren't you?

If Etta had merely been enraged before, this apparently flippant response pushed her over the edge. She searched for a rock or something heavy to throw at him. Unfortunately, none were close enough to grab before she noticed that he was looking at her expectantly. The request had been completely sincere without even a hint of mockery in his voice. Somehow, that only served to infuriate her more.

"I know what a *saw* is," she said through clenched teeth. "What do *you* want with one?"

He pointed to the snapped piece of wood still sticking out of the ground.

"The post didn't break cleanly. I need to cut it flat so the mailbox will sit straight."

She was silent, struck dumb by the absurdity of the sight before her. This boy had been sleeping off a drunken stupor in her family's barn moments earlier, and now was kneeling in the dirt, with his disheveled hair and crooked glasses and church clothes, asking for tools.

Etta shook her head, about to refuse his request, but then she noticed the mailbox itself had mostly been returned to its original shape, albeit without the door. This boy was making progress to fix it, using nothing more than a pair of rocks and his own hands. For a second, she felt a certain relief that at least one of the day's chores seemed to be taking care of itself.

Then, she reminded herself, *They were so drunk they smashed a mailbox with a car*. Etta's eyes narrowed as she mustered up some fresh resolve.

"I don't want you to…"

All else aside, he was doing a competent enough job, and she lacked for any better options. Shoulders slumped, Etta sighed with resignation.

"How long will this take?" she demanded.

He paused, eyes far away with his face scrunched up in thought. Briefly turning his attention to the half of the post still in the ground, he reached out and gave it a testing push. When it did not move, he nodded to himself and then turned back to her.

"If you have a saw, a hammer, and some nails, I think I can do this in an hour."

Etta pursed her lips, realizing that she would have to postpone her visit to town. It was not ideal, but she did not want to leave this stranger alone at her home. Besides, it would give her a chance to finish her chores and hard-boil the eggs.

I suppose I can suffer his presence for an hour.

"Fine. The tools are up in the barn," she said. As he stood up, she added, "But you are to leave the very minute it's finished."

He turned to face her, looked abashed again and then nodded. They walked up the dirt path in silence. She set a brisk pace as he followed, stopping only once they reached the doors to the barn. From the entrance, Etta pointed to her father's workbench.

"You should find what you need over there," she said.

He muttered thanks, and walked to where she had indicated. Before leaving, Etta looked back and watched as he methodically searched through the drawers. She told herself that it was to make sure he didn't slink back to the canvas and fall asleep, but she watched for longer than was necessary for that. Despite her dark mood, she furrowed her brow and smirked. He did make an odd sight, with his unruly hair and glasses. But at least he seemed to know what he was doing. Grabbing the egg basket, she left him to it and resumed her morning chores.

They labored separately for the next hour. At first, Etta glanced in his direction every ten minutes or so, ostensibly to make sure that he was still working and had not absconded with Papa's tools.

As she had feared, the birds were grumpy at being fed so late, and two of them were now missing feathers. Nothing too serious, but it was still annoying. However, it was nothing compared to the other calamity.

In all that had happened, Etta completely forgot about the coffee which she left sitting on the stove. While mucking the pen, she happened to notice the smoke rising from the chimney. A second later, she remembered why she had started the fire in the first place, and rushed back to the house.

It was too late. The coffee was burned, almost to the point of being undrinkable. Sighing, Etta poured a mug anyway, and winced as she drank it. It took three or four pulls before she decided that the morning's excitement left her blood pressure sufficiently high, and discarded the rest of it.

Now I'm mad...

Returning outside, she continued to rake up the old straw and droppings. Absorbed as she was in her work, she did not notice that the boy with the glasses had returned, and was standing just outside the pen. Startled, Etta inhaled sharply upon seeing him. At first, she did not say anything, but noticed that his eyes snapped up as she turned around. Almost as if they had been staring at something lower while her back was turned.

Well, that's rude.

"Can I help you?" she asked, hoping to conjure up some of her earlier venom, but not quite managing it. The young man blinked through his glasses and shook his head. Not in answer, but as if clearing away a distracting thought.

"Um... yes. Job's done."

At the mailbox, Etta tested the repairs by leaning against it. She pushed harder than was necessary, in a strange way, almost hoping that it would fail and give her an excuse to tap back into the animus that had left her. Once it was clear that the repairs were, in fact, holding true, she nodded.

"It would have been better if you hadn't broken it in the first place," she began.

The boy dropped his eyes back to his feet, and Etta silently chastised herself. That had been uncalled for. Somewhat. He was trying to make things right, after all. She let out a small sigh.

"But," she continued, "I suppose it won't fall over anytime soon."

He looked up, and gave a reserved smile of relief and satisfaction.

He does have a nice smile, she thought, and then shook her head to dispel the notion.

"I'm glad it's acceptable," he replied. They were both silent for a moment, before he finally continued. "I should probably get going then."

Etta nodded, feeling a brief flash of disappointment, which confused her. Instead of speaking, she simply nodded, and met his eyes.

He's staring at me again, she thought. *So rude*. But she gave no reprimand.

"I um... you never mentioned which way leads back to town."

"Oh." Now it was her turn to be abashed. Raising her arm, she pointed down the road where it curved around the copse of trees at the edge of the property. "Follow this way to the end. When you get to a fork, the left turn goes back to the lake."

He nodded, and muttered a quick "thanks" before starting in the direction she had indicated. Etta stood there a moment and watched the boy go.

No, not a boy.

From behind, his hair was still ridiculous, but without the eyeglasses to distract her, she noticed, for the first time, how broad in the shoulders he was. And there was just something about a man working with his shirtsleeves rolled up.

Shirtsleeves...

It occurred to Etta that he was not wearing his jacket. Looking around, she spotted it folded over the fence next to the mailbox.

"Wait!" she called, grabbing the jacket and walked toward him.

"Thanks," he said, accepting it and draping it over his arm. "I seem to keep doing that." The young man nodded and favored her with another smile, before turning to continue on his way.

"Are you hungry?" she asked without thinking.

He stopped, and turned around, a thoughtful look on his face. "As a matter of fact, I am."

"You could stay for breakfast if you want. I got a few extra eggs out of the ladies this morning. Some toast as well. Like my mother used to say, 'You work. You eat.'"

His expression was difficult to read, and Etta could not tell whether he was considering her offer or was simply fatigued. She felt foolish.

Ugh. That was too forward of me, she thought.

"Maybe something to drink?" he asked.

Etta nodded. "I've got some lemonade."

"That would sure hit the spot. Thank you, ma'am."

At least he's got manners.

Starting back towards the house, they soon fell into stride together.

"It's *miss*," she said. Then, a moment later, she added, "Well, Etta. Etta Wozniak."

"Art. Nice to meet you."

"Would that be short for Arthur?"

"Sort of. It's supposed to be Arturo, after my mother's father. That's what she calls me, but outside the house it's Arthur. My father thought it sounded more American."

"'Arturo,'" Etta repeated. "I like that. Do you get along with your mother?"

"Actually, I do." He paused a moment. "Aside from my one brother Thomas, I think she's the only one in my family that I actually like."

Art's mouth flattened to a straight line. For a moment, Etta wondered about the circumstances that led to him being separated from his brothers way out here in the farmlands and why they left him to walk back to town. It seemed a sensitive topic, and, despite her curiosity, she let the matter go as they approached the house.

Reaching for the door, she found that Art's hand beat her to it.

Surprised, she furrowed her brow but remained still as Art opened it for her. He smiled, thinking it was gentlemanly. A bemused smile crossed Etta's face and she had to concede that there was a certain, odd charm to it.

"I love a man with manners, but that might be the first time someone has held the door for me in my own house."

Chuckling, she touched his arm as she passed.

Once inside, Etta set to work, energized at the prospect of company and an excuse to have a full breakfast. It would not do to skimp for a guest. Luckily, there were just enough eggs for a decent breakfast as well as to hard boil and sell. She put a couple more logs on the simmering coals.

As the wood caught and the stove heated up, she remembered that she was parched from working outside.

She looked at Art. "I promised you lemonade, didn't I?"

Her guest nodded and Etta grabbed two mismatched glasses from the cabinet. The door shifted as she opened it, dropping even lower than usual.

It's getting worse, she grimaced, but carried on without pause.

Etta poured the first glass for Art, which he promptly downed before she finished making her own. An involuntary, contented grunt escaped him before he remembered himself. Once again, Etta was not entirely sure what to make of this man.

"Someone's thirsty," she teased. Amused, she poured him another. "If you drink like that, it's no wonder you ended up sleeping in a strange barn." The last she had intended to say more tongue-in-cheek, but it came out with a hint of rebuke, which she regretted immediately.

Then, she reminded herself, *They were so drunk they smashed the mailbox with a car.*

Etta's smile faded and Art's momentary relief fled with her darkened expression.

"For what it's worth," he began, "Last night was very unusual for me."

That, I might actually believe.

He struck her as a bookish type. Albeit one who knew his way around carpentry and was built like a farm hand. Still, she wagered that he would be more at home in a library than a saloon. She supposed it was mostly the glasses.

His hair though...

For some reason, it bothered her so much that she had to resist an urge to smooth it down for him. The two of them regarded each other.

At last, Etta returned her attention to the stove, which was now hot enough to cook on. Eager to move away from the previous topic, Art wandered as Etta worked. This did not take long, since the kitchen was fairly small, and he paused next to the icebox. She paid him little mind, focused as she was on the task before her.

"Is your ice man late today?" he asked.

Etta was busy scooping the eggshells into the refuse bin and did not look up. "Pardon?" she replied,

"Your Copeland here. It gets a fresh block of ice once a day, doesn't it?"

Brow furrowed, she looked at him. "Sometimes it does. But what's an 'ice man?'"

Art was confused. "Well... the fella who delivers your ice, of course."

Etta responded with a mirthless laugh. "That would be me. Hope you like your eggs scrambled."

Art stared blankly. "Scrambled is fine. You deliver ice?"

Etta answered distractedly, frowning at a spot on the pan where the eggs were sticking. They were out of butter again.

"Only to this house," she replied and glanced out the window. "But we hardly use it these days. We – ah – don't typically have much in the way of leftover food. Besides, the Fichners are charging an arm and a leg this year. It was a poor harvest."

"'Harvest?' Does your ice house only produce in the winter?"

She laughed again, but this time with genuine amusement. "Of course. How else would you do it?"

“Well... I suppose I’d recommend one of the newer, see-eff-see units. The meth-ill chloride cycle needs too much electricity. Plus, it's poison if you ever get a leak.”

What?

Head cocked to the side, Etta stared at him and tried to make sense of the gibberish he had just spouted. Art looked back, his face once again devoid of any humor. After a long pause, it occurred to him that she had not understood anything he just said.

“My – ah – family sells electric refrigerators.”

She nodded and returned to the eggs, which were nearly finished. Art resumed his walk. Having seen the entire kitchen, he continued through the opening to the living area.

“Well, I'll be.” he said loud enough for her to hear. “Nice Wurlitzer.” He returned to the doorway to the kitchen.

“Nice what?” Etta asked.

“Your radio,” he replied. “Looks like it's in great shape too. How’s the reception out here?”

“Oh,” she frowned. “Couldn't say, unfortunately. First time we plugged that in, it let out a puff of smoke and never did anything else.”

It was something of a sore subject in the Wozniak's house. Even secondhand, it had cost them most of a month's earnings. Her father thought he was getting a deal from a sheep farmer in the next town over, who even offered to deliver it. This was before they had lost Edward, when things were good. The idea of having music in the house was something that Etta, even then, was aching for.

To say she had been disappointed was an understatement. Papa had gone to the sheep farmer to ask for his money back, but the man had refused, insisting that it worked before the Wozniaks took delivery. For a short time, they considered getting it repaired, but after Edward passed away, it was put off indefinitely. Eventually, it sat forgotten, and simply became part of the room. Too heavy to casually move and not enough of a nuisance to warrant the effort. It sat there for years, collecting dust and the occasional, odd article of clothing.

Art replied with a grunt, as though his mind was tending to other matters. He returned to the radio, eyes fixed, as if he were seeing an old friend for the first time in a long while. Etta found him reaching out to turn a knob when she called him to the table.

“Food's ready.”

With a plate in each hand, she hesitated just a second. One went to her usual seat, naturally, but she could not immediately decide where to place her guest. After all, the rest of the spots around the table were already accounted for despite being empty.

Directly across from her would have been the obvious choice, but no, that was Irene's chair. In a hasty decision, she chose the next, adjacent seat, which had been Florence's. This put Art sitting diagonally across from her, which was mildly awkward, but she had already set down the plates, and decided to leave them.

As her guest took his seat, Etta lowered a batch of eggs, into the now boiling pot of water.

The bread was stale, but a light toasting and generous portion of jam helped with that. Etta suddenly felt self-conscious about it, but Art did not complain nor did he comment on the apparently odd seating arrangement.

"You ever call anyone out to take a look at the Wurlitzer?" he asked. "Shame for that to just be holding the carpet to the floor."

Etta took her own seat, but said nothing at first. "We've thought about it," she replied at last. "The nearest place we could find to fix it is all the way in Morristown. And we never had a spare day to drive it out there."

"Most reputable shops should have a trucking service."

"That's... more than we can afford," she replied. Her family's money troubles were something she tried to keep quiet. Friends were bad enough since they would offer to lend or worse, give charity. Strangers were a different matter.

"Oh," Art replied.

The table shifted as he leaned on it, and for the first time, Etta was all too aware of its modesty and the house's general state of disrepair. Moreover, her guest clearly had an eye for details and she was sure that he had noticed. She cringed as his eyes scanned the room.

The door to the icebox was held together with an ad hoc repair that threatened to break at any moment. Several of the cabinet doors were broken or missing entirely. There was no sink. No running water in the house of any kind. Even the electric lights were usually kept off, though that was less obvious at this time of day.

Etta slumped in her chair, feeling embarrassed by Art's silent appraisal. He seemed to realize what he was doing and returned his attention to the meal in front of him.

"These are really good," he said around a partial mouthful of eggs. Suddenly remembering his manners, he shot a hand up to cover his mouth.

The compliment helped to improve her mood. As did his mild embarrassment.

"Thank you. They could be fluffier, but we haven't been getting milk lately." Etta shrugged apologetically. "Still, freshness matters for eggs, and they don't come any fresher than that."

Art nodded before glancing at the empty seats at the table.

"Is anyone else joining us?" he asked.

"I expect not. Papa is out making deliveries and won't be getting back until late." Etta cleared her plate before returning to the stove to remove the now-boiled eggs.

"Just the two of you?" asked Art, still sitting at the table.

"Yes," she replied without elaborating.

"No brothers or sisters?" he ventured.

"Not anymore." This was another subject that she did not care to discuss with a stranger.

Art said nothing and silence lingered in the air. Etta was suddenly reminded of all the chores that needed to be done. The rugs were long overdue for beating, and the grass out back had grown tall.

First things first. She grabbed the usual basket and lined it with a hand cloth. Now cool, Etta set the hard boiled eggs inside along with a shaker of salt and pepper. It was not much, but it would be better than nothing.

At the table, Art stood up, and collected the plates. Looking over her shoulder, Etta grunted appreciatively.

"Thanks," she said. "You can just leave those on the counter." She covered the basket with another kerchief and glanced at the clock in the other room. "I need to get going."

"I won't keep you then."

Closing the dampers on the stove and making sure that the lantern was off, Etta led Art outside. Once again, she noticed that her guest was watching her. That he would avert his eyes when she turned to face him was a little too conspicuous.

You're not fooling anyone, she thought, but grinned anyway.

They started down the path toward the road, passing the mailbox without a word. Neither commented on the previous night's indiscretion.

The quiet remained for several more minutes, but as they admired the landscape, it became more of a companionable silence than an awkward one. The shadows of scattered clouds crawled across the wide valley floor. Neat and even rows of corn and barley swayed in the breeze.

"That sure is something," Art said eventually.

Etta nodded in agreement. This stretch of road was particularly nice, to be sure. The land had mostly been cleared for crops and pastures, and dotted with the occasional barn or house. Purple wildflowers had sprouted in a few errant spots that were too inaccessible or difficult to cultivate. The first bloom of the season had been the week before, and a pattern of green and purple stretched out for miles. Her eyes followed a train as it made its way along in the distance.

"And you get to see this every day?"

"Just about," Etta replied. "This is nothing though. In a few spots around town, you can see for thirty miles on a clear day. But without climbing a hill, this is about as good as it gets." She closed her mouth abruptly, catching herself. She had come dangerously close to mentioning the jalopy.

Art continued to admire the view as they walked. "You're lucky," he said. "This town is pretty swell. I can see why people visit." Etta glanced at him, but for the first time, he did not have to avert his gaze.

Is he playing with me? she wondered.

On the contrary, his attention was genuinely and fully absorbed by their surroundings. Perhaps still feeling put off by her last outing with a boy, Etta had a paranoid suspicion that his compliments were insincere or that he had some ulterior motive.

First impressions tend to last, especially when they involve trespassing and vandalism. However, Art remained quite the puzzle. Etta was starting to accept his claim that the previous night had been an errant one.

The first cottages provided evidence that they were getting closer to the lake and the town proper. Here and there, people were beginning their day. An elderly couple was out for a walk. The smell of morning meals wafted out of open windows.

They walked in silence for several more minutes, until they reached the lake. More early risers were coming out and walking along the waterfront. Luncheonettes were opening and various other recreation areas were setting up.

It was shaping up to be another busy day around town.

Abruptly, Art stopped walking, apparently recognizing where they were. Etta took another step before turning around.

"Um..." he nodded up the street. "This is me."

They stood, regarding each other once again. Both lingered, uneager to leave, though not sure of what more to say.

Finally, Art found words. “Thanks for breakfast. I'm sorry again about the mailbox.”

Etta bit her lip. Reminding herself of the circumstances that led to Art's arrival, annoyance was probably foremost in her mind. Surprisingly, she found that it was also fleeting.

“Thank you for fixing what you broke.”

She had intended to say it more harshly, but it ended up sounding more of appreciation than rebuke.

At last, Art nodded goodbye and turned up the adjacent street. Etta watched him go until he disappeared behind a cottage and out of sight.

Alone again, she turned around and adjusted her grip on the basket.

His hair is just ridiculous.

Chapter 14
Art

Upon returning to the cottage, Art was not entirely surprised to learn that no one had gone out looking for him. Nearing the house, he saw Junior and his son Georgie cleaning the Buick. The adventure from the previous night had accumulated a great deal of mud. While being ignored by Junior was Art's usual preference, the apparent lack of concern was strangely infuriating this morning.

"Well, I'm home," he said with all the contempt he could muster.

It was mostly lost on Junior, who at this time seemed only to mimic the appearance of being awake. Asleep on his feet, the motion of washing his car was possibly the work of some unseen puppet master.

"No worries, then. I'm fine," Art carried on, his voice rising.

Junior might have glanced in his direction, but only with his eyes. He did not even bother to turn his head. Strangely, Art felt his temper rising at the utter indifference. Even a glib remark would have been acceptable. A degrading name. Something.

I spent an hour cleaning up the mess you made, he wanted to say, but as soon as he closed within reach, Junior clamped the front of Art's shirt in a meaty fist. It turned out that he was in no mood for raised voices but remained fully capable of knocking Art square on his ass. After picking himself up from the dusty road, Art wisely let this particular matter go and continued into the house.

Inside was quiet, with only Allyson and Matthew sitting in the main room. They did not acknowledge Art as he walked in, as they were fully absorbed in a picture book spread out between them. Looking at the clock, Art was surprised to find that it was only mid-morning. It felt much later and he had to wonder about the lady farmer, Etta, and just how early she started her day.

The sound of someone descending the stairs caught his attention. It was Ralph, looking much like his typical morning self, albeit, slower than usual. With the poor outcome of his confrontation with Junior still fresh in his mind, Art regarded Ralph with a more reserved glare. Having presumably slept longer than Junior, Ralph was more alert, and acknowledged his younger brother's sudden appearance.

"Morning," he nodded, as casually and disinterested as if this were any other day. Clearly, he was not burdened with any crisis of conscience.

"'Morning' yourself," Art replied. His voice was low, and his glare was unblinking.

"Guess you made it home then," Ralph said. He flashed a wry, yet mocking smile.

Before Art could work up a retort to adequately convey his grievances, Allyson called from across the room.

"Good morning, Uncle Ralphie."

Through half-lidded eyes, Ralph smiled and waved back, ignoring his younger brother for the moment. Art's glare intensified. It was bewildering how Ralph could sustain his Devil may care, easy confidence when he was so blatantly in the wrong. On the other hand, Ralph's demeanor actually seemed to wilt under his younger brother's surly visage. Maybe Art was getting through to him after all.

"Say, ah..." Ralph continued. "Any chance you're going to have my car fixed by tonight?"

Art was speechless for a long moment.

"You're a real piece of work..." Art started to say, but Allyson interrupted him again.

"Uncle Ralphie, Nonna left breakfast out for you, and she said to please put it away when you're done." Ignoring the contempt that Art was trying to convey, Ralph smiled at Allyson again.

"Thank you, sweetie."

As Art considered a few choice names for Ralph that were decidedly not for children's ears, Allyson continued.

"She and Grandpa said they'd be out for a while. They walked down to the market to get the fish for tonight."

Ralph might not have heard the last part, since he was already turning towards the kitchen, but Art did.

Fish...

His eyes went wide, and everything he had been about to say to his brother promptly fled him.

"Is it Friday?"

"All day long." Ralph called from the kitchen in a tone that clearly indicated that this information should be obvious.

Art looked at the clock again. With everything going on that morning, he had completely lost track of things. He was about to run out the door, but before he could lift his foot, an idea occurred to him. Dashing through the kitchen, he plucked the breakfast roll out of Ralph's hand and continued out the back door without pause. It was still swinging shut as the older Adams brother cried out.

"Hey!"

Art arrived at the workshop in record time, but still extremely late. The partial recovery he had been enjoying quickly relapsed, and he was obliged to take the last mile more slowly. He was not accustomed to running for any amount of time, and especially not after a night like the one he had. Despite the haste, he detoured to the well pump adjacent to the house and drank his fill before entering the stone workshop. The sound of whatever Gregory was working on carried outside.

Wondering about what excuse to make for his tardiness, he cautiously approached. Gregory ran the grinder over a work piece without noticing Art enter. His eye and ear protection effectively made him blind and deaf to anything beyond what was in front of him. Still catching his breath, Art remained out of sight and waited patiently for a pause to announce himself. Just as he considered changing into his coveralls, Gregory stopped.

Thinking he had been noticed, Art was about say something when, to his surprise, the grinder slipped out of Gregory's hands. Art winced as it fell to the floor with a clatter. Gregory was usually so careful about his tools.

To his surprise, the older man made no response. On the contrary, he stood in place for a moment, leaning on the worktable with his elbows.

"You alright?" Art called to him.

Gregory made no response, but perhaps he not heard due to the cotton still in his ears.

Art moved around so he could be seen. "Gregory?"

This time, a pair of goggled eyes turned to face Art, and through them, Gregory blinked his eyes several times.

"Oh," he said, looking surprised. Confused and unsteady on his feet, he pulled the cotton from his ears and slid the goggles to his forehead. "Hi, Art. When did you get here?"

"Ah – just a minute ago. You alright?"

"Yeah. Why?"

"You dropped the grinder."

Looking at Art, he furrowed his brow, searching the table and eventually the floor where it still lay. He grunted, as if to say, "How about that."

"Reckon the heat must be getting to me. Hot as the Devil's ass in here. What time is it anyway?"

Art shook his head to clear it. Gregory was fine. As he said, it was probably the heat.

"It's mid – erm – late morning," Art replied. "Sorry I'm so late. I had something of an odd night."

With his usual sharpness returning, Gregory looked at Art with raised eyebrows.

"'An odd night.' Something fun, I hope?"

While Art had not intended to revisit the events of the previous evening, Gregory kept asking follow-up questions and eventually the whole story came out, including his breakfast with Etta. Even so, Art managed to keep mum on select details, such as the distracting way her hips moved.

Those thoughts were just for him, and remained safely locked away. He concluded his story with the part where Ralph had the audacity to ask about his car.

"So, my first impression of your brother was pretty spot-on: he's an asshole."

Taken aback, Art felt obligated to say something in defense of Ralph, but was unable to come up with anything.

"Most people seem to like him," Art shrugged.

"Yeah. That happens with assholes. Believe me, I've known more than a few." A mischievous grin spread across his face. "What do you say we dump that car of his in the valley? I know a couple places it'll never be found again."

Art considered it for a moment.

"No. That's alright," he replied, though he suppressed a grin at the thought.

"Well, your call, I suppose." Gregory shrugged, as though genuinely disappointed but trying hard not to show it. "Family can be tough," he continued. “When you can't just tell someone to go to Hell, it tends to limit your options. Although in the case of my sister, exceptions might be made. Messy business after our parents died. But if that's how Cheapskate Kate wants to be, then that's how it is.” The last bit was muttered, almost to himself, before he seemed to remember that Art was there. Shaking his head again, he carried on.

“I'll tell you this though: I know your brother's type. He's not gonna respect you unless you make him. Might be you need to bloody his nose over something before he gets the message. Just an old man's opinion.”

Art nodded politely, and suppressed a despondent sigh over the very idea of getting into a physical altercation with Ralph.

Gregory waved his hands, indicating he would say no more on the subject. “Enough of that. You skipped over the best part. Who was the girl?”

“Um. Just a girl. A... farmer girl.”

Gregory raised an eyebrow, sensing – quite correctly – that Art was withholding key details.

“Oh, come on now. She went from hitting you with a broom to cooking you breakfast and you're going to tell me nothing else happened?”

Art hesitated, which seemed to only confirm Gregory's suspicion.

When it was clear that Art intended to say no more, Gregory sighed. “Fine. I won't pry. But, if I were you, I'd keep her in mind. In my experience, a girl doesn't just make breakfast for you unless she's at least a little bit interested.”

Art believed his mentor was reading too much between the lines, but nodded anyway. Satisfied, Gregory pulled his goggles back over his eyes.

“Since you're here, better get properly dressed. Hope the Brandelsons’ gut-rot isn't bothering your head too much. We've got a ton of work to do.”

Chapter 15
Etta

It had been a productive day. After completing her errands in town, chores accounted for the rest of the afternoon. Her work clothes had been in desperate need of a wash. Likewise, the rugs looked practically new after she finished knocking the dirt from them. Tired but satisfied, she took a few minutes to appreciate the results of her labor.

Farms being what they are, there remained about a dozen other things that could be done, but Etta decided to leave it there. These days, she had more respect for her limits, and increasingly failed to see the point of fussing over the house. After all, Papa was hardly around anymore, and in a matter of months, she would be gone.

Closing up the barn, she glanced at the sun hanging low in the sky. The Saunders would be having dinner soon, and she decided to accept their standing invitation. Some familiar company was just the thing she needed.

It occurred to her that she should bring something. Invited or not, Mama would never have approved of her showing up empty-handed. Even so, the only thing she had worth sharing was a batch of lemonade that accounted for the last of the sugar. Still, it was better than nothing, and gave her an excuse to dawdle.

Frequently, she peaked outside, hoping Jakob might return home in time to join her. Since the painful night with her hands, she had started to make an effort. During their limited interactions, she spoke more than usual. Typically, it was about her own day, but she also asked questions about his daily trips across the state. Though his responses were short, he brightened at even this light conversation.

Seeing his usual melancholy disappear for even a few minutes would leave Etta feeling contented but also conflicted. It surprised her how moments such as these made her reconsider her decision to leave.

Dinner turned out to be a larger affair than usual with the Saunders playing host to several visiting relatives. Mildred's sister, brother-in-law, and their children were visiting from out of town and even Etta's cousin Robert was in attendance. This was in addition to the usual crowd of Helen's brothers and younger sister. It was fortunate that the evening was a warm one since the only way they could fit everyone at the table was to place it outdoors – church picnic style. To Etta's relief, the modesty of her contribution was not noticed.

As usual, the Saunders had plenty to eat. Peter had managed to coax an early harvest out of the potatoes and green beans. For years, Etta thought that Helen's father was distant and cold since he spent nearly all his time working. It was generally accepted that Peter was more likely to be found somewhere out among the crops or tending to the animals than at the house. After realizing that this meant none of the Saunders ever had to skip a meal, she could only admire him.

Looking at the bounty before her, it was with some restraint that Etta did not tuck into her meal immediately.

Silently and discretely, she said a prayer first.

The Wozniaks had never been a praying family. In fact, this was a habit Etta had picked up only after her mother passed away. It was around the same time she started making her visits to the cemetery, though not quite for the same reason. An expression of gratitude seemed appropriate when it came to be that she could sometimes count the number of meals in a given week on one hand. Helen had overheard once or twice, and asked her about it, genuinely surprised.

At the time, Etta had given a partial explanation, not quite comfortable revealing the depth of her and Jakob's poverty, even to her best friend. Hoping to avoid further questions, she only did it at dinnertime, and kept it quiet. At least at the Saunders' table.

Tonight, it might have gone unnoticed regardless. There were about a dozen conversations going on at once. Darting among them was the dog, Max, who seemed convinced that some of the new faces could be coaxed into handing him some table scraps. He poked his head into Etta's lap more than once.

Sitting across from her, Helen was catching up with her cousins, Megan and Sandra. The two girls were a few years younger than Helen and Etta, and to the latter's annoyance had recently discovered *boys*.

For the most part, Helen was happy to indulge them, while Etta rolled her eyes more often than not. Catching her friend's attention, Etta gave her a few pointed looks; a raised eyebrow, head cocked to the side. Such was the nature of their friendship that, even without words, Etta's teasing message was crystal clear: *Are you listening? This is what you sound like.*

Helen typically responded to such teasing by sticking out her tongue. This, in turn, earned her a rebuke from Mildred, seated at the far end of the table.

While Helen chatted with her cousins, Etta was glad to catch up with her own. She used to see a lot more of Robert and Daniel when they were growing up. However, the circumstances had been unfortunate. Their father, Seamus McCormick, had left the family shortly after Daniel was born, never to be seen again.

Etta did not remember much from those days, except that the two boys often stayed at the Wozniak's farm. The visits sometimes lasted for days or even weeks at a time. Young as she was, Etta was oblivious to the reasons, and did not probe Mama's explanation that Aunt Alicja was "busy."

For the children, it was fun to have additional playmates. That had been when all of Etta's siblings were still alive, and it was a happy time for her. For the adults, it was a wedge that created disquiet and misery.

It turned out that Etta's aversion to charity did not spontaneously appear out of the ether. To the contrary, it had deep roots among her mother's side of the family.

For Alicja, raising her boys was just about the biggest charity that the Wozniaks could give, and Lena only compounded the issue. From the very start, she did not like Seamus and said as much to her sister. After he left, she was not shy about saying "I told you so."

As Robert and Daniel grew older, their mother brought them over less and less. Despite having come to this country together, Lena and Alicja fought during the increasingly rare times they saw each other. Eventually, the rift became irreconcilable.

Thankfully, it was a small town, and there was no keeping the cousins apart.

As the years went on, Alicja, in her self-imposed isolation, grew more and more fond of the drink. Eventually, she too left town, and spoke to none of them ever again. Her grown sons stayed. This was their home after all. Whatever feud remained between their mothers, the cousins were family both in blood and affection. After Etta's brothers and sisters were taken, she and Robert had only grown closer.

On this night, they talked about the upcoming wedding. She wanted to congratulate him on the baby as well, but noticed that no one else had brought up the topic in the presence of the visiting relatives. Suspecting that they were not aware of Helen's delicate condition, Etta was careful not to be the one to spill the beans.

"Congratulations," she said with raised eyebrows. "For the wedding."

Her full meaning was quite obvious and Robert winked his understanding.

"How does Daniel feel about it?" Etta asked.

"Oh, you know... He's really excited to be an- uh... brother-in-law. Then, o' course, Mildred gave us the whole, 'you two are so young' and 'where are you going to raise... the crops?'" Robert stopped himself before the worst kept secret in town was completely out.

He replied to her parody of a scowl with a bid, toothy grin. She could not hold her pursed expression for long before it melted into a wide grin. No one could quite brighten her mood like Robert. He was a good sort; always ready to help, and quick to laugh. Seemed like there was very little that could actually dampen his mood. Even though his own parents had set a low standard, she knew Robert had it in him to be a great one.

The pleasantly warm afternoon gave way to a chilly evening. As the sky darkened and the first stars came out, Etta helped the Saunders clean up. Helen's oldest brother, Mark, had the lightest set of responsibilities since he had to get down to the lake for his shift at CasinO. Etta never got the chance to speak with him directly, but as far as she could tell, he had suffered no consequences from their formerly mutual employer, for which she was thankful. Before heading out, he started the family's turntable to play some music and brought in a few buckets of water from the well pump.

Peter, his son Michael, and Mildred's brother-in-law were out in the barn, making use of the last hours of daylight. There was plenty of work yet to be done on the honeymoon cottage, which they would need in less than a month. Max, evidently not a music lover, had gone to supervise.

Etta had seen the sketches of Helen and Robert's future home. Located on a far corner of the Saunders' property, it would be just far enough for the newlyweds to enjoy some privacy, but close enough that visits would not be a burden. Helen grumbled over the small size, but to Etta, it had all the makings of a cozy place to make a good life.

Everyone was busy after dinner, all doing their part. Even little Susie. She would turn eight in another month and was the youngest of the Saunders, but even she dried the plates and changed out the dirty wash water. Only Helen, Robert, and the cousins Megan and Sandra were unaccounted for. While Mildred never addressed it directly, she made more than a few annoyed sighs, and it did not take much effort to guess the reason.

Etta predicted that the others would remain out of sight until just after the chores were finished. It was just as well. Etta had some guilt after eating double portions but only contributing a meager bottle of lemonade. Taking up Helen's slack help assuage her conscience.

The Saunders did not have a radio, and only possessed four records for their turntable. Etta knew just about every pop and scratch on this copy of "Dark Was the Night." Still, it was better than no music at all.

Better still, was spending time with Mildred. They talked about the upcoming wedding, of course, and Etta could not help but marvel at the world of difference between mother and daughter. Their perspectives and concerns on this topic were about as opposite as night and day. Where Helen had been focused on the music and dress, Mildred was trying to figure out how they were going to feed over a hundred guests.

Despite Mildred's concerns, Etta found these moments comforting. Like how it might have been with her own mother. Most of the anecdotes and stories she had heard before. Like the time Mildred found Helen covered, head to toe, in flour. It used to be that she would roll her eyes at hearing it for the hundredth time, but now she could only smile fondly.

While the wedding was the biggest piece of news at the moment, it was certainly not the only thing happening around the Lake. Mr. Grayson had recently turned up after getting lost in his own apple orchard for two whole days. Lizzie Hunley was limping around after getting her foot under a cow's hoof. Bradley Heckel had been asking about Etta again...

As if the Saunders were not enough to keep her fully occupied, Mildred had long established herself as a pillar of the farming community. If a family was in need of help, Mildred was often the one to coordinate support. Never charity, of course. The family that provided aid one day might be in need of it on the next. Such was her way that she considered the Beckett's recent misfortune to be a personal failure.

Etta realized that she would miss moments like this.

While her hands had since healed, prolonged exposure to the soapy dishwater started driving them to itch. Itch. Not burn. Etta's grimace was subtle, but Mildred was an attentive sort.

"Are you sure those are healed enough?" Gently but firmly, she grabbed one of Etta's hands and inspected it herself, not trusting her to be honest.

In all fairness, it was valid concern. Etta probably would have attempted to help even if she was still wearing the bandages.

Satisfied, Mildred continued, "And where did you leave your father this evening? I hope he knows that there's always a seat at our table for both of you."

"By now, he's hopefully on his way home," replied Etta.

Mildred frowned. "Surely it doesn't take that long to get back from Morristown?"

"Actually, he's driving out to Newark now."

"You're joking. That far away?" Mildred shook her head with equal parts disapproval and disbelief.

Etta shrugged. "He was told that he could get a better price if he gets closer to New York."

Mildred pursed her lips. "And who told him that, I wonder? Someone in Morristown who didn't want the competition?"

Etta paused in her scrubbing. She had not considered that before.

"It *was* one of the other sellers, now that you mention it."

The idea of Papa having been tricked by unscrupulous individuals was frustrating, but it would not have been the first time. The radio and the sheep farmer he had bought it from briefly came to mind.

On the other hand, she and Papa were desperate. If he saw a better chance somewhere, it seemed unfair to fault him for trying. Of course, this line of thought brought Etta dangerously close to admitting the depth of their money troubles. Thankfully, Mildred had other concerns.

"And what about the farm? Are you taking care of the birds all by yourself?"

"Yes," replied Etta without hesitation, not sure where this conversation was going. At least this was a safer topic that she was far more comfortable discussing. She did, however, remain wary of how much to disclose to Mildred. While Helen had promised not to reveal

Etta's plans to leave town, there was always the chance that something had slipped.

"That's a lot of work for one girl," Mildred ventured. When Etta did not respond, Mildred was gracious enough to change the subject. "And especially for such a skinny one. Was this the first meal you've had all week?" Mildred gave Etta, what was intended to be, a well-meaning squeeze of her arm. Unfortunately, she had strong hands, and caused Etta to wince.

Despite the comment, Etta knew that Mildred would eventually come back around to the topic if it were not addressed.

"It's still early in the season." *True enough.*

"We're growing the flock, but it's manageable right now." *Mildly dishonest.*

"Papa and I have been talking about hiring some help." *True but misleading.*

The latter was Etta's hope, but she did not elaborate. Especially since the intent of it was to replace the work that she would have done. Mildred frowned again, sensing, quite accurately, that Etta was withholding much. It was no secret that several other families had been driven out of town in recent years, unable to keep up with the new property taxes. The Becketts were merely the most recent. On the rare occasion that he got into his cups, Helen's father would get himself riled up over it.

The various farming families in town were a close-knit community; a loss of one was felt by all. There were few among them who had not trudged through the snow to check on someone who had fallen ill or to borrow a cup of sugar.

Mildred was especially sensitive to this where Etta was concerned. The Wozniaks were no strangers to tragedy after all. Even if Etta would never admit her predicament, Mildred knew, or at the very least suspected that they were in trouble.

Just as she opened her mouth, about to press Etta on the things not being said, Helen and the others returned. Thankful for the interruption, Etta could not help but think that her friend was losing her sense of timing. Helen had returned before all the evening chores were finished.

Mildred frowned and shook her head. Helen was laughing so loudly that the conversation with Etta could not continue. Excusing herself, Mildred left to go and scold her daughter.

As the two of them got into a spat in the other room, Etta let out a sigh of relief. She had little doubt that if Mildred continued to scrutinize her it would be only a matter of time before she slipped and revealed a detail about her intentions to leave town. Something that could not be explained away or ignored. Even though she had promised Helen that she would do so, Etta was not quite ready to have that conversation.

Aunt Mildred had a big heart, but was prone to meddling. That was simply her way, and maybe she had the right of it sometimes. The incident with her hands had made that clear to Etta. While having a full belly had been nice, the loss of her independence to Mildred's intervention was a high price.

It seemed highly unlikely that Mildred would simply say "goodbye and good luck." On the contrary, it was almost certain that she would talk Etta out of it.

The evening was late by the time supper was cleaned up. Etta might have stayed longer, despite the morning that would come sooner than anyone would like, but the latest spat between Helen and her mother lingered. Etta doubted that anyone in the Saunders' home would find peace for the remainder of the evening. In that way, she was rather envious of the men still out, working on the cottage. By comparison, a few hours of swinging a hammer seemed like relative peace and quiet.

Robert was leaving for his shift at the firehouse and Etta accepted his offer to drive her home. Aside from the domestic tension, a ride in a truck was a seldom enough occurrence that she could not decline it.

Etta remained on the porch with Mildred, giving Helen and Robert some privacy at the truck. They were taking a long while to say "good night."

"Just a quick kiss," Mildred called.

Helen briefly regarded her mother with a scowl before turning away again.

Then, under her breath Mildred added, "Not that you could get any *more* pregnant."

Coming from Mildred, the comment was doubly surprising, both in its flippancy and lewdness. The latter struck Etta as particularly funny, and she snickered. At first, Mildred looked confused, but soon blushed, having not intended to voice that particular thought.

She composed herself while still grinning, and pulled Etta into a warm embrace. "Don't be a stranger now." She gave a quick glance toward the truck to confirm that Helen and Robert were still distant. Satisfied, she spoke her next words with care, making sure that only Etta would hear.

"My daughter has a good soul, but she's terribly lazy. For the life of me, I don't know how she's going to handle this baby." Gripping Etta's shoulder, she let the words sink in, her expression serious.

Etta was too surprised to respond. It was a frank assessment, especially coming from Helen's own mother, but Etta could not find fault with it. Certainly, she had thought much the same thing, but never allowed it beyond the privacy of her own thoughts. Though she had come dangerously close during her own recent spat with Helen.

Mildred continued, "I think she will do what she has to... eventually. But it will take time. I'm asking you to be there for her until she does."

In truth, from the moment Helen first broke the news, Etta had a sneaking suspicion that something like this would happen. Hearing it actually spoken, and asked of her directly and without ambiguity was unsettling. While it did not quite surprise her, the starkness of Mildred's admission did. It was no secret that Helen would avoid work whenever possible, but neither had it meant any consequences for Etta before.

The implications left her uneasy. Doing as Mildred asked would mean a delay of Etta's plans to leave town. That also assumed she and Papa had not lost their home by then.

What's another six months?

Maybe longer. And being a nanny on top of everything else.

Not for the first time, Etta thought about simply leaving without saying goodbye.

Like Alicja had done...

If her face betrayed any of these thoughts, Mildred did not acknowledge it.

Instead, Etta merely replied, "Of course."

Robert dropped Etta off in front of her house a few minutes later, and she was relieved to find that Jakob had returned. Approaching the house, the telltale glow of the kerosene lantern shone through a window. This was odd, since Papa was normally in bed by this hour.

Instead, she found him seated at his usual place at the end of the table, a chaotic mess of papers spread out before him.

"I was wondering when you would get back," she greeted.

Papa nodded, without looking up, but Etta noticed that he did curl his mouth up in a smile.

"I was beginning to think the same about you," he replied. "And how are the Saunders?"

Etta grinned, thinking, *He knows me too well.*

She was pleased that her recent efforts at conversation were having a positive effect. Small talk was coming more easily between them since her incident, and Papa's mood had taken a turn for the better. For that matter, so had Etta's. As a practical concern, they still had to talk about the latest thing that had broken, but even a transient discussion of a happier topic did wonders for the both of them.

"They're well," Etta replied. "Mildred was asking about you. Wanted me to remind you that you are welcome to supper as well."

"That's kind of her, but I've been eating in Newark. There's a man that sells fried cod in the stall next to mine."

"And how was the farmer's market?" she asked, sitting down in her usual chair.

Jakob looked up from the papers, still smiling, but now also looking tired. "Profitable. In some ways." Then, he sighed. "Less so in others." Eyes downcast, he spread his hands over the mess of papers. "We have only about half of what is owed the tax collector."

Etta frowned. "I thought Newark was supposed to give better prices?"

"It does. But after the fuel for the truck, the market fee, and other costs, it only goes so far."

She found herself with a sudden, nervous energy, and started to tap her foot beneath the table. This was not good news.

Etta had come to think of the upcoming tax payment as the conclusion of her responsibilities here. It was the only way she would be able to leave with a clean conscience. The day after it was paid, she planned to buy her train ticket and depart from town. That was, of course, before Mildred's request for her to help with Helen's baby.

She had long debated about how soon to tell Papa ahead of time, just to give him a chance to hire the help that he would need. It was only fair. With their improving relationship, she remained unsure how he would take the news. Much as it troubled her, Etta was willing to leave Mildred with only a goodbye letter if it came to it. That simply would not do for Papa.

"I'll take the job with the Van Dycks," she said suddenly, slumping in her chair with resignation.

Working at the butcher was not ideal, but she supposed that it could not be any worse than burning her hands at the hotel or being subjected to Mr. Mustache. Seeing his daughter's discomfort, Papa set down his pencil and raised a hand in a soothing gesture.

"As I said, it was profitable in other ways. While I was there, I came across another opportunity. A job actually. I think this may be the answer we have been looking for."

Even with her every intention of leaving, Etta had worried about Papa losing the farm. The very idea of some stranger buying their home, and using her mother's kitchen gave her a shudder. That Papa apparently would be able to keep it was a huge relief.

"What's the job?" she asked.

When Papa did not respond right away, she grew concerned. His eyes shifted as if the answer was uncomfortable and he was trying to be delicate. As the silence continued, a thought occurred to her.

Eyes narrowed, and giving her father a critical look, she asked, "Are you bootlegging?"

At first he looked at her in confusion, as if she just told him that she wanted to enter one of the chickens into the August Pageant. Then he laughed. Not a reserved chuckle either.

"No, nothing like that. I'll leave that to the Brandelsons. This is accounting work. I happened to meet the owner of a textile mill who needs help managing their book at the end of the week. I told them I would come back out tomorrow."

Etta visibly relaxed and nodded.

"That's good news. Are you going to sell the eggs beforehand?"

Jakob shook his head. "I won't be selling the eggs."

Etta resumed her frown. "So, then what are we going to do with them?" She trailed off as she realized that her daily trip to town was back on. Used to be that Etta enjoyed the walk since it was the only way she could get any time to herself. With Papa away for most of the day, she had an abundance of such. Now, hauling the wagon to Dominic's would just be another chore.

Papa continued. "If this goes well, we won't need to sell eggs at all."

Etta remained unconvinced. There was something he was not telling her. Recently, she was better able to read between the lines with her father, but in this case, he remained opaque.

What is he keeping from me? Is our money situation that bad?

"Some good news," he added. "We will not need to wake up in the middle of the night to load the truck."

That was something at least, but Etta's frown remained.

Sensing his daughter's unease, Jakob reached out for her hand. "This past year – well, these *years*, have been difficult. We have lost much. But... I promise you, things are going to get better."

There it was again. Papa smiled at her, but there was clearly something left unspoken. Etta would not pry. Just as there were things she did not want to tell Papa, she would leave him his privacy.

It hardened her resolve to continue doing her part. Just in case this new opportunity was not as profitable as Papa seemed to believe. After all, it would not be the first time he had misjudged something, or even been tricked. They regarded each other a moment. The last two people in a home that used to be much busier.

Ghosts and memories... and now secrets.

Papa suddenly furrowed his brow as a thought occurred to him.

"It was dark when I came home, and it could be that I'm imagining things... but did something happen to the mailbox?"

Of all the small jobs with which Etta had dabbled, her least favorite was helping at the butcher. This was due to a variety of reasons, but essentially came down to two. The first was working with knives, which made her uncomfortable and she avoided it as much as possible. Cutting vegetables at home often took twice as long due to her caution. Having seen her mother slip once and almost lose the tip of a finger made an impression that would stay with her for life.

The second was blood. Oddly enough, she could prepare a chicken from pen to plate without a second thought. Perhaps it was just something she was accustomed to, but it did not bother her in the slightest. The butcher was another matter. The last time she had worked there, they had prepared lamb "on the hoof."

That was something else that would stay with her for life. Unfortunately, she lacked for other options.

After the conversation with her father the night before, Etta was convinced that their finances were more desperate than he let on. Jakob remained a proud man who would never admit to being unable to provide for his family – small though it was these days.

If the money simply *appeared*, however, he would not be too proud to accept it. Thus, after seeing him off that morning, she had resolved herself to at least a few days – hopefully not more than two weeks – of working for the Van Dycks. Arriving at the butchers' store an hour before they opened, Etta let herself in.

Paul, the older brother, had been preparing the public side for business, but looked up at the sound of the tinkling bell. He was just a little older than her father but his hair was far more salt than pepper and his face had more lines. He greeted Etta warmly.

"Miss Wozniak! *Gut morgan*. Is it culling day already?"

He spoke with a substantial accent, Dutch having been his first language. Etta had been very young when he and his brother, Franke, had immigrated to her town just after the start of the Great War. Over time, they became a staple of the community, until eventually it was like they had always been here.

"Good morning," she replied. "And no, I don't have any birds."

Etta had, in fact, just sold the day's egg collection to Dominic, having beaten the Heckels again by mere minutes. The profits from the eggs seemed lighter than usual, with their tax shortfall still fresh in her mind. This had ultimately decided her on visiting the butcher.

Paul frowned and spread his hands apologetically.

"I'm sorry, but if you are here to buy, nothing is ready yet. We had not planned to open for business for another hour at least."

"Actually, I'm here to work if you'll have me. Does Franke need any help out back today?"

Paul's brother had dropped the second syllable of his name, and gone by "Frank" since he became a citizen. Paul still called his brother by his given handle, and Etta hoped this small touch might earn her a little more favor.

"Yes," Paul nodded. "Your father mentioned you might come to visit." Paul stared off into space with a thoughtful expression for a moment before nodding. "As it happens, we took delivery of some quarters of beef this morning, and I'm sure he could use help. At least until the morning rush is over."

Both relief and dread came to Etta in equal measure. Despite their situation, a part of her had been hoping for Paul to decline her offer. Instead, she nodded.

"And – ah – payment?" she ventured. She never liked discussing money, but it was necessary. Today especially.

Paul nodded, as if this was a matter of course. "Ten dollars for the morning. I will add a string of sausages if you can fill the display case before we open."

That was about as good as she could hope for. For a moment, she considered haggling, but it was already generous. And the prospect of something other than eggs for dinner was enticing.

"That's a deal," she replied and braced herself.

Where Paul was kindly and easygoing, Franke was stoic and quiet, with a near singular focus on his work. That was not to say he was unfriendly, but it took some time for him to warm up to someone. Even then, he did not say much. To Etta's mind, he was the ideal working partner. Without smiling, he acknowledged her with a courteous nod, and indicated an open place across from him at the wooden butcher's block.

With a sigh of relief, Etta noticed that the cows were already quartered and hanging from hooks in the back of the cooler. At least there would be no large eyes looking at her with accusation.

The processing room was cold though. Ice blocks lined one wall like bricks, and Etta was glad she had worn long sleeves this morning. Still, she shivered, and wanted to get an apron on for the additional warmth. A blue one and a white one hung near the door. Liking the color, she reached for the blue one, but Franke surprised her when he placed his hand over it and shook his head.

Without explanation, he picked up the white apron and handed it to her before returning to the table. Unsure what faux pas she had just committed, Etta sighed as she followed him to the cutting block.

The rest of the morning went quickly. Franke did most of the bulk portioning with an electric saw, while Etta's job was to trim the cuts into individual servings, wrap them, and set them in the glass display case in the storefront. She was immensely thankful for this, since the band saw terrified her more than knives.

Where her mother had almost lost the tip of one finger, Franke was down to eight digits. Testament to the hazards of working with equipment designed specifically to cut through meat and bone. The sight of his short hand never failed to give her a shiver. Not so much for what it was, but too vividly, she could imagine the mishap that had made it that way. Franke was not shy about it, especially when he felt Etta was not being safe.

"Slow down. People will wait." His accent was even thicker than his brother's, but there was no mistaking his words, especially when he wiggled his remaining fingers for emphasis. Etta nodded, took a breath, and carried on with more care.

It was a lot of meat to process, even for two people. Despite being accustomed to physically demanding work, her fingers ached, and her arms were burning by the time she finished getting through the first batch of cuts. More than once, she was thankful for Franke's lack of haste.

Eventually, it was time to make the sausage. Franke was especially grateful to have a second set of hands for this part, as someone had to turn the crank while feeding meat into the hopper, and – at the same time – let the casing run out. All this while also twisting it into individual links. It was possible to do alone, but two people made for a much smoother operation.

Paul, punctual as usual, officially opened for business at eight o'clock sharp. Though the storefront was out of sight, Etta could clearly hear everyone coming and going. For the regular Townies, Paul knew most of their usual orders from memory. Besides the locals, their business proved popular with the out-of-towners. Paul greeted them warmly, and listed the day's offering more times than Etta could count despite it being written on the chalk sign.

The morning rush was aptly named.

At first, Etta thought they were making great progress, but she and Franke quickly found themselves struggling to keep up with the orders. Paul would poke his head into the preparation room, call out the next order, and then disappear again.

"Half rack of prime rib!"

"Two briskets!"

"Three pounds ground chuck."

But we're in the middle of making sausage.

While she prided herself on a solid memory, even she lost track more than once. The orders from Paul were interspersed with the occasional warning from Franke.

"Cut away. Not into belly."

"Push too hard. Switch for sharper knife."

And so went most of the morning.

Eventually, things quieted down, and by noon, the customers came in one or two at a time until they tapered off completely. The store was quiet when Paul came back to lend a hand. The Van Dycks knew their business well; there were less than a dozen or so cuts that had not sold. To Etta's surprise, Paul frowned.

"A good day for earning," he said looking around the processing room. "But not a great one. We did not sell all of the prime cuts unfortunately."

Franke shrugged. "It is not too warm today. We might keep some on ice for tomorrow."

Paul's frown deepened. “Selling day-old meat is such *Franse slag*.”

“And salting a prime cut should be a sin,” Franke protested. Reluctantly, he sighed his agreement. “So be it,” he replied. “It will be better than nothing.”

He drummed his fingers on the preparation table, next to a few extra sets of sausage links. One of which Etta had claimed for part of her payment. Franke had been kind enough to add extra garlic upon her request and even used less organ meat than he had for the customers.

“Glad I could help,” said Etta, looking at him expectantly.

Paul held up a finger, as if remembering something. “Your payment, *ja*.” He disappeared to the storefront and returned with a small fold of greenbacks. “You are hard-working and always welcome here. Please do not be a stranger.”

She smiled and nodded in acknowledgment as he pressed the money into her hand. The wad of bills was comforting. It would go a long way to cover their tax burden.

A very long way, Etta thought, rubbing the money between her fingers with a growing suspicion.

Normally, Etta was very conscious of etiquette and manners, and had not intended to count the money, especially in front of the Van Dyck brothers. It was only when she noticed that the wad of bills felt thicker than it had a right to be that she splayed them out and counted them.

“We said ten dollars,” she said, looking directly at Paul. “This is almost twenty.”

“Yes,” he replied. “That is – what – bonus.”

What she heard was *charity*, and felt her hackles rising. Somewhere, a meek voice urged her to stop talking, and simply say “thank you.” Stubbornly, she ignored it and pressed on.

“This is not what we discussed,” Etta replied tersely.

“You were a great help today. When customers are served promptly, it is good for business.”

When she made no response, Paul’s expression turned from confused yet vaguely amused, to simply confused. Neither spoke for the span of several breaths.

The nagging voice was more assertive this time, and managed to prevent Etta from further protest. The Van Dycks did not deserve to be slapped in the face for their good intentions. Loathe as she was to admit it, she absolutely could not afford to pass up this generosity. Still, her pride was a damned, stubborn thing.

“If it's alright with you,” she continued, “I'd like to earn the bonus.”

Paul relaxed and exchanged a look with Franke who motioned to something behind Etta.

"Very well, *Missen*. If you insist." He pointed to the meat grinder that she and Franke had used to make sausage. "I think that could benefit from your attention."

Etta looked it over, thinking that it did not seem like any great task. "That's all?"

Franke let out a short bark, which took Etta a moment to recognize as a laugh. Again, the brothers exchanged looks, and laughed good-naturedly. At least a small part of it was at Etta's expense, but in a friendly way.

Franke explained, "You will see. That *lellebel* will keep you busy for an hour at least."

Paul shot his brother a look of clear disapproval, even though Etta was not sure what it was about. Franke caught the unspoken rebuke, and shrugged his shoulders, unconcerned.

Franke disassembled the grinder in a few well-practiced motions, and laid out the components on the butcher's block with bits of meat and fat still clinging to them. She had remained skeptical, and, true enough, the majority of the pieces were simple enough to clean. But as she looked inside the main housing, she saw the meaning behind the Van Dycks' earlier laughter. Franke had not exaggerated.

The inside of the housing contained tens of small, annular grooves to pull and tear the meat as a large screw pushed it through. They were small, difficult to reach, and an hour later, she was still fussing with it.

"Every one must be cleaned entirely," Franke explained. "There can be no pieces left inside to fester."

As it turned out, her long, slender fingers made this task somewhat simpler, even if it was still time consuming. At least the quietness of the shop gave her a chance to think. It occurred to her that she still had much to finish before the day was through. More than once, she silently cursed her pride for not simply accepting the well-meaning "bonus" despite its charitable taint. On the other hand, it was one of the few paying jobs she had come across that could be performed while seated.

Her thoughts were interrupted by the sound of the front door ringing as someone entered the store. Perhaps the Van Dycks would sell those last few portions after all. Paul spoke with the newcomer, who was a loud fellow, but Etta paid little attention. She hoped to complete this final task before midday.

The sound of a familiar name being spoken pulled Etta out of her idling thoughts.

Then, she heard his voice.

Chapter 16
Art

"For crying out loud, boy, stand up straight." George smacked Art's chest to emphasize his words. It was only intended to get his son's attention, but his meaty palm carried weight and knocked Art back a step. "Act like you have some answers. Show a little pride. No one is going to want to buy anything from some quivering slouch."

While he felt the word "quivering" was an exaggeration, Art straightened up all the same. Feeling both pretentious and awkward, it apparently met with his father's approval. This was their fourth stop of the day, and he had been hearing a variation of this "advice" all morning.

"Speak from down here this time," George said, pointing to Art's belly. "I could barely hear you at the general store, and I was standing right next to you."

For several days, Art's father had mostly ignored him, doting on the grandchildren instead. At last, he simply could not resist going back to selling his wares, and they resumed Art's second apprenticeship. His other brothers, as usual, went off on their own, making the case they would be more effective that way. Their father had agreed enthusiastically, praising his sons' keen sense for business. It was not until later that Art realized his brothers were old hands at this game, and had succeeded in getting their father to ignore them for the day.

Art was still salty about their abandoning him on the farming side of town, but at least they were leaving him alone. Perhaps they thought that if they did not talk to him, he would not confront them on the matter. To be fair, it was proving to be an accurate assessment.

Feeling extra confident as they left the house that morning, George decided that their first stop would be the Fichner icehouse. It was actually Art who had told his father about them, recalling what Etta the farmer, had mentioned. It turned out they were a rather big name in town. George reasoned that if he could sell to them, he could practically afford to buy the cottage they were currently renting. Or so was the claim.

Unfortunately, that venture had ended in a huge bust. Ostensibly, the oldest son ran the Fichners' business, but it was soon apparent that his father made the decisions. He was a spindly, bent-backed old man who went by the handle Old Sarge – having been a quartermaster in the Spanish American War. Unfortunately for the Adamses, he was skeptical of the whimsical gadget they were hawking.

Art thought their rationale was sensible, but wisely kept this judgment from his father. The Fichners' business had changed little in the past fifty years. Each winter, once the lake was frozen several inches thick, they would take a crew out to cut blocks. Once dragged back to shore, they were stacked in the insulated warehouse, which would preserve them for most of the year. Collection was both spotty – depending entirely on the fickle whims of nature – and also dangerous.

George had jumped on the second detail immediately, pointing out that this would eliminate the need for them to bring a crew out onto the ice ever again. In addition, they could manufacture year-round instead of merely harvesting. This detail actually intrigued the Fichner patriarch, who conceded that they had nearly lost a man on the ice just this past season.

Both father and son admitted that by late summer, supplies typically ran low, but they had recently made a significant investment to improve the insulation on their warehouse. Thus, the idea of spending even more money to completely upend their business model was utterly out of the question. Old Sarge had been firm on this point, leaving no room for debate. This clearly rankled George, though he tried not to show it.

Accusing George and Art of trying to put him out of business, Old Sarge grew more hostile as the meeting wore on. George, to the contrary, remained polite and businesslike the whole time. As soon as they returned outside, he dropped Sales Smile so quick that Art recoiled.

Through clenched teeth, George proceeded to speculate on several improbable, anatomical configurations. Specifically pertaining to the Old Sarge's head and its proximity to his ass.

Art, meanwhile, did his best impression of a statue, and thought about the workshop. This had been one of the days where Gregory was out of town, so nothing would happen with their current project in his absence. Thus far, Art had managed to balance his unexplained disappearances with his father's demands. With a vague unease, he wondered at how long he could maintain this dynamic.

That was a problem for another day.

During their next three calls they made one sale. Unfortunately, it did little to improve George's mood. He was more rattled by their bad showing with the Fichners than he let on.

"Remember, keep it simple. No technical jargon. Don't talk to your feet. And for Heaven's sake, no more of that 'your electrical bill will triple' nonsense."

Art nodded, waiting for his father to stop. Idly, he wondered for just how long he would be reminded of his faux pas at the Warren Hotel.

"Put your Sale Smile on," said George as he made a final adjustment to his necktie. With that, he pushed Art through the door.

"*Goedemorgen*," greeted the man behind the counter. "Can I help you gentlemen?"

"As a matter of fact, sir, I'm hoping I can help you. My name is George Adams, owner of Adams Refrigeration and Service. This is my son, Arthur. Are you Mr. Van Dyck, as it says out front?"

Sales Smile is weak, Art silently critiqued. His father must have been tired.

"I am Paul Van Dyck," the man nodded as he folded his arms across his chest. "What is it that you would be helping me with, George?"

Right away, Art could tell the man was not interested, and only let them continue so as not to be rude. Art had completed enough of these calls to sense when it was going to be a challenge.

"If we could have but a few moments of your time, I believe we can make you an offer on a product that will really enhance your fine business here."

"Ah, salesman," Paul said, as if to confirm a suspicion. "I will not waste your time or mine. Whatever it is you are selling, *dank u*, but no." He was firm on that point, yet polite about it.

Ever the optimist, Art was about to turn to leave. To his dismay, George continued, undeterred. Art had already accepted Paul's answer, but forgotten that his father's opinion was the only one that mattered.

"You speak plainly, and to the point, sir," George continued. "And I commend you for it. But to the contrary, it is not my intent to waste your time. In fact, I believe I can help you save a considerable amount of it, if you would be kind enough to make us a gift of two minutes now. At the very least, perhaps I can give you some food for thought."

Paul let out an exasperated sigh, his annoyance briefly overriding his polite exterior. He shifted his weight back and forth a few times, clearly debating how firmly he was prepared to ask them to leave.

"Very well, *Mijn Heer*. What is it you are selling?"

"As I said, our business is refrigeration. May I ask, how do you currently store your cold provisions?"

"We must keep the back room quite cold. It takes maybe five hundred pounds of ice each week." Paul replied.

George whistled, as if impressed and elbowed Art in the ribs.

"Five hundred pounds, he says. That's a lot of blocks to move, eh son?"

Art glimpsed a flash of irritation from his father's eye, and realized that he was slouching. He quickly straightened and his father turned back to Paul.

George continued, "That must take a toll on your back."

Paul shrugged. "It is not so bad. We move almost that amount of meat each day."

"Still, that must be time consuming," George insisted.

Paul's look of annoyance deepened. "It takes twenty minutes. The truck pulls up. My brother and I grab the blocks, and walk ten feet to the back of the store. We spend more time to salt and dry the unsold inventory each day."

George stumbled. The time-saver angle usually worked. Next he tried the maintenance strategy, also to no avail. Paul made an obvious glance towards the clock on the wall, checking whether two minutes had yet passed. George went through his usual list of questions, and tried to offer up scenarios where an Adams refrigerator would make the Van Dycks' life better. Each time, Paul shot it down. By the end, his composure was just beginning to slip.

Art started to fidget, growing more uncomfortable with every passing second. At least Old Sarge had managed to cut the pitch short with his refusal. It was better than letting it limp along as they were currently doing. Having already conceded defeat, Art's eyes began to wander the room, but his father carried on, determined. This, combined with their earlier failures would ensure George was in a foul mood for the remainder of the day. No doubt, Art would later have to endure a meticulous review of every detail that had contributed to this poor outcome.

Half-listening to the conversation, Art's eyes settled on a large slate on the wall behind the counter. Prices were written in chalk, and a powdery, white film indicated that the offerings were changed with some regularity. The main feature of the room was the glass-fronted display case. Mostly empty now save for a scattering of various high-end cuts. A thought gradually formed in his mind, and he found himself blurting it out before fully thinking it over.

"How much spoils before you sell it?" Too late, he realized that he had interrupted.

Both Paul and George shot him a dark look. In the case of the latter, he had been the one speaking, while the former had the look of a man deliberately insulted.

"*Pleur op!*" Paul barked.

Art had no idea what that meant, but there was no mistaking the tone.

Paul continued, "We sell no spoiled meat here!"

George switched immediately to damage control, attempting to smooth over the mess Art had made.

"I'm sure my son didn't intend-"

"What I mean was-" Art was so panicked that he cut off his father for a second time.

Paul remained on guard, fully prepared to take offense and George absolutely radiated displeasure. For a certainty, he would blame Art not just for this failure, but the rest of the morning as well. After all, who told George about the Fichners? They would lose this sale, Art was sure. In a distant, logical part of his mind, he wondered if his father would go with the "money doesn't grow on trees" lecture, or the "be more like your brothers" lecture.

His heart beat faster and his suit was suddenly stuffy and uncomfortable. A thin sheen of sweat appeared on his forehead, and he was now keenly aware that his shirt was stuck to his back. There was a momentary distraction as a second man in a blue apron emerged from the room behind the sales counter.

"What's this now?" the man asked.

Unlike Paul, this new man wore a scowl that must have been his default expression. His dark eyes turned to Art and George with unveiled animosity.

"*Zakkenwasser* asks if we sell spoiled meat," Paul replied.

Art thought he noticed movement in the back room, but could not see beyond the man in the blue apron. Having had enough, George cleared his throat, interpreting Art's silence as a concession of defeat.

In the time it took for him to draw a breath, Art jumped back in.

"I can save you two hundred dollars each year," Art blurted.

That got their attention. The three older men looked at him in surprise. Paul still carried an annoyed expression, but it was now tempered with curiosity.

"Explain."

"Yes, *please* do," added his father. The Sale Smile was hanging on by a thread.

Art gulped.

"This is just a rough guess, but your display case is about one tenth full. Mostly the expensive cuts, right?"

Paul nodded a hesitant concurrence. The other man merely narrowed his eyes.

Continuing, Art said, "From your sign, those fetch a much higher price than dried meat, which you said is what happens to leftover inventory, right?"

Art inflected his voice, making it a question. To his relief, Paul and the other man both nodded.

"An electric refrigerator is much colder than ice, and the leftover inventory would stay fresher for longer. You wouldn't need to dry it." He began to rattle off some numbers, but stopped at a look from his father. "Bottom line, you could sell more prime cuts without risk of spoi- without wasted opportunity. That could be well over two hundred dollars in a year based on your prices here. Our refrigeration unit could practically pay for itself. In time."

The "opportunity" bit and the "pay for itself" angle were two of George's favorite key phrases, which he had pressed Art to learn from the beginning. This was the first time he had actually used them. The "in time" qualifier was something that he added on his own; feeling dishonest otherwise.

A thoughtful expression played on Paul's face. He looked over his shoulder at the display case, rubbing his chin in thought.

During the pause, Art glanced over at his father, whose visage was much softened. For a moment, the Sale Smile had dropped, and was replaced by something Art was simply not accustomed to seeing on his father. At least, not directed at him. It was an actual smile. Art stood a little taller without needing to be instructed to do so.

Paul and the other man exchanged a look. They did not seem quite convinced, but it was a near thing. Sensing this, George provided a gentle, verbal nudge.

"We have sold a few of these units to other businesses around town. Perhaps you know Maggie Warren or the Fichners?"

Art winced, unsure why his father had mentioned one of their conspicuous failures. From the uncomfortable expression that followed, George had not intended to do so. It must have rattled him more than Art originally thought. However, his nudging had the desired effect.

"What you say, Franke?"

The second man cocked his head and shrugged his shoulders in what must have been affirmation. Paul nodded once in response before turning back to Art and George.

"You mentioned the Fichners. What did Old Sarge say?"

This time, George answered, trying to gloss over the inconvenient parts of their earlier interaction. "He was interested. I believe he had a near accident on the ice last year, and the idea of never harvesting again was very appealing."

That is a generous interpretation, thought Art, but he had to concede that it was a good recovery. The facts would hold up to scrutiny if not the spin.

Art was finally beginning to understand the hazards of being too honest, and made no attempt to correct his father. Besides, his own thoughts proved distracting.

Did I really just make a sale? Is this what my brothers feel like all the time? No wonder Ralph was always strutting around. The feeling was intoxicating. Euphoric.

Paul returned his attention to Art. "You make some excellent points, *Jonge Heer*. My brother and I consider waste to be a grave sin, but we will need time to consider. Could you leave us with an estimated cost that we may consult our books?"

Both George and Art replied in near unison, "Of course."

George slapped his son on the back affectionately, but it still caused him to stagger. George pulled out several sheets of paper bearing the company letterhead and began to write. His earlier scowl had practically disappeared. This was his element now. Meanwhile, Art continued to bask in the glow of success, and actually looked forward to dinner with the family. Without a doubt, his father would talk about this for at least the next two evenings. And for once that would be a good thing.

"With regards to capacity," George started. "I believe you would want something large enough to walk inside. This would be too large, I think, to fit within the store itself. Fortunately, we offer outdoor units based on the ammonia cycle-"

"If it's going to be outside, you might as well go with a Freon unit," Art offered. "It will be larger, but if it ever leaks, you won't have to worry about ammonia poisoning."

George stopped writing, his face wincing in anticipation.

Both Paul and Franke's eyes snapped to Art.

"What's this about poison?" demanded Paul. "Is the product dangerous?"

"No!" George answered quickly. "Absolutely not. My son is referring to a handful of incidents with very *early* models which are no longer in service." His face darkened as he turned to Art. "Isn't that right?"

The pride Art had been feeling only a few seconds earlier vaporized. Indeed, all powers of speech had fled him at that exact moment.

"I ah – well..." Art hesitated.

Desperately, he searched for the right combination of words to fix the situation, but was unable to condense a vast pool of information into a single thought. He might have simply said "No," which at least would have been concurrence with his father, but instead he said nothing.

It turned out that was the worst thing he could say.

"I think we have heard enough," said Paul. "Good day, gentlemen."

The air had turned brisk. A steady breeze carried across the water, chilly by the time it reached the shore and crossed Route Six. Overcast clouds, stole away any warmth the sun might have provided. For several minutes, neither Art nor his father said a word. Art was slouching again, and stared at his feet with determination as he anticipated the inevitable. Surprisingly, his father did not appear angry anymore, which actually gave him some concern. At least if George was yelling, his intentions were clear.

Eventually, the feeling of dread subsided, and Art just awaited the verbal lashing that was surely on its way. As the silence dragged on, the dread shifted to boredom.

Just yell at me already. Something.

"You go for days or weeks without saying two words. But then you torpedo a sale because you talk too much." George shook his head, and upon realizing he was still holding his pen, returned it to his pocket. "I am going to continue on alone and see if I can salvage the day. Don't bother coming back to the house before suppertime. You need to get a little perspective on what it means to not be employed."

And there is it: money doesn't grow on trees.

"You know, on Junior's first sale, he sold two whole units to that restaurant in Brooklyn. And Thomas was doing solo runs by the time he was your age."

Followed immediately by: be more like your brothers. Art could not recall getting both reprimands consecutively before. His father must have been truly livid. Eventually, George shook his head one last time and walked away.

Alone again, Art turned his face into the breeze. Thinking about the sale and how close he had been to success only underscored the disappointment.

Though he had the rest of the day to himself, he had no idea what to do with it. Some reading would be nice, but of course all his books were in the room at the cottage and thus off-limits. Likewise, the shop was closed to him while Gregory was out of town. Sighing, Art remained staring at the lake for a long moment until a voice interrupted his thoughts.

"Don't beat yourself up too much."

Art turned his head, though he was not immediately sure if he was the one being addressed. It was a woman's voice and familiar.

"The Van Dycks haven't bought anything new for as long as I've known them. Pretty sure their knives are from the 1800's."

Art's expression was blank for a moment before his eyebrows went up in recognition. "Oh. Hi Etta."

Her smile gave an immediate boost to his spirits. Unfortunately, it was also fleeting.

"So, you heard all that, huh?"

Etta nodded, shifting a black bag on her shoulder. "To be honest, I think it was incredible that they even considered it. I heard Franke once tossed an insurance salesman out the door. I mean, actually *tossed* him."

That cheered him up just a little bit. A half smile flashed across his face, but his glum mood stubbornly remained.

"I meant, you heard that thing just now... with my father." Art had been standing straighter with Etta's praise, but now resumed looking at his shoes.

"Oh. Well, yes." She waved a hand, dismissively. "I still say it was impressive. Did you really do all that math in your head?"

He looked up, nodding.

"Where did you learn to do that?"

Art shrugged. "Numbers just always came naturally to me. People, not so much." A thought occurred to him as he changed the subject. "So, you work here?" He asked, indicating the butcher's shop.

"Some days I do," she replied simply but evasively.

"I thought you worked on a farm?"

Etta shrugged and turned away, suddenly looking as bashful as Art. "I do that also."

"That sounds exhausting," he replied sympathetically.

Turning back to him, she smiled and said, "It certainly can be." By the look in her eyes, it was clear that what she meant was, *You don't know the half of it.*

Encouraged, Art grinned back. "What are you doing now? I was going to find a place to get lunch, since-" he waved his hand in an inarticulate gesture, "I can't go home yet."

Etta perked up at this, about to accept the offer, but her lips formed a line, and she shook her head.

"I have to be going," she said, a rueful expression on her face.

Art's smile gave way to a mild grimace. It had been the answer he expected, even if it was not the one he hoped for.

"But," she quickly added, "You could walk with me you want."

Looking up, his smile returned, and the two of them left the butcher shop. Following the shoreline, they walked side-by-side and passed a row of newer cottages. The trees were full by this time of the year, and formed a green tunnel as they traveled the packed dirt road.

Art stole a few glances in Etta's direction. She was pretty. That had been clear from their first meeting, but he had been out of sorts at the time, and distracted in a variety of ways. Now that the two of them were considerably more relaxed, he noticed details that had escaped him before.

Her blonde hair was longer than most, and only loosely tied back. It bounced on her shoulders as she walked. Her hawkish features, which had given her a stern appearance when she discovered him in the barn, seemed softer now. She glanced sideways then, and caught him staring. While he was still too shy to hold her gaze for long, he still held it, albeit briefly. All of a sudden, he was self-conscious of his own hair and made an effort to smooth it down.

"So, where are you from?" she asked, breaking the silence.

"At the moment? About three streets over." He gave her a wry smile.

"I meant, of course, originally."

Art was about to say "New York," but that was not entirely right. After thinking about it, he eventually replied, "Most recently I'm from Philadelphia. Been living there for the last four years. That's probably longest I've been in one place since I was a kid."

Etta cocked her head, inviting him to elaborate.

"My family moved around a lot when I was growing up. Dad's work took us all over. Most of us live in New York now. But I suppose originally we're from Boston, or rather, one of the smaller towns outside the city."

"Wow. You get around."

"Yeah, I hate it," he muttered.

Etta pushed on. "What's Philadelphia like?" She looked him square in the face.

At first, Art was mildly intimidated by her sudden attention, but soon embraced it. She was eager for information on a subject with which he happened to be quite familiar, and he was eager to hold her interest.

"Oh, it's..." He bit his lip, searching for something positive to say. She was probably not interested in what the inside of the academic buildings looked like, or of the immature antics of a dormitory full of young men. "It's not like here."

She frowned.

Quickly, he added, "I mean to say, there's hardly any trees. And no lake views for sure. Best I had was the Schuylkill River, and on some days I couldn't open my window because of the smell."

Her frown deepened in apparent disappointment. "Surely the whole city isn't like that?"

Art shrugged. "Couldn't really say. I stayed on the university campus mostly."

She raised an eyebrow. "A college man?"

Thick headed as he might be with social cues, there was no mistaking her impressed tone. Art puffed up just a little. "Not anymore. I finished my exams last month."

"Congratulations. So, is that why you're in town? This is a celebration holiday?"

He nodded again, encouraged by her continued interest. "In part. But mostly it's for my-" he almost said the word *engagement*. "My family's reunion. I have three brothers and five nieces and nephews that I haven't seen in a few years. I don't think my mother has seen them much either, so this was the solution."

Etta looked off, smiling. "Five grandchildren. Your mother is very lucky." She was quiet a moment, looking thoughtful.

Art took the opportunity to steal another glance in her direction. A rebellious strand of her own hair had gone off in its own direction and she casually tucked it back behind her ear, angling her head up as she did so. Despite a haggard expression that spoke of perpetual exhaustion and long hours of hard work – one that Art well recognized – he thought, not for the first time, that she was quite lovely.

"How long have you lived here?" he asked after a moment.

"My whole life," she replied. "My parents bought the farmhouse first thing after they immigrated, and that's where I was born." She paused a moment before sighing heavily. "I don't plan to stay much longer."

"Why?" Art asked, genuinely taken aback.

She looked him full in the face, and replied, "Because I can't wait to leave. I'm tired of it here and I want to be somewhere where I don't have to wake up with the chickens and scrape in the dirt all day. And music. Music would be nice," she added, almost wistfully, before looking off into the distance.

She opened her mouth to say more, but held back. From the contented look on her face, it seemed she had a particular vision of what life in the city was about. Art suspected that it contrasted with his own experience.

"I'm not sure the city is going to give you those things."

She shot him a look that contained more than a hint of annoyance. This was mostly lost on him, as Art had momentarily withdrawn to his own thoughts, and remained oblivious to her silent rebuke.

"Except the music," he conceded. "I suppose it can deliver on that."

"And how would you know? You said you hardly left school."

"Well, yes. But that doesn't mean I *never* got out. I mean maybe once you got past the soap factory, things were nicer."

She frowned. "So, what's past the soap factory? You're skipping the good part."

Art waved his hand. "I don't know… most places had some kind of music a few nights a week. But they have that here too, don't they? I saw couple restaurants in town with live entertainment. What's that one place?" He snapped his fingers, trying to think of the name of it. "Had an odd spelling. CasinO? Is that it?"

Etta seemed to tense. "They do," she responded crisply. Her lips pressed into a thin line.

Unsure of what he had said to ruin the mood, Art remained silent. After a few breaths, her expression softened and she nodded past his shoulder.

"That way will take you to the lakefront. The only luncheonette I can recommend is Jimmy's. He's an old family friend. Makes a great corned beef hash."

Sensing the conversation was over, Art smiled one last time despite his disappointment. "Thanks," he said with a nod.

They both lingered. Hoping to prolong the moment, Art added, "It was good to meet you again under better circumstances."

To his surprise, she smiled. Genuine but weary, as if she was pleased but simply exhausted. He took it as encouraging.

"Be seeing you," she said, and turned to walk away.

Art watched her go. The motion of her skirt where it hugged her hips drove all other thoughts from his mind. He looked away and shook his head. Regaining his wits, he stopped as a spark between his ears formed an idea. Having been relegated to the back of his mind until just this moment, it jumped to the forefront. Where before, he was unsure how to fill the rest of the day now he only hoped there was enough time.

Checking his watch, he nodded to himself. If he left now, he might just be able to pull it off. Mentally listing the things that needed to be done, he strode off but not in the direction of Jimmy's. A sudden energy carried him along, and his plans for lunch were forgotten.

Chapter 17
Etta

The new billfolds were reassuring, and the sausage links promised a good dinner. By all rights, Etta should have been completely at ease for the rest of the day. Before she left, the Van Dyck brothers had thanked her again and reminded her that she could work as often as she cared to. Soon after that, they fell into an animated conversation about the cheeky out-of-towners that had just left. As half the conversation was in Dutch, Etta took the opportunity to excuse herself.

The prospect of steady work was even better than the money already in her pocket, which she hoped would help with the tax burden as well as pad the leaving-town-fund.

Seeing Art again had been something of a mixed bag. He looked sharp in his business suit. Certainly, he was more put-together than their first meeting. Despite that unruly mass of curls on top of his head, the way he handled himself was genuinely impressive.

And well traveled too. That was intriguing, even if he was more negative about it than she would like. As with their first meeting, Etta had caught him looking at her more than once. Instead of finding it rude, this time she started to explore possibilities. Frowning, she realized that they had not made any plans to meet again. Maybe they would cross paths again on one of her visits to town.

Ever since Helen had revealed her pregnancy and engagement, she and Etta often talked about what everyone would wear. Helen had given a great deal of thought to the details of her wedding day, and had a very specific picture in mind. One that was at odds with her family's means. Compared to Etta, they were quite well off, but in absolute terms, they were not particularly wealthy.

As usual, it was left to Mildred to confront her daughter's lofty dreams with practical reality. This led to a number of disagreements that sometimes turned heated. At least on the matter of clothes, Helen's vision of a bridal party with all matching dresses was something attainable. This was only possible for two reasons: Mildred and Etta both happened to be proficient with a sewing machine, and they had time in greater abundance than money.

Despite the fuss, an afternoon at the Saunders' house, doing needlework was something she had been looking forward to. Dragging out the dusty old Singer sewing machine was something of a hassle, but she was happy to do it. There was a certain satisfaction in seeing someone wear clothes that she had made, and it had been far too long since she had an opportunity to do it.

At first, this talent had been born out of a certain, practical, necessity. Even in the days when the Wozniaks did not have to worry about their next meal, they had practiced "Use it up. Wear it out. Make it do, or do without." Farm work was rough on clothing, and being able to mend them was vital. As a result, Etta had developed a deft hand for stitches. One day, she started to experiment with one of the two dresses she owned. It was second hand, and hung loosely from her shoulders much like a potato sack, but by the time she was finished, it fit like a glove.

"Tight" was the word her mother had used, and it was made clear that she was never to wear it outside of the house. Still, the experience had kindled an interest, and soon it became more of a hobby than a chore. She even started making adjustments for her mother and sister.

Etta's buoyant spirits were promptly squashed upon her arrival at the Saunders' house. She was about to let herself in the front door, as she usually did, when Helen opened it first.

"You're late," she accused. Helen rested her hands on her hips and blocked the entrance.

"I beg your pardon?" Etta replied, genuinely confused. She had not yet stepped foot in the house.

"We said 'late morning,' didn't we?"

"Sorry. I was working at the butcher. What time is it?"

"Noon," Helen said with emphasis. She scoffed with frustration and stomped back into the house.

Etta followed, but with some hesitation, and seriously debated whether to turn on her heel and go home.

The reason behind her friend's foul mood soon became apparent. Aunt Mildred had set up their main room as a work area, and a white dress was laid out on the table. With a tired expression on her face, she nodded in greeting before Helen resumed the argument they had been having prior to Etta's arrival. It took only a few minutes of listening to gather what it was about.

Mildred had offered her old wedding gown, which she had made herself. To Etta, this was a sweet gesture, and something she would have appreciated from her own mother. Unfortunately, Helen's very particular vision did not include a *used* dress.

"I thought we were going to make something new," Helen said.

Mildred shook her head, as if she were repeating an argument she had already made. "We have to make two new bridesmaid dresses and we only have a few weeks to do it," Mildred countered.

"We're making two dresses, and the *bridal* gown can't be one?"

"This one is already finished. It just needs to be adjusted a little."

"It's old."

"It was good enough for me. Stop being so difficult."

Etta watched the argument continue for several more minutes. All the while, she found it remarkable that Mildred's famous composure seemed in real danger of faltering.

"How about this?" Etta interjected. When Helen and Mildred looked to her, she continued, "We let the dress out a little bit. Then, we'll trim with lace, and add a belt. For a little bit of work, it'll look completely new."

Mildred gave the slightest nod of concurrence, but said nothing. Helen maintained her frown, perhaps more disgruntled at her mother winning the argument than she was opposed to Etta's idea.

"It smells like mothballs," Helen muttered.

"We'll air it out then," Etta countered.

Helen fidgeted, looking at the dress on the table. Try as she might, she failed to come up with any good reason to deny the suggestion. Eventually, she agreed with the condition that they include a beadwork pattern.

Despite her current robust build, Mildred had been a petite thing in her youth, and much shorter than her daughter. The dress needed to be altered. Regarding Helen's delicate condition, there was some debate as to how much to let the waist out. There was no telling how much she might be showing after a few more weeks. In the end, they resolved to err on the looser side, and hide with a large bouquet if necessary.

As Mildred took Helen's measurements, Etta carefully ripped the old seams on the bodice where it would be expanded. It was painstaking work but thankfully, peace had been restored to the house. At one point Mildred caught Etta's eye, and made an expression that clearly said "Thank you."

Helen continued to loosen up and eventually began talking about her hopes for wedding day – mostly fussing about the weather and food.

Mildred, carefully but repeatedly, attempted to steer the conversation towards practical matters like things for the baby and the new cottage. This, in turn, caused Helen to dig in her heels. Thankfully, Mildred backed off before emotions could get heated again. At one point, she left the room to see what she might already have in the way of beads.

Once they were alone, Helen turned to Etta. "She's been on my case about the baby all day. I'm not due until Christmas for goodness sake."

Etta considered her next words with extreme care. "With fairness to your mother, it is a matter of some concern."

"You're going to take her side again?"

Etta bit her lip, sensing the precariousness of the situation. "She made a good point is all."

Helen's frown deepened, but her tone was deceptively conversational. "'A good point,' eh? Is that what you'd say if she told you that you shouldn't leave town?"

Etta shushed her, keenly aware that the door was still ajar.

Helen was genuinely taken aback. "What, you haven't told her?"

"Not... yet," Etta replied, frequently glancing back at the door.

"You have to tell her eventually," Helen added. "What, were you going to leave a note?"

The thought had crossed my mind...

Helen was about to say more when Mildred returned, and the subject was dropped.

By the time Etta left, she and Helen were back on good terms – the initial curt greeting and later disagreements were mostly forgotten. They made tentative plans to visit the swimming pond the following day, and Etta left their house with every intention of returning for supper. Naturally, she had work to finish before then.

However, after a full morning at the butcher, followed by dress work, Etta found she simply could not face the day's remaining chores just yet. While not exhausted to the point of fainting, as she had been a couple of weeks before, she now had a respect for her limits.

In need of a quiet place to sit, it was the perfect excuse to visit her favorite spot.

Clouds covered nearly the entire sky today except for a thin line of blue at the horizon. Still, the view from the jalopy was good as it always was. The blanket of clouds moved across the sky quickly, as if in some kind of rush. The day was hot, but a strong, persistent breeze, passed over the hilltop, making it pleasant.

Off to her right, she could see all way to the lake's northern shore and in the far distance, the rolling hills of the Heckels corn field. To the left, Route Six snaked along the landscape, carrying a handful of automobiles going about their business.

From up here, they might as well have been ants, but she started wondering about where they might be going. Eventually, her thoughts turned to her plans of escape, and she retrieved the map. Carefully, she spread it out on the blanket that served as the seat cover.

The previous autumn, she had intended to sew a proper one that fit better than the blanket. About the same time, the store in town had a fabric pattern that caught her eye: red flowers on a taupe field. She had gone so far as to take measurements, and figured out how to match the contours of the seat.

Months passed and she never quite found time for the little side project. Neither could she justify withdrawing the cost of material from her then small nest egg. Eventually, the fabric was moved out of inventory, and nothing else had quite the same appeal.

On the map, she mentally traced the route she had come up with to get to New York City. She had long since memorized the name of each town along the way, having never actually seen most of them. She wondered what they might be like, and imagined the drive to get there.

Realistically, her journey this fall would be by train, but after a few months of working, maybe she could afford a real car. That is, one that she could actually drive. The jalopy itself would never run again, but maybe Etta could get one like it. Perhaps even the same model. To be able to go wherever she wanted; that would be the life.

Even driving the truck would be something, but Papa would not allow it as long as she lived here. While he had done much to try to reassure her, Etta just knew that he secretly blamed her for what happened to Irene. More and more she wondered whether he had left something out of his explanation that the other driver was the one at fault.

Perhaps he was only trying to spare her a guilty conscience. After all, why else would he not let her drive?

Sometimes she wondered if maybe it was true. Maybe it was her fault. She had bumped her head in the accident, and the details from that time remained fuzzy to her. Many things she only remembered from seeing them after the fact. The steering wheel was bent around where Etta braced against it during the impact. The broken glass in the road. Her sister lying prone and covered by a sheet. That was something she could not forget if she tried.

The loss of little Irene had been raw at the time, and everyone was utterly consumed with grief. She was only a few weeks past her eleventh birthday. It had been a time for mourning, and Etta had spared little thought to the full details of the events leading up to the crash. For a while, she never second-guessed her father's original assessment.

That was until her mother began to act strangely.

Lena never spoke about the accident and her silence eventually gave Etta cause to doubt the version of events she had been led to believe. Never did she accuse Etta, but neither did she offer reassurances. Lena only grew distant. It was the fourth tragic loss in their family in as many years, and for Mama it was the hardest.

An unusual sight interrupted Etta's dark musings. Leading a plume of dust, a single car made its way along the dirt road coming from the direction of town.

The damn taxman is making the rounds again, she grimaced.

Tracking its progress, she wondered who would be the unlucky one today. As the car began to slow, her pulse quickened. The taxman was looking for something. She breathed a sigh of relief as he passed her house and kept going.

Not us then.

The thought made her feel immediately guilty, but it was soon replaced by alarm and dismay as the car slowed to an idling speed. It occurred to her that the Saunders were the next closest neighbor. Eyes wide, her blood practically ran cold at the thought.

No. It can't be. Anyone but the Saunders.

The car stopped. Etta's mouth went slightly agape as it drove in reverse back to her driveway. Then, with utter horror, she watched as it rolled up towards her house. She held out a forlorn hope that perhaps it was a mistake. Maybe he was only turning around.

Those hopes were dashed as a lone figure emerged, and approached her front door. Etta let out a dejected sigh, and began scolding both herself and her father. He told her they had months to make up the payment. He told her she did not have to work. Now they might lose the house *today*.

She could have done a few extra small jobs around town if time was so short. Why had she not started working at the butcher sooner? That was just like Jakob, trying to protect her to both their detriment.

When no one answered the door, the lone figure walked back over to the car and leaned against it, making it clear he intended to wait. Sighing heavily, Etta realized that any chance she had for relaxing was now gone. There was no telling how long the man would stay, and she would be unable to ignore him. Collecting her bag, she left the car and began to walk. While she made no particular rush to get home, neither did she dawdle.

Down in the valley, she lost sight of the taxman. Even so, he remained at the forefront of her mind. She hoped that he would simply disappear by the time she arrived home. Ten minutes later, she reached her mailbox, its recent repairs holding fast, and the strange car was still in her driveway.

The details of it were clearer now, and she realized that it was of finer quality than the one he had driven on his previous visit. Oddly, it was missing its roof. The man leaned against the side opposite from her approach. Mentally, she girded herself for what was to come. Would she have to leave the house today? Where would she put her family's old things? Why did this have to happen while Papa was out? She scolded her nerves as she walked up the hill.

Each heartbeat thumped loudly in her temples. Her mouth was suddenly dry. She had not been this nervous even around Walter. He had merely been a bully and a pig; two things she knew how to deal with. But how do you fight the taxman?

Oh, Papa, what have you not told me?

Hearing her approach, the man stepped out from the far side of the car, and Etta nearly dropped her bag.

"Oh, it's you," she said simply.

"Hello again," greeted Art. "I hope you don't mind my stopping by," he continued. "I would have called ahead, except I know you don't have a phone and-" he trailed off.

Etta put a hand to her mouth as her eyes welled up in relief.

We're not losing the house today.

The realization left her oddly shaken. Even more than she had been a moment earlier. Art raised his hands in a calming gesture, clearly thinking that his intrusion was the cause of her distress. “Alright, look, I shouldn't have barged in like this. I'm sorry. I'll leave.” Not waiting for a response, he retrieved a box from the hood of the car.

“No,” she said. “It's fine. I just thought... you were someone else.” Her breathing slowed back to normal as her anxiety faded. She motioned to the box he was holding. “What's that?”

Art stopped and his eyes fell to the box in his hands. “It's ah...” Her reaction had damaged his composure and he was about to say more before he stopped himself. A sheepish grin spread across his face and he cleared his throat. “Well, it's kind of a surprise.”

“A surprise?” Curious, she cocked her head to the side and raised a questioning eyebrow. He had her attention now.

Encouraged, Art pressed on. “Thing is... I need about an hour in the house to get it ready. Would that be okay?”

Her expression switched from an arched eyebrow to a narrowed gaze. After all, it had only been a matter of days since Etta discovered this young man sleeping off a drunken stupor, and now he was asking to be left unattended in her house.

She thought about Walter, and how he had turned out to be both a pig and a cad. Trying to work up some suspicion, Etta was at a loss. Art struck her as both frank and honest. Besides, if this was some ruse to get her out of the house so he could rob it, he was in for disappointment.

Ultimately, and for reasons she did not fully understand, Etta nodded.

“Sure. I have a few chores to do before dinner. Let me just change into my farm clothes and you can work on... your thing.”

He smiled, and marched off towards the house, carrying the box against his hip with one hand. Whatever it was, he was boyishly excited about it, which struck her as amusing coming from someone his size. Grinning, she shook her head and followed him to the front door. He reached out, as if to open it for her again, but abruptly stepped to the side.

“Silly of me,” he said. “I don't have the key.”

She paused, looking at him, then reached across to grab the doorknob. As she brushed his chest with her shoulder she was keenly aware of their proximity. Looking from the open door and back to her, Art was confused.

“We never lock our door,” she explained. “No need around here.”

He nodded. "My first year at school, I forgot to lock my door just once. As a prank, the other fellas raided my wardrobe and I had to wear the clothes on my back for a solid week. Then, for the next month they scattered the rest around campus."

Etta snickered, and could not help but grin. "That sounds unpleasant."

"You don't know the half of it. They made sure to hang my unmentionables from a statue outside the women's college."

A full, hearty laugh burst from Etta as she turned to face him. Without particularly thinking about it she reached out and gave his shoulder a sympathetic squeeze.

"You poor dear. That will teach you to trust boys. My brother Edward used to put one of the chickens in with John when he would sleep too late."

Art chuckled as Etta disappeared into her bedroom.

"Be sure not to mention that story around my brothers," he called. "I have every confidence that Ralph might try to outdo it. Although, considering he abandoned me out here, maybe I should use it on him. Got an extra chicken I could borrow?"

Leaving the door partly ajar, Etta slipped out of her clean – or rather, less dirty – clothes, and into something more suitable for farm work.

"If you decide to visit any misfortunes on your brother," she called, "I'll thank you not to involve me and mine." Much relaxed from her earlier episode, Etta's tone was playful.

Art responded in kind. "Not to worry. I won't sully your good name."

She emerged while still tying her hair back with a kerchief. Art was unpacking the box on the kitchen table when he met her eyes. Suddenly, Etta wished that she had remained in her other clothes despite the extra laundry it would create. The dark stains on this apron and skirt were conspicuous in her mind. Even so, her guest did not seem to notice, despite his customary attention to detail.

Briefly, she glanced over the items scattered across the table, not recognizing any of them. There was something that looked like a pair of short, stubby scissors, and a small knife next to a part she had no idea what to make of. Art made an unnecessary attempt to cover them; as if there was any chance she might recognize it and spoil the surprise.

"Well," she said, walking towards the door, "I will leave you to it."

Art flashed her a quick smile. "Shouldn't take more than an hour, if I remember correctly."

She glanced back at him, not sure of his meaning, and disappeared out the door.

Art's assessment had been close, though it had taken slightly longer than the hour he had given himself. Etta was working in the barn when she heard something. Howler detected it as well. Lying on top of the rain barrel near the door, her ears twitched at the disturbance. The rest of her body remained still. Having decided that the matter was beneath her, Howler fell back asleep, continuing to soak up the afternoon sun. Etta went to investigate.

It was a woman's voice, and familiar. Thinking there might be another visitor, Etta first looked to the driveway, but there was only the car that Art had arrived in. Frowning, she continued to look and realized the voice was coming from inside the house. As she approached, it grew louder and Etta did, in fact, recognize it.

Not talking, she thought. *Singing*.

Opening the door, she could hear it clearly, but almost did not believe it. Making her first appearance inside the Wozniaks' home was Ruth Etting singing, "Ain't Misbehavin'" from the old Wurlitzer.

Etta walked into the main room, finding Art standing next to the radio with his back to her. Unaware of her presence, he nodded to himself as he continued fiddling with something unseen. The volume briefly rose and fell as he adjusted a knob. Etta was speechless. There was actually music in her house. Entranced, she listened and watched him work. Art, still unaware that Etta was in the room continued making adjustments and the music was briefly replaced by static.

"Wait!" called Etta. "Can you go back?"

Art was startled by her sudden outburst, but soon recovered and quickly reversed whatever change he had made. The sound returned, loud and clear. He nodded with satisfaction and then looked up at Etta who stood transfixed. He left her alone for the remainder of the song, and returned his tools and spare parts to the box.

Her expression remained a mix of incredulity and awe as she stared at the radio. Art grinned as he moved to her side.

"How does it sound?" he asked when the song ended.

She had almost forgotten there was another person in the room, she was so transfixed.

"It's... perfect," was all she could manage. After recovering her powers of speech, she continued, "I can't believe you got it working."

Art put his hands on his hips, apparently satisfied, and rightly so.

"I take it that you're pleased?"

"Very much so." Etta looked away from the radio for the first time since she entered the room. "What did you do?" she asked, still trying to work it out.

"Based on what you said, I figured it was probably the amplifier. I was hoping it wasn't one of the vacuum tubes since I couldn't find one at the repair shop. Normally I'd-" he trailed off suddenly, noticing Etta's blank expression. Grimacing, he nodded to himself, as if recalling something.

Amused by his befuddlement, Etta ribbed him just a little bit. "Was I meant to understand any of that?"

Art bit his lip, as if scolding himself. "Not at all. It's a fancy way of saying I swapped out the parts that were making smoke. I've made similar repairs before. The hardest part was just finding a place that sold spares. I had to go two towns over, and must have driven up and down half the streets they had. Passed the hospital twice."

Etta continued to stare as her mouth curled up into a smirk. After a minute or so of the radio announcer speaking, another song started to play. This time, it was Cliff Edwards and his ukulele singing, "It Had to be You."

"Whatever you did, this is the first time we've had music in this house." Without particularly thinking about it, she looped her arm through his. "And I like this song." It said much that she had momentarily forgotten that she was still wearing her work clothes. Had she not been so distracted, she probably would have felt too grimy to be this close.

They listened and Art remained absolutely still. Afraid he might scare her off if he so much as shifted his feet. Even though she was focused on the radio, Etta noticed that he sneaked a glance or two in her direction. Grinning, she leaned into him.

As the song played out, the broadcaster announced the end of the afternoon music block, and that listeners should tune in again in a few hours. At that, the spell was broken and Etta remembered the state of her clothing. Unwrapping her arm from his, she pulled away. Turning the radio off her fingers lingered over the dial, fearful that it might not turn back on again.

She could scarcely believe it; music in her own house. It reminded her of how much she had missed it. True, there was singing at church most Sundays, but it was not the same thing. There was no Ruth Etting at church. There was no Cliff Edwards. The Saunders' turntable, with its grand total of four different records was nice, but nothing like this. Her eyes welled up, and she put a hand to her mouth, fighting to keep them dry. Art misinterpreted her reaction entirely.

"Geeze. I'm sorry. Is something wrong?"

"No. Not at all. It's just... this might be the best thing someone has ever given me," she said quietly.

As Etta composed herself, she suddenly realized that she had walked into the house wearing her mucking boots. A trail of muddy prints tracked all the way back to the kitchen door. Realizing that she had just added at least a half hour of work for herself, her shoulders slumped. Art remained standing where she had left him. While his hands were still on his hips, he was less sure of himself.

Inwardly, she cringed when she realized she had been leaning against him wearing her work apron. Sure enough, a dark smudge on his shirt marked the exact spot where they had been touching. Her anxiety must have been obvious, because Art dropped his hands, and suddenly became equally dismayed. His easy confidence from a moment ago had vanished.

Etta took a breath, at a loss for something to say.

"I can't pay you for this."

He relaxed somewhat, relieved to not be the source of her discomfort.

"Think nothing of it," he waved her off. "This one's on me."

Etta frowned. "This is too much," she insisted. A subtle but harsh edge had crept into her tone.

Strangely, it was both familiar and comforting, but she disliked it all the same. Art's dismay deepened, and she felt a pang of regret. Neither of them spoke for a long moment.

"Listen," Art started. "I still feel pretty bad about the thing with the mailbox. And sleeping in your barn. You were a really good sport about all that." He nodded towards the radio. "This is a gift, freely given. And maybe I'm hoping it evens the scales just a bit."

She cleared her throat, feeling much of her anxiety let go. It finally occurred to her that she had not actually thanked him.

"I'd say it does just that. And thank you."

A smile tugged at the corner of his mouth. For the first time, she noticed that he had been working with his sleeves rolled up again. Better still, his hair bore signs of a passing affair with a comb. Perhaps not as neat as it was during his business call to the Van Dycks, but worlds better than their first meeting. She had to admit that he looked quite sharp. Later, she would remember this as the exact moment that her wits took leave of her, and the likely reason for what she said next.

"I can't wait to see what I get when you sleep in my bed."

What she had intended to say was, "my house," but in the instant before she spoke, she thought that "house" was too general. After all, the cat slept in the house. And so, Etta intended to be more specific by offering "a bed."

Instead, she ended up with a rather frank invitation.

This realization occurred in the span of half a heartbeat. By then it was too late, and all she could do was hope to die on the spot. Unsure of what he had just heard, Art squinted as his brain attempted to make sense of the words in their present arrangement.

"*A* bed. I mean," she quickly amended, hoping to cover up her blunder before too much time had passed. The smile that had been tugging at his mouth erupted into a full-fledged grin. Gentleman that he was, he was kind enough to stifle the laugh that attempted to follow, but still shook with the effort. Etta's face grew hot, but eventually they both had a good laugh over it.

"Well..." Art began, after the two of them recovered. "On that note, I should probably go. Need to get the car back to Gregory's shop before he thinks I was using his tools without him."

Etta followed as he started making his way towards the front door.

"Gregory?" she repeated.

"Yeah. Robbins? He owns a repair shop on the far side of the lake. Not sure if you know him."

"Sure, *I* know him. I'm just surprised that *you* do."

"Oh, yeah. Been working with him for the past month now."

"I thought you were a refrigerator salesman."

"Some days I am," Art replied, and smiled coyly.

Etta recognized her own words and narrowed her eyes in amusement.

Following Art outside, her thoughts abruptly shifted upon seeing the car. At first, she had assumed it belonged to the taxman and thought little beyond that. Then, with everything else going on, it had likewise escaped her notice. Without a more pressing concern, it was as if she was seeing it now for the first time. Its shiny paint caught the afternoon sun. With a renewed interest, her expression turned serious but also curious.

"So, why do you need to get it back to Gregory's?"

“That's where it's staying for now. It's been fixed for a few days, but my brother has been a complete ass lately and we're holding it back until he learns some manners.”

“So, it's your brother's, not yours?”

Art pursed his lips, clearly interpreting her tone as disappointment. She frowned, as that had not been her intent, but he answered before she could correct it.

“It's not. But I'm going to get one,” he quickly added. “Didn’t really have much use for a car while I was in Philly.”

She tried to rephrase what she had been trying to convey. “It's just – um – well, long story, but can you keep it for a little while?”

Ugh, she cringed. *That was too blunt.*

Art, however, did not seem to mind. On the contrary, he was happy to oblige.

“Would you like to go for a ride?” he ventured.

Her eyes were wide with intensity.

Music and a car ride? And on the same day? It was almost too much.

“Could we?” Her excitement was palpable. She had never ridden in an open top car before.

This was not lost on Art who cleared his throat and intentionally prolonged the moment before answering.

“I suppose we could take it up and down the block real quick.”

Etta dashed to the door, about to let herself in, but stopped short. Instead of opening it, she took a step back and folded her hands behind her back. Striking a pose of mock formality, she motioned towards the door with her head.

“Good sir, would you kindly get a door for a lady?”

Art let out a good-humored sigh. “It's a Model T, not a Duesenberg,” he replied, grinning. Shifting the box under one arm, he matched her affected formality.

“My lady,” he said. With a bow and flourish, he opened the door. She picked up her work apron as if it were an evening gown, and curtsied before stepping up.

Leaning in from the side, Art made a few deliberate adjustments to the knobs and levers before moving to the handle on the front of the car. With a few cranks, the engine was running. A steady put-put-put vibrated through the chassis.

They resumed the game after he got into the driver's seat next to her.

“Where to, Miss?”

"Anywhere but here," she replied.

A moment later, they were bouncing down the dirt road.

With no top, the wind rushed over them and inflamed Etta's excitement. Growing more confident, and sensing her enthusiasm, Art ticked up the throttle lever and they sped through the farmland. He hesitated at the first few turns, unsure of where he was going before Etta would point in a direction. She, of course, knew every one of these roads by heart.

After finding their rhythm, she began to point out the turns early enough that Art did not have to slow down. Already sitting close on the narrow bench seat, each turn pressed them together. Etta gradually navigated them towards an area of town that was flat and open.

"You could drive faster, if you wanted," Etta said over the rushing wind.

Art, bit his lip, hesitating. "I should probably take it easy. It *is* my brother's car."

"Didn't he abandon you out here in the middle of the night?"

"You make an excellent point."

With that, the Model T lurched forward, barreling down the road. A wide smile remained fixed on Etta's face for the entire ride. This was incredible. Her recent car experiences had been limited to a slow and sensible transit in a rumbling truck. They were nowhere near as nimble or quick as how she and Art were driving now.

For months, she had sat in the jalopy, imagining a ride just like this. Now that she had the real thing, she realized there was no comparison. Of course, in her pantomime, she had been the one behind the wheel.

"Could I drive?" she asked suddenly.

The road and the wind pulling at her hair also made her considerably bolder than she might normally be. Art hesitated, and for a moment, she feared she might have asked for too much. There was a delay of a few seconds before he slowed down. Such was her excitement over his presumptive "yes," that they were still rolling when she stood up and started to shift into the driver's seat.

Art could only react, barely able to engage the brake lever before he moved beneath her. As he shifted across the seat to swap places, Etta briefly sat on his lap in a way that might have made them both blush had they time to think about it.

Having successfully traded seats, Etta gripped the steering wheel. It was the first time she had been in the driver's seat of a running automobile in four years. She soon noticed there were more pedals and levers than on her family's old Studebaker and was intimidated for a moment, despite her excitement. It took several minutes of Art pointing out their function and purpose before she felt ready to try for herself.

All thoughts of restricting this outing to "up and down the block real quick," were soon forgotten, and they spent the better part of an hour exploring parts of town that Etta had not been to in years. Places much too distant for her to reach on foot. Most of the roads out here were farmland, and they passed only one other car over the course of their adventure. She wanted to savor every moment.

At one point, Etta was surprised to find Art's hand on her upper thigh. For the first time since meeting him, she thought he might be getting fresh. The idea actually surprised her more than anything else. Indeed, it turned out he was only checking the sight glass for the fuel tank beneath the seat. When he realized what he was doing he blushed and quickly pulled his hand back. Clearing his throat, he asked her to start making her way back to town.

After fueling up, Art reluctantly said that it was time to get the car back to the shop, but he offered to drive her home.

"We're closer to Gregory's than my house," Etta replied. "Why don't we drop it off first?"

"It's kind of a long walk to town," he replied.

Etta shook her head. "Only if you stay on the roads. Let me drive to Gregory's and maybe I'll show you a shortcut."

Art agreed and Etta eagerly jumped back into the driver's seat. As they neared the workshop, Art motioned for her to slow down as he craned his head, apparently checking for signs of his mentor. Confident that it was all clear, he waved her on.

"Are you sure you work for Gregory?" she asked. "And didn't just borrow this car without permission?"

"I most certainly do work for him, but I can guarantee he'd show me the door if he found out I let myself into the shop without him around. He's a real stickler for safety, and doesn't quite trust me to work alone yet."

Etta nodded sympathetically.

"But as far as borrowing the car without permission..." He gave her a smile that seemed uncharacteristically mischievous. "The way I see it, my brother owes me."

Art opened the shop, but continually looked to the road; paranoid that Gregory might return at any moment.

With the car safely returned, Art locked up, and Etta led the way home. Her shortcut took them through a couple of neighboring farms. For much of it, they cut through cornfields and were obliged to walk single file. At this time of the year, the stalks were about the height of Etta's waist.

"Are we okay to be here?" Art asked at one point, strangely apprehensive.

"Sure," Etta called over her shoulder. "Most farmers around here are used to us cutting through. Otherwise it would take all day to get anywhere. Just don't go picking any corn or spit on anything and you'll be fine."

"Good to know." Art replied, conspicuously clearing his throat.

Eventually, they arrived back on the dirt road leading up to Etta's house. Pausing at the repaired mailbox, she smoothed down her hair. For the first time, she noticed that her kerchief was missing. Unsure when the wind had claimed it during their drive, she shrugged.

Small price to pay.

They were both quiet for a moment before Art nodded toward the house.

"I'll leave you to your chores then. Enjoy the radio."

"What are you doing later?" she asked without preamble.

At first, Art thought it was a casual inquiry, and his response was flat and without inflection.

"Probably dinner with my family. I would- oh," Art stopped abruptly. As understanding came over him, he went so far as to stand a little taller. "I mean, 'no plans.' Why?"

"You should come over for supper."

"I... would like that."

Chapter 18
Art

Letting his mother know that he would not be staying for dinner was a tricky matter. Disappearing for most of the day was one thing, but mealtime in the Adams' house, and dinner especially, was sacred. A carryover from the days when it was the only time that Luciana could see her whole family at once. Begging off today was especially difficult, since she had been talking about the veal all week.

Playing off his father's lecture from earlier that day, Art gave a vague explanation that he was trying to make up for his poor showing at the butcher's shop. Mother would undoubtedly confront George on it when he returned home, and Art hoped the scant details he provided would hold up under scrutiny. Even so, he dashed out the door before she could ask too many questions.

While he and Etta had not agreed on an exact time, he did not want to be late. Besides, his mother did not raise an unwashed miscreant and he needed to find a store first. It would not do to show up empty-handed. Problem was he had previously visited most of the ones nearest to the cottage with his father. Worried about being recognized, he was obliged to venture further out, which cost time.

It took the better part of an hour to find what he considered a suitable gift for his hostess. The shop owner was a meticulous type, and fussed over rearranging each piece of inventory that Art had touched. After finally ringing up his purchase, Art was happy to leave, feeling that his very presence was somehow disrupting some unseen order.

The sun was low by the time he returned to Etta's house. The deepest parts of the valley were lost to shadow. The only sounds were crickets and the wind as he passed the mailbox. With some satisfaction, he noted that his repairs were holding true. In doing so, he almost dropped the dessert and cider for the umpteenth time. Once again, he wished he had grabbed a bag or something before leaving the house. It would have been smart, but he had been in a hurry to get out the door.

Arriving on the front porch, he heard pieces of music escape from the open windows. Art smiled to himself, in part because the radio was still working, but mostly that Etta was enjoying the gift. Raising a fist, he knocked just loud enough to be heard.

There was a brief delay before Etta called from within.

"It's open."

Of course, he thought.

The concept was strange to him: a place where one did not have to lock their doors at night. Reaching for the knob, he hesitated with a sudden pang of nerves.

I'm about to sit down to dinner with a girl.

Despite their drive earlier that afternoon, and their breakfast the other day this was different. One might take their mother out for an afternoon car ride. Dinner, just the two of them in the dark, was another matter entirely. Having thought about little else for most of his walk from town to the farm, only now did it seem real. Steeling himself with a breath, Art stepped inside.

The room was dimly lit, and it took his eyes a moment to adjust. The house smelled of cooking meat, thyme, and garlic. In the kitchen, the lone, west-facing window captured much of the fading sunlight as it transitioned from blue and gold to orange and purple.

Etta was busy at the stove as he entered.

Glancing over her shoulder, she flashed a welcoming smile at him.

"Hello again," she greeted.

Giving a final toss to the sizzling pan with a wooden spoon, Etta set it down and walked over to give him a hug. Art did his best to hide his surprise. He returned the greeting, even though he was holding something in each hand and the motion was awkward. Etta's hair brushed his face and he realized that she was wearing perfume. A dress as well. Art swallowed, feeling as though the stakes had been raised again.

It occurred to him that this was the first time he had seen in her in anything other than work clothes. Her dress was simple, yet flattered her: a pattern of small, white dots on a navy blue field. One would never suspect she had been mucking chicken pens, and toiling all day. Art was suddenly glad he had worn his tan suit this evening instead of just shirtsleeves.

"Good to see you," he replied after a moment's hesitation. "Sure smells great."

"Thanks. Hope you like garlic."

"Wouldn't be much of an Italian boy if I didn't," he replied.

With a coquettish grin, Etta nodded toward the parcels he carried. "And what do we have here?"

"Dessert and something to drink," Art replied, presenting both for her inspection. "Didn't think it was right to show up with just an empty stomach."

Thanking him, she accepted the bottle and squinted at the label. Holding it up to read in the fading light, she snickered and grinned. Art had a fleeting bout of panic. There had been only two brands on the shelf at the store. This was one and the other featured a suggestively dressed woman on the label.

He had chosen this one, not wanting to give Etta any wrong impressions. Now, he was less sure, but neither could he understand what she found so amusing. All else aside, it was received well. Confused, and hoping to move on, Art held up the dessert.

"And fruit pastry for after."

This time, her reaction was more in line with what he had hoped for. Her eyes lit up.

"I absolutely love fruit. We – ah," a mirthless laugh escaped from her lips, "Don't get that very much." Recovering, she motioned to the counter. "Would you set that over there?" She placed the bottle on the table and moved back over to the stove, giving the contents of the pan another flip. "And thank you. I do appreciate manners."

"My mother was always a real stickler for that kind of thing. 'The part of my education that I wouldn't get in school' was how she put it."

"Well, in that case, I'll be sure to thank her." She turned back to the stove. "Dinner is just about ready. You want to open the cider?"

The table had already been prepared, so he poured out equal portions in each of the two glasses present. Afterward, he scrutinized the label again, trying to see what he missed.

Noting his inquiry, Etta explained, "Mr. Shaw makes that. He lives a couple of farms over from here. Usually, he brings it to the church picnics. I've never actually gotten it from the store before."

"Oh," was all Art could say. A feeling of mild embarrassment came over him, though he was not exactly sure why. Setting down the bottle, it occurred to him that the room had gotten darker since his arrival. Without particularly thinking about it, other than feeling a sudden urge to keep busy, Art spotted a switch on the wall and flipped it on.

"Oh!" Etta was genuinely startled. "Could you turn that back off?"

He did so immediately, spurred by the urgency of her tone. "Sorry," he said quickly.

"It's fine. It's just that the electrical bill- erm..." she trailed off, then quickly added, "I thought the lamp would be nicer."

Art considered mentioning that if she was concerned about the electrical bill, the radio was a much greater power draw. Not wanting to spoil the mood, he remained silent. He had adored the smile it put on her face the first time she heard it working. Besides, how much could it really cost to run for a couple hours?

Giving the pan another stir, she pulled a thin piece of kindling from the metal bin next to the stove. In series of smooth, well-practiced motions, she opened the firebox door, ignited the stick and held it out with one arm while stirring dinner with the other. "Here. Would you mind?"

It had been several years since he had cause to use an oil lamp and he took a minute to remember how. The room was soon bathed in golden light, which shone especially bright in the small space.

"Dinner's ready," Etta called as Art lowered the glass cover back in place.

Doling out equal portions of sausage and potatoes to each plate, she motioned for Art to sit. He did so, noting that they were seated directly across from each other this time, and fought the urge to immediately dig in. In truth, Art was famished. It had been a long day of walking, and a certain degree of willpower was necessary to leave the steaming, aromatic food untouched. As it was, Etta had barely settled into her seat, before Art snatched up his fork and scooped up an improbable amount of sausage and potato. It nearly reached his lips before the sound of Etta clearing her throat stopped him mid-motion.

Once again, it was her tone that immediately grabbed his attention. Freezing in place, Art looked up to find Etta with her hands facing up, outstretched on the table. Head bowed, she looked past her eyebrows at him.

"I'd like it if you would join me."

He remained motionless until she waved her left hand at him in invitation. Understanding now, he quickly lowered his fork back to the plate.

Less quickly, he reached out to accept her outstretched hands. Despite the fact that she was inviting him to do so he could not help but feel a sudden pang of nerves at the thought of holding her hands. He reminded himself that this was to say Grace and not a romantic gesture and did as she asked.

It was the first time he held hands with a young woman in nearly a year. He was suddenly keenly aware of the dirt and grease he had failed to scrub from the deepest parts of his fingernails. Her hands, by contrast, were clean and smooth despite an abundance of calluses that spoke of long workdays.

After she finished speaking, Etta nodded at Art and let go his hands. Only after she picked up her own fork and started eating did he do likewise, lest he commit another social faux pas.

"And here I thought I was dealing with a man with manners," she said with a wink.

Art was about to say something in his defense before he realized she was teasing him. Composing himself, he took a few bites of dinner before responding, careful to make sure his mouth was clear first. The taste of food did much to help him relax.

"I have three older brothers. Growing up, if you didn't act quick, you might not eat."

Etta wrinkled her nose. "Your mother allowed that sort of thing?"

Art shrugged. "Not usually. She wasn't shy with the wooden spoon, that's for sure. Junior caught it upside the head fairly often, but Father thought it was good for us to compete. Eventually, she mostly gave up trying to civilize us." He chewed a moment, thinking. "My oldest brother was probably the worst offender. Things got much better once he moved out, but Ralph made up for the difference."

Etta frowned, apparently confused. "Do you not get along with your brothers?"

That would be putting it mildly, he thought.

Not answering right away, Art worked another portion of sausage and potatoes onto his fork as he attempted to come up with a more tactful reply. Forgetting himself, he nearly put an elbow on the table, but covered the misstep with a shrug of his shoulders.

"I suppose we had our good days and bad days. Thomas was alright until recently, maybe. But he kept to himself. Junior and Ralph did whatever they wanted. Things are better now. Mostly because I hardly see them anymore." He intended the last remark to be half in jest, and flashed a wan smile at Etta.

She did not return it – and in fact responded with a frown. "Maybe things are different now that you're all grown. You're in town for a reunion, aren't you? Have you spent any time with them?"

"After the other night, I think I've had my fill."

"That's a shame," Etta replied. "You might find that one day, when you no longer have the option you'll wish you had done things differently."

Abashed, he returned his attention to his plate. She also looked away, eyes focused on something distant or perhaps unseen. Art let the silence hang a moment, suddenly reminded of what she had said during their first meal together.

He grew somber. "Your brothers aren't around anymore, are they?" Though he suspected that he already knew the answer.

Etta shook her head.

"How many did you have?" he asked.

She looked back to Art, but did not answer right away. "Two brothers and two sisters as well. A mother too, for that matter. Now it's just Papa and me."

"I'm sorry," was all he could think to say.

She waved him off. "Not great for table talk," she said. "It was a long while ago." Etta took a sip of her drink and let the music substitute the conversation for a moment. Finally, she continued. "That was some trick you pulled with the radio. Where did you learn to do that?"

"I was probably about eight or nine. We were still living at our place in New England, next door to Father's repair shop. It was just a tiny house on the edge of a small town. Six of us crammed into two bedrooms. I actually liked it, but then I'm the smallest in the family."

"You're the smallest?" Etta blurted out.

Art smirked, and nodded. "Now you see why I had to fight for my meals. My brothers and I spent a lot of time in the shop. At first, it was just a good way to get out of the house for a while, and we watched Father take things apart and put them back together. Eventually, Junior and Thomas got to help with some of the lighter work, while Ralph and I were only trusted to break down junk to sell for scrap. Mostly small appliances, radios, things like that. Graduating to a particular tool became a kind of right of passage for us.

"Father was real grumpy in those days – not that he's a whole lot better now. I remember distinctly, Junior lost a screw to a washing machine once. You thought the earful that I got today was bad?" Art shook his head to underscore his point. "I'll bet Junior has a permanent dent in his head.

"So then, one day, a salesman from Frigidaire comes into the shop, looking to hire us on a long term basis to service his customers. Father started making house calls, then after a while, he gets the idea that we should be selling things and not just fixing them. Turned out he was really onto something. For a couple years, we moved around a lot, trying different towns with better prospects. The houses got bigger. The towns got nicer. My mother got her own car, and eventually we moved to New York."

"That must have been great," Etta commented.

"Actually, it was awful," Art replied.

"Why?" Etta asked, clearly not seeing the problem.

"We never stayed in one place for too long, so I never really got a chance to make friends. Plus, I was actually pretty good at fixing stuff. It was something I could do even better than my brothers. Once we started making sales, Father sold the shop and his tools. We never bothered with repairs again. My brothers were all better at talking to people than I was. Junior especially. He didn't even have to finish high school. Just went straight into business with my father. Though I suppose New York had its perks."

"Now there's a place I'd like to visit." Her tone was much more lighthearted and positively brimming with interest. "What's it like? Or did you never see anything outside of school?" She arched an eyebrow at him, referencing his comment on Philadelphia.

Art was encouraged. Remembering how their previous conversation soured on this topic, he searched for something positive.

"Yes, I was still in high school. And I did focus on my work..."

Her expression faltered just enough for him to notice.

Concerned that he was losing her interest, he quickly added, "But my brothers certainly made use of their time there. Let's see... Junior and Ralph went out most evenings, and came back late, usually smelling like tobacco and alcohol. They got into a lot of fights with my parents. Usually woke me up. One time, the police actually got called."

Art chuckled at this, but Etta simply looked horrified.

Clearing his throat, he continued, "I mean, not to say we were like that all the time. We had our good moments too. Meal times were always a big deal, and saint days especially. I'm sure your family had its own share of disagreements."

Etta looked as though she were about to take offense at that, but remembering something, she closed her mouth.

"The police were never called, I can tell you that much."

Art nodded, feeling the rebuke, but less so than before. "Not out here, I suppose. Your neighbors are pretty far away."

"They are, but that's not what I meant. My family never shouted at each other. Maybe we had disagreements, sure, but we didn't *fight*. And we always sat down to dinner together and walked to church together. My parents never had to 'put a dent' in anyone's head."

"As to that, if you met Junior you'd understand. Still, sounds nice that your family got along so well."

"It was, while it lasted." She sighed. "I remember it wasn't until Irene, my younger sister, was maybe five or six before things really picked up. We all did chores from the time we were old enough to hold a bucket. No one takes a day off on a farm. Back then, we had a huge flock of chickens. Crops too. Nearly the whole of the property, all the way out to the rock wall."

"Gosh. You folks were doing well."

Etta nodded, looking around the room as if in wistful remembrance. "Oh yes," she nodded toward the other room. "That radio was a luxury we could finally afford even if we couldn't afford to fix it. We had two cars, and never thought twice about turning on the lights."

Etta fidgeted, having momentarily forgotten that her excuse for leaving off the electric lights was ambiance.

"So, what happened?" Art asked.

Etta attempted to dodge the question again. "Oh, you don't want to hear about that. Not much of it is pleasant, believe me."

"I don't mind," Art replied. "It can't be any worse than my family's nonsense."

Her mouth remained a thin, flat line, as she considered this. Letting out a slow breath, she opened her mouth to elaborate when she was cut off by a knock at the front door. Brow furrowed, she craned her neck to look past Art's shoulder into the next room.

"Are we expecting company?" he asked.

Etta frowned, shaking her head "no." She pushed her chair back from the table, and quickly dabbed her mouth with a napkin.

"Would you excuse me for one moment?" she asked only after leaving her seat.

Art nodded, not sure what to make of her reaction. Her frown remained, and her eyes betrayed a mix of concern and apprehension. Whatever her feelings, she was making some effort to conceal them.

"Not sure who that could be at this hour." she said in a carefree tone that was forced. Then, she muttered under her breath, "People don't usually bring good news after dark."

Art remained seated, idly poking at his dinner and waiting for his hostess to return. Alone, he reflected on the conversation thus far. He shook his head as he scolded himself.

Why did I say that part about the police being called? Stupid of me.

In the other room, Etta answered the door for their late caller. Without particularly trying to eavesdrop, Art heard the entire exchange clear as day.

"Oh," said Etta with both relief and surprise. "Hello, Susie."

"Hi, Etta," replied a young girl, who sounded maybe a couple of years older than Allyson. "Mom made extra tonight since she thought you were joining us."

"Thank you. Please tell Aunt Mildred that was very kind." There was a pause.

"You look nice," the younger girl said. "Is that your church dress?"

Etta cleared her throat, as she considered her response. "It is, actually," she said simply.

Susie barreled on. "And are you wearing... lipstick?"

"Yes, Susie," Etta replied. From her tone, she was trying to shoo the young girl away as politely as possible, but failing to do so. The door squeaked as she attempted to close it.

"I wish I could do that, but Mom won't let me. She says harlots paint their face."

Art nearly laughed out loud at that, but managed to keep it quiet.

"When did you get a radio?" she continued. Before Etta could answer, Susie peppered her with more questions. "Do you have company? Is it a boy?"

Etta sighed.

"Yes, I'm having dinner with the boy that fixed the radio." Her tone was resigned, as if she were making a guilty admission.

Young Susie ran out of questions, but only for a short moment. "Are you going to have a baby, like Helen?"

Unable to withhold the laugh this time, Art only hoped that it was not loud enough for Etta to hear. He cleared his throat in a poor attempt to conceal it.

"Good night, Susie," Etta said with finality. After shutting the door, she walked in and set the plate on the counter. With a sigh, she returned to her place across from Art and sank low in her chair. Neither of them made eye contact for a long moment.

Art spoke first. "So, ah..." he began, "That your cousin?"

Etta looked confused.

Art elaborated, "You said, 'Aunt Mildred.'"

She nodded with understanding. "Mildred is my best friend's mother. It's just what I call her."

"Your best friend is that little girl?" he asked with genuine sincerity.

Etta gave Art a bemused smirk. "No. I mean her older sister, of course, but I'm pretty close with their whole family. Mildred is more of a second mother than an aunt, really." She sighed. "And I'm sure I'll have to answer some questions about you once Susie tells her."

"So, the older sister is Helen? She's the one having a baby?"

Etta nodded, as she scooped up the last of her dinner.

Art continued, "That must be exciting."

"That's a word for it." Etta took a long moment to chew. "Personally, I think she's too concerned about the wedding, and not enough about what it's going to mean to have a baby."

"Oh, so she's not married."

Etta shot him a look, unsure of his tone.

Art held up a hand. "I mean no judgment."

Etta relaxed, and let out a sigh. "It's fine," she continued. "I just have doubts about how she's going to handle this. I know she'll need help, and, of course, I'll do it because she's like family. And Robert *is* family. Neither of them are especially responsible. God knows I love them both, but did she do anything to help me when my mother died? Of course not. I don't hold it against her, naturally, but I just don't need any extra work."

Her volume had gradually increased as she spoke. By the last sentence, she was louder than was necessary for how close Art was sitting. Etta bit her lip, cutting off the verbal purge. Withdrawing from the table an inch or two, she blushed with embarrassment over the outburst. Art remained quiet.

"I'm sorry," she said at last. "I don't usually do that."

"It's fine." Art shrugged.

"Helen really is like a sister. It's just that she's been driving me a little batty lately."

"In my experience, it's family that drives you batty more than anyone else." He curled up the corner of his mouth in a reassuring smile. "Not sure you need to worry about your friend though."

"How's that?" Etta asked with a furrowed brow.

"You said it yourself: you don't plan to stay around town for much longer. You can't be expected to do much if you're not here."

That brought her up short. "Well, I wouldn't..."

She trailed off, eyes darting back and forth in a way that Art recognized. It was the same look he would make while trying to solve a particularly troublesome problem. From the way she blew air out of her nose, she had not come up with a satisfactory solution.

"It's not like I would *abandon* everyone here." She folded her arms and frowned

At first, Art got the sense he had stumbled, yet again. Then, it occurred to him that this time, her posture was defensive.

"This is only temporary," she explained. "We're having some trouble with town hall just now. Once we get past that, Papa is going to bring on some hands to help with the work. I might stay around a few extra months, just until the baby is old enough that Helen won't need me."

Art replied, "I've found that the longer things get put off, the less likely they are to happen."

Etta's frown deepened, and Art spread his hands, apologetically.

This is not going well. Looking away and clearing his throat, he tried a different track.

"Where will you go?" he asked. "When you do go."

"Well," she said thoughtfully, "I had been thinking New York or Philadelphia. But you don't seem to think much of those places. I suppose anywhere with a flushing toilet would be an improvement." Etta smiled wryly.

"There you've got some options. Though I would argue that the scenery around here is worth the sacrifice."

"It has its moments," she allowed. "But it's mostly wasted on me since I'm working all the time."

Art followed her reasoning, but could not help but question her tacit assumption. "You won't be getting away from work, especially if you're on your own. Cities tend to be expensive places. You might end up in the garment district, and a typical shift is twelve hours. I've met a few girls who go weeks without going outside during the day time."

From the way she frowned, this was not something she had considered until just now. Instead of responding directly, she narrowed her eyes, and curled up the corner of her mouth.

"Oh. So, you knew a *few girls* did you?"

At first, Art could not tell whether she was teasing him or not. Her full grin suggested that she was.

Etta continued, "Why do I get the impression that there is a lot you aren't telling me?" The orange glow of the lantern caught the side of her face, and made her eyes sparkle.

Art became distracted, and nearly forgot what his point had been. He opened his mouth, about to continue, but pulled back at the last moment. Saying too much had gotten him in trouble a few times in the past month, and even he realized that throwing darts at the dreams of his hostess was a sure path to trouble. Instead, he grinned back, remembering something she might find interesting.

"Alright, I've got one story from Philly: do you want to hear about the time I went to a speakeasy?" Art raised his eyebrows in, what he hoped, was an enticing manner.

Etta looked at him skeptically. "*You* went to a speakeasy?" Her tone was incredulous.

Art did not quite appreciate her emphasis on the word "you," as if it were completely implausible that that he would have an adventure. Still, he had succeeded in renewing her interest.

"That's right," he said, chest puffing up with pride. "You're having dinner with a regular bootlegger."

She chuckled at that. "Doubtful," her tone was serious for a moment. "I know a few bootleggers."

Art nodded, remembering the shady cabin distillery he had visited with his brothers.

Etta motioned for him to continue, her interest plain. "What was that nonsense about spending all your time at school? Come on. I want details. Did you drink bathtub gin and listen to a jazz band?" Her tone was playfully mocking, but her eyes were intent on his answer.

"It wasn't gin, it was whiskey. Though it might have been kept in a bathtub for how much it was watered down." He shook his head, remembering. "Let's see, this was during my first year at school. One of my classmates learned the password to a place in West Philly, so a bunch of us went out one night. We walked through an indescribably bad neighborhood to get there, and it was a genuine speakeasy. They had the hidden door with the small window to say the password and everything.

Then, once inside, I spent a whole dollar on my drink, and I didn't even finish it. The police came in five minutes later."

Her eyebrows went up at that.

"Wow. A bootlegger and an outlaw. Did you go to jail?"

Art considered embellishing, but decided not to press his luck. "No. I mean, not behind bars or anything. They held us at the station until our parents came to pick us up. In my case, that was the following morning. So, I suppose, in the literal sense, I spent a night in jail. Considering Father's mood when he arrived, I might have taken my chances behind bars. Well... not really."

Etta nodded sympathetically, but chuckled all the same. "He must have been furious."

"You better believe it. He was ready to drag me back home then and there, but I managed to talk him out of it. Barely. He didn't even want me going in the first place."

Etta furrowed her brows. "To a speakeasy?"

"To school..."

"Why not?"

"The business was really taking off at that point. He and my brothers had their hands full and he saw my schooling as a distraction."

"That's hardly fair. It seems to me your time was well spent."

"I'd like to think so."

After finishing dinner, Etta suggested they move to the rocking chairs on the front porch to have dessert. Things were quiet for a while, save for the tinkling of forks on plates.

"Can't remember the last time I had dessert," she said, clearly savoring each bite.

"Now, that's a sin," Art replied. "As my mother is fond of saying, 'never let a day go by without a cannoli.'"

Etta frowned. "What's a cannoli?"

From the front porch, they could almost see the northern edge of the lake off in the distance. It was difficult to make out through the trees, but as the sky continued to darken, the lights from the Oasis stood out just enough to see. Directly in front of them were the rolling hills and farmland in the valley. Twilight had recently given way to the dark of night, and fireflies darted back and forth in the tall grass beyond the porch.

The conversation had mellowed with the two of them falling into a pleasant back and forth – mostly about the town and Etta's extensive knowledge of it. They left the window to the living room open, and the radio filled in what brief gaps existed in the conversation. At once point, a black and orange cat sat down nearby and cried at them. It conveyed an obvious sense of annoyance, which Etta returned.

After letting the cat back into the house, Etta sat back down and continued to explain the quasi feud between the lakeside residents and the farming community. Both groups maintained a love-hate relationship with the out-of-towners – present company excluded of course. The latter had actually been a slip. Etta had become so comfortable that she momentarily forgot that Art was not from around here.

Eventually, stars replaced the dancing fireflies, and they reluctantly admitted that the evening was over. Art was more familiar with the area than he had been a few days prior, but expected that it would take him some time to find his way back to the cottage in the dark. Likewise, Etta intended to be up again before sunrise and would turn in soon. With everything put away, she followed him to the front door to say good night.

"Thank you for dinner," Art said.

"Thank *you* for dessert."

They stood for a moment looking at each other. Having only done this sort of thing a bare handful of times, Art wondered if he should try for a goodnight kiss. He froze at the thought. She looked at him with what might have been expectation. However, a nagging doubt kept him firmly rooted to his side of the porch. Limited though his experience was, he did not get the idea that she was in a rush for him to leave.

Instead, he asked, "Do you have plans for tomorrow? Besides work I mean?" He smiled to show he was only teasing.

"As a matter of fact. My friend Helen and me were planning to go to the swimming pond. You should come with us. I'm sure that Susie has told her all about you by now, so maybe introductions are in order."

In the end, they only hugged goodnight, but Art noted that she held on for longer than mere courtesy would call for. Contently, he began his walk back to the cottage. It had been a lovely evening.

The following day was hot and muggy. There was not so much as a gentle breeze for relief. The sun had barely passed above the trees before things became unbearable. People flocked to the water, and anywhere else with shade. The Oasis and every sandy beach were as crowded as they had ever been. Those selling ice cream and cold drinks were in high demand. It was nearly July, and if a scorcher like this was possible now, one could only imagine what the rest of the summer might bring.

For Art, it was another reason to look forward to his swimming date with Etta. As if he needed one. The thought of seeing her again buoyed his spirits, and insulated him from his brothers' usual jabs. It was less effective against Luciana's poorly concealed frown. As expected, there would be a price to pay for the dinner he had missed. Somehow, he failed to work up any concern over it, as the pretty blonde girl pushed most of everything else out of his head.

Much like Art, George was practically bouncing with enthusiasm, but for an entirely different reason. With the whole family gathered in the backyard of the green cottage for breakfast, his voice boomed across the table.

"This unbearable weather is a gift from the Almighty. If we were going to sell these rubes on cooling equipment, this is the day for it. I want four hours of sales work out of everyone. Art, you're with me again. Thomas, you and Ralph should team up for the new places in Hackettstown-"

"Actually, Dad. I made a new contact yesterday that I was going to follow up with." Art blurted it out before George could move too far down his itinerary.

Despite his distraction throughout the morning, Art had anticipated that his father would want to get some work done and realized that he needed a plausible excuse for his absence. This was his first time playing this game, and decided the simpler the ruse the better. Taking inspiration from the vague excuses usually given by his brothers, he decided that it should also be grounded in at least some truth.

Not accustomed to being interrupted, the announcement caught George off guard and he faltered.

"I- what? When did that happen?"

"After the butcher. You told me not to go home, so I made a few calls."

Just enough truth to be plausible. It seemed to be working.

"And?" George was watching him, not sure whether to be suspicious or impressed.

"There was interest. I said I'd come back with more information."

A complete fabrication, but not bad for being completely off-the-cuff. Still, it was enough to push George over to "impressed."

"How about that? Good man!"

It took Art a moment to understand what he was feeling, since this was one of a handful of times his father had said something that might be considered praise. It turned out that he liked the feeling of approval... even if it was based on a lie. Turning to his oldest son, George continued. "I suppose that means you're with me today."

Junior furrowed his brow. Hesitantly, he cleared his throat. "Ah... I was going to meet with some new clients in the next town. I scheduled a follow-up appraisal with them yesterday."

"I'll come with you. It's been too long since you and I have done a sale together. It will be just like the old days."

Without waiting for him to accept, their father moved on, leaving Junior and Martha to exchange some looks. From her, it was an annoyed glare. From him, visible discomfort.

Catching a few snippets of their subdued conversation, Art gathered that their family had plans to spend the day on the water. Plans that were now on hold. On top of that, Art suspected that his brother had never met any clients as he had claimed, and was desperately trying to come up with a plausible way to hide this fact.

His father's praise had been pleasing to Art, but seeing the colossal prick that was his oldest brother, made uncomfortable was even better. He struggled to suppress a smirk. Thomas and Ralph, hoping to avoid their father's attention, silently nodded at the remaining marching orders.

Mother mentioned something about preparing for a big dinner the following day and the need for a larger table. By that point, however, Art was barely listening.

After breakfast had dispersed, he slipped away quietly, feeling a certain rush at successfully dodging a sales run. Such was his distraction that he made it to the end of the road before it occurred to him that he had to do some shopping first. Despite the heat, the prospect of seeing his new lady friend put a certain spring in his step.

The day was off to a great start.

Chapter 19
Etta

"How deep is it?" Art called from the largest boulder.

"Oh, it's plenty deep," Robert replied. "Just don't let go too early, or you'll break your neck and drown." He let the words hang for the span of a breath before breaking out in a hearty chuckle.

Etta smiled too. Her cousin was such a tease, but never mean-spirited. In fact, it was a sure sign that Robert liked him, and that Art was part of the in-group.

From the top of the rock, Art took in the slack of the rope and pulled to test it. At first, Etta thought he might be stalling for time, but decided he was more likely calculating something. He was a cautious sort, not a coward.

She floated next to Helen. The pair of them had taken the only rubber tubes on the pond while Robert and Daniel sat closer to the rope. Frowning suddenly, Etta considered moving closer. Just in case. While he had not said as much, it was clear that Art did not know how to swim.

Oddly enough, he was the only one to show up with an actual bathing suit. Everyone immediately recognized it from the store in town; one of the Atlantic City styles that covered most of the body. After some friendly teasing over the matter, Art followed suit – so to speak – and stripped down to his underclothes like everyone else.

"Come on," called Robert. "We had a lady with a baby on that thing an hour ago."

The lady in question splashed water and shushed him too loudly. Etta had to laugh and responded to Helen's look of mock indignation by sticking out her tongue. The term "worst-kept secret" had been used so many times already that it need not be spoken again. Helen's bump was not terribly obvious, but it was there. She might have been able to hide it, except for the shift that stuck wet to her body.

Without further preamble, Art picked up his feet and held fast to the rope. Perhaps too well. He did not let go until just beginning the return swing. A huge splash followed as he struck the water with his back. Etta cringed. Thankfully, he landed near enough to the shallows that he was able to stand. Recovering, Art pushed the wet hair from his eyes and made a satirical half-bow as everyone applauded. Robert not least among them.

Bobbing in her tube, Etta watched as Art waded out toward her. Bared to the waist, he was quite a sight. The water had flattened his hair, giving it the appearance of being tidy. Best of all was seeing his brown eyes without glasses for the first time. As the odd circumstances of their initial meeting grew more distant, Etta had found herself becoming quite fond of him.

Another step pulled him lower so that his under clothes disappeared below the waterline.

Almost looks like he could be naked.

Surprising herself, Etta turned her gaze toward Daniel who had reached the top of the boulder with the rope in hand. Without any of Art's hesitation, he kicked off the rock and smoothly brought his feet up over his head. Making a slow turn, he executed a perfect release, and struck the water feet-first. Robert applauded again, but genuinely and more loudly than before.

"We got us a trapeze performer over here. Where did Mama pick you up from? The circus?"

Etta applauded as well, genuinely surprised. It had been nicely done. Quiet as he was, it was easy to forget what Daniel could do. Art soon arrived at her side. Having removed his glasses for swimming purposes, the precise range of his nearsightedness became apparent. Closing within a few feet, he conspicuously shifted his eyes away from her wet clothes and how they conformed perfectly to her body. His efforts to avoid looking were so obvious they were comical and Etta could not help but grin.

Most of the locals, except for the most ardent bluenoses, understood that the swimming pond was a place of relaxed social norms. Hence, the lack of bathing suits. Art's attempts at being a gentleman, while endearing, were entirely out of place. A sudden shout from Helen called their attention.

"Robert McCormick! Don't you dare do any of that daredevil nonsense!"

Instead of carrying the rope up to the rock like the others, he was preparing to leap out and grab it mid-air. A silent back-and-forth ensued between Robert and Helen, as he dared her to give him an "or else." Art stood next to Etta as they watched the drama unfold.

"You didn't break your neck or drown," she remarked lightheartedly.

"No, I did not," he agreed. "Though if I broke my neck, I'm not sure how drowning would make a huge world of difference."

"The difference between horrible and catastrophic?" Etta offered.

"That seems about right," Art replied, in what might have been an attempt at a smile, but ended up as a wince.

"How was that landing?" she asked sympathetically.

He grimaced. "Held on for too long, I think."

Before she could reply, they were interrupted again by Helen's shouting. Robert sprinted for three strides before leaping off the top boulder. Arms outstretched, he snatched the rope as he sailed through the air. A word not for polite company escaped him when his hands slipped an inch or so, but he held true. Letting go a moment later, just before the rope began its return swing, he dropped into the water with decidedly more grace than Art or even his brother.

Daniel let out a whoop and Helen crossed her arms. Her scowl was intended to be a rebuke, but the way she was bobbing in the water with her feet dangling in the air did much to undermine her intended severity. However ridiculous her appearance, her intent was serious. Robert swam over to her, clearly pleased with himself. This only served to deepen Helen's attempt at reproach, and Etta knew that a terse exchange was forthcoming.

In part because she was at risk of laughing at her friend's ridiculous, albeit completely serious expression, but mostly because she did not want to get involved in the couple's bickering, Etta caught Art's eye, and nodded toward the deeper end of the pond.

As the ground fell away, Art struggled to keep his head above water. To his credit, he did not panic or complain, though it probably would have been wise for him to ask for help. Having momentarily forgotten that he could not swim, Etta slipped out of the tube. With an arm looped around one side, she offered the other to Art.

He accepted without hesitation and not a moment too soon. Hugging the tube to his chest, he pulled his head clear of the water in the same way as Etta. He must have been more concerned about drowning than he let on, because it was not until he had settled that he realized how close they were. The inner tube was not large and hugging opposite sides brought their faces inches apart.

Floating into yet deeper water, their dangling legs brushed past each other in a way that might be considered inappropriate somewhere other than the pond.

Art's eyes wandered again, this time looking at the surrounding scenery and nature. At first Etta thought he was trying to avert his eyes again in a well-meaning way. However, she soon suspected that his interest might be genuine.

"It's so quiet out here," he said after a moment.

Likewise, she turned her attention to the trees and greenery. The dogwoods on the far side of the pond retained most of their spring blossoms, and the towering willow cast a shadow where it extended over the water.

"One of the best local secrets in Bott's Lake," she agreed. "There are usually more people here, especially after mid-summer, but only locals. And not those heathens in town mind you. Just us farmers."

Art looked back at her and grinned, recalling the mock rivalry she had mentioned the previous evening. "Oh right, those darn lakeside types,"

"'Townies,'" Etta corrected. "Many of them – I'm sure – are fine people," her tone dripping with mock sincerity and her eyes rolling too obviously. "You just wouldn't want your daughter marrying one."

"Aren't Robert and Daniel Townies?"

"They are," she conceded. "And Helen, isn't my daughter. What's your point? Still, better a Townie than one of them out-of-towners." Her eyes widened for a brief moment and she flashed a teasing smile at him.

He pretended to glare at her; grinning but with narrowed eyes.

"Don't worry," she continued. "You're one of the good ones." More quietly, she added, "Too many of them are not."

It took Art a moment to notice that the mood was no longer playful and his brow furrowed.

"You're serious."

Etta bit her lip. "Like I said, it's kind of a love-hate relationship. Visitors bring money into town, but a lot of them are rude and disrespectful. Then they leave, and we have to clean up after them. Since they're only visiting, they don't have any reason to mind their manners. Sometimes they're even dangerous."

"How so?" he asked.

Like Walter. Etta had thought about her unpleasant evening with the musician a few times since it happened. In hindsight, she realized that a number of things about Walter's behavior should have warned her to keep away but she had ignored them. For a variety of reasons, she did not share these thoughts with Art. At least not yet.

By contrast, it occurred to Etta that she had no such misgivings about Art. The circumstances of their first meeting had been unfortunate, perhaps, but since then she always had the sense that he was honest. He had never asked for anything that was not freely offered, and genuinely behaved like a gentleman. Hence, his bashful reaction to her swimming in underclothes. Of course, she had caught him sneaking a few looks, but frankly she would have been worried if he did not.

That was all fine. However, it was the matter of what he had been doing before she found him in the barn that had been a fly in the ointment. The same circumstances that had resulted in the mailbox being broken; what she really meant by "dangerous." Frowning, Etta hesitated before continuing.

"My mother was killed a few years ago by someone driving a car while they were drunk."

It was a blunt admission, and so completely unexpected that Art did not react for a long moment. Gradually, the full implications of this revelation set in, and he backed away as much as he could while still maintaining a hold on the floating tube. Etta sighed. Clearing his throat, the expression on Art's face was utterly guilt-stricken. While this subject had been weighing on her mind for some time, she had not intended for it to come up just yet. But there it was, all the same.

"I'm sorry," he said eventually. Though it was not clear whether he meant it as an apology or in sympathy. Eventually, he added, "I hope you know I wasn't the one driving that night."

Gritting her teeth, Etta resolved herself to the discussion now that it was upon them.

"I've actually given this some thought," she began. "Yes, you and your brothers were not acting responsibly, but... neither was anyone hurt. I was angry about it, and maybe I still am, but you tried to make good on it. So, I think I can still be angry at your brother, but not at you."

Finished, Etta looked at him as he mulled it over. She left it unspoken that if someone had been hurt that night, these terms would be null and void. In general, Art was an expressive sort, and prone to a guilty conscience, not unlike herself. She thought it unlikely that he could conceal much even if he tried. Thus, she believed him when he said that he had not been the one driving, and that made her decision considerably easier.

On top of that, she decided that it would have been hypocritical to hold it against him. After all, no one had been drinking the day Irene died. She suppressed her own guilty shudder. Thankfully, Art spoke before the subject of her thoughts became too dark.

"Well, I'm glad someone else finally agrees that my brother is a jerk." He flashed a weak smile, clearly trying to lighten the mood, but being cautious about it.

Etta was glad for it, but likewise, could not move on right away. Much time passed and neither of them said anything. They floated in silence until the sun disappeared behind a mass of clouds, taking its light and warmth with it. The chill of the lake returned with a fury, and within a minute, Etta and Art were shivering, despite the earlier heat.

To hasten their exit from the water, the rumble of thunder in the distance finally urged them along. In trying to return to shore, they found themselves in a predicament.

They had drifted out to the middle of the pond where neither could touch bottom. With Art unable to swim without the inner tube, and Etta unwilling to let her hair get wet, they made little forward progress. After some trial and error, much of which saw them, literally spinning in circles, Art shifted to the same side as Etta, and they began to make headway.

The physical effort had an additional benefit of pulling them out of their emotional slump. The bare skin of their arms and shoulders pressed together as they kicked toward shore, and they resumed a light banter as the earlier tension faded.

Helen, Robert, and Daniel were already out of the water and drying off next to a tree. Their clothes draped over a branch. Reaching the shore, Etta's feet touched ground first. She and Art rose from the water as both kept their grip on the inner tube. Probably without thinking, Art started to pull it towards himself. Instead of letting go right away, Etta pulled back.

Art looked at her, and frowned a moment before understanding. A brief tug-of-war ensued, with each of them holding a side one-handed. Grinning, Etta escalated by grabbing with both hands and leaned away with all her weight, but Art held firm. Suddenly, her expression changed, turning almost mischievous. Before Art could understand what to make of it, she let go. While he stumbled, he ultimately managed to keep his footing in the water.

"Dirty pull," he chided.

Grinning, Etta stepped out of the pond while Art's eyes drifted downward. With a start, he pointedly looked in a different direction and climbed out of the water. Etta frowned, but then looked at herself and noticed that her wet shift was clinging to her skin in an especially provocative way.

Following him, Etta pulled the fabric away from her skin and returned a semblance of modesty. She did, however, feel a certain satisfaction from making Art blush again.

Beneath the large tree, the others were already tearing into the picnic lunch. Helen pointedly looked between Etta and Art, and raised an inquiring eyebrow. Meeting her gaze, Etta dismissed her with a waved. Still, Helen grinned at the apparent reversal of their typical roles. For years, it was Etta who teased Helen about her romances.

They all gathered around the picnic basket, eating and drying off. After buying his absurd bathing suit, Art had also picked up bread, cheese, and fresh fruit before arriving at the farm that morning. It was nothing especially fancy, but to Etta, having skipped breakfast again, it was a feast.

Robert had taken to referring to Art as “College Boy.” From anyone else, it might have come off as mean-spirited, but her cousin made it sound endearing. Daniel, while mostly quiet, emerged from his usual shell as the conversion turned to cars. It turned out he and Art had a mutual interest in machines. Etta only caught bits and pieces of the boys' conversation. She and Helen were discussing the church ensemble and how best to approach them about performing for the reception.

“Ellis Young and Roy Paddock both owe my mother a favor, so they're a shoe-in. That means Grace Ayers will come too.”

“The organist? I heard she quit.”

“Salacious rumor. That's just the word that got around after she called Pastor James a drunkard and an ass in front of the whole congregation.”

“In fairness, he's not a drunkard. We'll need some string players if this is to be done right. Have you spoken with the Sullivans?”

“Strict teetotalers, and they backed out when they discovered Enoch Pershing would be there.”

“Rotten luck.”

“They are close friends with the Heckels. Maybe if you asked Bradley to put in a good word…”

“No, Helen.”

All the while, the clouds continued to darken, and thunder intermittently rumbled in the distance. Whatever storm was coming steadily drew closer. Soon, they started back down the trail leading home. As it happened, they were caught by the rain, but only for a few minutes. The leafy and ample tree cover spared them the worst of it.

Upon reaching the road again, they ran into Martin Kovaks, a young man of an age with them. He lived a few farms over from Etta and was friends with the McCormick boys. Robert, of course, greeted him with a casual joshing.

"Haven't seen you since that barn party last October where you drank enough cider to knock out a horse," Robert said.

"For sure," Martin replied. "We should get together more."

"What are you doing tonight?"

And that was how the first barn party of the season began.

It was still early, which permitted some time for word to spread. A plan was soon formed to meet up at the Kovaks' farm along with the rest of the local families shortly before sunset. Briefly, Etta thought about begging off, as there was no shortage of chores she had to get done. Coming to her senses, she decided that she could not rightly pass up a barn party.

Helen and the McCormicks separated from Etta and Art as they all passed the Saunders' farm.

"Make sure you bring your new man," Robert called. "I want to see what this guy is like after a couple beers."

Art and Etta continued on to her house, walking around a handful of newly formed puddles.

"Guess I have to go," he said with a wink.

"Of course. You wouldn't want to disappoint my cousin," she replied, grinning. "I just wish they'd picked a different day is all. There's a bunch of work I've been putting off."

"What needs to be done?" he asked.

Etta raised her eyebrows. "You really want to stay and help?"

"Unless you'd prefer to do them by your own self." He was teasing her again.

"Let's not get hasty now."

Etta proceeded to rattle off a laundry list of tasks – one of them actually being laundry – which they split up. Burning the garbage and heating water for the laundry both called for a fire, so Art split wood and built a kindling pile. Etta mucked and fed the chickens, and was pleased to find about two-dozen eggs. Not a bad haul for the evening.

By the time she was finished, Art had the fire burning hot enough that it was producing hardly any smoke. Etta smiled, relieved that she had been spared a whole hour of work as well as the need to use the ax.

Not wanting to spoil the clothes Art arrived in, Etta loaned him a shirt and pants that once belonged to her brother Edward. They were of similar build, though Art was noticeably taller. The pants came up short by a few inches, which they had to laugh at. As the water for the laundry heated up, the two of them gathered the washtub, ringer and scrub board.

"I haven't seen one of these in a while," he commented.

"We have an electric Maytag," she replied. "But it stopped working a few years ago."

"Guess I found my next project," Art said, mostly to himself. Then, to Etta, he continued "How do you do this on your own?"

"It usually takes longer," she replied with a shrug.

Art's question made her think about Jakob, who should have been back by now. In a fleeting thought, she wondered about the reason for his delay, but did not dwell on it. He had been returning home later and later in recent days. At first, this had been distressing, but now it was reassuring that Papa was unlikely to arrive at an inconvenient time. Although she and Art were only doing laundry, she was not especially keen to be found alone with a strange boy.

"That's one way to fill the day," Art called over his shoulder as he went to retrieve the burn barrel. It took the better part of an hour to get through the week's refuse and about the same for Etta to do the laundry. After putting the last article through the ringer, she hung it on the clothesline and joined Art by the fire.

"All finished?" he asked as he watched the flames and rested his hands on his hips.

"Amazingly, yes," she replied, frowning in mild puzzlement. "So, what college class taught you how to properly set up a garbage fire?"

He grinned. "Our home in Massachusetts was much more rural than where my parents live now. This was my weekly chore for a few years."

"You're just a man of many talents." The realization that the chores were done so early in the evening left her feeling lighthearted and carefree.

"Everything from appliance repair to garbage disposal," he said in a parody of his father's salesman voice. "Arturo A Adams, here for all your basic needs."

Etta had to chuckle. The impression of Art's father was spot-on. As they stood next to each other, watching the fire, and feeling contented,

Etta was surprised to notice a hand casually resting on her opposite shoulder.

It was unexpected but not unwelcome. However, Art did not pull her close, or even rest the full weight of his arm on her. His hand was just there. Almost as if he was unsure about this sudden act of boldness. At first, Etta had appreciated his unassuming manners, but sensed he could probably do with some encouragement.

Ever so slightly, she leaned into him with her hips and shoulder. As she had been hoping for, the weight of him arm rested more firmly across her shoulders, and the pair of them forgot that they were both wearing dirty work clothes. Contentedly, they simply stared at the fire and enjoyed the well-earned respite.

As the sun dipped below the tree line, the barn and chicken runs sank into shadow. Eventually, the fire burned down to ash and smoldering coals. It was almost time to head over to the Kovaks' party, but Etta was not quite ready to separate from Art. Without moving, she turned her head up to his, their cheeks almost touching.

"Hungry?" she asked.

"Starving," he replied.

With mutual reluctance, they slowly parted before heading back to the house. They had a simple dinner of half a loaf of yesterday's bread, a small wheel of cheese, and a pair of peaches left over from lunch. Art and Etta had worked up a considerable appetite, and ate in companionable silence. Sitting in the pair of rockers on the front porch, they watched the sky gradually change color.

The storm clouds from earlier had cleared away entirely, so the sky simply turned from light blue to dark blue as night descended. Etta checked the clothes drying on the line, hoping to bring them inside, but frowned upon discovering they were still damp. With the sky clear, she reckoned there would be no harm in leaving them out to dry overnight.

Art asked about a spare room to change his clothes, but Etta reassured him that he was best as he was and they started to walk. In the front field, the fireflies had come out and were now darting around in the air.

The revelry from the barn could be heard before it was even in sight. As they turned the last bend, the party came into view.

"Good turnout," Etta said. "That might be just about every farmer on this side of town."

The Kovaks' place was teeming with activity. Outside the main barn, some young men were splitting logs and feeding a large cook fire while a couple girls tended chickens on a roasting spit. To one side, three dogs sat on their haunches, watching the birds turn with rapt attention.

All were familiar faces, and Etta greeted them as they passed. Larry Summers, who had the unfortunate reputation for snoring during church, split wood alongside his cousin Harold. The latter was particularly specific about his name. It was “Harold” not “Harry.” Since the boys were most often seen together, it was all too easy for them to become “Harry n' Larry.” They smiled and nodded back at her, casting an incurious glance at Art before returning to their work.

“They need about another half hour,” called one of the Turner girls. She brushed the roasting birds with some of their famous sauce while her younger sister turned the spit. The pair of them were well known for two things: a spicy and sweet cooking sauce that quickly disappeared at every church picnic, and singing voices that were even sweeter.

Carrying a small bundle of wood, Bradley Heckel stopped and looked between Etta and Art with furrowed eyebrows. Slumping his shoulders, he sullenly dropped the wood onto the fire. Certain dreams might have just been dashed for good. Etta felt just the least bit guilty, but mostly relieved that she would never have to endure any more of his attempts to woo her.

The main barn was a large thing. From the lower level, it towered above the cook fire and scattered crowd. Etta and Art made their way to the far side where an earthen ramp rose up to a pair of large doors. A tractor and a few other pieces of equipment had been moved out of the main room and to the ground level. Over the years, these large gatherings had become a staple of the community and the Kovaks had developed a system for transforming their barn from a place of work to a place for play.

In the main room, several young men were still setting up tables and chairs. Having been collected at odd times over the years, only about two or three of them matched. The center of the cavernous room featured a clear area where there would in all likelihood be dancing before the evening was through. Everything was cast in the yellow-white glow of electric lights which dangled from the large rafters that spanned overhead.

A recent addition, they remained a topic of mild controversy. Mr. Kovaks had done the work himself, and one small fire had resulted from a faulty connection. It was decried as dangerous among several of the farmers, who were old-fashioned types, and knew too well how fast any fire in a barn could become catastrophic. Even after it was fixed, and years had passed without calamity, they refused to enter the barn on principle; a few tables were set outside for their benefit.

Etta explained much of this to Art, who was no doubt trying to diagnose, precisely what Mr. Kovaks had done wrong. All the while, she continued to exchange greetings. After the fourth or fifth one in the span of a minute, Art chuckled.

"You the mayor or what?"

"None of us really travel too far from home," Etta explained. "You tend to get to know your neighbors."

As they passed through the big room a few looks were directed at Art that ranged from curious to bordering-on suspicious.

"I suppose I'm the only 'out-of-towner' here?"

She placed a reassuring hand on his arm. "Don't worry. At least you're not a *Townie*."

They descended a steep and narrow set of stairs that was almost a ladder and emerged into the lower level. At last, Etta found Helen, who had changed into something more concealing since their outing at the pond. However, it still managed to show off her ample décolletage.

Robert and Daniel were there as well, helping another young man set up a pair of crates in an alcove. Enoch Pershing was a few years their senior, and another close acquaintance of the McCormicks. Robert, like Helen, had a habit of collecting friends.

Approaching, Etta noticed the crates were filled with dark-colored glass bottles. Robert, Daniel and Enoch each pulled one out and thumbed open the swing-top with an audible pop.

"You hit it right this time," Robert said after his first pull. Looking up, he noticed Etta and broke out into a smile. "Hey cos. Long time, no see." Then, grinning at Art. "And glad to see you brought College Boy."

Robert turned around to fish out another pair of bottles while Etta greeted Helen. Her friend was clearly annoyed about something... again. Thankfully, at least this time, she was making an effort to keep it to herself.

Returning to Art and Etta, Robert offered the bottles. "To your health," he said.

She thanked him and thumbed open the top while Art hesitated.

"Is that beer?" he asked.

Etta had a sudden, but fleeting bout of panic at his reaction. His earlier behavior at the pond she had written off as nerves, but now she was suddenly worried that he might be a genuine prude. Almost at once, she dismissed it, recalling that their first meeting had been the result of him sleeping off a bender.

It occurred to her that the revelations about her mother and general feelings on irresponsible behavior might be the reason for Art's current hesitation. Raising her own bottle and taking a sip, she gave him a pointed look. Apparently receiving the message, Art thanked Robert and accepted the drink.

"Yes, sir," replied her cousin, who had not noticed the exchange. "Courtesy of Master Brewer Enoch here. Enoch, this is Etta's new man, Art."

He said it so matter-of-factly that Etta barely had time to cast an annoyed glance at her cousin. While she was growing fond of Art, she had not quite started thinking of him as "her man."

At least not yet.

Art made no reaction to the handle Robert had applied him, other than to take a quick sip while shaking Enoch's hand.

"Never officially made it to 'Master'," Enoch explained taking a thoughtful pull. "What with the brewery closing and all. Officially, we make *bread* yeast now. But..." he indicated the crates of beer bottles. "Dad said another couple of years and I would have been the youngest one to do it."

"I bet you would have," Etta chimed in. "This is delicious."

Enoch nodded his thanks and idly stroked his ample beard.

"I lagered this batch for much longer than usual. Brewed it back in February actually. Couldn't get my hands on any hops so I used spruce tips. Was afraid it might have come out too piney. Oh, make sure you save the bottles please."

Etta took another swig, savoring the flavor and found it lightly tart and crisp. After working outdoors for most of the afternoon, it was refreshing even warm as it was.

As more people arrived, Etta and Helen drifted outdoors, meeting up with another group of girls. Many of them, Etta had not seen since the previous barn party nearly eight months ago. Helen, on the other hand, was much better about keeping in touch with people, and her greetings were far more familiar that Etta's. All in all, it was a genuinely pleasant reunion for Etta with one notable exception.

Mabel Flanders and Etta had something of a rocky history, though the exact origins for their dispute were long lost to memory. While Etta was generally too busy to give Mabel a second thought, the other girl had carefully nurtured the old grievance. Thus, a poorly concealed jab at Etta's working clothes caught her completely unaware.

"I actually saw you a few weeks ago, Etta. Yeah, I recognized this apron and skirt. Though you've got a few less flies about you now."

This remark was mostly met with scathing looks among the other girls, but also no small amount of tittering. Etta opened her mouth, intending to say something in response, but too ruffled to think of anything.

"Mabe," Helen jumped in. Her voice was far sterner than normal. "If you can't mind your manners around the Maid of Honor, I'm not sure there's a seat for you at the wedding."

The conversation continued in a more cordial direction, but still, Etta made sure to note which girls had found the jab amusing. Not long after, she left the circle and went looking for Art, who was not with Enoch and Daniel where she had left him.

Coming around one of the outbuildings, Etta saw that the rest of the Saunders had finally arrived. Max immediately ran off, barking at the other dogs in greeting and wagging his tail. Peter, Susie and Michael looked fresh from the field and Mark was, no doubt, at work. Mildred held a tray of food, which was the apparent reason for their tardiness.

Etta waved to them, and had a passing exchange with Mildred who asked about Helen. Unsurprisingly, she had left chores undone before leaving for the party. It was soon clear that this was the reason for Helen's earlier annoyance. Sensing that another tense exchange between mother and daughter was forthcoming, Etta continued looking for Art.

At last, she spotted him chatting with Mr. Shaw. Or rather, Mr. Shaw was chatting *at* Art. For his part, Art mostly stood still and looked uncomfortable, barely making eye contact. Confused, Etta made her way over to the two of them. She had not seen the older, gray gentleman for a while, but he had always been a lighthearted soul and quick with a joke. Most everyone found him to be personable. The only thing that might be said against him was his excess of gab, and an unfortunate tendency to interrupt.

Still, Etta could not imagine the cause for Art's apparent discomfort. As she walked over, she caught a few snippets of their conversation.

"-not like you. You seem a decent sort. A proper young man, dressed like he works for a livin'. But most these out-o'-towners I tell ya...'bout a week ago, I caught three of 'em on my property. Drove right across my field, and – if you can imagine – they just pissed all over my-" He stopped abruptly upon Etta' approach.

"And what are the two of you talking about?" she asked.

Art said nothing, but his eyes spoke of relief at seeing her. Mr. Shaw blushed.

"Nothing that's polite to discuss in mixed company, Etta." He looked around, as if a thought had just occurred to him. "Haven't seen your father today. He feeling unwell?"

"Papa is out of town tonight," she replied simply. "He-"

"Out of town? Are you working the farm by yourself?"

"Actually, the fella you've been talking with has been helping me." She stuck her chin out towards Art for emphasis.

While he had grown more comfortable with her arrival, now Art was distracted by something. Etta frowned, wondering at his odd behavior. Mr. Shaw, however, replied to Etta.

"I figured him for the type." He nodded approvingly.

"He's been working with Gregory Robbins as well," she said, trying to give Art an opportunity to join the conversation. When he did not do so, she added, "Even fixed our radio." Still, Art did not respond, and continued to look past her shoulder.

"What are they doing here?" he asked. Though, it was quiet enough that he might have been saying it to himself.

Etta and Mr. Shaw turned to look in the same direction. A battered green truck had stopped on the main road, just on the other side of the fence that bordered the property. Two young men stood, watching from beside it but made no move to approach. After a moment, the oldest Kovaks boy, Martin, walked down to meet them, and exchanged pleasantries.

It took Etta a moment to recognize Tim and Jeff Brandelson. After all, the town's most infamous moonshiners wisely kept a low profile, and it had been a few years since she had seen them. Not quite able to place it, Etta found herself with a strong sense of something familiar, beyond simple recognition of her elusive neighbors. She did not have time to dwell on it for long.

Mr. Shaw must have recognized them around the same time. He made a sound of contempt and spat on the ground, momentarily forgetting his own policy on "mixed company." Clearing his throat in embarrassment, he looked sideways at Etta, perhaps hoping she had somehow not noticed.

"Haven't seen the Brandelson boys in a while," he said, making no effort to hide the disdain in his voice. "After that incident a few years back, I figured they never left their shine shack." He shook his head.

"What's Martin Kovaks doin' associating with those types? I figured him for a fine, upstanding young man." He took a swig from his beer bottle, disapproval plain on his face.

Art looked from Brandelsons, to the bottle, to Mr. Shaw. "You disapprove of moon shining?"

The older man flattened his lips in a scowl and shook his head. "Not at all. Making hooch is a fine and noble profession," he lifted Enoch's bottle to underscore his point. "I don't even so much mind the gut-rot those boys and their father sell. But they're a damned pair of arsonists. Wouldn't be the least bit surprised if they burned down their own house tomorrow."

Etta watched Mr. Kovaks make his way to where his son was standing with Tim and Jeff. She could not make out what was said, but from the motion of his arms, and the way Martin wilted, it was clear that he was not pleased. Over the sound of other conversations, she could make out the words, "-not on my property." Jeff and Tim put up their hands in faux deference, and slowly got back into their truck. Mr. Kovaks cuffed his son and shooed him back towards the barn.

The general atmosphere of the party recovered only after the green truck was out of sight. It was not so obvious at the time, but several conversations had been momentarily suspended. After the incident was over, they resumed, no doubt discussing everything from illicit hooch to unexplained fires.

"Really take the air out of a room, don't they?" asked Art, trying to be conversational.

Etta replied dryly, "When the schoolhouse catches fire while school is in session, people tend to remember."

The three of them were silent for a long moment.

After taking another sip of beer, Mr. Shaw loosened up, and asked, "You do any fishing, Art?"

Etta inwardly groaned, immediately recognizing the beginning of Mr. Shaw's infamous trout story. Knowing this topic could go on for at least an hour if left unchecked, she looked around in desperation. Spotting Helen and Robert by one of the outbuildings, Etta grabbed Art and hastily pulled him along.

"Good seeing you, Mr. Shaw," she called over her shoulder without breaking stride.

Etta glanced at Art who nodded a sincere thank-you. He had the look of someone spared more than an old man's fishing story. Etta was puzzled.

"What's the matter? You and Mr. Shaw get along alright?"

Art cleared his throat. "Long story. Ask me again some time."

They stayed with Helen and Robert after that, with the conversation only interrupted by the occasional well-wisher. News of the couple's engagement had made the rounds, and the evening had turned into a sort of ad hoc engagement party. One or two of the older women also gave Helen a second and more hushed congratulations.

Most poorly-kept secret in town, Etta thought.

Eventually, the roasted chickens had been eaten and the beer had been drank. The empty bottles, for the most part, returned to their crates. As the evening wore on, the crowd had broken up into several little islands of conversation, mostly gathered around the fire, but a second crowd formed in the main barn where a fiddler and a guitar were warming up. Several of the younger children ran around, chasing the dogs among the clusters of adults.

A distant rumble of thunder caught the attention of all present, especially those sitting outside. The telltale flash of light shone unusually bright in the evening sky and made clear what was coming. A few of the dogs barked, warning the clouds to stay away, while another whined. Like most farmers, the Kovaks were keenly aware of the whims of nature and weather, and rearranged the tables in the main barn to make room for everyone inside.

Most folks proceeded under cover, except for the stalwarts who remained skeptical of the electrical work, and were determined to stay outdoors for as long as possible.

Etta was standing with Helen just inside the main door, listening as the Turner girls joined the guitar and fiddle. She took two steps inside before she froze. Eyes going wide, she said a hasty goodbye and grabbed Art by the arm.

"We have to go," she said with a hint of alarm.

Art picked up on her urgency and followed. "What's wrong?" His tone mirrored hers.

"The laundry!" she called over her shoulder as she picked up her pace. "It's still on the line!"

Art furrowed his brow as if her reaction and her explanation were incongruous. Halfway to the road, she realized that he was not following. Turning around to see what the matter was, she found him still at the bottom of the earthen ramp, looking confused.

"And?" he asked.

Etta cocked her head to one side, unsure if he was making a joke. When he did not grin or give any sign of insincerity, she motioned up at the sky and then looked back at him. Finally, he nodded understanding, but still failed to share her urgency.

Another thunderclap ushered them along – this one much louder than any before it. They continued at a brisk walk, making it to the end of the property before the first drops of rain came down. Not many at first, but they were heavy.

The air itself grew thick and promised more to come. Etta groaned. She did not care to start the next day with sopping wet clothing. She hitched up her skirt with one hand as their brisk walk increased to a jog. Not for the first time, she was glad to be wearing practical boots instead of something dressier.

By the time they reached the house, the storm was right on top of them. Rain was coming down in earnest and punctuated by frequent thunderclaps. So close was the lightning that hardly any delay existed between flash and thunder.

Blinking water from her eyes, Etta found her clothes right where she had left them. They flapped and whipped, trying to break free of the rope. Not bothering to get the laundry basket, she and Art hastily snatched up as many articles as they could and hugged the disorderly heaps close to their bodies. By this point, much damage had already been done, but there was still hope. With everything in hand, they dashed to the house. Etta's hair was clinging to her face. Rivulets of water streamed into her eyes and down her back.

With the two of them each holding a full armload of increasingly wet clothes, they fumbled with the kitchen door for an interminable couple of seconds. Bursting inside, Etta cursed as she tripped over the cat, who must have been waiting by the door. Etta and Art dumped their bundles on the kitchen table.

As they caught their breath, Etta quickly lit the kerosene lamp with dripping wet hands. All the while, she prayed that somehow they had been fast enough. With the room properly bathed in gold light, she looked for her apron in the sopping wet heap. Alas, it had not been spared.

"Well," said Art still catching his breath. "We tried."

Looking at him, Etta laughed. His hair was plastered flat against his head, covering everything above his eyes, and his glasses were completely whited out with fog. This was in stark contrast with his deathly serious expression.

For reasons she could not explain, this combination was hilarious. Covering her mouth she started to laugh and soon found she could not stop. Art's expression took on a mixture of confusion and borderline offense, but soon decided she was not quite laughing *at* him.

"What?" he asked, cracking a smile in return.

Still laughing, she reached out to push his hair to the side.

"You look like a mop."

"I do not," he protested, but grinned all the same. He removed his glasses, and made a halfhearted attempt to wipe them off on his shirt but was unable to find a dry patch.

Still laughing, Etta felt her own hair, and grimaced at what she found. "Ugh. I must look like a blonde, drowned rat."

"No. Not a rat."

She shot him a look.

"More like a drowned cat."

He appeared completely earnest before he gave it away with a single laugh.

"Now, that's just mean," she said, broad smile still planted firmly on her face.

Etta was soaked through. Her blouse stuck to her arms and chest. Sighing, she considered the certainty that tomorrow would find her doing the morning chores in cold, damp clothing. Pulling her wet clothes away from her skin, her thoughts steered toward what she might do to get something dry by morning. Distracted as she was, it took a few beats for her to register what Art said next.

"Still, probably the prettiest drowned cat I've ever seen."

Blinking, Etta looked up at him. As far as compliments went, it was rather ham-fisted, and his delivery could charitably be described as clumsy. But coming from him, it was endearing in a way that she could not quite put her finger on. His glasses, still fogged over, rested on top of the pile of laundry, and for the second time today, she saw his eyes unobstructed.

Later on, when she reflected on this moment, she would be unable to say who moved first. Pride would say that it had been Art, summoning some previously unseen courage. Self-doubt would insist that she had been more eager than a lady should be, and leaned in. It may be impossible to say with any certainty what the truth was. The indisputable fact remained that they shared their first kiss in her family's kitchen on the first major thunderstorm of the season.

When their lips finally separated, it was only by an inch, and their noses remained nearly touching. They stayed that way for a long moment before Etta even opened her eyes. As she did so, she noticed another source of light that the lamp could not account for. At first, she thought it was another lightning flash, but it lasted for too long and there was no accompanying thunderclap.

Realization struck her. As one, they both turned to the front window, seeing the unmistakable presence of car headlights.

Of all the times...

"Who-?" Art began.

"My father," Etta cut him off. "You have to go."

"Well. Shouldn't I meet him?" Art asked.

Etta furrowed her brow, once again, not quite sure if he was serious. Mirthlessly, she let out a single laugh before continuing to shoo him out the door.

"Not tonight."

He turned to go out the back door before Etta pulled him back. "No. Not that way."

She ushered him through the living room towards the front door as the headlights extinguished. He stopped short, and bumped into her as he turned on his heel.

"My glasses." The torrential downpour from a few moments ago had given way to a light drizzle, and they could clearly hear the sound of Jakob's footsteps squishing through some newly formed puddles on the far side of the house. Grabbing his specs off the laundry pile, Art returned to the front door.

The footsteps had almost reached the kitchen as she pushed Art through.

"What are you doing tomorrow?" he whispered just as he passed the threshold.

Back in the kitchen, the doorknob started to jiggle.

"Farmer stuff. Come by if you can."

Art slipped outside and Etta closed the door behind him just as Jakob entered the house.

Chapter 20
Art

The golden bright of dawn was harsh. Having woken up before sunrise every day since his arrival, Art was not previously aware of just how perfectly the sun aligned with the bedroom window. Instead of the gentle line of changing colors along the horizon there was a white-hot nail of light fired straight into his face. Blinking several times and finding that his eyes stubbornly refused to adjust, he pulled the sheets up over his head.

How late is it?

Covering his face with the blanket turned out to be too stuffy to be comfortable, so he flipped around, trying to find a new position where the glare was not quite as bad. In this, he found some minor success, but there was no escaping it entirely. Gradually, he became aware of someone else in the room. Whoever it was, they were speaking, but they had to repeat themselves before their words started to make sense.

"I said, 'Get up.'"

The voice, which Art now recognized as Ralph's, dripped with contempt. The next command was accompanied with a shove that was impossible to ignore. Art blinked his eyes until his brother came into focus. Ralph stood over the bed, regarding Art with a glare that mixed his usual, baseline scorn with a fresh strain of annoyance. Not only was Ralph awake before Art, but he was also dressed.

Damn. It is late.

"What time is it?" he asked, dragging himself to a seated position. Art could not remember the last time this had happened. He must have gotten to bed even later than he thought. The events of the previous evening slowly came back to him. The party. The rain. The taste of Etta's mouth on his.

Oh my God, did we really kiss?

Eyes still half-lidded, he smiled at the memory, despite feeling otherwise out of sorts.

"Almost eight," Ralph replied. "Get dressed. We're supposed to pick up food for the big dinner."

"What big dinner?" Art asked, rubbing his eyes.

Every dinner this summer had been big. With grudging compliance, his legs found their way to the floor, and he began searching for yesterday's pants. Yawning, he remembered that he had worn Etta's brother's clothes home, which remained in a wet heap beside the bed. Grimacing, he went to the dresser to find another pair while Ralph sighed impatiently.

"For your lady friend, of course. It's all Ma's been talking about."

Art's jumbled thoughts snapped into line as quickly as if Ralph had doused him with cold water – which he had in fact done more than once. They knew about Etta? How was that possible? They had not even kissed until last night. Did someone spot them walking together? When did they plan a big dinner?

Such questions flooded his groggy mind, and overwhelmed his powers of speech. Attempting to compose himself, Art grabbed the first pair of clean pants his hands could find. Hopping in place, he attempted to pull them over his legs.

Clearing his throat, he replied as casually as he could, "She knows about that?"

Ralph cocked his head, confused by the question. "I'd say so. You two have been engaged for months now."

Art blinked, not comprehending. *We met barely a few weeks ago.*

"Who are you talking about?" he asked, genuinely perplexed.

Leaning towards the theory that Art had been struck dumb, Ralph spoke slowly. Not out of any particular concern for his brother's wellbeing, but out of a desire to not repeat himself.

"Dorothy Kennedy." Interpreting Art's wide-eyed expression as a lack of comprehension, Ralph continued, and annunciated each word. "Your fiancée. Is arriving. Today."

George was pacing, and Art did his best to remain invisible. If there was anything worse than his father working, it was his father idling with nervous energy. He checked the station clock yet again, and compared it against his own watch.

"Damned country trains running late," George said louder than Art would have liked. "They'd be out of business tomorrow if there was anything resembling competition around here."

Thankfully, the platform was mostly empty of people. The few that remained politely ignored the ramblings of the mustached, well-dressed man attempting to wear a rut into the platform with his feet.

Luciana fussed with Art's necktie for the third time in as many minutes. Despite her outwardly calm appearance, Art knew his mother well enough to tell when she was on edge. The realization did not help his own nerves, but at least she expressed it more quietly than his father. Gently, Art pushed her hand away, and considered saying something to dissuade future attempts. He carefully avoided doing anything to attract his father's attention. With no one else around besides his brother, Art expected that any grief would fall squarely on him. For his part, Ralph was also quiet, but it was due to lack of interest than nerves. His folded arms and slouched posture gave evidence to his resentment for being there.

The rest of the family was back at the cottage, making preparations for dinner. This was to be the engagement party for Art and Dorothy, and the whole afternoon and evening was set-aside for it. Earlier in the day, Art and Ralph had been tasked with driving around to acquire provisions for the evening. Hence the unpleasant wake-up call.

After their poor showing with the Van Dycks, George had insisted on a butcher in the next town over for the meat. For this at least, Art was thankful, as he now had concerns about being recognized around town. While there probably had been no "Townies" present at the barn party, he saw no need to temp fate.

Ralph said little to him during their morning errands, which he might have preferred to do on his own. Likewise, Art would have been happy to let him, but it was Father's opinion that this was a two-man job and that was that.

Quietly, Ralph asked to borrow Thomas' car since his own was still at Gregory's shop. Yes, it was working, but Art felt no need to inform his brother of that particular detail. He was still feeling salty over being abandoned at – what he now knew to be – Mr. Shaw's farm. Despite the fact it had led directly to his meeting Etta, one thing did not cancel the other.

Besides, for the first time in his life, not only did Art have something that his brother wanted, but it was something he could not take by force. Ralph did not want their father to learn about the damage done to the car.

Thus, he would not press the matter, even when it was clear that he was growing impatient.

Only after they were alone did he ask Art about the status of the repairs.

"About two weeks," Art replied.

"You said that last week."

"Did I?"

Ralph frowned and started to work his jaw, but let the matter rest. After that, they drove in silence, with Ralph making it clear that he did not care to interact any more with his younger brother.

The feeling was mutual. More importantly, it gave Art time to think. His tentative plans to visit with Etta were now postponed. He only hoped that she would give him a chance to make it up to her later. Maybe he could sneak away after dinner. Briefly, he considered asking Ralph to drive past the farm, but that would have raised questions to which he had no good answers. Not to mention that Art knew better than to give his brother any leverage over him whatsoever.

In a moment of temporary insanity, he considered simply explaining the situation to his parents: he had met someone, they had really hit it off, it was nothing too serious yet, but he wanted to continue their courtship and see where it goes.

And yes, I'm afraid this will mean my engagement to Miss Kennedy will be broken off.

Absolutely out of the question. Both his parents were in agreement on this arrangement.

At breakfast, George had spoken almost without pause about the benefits of a partnership with the Kennedy's business. Luciana, of course, had arranged the union in the first place and believed she was doing right by him.

"I want what's best for my son. You are thoughtful, and quiet... wonderful attributes, but they won't help you get a wife."

Somewhere in there, he supposed, was intended to be a compliment.

"This is how things were done in the old country. You trust the village matchmaker. Else, how do you know if someone is good for you?"

Art considered this. "Okay... but you met Dad met at the dance hall in Quincy."

"Yes, but that was different. This way is better."

Art might have challenged her on that, but backed down at a thinly veiled reference to Sarah. "If we had done this sooner, you wouldn't have had to bother with that mousy nun and her awful parents. That family was no good."

The Grant family, in an unfortunate twist, happened to have connections to many of the same social circles that his parents had recently joined. Art's little indiscretion – as it was referred to – had the consequence of closing certain doors to them.

If the incident in itself was not embarrassing enough, the version that ended up getting around, and what Luciana heard, was that Art had lured Sarah to the men's dormitory under false pretenses. They smeared him as some kind of unscrupulous seducer. An idea so patently ridiculous that Art had discounted it. Unfortunately, it was the story that stuck.

Moreover, he had lacked the fortitude to correct such assertions, and was perhaps too eager to put the matter behind him. For the same reason, he never pushed back on the arrangement with the Kennedys and tried to ignore the matter until now. Most of the details and the origins of it were opaque to him. He knew only that Luciana and Dorothy's mother were recent friends. Now, the matter was all but decided.

The sound of a steam whistle somewhere in the distance pulled Art out of these thoughts and back into the present. To his surprise, he had taken several steps in the direction of the lake without thinking about it. A few seconds after the initial whistle, a rhythmic hissing and rumbling sound heralded the approach of the locomotive. Sighing, Art returned to stand with his family.

"About damned time," said George.

"Language dear. You're about to make a first impression."

George nodded, taking a calming breath, and straightened his jacket and vest to present to Luciana for final inspection. She lifted up on her toes to make a few minute adjustments to his tie, which he wore despite the summer heat.

Art had seen his father restless before, but this was one of only a few times he would have described him as nervous. It was oddly disquieting. A moment later, he realized he was feeling likewise. Ralph, the only one among them who remained unaffected, was clearly unable to resist the urge to ruffle Art's feathers. His tone was casual, as if he were remarking on the weather.

"Don't know if Ma told you, but she brought me along to hold you down if you try to run. I'm guessing she's seen the face of your betrothed, and considers it a possibility. After all, why would a girl agree to an arrangement if she had an abundance of suitors?"

Art refused to make eye contact, as it would only encourage Ralph. However, that last point actually made some sense. On the other hand, he was somewhat grateful to have something to focus on besides his own anxiety. Dutifully, Ralph continued, careful to pitch his voice low enough that neither of their parents could hear.

"Now, in all seriousness, I think I have some helpful advice, drawing from my extensive experience."

Distantly, Art was impressed. Ralph's sarcasm had improved to the point where he almost – almost – expected the next words to be genuine advice.

"If she's merely ugly, make love to her from *behind*." He wagged a single finger in the air and inclined his head, as if this were some profound and helpful observation. "No sense in spoiling the whole experience. Now, if she's ugly and smells like a week-old fish, well-"

Any further vulgarity was cut off at a call from their father. "Boys! Front and center."

George and Luciana had moved to a more open location on the platform, making themselves easier to spot. The smoke plume mixed with steam in the air as the locomotive rumbled past.

Ralph glanced over at Art, eyes narrowed, and his mouth turned up in a mocking grin. Art met his gaze, once again oddly thankful for the distraction.

With a mocking grin of his own, he whispered, "Two weeks."

Ralph's smile vanished, and the two of them watched the train with no further interaction. The noise intensified to a din. Steam vented from the engine as it gradually slowed.

George straightened up, trying to peer through the passing windows for a glimpse of the Kennedys. Luciana then turned to Art for a final adjustment to his hair, which remained stubbornly non-compliant. A fluttery sensation in his midsection distracted him to the point that he almost let her do it unchallenged.

One, final time, Art pushed her hands away, and she sighed heavily, accepting the unruly mop adorning his head.

"Didn't this suit come with a hat?" she asked.

Art said nothing.

The conductor stepped down to the platform, followed by the first of the passengers. This was it. For the first time, the reality of the situation settled on Art. Until now, the idea of being engaged had been in the abstract; it was something he dimly acknowledged, but somehow, never thought would have any actual consequences. Now, confronted with the stark reality that in a minute or two, his future wife would exit that train, his anxiety was palpable.

Once again, he thought about Etta. Things with her were going well – so he thought. On the other hand, he had been wrong about such things before. And they did have something of a rocky start. Did his mother have it right? Maybe someone older and wiser should make such a life-altering decision on his behalf. The idea provided little comfort him, and Art remained ill at ease. Not even the mess of pistons and linkages on the side of the locomotive could hold his interest.

The sensation only worsened as people disembarked. He had never met any of the Kennedys before, so he was waiting for some kind of indication or acknowledgment from his parents to point them out. There were a few false starts. His mother shifted her weight as a girl of no more than thirteen years stepped down to the platform. He almost fell over in panic. Even after he realized his mistake, Art's leg began shaking of its own accord.

Art clasped his hands together to keep from shaking. He found that looking at the ground helped to ease his trepidation to an extent. Minutes went by with no indication that his parents had spotted the Kennedys.

The train eventually let out another whistle as it built up power to depart. It pulled away from the station, and Art's parents still had not recognized anyone. He began to hope. Perhaps the Kennedys had missed their train. Maybe they had even canceled the engagement entirely. For a moment, Art dared to think he might actually be off the hook.

It was extremely short-lived.

"Ah, Lucy! There you are."

The Adamses turned to find a middle-aged couple leading a small group from the far end of the station platform.

"Gertrude! Good to see you again," replied his mother, who moved to embrace the other woman. Art noted that any vestige of her accent had disappeared, and she was, apparently, going by "Lucy" again.

George greeted the man next to Gertrude. "And Franklin, I presume?" He grabbed the man's hand, and clapped him on the shoulder affectionately. "Good to finally meet you, Old Sport. How was your journey?"

The man was small. Although, most people appeared so when standing next to George. Despite Franklin's diminutive stature, he had a steely-eyed gaze and conveyed the sense that he was not to be dismissed lightly.

As they shook hands, George spoke in an affected tone, which Art recognized and thought of as Fast Friends. He often did this when meeting new people. To Art, it was the obnoxious older brother to Sale Smile. At least with Sale Smile, he only wanted someone's money. With Fast Friends, one was meant to think it was genuine affection. Like Art, Franklin was mildly put off by the overly-familiar tone. Though he did not object, he narrowed his eyes at George in disapproval.

"Long. Dirty," he responded as he withdrew his hand. Franklin's voice was far raspier than his apparent age might suggest. "The soot from these coal burners disagrees with my sinuses." Immediately, he pulled the handkerchief out of his vest pocket and blew his nose right in front of George, who backed away as far as he could without shifting his feet.

While he was tactful enough not to say anything, it was clear that he was now the one put off. With some effort, Fast Friends remained bolted in place.

Franklin carried on as if nothing were amiss. "Very kind of you to meet us."

Recovering, George replied, "Think nothing of it. It's such a fine day, we would have been out for a family walk anyway."

What a damned, dirty lie, thought Art. He glanced up from his feet long enough to shake his head.

A flash of annoyance at his father's insincerity helped to quiet the trembling in his arms. At last, he noticed the three young women who had been following Gertrude and Franklin. Their feet anyhow. He was still too shy to look at them directly. More pleasantries were exchanged between the parents before George turned to face Art and Ralph.

"I think introductions are in order," said George, smiling and resting his hand on Franklin's shoulder, which was unwelcome by the latter. "My older boys – both family minded men – are back at the house making preparations. But these are my younger sons Ralph, and the bridegroom to be, Arthur."

Mr. Kennedy nodded acknowledgment to Ralph before extending his hand to Art.

"Nice to meet you, sir," was all Art could manage as he focused on standing up straight.

Franklin had both a strong grip and severe expression as he regarded his future son-in-law. Despite the fact that he had to incline his neck to look up at Art, his visage was both intimidating and conveyed the notion that everything in sight was failing to live up to his expectations.

"Arthur," he greeted curtly. "So, you are to marry my Dorothy."

"Ah, that's right, sir."

"Hm. Your mother has convinced my Gertrude that you are an upstanding young man, of good moral character." He paused significantly, as if it were a merely a rumor he had heard and expected Art to provide evidence.

Art said nothing, his wits retreating under Franklin's glare.

The older man continued, "I know we live in a liberated time, but my daughters are my treasure. I tell you here and now: there is to be no fornication before the wedding."

Art blinked. *What did I just hear?*

"Dear," interjected Gertrude in a tone that was careful but firm. "They haven't even met yet."

Poorly concealed tittering could be heard from behind the couple. Art did not break eye contact with Franklin, but still noticed movement, as if one of the girls was shushing the others. Franklin's expression softened by a shade, and he nodded.

"Yes. Quite right. We have not finished introductions." He turned halfway, standing beside Art, and motioned for the three girls to step forward. He briefly added that their oldest daughter Emmie was away at the moment, but would join them later in the summer. Then, in order of youngest to oldest, he introduced Irving, Agnes, and finally Dorothy.

She stepped forward, and it occurred to Art that he had been avoiding eye contact again. After an interminable moment, he forced himself to look up.

Dorothy Kennedy, while not Venus reborn, was nothing like the unfortunate picture Ralph had been attempting to paint. A tumble of ginger-red hair stuck out from beneath a floppy, brown beret. So curly that it bordered on wiry. It was cut in a short bob, as was the style in certain circles. Tall for a girl, though still shorter than Art, she had an abundance of freckles that stood out against her pale complexion. Her heart-shaped face was otherwise unadorned by any kind of cosmetic or lipstick. About his own age, she looked at him with sharp green eyes, which only emphasized the redness of her hair. Her expression betrayed a certain, general anxiety, which, Art suspected, mirrored his own.

Instead of a dress, as her mother and sisters wore, she had opted for a sporty look: knickers, argyle socks, vest, and a man's necktie. It was not a rare ensemble, though certainly a less conventional one. Art had seen it often around his old university campus. From Gertrude Kennedy's look of consternation, Art surmised that this wardrobe choice was a recent point of contention.

The pair of them stood awkwardly, breaking eye contact as they fidgeted under the pressing stares of their assembled family. Based on the silence from everyone else, Art thought they were expected to do something. He struggled to come up with anything to say, too aware of Ralph standing just behind him. The anticipation of his brother loosing his sharp tongue rendered Art incapable of using his. Dorothy was at a similar loss for words, hands clasped in front of her.

To Art's relief, Luciana broke the silence.

"Let's walk, and give Art and Dorothy some time to talk without the rest of us listening in."

Heads nodded in agreement.

"Supervised, of course," shot Franklin.

"Of course..."

After gathering the luggage, they assembled themselves in a loose train per Luciana's suggestion. Art's parents and the rest of the Kennedy's led the way towards the lake, while he and Dorothy lagged behind. Just out of listening range but never out of sight, it was enough to give them a semblance of privacy. After some prodding from his mother, Art picked up Dorothy's suitcase.

George, of course, was still loud enough for Art to pick out every third or fourth word. Meanwhile, Franklin continuously glanced over his shoulder, ostensibly checking to ensure that Art had not begun to ravage Dorothy in the middle of the street in the past forty-five seconds.

That left Ralph, who hovered somewhere between the two groups, carrying another pair of suitcases. He also looked back toward the couple more often than was necessary. Art's anxiety returned as he anticipated what Ralph would do. Though, to his surprise, he found he was almost hoping for some kind of embarrassment. Best-case scenario, his taunting would cause Dorothy to call off the engagement.

Alas, Ralph had stubbornly remained silent for a change. His expression was unwell, and Art felt a brief pang of concern for his brother's health. That he was carrying both Agnes' and Irving's suitcases might have accounted for this, and Art pushed it from his mind.

Next to him, Dorothy walked with a straight back and her head held high. This gave the impression that she was looking down her nose at the surrounding greenery and open space. In a certain sense, she was, but from the way her eyes darted around, and the way she fidgeted with her hands, Art suspected this was mostly nerves. Neither of them had yet said a word to each other.

Shifting her suitcase to his other hand, Art undid the top two buttons of his shirt and loosened his tie. Silently, he scolded himself for not challenging his mother on her insistence that he dress up for the occasion. Franklin happened to glance back, yet again, and witnessed Art in the apparent act of disrobing. Eyes going wide, he looked as though he would start a fuss before Gertrude put a restraining hand on his shoulder.

"Your father keeps a pretty close eye on you, doesn't he?" Art remarked.

Dorothy was almost startled, as if she had forgotten he was standing there. It took the span of several breaths for her to respond.

"He's very attentive. I think he's making up for the past couple of years while I was at school." Her New England accent was mild, but especially noticeable on the words "past" and "years."

"So, you're a college girl?" he asked, trying to keep the conversation moving.

"Bradford College at Haverhill," she replied proudly. Before Art could respond with a follow-up question, she continued, "Does that surprise you?"

Her tone was defensive, as if challenging him to deny it. A moment ago, she had been aloof and the sudden shift caught him off-guard.

"Why would-? No." he stammered. He shook his head to recover. "I'm not familiar with that one. What did you study?"

"Psychology with a minor in sociology. I find human behavior fascinating. Even if the coursework was a bit too heavy on Freud for my liking. I mean, really, at a women's college, the curriculum couldn't include a few books by Margaret Washburn?"

"Who's that?" he asked, trying to follow along. She shot him a look, as if he had just broken wind in front of her.

"Why only the *President* of the American Psychological Association," she replied, as if this were common knowledge. Her minor outburst had caught the attention of her father, whose next glance lingered on Art just a bit longer than his previous ones.

"Of course," replied Art.

"It's true she attended Harvard, though I would never hold *that* against her." The last part appeared to be a joke, since she favored Art with a half-smile as she said it.

Art remained silent, wary of committing another misstep.

"Are you a college man?" she asked eventually.

He nodded at first, not eager to speak. "Yes. Well, *former*. I graduated a month ago."

She nodded acknowledgment, without looking toward him. "And how have you been making use of your time since then?"

He opened his mouth to respond, and just in time, remembered to prune most of the compromising details. "For the most part, I've been here. Working with my father. Picked up a few odd projects here and there."

"Projects?" she asked with – what Art thought was – genuine interest.

"I fixed a radio recently. There was also some minor carpentry."

"So, you went to college to become a maintenance worker?" While she was using the same tone, it was clear that it was not curiosity he was hearing. This was a rebuke. Once again, Art found himself unsure how to respond and simply said the first thing that came to him.

"No. This was just something that came up. I do enjoy that kind of thing, though."

She sniffed, pursing her lips in clear disapproval. Sensing this topic was a dead-end, Art attempted to shift to something else.

A pattern emerged as he group made their way to the cottage. Franklin repeatedly cast scrutinizing looks back at them. George regaled his new best friend with stories of sales past, or whatever the man talked about when he was pretending to like someone. Dorothy's sisters migrated off on their own, just far enough that Luciana and Gertrude were unable to pull them in to their own animated conversation.

The younger girls clearly preferred to keep their own company. Occasionally, they would erupt in a fit of giggles as they looked over at Dorothy and Art, but more often they made big eyes at Ralph. Even carrying two suitcases, and puffing along in the summer heat, the bastard somehow managed to look dapper. As they walked, he would drift closer to Art and Dorothy until caught by Luciana who would motion him to back away again.

Art, meanwhile, only managed to verbally limp along with Dorothy. Thus far, the alleged conversation had consisted of dead-end topics or something that sent her off on a monologue. They had never quite committed to anything that might be rightly labeled a back-and-forth. It said much that by the time they reached the house, Art was actually glad to see Junior.

Introductions were made with the rest of the family and Art was more than happy to let others talk for a short while. For her part, Dorothy watched the nieces and nephews chase each other around the cottage yard and beyond. Art noticed there were more children than his family alone could account for. Whatever game they were playing had since pulled in others from the neighborhood.

Dorothy and her sister, Irving, moved closer to the road, and Art saw it as an opportunity to catch a break. He drifted towards the conversation between his parents and the Kennedys. When Luciana saw him alone, she shooed him back towards his intended. With a sigh, he joined Dorothy at the fence.

As she spoke with her sister, watching the children at their game, Art noted the contrast to how she had been acting before. With her sister, Dorothy was smiling, chatting, and – for all appearances – enjoying herself. Art watched for a moment, trying to reconcile this apparently different person. For the entirety of their walk, she had either been reserved or dismissive. Now, she was downright pleasant.

Art frowned, feeling slightly guilty. Maybe he had her all wrong, and they had simply gotten off to a bad start. After all, he was no stranger to how poor and inaccurate first-impressions could be. She acknowledged him as stood beside her. While she said nothing, her smile, at least remained.

Some minor drama ensued when two of the children ran into each other at full tilt, falling to the ground in a tangle of limbs and a cloud of dust. Crying and heated disagreement followed. His oldest niece approached before their tiny fists could start swinging. Though she was no more than seven, she successfully separated the two.

"Isn't it funny how they organize their own rules and social order?" asked Dorothy, eyes still on the scene in front of them. "This older girl here has taken it upon herself to break up two separate fights."

"That's Allyson," Art offered. "My brother Junior's oldest daughter."

Dorothy nodded without turning her eyes from the children's game. Her face was both curious and intent. Art knew the look well. It was the same way he would examine the workings of a clock or a radio and attempt to understand its operation.

"You really are fascinated by people, aren't you?"

Her smile broadened as she turned to face him. "There's plenty to see if you bother to look, especially when it comes to roles in social groups. This is interesting to see in children since they're less affected by social conditioning than adults."

She pointed to Allyson. "Take your niece for example. She found a role in deescalating conflict. Women are naturally inclined to matters of emotional health, you see. Men tend to be handicapped in this regard. Frankly, if women's suffrage had come first, we would have gotten the Prohibition that much sooner. Both of which, I might add, were long overdue."

Art blinked.

After thinking about it for a moment, he was unable to make the connection between the children's game and Prohibition, and ultimately gave up. Hoping to avoid another dead-end, he attempted to follow this thread as best he could.

"I suppose there's something to that," he ventured, noncommittally.

She regarded him with a smile, which he interpreted as a good sign of sorts. Emboldened, he attempted to continue.

"Though as far as women being tenders of emotional health, you might feel differently after you meet my sisters-in-law."

He flashed a grin at Dorothy, attempting to signal that it was a joke, but she only returned a look of clear disapproval.

"I don't cotton much to gossip, Mr. Adams."

Now Art felt like the one making a poor first impression. The rebuke stung more than he would have thought and he felt compelled to try and recover.

"I'm just being humorous," he replied. "They're not so bad after a glass or two of wine."

He smiled again, hoping to smooth over his earlier stumble. This time, Dorothy frowned and even Irving shook her head. Art realized that he had somehow said the wrong thing again. To indicate the level of her displeasure, Dorothy adorned herself with pursed lips and a narrowed gaze.

After Art's smile wilted entirely, she simply said, "Well, that won't be happening. Might I humbly suggest that you not rely on alcohol as a cure-all for your relationship woes?"

"I-" Art was about to say something to the effect of "That's not what I meant," but instead, remained silent, hoping to simply quit while he was ahead. For her part, Dorothy returned her attention to the children with her arms folded across her chest.

Then again, he thought, *first impressions can be quite telling.*

Dinner was the typical chaotic affair. Ten different conversations overlapped each other and were often shouted. Of those, only about a third could be blamed on the young ones who had been pushed to a smaller table. This included Irving and Agnes who preferred the younger children's company despite the difference in age.

As usual, the tables were set up outside, the only place where everyone could fit. The Kennedys proved more than capable of making themselves heard. Not least of all was Gertrude who, combined with Luciana, were the liveliest of the bunch. Still, the strict banning of wine at tonight's dinner ensured that the overall chaos was less than it might have been. It was revealed that Franklin Kennedy was a strict teetotaler – a piece of information that Art might have benefited from an hour earlier.

At that moment, he could have done with a drink. Or three. Of course, Art had been seated next to Dorothy as to give them yet more time to become acquainted. Mercifully, the critical looks from her father grew fewer and the time between could be measured in minutes instead of seconds.

Meanwhile, any reticence or shyness Dorothy had exhibited upon their initial meeting was completely melted away. It turned out that once she felt secure, she was more than happy to go on about everything from current events to her time in school with great detail.

She soon covered much of her academic career, most of which had been spent living in a boardinghouse with several other girls. She then proceeded to describe the various cliques and a number of emotionally vindictive acts that had ensued. Art could not help but consider himself fortunate that growing up with brothers had merely resulted in physical torment. More than once, he felt inclined to point out the apparent contradiction with her "matters of emotional health" remark, but was wise enough not to bring it up again.

As dinner wrapped up and dusk settled, the Kennedys made their goodbyes. Tentative plans were made for later in the week to allow Art and Dorothy to resume their courtship. As usual, the mothers arranged this on behalf of the couple-to-be.

Under the scrutiny of their respective families, Dorothy and Art shook hands – though he thought it an oddly formal farewell gesture. As they left, Art was relieved that the evening was finally concluded, but it was tempered by an emerging anxiety. Two things were certain: this match would not work and he had no idea how to get out of it.

Chapter 21
Etta

This is excruciating.

It was the third day of dressmaking at the Saunders' house, and Etta fully intended for it to be the last. Initially, she thought the new routine would be something she would enjoy. It gave her a chance to both spend time with Helen and get off of her feet for a few hours. However, she had failed to appreciate just how dysfunctional the relationship between mother and daughter Saunders had become.

Another argument had started, albeit less overt than the last one. This time, Etta was happy to pretend to ignore it while she worked on her bridesmaid dress. These spats were becoming a regular occurrence; far more frequent than she could ever remember. Ironically, whereas the previous fight was because Helen was loathe to wear her mother's old dress, now she refused to take it off. That the adjustments and lace were only held together by pins was of no concern.

Aware of everything else that needed to be done, Mildred was eager to finish this particular task, and grew increasingly annoyed at her eldest daughter's petty defiance. Not accustomed to seeing Mildred flustered, Etta was surprised by how much Helen was able to get under her mother's skin. Indeed, Mildred became so riled up that she was desperate for Helen to comply with *something*.

"Can you take the dress off, please? We need to sew the lace on properly."

"I'd just like to wear it a little longer."

"Would you kindly take your feet off the table?"

"Oh, but the baby... This is much more comfortable for my back."

"It's hot today. Drink some water."

"I'm not thirsty."

Even Susie, sitting next to her mother, grew confused at the on-going test of wills.

The tables were soon turned when Helen could no longer ignore an intensifying compulsion to visit the necessary. Mildred helped her out of the dress, and waited until Helen slipped outside before switching it for the one currently on the sewing machine. With the gown committed, she grinned to herself. As Helen had come out ahead in most of their recent disputes, Mildred was contented by even this small victory.

Thankfully, Etta's own bridesmaid dress was nearly finished. It had been many years since she had operated a sewing machine for so long, and her leg was getting sore. The treadle on her old Singer had been poorly maintained and took some effort to keep moving.

Helen's cousin, Megan worked on her own dress beside Etta. While they had met previously at dinner, they had not spoken much at the time. For the sake of being polite, and since Helen was decidedly preoccupied, Etta made an effort at small talk. There was something of an age gap, which soon became obvious. Any sporadic conversation that was not interrupted by Helen and Mildred often returned to gossip that was only of interest to Megan. Etta soon gave up, and only spoke to provide instruction. At first, it was simply out of a desire to prevent Megan from making a mistake that Etta would have to help repair.

"Cut outside the pattern, or you won't have enough material."

"No, don't pin it in your lap, that's what the dressmaker's dummy is for."

"Add some material up here, or your breasts will be out for everyone to see... yes, I'm sure you are proud of them... no, you're a bridesmaid, not a flapper."

For the younger girl, this was no more than a chore that needed to be done. Not unlike how Etta would feel about cleaning the chicken coop. After some time, enough pieces of the bodice came together to form something that could be recognized as part of a dress. Seeing it take shape, Megan found her motivation and more actively sought Etta's advice. The peppering of questions had been annoying at first, but gradually, Etta found that she liked this role as mentor.

"You sure know a lot about this," Megan said at one point. "Have you made a lot of dresses?"

Before Etta could answer, the door opened, and Helen sauntered back into the room. Not finding the gown on the chair where she had left it, she cast a suspicious look toward her mother who was busy at the Singer. Reluctantly, she conceded this round to her mother and flopped into the vacant spot next to Etta. Mildred, in turn, pointedly ignored her daughter and did not bother to conceal a smug expression.

"So, do you make a lot of them?" Megan asked again.

"I used to adjust dresses from the second-hand store so they fit better. But not lately. You can see this takes a lot of time."

"That sounds fun, though. Is this the first time you've made an entire dress before?"

"Well... no."

When she did not elaborate, Helen filled the silence as she often did. "There was the one you made for Irene-" She quickly trailed off at the word "Irene." Too late, Helen recognized her indelicate stumble and fell silent.

Across the room, Mildred's foot conspicuously paused in working the sewing machine treadle.

"Yes, there was that one," Etta said evenly.

Megan looked between Etta and Helen a few times, expecting someone else to speak. When no one did, she continued.

"It must have been nice. I'd love to see it."

Etta bit her lip, saying nothing, and her hands stopped moving as she tried to form an appropriate reply.

"Oh, I remember Irene," Susie offered. "She was always nice to me."

Etta still had not said anything. Staring at the nearly completed dress in front of her, she was oddly calm. No, not calm. Numb, maybe? Fatigued?

Guilty.

Somehow, Mildred's subdued attempts to shush young Susie only underscored the uncomfortable turn in the room's mood. Helen bit her lip and began to fidget.

With a sigh, Etta calmly explained to Megan, "My younger sister. It was her burial dress."

Megan was dismayed and appeared unsure of how to respond. Hoping to simply move on, Etta returned her attention to the dress in her lap. There was still a chance to finish it before leaving, and she could hopefully forgo the next uncomfortable sewing circle.

However, Susie spoke up in the silence that followed. "It was a car accident, right?"

Mildred was more overt this time. "It's not polite to talk about."

Etta bit her lip. "No, Mildred, it's fine." Turning to Megan, she continued, "It was years ago."

As if that's any time at all.

Helen started bouncing her foot. Having blundered onto this topic in the first place, she was compelled to try and smooth things over.

"Everyone knows it wasn't your fault, Etta. That damned out-of-towner crossed over the road. He's the one to blame."

"Helen..." Mildred said from across the room. That single word conveyed warning without ambiguity. For the first time that day, Helen listened to her mother without argument and clamped her mouth shut.

"I-I'm sorry. That must have been hard for you," Megan offered.

Etta looked at her, and recognized genuine pity in the younger girl's eyes.

"No worries," she replied eventually. She gave Megan a weak smile that was meant to be reassuring. "You're doing well. It's coming along really nicely."

With that, Etta decided that it was time to leave. She made a small bunch in the material, and stuck the needle through, keeping it safely out of the way. Draping the nearly finished dress over one arm she stood up and made for the door.

"I- I didn't mean to-" Helen stammered. Trailing off, she bit her lip again.

Sighing, Etta stopped at the door and turned back. "It's fine," she said quickly. "I just have some chores to finish while the sun is still up. I'll see you at the Kovaks' tonight." Without waiting for a reply, she let herself out.

The kitchen was silent, and the only room bright enough to see without lights. Finished at last, she appraised her work with satisfaction. The feeling lasted for only a few moments before she grew restless. Irene remained in her thoughts. Without something to keep busy, the quiet house only reminded Etta that the once lively place was now empty.

It was worse at night when none of her daytime chores could distract her. In those moments, she would look around and remember. Edward used to sit closest to the window at the dinner table. Mama would read to them by the fireplace. Irene walked around too loudly and too early in the morning. Every time she remembered, she was inevitably reminded of what had been lost.

Ghosts and memories.

The radio had made things bearable, providing her with a pleasant distraction. At least, while it lasted. That loss had been a particularly hard blow. In the days after Art fixed it, she played it almost without pause.

With Papa away for most of the daylight hours, and Art making only a few appearances in the past week it had been a balm for her spirits. One, it turned out, she had sorely needed. Having music somehow made her other problems less so.

This was especially true of the kitchen. Out of all the rooms in the house, it had most often seen the family all together. Thus, it had more than its share of ghosts. On the other hand, it was the only one that had a few pleasant new memories to elbow out some of the more painful ones.

Whereas every other room in the house only served as a reminder of those who had been lost, here she could remember kissing Art next to the heap of wet laundry. Or having dinner together. Or even their first breakfast.

With the music, it was hard to imagine what her life would be like without it. Unfortunately, she found out all too soon. In an unlucky coincidence, the electricity bill had arrived soon after and Papa was aghast.

At first, he thought there must have been some mistake, until Etta's guilty conscience compelled her to come clean about the now-working radio. Conveniently, she omitted many of the details about the boy who had fixed it and shared a kiss with her. That was a conversation for another time. If ever.

Jakob was not angry. Although, he was just a little annoyed that she had kept the secret from him. After all, the radio was finally working.

"Let that sheep farmer be damned!" he exclaimed.

With an almost boyish excitement, he turned it on for himself, and the two of them stood before it, listening. After just one song, he sighed and shut it off, then unplugged it from the wall for good measure.

"We simply cannot afford it," he said apologetically. "As it is, we are already a month behind." The radio, once again, resumed its role of holding the carpet to the floor.

Thus, the house had remained silent as well as empty. Dirty too. Basic upkeep had suffered as Papa spent less and less time at home. Two of the cabinet doors had been hanging at odd angles for months and the roof had sprung a new leak. Or rather, it was an old leak that Etta only recently discovered in Edward and John's old room. The most consideration given to it was a bucket, which had to be emptied twice each hour during bad rainstorms. A persistent moldy smell assaulted her every time she went in.

As a result, there seemed little point for Etta to keep up with cleaning. Several articles from last week's laundry were still hanging in the main room, having long since dried. Cobwebs were going untended in most all corners of the house, and the floors had not been swept in so long that she would be hard-pressed to find the broom.

It was frustrating how a nearly empty house could get so dirty, but in a few months it would no longer be her problem.

Etta supposed she could not entirely blame Papa for letting his side down. The new routine was taking its toll, and the daily drive wore him thin. The bookkeeping job tended to run into the evening, and after the return trip to the farm it was even later. After one incident where he fell asleep while driving and nearly ended up in a ditch, he decided something had to change.

For the past week or so, Jakob had been staying in Newark overnight, only returning home every second or even third day. For the first time in her life, Etta slept in the house by herself.

The days had not been all drudgery. Art's visits were becoming more frequent. While he never stayed too late, he always brought food and helped make the daily chores go much quicker. True to his word, he had made a point to fix the washing machine, though she did not have the heart to tell him that they were no longer using the electricity.

They always took their time saying goodbye. She savored the taste of his mouth, and the feel of his hands running through her hair. She wondered if he was intentionally teasing her when he touched her lower back and hips, but never advanced any farther.

Once or twice, she considered moving his hands, hoping that he would finally take the hint and pull her off clothes for her. With some frustration, they had done nothing more than kiss, but he always left before it got dark. Even alone on the farm, with practically no chance of being interrupted, she was reluctant for these trysts to escalate while the sun was up.

Looking at the completed dress for another long moment, Etta sighed. Despite what she told Helen, she had finished her chores that morning, planning to be at the Saunders for the rest of the day. For the same reason, she did not expect Art to come over until later when they would leave for the Kovaks' party. An unusual problem: Etta was burdened with a lack of pressing obligations.

Normally, the jalopy would be her top destination in such instances, but she did not feel up to climbing the big hill just now. Besides, seeing the dress finished, she wanted to try it on. And for that, she needed a full-length mirror.

I think we are due for another visit.

Standing in the street, Etta looked around to make sure that she was still alone. It was more an excuse to delay than a genuine concern. Nervously, she adjusted her grip on the two garment bags she carried. Even if it did not truly count as trespassing, she had an irrational fear at being caught. Although, with each subsequent visit her hesitation diminished.

Seeing the Beckett's former house stand empty was odd. Physically, it looked no different than the countless other times she had previously walked past it. As if any moment now, Bridget might walk out the front door and give her a wave. But it was different. This was no longer anyone's home. It was just an empty house. Yes, perhaps it had its own ghosts and memories, but at least they were not Etta's.

With a sigh, and a final glance up the road, Etta approached. The other thing she had come to appreciate about this place was the full-length mirror. Once or twice, she had considered dragging the heavy thing back to her own house, but never did. Despite having been abandoned, it felt too much like stealing and she was also afraid of breaking it in transit. Besides, leaving it at the Beckett's gave Etta an excuse to get out of her own house for a short while.

As she had on previous visits, she made her way around back. The grass had grown taller, but still short enough that she was walking over it and not through it. The back door was unlocked, of course, but tended to stick. Its token resistance to Etta's intrusion was as though the house longed for its original occupants. Anticipating the issue, Etta shouldered it open, and it gave way immediately. Her trepidation vanished once she was inside, as it usually did.

This was perhaps her fourth or fifth visit since the night she met with Walter. Each time, she found a few more of the Beckett's old things that had been left behind. A vase. An extra lamp. She would rearrange them, making the place a bit homier. In truth, she was not sure why she kept coming back. After all, she had a perfectly sound home just up the street. By all rights, it should have kept her entirely occupied. It was the memories, perhaps more than the ghosts that drove her away.

The best part about the Beckett's house was that it had none of that.

Draping the two dresses over the only chair in the room, she wrinkled her nose. Her eyes fell to the vase sitting on the table. On her last visit, she had picked some wildflowers to spruce up the place, and cover up some of the musty smell. That had been a while ago, and now the flowers were wilted and smelled foul.

Edgar and Bridget had taken their kitchen table with them, so Etta had improvised with a small end table from one of the bedrooms. She moved it here during a previous visit, same as most of the remaining furniture. This one room had the appearance of being lived-in, despite the rest of the house being empty. Like her pantomime in the jalopy, she liked to pretend that this place was hers, if only for a short while.

Her eyes fell on a ceramic jar tucked into a corner by the only window in the room. While confident that no one else had intruded, she was compelled to check that the contents remained undisturbed. Tipping open the lid, she stole just enough of a glance to verify the contents before returning it to its place.

Sure enough, her "take" from the CasinO safe remained. After getting away from Walter, her long walk home had given her plenty of time to think. The greasy, blonde pig had been right when he said that she could not simply return the money without appearing guilty herself. But neither did it feel right to keep, despite how much it could help her. Turning on the electric lights would not have to be a luxury. It was certainly enough to knock the tax bill down to a manageable sum. Not wanting to mingle it with her honest nest egg, she needed a place to stash it so Jakob would not come across it by accident.

As she had returned to the Beckett's house that night to collect her busgirl clothes, she dropped the money into a random jar on the counter, and there it remained. More than once, her will had been tested, and she seriously thought about simply giving it to Papa. Each time, she ultimately decided to leave it be.

Satisfied that the illicit cash was where she left it, Etta grabbed the vase and headed outside. The rear of the house led to the barley field – or rather what would have been the barley field. Already, grass and weeds had taken over and grown up to the height of her knees.

Making her way over to the well pump in no particular rush, she admired the view. It was the same valley she had seen her entire life, but the angle was just different enough to make it new. Better yet, from here, she could more fully see the hill where the jalopy was. Even though the car itself was not visible, just knowing that it was up there gave her comfort.

Etta spent some time collecting a fresh bundle of flowers. Some purple things were growing at the edge of the former barley field, which caught her eye. After returning the vase back to the kitchen, Etta did something she rarely did at her real home; she sat down.

Another random article of furniture was a wooden chair, which she had previously set on the small deck. The structure was clearly a recent addition, and Etta hoped Edgar and Bridget had a chance to enjoy it at least a few times before they were forced to leave. Looking across the valley, her thoughts inevitably drifted back to the events of the afternoon.

Four years was not nearly enough time to get past her sister's death. Not for her, and certainly not for her father, who refused to let her drive a car to this day.

On the other hand, it had been so long ago that there were times she could hardly remember what Irene looked like. The same was true for Edward... and John... Florence… Mother. Only two photographs existed in the house. One of them was a family portrait, taken years ago. Etta had still been a baby, and Irene was not even born yet. The other was from Jakob and Lena's wedding.

Etta's visits to the cemetery helped, and were vital to coping with the thoughts that would intrude on her peace. Mostly guilt, especially when she was alone. That happened often these days. Despite Helen's earlier insistence that Etta had not been the one at fault, it was a version of events that she had become less sure of recently. It was certainly not what Lena had believed.

Etta shook her head. Troubling as these thoughts were, they had been handled often enough to wear down the worst of the barbs and sharp edges. It was a rare occasion that Etta would break down in actual tears. The family plot was her place for reflection and mourning.

It was not Helen's clumsy treatment of a delicate subject that had ultimately driven Etta from the Saunders' home. It was the looks of pity from everyone, and the knowledge that they would treat her like a porcelain doll for the rest of the afternoon if she stayed. Had it only been Megan, she might have tolerated it, but not from Mildred and certainly not Helen. For Etta, pity was nearly as bad as charity.

She absolutely detested the idea that she could not get by on her own. For over two years, she had increasingly relied on herself and managed her own affairs. Yet everyone was keen to hold her down in some way or compel her according to their own wishes. Papa would not let her drive. Mildred wanted her to be a nanny. Only Art was content to walk beside her rather than push her along or hold her back.

Sitting in the chair, Etta basked in the quiet for perhaps half an hour before heading inside. Trying on the bridesmaid gown, she gave it a proper assessment in front of the mirror. It had turned out well, all things considered. There were flaws, of course, but even Etta had difficulty in spotting them.

The fabric Mildred had provided was simple and without a pattern, but Etta knew a few techniques for smocking that gave it a little bit of texture. Since Helen and Robert would not be getting married at church, she had hemmed the dress higher than she normally might have. More importantly, it had allowed enough of her back to be exposed so she would not bake in the July heat. The summer had already seen a number of days that were absolutely brutal, and she suspected this particular detail was going to be a lifesaver.

Seeing it all come together after weeks of effort was remarkable and Etta sighed contentedly. From a bolt of unremarkable fabric had emerged something she was quite proud of.

Chapter 22
Art

"Penny for your thoughts?" Etta said, by way of greeting.

Art blinked in surprise, having not seen her approach. He had arrived at the house early, and was mildly surprised to find that she was not there. Content to enjoy the view and let his thoughts wander, he plopped down in what had become his usual rocking chair while he waited for Etta.

"Just thinking," he replied.

"You do a lot of that," she said, grinning playfully.

"Some things need a lot of thinking about." Art melted, just a little, seeing her smile. "You look nice. Is this *the* dress?"

"Not this one," she said, indicating her current attire. "This is." She lifted the protective bag so he could see it. "I need to trim a few hanging threads, but it's finished."

Art did not have much of an eye when it came to clothing, but he recognized craftsmanship when he saw it. He also knew what it was like to create something, and have pride in one's work.

"This is amazing. You must have put a lot of work into it."

"It's just fine," Etta replied, but blushed prettily all the same. Soon recovering, she changed the subject. "You're early. The Kovaks won't be getting started for another hour or two."

"Oh..." he replied thoughtfully. "Can I assume there's no laundry or garbage that needs tending to?"

"I'm afraid not," she said with mock severity. "I'm the very picture of leisure."

"While I'm the very picture of a man under-dressed for a fine shindig." Art raised his arms to emphasize his point. It was one of his more worn shirts, but it was clean, and his sleeves were rolled up, tight and neat just above the elbow.

Etta looked him over with approval. “No. You look just right,” she said. “The tax man wears a suit, and you don't want to be mistaken for him. Or – God forbid – the census taker. You're likely to get chased off at gunpoint.”

“Yes... we wouldn't want that to happen.”

Again.

“Besides, what if someone needs an emergency tractor repair, or some last-minute carpentry work?”

“I had brought dinner, but if you're going to be like that...” Art reached behind the chair and pulled out a basket. As he did so, the aroma of meatballs in tomato sauce wafted out, causing both their stomachs to rumble.

“Now this is a surprise.”

Opening the top revealed enough food to easily feed five people, which was, in fact, its original intent.

“Goodness,” she said, eyes wide. “Are you sure you brought enough?”

Art chuckled. “Kind of a long story. In a nutshell, it was my sister-in-law's turn to prepare dinner, and my mother didn't trust her to do it. This was the backup meal.”

Mostly the full truth. He left out the part where the Kennedys were supposed to join them. Franklin's sinuses were not taking well to the country air, and they canceled at the last moment. Art's pretense for leaving with the meatballs had been to deliver them in person. If he was lucky, Luciana would never ask Gertrude about it. The thought made him nervous all of a sudden. Despite his decision to cancel the engagement, he had failed to bring up the matter with his parents. It would most certainly cause a fight, and Art doubted his resolve to see the matter through. He could, however, drag his feet with the best of them.

Etta regarded him with some suspicion, and Art realized that he was fidgeting.

“Don't worry,” he continued. “It won't be missed. Neither will I probably.” The last part was more muttered to himself than her.

Etta let the matter drop, and said, “Let's dig it then. I'm starving. I was going to eat at the Saunders but... I didn't end up staying.”

This time, she was the one fidgeting, and Art suspected that there was more to the story. With a hand on the door, she was about to go inside, but hesitated. At first, Art wondered if she had locked herself out by accident, but remembered that she never did that.

"Thought you were hungry," he said. "Something wrong?"

Etta frowned. "It's just that my house is a bit of a mess right now. I haven't been keeping on top of it."

"You're talking to the guy who slept in the barn, y'know."

Unsure why he had gone for that particular joke, he was immediately afraid that it was treading on a dangerous topic. To his relief, her look of mild annoyance was tempered by clear amusement. Art continued to grow more comfortable around Etta, but determining acceptable boundaries of conversation was ever his weakness.

Looking at the basket, Etta brightened with a sudden idea.

"Are you wearing your walking shoes?"

The shadows were long by the time they reached the top of the hill. According to Etta, they still had a couple hours of daylight left so they were not at risk of finding their way out in the dark. Nearing the summit, the narrow footpath opened up and they were able to walk side-by-side again. Art was breathing heavily, though not quite panting.

"You sure like to work up an appetite before dinner," he said, shifting the food basket from one arm to the other.

"With all the food you brought, I think we need to work up all the appetite we can," she replied.

"Is this a different way to get to the pond?"

"We're not going to the pond. This is... something else." Etta cast another glance back at him. She had been doing this with increasing frequency since entering the forest. It was odd, but her expression was almost nervous.

"What?" he said between breaths. "A five-star restaurant in the middle of the wilderness?"

"Oh, hush. We're almost there," she replied. "Actually, I think it's something you'll appreciate."

Reaching a wall of boulders, Etta hesitated one last time before entering a hidden path. Art followed. A minute later, they emerged into a clearing and she waved her arm proudly.

"I give you the best seat in Bott's Lake with the third best view." Etta sighed contentedly.

Still catching his breath, Art's eyes went straight for the edge of the clearing. The ground dropped away and gave way to a commanding view of the valley. She did not oversell it.

"I gotta admit that's a nice- oh."

The sight of a car brought him up short, and he blinked a few times to make sure that it was not some hallucination. Art stared, saying nothing until he finally remarked, "Gee... how about that."

Etta grinned at his perplexed expression. "Well, this is my car," she said with a shrug.

She was even more nervous than before. In fact she was downright bashful. It was the way she might have acted if they were about to see each other naked for the first time. His attention was soon fully absorbed by the fact that a car had contrived to get itself onto a hilltop in the middle of the forest. This was especially perplexing, considering the narrow and steep footpath they had just taken in order to reach it.

Looking around he quickly ruled out the footpath. Likewise, the car did not climb up the sheer drop towards which it was pointed. That left one of the remaining sides. The wheels were turned at a slight angle, which suggested one direction over the other. While it was thick with brush Art reasoned that it was the most plausible point of entry.

"I see," Art said, distractedly. Setting the picnic basket down, he walked a slow circle around the old car. It was not a model he was immediately familiar with, but the initials "REO" were displayed prominently on the radiator. The model year was probably around 1914 or so, with a canvas top that did not even have side coverings.

"How on Earth did you get it all the way up here?"

"It's not *really* my car. Or at least it wasn't originally. I just found it here one day."

Accepting her explanation, though not quite able to believe it, Art continued inspecting this oddity. Save for a few patches of rust, the paint was shiny, giving the impression that it was in nearly working order. Here and there, he noticed telltale signs of neglect. The weathering of the interior and canvas top made it clear that it had been outside for a while.

With some exploration to discover the unlatching mechanism he managed to get the cover open. Like the exterior, he found nothing visually wrong with the engine aside from a mouse that had taken up residence between some cables. The radiator was dry, but he found that he could move the fan by hand, so at least the pistons had not seized.

The front passenger-side wheel was the only mechanical problem he could immediately spot. While conspicuously bent at an odd angle, it was simple enough in terms of repairs. Etta moved to join him where he squatted next to the damaged wheel.

"Well?" she asked, almost shyly. "What do you think?"

"Looks to be mostly cosmetic damage," he replied without hesitation. This had been a fairly routine exercise from his time with Gregory and he rattled off the tasks almost without thinking about it. "The steering linkages here all need to be replaced, but the frame is alright. Assuming the engine still works, I'd say probably six to eight weeks to get it running. That's if nothing else comes up, which it probably will. Of course, how to get it back through the woods is another matter."

Etta chuckled. "Hm. Well that just won't do. I'll need this for the Bovine Debutante Ball next week."

Engrossed as Art was with the jalopy, Etta's tongue-in-cheek remark went right over his head. He frowned, mistakenly thinking that her response to his estimate was in earnest.

Spreading his hands apologetically, he continued, "That's a little unrealistic. It might take a week just to get it off this hill."

Etta blinked. Prolonged silence followed as she searched for any signs of insincerity or humor. Finding none, all vestige of her amused grin faded, and she stared at him with intensity. It went on for long enough that Art began to feel uncomfortable.

"You're serious," she said at last.

Once again, Art mistook her expression for disapproval. "There are just a lot of unknowns. Sitting outdoors like this, I suspect there's water damage somewhere we can't see. Not sure how easy it'll be to get all the parts either."

"Are you saying... you can fix the jalopy?" she asked in a voice just above a whisper.

Brow furrowed, he shrugged his shoulders and nodded. "Sure. Anything can be fixed."

Mouth agape, Etta was astounded to the point where she could have been knocked down with the feather. As it turned out, it was Art who was knocked down when she wrapped her arms around him.

"Wha-?" was all he could say as they fell together.

The pair of them landed in a tangle of limbs as Etta hugged him tightly and giggled in a way that Art had seldom heard from a grown woman. She continued grinning, apparently oblivious to the fact that she was now resting on his chest.

His own expression changed from startled to bemused, and he ignored the fact he was lying in the dirt. They were close enough that her hair dangled in his face. Reaching up, he tucked it back behind her ears before resting his hands on the small of her back.

Unable to think of anything else to say, he fell back on something he felt sure of. "Eight weeks. I can't promise any sooner than that."

"And you have no idea how it got here?" Art asked between mouthfuls of food.

Etta shook her head as she tucked into her fourth meatball, held between a couple pieces of bread. Sauce dripped from the ragged edge where she had torn it off the loaf. Everything was cold by this point, but per her own words, it was the most delicious meal she had had in recent memory.

After reluctantly untangling themselves, they had moved to sit inside the car for their picnic. Etta took the driver's seat, as she was more accustomed to eating around the steering wheel. The front bench was cramped with the two of them plus the picnic basket stuffed between. While the back seat was more spacious, the view was simply not as good.

And what a view it was. The few clouds above the distant lake were starting to change in color, foretelling of the impending nightfall. Art remarked that if this the third best view in town, he would have to see the first two for himself.

Finishing another bite, Etta replied, "All I know is that it got here sometime between spring and fall last year. Never found any tracks or anything obvious. It's better than the usual junk the out-of-towners leave behind. No offense."

"None taken." Art craned his neck forward. "Lucky they stopped when they did. Looks like the drop is pretty steep over there."

"I thought the same thing, first time I found it. Once, I walked around the bottom, just to see if anyone had fallen down. Nothing... thank goodness," she quickly added the last bit and grinned.

Her usual remarks about out-of-towners notwithstanding, Art had to wonder about her sincerity on the matter.

"Y'know, you got my hopes up with all your talk of fixing it. Did you really mean it?"

Art nodded seriously. "Just a matter of how much time you care to give it."

She was thoughtful and hesitated before she spoke next. "I always thought of it as my car, and imagined driving it, but it was just fantasy. I never seriously thought it could happen."

Art watched her. Biting her lower lip, Etta's expression was one of wonder as she pondered a world of new possibilities. He had to admit that it was a look that he enjoyed seeing. It made him not want to disappoint her.

Clearing his throat, he asked, "So, where are you going to drive?"

She glanced sidelong and bit her lower lip.

Does she know how cute that is?

She reached past him to a box under the console. Clearly not a stock component, Art had bumped it with his knees throughout dinner but otherwise paid it little mind. He was obliged to move clear so she could withdraw a folded-up piece of paper. After maneuvering the picnic basket behind them, she leaned into Art and unfolded what she held. It was a map.

Etta pointed out New York City and Bott's Lake, and Art got his bearings. A few thick lines – clearly drawn by hand – loosely connected the town with the city. The routes meandered back and forth, taking a sometimes circuitous path but inevitably led to the same destination.

Several other markings, and little notes had likewise been added here and there, carefully tucked into blank spots. He nodded to himself, thinking that some of her earlier questions and reactions now made just a bit more sense. New York itself was circled twice, centered over, what he recognized, as Midtown.

"You shoot for the moon, don't you?"

"How's that?"

"You're circled right around Manhattan. That might just be the most expensive place in a very expensive city."

She frowned, clearly taking his comment as an unwanted rebuke.

"What I mean is-" he quickly added, and pointed to a spot just to the East. "You might consider somewhere nearby, but slightly more... accessible. My parents' house is in Queens. It's not exactly Midtown, but it's still pretty nice."

Tentatively, her frown disappeared as she considered this.

"Is there music and dancing there?"

"I can't rightly say that there it. Some halfway decent libraries though."

"You know a lot, but you don't seem to understand how dreams work," she said with a smirk.

Now it was Art's turn to narrow his eyes. "I know just fine, but I thought you were serious about living in the city one day."

"Sure, I am. But you've been to be telling me all the reasons why I shouldn't. 'It's expensive. It smells bad.'"

"I like to have realistic expectations and it is those things."

"There you go again. If it were up to you, I'd be mucking chickens for the rest of my life."

"Untrue. I just don't want you to trade it for a day-long shift in a room with no windows."

"I'd find something else to do."

"You could sell refrigerators."

"Oh, is your father looking for a saleswoman?"

"I don't know. Can you meet the quotas?"

"Can you?" Etta shot back.

"No, I've been too busy fixing mailboxes and doing laundry."

"And dirtying your hands at Gregory's."

"At least Gregory's shop has windows."

Etta paused. "You said 'windows' already."

Art grinned as he worked on another bite and considered his reply.

"I'll grant you, the city has a good side, but I still wouldn't want to live there."

Etta was quiet for a long moment, frowning as her eyes drifted beyond the cliff. Concerned that his last gibe, which had meant to be friendly teasing, was too on the mark, Art felt he should add something. He spotted a pen in the console box.

"Ah – may I?" he motioned to the map.

Etta's breath caught as if he had just asked to take her to bed. Hesitantly, she nodded, but watched him carefully. This was not lost on Art, and he made sure to move slowly.

"The nice thing about a car," he said while writing, "Is that you can visit someplace without living there. Think of it as the best parts of both."

Etta followed his hand with her eyes, reading his blocky text alongside her flowery script. Next to what he had identified as Manhattan and carefully written within the blue of the East River were the words: "Day trip." Then, moving westward, he added the word "Home," in the same blocky text in the middle of a blue patch that was the Lake.

Etta regarded his words for a moment before looking back at him. While not wholly convinced, at least she was no longer annoyed with him.

"You've got a very practical way about you, Arturo," she said as she carefully refolded the map.

It was not immediately clear whether she intended it as a compliment or not. From the way she used his proper name he suspected that it was.

After finishing their picnic dinner, Etta and Art left the jalopy and made their way back down the hill to the dirt road. Despite what Art had initially thought was a stumble on his part, Etta was in a good mood. At first, he accounted for this as simply her being content with a full meal and the prospect of a barn party. Then, she bumped into him.

He thought little of it. They were walking close together, and it could have been random. Then, it happened a second time. Glancing over, he noticed that she was looking right at him, and it was a tell that even he could not mistake. Despite the fact they had kissed several times before, it was with no small amount of trepidation that he reached his hand out to hers, and a similar degree of relief when she clasped it in return.

They were not in a particular rush, and their walk to the Kovaks' farm was leisurely. It was early twilight by the time they reached the party, which they could hear long before they saw it. There was a solid turnout. The barn was overflowing, and extra tables were set up outside.

Those few who had missed the previous shindig had made sure they would not miss the second. Inside the main room, someone was warming up on a guitar; the sound of a few experimental chords drifted outside among a few dozen conversations.

Etta and Art exchanged greetings with a few familiar faces as they approached. This being his second appearance at one of these events, the odd looks he received were fewer and lesser in intensity. In fact, there were more than a few friendly greetings, mostly from people he had met through Gregory. Some of the dogs even came by to give him a passing sniff.

To Art's surprise, Mr. Shaw actually clapped him on the shoulder in a warm greeting. In the back of his mind, Art could not help but reflect on the odd turn of events. After all, it was only a matter of weeks since this man had unknowingly shot at him.

Robert soon found them and gave them both an enthusiastic hug, nearly spilling some of his beer. By his exuberance, Art guessed it was at least his third. Maybe even fourth.

Robert draped an arm over each of their shoulders and Art had to stagger his feet to keep from being pulled over. It was apparent that Etta's cousin was less being affectionate and more trying to remain upright. Briefly, Art wondered if his estimate of four beers might have been low.

"And where have you two been?" Robert asked. His eyebrows were raised in a salacious manner so there would be no mistaking his full meaning.

Art was about to protest their innocence, but Etta replied first.

"A gentleman never asks and a lady never tells, Robert," she said casually.

"Good thing neither of those types are here," he winked. Looking at Etta, there was something odd about his expression beyond his glazed eyes. He grimaced slightly, which was odd, considering his otherwise jovial demeanor.

"So, only a week until the big day," Art said after pointedly clearing his throat.

Robert's odd expression disappeared and the broad smile returned. "That's right! Helen and I- hey, where is she?"

A moment later, Helen approached from behind and tapped him on the shoulder. Releasing Art and Etta, Robert returned to his sweetheart before he could become too imbalanced.

"Helen and I talked to Old Man Kovaks. He's gonna set us up in the main room of the barn." Robert pointed with his beer hand, extending a single finger.

Helen looked skyward. "Send a few prayers this week that the weather holds out."

"You didn't want to get married at the church?" Art asked.

Robert and Helen exchanged glances.

"Sure we did," Helen answered. Then, putting an almost casual hand over her belly. "Pastor James felt differently."

Etta frowned, and made an annoyed sound. "Seems like him," she said. "The Sunday service has really suffered since he took over. Prudish even for a priest." She furrowed her brow suddenly, and pointedly looked at Helen. "How did he find out about the 'worst kept secret,' by the way?"

Helen shrugged. "Good news travels, I guess."

"It sure does," Etta grunted in response and frowned.

A silence followed as the two women stared at each other. Art suspected there was more going on here that he was not privy to, and thought it best to move on. Robert came to a similar conclusion, and cleared his throat.

“As luck would have it,” Robert started. “Carl, down at the ladder company, has an older brother who was an Army chaplain. Still ordained and all. He's not Catholic, but he said he would marry us.” He grinned again. “We just have to keep him sober long enough to get to 'I do.'”

Chapter 23
Etta

She was probably more annoyed than she had a right to be. On the one hand, it did not affect her, but Etta strongly suspected that Pastor James' refusal was due to Helen's loud mouth. Maybe not directly. But Helen had a great many friends, and she most certainly had not been shy about telling most of them.

The conversation moved in a different direction with Daniel's arrival. He and Art greeted each other warmly, which surprised Etta. She was accustomed to seeing the younger McCormick more quiet and sullen than he was now. Before Etta could wonder about it for too long, Helen gently grabbed her by the arm and led her away from the boys.

Unsure what to make of this strange behavior, Etta followed. When she asked what it was about, Helen shook her head. Whatever it was, she was keen to discuss it only after reaching the privacy of the lower barn.

"Listen, about before…"

She had to speak up in order for Etta to hear over the music. Upstairs, the Turner sisters had joined the guitarist and the three of them were performing a rendition of "After You Get What You Want, You Don't Want it."

Etta cut her off. "Really, it's fine." Up until a moment ago, her spirits were still buoyant from her picnic dinner with Art. The uncomfortable events from the Saunders' house were not something she cared to retread.

Letting out a breath, Helen bit her lip. "Alright," she replied. While reluctant about it, she was prepared to drop that particular subject. However, her expression remained tense. Sure enough, she continued. "Thought I should tell you that Robert knows."

Etta's brows furrowed. "Knows about what?" she asked, suspecting the answer.

"About you leaving town."

Etta groaned. "Helen..." It did not need to be stated just how Robert had come into that knowledge.

"I'm sorry, it just slipped out."

"That happens a lot with you. Who else have you told?"

Helen had been abashed, even apologetic before, but quickly became defensive. "No one. Goodness, I'm not *that* much of a gossip. For that matter, why didn't *you* tell Robert? Or anyone else?"

Etta did not reply at first. In part, because she did not have a good answer, but also because there were still ears present, even in the relative privacy of the barn. After several breaths, she turned back to Helen.

"Alright, look," Etta started. "I'm going to tell your mom, and everyone else. There's just been a lot going on lately."

Helen said nothing, but from her expression, she was clearly unconvinced. In that moment, the resemblance between her and Mildred was downright uncanny.

"After the wedding," Etta said at last. "I promise."

It took a moment, but Helen finally relented, and let out a heavy sigh. "Okay, Chicken Farmer," she said as she pulled Etta into a hug. "No more of this fighting nonsense. It's bad enough with my mother. I don't want to spend our last summer bickering."

To her surprise, Etta felt her own annoyance vanish.

No one can quite avoid a grudge like Helen, she mused.

Arms draped across each other's shoulders, they left the barn and slowly made their way back toward the boys.

"I won't be 'Chicken Farmer' for much longer," Etta said.

"And in a week, I won't be 'Madame Spinster.' Guess we'll just have to figure out something else."

Eager to avoid any more troubling topics, they grinned at each other. Etta's spirits were much improved, but she was also distracted. In their absence, Enoch had arrived and Robert naturally made sure that Daniel and Art both had drinks.

Etta remained quiet as she grappled with Helen's revelation. Now in context, the strange look from Robert made some sense. There was also the realization that she had just promised to tell Mildred about her plans. Knowing how she was likely to be challenged, it was not a conversation she looked forward to.

Then, Robert said something that pulled her out of her thoughts, but she had only half-heard it.

"Pardon?" she asked.

"I said, 'The Hunleys are here,'" he pointed across the yard with his chin.

Etta perked up at the familiar name. "Oh! I haven't seen Lizzie in such a long time." Looking in the direction her cousin had indicated, Etta spotted them quickly.

They were dressed considerably better than most everyone else present. Etta and Helen had gone to school with Lizzie, the oldest daughter, and the three of them had been good friends at one point. Gradually, she and Etta had drifted apart, as tends to happen when priorities and life go different ways. Helen, being who she was, had remained close with her.

"Looks like the dairy business has been treating them well," Etta remarked.

"You're not kidding," Helen said. "They've started selling ice cream from a few of the stores around town. Really popular with the summer crowd. After I asked Lizzie to be a bridesmaid, they offered to make extra for the wedding reception, as their gift."

"That's quite a gift," Etta said with raised eyebrows.

Robert took another pull from his beer and said, "I heard they go through a truck load of ice each week since they're making so much. The Old Sarge didn't even want to sell it, since it was so early in the summer. They had to go to two different towns to get enough."

"So that's what that was," Art said, almost to himself. "Gregory and I fixed something for the Hunleys the other week. I wasn't sure what it was at the time, but it would make sense if it was an ice cream maker." He thought another moment and shook his head. "They must be using ice and salt though. That seems really inefficient."

"How's that?" Robert asked.

"You can only do so much with wet ice. Electric refrigeration is the way to go."

Eyes still glazed, Robert looked at him blankly.

Art quickly added, "My family's in the refrigeration business."

Daniel chimed in. "Oh, yeah. We've got one of those at the station house. Always wondered how it works."

Art opened his mouth, as if about to reply, but caught himself. "Money goes in, cold comes out," he said simply.

This pulled a chuckle out of both McCormick brothers.

Etta looked from Art and back to the Hunleys. A thought formed.

"Let's go say 'hi.'"

She grabbed him by the arm, to his surprise, and pulled him towards Lizzie who was on her own for the moment.

In addition to being the best-dressed ones in attendance, the Hunleys stood out in a crowd. They were a handsome lot, all of them having chiseled features and wavy, raven black hair. Except for Lizzie's father, Owen, whose head was streaked with a dignified amount of gray. A handsome devil, he certainly turned more than a few heads. It said much that the fact he was missing his right arm was not the first thing someone would notice.

Just so, Lizzie and her mother, Bethany, commanded the attention of just about every warm-blooded man with eyes to see. The resemblance between mother and daughter was unmistakable. They both had the same, lithe build and high cheekbones, making it difficult to comprehend that they tended cows for a living.

By Etta's recollection, Lizzie had been popular when they were in school, and suspected that seeing her alone now was unusual. Despite their natural good looks, the whole family was remarkably humble, and generally well liked around town. Never did they flaunt their money or other positive attributes.

Etta caught Lizzie's attention as she and Art drew close. The other girl brightened with recognition.

"Etta! Hey there." To her surprise, Lizzie actually greeted her with a hug. "I haven't seen you since..." she stumbled. "Well-" Left unspoken was that she was referring to Lena's funeral.

"It's been a while," Etta quickly added, hoping not to dwell on the subject.

Lizzie nodded, happy to do likewise. "How have you been?" she asked.

"Keeping busy. Up with a chickens every day."

Lizzie smiled, sympathetically. "Yeah. I can relate." Looking past Etta, she cocked her head to the side. "And who is this?"

Art had been standing behind Etta, not yet sure if he was a part of this conversation. With an encouraging look, she motioned him forward and made introductions.

"How do you do?" he offered his hand to Lizzie, though he looked as though he wanted to be anywhere else just that moment.

"I do just fine, thank you." She accepted his offered hand, but also batted her eyes in a way that Etta did not quite appreciate.

Art did not notice, as he was concentrating on not slumping his shoulders or looking at his feet. It had the effect of making him even taller than usual.

"Are you from out of town?" Lizzie asked.

"Originally, sure," Art replied.

Etta knew him well enough by this point to realize that his answer had intended to be sincere, but Lizzie apparently thought he was being funny. At first, he frowned, thinking that she was laughing at him, but started to warm up when it was clear such was not the case. Etta had noticed something similar occur when he met Helen and Robert for the first time. His shyness was only conspicuous now since he was never so with her.

"We've met before, actually," Art continued. "When you and your father dropped off the ice cream maker at Gregory's shop."

Lizzie's eyes widened in recognition. "That was you? Yes. Gregory mentioned that he had a fella working for him."

Art nodded. "I'm the fella. I was wearing a welding mask at the time so you probably didn't see my face."

"That was unfortunate..."

Alright, that's enough, Etta thought, narrowing her eyes.

"So, the ice cream." Etta cut in, as subtly as she could. "I'm looking forward to that."

"Oh, yes," replied Lizzie, as though she had forgotten that Etta had been standing there.

She recovered so quickly, Etta might not have noticed had she not been paying attention.

"As if the days weren't full enough," Lizzie continued. "My brothers usually work the machine but we've been making so much that I had to take a few shifts myself. Mostly, I drive around with Daddy to deliver to the shops."

"Is that the truck with the picture of the cow in front of the fence?"

Lizzie nodded. "That's the one. Mama painted it herself. It's just a shame that the silly things make such a mess of it. This last week with the heat was especially bad. I swear I spend more time cleaning up melted ice cream than anything else.

"Well that's funny. You'll never guess what Art does..."

In hindsight, Etta could not rightly say where the sudden urge had come from. Part of it had been a genuine desire to talk with an old friend, but there had been little in the way of catching up. Neither had she intended for it to become a sales pitch, which it nearly had. She simply suggested that the Hunleys would have an easier time of moving their wares in a truck that could keep things cold.

That such a product did not currently exist was of little concern. After all, she happened to know a young man who was quite capable in such matters. While Etta had not *sold* anything, Lizzie was confident that her father would be interested in what Art had to say. By no means was it a sure thing, but it was certainly encouraging. The sudden appearance of Mabel Flanders dampened Etta's spirits, but only temporarily. Before Lizzie could be pulled into a new conversation, she and Etta made tentative plans to meet for lunch sometime soon to discuss more.

Art shook his head with a half-smile on his face.

"I was only kidding before about meeting quota," he teased. "I wouldn't recommend going into business with my father."

"It can't be worse than selling eggs," she replied.

"You might feel differently after you've met the man."

Etta was almost giddy as she looped her arm around Art's. "I think I might like being a saleswoman. Does he have an open position in the City?"

"Sure. You can have mine. Think I'd rather stay here, anyhow."

Grinning, Etta dismissed the remark as nothing more than playful banter. Had her head not been in the clouds at that moment, she might have noticed his serious expression. Her attention was further divided by a sudden thought, and she turned back around.

"Be sure to say 'hello' to your sister, Ros, for me," she called. "I hope she's doing well."

Lizzie turned from Mabel for a moment, looking confused. With a shrug, she replied, "You can tell her yourself. She's just over there."

That's odd. How did I miss her?

Still grinning, Etta hugged Art's arm more tightly and began searching in the direction Lizzie had pointed. It took a moment, but eventually she spotted Ros.

Her grip on Art's arm tightened, but not in affection this time. Etta froze and her smile vanished. At first he must have thought she was trying to get his attention, because he was smiling when he turned to face her. It was only after he noticed her expression of disgust and fear that he turned serious.

"Something wrong?" he asked.

It can't be... she thought, still staring across the yard.

Ros was over by the lower level of the barn with a group of other girls, carefree and enjoying herself. Standing next to her, casually drinking one of Enoch's beers was a handsome, young man, with slicked blonde hair.

"Etta, what is it?" Art asked, growing concerned.

Walter was at the party.

She did not respond immediately, and continued to stare at the musician. For his part, Walter was having a drink, laughing, and joking with an easy smile on his face. A smile that faded as soon as he made eye contact with Etta.

At first, she stared back, unable to move. Then, realizing what was happening, she was suddenly compelled to get out of sight. Turning, she quickly walked to the far side of the nearest outbuilding. Art followed, confused. Once more, he asked her what was wrong.

The man that robbed CasinO and attacked me is having a drink.

That would have been the short answer and she almost said it. Instead, she said nothing. She had hoped to keep that whole matter quiet and let it lie without further incident. The conversation with Officer Hoffman and his veiled threat was still fresh in her mind. Beyond that, she knew the violence that Walter was capable of.

Meanwhile, Art continued to watch her, concern plain on his face. Etta remained frozen with indecision, glad to remain concealed behind the smaller barn.

"I – ah – just felt ill for a moment," she lied. "I'm better now."

Art looked skeptical, but did not press the issue. Once Etta had composed herself, she suggested that they get back to the party. Careful to steer away from where she had seen Walter, they eventually met up with Helen and Mildred, who were back on smiling and laughing terms. Daniel and Robert were next to them but having a separate conversation. Art joined them as they pressed a fresh beer into his hand.

Etta saw Walter again a few minutes later, but was less stricken this time. This town was her home after all, and she was surrounded by friends. At first, she kept a vigilant eye on him, making sure that he remained on the far side of the party. If he was watching her, he was not being obvious about it. Gradually, Etta looked for him less and less until she eventually lost sight of him altogether.

The evening carried on, and everyone grew more relaxed. So much so that Robert began telling jokes of mildly questionable taste. Still, they got a laugh out of everyone who was not sober, prudish, or both. The sky grew darker, and everyone began to migrate toward the ring of stones that contained the cooking fire.

With evening darkness upon them, someone tossed a few logs on the cherry red coals. They charred and smoked and were soon wholly engulfed. Orange and yellow light illuminated the yard and cast flickering shadows against the walls of the barn.

In a genuinely casual motion, Etta leaned into Art while they stood, watching the flames. He responded in kind, looping his arm across her shoulders and gave her an affectionate squeeze. Etta noted with some satisfaction that she did not have to be quite as obvious about her hints. Helen stood on her other side, likewise leaning against Robert. After a few moments, she reached out and squeezed Etta's hand, favoring her with a wink.

They all watched the fire for a short while, listening to the steady rush of air, punctuated by random pops and hissing from the burning wood. It served as a prevailing backdrop for the scattered islands of conversations.

The crowd had started to thin by this hour. After all, dawn was inevitably coming, and sooner than anyone might like. Helen yawned loudly and said she was ready to go home. Robert nodded and quickly downed the last dregs of his beer. The sudden motion caused him to stagger his feet. Etta frowned. Seeing her look of disapproval, Robert waved her off in a pacifying manner.

"Not to worry. I'm staying at the Saunders' place tonight," he said.

Etta nodded and bid them a good night.

Before leaving, Helen approached Etta and gave her an affectionate hug. "G'night, Chicken Farmer."

Etta sighed, glad that they had moved past their most recent tiff. She watched her friend and cousin walk away together, the very picture of contented bliss.

Leaning against Art, she let all other concerns fall from her mind, save for the time. It was growing late and it had been a long day. Tomorrow would be more of the same, and she just wanted to enjoy the next few hours to their fullest.

"You're quiet," she said to Art. Around the fire, the various conversations continued, so they might as well have been alone.

"Just thinking about how to stick a refrigerator on a truck," he replied. "Far as I know, it hasn't been done before." He scoffed. "I'm not sure what good it is, to be honest."

Etta frowned since it had largely been her idea. "And, pray tell, just why isn't it any good?" she asked defensively.

Rightly suspecting that her offense was insincere, Art cleared his throat and gave her another affectionate squeeze.

"Not to impugn your idea. Just seems like the Hunleys could make do with a few extra blocks of ice if they're just delivering around town. Doesn't seem worth the effort."

She shrugged, still leaning against him. "Maybe the Hunleys want to deliver *outside* of town. Just because you know how to make the thing work doesn't mean you understand what someone will do with it."

Art looked at her, grimacing in mild horror. For a second, Etta was not sure if he was serious or not – as she found was often the case with Art – until he burst out laughing. "Dear God, why is my father speaking in your voice?"

Etta snickered. "You mind your tongue, now." She was quiet for a moment, before continuing, "Speaking of fathers... mine is out of town."

"Mm hmm," he replied distractedly, eyes intent on the fire.

"For the night," she elaborated.

Etta stared at him meaningfully until he blinked with apparent realization. While the flickering light made it difficult to tell, Etta swore he blushed just then.

"Well, then." He cleared his throat. "Excuse me for just a moment, then shall we start walking?"

She nodded. Art tried in vain to hold his composure, but Etta could see him grin as he turned away. Alone again, her own nerves flared up with excitement. It had been a rather frank invitation on her part, the more she thought about it. Briefly, she rebuked herself, wondering what her mother would think, but eventually decided that, had she been around, Mama would have liked Art. For that matter, Papa would too... once he was around long enough for the matter to come up.

Etta continued watching the fire, thinking about the evening ahead when someone stepped next to her. From his bold familiarity and how close he stood, she assumed that it must be Art.

"That was fast," she said. "I thought you'd be-" Etta cut herself off as she suddenly recognized the oily smell of Vaseline.

"Thought I'd be what?" Walter asked, standing so close that she felt his breath puff against her hair. Etta refused to look at him, hoping that he would somehow just disappear on his own accord. Perhaps it was some other overly bold young man with cheap hair product. But she knew that voice. Glancing out the corner of her eye, she caught the unmistakable shine of blonde hair, and there was no denying who it was.

Arms folded, she leaned away, but her feet remained stubbornly rooted to the spot. Silently, she cursed her legs for failing to obey her commands. For good measure, Walter hooked an arm around her back and held her tightly, in a parody of how she had been standing with Art a moment earlier. Looking around, she tried to catch the attention of a familiar face, but everyone was otherwise distracted. The solitude that she and Art had been enjoying a moment earlier now served to isolate her.

In the back of her mind remained an overpowering urge to avoid a scene. She did not want the details of her last meeting with Walter to be known. At the same time, she could not resist a natural urge to try to squirm free of his grip.

"Relax," he continued, sounding annoyed. "I just want to talk. Let the other rubes enjoy their night." Still holding her fast, he turned his head away to take another swig of beer.

Enoch will have to burn that bottle. There's no saving it.

Etta stiffened, and craned her neck away as much as she could.

"Don't call them 'rubes,'" she shot back, teeth clenched.

Walter smirked. "Why not? They are." His voice was mildly slurred and he leaned on her as much as he held her in place. "I don't mean it in a bad way. A lot of my favorite people are rubes. My cousins, who make great moonshine. And my uncle... who I think you've already met."

Etta felt her heart start beating faster. Already, she sensed the direction this conversation was going and did not care for it.

Taking her silence for a denial, Walter continued. "No? You'd recognize him if you saw him. Blonde like me. Uniform. Badge. Told me an interesting story a few weeks ago. Apparently, someone had ideas about the CasinO's recent misfortune. He said some skinny, blonde thing came in pointing fingers."

Walter finished his beer before tossing the bottle in the fire. Sparks and embers flared up from the place where it landed. While his attention was off of her, Etta took the opportunity to try and push him away. She earned a few inches of space, but quickly lost it when he pulled her back.

"None of that now," he said, more annoyed than before. "Just sit tight. I want to make a couple of things clear. I'm still a little salty about that matter with my trumpet case. Spent a few hours in the water, looking for it. Thought I'd lose my teeth for how they were chattering. Now, I'm willing to let that go, but if you can't keep your mouth shut about what you *think* you know, I-"

"Help you?" a new voice interrupted.

Walter sighed in frustration. "Listen friend, can ya piss off for a minute?" he said over his shoulder without paying any particular attention to the new speaker. "I'm havin' a conversation with my lady friend here."

"Etta? You know this guy?" She recognized the voice now, though it was pitched deeper than she was used to.

As Walter turned, his grip loosened and she looked as well. It was Art, but there was none of his usual quiet shyness. Something stirred behind his eyes that Etta had not seen in him before. Unsure whether Walter was a friend or not, Art hesitated to act, but rightly suspected that something was wrong.

"Matter of fact, she does know me," Walter answered.

"I'd like to leave now," Etta said at the same time.

"Excuse me," Walter said as he tightened his grip on her shoulder. "I wasn't finished."

Art stepped closer as Etta's discomfort became obvious.

"Matter of fact, I think you were," Art replied as he reached out to grab Walter's shirt collar.

The instant that Art's hands touched Walter, his eyes went wild. Immediately forgetting about Etta, he released her and gave Art a hard shove in the chest with both hands.

"Don't touch me!" he snarled.

Not expecting it, Art stumbled backwards but managed to keep his grip. It happened so quickly, Etta could do nothing but remain still. Walter tripped over her feet. The two men went to the ground in a tangle, which caught the attention of nearly all those present. Just about every conversation around the fire abruptly stopped at the same time.

So much for not making a scene.

At first, there were a few quiet chuckles from the other attendees. They clearly thought this was some good natured tussle among friends; a minor grievance combined with alcohol. Not exactly good manners, but neither was it cause for alarm.

"Get off me!" Walter yelled.

That's when the first real punch was thrown. As it landed, Etta was reminded of working at the butcher shop. It was the same solid, wet, *thunk* sound a side of beef would make from being dropped onto the cutting block. Art had a distinct advantage in size, but Walter made up for it with sheer ferocity. The two of them grappled, rolling on the grass and arms swinging. It continued until Art realized that Walter was smaller than he was. Getting his arms between them, he delivered a solid shove, sending Walter skidding along the ground.

By now, Daniel McCormick and the Kovaks boys had approached from the other side of the fire. Getting between Art and Walter, they eyed the latter with caution. Walter prepared to charge again, but seeing them, he hesitated. His chest was heaving as he rose to his feet. He was almost ready to keep swinging, despite being outnumbered, but relented in the end. Contenting himself to spit at their feet, Walter stormed off. Before disappearing into the night, he detoured to an out-of-the-way tree, and angrily snatched up his trumpet case. Only then did he leave for good.

After Walter was finally out of sight, Etta looked to Art. She found him in the same spot, covered in dirt with blood dripping out of his nose. Leaning with his hands on his knees he swayed in place, as his eyes swept over the ground. Confused, but still shaken up from the recent excitement Etta took a step towards him.

"You alright?" she asked.

"My glasses fell off," he replied. "Can you help me find them?"

She nodded, even though he was not looking at her. Turning her own eyes to the ground, her shaking hands touched them a moment later.

"Here," she said. "I think the frame is bent though."

Art frowned, taking them from her. After briefly trying to bend them back into shape, he returned them to his face, wincing as they came to rest on his nose, which still trickled blood.

"At least the lenses are okay." Art sighed, beginning to resemble his old self.

Daniel approached and handed a handkerchief to Art.

"Hey, what happened there?" he asked.

"To be honest, I'm not entirely sure," Art replied, bringing the handkerchief to his face and giving Etta a pointed look.

Daniel followed his attention, and Etta froze where she stood. Looking between the two of them, she was still not quite ready to explain the entire story and gulped.

"He was getting fresh," she replied simply.

When it was clear that she was not going to elaborate, Daniel grunted. "Dirty move, hitting a guy with glasses. Should've at least given you a chance to take 'em off."

"Yeah, I got lucky there. They fell off when I hit the ground."

"Should have shoved him off sooner than you did," Daniel said. "That guy was smaller than you, but he really had the anger behind him."

"I'm a little out of practice. Haven't had a fight with one of my brothers in a few years." Art gave Daniel a wan smile to let him know he was joking as he dusted himself off.

Daniel chuckled. "I hear ya. You'd never guess it, but Robert and I used to fight like cats."

Etta frowned as Art worked his jaw, as though testing it.

"Come on," she said. "Let's get you cleaned up."

Daniel nodded and clapped Art on the shoulder as the couple left.

Art did not limp, but his movements were sluggish. Etta only hoped that it was more due to the beer he had been drinking than a knock to the head. The normal walk back to her farm took longer than usual, and they remained silent for most of it. It gave her a chance to reflect on just how random and unexpected Walter's appearance had been. After their altercation outside CasinO, she thought that he would continue traveling with the band and that would be the last she would hear of him. Apparently, not only was his uncle a cop, but he was also cousins with the Brandelsons. The uncertainty of it all left her with a lingering disquiet.

Finally reaching the house, Etta guided Art to the kitchen, where she used one of her precious matches to light the kerosene lantern instead of attempting to light a stick from the fire. In the yellow glow, she could see that Art's face was red and puffy. Crusted blood stuck to his upper lip. Fortunately, now that she could see it more clearly, it looked like it had not actually been broken. On the other hand, she could also see his clear look of annoyance.

"So, what was that really about?" he asked directly.

Etta sighed. Instead of answering, she grabbed a clean rag and dunked it in the water pitcher. Ice would have been better, but of course they had none. Wringing it out, she handed it to Art for his face. He nodded thanks before resuming an expectant stare. Etta sat down, and after another long moment, finally relented.

"His name's Walter. I met him last month when his band was playing in town. The short version is: he robbed CasinO and threatened me to keep quiet about it."

"You didn't go to the police?"

"Actually, I did. Turns out, his uncle is a cop. Basically told me to keep quiet too."

"Yikes. That could cause some grief for you." Art shifted his elbow so that he could rest his head on his hand while holding the wet rag to his face. He sighed as he settled into the new position. "I guess I don't blame you for not wanting that known."

Etta retrieved another rag, and gently wiped the dried blood from Art's lip.

"Sorry you got punched," she said.

Art shrugged as much as he could manage without disturbing the position of his head.

"It was a nice evening up until then," he smiled weakly and extended his free hand across the table. Etta reached out to clasp it. Despite the unfortunate circumstances, she appreciated the moment. Art was a good catch. Never pushy or presuming. Perhaps it was misplaced, but she felt guilty over his injuries. Maybe they would not have happened if she had done something differently.

Art's expression suddenly changed as a thought occurred to him.

"Does the owner of the restaurant know?"

"I don't think so," she replied, frowning.

"You didn't tell him?"

"We're not on great terms," Etta shrugged. "He's kind of a prick, actually."

Art raised an eyebrow at that. She was mildly surprised herself. Apparently, her tongue was looser than usual. Not that she was a prude, but neither had she spoken like that in front of him before.

"Language," he scolded playfully.

Etta grinned at the look he gave her: taken aback yet mildly impressed. Art's face turned thoughtful and serious again.

"I figure the owner could be in a better position to make life difficult for Walter. And no one ever need know how he found out. Could have been one of the kitchen staff or a customer overhead."

Etta had not thought of that before, and it was worth considering.

"I should get going," Art said as she yawned.

"Maybe you should stay here. I'm not sure you ought to walk back home tonight," Etta replied.

"Really, it's not as bad as it looks."

"I mean, if you don't want to..."

Her voice trailed off meaningfully and a goofy grin returned to Art's face, as her full meaning set in.

"In separate beds," she quickly added.

His grin evaporated. "Of course," he replied after a heartbeat.

She nodded, satisfied, but then made it clear that she had left unspoken, the word “after.”

Chapter 24
Art

At first, he felt surprisingly good, and wondered if perhaps he had dreamed many of the events from the previous night – both the good and the bad. It was not until he started moving around that each and every new ache began to assert itself. Despite the discomfort, he could not help but smile at the memory.

The evening had ended well. Having only kissed until now, it was clear that both of them were craving an opportunity to be alone without interruption. And they certainly made the most of it. Art's pains were soon forgotten as Etta guided his hands to her body. Any lingering timidity or undo caution was soon dropped along with their clothes. Her dress, his shirt, and soon his pants all mingled in a disorderly heap on the bedroom floor.

In the darkness, Etta had not been shy about her own hands either. While Art had only done this sort of thing a few times before, the way she responded to his touch and clutched his hair in her fingers just felt right. No thoughts were spared for troubling distractions. For a time, the rest of the world might as well have not existed except for two people. There was only Etta's body, soft and warm, pressed against his.

Art's nose suffered one or two errant bumps, but it was a small price to pay.

True to her word, Etta had moved to the adjacent bed, but not before they initially fell asleep together, limbs tangled, and contentedly spent.

She was well into her chores by the time he awoke the next day. Despite the physical discomfort, Art felt better than he had in a long time. Finding Etta out by barn, he protested that he would have helped if only she asked. Etta claimed to still harbor some guilt over his recent injuries, and letting him sleep helped to balance the scales in her mind.

An urgency seized him when he realized the time. He had to get back to the cottage. Even so, they took their time saying goodbye. In fact, what was intended to be a single kiss quickly escalated. If not interrupted by the crowing rooster, maybe ten paces away, they might have returned to the house to act on it.

They resolved to meet later. With an affectionate yet restrained, goodbye kiss, he started down the road at a brisk walk.

Returning home after being out all night was one thing. Ralph had done it more than once. Even though Art had none of his brother's so-called charm, he was reasonably confident that his parents might let the matter go. On the other hand, they would not so easily dismiss his new menagerie of bruises. It was abundantly clear that he had either been in a fight or fallen down some stairs onto a dirt pile. His nose, especially, remained swollen and declared for the entire world that it had recently been punched.

Over the course of his trek back to the cottage, he came up with an explanation that retained just enough truth to be plausible, yet glossed over some of the more incriminating pieces. Specifically with regards to his lady friend. While he was beginning to realize that such a conversation would need to occur at some point, it could wait until his head was not so out-of-sorts.

The sun continued to climb and his pace steadily increased as he drew closer. It was full light, but still early enough that there was a chance, however remote, that he might sneak in and hide the fact that he was out all night.

To his dismay, he found the front door locked. Noticing that the upstairs bedroom window was open, he considered attempting to climb up. Sighing, he dismissed the idea, and resigned himself to the original plan. Going around back, he reviewed the story he had cooked up during his walk, and focused on the key details. Approaching the kitchen door, there was no mistaking the sounds and smells of breakfast being cooked. Dread mounted as he anticipated his parents' reaction.

This was it. Both his mother and father looked up as Art opened the door. Their expressions simultaneously went from surprise, to scathing, and finally to concerned in a matter of seconds. Stunned silence ensued as they took in the state of his face.

“Good morning,” Art said, in a tone that he hoped sounded pitiable.

"And what happened to you?" his father asked, not sure what to make of the sight before him.

"Got in a small fight," Art said simply.

George grunted, as if to say, "A fight? You?"

Up to this point, his parents were acting in near unison. It was only now that their responses changed. His mother remained concerned yet horrified, while his father appeared mildly impressed.

"Who did you get in a fight with?" George asked, a subdued grin on his face.

Art shrugged. "Some local." He hoped his short answers and reluctance to elaborate would head off additional questions.

"Heh. How about that?" George was clearly more amused than anything else.

Luciana gave him a sharp look of rebuke. "George! This is no laughing matter. Just look at him."

He waved her off. "Oh, he's fine. Back home, safe and sound. Adams men are made of harder stuff." George's grin only broadened as he regarded their son.

Of the two of them, Art had been expecting more interrogation from his father. However, he had underestimated the tenacity and fire of an Italian mother whose child had been threatened. Luciana remained implacable, working herself into a veritable froth as she fussed over Art's discolored face.

"Really now! Our son was accosted by some local."

George sighed, but toned down his grin at least. "So, how about it, boy? Who did it?"

Art shook his head. "It was dark." This was technically the truth.

George held his hands palm-side up, and looked to his wife as if to say, "What more do you want?"

Her scowl remained, but at least she was unlikely to raze the town over it. "And how is this going to look to the Kennedys?"

George was taken aback, having not considered that. Attempting to close the matter, he finished by saying, "Alright then. Art, let's keep future hell-raising to a minimum, shall we?"

With relief, though trying not to show it, Art reluctantly nodded. "It won't happen again," he muttered, eyes downcast.

His mother sighed and shook her head. Gently but firmly, she turned Art by his chin in examination. Suddenly, her brows furrowed.

"So is that why you never dropped off the meatballs with Gertrude?"

Art's breath caught. He had completely forgotten about the food basket. Realizing that his mother had offered an explanation, he jumped on it.

"Yeah. Sorry."

Rightly sensing that he was not telling the whole story, Luciana squinted. Art's relief briefly turned to guilt under her probing gaze. Lying was not something he was accustomed to, especially to his mother. Still, as she returned to the stove, his father gave him a wink, as if this were a milestone worth celebrating.

With her back to them, his mother continued. "Franklin is much improved so we're going to have dinner with them tonight. Do clean yourself up before Dorothy sees."

Art frowned. That complicated things. It was a major snag in so many of his plans, and he had no clean solution for it. Once again, he scolded himself for procrastinating and considered calling the whole thing off here and now. It would cause a mess, certainly, but perhaps it was one he could simply endure.

"Before she sees what?" Ralph asked, entering the kitchen still wearing his nightclothes.

He was up early today. That was odd. No one spoke, but George motioned towards Art and resumed beaming with pride now that Luciana was not looking.

"What, you get in a fight or something?" Ralph asked, in what might have been concern, but his tone suggested otherwise. More likely, he was still half-asleep.

Art said nothing, but shrugged, figuring the less he spoke, the better.

"Good for you," Ralph responded in an automatic tone without inflection that conveyed an utter lack of interest. Ralph rubbed his eyes and yawned. Thankfully, he was in no mood to pry.

Art breathed a quiet sigh of relief and then returned to his thoughts. The news about the evening's dinner plans put a wrench in things. Maybe this was as good a time as any. After all, he had survived the inquiry over his face and all-nighter. He opened his mouth, about to state his intentions, but Ralph spoke first.

"Hey, Art, is my car going to be finished soon, or what?" He stifled another yawn.

Dammit.

Ralph looked up, blinking, and too late noticed their father's abrupt change in demeanor. No longer was George beaming.

"What's wrong with your car?" he asked, in a tone that was deceiving in its candor.

"Well, it-" Ralph started to answer but George cut him off.

Abruptly, he turned his attention to Art. "And why is he asking you?"

Art froze, staring at the table with his lips pressed into a thin line. He had not anticipated this turn of events.

Stupid. Damn. Ralph.

"He-" Ralph attempted to answer, but George cut him off again.

"I'll get back to you," he said, maintaining an icy stare at Art. "You wreck his car or something?"

Art gulped, unable to come up with a lie. He had managed, up until now, by providing only limited information, and letting his parents reach their own conclusions. Such goodwill was now gone. This was a direct, compelling question.

Without thinking, he just responded. "Actually, I'm fixing it."

George set down his newspaper, and looked Art full in the face. Though his expression remained neutral, it was clear that he was tense.

"And how did you come to be fixing Ralph's Ford?" he asked evenly, despite his apparent suspicion.

"Because he took it to the shop I'm working at." Art surprised himself with just how much he did not care about what happened next. When Ralph had threatened to intentionally reveal the nature of Art's employment to their father, it had carried real weight. That had only been a few weeks ago. Now that it had actually happened, he found he was more concerned with the shiner on his face, his bent nose, and when he might get another chance for some time alone with Etta.

"You're turning wrenches again?" George demanded.

"I am," Art replied simply. Beneath the new assortment of aches and bruises, he noticed just how hungry he was. Without further elaboration, he snatched up one of the small sausages from the table and popped it into his mouth.

While Art did not look at his father, it was clear that George was glaring at him. His face turned red at this apparent act of defiance, yet he was unsure of how to respond.

"So that's where you've been disappearing to all day without explanation?" It was his mother now. "You know, you missed more than a few family dinners. Not to mention time with Dorothy."

That reminded George of another thing to scold Art for. "That's right. And she isn't marrying a blue-collar assembly line worker. I've told you, we don't do that kind of work anymore."

Art stopped chewing for a moment, and turned his head up to face his father. George was an alarming shade of red, but Art only shrugged.

"You're quitting," George said in a much louder voice. "Today." Confident that his orders would be followed without any further prodding, George returned his attention to his morning newspaper, which might as well have been a brick wall.

The table was quiet for a long moment before his mother turned around, and regarded the newspaper wall with an icy stare.

"Your youngest son walks in the house, covered in bruises after being out all night, and you laugh it off. Someone mentions a damaged car and suddenly you're concerned?"

A poorly concealed sigh escaped from the far side, but the wall remained in place. Shaking her head, Luciana returned her attention to the stove.

As expected, George had forbidden Art from working at the shop any more. For a brief moment, he was genuinely concerned. It faded as soon as he actually thought through what it would mean to defy his father. What was the worst that could happen? He would get kicked out of the house? Unlikely as that was, it seemed he had some options to call upon that he did not have before. It was a strangely liberating feeling. Of course, it was by no means ideal, especially long term. In a truly strange way, Art found that, despite everything, he actually wanted his father's approval.

Dismissing the issue of his fiancée for the moment, he focused on how to remain at Gregory's. He liked the work, and promises had been made that he intended to fulfill. There was also Etta's refrigerated truck idea. That would be a fun challenge. Not just the technical aspect but also the scale of it. Though, getting a small refrigeration unit from his father could be an issue... or would it? Suddenly, it occurred to him that, a neat solution might just have presented itself.

"I can't quit," Art said simply.

George slowly lowered the newspaper, clearly reluctant to do so after having already decided the conversation was over.

"Excuse me?" he said, tone implying that Art should reconsider this subject.

"This is going to hinder some local prospects for Adams Refrigeration," Art replied. He had chosen these words carefully, knowing their particular importance to his father.

This was not lost on George, whose eyes narrowed. Suspicious, but also curious.

"Explain."

"I *have* been turning wrenches, but it's part of a local opportunity that I've been running down. As a matter of fact, I planned to bring it up with you today."

"Is that so? One might say that's rather convenient."

"I wasn't sure it was going to work out before, and didn't want to come to you with a half baked solution."

"But now you have a *whole* baked one?" George was still skeptical.

Art nodded. "Yes. Well... most of one. The – ah – *clients* are ready to commit, and Gregory can begin work just as soon as we get one or two current obligations fulfilled."

Art cast a meaningful glance at Ralph, who was looking for an opportunity to leave the table, and did not care for being drawn back into the conversation. George spared him only a quick glance, remaining focused on Art. He had heard all manner of poorly conceived business plans and outright scams over the years, and Art had no doubt that he was, at this very moment, preparing to root out every flaw.

Art proceeded to describe the concept for the refrigerated truck, and his rough plan for how it might work. George was ready to dismiss the idea as too much of a risk and Art was afraid it might be dead in the water. After sketching out some crude drawings to describe the operation, he held his breath while his father considered it.

After an interminable pause, George nodded. "Alright then."

Art could hardly believe it, and almost thought he had misheard. "Really?"

His father took a long pull from his coffee before looking at him. "Yes. Of course, you're a little fuzzy on some of these details, and I'll want you to get it from the customer in writing, but this is a good start."

Then, in a moment so rare that Art was stunned, his father actually smiled at him, and clapped him on the shoulder in genuine affection. Unfortunately, it was on the shoulder that had been slammed into the ground barely twelve hours earlier, and he winced in pain. But his pride was a powerful salve. George's smile only faded when he returned his attention to Ralph who had born witness to the entire exchange with incredulity.

Art knew all too well the look that Ralph made then: shoulders slumped and bordering on shame. He almost sympathized with him. On the other hand, in all their years together Ralph had never missed an opportunity to rub salt in any of Art's wounds. Not once. Thus, it was with a certain satisfaction that when Ralph met his eyes, trying to come to terms with what had just happened, Art simply grinned.

"No." Gregory offered no caveats or explanation.

As he was with most things, he stated it simply and directly. Clearly expecting that to be the end of the discussion, he returned his attention to the drawer he was leafing through. Frankly, Art was surprised more than anything.

"You haven't heard the whole thing," he replied.

"I think I know enough to make a decision. You need to cut apart a truck, which we don't have, to tie in a refrigerator, which I don't know how it works, to build a contraption that seems unnecessary. That's a lot of unknowns, and I've got plenty of work as it is."

Art's earlier confidence was slipping. After the successful pitch to his father, it occurred to him that Gregory and the Hunleys also needed to agree to the deal. If either refused, the whole thing was off, and he had no excuse to continue working at the shop. Of the two, he considered Gregory to be a sure thing and was not prepared for an argument. Thus, he struggled to come up with something on the spot.

"I just… I thought this would interest you."

"Oh, it interests me plenty," he replied, closing the drawer and returning to the workbench. Frowning, he patted down his pockets, growing more annoyed as whatever he was looking for failed to materialize. At last, he touched his head and found his goggles resting there. With a roll of his eyes he muttered, "Of course."

They were nearing completion of the hay baler. The Anchor had been finished the previous week, and much of the time since then was preparing the machine to accept it. Then, realizing the Anchor had become too heavy to lift by hand, they spent another day rigging up a block and tackle on one of the overhead timbers. Once Gregory finished grinding down a few tight spots, they would be ready to install it. Or, as he had put it, "Just need to massage it a little bit."

Gregory continued, "Three days each week isn't nearly enough time for something like what you're saying."

Art was growing frustrated by his mentor's intractability. "I can work more," he offered, sensing an opportunity. "I'd come here every day if you let me."

"I know you would. And you've been doing great work, but-" he was quiet for several seconds. At first, Art thought he might be composing his thoughts, but his expression was oddly vacant and his eyes were unfocused behind the goggles. For a moment, Art nearly forgot about their conversation and wondered what was happening. Before he could become concerned, Gregory shook his head and carried on as if nothing was amiss. "I don't want you in here alone."

"What if we hired someone? I'd even take a cut in pay."

Gregory sighed. "Listen, Art. I do this to keep busy. I don't need to work full time anymore, and I don't want to. I like seeing my daughter and granddaughter. Plus, I do repairs, not new inventions. And – *and* – you haven't even spoken to the Hunleys about this, have you?"

"As a matter of fact, I have," Art replied. Strictly speaking, it was true. Then, without even thinking about it, he added, "Owen Hunley is ready to go."

That was stretching the truth to the point of breaking. Lizzie had been fairly confident that her father would be interested... after she told him about it. Which she very plausibly *might* have done by now. Nothing approaching a commitment had even been mentioned. Immediately, Art feared he had overplayed his hand, and Gregory was going to call him on it. Instead, and to his surprise, Gregory considered it.

"Has he? Hm."

For a second, Art thought of backing out and apologizing for his exaggeration. Something made him keep his mouth shut. Eventually, Gregory assumed a thoughtful expression and nodded to himself.

"You know, he's a former Navy man, same as me. Not prone to taking odd risks or doing things out of the ordinary."

Again, Art made no reply, sensing that Gregory was close to agreeing. Close, but not quite there yet. Art chose his next words with care. One last card to play.

"If you bring on another worker, the two of us can do practically all the work, leaving you to spend more time with your granddaughter. You'd be our manager, and could get your hands into the mechanical stuff as much or as little as you care to."

For years, Art had quietly rolled his eyes at his father's patented Sales Smile and the disarming grin that accompanied it. He always considered it insincere. Now, so close to achieving his own small victory, he could not help but see the utility of it.

Instead of answering right away, Gregory motioned for Art to insert the pin to retain the Anchor to its place in the hay baler. Art did so and waited patiently for Gregory to finish thinking it over. It went on for so long that Art was mildly concerned that he had forgotten about it. With some effort, the two of them rolled the hay baler outside where there was more room.

A moment later, Gregory was in position next to a lever and motioned for Art to start the engine. Art had been looking forward to this moment since the beginning. Now that it was upon him, however, he was almost too distracted waiting on Gregory's reply to enjoy it.

That changed as soon as the engine kicked over. Loud as it was, it was impossible to think about anything else. Gregory slowly pulled the lever, and the large leather belt started to turn. He backed off once or twice, concerned that the Anchor would live up to its name, and get stuck. Unable to talk over the din, Gregory pointed to the oilcan, which Art picked up.

Squirting a generous amount into the Anchor's track, Gregory waved him to stand clear, and resumed pulling on the lever. The belt started to turn again with no binding or any other snags. The Anchor moved back and forth along its track in smooth operation.

Grinning wildly, Art looked at Gregory, who was laughing. Victory. After a few minutes of letting the machine run through, and satisfied that it was working again, Gregory disengaged the lever, and Art shut the engine off. Standing back, the two of them folded their arms and took a moment to savor and appreciate what they had accomplished.

"So who did you have in mind?" Gregory asked without preamble.

Art had gotten so wrapped up in the hay baler that he was the one who had forgotten what they were talking about. "Pardon?" he replied.

Gregory looked at him. "I'll agree to bring on more help. But did you have anyone specific in mind? I know you're new in town and all."

"As a matter of fact, there are one or two fellas I could suggest. Pending your approval, of course."

Gregory paused. "Okay. If the Hunleys are on board, so am I."

Art breathed a quiet sigh of relief.

That's two, he thought, and it had been a near thing. Everything depended on the Hunleys being willing to commit to the promises Art had made on their behalf, which seemed no small challenge. With the whole deal at stake, he decided that he could not do it without help.

Chapter 25
Etta

The week leading up to wedding day was long and taxing. Everyone was busy doing their part, and there was much to do. Etta spent a great deal of it biting her tongue.

Most of the last-minute details had fallen to her and Mildred as maid of honor and mother of the bride, but there was plenty of work to go around. While Mildred dealt with the food and prepared the barn, Etta applied the final details to Helen's dress.

Megan continued to seek out Etta for guidance and direction. For sheer practically, Helen's cousin was indispensable for getting everything ready. Beyond that, Etta was growing fond of her company. The difference in the younger girl's disposition from a month earlier was stark, and Etta felt a certain pride at the knowledge that she had contributed to it in some way.

"Thank you so much," she had said to Megan. "We couldn't do this without you."

The younger girl had beamed with the praise, and for a moment she had reminded Etta of Irene. It surprised her just how much she had missed this sort of relationship. On the other hand, Helen was getting the jitters in a bad way. Etta's nerves had been improving in recent weeks, but were strongly taxed in those final days.

"Why are you letting it out so much?" Helen demanded. I haven't gotten *that* big."

"Can you believe Robert wants to ride the ladder truck to the wedding? I told him absolutely not. It's ugly and has no place there."

"Isn't Pastor James just charming? Did you notice that little quip about 'the virtues of chastity?' Gee, I wonder who *that* was meant for?"

The last, Helen had said during the walk home from church, but on that particular topic, she happened to have Etta's sympathy. Pastor James had already refused to marry them, but Etta's least favorite member of the clergy could not let that be the end of it. Mildred must have noticed the thinly veiled, but very public rebuke. Still, she remained silent over it.

Robert of course, had an alternative explanation. "He's bitter about the lack of sex. That's what it is."

"Robert!" cried Mildred. The rebuke was more of a reflex than anything else, as evidenced by the grin she wore.

"No, I'm serious. Freddy down at the station house said he and his wife went to Pastor James for marriage counseling. The man was focused on *very* specific parts of their relationship."

While Etta suspected that her cousin was exaggerating for the sake of a good anecdote, she had to wonder if there was more than a little truth to it. Frankly, she was glad for any distraction from the other concerns in her life. Walter's appearance at the barn party had forced her to acknowledge that he could appear without warning.

For a few days, she considered Art's suggestion to go straight to Mr. Mustache, and tell him what she knew. Inevitably, one excuse or another stayed her feet. It would have been nice if the whole thing simply went away on its own.

Then, during one of the working sessions at the Saunders' house, she overheard Mark talking about how his hours at CasinO had been cut again. According to him, Mr. Mustache was looking quite ragged these days, and was even less enthusiastic about berating his employees.

Despite her poor opinion of him, Etta spent some of her precious leisure time one afternoon to walk over to the restaurant.

On first glance, CasinO was much the same as the night she worked. Upon closer inspection, she noticed telltale signs: there was debris on the floor, as if they were only sweeping a few times a week instead of every night. The tables showed stains that had not been dealt with right away. A single waiter ran around in a near frenzy, apparently the only one on staff. Etta recognized him as the one who knocked into her the night she dropped the plates.

Heading to the office, she thought she would find her one-time boss there, but there was only an empty desk. Looking around, the room showed much of the same neglect as the rest of the restaurant. The safe was closed, though she now knew that it did not actually lock.

Not caring to wait around all day, Etta looked around for a pen and paper, thinking she would leave a note and be gone. The door to the office remained open so she did not hear anyone approach.

"Hey!" cried Mr. Mustache, as he entered the small office.

Etta jumped in surprise.

"What are you doing in here?" he asked, recovering. Recognition slowly formed on his face, followed by a triumphant "Ah ha!" As if he had caught her doing something untoward. "You won't find the safe sitting open for you anymore, Missy. I can promise you that."

Etta was confused. "Beg pardon?"

"Oh, you'll beg alright, once I call the police. They've been pretty useless thus far with apprehending the thief. Seems I have to do their job as well as every other job around here."

Thief?

It occurred to Etta that Mr. Mustache had misinterpreted the sight of her apparently rifling through his desk. On the other hand, she did not have much confidence that the police would give her the benefit of the doubt if called. Especially if Officer Hoffman was the one responding.

"I was only leaving a note," she said, in what she hoped was a disarming tone.

Mr. Mustache scoffed. "Oh, I'm sure. 'Thanks for the cash. See you next month to clean house again.' Didn't think you would be so bold as to try it during the day though." He was quickly becoming agitated and erratic. Etta wanted to simply leave, but he was blocking the door. Furthermore, if she left without first talking him down, she suspected that he would go straight to the police. With her poor luck, Walter's uncle would jump at the opportunity to pin his nephew's crime on her.

Etta raised her hands and spoke as she would to a spooked horse. "Let's just calm down."

He was still red in the face and breathing heavy, but at least he was listening. Now that he was more or less still, Etta could see that Mark had not adequately described the man's sorry state. His signature mustache lacked its usual wax, there were bags under his eyes, and he was harried and exhausted.

"Good," she continued, speaking in a deliberately quiet voice that forced him to relax in order to hear. "If I was here for the money, why would I be fooling around with your desk in the middle of the day? The fact is I was going to leave a note telling you who did take your money."

He frowned, still ready to pin her for the crime, but less confident than he was before. "Well? Out with it," he said.

"I'm willing to bet that you haven't had anything go missing except for when the Rick Leonard band is in town, right?"

Mr. Mustache frowned again, in apparent confirmation. "Are you saying Rick has been robbing me?"

Etta shook her head, continuing. "It's the trumpet player. His name is Walter, and he's the one who took your money. Far as I know, none of the others even know about it."

His expression changed from suspicious to concerned. "The safe is just for show. It doesn't actually lock," he muttered, almost to himself. Then, more loudly, "They're playing here again tonight. If what you say is true…" he trailed off, thinking.

For a moment, Etta was relieved, thinking she had gotten through to him. It was short lived, as his face darkened again.

"That seems like just the kind of nonsense a kleptomaniacal hussy would spout in order to get the heat off of her. Now, get out of my office before I have the police put you away."

Etta groaned in dismay, more frustrated than actually concerned. He moved to one side, allowing her to freely exit the small office. Unlikely as it was that he would actually call the police, it still weighed on her mind for the rest of the day. The walk home was stressful, but if nothing else, at least she had tried to do the right thing.

Helping to make it bearable were Art's visits, which had been increasing in frequency. They often spent the afternoons together, getting the chores done early enough to walk up to the jalopy for a picnic dinner. The two of them had been hitting their stride, often falling into a pleasant banter, while enjoying some much needed rest and – in Etta's case – venting.

It was such a relief to have the ear of someone who was not directly involved in all of the nonsense that was going on. Normally, she could talk to Helen about these things, but that was no help when Helen was the increasingly the cause of them. Etta had been so distracted by her own troubles that it took her some time to recognize that Art was quieter than usual. Which was to say, nearly silent.

"Something on your mind?" she asked casually while they sat in the front seat of the jalopy, watching the landscape. His left arm was draped across her shoulders, and she fit comfortably against his side. He did not answer right away, which she took for a tacit, "yes."

"As a matter of fact, I seem to have a problem that I'm not sure how to tackle."

"If you need me to fix something, I'm afraid you may be in trouble." She grinned at him.

Art made a show of grinning back, but was clearly troubled. "So, what's the matter?" she asked, gripping his free hand with hers.

"Well," he began, "I need to talk to the Hunleys..."

At last, wedding day was upon them. Etta had woken at her usual time to tend the chickens and get a few essential chores out of the way. With Papa's new bookkeeping job, and Etta working for the Van Dycks a few times each week, they had not grown flock this year as they normally would and even sold some of the pullets for extra cash. They had kept just enough egg-layers for Etta to have a respectable breakfast and to start building again once this matter with the taxes was past.

In the privacy of the barn, Etta stripped out of her work clothes and dipped into the washtub. It was usually intended for laundry, and she was only able to fit by sitting with her knees pulled to her chest or dangling her feet over the side. The day was already hot, and her morning work had gotten her sweating something awful. The water was cold enough to make her gasp, but still refreshing.

There would be no avoiding kicking up road dust on her trip to the Saunders' house, so she put on a set of fresh walking clothes and covered the folded dress in a sheet. Before leaving, she stole a quick peek into her usual bag, checking that she had remembered the sewing kit and a few other items for unforeseen emergencies.

As she stepped onto the dirt road, Etta frowned. Papa had not yet returned from Newark. These days, he was only at the farm once a week, or even less. The bookkeeping work was keeping him quite busy. In fact, he skipped last week's visit altogether, but promised to come back for the wedding. After all, the Saunders were practically family.

While there still remained a few hours, Etta wondered if he might not show up and the thought disappointed her. Her recent efforts were paying off, and she and Papa were getting along better than they had in years. Even seeing each other just one day each week, they talked and laughed more than ever.

Maybe now, he would be willing to discuss getting help for the farm He would need it once Etta left. One way or another. While she and Art had not explicitly talked about what would happen after the summer was over, he consistently used the word "we" when discussing his future. Etta still had not told Papa about her plans, but she resolved to do so soon. Not today though. Today was to be a happy occasion.

Such thoughts evaporated upon her arrival at the Saunders' house. Indeed, it was near impossible to think about anything beyond what was immediately before her. As she had predicted, it was a veritable state of chaos, with quite possibly every one of Helen's aunts and female cousins in various states of dress and primping.

Bags and random articles of clothing were draped over practically any surface that could support them. The single mirror in the master bedroom was a highly contested location, with most every woman pressing in for a spot. Helen's cousin Sandra was in the kitchen, applying her makeup using a large metal spoon for a mirror. An act of apparent desperation.

Making her way to Helen's bedroom, Etta was glad she had taken an extra few minutes to do her own makeup at home. Inside, her friend was pacing restlessly.

"*There* you are," Helen said. "Where have you been?"

"Good morning yourself," Etta replied, taken aback by the curt greeting, but willing to let it slide.

As had been the case all week, Helen had nervous energy. With a forlorn hope, Etta attempted to calm things down before they could progress into another fight. After gently laying her dress down on the bed, she turned back to Helen who was determined to provoke a reaction.

"Can we get started already?" she demanded.

"Alright," Etta replied evenly. "What needs to be done?"

Helen looked at her, exasperated. "Everything! I'm still in curlers for goodness sake!"

Etta slumped her shoulders and nearly rolled her eyes in aggravation. "You couldn't even do that much on your own?" She fought to keep her voice even, but could not entirely hide her annoyance.

"Don't use that tone with me. You said you were going to be here early."

"And it *is* early. Instead of complaining, why don't we get started?" Etta's composure slipped, but she was still willing to move on.

Helen, unfortunately, was not finished saying her piece. "I've been waiting here all morning and you just seem completely unhurried." Helen's eyes narrowed as she looked at Etta. "I see you found time to do *your* makeup."

What remained of Etta's calm was quickly breaking down. Had she not been frayed by similar interactions all week, she might have had a chance of keeping her temper in check. Unfortunately, that was not the case.

"You've got a lot of nerve, you know that? Sorry if you couldn't help yourself for one hour while I took a bath so I don't have to come over here smelling like dirt and chicken shit!"

As had happened before, Etta's voice rose as she spoke. From Helen's expression, she was concerned that she had pushed too far again. After all, it was an exceedingly rare occasion that she cursed. Soon, it was clear that Helen was not looking at her, but at something past Etta's shoulder. Groaning, Etta turned around to find several faces poking in, observing the girls' tiff.

"Mind your business!" Etta snapped, slamming the bedroom door closed. Returning to Helen, they regarded each other for a long moment. The interruption had reigned in their respective tempers, but only just. No longer were they yelling, but not for lack of want.

"Sit down. I'll take out your damn curlers," Etta muttered.

For the next hour, they mostly remained silent as Etta tended to Helen's hair and makeup. When they did speak, it was to exchange verbal jabs, which became more creative as time passed. Each of them brought up grievances that neither had thought about in years. Etta herself dug up something from as far back as grade school. To their credit and despite the heightened emotions, it never quite got *mean*.

At last, they ran out of energy for it, and when Helen spoke next she only sounded tired. "Why'd you even bother?" she asked.

Etta had no more desire for a fight and muttered a reply. "Look, I already told you, I was just trying to finish up, so I could focus on you when I came over. I'm sorry I was late."

Helen was shaking her head before Etta even finished. "I meant... it's not like you're going to be here for much longer. Why even wait 'til the fall?"

Etta glanced to the space beneath the door, checking that no one was eavesdropping. "That's uncalled for. I'm here because I want to be. Anyway, you said yourself that you're going to disappear after today."

"That was a joke. Robert and I are only going to be on the other side of the potato field. You're leaving town."

Etta looked to her friend, wondering why she was bringing this up now. After all, Helen had no shortage of friends, and neither had she been particularly concerned when Etta first broke the news. Though Etta thought it was odd at the time, she had ultimately paid it little mind.

Helen continued, “Jakob is hardly around anymore, and Art's place in New York is even farther away than that.”

Etta finally understood. Of course Helen would assume that she only meant to leave town in order to be with Art. Although that had recently become her assumption as well, it was certainly not the main reason. Etta was about to correct Helen when she continued.

“Besides, what if my new neighbors are jerks?”

Etta closed her mouth, and the words she had been forming died on her tongue. Instead, she replied, “What do you mean, ‘new neighbors?’”

Helen turned in her seat to face Etta who remained too surprised to speak.

“Your father is already living in Newark. Why would he keep that house if you leave too?”

In truth, it was not something Etta had considered. All this time, she had assumed that Papa’s trips out of town were temporary. So focused was she on the issue of the tax bill that it had not occurred to her Jakob might have his own plans. Etta grew distressed, suddenly unsure of the very ground she was standing on.

“But that was our family’s house. He can’t just get rid of it.” She said it as if the act of speaking it might make it so.

“Etta...” Helen started, taking care to speak delicately. “It *used* to be. The two of you are all that’s left. Jakob can’t work it all by himself. And he lost his wife, for goodness sake. I don’t think he wants to stay there any more than you do.”

Etta grew more uncomfortable at the mention of her mother. Doubly frustrating was that Helen’s explanation was completely in line with the way her father had been acting. He was not even eating meals in their house anymore. On the increasingly rare occasion that he was around, it was like he was visiting.

Despite all her efforts, they might not be forced from the house, but they would lose it all the same. The very thought of someone else sleeping in Irene’s bed got Etta’s blood running hot.

“You don’t know what you’re talking about,” she said at last. “Papa said he’s going to keep it.”

Helen, sensing Etta’s growing distress, spoke with maddening calm. “You can’t honestly believe that. I mean, if the house is that important to you, why don’t you stay. I’m sure my parents could help you.”

Etta realized that she was clenching her teeth and made an effort to stop. “Do you and Mildred just gossip about my family’s troubles all the time?”

"What?" Helen was taken aback. "What on Earth has gotten into you?"

Etta cinched down the bodice, with more force than was necessary. Helen let out an "oof!" Apparently both in response to the discomfort, but also in surprise that Etta would do such a thing. She was surprised herself, and immediately felt guilty about it.

"You're all done," Etta said tiredly.

Helen made no reply, save to shake her head and leave the room. Alone, Etta stewed in silence.

Helen disappeared into the throng of her female relatives who showered her with compliments and asked about the baby, not even bothering with the pretense of a secret any longer. Etta, not in much of a mood for company, remained in Helen's room, which was the only quiet place in the house. All the while, she continued to think about what her friend had said.

Helen's wrong, she thought at last. *Papa said we would keep our house and that's that.* Etta had nearly convinced herself and pushed the lingering doubt from her mind. What replaced it was guilt over taking it out on Helen. It was her wedding day after all.

Etta might have sought out Megan's company instead, but Helen's cousin was out with the rest of the women. With Mildred running around doing last-minute arrangements, that left Susie, who had latched onto Etta as the only familiar face.

"Are you and my sister fighting?" Susie asked without preamble.

Etta sighed. *Kids...*

"Why do you ask that?"

Susie shrugged. "You usually talk more. And you were yelling."

Etta started to formulate a response, but failed to come up with a short explanation that the young girl would understand. Instead, she simply said, "That happens sometimes. It's grown-up stuff."

"Oh." Susie nodded seriously, as if that explained it completely. They were interrupted as someone else burst into the room.

"Sorry. Sorry. I know I'm late." Lizzie Hunley dropped a bag on Helen's bed and went directly for the mirror. "I had to help my father pack the ice cream for the reception and we got a late start-" she looked around, apparently noticing for the first time that the only other people in the room were Etta and Susie. "Where's Helen?" she asked.

"Out showing off her dress," Etta replied, nodding toward the door. "I'm surprised you didn't see her."

Lizzie shook her head, as though trying to force her thoughts into a semblance of order.

"Right. I'm all frazzled. One of the heifers went into labor, and it was not an easy one. I was up with the veterinarian half the night."

Etta raised her eyebrows at that. Now that she noticed, Lizzie had not yet changed out of her work clothes, which smelled of animal musk. She was barefoot and Etta suspected that there was a pair of mucking boots sitting just outside the front door. The harried girl before her was at complete odds with the well put-together young woman Etta had seen at the barn party.

"Can I get you something?" Etta asked, sympathy plain in her voice.

"Oh, don't mind me," Lizzie protested, but it was halfhearted.

Leaving for a moment, Etta retrieved a small washbasin from the kitchen. Such was the closeness of the house that she and Helen could not help but pass each other, but neither acknowledged the other. Etta sighed, frustrated with the knowledge that it was her own doing.

Growing up, they had often talked about this day, and had such high expectations of it. They were supposed to be sipping wine together, laughing about nonsense, and making bawdy speculations about the honeymoon. Instead, they were avoiding each other at best, and fighting at worst.

Etta returned to the bedroom where Lizzie had changed into her dress. She had, of course, been able to *buy* hers. Calmer now, she thanked Etta for the washbasin and quickly rinsed before starting on her makeup. Outside, the first truck had arrived to ferry women from the Saunders' house to the barn and Etta realized how late the hour was. Ostensibly to save time – but really looking for something to distract from her thoughts – she offered to brush the other girl's hair.

Lizzie grinned and chuckled. "Now I know what the cows feel like."

"I didn't know cows needed to be brushed," Etta replied.

Lizzie started to nod before she remembered that Etta was holding her hair. "It makes them calmer, especially when we have them in the barn for too long."

"I should try that with the chickens," Etta replied. "Maybe they'll be quiet for a change."

The girls commiserated about their respective workload for a while, until Mildred came in to check that they were ready to go. Her gaze lingered on Etta for a few seconds longer than necessary. Cringing, Etta assumed she had heard about the latest fight with Helen.

Soon, the last of them were on the truck heading to the barn.

Upon arriving, Susie, Mildred, and Lizzie went to find Helen, who was basking in the adulation of the other wedding guests. Etta was not quite ready to face her friend yet, knowing that an apology was in order, and instead went off on her own. Most of the other guests had already arrived and she tried to search out some familiar faces.

Suspiciously, a clutch of men gathered around Enoch's kegs, which, they claimed were still mostly full. The Kovaks had set up a simple altar in the main room of the barn where the ceremony would take place. Mildred had also added her own modest but elegant decorations among the rafters and walls. Considering the little bit of money that the family had been able to spare, Etta was impressed by the result.

After exchanging pleasantries with a few family friends, Etta quickly found she was still too distracted for small talk. Hanging off to the side by herself, the minutes dragged on. Normally, being alone did not bother her, but without something to do she grew restless. Compounding this was the fact she had not eaten since dawn.

Thankfully, she spotted Art at last, but barely recognized him. His suit was new and quite dapper on him. Unsure why he went to the trouble to have a suit tailored for the wedding, the effect was dashing all the same. Best of all, he had even gotten a proper haircut.

“Look at you,” she greeted. “Really went for the nines, didn't you?”

Smiling, he returned the compliment with a grin. “Back at you. If I were Helen, I'd put you somewhere out of sight.”

Etta frowned. A moment later, so did Art.

“I mean, because you look nicer than she does.”

Putting a reassuring hand on Art's chest, she replied, “No, I understood that part.” It was her first laugh all day, and it felt good. She attempted to come up with a short, but adequate explanation. “Ah... Helen and I are not talking just now.”

“Something happen?” Art asked, looking confused.

“Nothing exceptional. Just-” She was cut off by the sound of a blaring siren. Rolling up the road alongside the property fence was the fire company's ladder truck. Instead of heavy coats and helmets, the men aboard wore suits. As they came to a stop, the blaring siren was replaced by whooping and hollering from the groomsmen.

Helen's not going to like that, Etta thought, recalling that her friend had specifically forbidden this exact thing.

As the groomsmen hopped to the ground and approached the barn, their unsteady gaits became apparent. Their greetings were too loud, and one of them stumbled a couple times. It was quite clear to Etta, and indeed, anyone with eyes to see, that they had already started the reception wherever they had come from. Robert was in front, walking with his arm draped over Daniel's shoulder. As the truck went to leave, the groomsmen waved and called out to the driver.

"Have fun on your shift. Don't worry, we'll drink your share."

"Don't let the town burn down!" another yelled.

In response, the one on the truck blasted the siren again as he pulled out of sight. Etta allowed herself to smile at the shenanigans once she realized that at least the driver was sober.

One groomsman called out, "Hey, where's Helen? We've got your man here."

"Yeah, better marry him quick, before he falls asleep."

The two laughed raucously. At first, Etta dismissed it as an offhand remark, but then she noticed that Robert was quite unsteady on his feet. The arm over Daniel's shoulder was for support and not simply an act of affection.

"Oh no," Etta groaned, mostly to herself, but loud enough that Art could hear.

"You can say that again," he replied, mirroring the dread in her voice.

Mildred appeared suddenly, grabbing Etta by the arm and ushered her away to relative privacy. Etta had just enough time to steal a final glance at Art, whose concerned expression matched her own.

"The groom is drunk before the wedding has even started, and my daughter is having a fit," Mildred said to Etta in a hushed but imperative tone.

"I believe you are correct on both counts," Etta replied evenly.

"Can you try to calm her down while I get Robert to sober up?"

Etta sighed. *Why do you give me the harder one?*

"Erm... Let me talk to Robert," Etta replied.

Mildred looked to her, and her eyes narrowed with understanding.

"Don't tell me you and Helen are fighting right now."

At first she was surprised, having assumed that Mildred knew about their latest flare-up. Then, Etta wilted. She was not accustomed to being on the receiving end of Mildred's gaze. While she made no overt reply, her silence was clear admission.

Mildred scoffed, and released her arm. "You girls pick the damnedest times to pull this shit!" Storming off towards the barn, she called over her shoulder. "Fine. Go talk to my lush of a son-in-law."

Etta had rarely seen Mildred so worked up. Usually, the older woman was the stout, emotional anchor of the Saunders family as well as Etta's. In twenty years, Etta had never heard her curse and the break in composure was unsettling.

Art approached Etta while she considered what to do next. Looking at him, she held out the bouquet.

"Can you hold this, please?" she said while pushing it into his chest. "I have to try and get the groom sobered up in a hurry."

"What's your plan?" he asked, fumbling with the flowers.

She shrugged. "Coffee, I suppose." It usually served to get her own head on straight.

Etta looked around for the reception area and hoped that it had already been brewed. She was about to walk away, but stopped as Art cleared his throat hesitantly.

"If I could make a suggestion. Try walking him around. Get him breathing heavy if you can. That helps."

Etta regarded his sheepish expression and wondered about his sudden bashfulness. Understanding at last, she cocked her head to one side.

"Recent experience?" she asked, raising an eyebrow.

He shrugged and looked away. "I mean it did help."

Distractedly, she nodded and looked for her cousins. The groomsmen were at the edge of the grassy yard beneath a large tulip tree. Robert sat on a bench cut from a fallen log and held his head in his hands while Daniel watched him with concern. The other two groomsmen stood nearby, clearly untroubled as they shared a hip flask. Etta resisted the urge to scold them and focused on her cousin.

"Robert? You alright?" she asked.

Eyes glazed, he looked up and smiled. "Hey cos. Yer lookin' nice."

"What happened?" she demanded, hands firmly on her hips. "Isn't the stag party supposed to be the night before the wedding?"

"Oh, it was," he replied. "I jus' had a little drink this morning." He held up a hand with his thumb and index finger about an inch apart to indicate just how *little*.

"Yeah," added one of the other groomsmen. "Just a hair from the dog that bit him, y'know?"

He held up the flask after taking a swig as though his meaning were unclear. Now that she was standing closer to him, Etta better recognized Carl Dickerson. She had been unable to place him at first, unusual as it was to see him without his customary bandages. Narrowing her eyes, the events of the previous night started to make sense. Robert was naturally prone to foolishness, but Carl made him look downright cautious by comparison.

Growing up, he was often to be found with one of his arms in a sling, or getting along with crutches. On rare occasions, it was both. Such was the frequency of his injuries that he had the dubious distinction of being able to write with either hand, depending on which one was out of commission at a given time.

Putting him and Robert together, in hindsight, could not help but be a recipe for disaster. Thus, Robert's "little drink" was likely the result of some show of bravado initiated by Carl. With this in mind, Etta thought it was lucky that Robert could even able to keep his eyes open.

Etta glared at Carl, making it clear that no additional input was needed from him. Instead of recoiling as she had hoped, he merely shrugged his shoulders unconcerned. Briefly, Etta wondered what Mildred's secret was, as she probably would have had him cowering in fear. At least he remained quiet.

Turning back to Robert, she was barely able to contain her frustration. "What were you thinking?" she demanded. "You couldn't wait until the reception?" Immediately, she recognized her scolding tone, and hated it. In response, Robert rolled his eyes.

"Geeze, cos. You're not usually such a flat tire."

"Did you know that your bride is inside, crying right now?"

This caught his attention, and the shock served to partially sober him up. It was fleeting and after an unsteady attempt to rise to his feet he sat back down – hard.

"I should go talk to her," he said.

"No. You should dry out enough to say your vows."

Turning to Daniel, she breathed a sigh of relief to see that he was sober, albeit exhausted. He had the look of someone who had been minding his brother for many hours. Forcing calm into her voice, she said, "He needs to be on his feet, in front of the altar in thirty minutes. Can you please walk him around until he can stand on his own?"

Daniel nodded with a tired grimace. Gently but firmly, he patted his brother on the back and urged him to his feet. Robert complied only grudgingly, and shot a look of resentment toward Etta that she had never seen on him before. He mumbled something she could not make out, but strongly suspected that it was unflattering. The look alone cut her deeply.

So, now the bride and groom both hate me.

To Carl and the other groomsman, she said, "Do you know where the chaplain is?"

They had been talking to each other, clearly ignoring Etta. After she made it clear that she was not going away, Carl turned his head just long enough to point somewhere near the barn. Turning around, she spotted the white collar and was relieved to find that the Chaplain was thoroughly un-inebriated.

At least there's that, she thought.

Etta started walking back towards the barn and suddenly remembered her bouquet. A heartbeat later, Art appeared and held it out for her. His expression was sympathetic.

"Everything well?" he asked, handing back the flowers.

"Much as it can be," she replied. "I think I've succeeded in making just about everyone mad at me... except you, I suppose."

Art shrugged. "My brothers have given me a high tolerance. I'm sure, given time, you'll manage." He said it with his usual sincerity.

Even accustomed to it as she was, it took Etta several seconds to realize he was teasing her. She shook her head in disdain, but cracked the tightest of smiles all the same. It faded as Mildred stormed over to her, face twisted with fresh worry.

"What did you say to him?" she demanded. "Why is Robert leaving?"

"It's fine," Etta protested. "I told him to walk around to sober up. He should be dry in a little while."

Mildred took a breath to steady herself. "Alright. Sorry. Helen was absolutely beside herself, but I've gotten her to mostly calm down. I don't know what's going on between the two of you, but you shouldn't spend this time on bad terms."

Etta was about to disagree, but something in Mildred's expression kept her mouth shut. Instead, she nodded and followed her back to the farmhouse. Etta cast a parting look at Art who silently mouthed the words "Good luck."

The Kovaks' had set up the inside of their house for the bridal party to wait out of sight until Helen would make her entrance. While she had already made a point to see as many guests as she could, it now provided a quiet place for her to compose herself in private.

Also in the room were Megan, Lizzie, and Susie. All of them were flustered in appearance, and Etta wondered if Helen's current state of calm was only a recent development. She perked up as Etta and Mildred walked in.

"Well?" Helen asked.

"Everything's fine," Mildred assured her.

Helen was skeptical, but took her mother at her word. For a while, conversation was sporadic. Mildred left once or twice to check on Robert's progress.

"He's getting better, but we should probably delay a few minutes."

Helen did not like that, but at least things would soon be back on track. After a short while, her expression turned from annoyed to uncomfortable and mixed with just a little embarrassment.

"I need to use the necessary... could someone help me with the dress?"

Still feeling guilty over the earlier incident, Etta stood up first. Thankfully, the Kovaks had indoor plumbing. While the washroom was small, it was better than squeezing into an outhouse together. Once they were alone, Helen let out a breath.

"I told him, 'no fire truck.' And then on top of that, he shows up, falling-down drunk."

Relieved to not be the source of Helen's current anxiety, Etta was nonetheless compelled to defend her cousin.

"I suspect you might have Carl Dickerson to blame for both matters."

"I figured as much. Those two are trouble together." Helen shook her head in resignation as she gathered up her skirt and long veil.

She handed the bundle to Etta, who pointedly looked in another direction. After sitting down, Helen was quiet for a while.

In the near silence, she let out a single laugh. "When I pictured how today would go, I never thought about this part."

Etta cracked a grin. "I was thinking something similar before." She frowned, remembering the context and felt guilty again. "Listen... I'm sorry."

Helen frowned, but nodded. "I appreciate that. You have to admit, you've been a little touchy lately. And Mom and I don't gossip. You know how she is. She just worries about people. You especially."

Etta nodded, feeling relieved. She never liked leaving things unsettled with Helen.

"Don't forget your promise," Helen continued. "You're going to tell her." Her expression was serious. While somewhat undermined by the fact that she was sitting on the commode, she gave Etta a hard look.

"I will," Etta replied.

To the relief of the bridal party, Daniel got his older brother to the altar – mostly under his own power. Though, coming up the earthen ramp was a near thing, the ceremony itself had somehow gone off without a hitch. Once the newlyweds said, "I do," they proceeded to make their rounds greeting everyone.

Etta and Art found each other a few minutes later and her fatigue from the morning must have been apparent.

"Doing alright?" he asked.

"Ask me again later."

The rest of the afternoon was not, by any means, a dull event. The entire church ensemble had turned out, playing a much more upbeat set than their usual Sunday repertoire. Enoch's kegs drained quickly and he was obliged to bring out the cases of bottles he had brought in reserve. To her surprise, one was pressed into her hand by Robert. He was much improved from earlier, and favored her with a tight smile before moving in to give her a hug.

"Helen told me about you and College Boy," he said. "New York is a far drive."

Like Helen, Robert assumed she was only leaving because of Art. The full explanation would have taken too long, and it changed little. Instead, Etta just hugged him back.

He continued, "I'm gonna miss you, cos."

She had made a point to avoid thinking about everything and everyone she would leave behind. It was moments like this that reminded her about what she would be giving up in exchange. Helen's words from their fight that morning suddenly came back to her. For the first time, Etta wondered if leaving town was really the solution she thought it was.

Robert let go and stepped back. Seeing him in his wedding suit, Etta was certain of one thing: things would be different after today, whatever she decided.

In that moment, all she could think to say was, "Take care of my best friend for me."

The food was another matter entirely. Taking up several large tables, it must have accounted for nearly all the money Mildred and Peter had been able to spare. There were small sandwiches, fruit, meat pastries, and that was just the hors d'ourves. On top of that, the Kovaks and Turners were roasting a dozen or so chickens and even a pig over the big cook fire.

For Etta, who had been on a strict diet of eggs and whatever else she could find, which was often nothing, the bounty of options was staggering. She might have eaten her fill and more within a few minutes, but she was pulled into one conversation after another.

At first, she had assumed that Art was following her around, but at one point, she looked up to find him having a beer with Daniel who was visibly relieved to no longer be serving as his older brother's third leg. The two of them were clearly enjoying themselves, and she left them to it. Etta met with old friends and distant relatives. Some she had not seen since her mother's funeral. This led to some initially awkward greetings before she was obliged to change the subject.

Others were relatives of the Saunders that she had only met once or twice before, and knew by sight if not by name. For someone who did her best to avoid crowds, she was surprisingly at ease. Maybe it was because most of the faces were familiar or maybe her full belly put her in an agreeable mood.

For a short while, Etta spoke with Helen's cousin Megan and one of their aunts. The younger girl was very proud of the dress she had made, rightly so, and was taking every opportunity to show it off. Etta could not blame her. For someone with no previous experience, it had turned out well.

"Aunt Amelia owns a boutique," Megan explained.

Amelia was a handsome woman, of middle years, with well coiffed, dark hair, several long necklaces, and dressed far nicer than was necessary for a barn wedding.

"Oh, that must be nice," Etta said politely but not with interest.

This was the third conversation delaying her return to the serving table. Her stomach, now teased by the unusual abundance, compelled her to seek out more of those delicious beef pastries.

"Have you made many of these?" Amelia asked Etta as she eyed Megan's and then Etta's dress with a professional eye.

"Maybe two or three," Etta replied, distractedly.

I hope those pigs in a blanket aren't gone yet.

She continued, “This was my first time teaching someone else, but Megan picked it up quickly.”

The younger girl smiled with fresh pride.

Aunt Amelia replied with a critical, “Hmm,” as she continued to appraise the dress. No one spoke for a few seconds and Etta thought she might take the opportunity to excuse herself. Amelia looked up just as Etta took her first step away.

“You know, I'm always looking for help at the boutique, especially someone who can supervise the other girls. If you're interested, you should stop by.”

Etta paused, surprised by the offer, and forgot about her nagging appetite. For all the different jobs she had had, this was a possibility she had never considered before. The thought was appealing; something that actually interested her, and was not utterly exhausting, or dirty, or dangerous.

“I might just do that,” Etta responded. “Where are you located?”

“In Denville,” Amelia replied.

Etta tried to hide her disappointment. It was several towns away. She would never be able to walk the distance on a daily basis.

Instead of declining, Etta merely smiled and said, “Thank you.”

After filling a plate with more food, Etta sat down with Lizzie and they resumed their conversation from the morning. Now that they had become reacquainted, Etta could not understand why they had drifted apart in the first place.

It was such a relief to be able to talk to another girl who actually had to work every day. While Helen was a lifelong friend, the best she could do was listen attentively. She could never relate to something like going out in freezing weather to break the ice as it formed in the animals' water trough. With Lizzie, it was clear that she understood, because she had done it herself. They were soon discussing the unique challenges of working with cows versus chickens.

“I wasn't even sure I'd be able to wear these shoes today,” Lizzie said. “One of the ladies stepped right on my big toe last month. It swelled up something awful for a solid week.”

“I call the chickens 'ladies' too,” Etta replied. “Glad it healed up, but how are you able to walk at all? Don't cows weigh something like a thousand pounds?”

"It was only one of the calves," she explained. "But you're right. My brother got his hand caught between a full heifer and the wall of the barn a few years ago. It still doesn't work right." Lizzie shook her head. "We've got two farmers with only two working hands between them."

Etta shivered. "Yikes. At least with a foot, you can hobble around. Losing one of your hands is tough. I had both of mine in bandages for a week last month."

Lizzie nodded, eyes wide with understanding. "I heard about that. Something to do with a girl at the Hatakawana. That was you?"

Etta nodded, taking another swig of Enoch's beer.

"So, you were doing laundry at the hotel and caring for your chickens too?"

"It was what we had to do," Etta shrugged. "I think Papa has it worse though. He's been spending a lot of time in Newark since the work pays better. He wasn't even able to make it today."

Lizzie furrowed her brow, confused. "But isn't that him right over there?" She pointed.

Looking over, Etta spotted Papa standing in the yard. There were enough people between them that she did not have a clear view, but it was definitely him. She smiled, glad that he had been able to put in an appearance, and also that he was enjoying himself. For months now, she could hardly think of a single occasion where he was not stressed over something, particularly money.

Then, to her surprise, he actually laughed. Not a restrained chuckle either, but loud enough for her to hear it across the distance. As she wondered who had managed to draw that kind of reaction, the crowd shifted enough for her to see.

Standing with her father and sharing a beer was Art.

Curious as to what they could be talking about, but also wary of joining a conversation between her father and boyfriend, Etta tried to continue her conversation with Lizzie. After a few minutes, it was clear that she was too distracted for it and excused herself.

"By the way, Daddy was interested in that thing you mentioned," Lizzie called in parting. "Be sure to come by for lunch."

"We sure will," Etta replied, and felt doubly content. It had been a while since she made a new friend.

Etta slowly walked over to where Papa and Art were standing. Approaching, she felt a genuine trepidation and was unsure how to enter the conversation. As it turned out, Art excused himself and walked away just before Etta was close enough for Papa to notice her. When he did, the two of them regarded each other for a long moment. They had seen so little of each other recently that this was practically a reunion.

Papa spoke first. “So this is the famous dress you have been working on?” He nodded approvingly. “You certainly have your mother's knack for stitch work.”

Etta smiled at the compliment. “And you,” she motioned to her face. “Do they not have razors in Newark?”

Papa was sporting a new beard that was still somewhere in the transition between negligent stubble and looking respectable.

He nodded almost sheepishly. “Do you like it? Thought I would try something new.”

Etta made a show of looking it over, before giving her approval. “It suits you. You could be the King of Warsaw.”

He nodded thoughtfully. “If only...” Jakob glanced over at Art, who was now across the yard. “I was speaking with our recent handyman. It seems that you two have been spending a great deal of time together.” He let the unspoken question hang between them.

Etta nodded slowly, but said nothing. She was actually quite anxious. Not just because of Art, but also because of what Helen had said about the house. It had preyed on her mind despite her own self-assurance. Looking at Jakob now, it seemed that Helen had the right of it. This beard was not the only change in his life.

While she had been making grand plans to go her own way, and make it on her own, it appeared that Papa had already done so. On the other hand, if she wanted her independence, it seemed she might no longer need to leave home in order to get it. When it was clear that she was not going to say anything, Jakob continued.

“I’m glad the house is being taken care of, since I've been away so much. The quality of his work speaks for itself, but...” Papa had a strange look then. For the past year, Etta was accustomed to her father appearing stern, melancholy, and above all – exhausted. Now his face was an odd composition of relief tinged with regret. It was as if he had just made a bittersweet realization.

“He will need to learn the proper location for my tools. We have been discussing at some length, but I think you will need to teach him. Especially if he’s going to stay for a while.”

Etta grinned. “I will.”

“Promise me,” he said with mock severity.

She nodded and he grinned back.

Chapter 26
Art

"Stop pacing already," Mother scolded. "You'll wear a hole in the floor."

Art did so, but his nervous energy soon needed another outlet, and he started picking at his fingernails.

Luciana sighed. "If you need something to do, go and set the table. The Kennedys will be here soon."

"Breakfast is fine, but do I really need to take her boating?"

George looked up from the home office report and frowned. "What's wrong? You tired of your future wife already?"

Good God, if you only knew.

His mother scoffed. "They'd have to spend some time together before he could get tired of her. I don't understand this. She has a nice figure. She's from a good family. Why don't you like her?"

Ralph, never to miss an opportunity to take a jab at his brother, interjected. "What, you got another girl or something?"

Everyone looked at Ralph and the smug, mocking grin firmly planted on his face. Art was annoyed at first, but in fact it was a topic he needed to discuss and was hesitant to bring up himself.

Simply put, he had had enough. After the wedding, his thoughts turned towards the future, and what the rest of his life might look like. While it was nowhere near a complete picture, it did not include Dorothy Kennedy.

Out of reluctance to confront those involved, Art had allowed their supervised courtship to continue. Each time they met, he was put off just a little bit more. Dorothy tended to dominate their conversations, which by itself was not an issue. Art had a natural tendency for being quiet and liked to learn new things. While psychology was not his first topic of interest, it was something she was passionate about and he was mostly able to follow along.

Too often, when he tried to participate, she would grow annoyed by his questions. He frequently had to ask for definitions to clinical terms. On the rare occasion that he voiced his opinion on a particular theory or concept she was keen to take it as a personal insult. Dorothy's reaction would grow increasingly hostile until Art would decide it was simply not worth the argument and thereafter remained silent. As his mind then wandered, she would become annoyed for a second time.

Compounding this, every one of their interactions had been chaperoned by at least one family member. Thus, each one of Art's stumbles featured multiple witnesses. Usually it was Luciana and Gertrude. The mothers held their own conversation, and generally maintained a respectful distance. However, Luciana had grown fond of further meddling, calling out what she considered helpful suggestions.

"Oh, Art, Dorothy seems interested about that topic, you should ask her about it."

Strangely enough, Ralph had even volunteered a few times. At first, Art thought this was simply for the purpose of collecting more embarrassing details, but amazingly, he kept a civil tongue. In fact, he actually smoothed things over once or twice after Art had bungled the conversation. While not sure what to make of that, he doubted that Ralph had suddenly turned virtuous.

For all intents and purposes, Dorothy and Art were going to get married, so the topic of where they would live would often come up. It was clear that she had already decided upon a New York address.

"Perhaps I could be persuaded to suffer Long Island but certainly not New Jersey," she had said with a wink.

Art, momentarily forgetting his aversion to argument replied without thinking. "Actually, I've come to like this town. I was thinking about making the move permanent."

She had actually laughed at that, as if the thought were preposterous. "Indeed! Shall we farm chickens as well?"

It was in stark contrast to how things were progressing with Etta. With her, things just made sense. Once again, it occurred to Art that this delicate balancing act was untenable, not to mention unfair to all involved.

Making up his mind was one thing. Openly defying his parents was another, and took no small amount of courage. In a moment of temporary recklessness, and presented an opportunity on account of Ralph's intended jab, Art was about to do it. He opened his mouth, fully prepared to break off the engagement then and there. He got two words out before his father interjected, talking right over him.

"Of course he has a mistress," George said in response to Ralph's earlier quip.

Art was momentarily stunned into silence. He looked at his father, thinking that his grin was odd.

Then, George clarified, "A new business venture is not much different from a new wife after all. She demands most of your waking hours and then some. If you grant it, she'll make you a happy man. If you neglect her, she'll make you sorry." George winked then.

It would have been so easy to accept this explanation. Practical as well. At least in the short term. Art shook his head. Still feeling brazen, he attempted to press on. This was the time. Despite his awful habit of putting things off, he realized that this needed to be addressed. It might as well be now. Once again, he opened his mouth to say so and once again George interrupted him.

"By the way, how is the refrigerator truck coming along? Has the customer committed to a down payment yet?"

The sudden shift in topic was jarring, and Art's argument for breaking off the engagement dissolved. In truth, he had been hesitant to take the next step with the new project since it would require him to get the Hunleys to agree to the deal. An act that he believed had a moderate probability of failure.

Where breaking things off with Dorothy was a topic he was hesitant to discuss, the refrigerator truck had become one that he was eager to avoid. He was actually quite thankful that Etta had urged him not to bring it up at the wedding, despite the fact that Owen and Bethany would both here there. It gave him an excuse to postpone.

Still, Art did not want to admit that he had made no progress yet.

"We made a handshake agreement, but... I still have to get their signatures. It's been difficult to find a meeting time where everyone was available." A lie of course, but plausible. Recently, it had started to bother Art just how fluidly the words came out of his mouth.

George frowned at this explanation, and Art spoke again without particularly thinking.

"I had planned to meet with them today. Only I'm supposed to go boating with Dorothy."

"You've missed several dates already, Arturo," his mother chimed in. The hint of her old accent and use of his proper name gave evidence to her smoldering annoyance.

George considered this. "What if Ralph goes boating instead?" he ventured.

"Sure," both Art and Ralph replied in unison. Art looked at Ralph suspiciously, wondering about the eagerness of his reply.

Mother made a decidedly unladylike noise in response. "And is that the kind of thing you want to encourage? That she should seek out the attention of other men?"

George thought it over before nodding concurrence. "Quite not. Art, explain the situation to her. Reschedule if that's what you need to do, but make good on your promises."

Art nodded, though he was not entirely clear on which promises he was supposed to make good on and which ones should be rescheduled. He decided not to ask any follow-up questions since his father had provided him an exit from the conversation. Stealing a glance at Ralph, he could not help but notice the look of disappointment.

The Kennedys soon arrived for breakfast. Art and his brothers carried out the second table in order to fit everyone and the yard was crowded. As customary for these shared meals, Art and Dorothy were placed next to each other at the corner of the table, well in visual range of both sets of parents, but sufficiently buffered that they could speak freely. Not expecting much from this conversation, he politely – almost automatically – asked how her summer was going.

"The Haverhill Temperance Society seems to have finally recognized my forwarding address, and sent me all the back issues of their newsletter. I've been enjoying a considerable amount of leisure time as of late. Mostly reading but I've been sampling the local nature as well. I never had much time to relax during the school term. Surely, you had a similar experience."

She paused and looked at Art expectantly. It had not been a question, but she gave every impression of inviting him to speak. He knew what came next, but stubbornly held out hope that maybe this time it would be different.

"Yes, I ah-" he started to reply, but made it no further.

"A demanding curriculum can certainly seem like an occupation, can't it?" she interjected.

"Absolu-"

"Now, my first semester was probably the lightest in terms of course work..."

This continued for some time. Art tried once or twice, in vain, to contribute anything of substance to the conversation, but Dorothy would inevitably and heedlessly barrel on. While she would pause in her monologue from time to time, giving all appearances that she was looking for a response, he decided it was easier to simply nod agreement. Not for the first time, he regretted that he had not called things off when presented the opportunity earlier.

At one point, a lock of her wiry, ginger hair was knocked loose from her beret and fell across her face. Making no attempt to tuck it back, she decided instead to blow out a puff of air to keep it at bay.

It happened to be on the same side as Art, and due to their proximity, it had the effect that she was blowing air almost directly into his face. Her monologue continued, punctuated by the regular sharp puff. The exercise, at first, was simply distracting, but soon transitioned to obnoxious.

More than once, he fought the urge to tuck her hair back for her, but Franklin's perpetual grimace stayed Art's hand. While this surly gaze had been unsettling on their first meeting, now Art was only annoyed by it.

My hands are on the table, right where you can see them, jackass.

While Dorothy continued to blow air in his face, Art returned Franklin's glare without blinking. Eventually the older man stopped doing it. Art was both relieved, as well as surprised that his directness actually had the desired effect.

Dorothy grew tired of dealing with her hair in half-measures, and finally tucked it back under her hat. Fighting the urge to sigh, Art finally relaxed. No longer distracted, he noticed that Ralph, across from them in his usual seat, had started talking with Dorothy. Art thought little of it at first, and was glad for her attention to be directed at someone else for the moment. On the other hand, Ralph's natural tendency to lay it on thick caused Art to roll his eyes.

"You have a real passion for this subject," Ralph said, smarmy as ever.

"Quite so," she replied.

Dorothy was about to continue as she usually would with Art, but Ralph spoke first.

"You mentioned some interesting points," he said. "Could you recommend some reading material for a fella with an interest?"

That was odd for Ralph. Art suspected his brother could count the number of books he had read on one hand. If not for his eager response to their father's earlier suggestion, Art might have disregarded it.

"Certainly," Dorothy responded. "In fact, I happen to have a copy of an introductory text which should do nicely."

"I'd be much obliged," Ralph replied, staring at Dorothy intently. "I'm always keen to learn something new."

Dorothy was uncharacteristically flustered, and stumbled on her next words. "Well, ah – I hope you find it worthwhile."

"Surely I will. I doubt an intellectual such as yourself would waste her time on an unworthy subject."

Dorothy brightened at the inferred compliment, for once at a loss for something to say. Several seconds passed as they stared at each other.

Art looked between the two of them before chiming in. "Just make sure it's book with lot's of pictures."

Dorothy, who had been grinning, suddenly frowned as she turned back toward Art. "Oh, Arthur. Bad form," she chided.

"Yes, Arthur," Ralph added. "Bad form." His mocking grin went unnoticed by Dorothy.

Confused at how he had somehow ended up looking the fool, Art retreated even further into his own thoughts. Dorothy resumed speaking, but he was no longer listening. Instead, he fell into a pattern of nodding at the appropriate cues. This went on for some time. Then, Dorothy paused again and Art nodded. Instead of continuing to speak, as Art would have expected, she made an annoyed sound and remained silent.

Damn, that wasn't a 'nod' question.

"Ah... Beg pardon?" he said.

Dorothy scoffed. "I asked, 'What are we doing today?'" She continued. "I believe there was talk of sailing. Or perhaps a rowboat? Something on the lake, to be sure. It's a fine day for it."

The issue had come up at last. She was looking for a direct answer now, with no hope of the conversation moving on without him. Composing himself, Art tried to get out of the date as delicately as he knew how.

"Ah... the thing is, Dorothy, I have to work today." Granted, his most delicate was still quite blunt.

She wrinkled her nose, clearly put off by his answer. "Work?" she repeated, in equal parts skepticism and distaste.

"I've been trying to reach a deal with a new customer, and today was the only time they had available."

"But it's Saturday," she protested.

"Yes, well..." he fumbled before remembering something she had said previously. "You know these rustic types."

Immediately, he felt bad for calling the farmers "rustics," since he certainly knew many of them better than he did the Kennedys. However, his choice of words had the desired effect. Dorothy nodded as though that explained everything.

Sighing loudly, she said, "You do what you want."

"Oh. Alright then. Thanks," Art replied naively.

That had been easier than he thought it would be. Although, now he was the one that was confused since she had suddenly turned uncharacteristically quiet. At the same time, Art caught Ralph rolling his eyes and shaking his head.

Confused, Art excused himself from the table. The day was already getting late and he could only hope that the Hunleys were, in fact, available. Etta too, for that matter. Still, if he did not deliver today, there would be uncomfortable questions and he resolved not to return home until he had figured out a solution.

"Remember, they're not strangers," Etta said. "You were sharing a beer with them a couple weeks ago. This is like a visit with old friends."

Art brought his brother's car to a stop, but remained with his hands on the wheel for a few more seconds. Up until now, he had focused on the act of driving so that he did not have to think about the task that lay ahead of him. Now arrived, his gut had turned fluttery.

It was not his first sale, but it would be the first one without his father. Etta's presence helped, and her words gave his confidence just enough of a boost that he believed they could pull it off, but it was not the same. If George were here, Art had a fallback. That man could swoop in and rescue the sale if he bungled it too badly. Today, it was on him.

"Nervous?" she asked.

Art nodded. "If I don't pull this off, I'll be working for my father."

She clasped his hand reassuringly, and fixed him with her eyes. "You're gonna do great."

She leaned in and kissed him full on the lips, just a shade longer than would have been necessary for "good luck." Now he was no longer nervous, only distracted. Grinning at each other, they stepped out of the car.

Art adjusted his grip on the sheaf of papers he had brought. Mostly specifications for various models of refrigeration units that were small enough to fit in a truck. Etta had cautioned him not to dwell too much on the technical details, echoing advice his father often gave him, but the papers gave him a certain comfort all the same. The numbers were solid. He was confident in them. Also, they had taken some time to put together and, he was determined to show them off.

Etta was dressed in her slightly less ratty set of work clothes, which were freshly laundered. Art had shown up to the Wozniak's farm in his formal business suit, and Etta quickly argued against it. On the one hand, the suit felt like a costume of sorts, which liberated him to fall into his sales voice with more ease. They had compromised on wearing the pants, but Etta insisted no jacket. His shirtsleeves were rolled up for good measure.

Art knocked on the Hunleys' front door. A moment later, Lizzie answered, dressed in work clothes similar to Etta's and greeted her with a wide smile.

"Hey, Stranger. I was wondering when you were going to visit." She cocked her head at Art and favored him with a slightly different smile. "And good to see you again, Art."

He took a steadying breath. "Hi. I was hoping we could talk about that refrigerated truck your father was interested in."

Lizzie hesitated. "I'm not sure today is the best time for it. He was up late last night."

"Oh. Ah..." Art froze. This had been unexpected.

"Maybe we could just sit down together then," Etta suggested. "No need to talk business right away. We brought a peach pie."

This had been Etta's idea, and had taken them an extra twenty minutes to drive to a market on the other side of town. At the time, Art thought it unnecessary, but now he was glad for it. He quickly agreed to Etta's suggestion of sitting down together, thankful for the diversion. Lizzie cast another odd look at Art, but ultimately nodded at Etta. A vague unease came over him.

The three of them passed through the house to join the rest of the Hunleys in the back yard where the table was set up. Greetings were exchanged, and Art could not help but notice Etta was greeted far more warmly than he was. In fairness, he was an outsider here, but recently he had come to feel less like one. Oddly enough, what ended up helping was Lizzie's younger sister Ros. In a move that surprised Art, she gently cupped the side of his face.

"Looks like it healed up alright. I am so sorry about that. Walter seemed much nicer before we got to the barn."

It took him a moment to remember the shiner he had received at the Kovaks' party. The bruising had long since faded, and Art had nearly forgotten about it.

Briefly, he considered a show of how much it still pained him, thinking that a little sympathy would help the sale. Remembering what Etta had said about staying honest, he dismissed the idea. Instead, he made a nonchalant wave of his hand.

"Not to worry. All water under the bridge. Though, if you don't mind my saying so, you could do better in your choice of men."

"Hmpf. You sound like my father," she accused. Her words were scolding, but her tone was playful. "I'm sure the two of you will get along great."

"And why not?" called Owen. He was already sitting and nursed a large cup of coffee. "Seems like sound advice to me." He spoke in the same friendly and teasing way as Ros, but his grin was tired.

The hair plastered to his head was evidence of a long morning working and sweating in the summer sun and his half-lidded eyes spoke of a long night before that. Owen took a pull from the mug in front of him, and Art felt a pang of doubt that this was the right time for his pitch.

"You flatter me, Mr. Hunley," Art replied, offering his hand. Owen did not reach out right away, leaving Art feeling like a statue. A second or two passed, and he grew more uncomfortable before he finally understood why.

I'm an idiot.

Art switched hands quickly, offering his left one this time. Unfolding his arms, Mr. Hunley nodded in acknowledgment, and shook Art's offered hand.

"It's Owen," he replied.

With some effort, Art made sure to look Owen in the eye, not trusting his gaze to stay away from the man's right arm, which ended in a stump just below the elbow. If he noticed Art's near stumble, he gave no sign.

"And I don't flatter. You and Gregory do good work. Be sure to give him my best, next time you see him."

"I will," Art replied.

"Not sure if he's mentioned, but he and I go way back. When I was in the Navy, we were both stationed at the Depot over in Dover. Spent a lot of hours together, counting stacked artillery shells." He grinned at the memory. “Used to play a game on me where he would drop a hammer or something in the quiet of the powder magazine. Practically made me jump out of my own skin on more than one occasion.”

Art let out a chuckle, which put him more at ease. “I'll have to ask him about that. Seems like something he might do. By the way, I hope that ice cream maker is still holding up.”

Thinking this might be a good segue to bring up the refrigerator truck, Art opened his mouth to press on, but he was interrupted as Bethany and the rest of the family joined the table. Lizzie's mother and Etta shared pleasantries, and Art was introduced again.

The conversation shifted to other topics as the family sat down to eat. Although they were supposedly already interested, Art lacked his father’s gift for gab, and was unable to steer the conversation. A few opportunities teased him as they passed, but each time he opened his mouth, someone would speak first, and he would back down. Each time, a small chip of his confidence was knocked away. As the minutes passed by he grew more disheartened. Even Etta's efforts to bring up the subject came to nothing.

Eventually, the meal drew to a close, and Art's anxiety gave way to resignation, as he accepted his inevitable failure to close this deal. He told himself, unconvincingly, that they might be able to try again another day. Then, Owen said something in passing about all the work they had to do in the next few weeks. Art realized he was not likely to get another chance before it would be too late.

His thoughts turned sullen, convinced he would end up working for his father in the city. Fatalistically, he started to think that it might not be so bad, but there was no fooling himself on this. Art's slice of pie and fresh cream remained untouched in front of him, stressed as he was.

Only half-listening, he was startled as Etta elbowed him in the ribs. Art looked up as she raised her eyebrows, as if to say, “Are you listening?” She motioned towards Owen. Now paying attention, Art saw his opportunity.

“...drive all the way to down to Hackettstown each day this week to buy ice,” Owen continued. “The Fichners won't sell to us anymore. The old curmudgeon says he needs to save it for his regular customers.”

“That man...” Bethany shook her head and made an annoyed sound. “Still thinks there’s a war going on and he has to ration supplies. I’ve never heard of someone wanting *less* business.”

Owen nodded his agreement and grumbled, “Huge pain in the neck is what it is.”

"You might make use of a refrigerator," Art said as casually as he could, desperately hoping that his voice sounded steadier than it felt.

"Sure, but I need something to go with the truck, and there's nowhere to plug it in."

Art nearly laughed. He could not have hoped for a better set up.

"Actually, I might be able to help you with that."

In the end, Art's pitch lasted for maybe five minutes. Once or twice he nearly prattled on about the technical intricacies involved with how it would work, but a subtle headshake from Etta cued him to stay on topic. Afterward, Owen and Bethany discussed between themselves, and ultimately agreed with the bones of it. While initially skeptical of trusting this young stranger with their property, it was Gregory that decided matters. By Owen's rationale, if Gregory was involved, that was quite the endorsement.

The details of payment and a delivery date would be decided later, but the Hunleys agreed to offer up one of their two trucks to be converted as well as a modest down payment. This was with the understanding that the project would be completed sooner rather than later.

That meant a lot of work for Art in the near term, especially since he only had a notional idea for how everything was going to work. Strangely, in that moment he found himself unconcerned. More that anything else, he was elated, having actually struck a deal, more or less on his own. He managed to hold his composure while they all said their goodbyes, but as soon as he and Etta were out of sight, a huge smile spread across his face.

By they time they reached the car, he was practically giggling. Etta looked at him, astonished, especially after he pulled her into a tight embrace and kissed her full on the lips. She chuckled in surprise, and looked at him with a bemused expression.

"I gather that you're happy with how that went?" she asked.

Still grinning wildly, Art nodded. "You have no idea. That's the first sale I've ever made without my father."

She cocked her head to the side, looking at him expectantly.

"Not that I did it all on my own." he quickly added.

She smiled. "I have to say, this sales business doesn't seem all that hard."

Art looked at her, unsure if she was playing with him. While he had become reasonably adept at picking up on her particular body language, there remained times when she surprised him. He came to the conclusion that she was mostly trying to get a rise out of him, but still believed what she was saying.

"Oh, okay," Art said, rising to the implied challenge. "You just sat down to lunch with a family you've known your whole life, who like you, and they already wanted what we're selling. Now, imagine you have to do that with a complete stranger, who maybe just wants a free lunch from you. And even if they do agree, they're fully prepared to nickel-and-dime you for the duration of the exchange. Try doing that over and over again, every day of the week."

Etta opened her mouth, ready to double down on her claim, but held back at the last moment, thinking it over. "That... actually seems like a lot of work," she muttered with grudging agreement.

Art nodded, just a bit smugly.

"Still, you get lunch out of it," she added as a final throw.

"I suppose there's that."

As the initial excitement over their shared victory subsided, it gave way to contentment. They embraced again, more calmly this time, and savored their mutual achievement with a long kiss.

While there had been many kisses between them already, this one was somehow different. Before, their emotions had been driven by the energy that all new romances have. This time, there was something else. Though neither Art nor Etta would quite be able to articulate it, on some level they understood the potential of what they could accomplish as partners.

"So where are you taking me to celebrate?" Etta asked after they got back in the truck.

"Nowhere until the Hunleys deliver the down payment. Do I have to tell a chicken farmer, of all people, not to count her eggs before they hatch?"

Etta grinned at that.

"Besides, they said they want their truck back soon. There's a lot of work to do first."

Dropping Ralph's car off at the shop, Art was about to tell Gregory the good news. Thankfully, he stopped himself, remembering that he previously claimed the Hunleys already agreed. Instead, he told his mentor a truncated version. Gregory, as usual, took it all in stride, but seemed to pick up just a little of Art's excitement. The two of them spent the rest of the afternoon wrapping up a few projects for other customers that were taking up valuable shop space.

This included the Model T. Once again, Gregory offered to disappear Ralph's car somewhere it would never be found or use it for scrap, but Art decided he had made his point with his brother.

"You're a better man than me," Gregory went on to say. "If I ever had the chance to pay back Cheapskate Kate for all the grief she's visited on me, not sure I'd be able to help myself."

With spirits riding high, Art proceeded to tuck himself into a notebook and began to write numbers down. After making some general assumptions, he came up with a rough size for the refrigerator unit he would need to request from his father. Gregory looked over his shoulder once or twice with passing curiosity. Art barely noticed, fully engaged with the math and sketch work before him.

Once finished, they had a lengthy discussion about the general tasks that would need to be done, and had to make some guess work about how long it would take. Gregory reminded Art that if he planned to bring on help, he should add at least a few weeks to get them up to speed.

"Don't forget how useless you were for the first week or so," Gregory chided.

While Art had grown more familiar with the faux insults often exchanged between men, he was most accustomed with the genuine ones delivered by his brothers. When he frowned at the word "useless," Gregory winked and clapped him on the shoulder, taking off some of the sting.

Knowing his family's product line, Art had a rough idea of how much the unit would cost. With a grimace, he realized that it would take a substantial chunk from the down payment.

To his utter astonishment, George offered him something free of charge, albeit slightly smaller than the one he wanted. True enough, it was one of their less popular models, but he considered it to be of mutual benefit, as it had been taking up valuable space at the warehouse. Even so, the idea of his father parting with it free of charge was remarkable.

Of course, particular strings were attached. Before agreeing to call the home office to arrange delivery, George instructed Art to pay a visit to the Kennedys at the Hatakawana Inn.

"I'm proud that you're starting to make your contribution to the family business, but you're going to have a family of your own soon, and I won't have you start out by neglecting your wife. Besides, it's important to your mother."

Art started to object, but it occurred to him that if he tried to get out of this direct request, it would most likely open up the discussion to the whole premise of the engagement in general.

His willingness to buck the arrangement had evaporated for the moment, but he told himself that he would bring it up just as soon as things with the new project were less fragile. The truth, which he was barely willing to admit, was that he was still terrified of directly challenging his parents.

Art arrived at the Hatakawana Inn without specifically knowing which rooms the Kennedys were staying in. He had been here once before, on a sales visit. The owner had brusquely made clear his lack of interest and chased them off. Thus, even though his appearance was different than from their first encounter, Art recognized the man sitting behind the front desk in the lobby. While in their first meeting, he had been generally well put-together and calm, now he was agitated and fidgeted almost constantly.

The owner puffed away at a cigarette with determination, bouncing his leg up and down, as if he could be pacing the floors instead of manning a desk.

Art approached with hesitation, wondering if it would not be better to try and find the Kennedys on his own. While he had a passing familiarity of the hotel's layout from his previous visit, he ultimately dismissed the idea, and resolved himself to speak with the owner. The man glanced at the guest ledger and provided Art with a room number before he resumed staring into space. Art muttered a "thanks" and left him to troubles.

The conversation with Dorothy had been a little more involved. She answered the door, but upon recognizing her caller, refused to speak with him until someone else could be present to chaperone. While annoying, it was not entirely unexpected. Art was about to follow her down the hallway to locate a suitable family member, but remained where he was at her insistence. Resisting the urge to roll his eyes, Art waited patiently in front of Dorothy's room for her to retrieve her older sister, Emmie, who had recently arrived in town.

The three of them took a short walk to the waterfront, which mostly consisted of uncomfortable silence. While Art was glad he would not have to endure Franklin Kennedy's usual scowl, Emmie proved more than capable of providing one in his absence. Ironically, while their father was wary of Art getting too close with Dorothy, the source of her sister's ire was that he was too distant.

"Glad you could be bothered to get to know your fiancée," she spat.

"Really now!" Dorothy chased her sister back to a respectful distance.

Even so, Emmie remained no more than ten paces behind, and folded her arms to underline her displeasure with Art. Now confident that her sister could appropriately verify the lack of shenanigans, Dorothy spoke.

"This is a surprise. I'm glad you decided to visit."

Her tone was pleasant, but also poorly concealed a rebuke. It took Art a moment to realize that she was also uncharacteristically quiet. As if this was an invitation to speak. On the other hand, he had been fooled before. Art could think of nothing to say, unaccustomed as he was with a quiet Dorothy, and resumed his usual practice of nodding. Dorothy frowned but did not continue. They walked in silence for several steps as Art waited for her to say something. To his surprise, she did not.

"Did you end up going sailing?" he asked at last.

"I did. Or rather, we did. Emmie arrived in town the other day and we've been catching up." Dorothy bit her lip, thinking for a moment. "You know, my parents trust her to chaperone. If she accompanied us, I think we might be able to enjoy a dinner together without the whole family watching us under a microscope."

Art's attention had been wandering, but he recognized the implied invitation. "Ah, yes, that sounds nice."

Dorothy looked at him for a moment, again, waiting for him to respond with something more. She genuinely seemed to be making an effort to get him to talk more, which struck him as unusual. Her nostrils flared as she let out a long, frustrated breath. Art grew increasingly uncomfortable.

"Did you *want* to have dinner together?" she asked.

"Oh, for goodness sake, girl, don't come off as desperate!"

Emmie had closed the gap between Dorothy and Art without either of them noticing. Dorothy's eyes went wide as she turned on a heel to face her sister. Then, with greater speed than Art had seen in her before, Dorothy pushed Emmie, not gently, back to the distance she had previously established before returning to Art. Grabbing him by the elbow, she ushered him along to increase the gap, while watching her sister over her shoulder. Just as abruptly, she withdrew her hand, blushing a furious shade of red at the unintended physical contact.

"Well, then," Art started, and cleared his throat. "Dinner sounds great." He paused. "The thing is I have to get a lot of work done this week."

Dorothy abruptly stopped walking, but Art continued another step before he noticed. She stared at him blankly, her face betraying no emotion and returning to its usual pale color.

"Of course," she said flatly.

Emmie remained at the distance Dorothy had assigned, but wore a look of clear disdain and stood with her arms folded.

"Thank you for the walk, Arthur. I hope you enjoy your work." She turned on her heel again and joined her sister. "No need to accompany us," she called over her shoulder. "We can make our own way."

Okay, off the hook. Art breathed a sigh of relief, but his feelings were quickly tempered by a pang of regret. Or was it guilt? It was complicated and unsettling. As Art walked alone, he attempted to return his thoughts to the project. For the first time, it was failing to hold his attention.

His mind continued to trouble him for the rest of the day. It did not help matters that Ralph was spending more time around the house than usual, despite having his Ford again. Art had returned the car earlier that afternoon, but strangely, Ralph was unconcerned. His attention was fully absorbed by the psychology book loaned to him from Dorothy. He merely nodded at the news, and kept his eyes on the page.

Shrugging his shoulders, Art turned to leave, but stopped at the sound of his brother's voice.

"Brother mine," Ralph said. "When a woman says to you, 'Do what you want,' never, ever, actually do what you want." He might have also muttered something about how it was no wonder that Art was still a virgin, but that could have been his imagination. Ralph fell quiet after that and Art took the opportunity to leave.

His parents, of course, soon learned about Art's latest poor showing with Dorothy, and were displeased – or rather, Luciana was. She gave him an earful about it before he walked away. Father was playing with a couple of the grandchildren at the time, and his rebuke was lackluster.

The weather was foul for much of the next few days, driving everyone indoors. That suited Art just fine, as he had to rethink much of his original design, based on the unit his father agreed to provide. Unfortunately, with everyone else likewise indoors, there was no shortage of distractions. Thus, he mostly remained in the bedroom he shared with Ralph, hoping to find some quiet.

In this, Art was only marginally successful. Ralph was often to be found in the room with him. Mercifully, he remained quiet as he read Dorothy's book. But even so, the close proximity divided Art's attention. At any moment, he expected some biting remark or verbal prodding.

In fact, Ralph only spoke once.

"It says here that conscious aims are often a cover for unconscious desires. Are you avoiding Dorothy on purpose?"

Art furrowed his brow, unsure how to respond. While it was clear that Ralph was reading verbatim from the text, and probably had only a vague grasp on what he was saying, it was fairly spot-on.

Instead of responding directly, Art replied, "Aren't you punching above your intellectual weight class?"

Ralph set the book down on his lap, clearly not expecting a response of this kind. Looking as though he might start something, he eventually settled for narrowing his eyes.

"Wimp."

After enduring this nonsense for most of the summer, Art shot back. "Prick."

The petty insults ended when Ralph tossed his shoe into the back of Art's head.

When Art finally went to sleep that night, he remained generally perplexed and distressed at the behavior of just about everyone in his life. Everyone, except for Etta.

The next day, he left the house without even waiting for breakfast with the family. That he was going to pick up the truck from the Hunleys was merely a convenient excuse. He needed a break from the lot of them. Though, about halfway to Gregory's, he regretted that he did not snatch a bread roll or something to chew on. At least the weather was fair again.

After borrowing Gregory's truck, Art made a quick stop at the bakery in town before going to pick up Etta. Already dressed and waiting outside, she was genuinely conflicted about whether to eat first or to get underway as quickly as possible. Indeed, Etta had practically jumped at the opportunity to be the second driver when asked.

After picking up the Hunleys' truck and the down payment, Art and Etta drove the vehicles to the workshop. With Gregory's truck returned to its usual spot, Art approached Etta in the project vehicle. Still in the driver's seat, she claimed that it was making a strange sound, and Art moved to hear for himself. She stopped him with a hand on his chest.

"It only does it when I do a particular thing. I should probably drive so I can do it again."

Shrugging, Art got into the passenger's seat. Etta took them along various back roads. They rolled up and down hills and their surroundings alternated between open farmland and pristine views of the lake.

The day had been hot and humid, even for late July, and gave no indication of letting up. Obliged to open the windows for some much needed airflow, Art poked his head out to try and listen to the engine, or the wheels. Anything that might be the source of the offending "strange" noise. Some time later, the sound had failed to materialize, and he turned back to Etta.

"Have you heard it again?" he asked.

"Heard what?" she asked, grinning.

"The sound you... oh. Of course."

She shook with silent laughter.

Art slowly nodded in understanding. "You could have just said that you wanted to drive," he chided, but also grinned.

Etta shrugged.

"Since I have no idea where we are, I suppose I'm at your mercy, then."

"Right you are," she agreed.

"However..." he stretched out each syllable for effect. "If you take too long, we might be late for dinner." He meaningfully patted his pocket that held the down payment. "I find myself with a little more cash than usual, and I think a celebratory dinner with my new business partner might be in order."

She made a show of considering this. "Hm. Drive or eat. I might actually have to think about that one."

He thought she was merely playing coy, but it actually took her several minutes to make up her mind.

They arrived at the Wigwam restaurant late in the afternoon. The air was still heavy with moisture and the heat remained oppressive, but the distant rumble of thunder promised a storm that would cool things off. At least, that was Art's hope. In hindsight, he might have suggested a dinner venue, which did not warrant a jacket and tie, but at least they had decided not to walk.

While the Hunleys' had loaned their truck for the purpose of the project, Art reckoned there was little harm in borrowing it for just one evening. That the walk to the restaurant would have had him sweating buckets helped decide him. Etta was wearing her blue dress tonight, and had even dug up a pair of short heels for the occasion.

Where to go for their celebratory dinner was a discussion that took some time. Much of it occurred through the partially ajar door to Etta's bedroom while she dressed. Art initially suggested going to CasinO since it was the only restaurant in town that he knew of which met Etta's criteria of live entertainment. However, he was immediately reminded of its particular significance to her.

They eventually settled on a place further down the same road called the Wigwam. As they passed the boxy, white building, that was CasinO, two workers were in the process of placing boards over a couple of the roadside windows. The one not yet covered was clearly broken. Most of the glass was missing and the little that remained was spider webbed, with jagged, broken edges.

Art spared it a passing glance, but remained focused on the road. Etta said nothing, but continued to stare out her window until the sight of the building and the workers was long behind them.

Arriving at the Wigwam a minute later, she remained distracted, but less so than before. With an encouraging smile, Art offered his arm. The sound of music drifted out to the parking lot and her smile returned at last.

After getting a table, they barely spent any time sitting. The restaurant was filling up quickly, and the bandleader wasted no time in stoking the crowd's excitement. Etta's reticence from earlier all but disappeared once the band started to play. Noticing that most of the other men were removing their jackets in the heat, Art was happy to do likewise. Similarly, Etta and many of the other women did away with their heels as most all congregated on the dance floor.

It was some time later, when they sat down for the first course and decided it was time for drinks.

"I'm surprised that they just have the bottles out like that." Art motioned towards the bar, where a row of various liquor bottles was on display. "Won't they get in trouble?"

Etta shook her head, explaining that this was a common trick. "It's just for show. Those bottles are filled with water. But they do serve if you ask right."

"And how do you ask right?" He was thinking about the fictitious password his brothers had attempted to use during their call on the Brandelsons.

"You say 'please' of course," she winked. "What do you think? Champagne? We *are* celebrating."

For the next hour, they danced, drank, and took the occasional break to eat. Their fellow patrons were quickly losing most inhibitions about physical contact. Taking a cue from their example, Art and Etta felt more comfortable getting close. So comfortable, that they almost kissed more than once. Each time, they exchanged a little, knowing look that promised to be revisited later in the evening.

Etta had made it known that her house was currently empty, and would be for the whole night. The implications were distracting, to say the least.

The band took a short break, and most everyone sat down for the main course. Etta found her shoes again, and excused herself to use the rest room, leaving Art at the table by himself. Now that the music had stopped, he noticed the rumble of thunder was less distant now, and accompanied by the steady roar of heavy rainfall. The wait staff had opened the windows to let the cooler air inside, for which Art was thankful.

His head pleasantly buzzed with the champagne, and he thought about the evening ahead. However odd the behavior of his own family, at least with Etta and his work, things just made sense.

Feeling content, Art took in the scene. Such was his light mood that the crowd did not even bother him. The other patrons were laughing and calling out to each other, their volume increasing with their lowered inhibitions. Two girls were still dancing together, despite the lack of music. Coupled with their flushed appearance, the empty glasses they were holding provided a likely explanation.

Plenty to see if you bother to look.

Art frowned. That was something Dorothy had said. Yet again, he had pushed the issue of the engagement from his mind, and his thoughts turned from contented to sullen with its return. Their latest exchange was fresh in his mind, and he realized that things had gone on long enough.

It was time to end it, with no more beating around the bush or further delay. Granted, he had intended and failed to address it multiple times already, but this was different. It was clear now, that this issue would not simply disappear of its own accord, and his opportunity to do something about it on his own terms was closing.

The recent foul weather had driven Junior and Martha to cut their vacation short, reminding Art that the summer would soon be ending for all of them. First thing tomorrow, he would tell George and Luciana two things: he would not marry Dorothy, and he would not return to New York. Briefly, he wondered which point would cause the greater controversy.

These thoughts were interrupted as his eyes settled on a familiar face across the room. At first, her name escaped him and he could not place her, but knew that he should. There had been a lot of new faces recently. Perhaps someone from the wedding? He was never great with names, and his thoughts were just a bit soggy, thanks to the wine. Not the wedding, but certainly a recent acquaintance.

All of a sudden, it hit him: Emmie Kennedy. It was the smile that threw him. When they met, she had scowled the whole time. Now, she was positively giddy. His first thought was a certain satisfaction at recognizing her. A heartbeat later, his grin disappeared, and he slowly turned his face away, trying to remain inconspicuous.

Still a bit sluggish, it occurred to him that if he was recognized, it would result in a lot of questions. Questions with inconvenient answers.

"Are you here alone?"

"Who is the pretty, blonde girl?"

The chance of that happening would only increase the longer they stayed. Not a minute earlier, he had decided that the engagement needed to end, but not like this. Not by being discovered out with another woman.

All else aside, he found a compelling desire to at least try and treat the matter delicately. Of course, this was to say nothing of Etta, and how she might respond to the fact that he was engaged. While the whole thing had been arranged without his consent or even knowledge, he did not care to take a risk on that nuance.

They had to leave, but how to tell Etta without raising questions of a different sort?

Art started thinking through what to say. The main course had only just been served. Dinner could last another hour. Maybe after eating, she would consider leaving early. But surely she would want to dance again once the band resumed playing.

Sliding low in his chair, he tried his best to remain invisible as he thought through different scenarios. Perhaps they could get through the evening without his being recognized. After all, he had made it this far. Keeping his head down and his gaze averted, Art failed to notice a young redhead make her way to the restroom.

Chapter 27
Etta

Everyone descended on the ladies' room at once. It was as if the music had cast a spell that caused all to forget their bodily needs, and once lifted, they remembered at the same time. As she waited, Etta wished she had taken at least a few bites of her meal before dashing away from the table. The effects of the champagne left her with a pleasant distraction from her nearly empty stomach and full bladder.

As she waited, she was dimly aware of the woman in line behind her fidgeting with her dress. Briefly, Etta glanced back, but paid the woman little mind. Her thoughts remained on the current evening, which was shaping up to be one of the best she had had in a long while. A full dinner, which she neither had to prepare for or clean up after and on top of that, real music. Then, of course, was the situation with Art. His particular choice of words from earlier, about being partners, and its various interpretations was enticing.

The woman with the dress continued to fool with it, and actually bumped into Etta this time.

"Sorry, Miss," she said quickly. "This dreadful thing had come undone."

From the way she spoke, Etta immediately placed her as an out-of-towner. While this was expected, as the restaurants in town were patronized almost exclusively by visitors, her accent made it even more conspicuous. Old habits are hard to break, and Etta's immediate reaction was one of disdain. Sparing her only a casual glance, Etta resumed waiting in line. Art remained a special case for out-of-towners, though Etta recognized the dissonance.

The woman continued to fuss, and her frustration mounted. At last, she sighed in exasperation and touched Etta on the shoulder, but more gently this time.

"Excuse me, I'm having the most difficult time with this. Would you care to oblige me?"

Etta let out a slow, annoyed breath. The pressure on her bladder was becoming difficult to ignore, and made worse so by moving around. Still, she did not have it in her to be openly rude even to an out-of-towner.

Upon seeing her, Etta's annoyance turned to sympathy. The dress had torn along the shoulder seam, completely out of reach. She motioned for the woman to turn around and went fishing through her black bag. She had not unpacked it since Helen's wedding, and so the sewing kit had remained.

"It's your lucky night," Etta said to her. "Sorry, but the thread color isn't going to match."

"That's fine. As long as it keeps all the lady parts covered."

Seems like they're plenty covered already. Where did you get this thing? A convent?

Etta said none of this out loud, but the other woman's dress was certainly more modest than most of the others on display. Despite the heat, it fully covered both shoulders and featured a neckline that practically came up to her throat. Though, Etta had to concede that the material was nice enough, and someone had certainly spent some time on the beadwork. She worked quickly, reminding the woman to hold still if she did not want to get a needle in her back. Thankfully, Etta did not have to hunch over in order to work since the woman was quite tall.

She finished about a minute later. "That should hold you."

As Etta put her sewing kit away, the tall woman shrugged her shoulder, testing the strength of the fix. Satisfied, she sighed with relief.

"Thank you so much, Miss...?" She extended her hand, and Etta had to concede that at least she had manners.

"Wozniak. Call me Etta."

The other woman grinned. "I'm Dorothy Kennedy."

Dorothy turned out to be a talker, and Etta was doubly thankful when her turn in line was up, giving her an excuse to walk away. Undeterred, Dorothy continued talking to her new friend from the adjacent stall.

"It's a nice enough establishment, but their flagrant disregard for the law leaves me just speechless. I mean to have the liquor bottles just out on display like that."

Etta considered correcting her, but was trying not to encourage Dorothy. Simple annoyance transitioned to embarrassment, as Etta was not accustomed to holding a conversation with her undergarments around her ankles.

What is wrong with this woman?

Trying in vain to do her business with all possible haste, she strongly considered leaving the restroom without washing up. However, several women remained in line, and their judgmental stares urged her back to the sink. Gritting her teeth, she silently cursed as Dorothy took up the spot next to her.

"That was lucky about the sewing kit," she continued blithely. "Do you always carry one?"

Etta sighed, realizing that Dorothy was not taking the hint. "Not usually. I happened to be at a wedding recent-"

"Is that so?" she barreled on, before Etta could finish. "Oddly enough, that's why I'm in town. Not for the wedding, I mean. We're still in our courtship."

Etta washed her hands quickly, hoping to get out of the room before Dorothy. If they left together, she doubted that she would ever be rid of her.

"Though, if I'm being honest, he's been terribly aloof lately. But, I'm told these Adams are all about their work."

Etta was turned halfway from the sink when she pulled up short. "I'm sorry. Did you say 'Adams?'"

Dorothy looked at her blankly. In the time it had taken Etta to respond, Dorothy had already moved on to another topic. She needed a moment to recall what Etta was referring to.

"Why? Do you say 'Adamses'? I've been struggling with that myself."

Etta shook her head. "No, I didn't mean... You said you were engaged?"

"Oh, yes. Arthur Adams. My fiancé."

Etta froze, trying to make sense of what she was hearing. Was it possible that it was just a common name? "Tall fella? Glasses? Unkempt hair?"

Dorothy's eyes narrowed, and she was suddenly quiet for the first time since she and Etta met. “Yes,” she replied slowly, voice heavy with growing suspicion. “Do you know him?”

It can't be...

For a moment, Etta considered saying, “yes,” but there remained the barest shred of doubt.

“A friend of mine lives on a dairy farm. There's an Arthur Adams doing some work for them.”

Dorothy seemed to breathe a sigh of relief, assuming that Etta's association was safely distant. “Ah, yes. The refrigerated truck. He's been very busy with it lately. Sometimes I wonder… Miss? Where are you going?”

The door was already swinging shut before Dorothy could get the words out.

Her thoughts jumped from confused to hurt and then to furious. With each step, she could hardly decide if she wanted to scream or break down in tears. Arriving back in the main dining area, the crowd gave her pause. Whatever she was feeling, the thought of making a scene in front of this many people was like a bucket of cold water.

Breathing heavily, she clenched and unclenched her fists to keep them from shaking. Casting her eyes to the table she had been sharing with Art, Etta stared. As he was facing away from her, there was nothing to help her determine the validity of her suspicions, but the sight of him gave fresh fuel to the storm raging in her mind.

Staring at the back of his head, she remained fixed in place with indecision. The blabbermouth had said *Arthur*. Not *Arturo*. Maybe there was a chance. He was sitting low in his chair, which was odd. Confusion momentarily tempered her other emotions, until it occurred to her that he gave every appearance of hiding.

You saw her, didn't you?

This seemed only confirmed when Art looked surreptitiously over his shoulder in her direction, and only upon recognizing her did he pick up his head and wave. Etta jumped back to furious and glared at him.

They stared at each other across the busy room for several seconds. Art's smile gradually faded as understanding took hold. Working her jaw to fight the urge to scream, she turned away. The sounds of the busy room suddenly felt constricting, and she did not want to be here any longer. Finding the exit, she stomped toward it without hesitation.

Outside, the rain was heavy and punctuated by thunder. The dull roar of the Wigwam crowd became muffled as the main door closed behind her. Somewhere in the distance she could hear sirens, but they soon faded into the steady drone of rainfall. Protected from the worst of the rain, she stood in the front awning and took a moment to collect her thoughts. Everything had happened so fast. Maybe an innocent explanation remained possible.

The muffled sounds from inside the restaurant rose and fell as the door opened behind her. Without looking, she recognized Art's voice.

"Hey, ah... W- what's going on?" The unease in his voice was almost palpable, and his casual tone was clearly forced.

While little doubt remained, Etta still needed to hear him say it.

"Are you engaged?" She was surprised by how steady her voice sounded, considering the whirlwind from a moment earlier.

Tellingly, Art was silent for longer than it would take to simply say, "No."

"Well..." he started. "I suppose the short answer is, 'yes.'"

Etta was already walking before he reached the last word. Heedless of the weather, she marched straight ahead. Somewhere in the back of her mind, she retained an odd clarity, and it occurred to her that walking through puddles would ruin her mother's shoes. Almost without thinking about it, she stopped to remove them. That's when Art caught up with her.

"Hold on. There's a longer answer to that."

"I don't want to hear it."

"Would it make a difference if I told you that I didn't plan to actually marry her?"

Now that they were alone, she was unencumbered by the desire to avoid making a scene. This time, when fury pushed her gloom aside, she indulged it. Rounding on Art, she underestimated how close they were and found herself unintentionally shouting in his face.

"And what would that prove? That you're a liar and you can't be trusted!?"

He stopped short, but remained where he was. The volume of Etta's rebuke surprised even her and the whirlwind of thoughts returned at once. Briefly overwhelmed, Etta decided that she had said her piece and turned to leave.

"That's not exactly what I was going for." Art started to follow. "Listen, there's a couple other things going on here. Believe me, if you knew my mother, you'd understand."

Every spoken word only inflamed her rage. His attempts at an explanation drove her to want to hit him as hard as she could, and culminated when he touched her arm.

He continued, “Let me drive you home and we can talk about this.”

She wrenched her arm away from him as if touching a hot stove. Without thinking, and much to her surprise, she let her hand fly. Etta had never actually struck someone in anger before, and frankly it showed. Her hit was wild and full of emotion. To both their benefit, Art leaned away, and Etta's hand landed harmlessly on the meat of his arm. Surprised, more than anything, Art remained standing where he was. Her intent was clear.

Frustrated as he held his ground, she pressed close. Her face inches from his.

“Do. Not. Follow. Me!” She spat each word. “Go marry your damned blabbermouth, and get out of my town.” With that, she turned on her heel and stormed off down Route Six.

During the two-mile walk back to her house, the anger that had been keeping her warm gradually faded. The pleasant, dizzy feeling from the champagne likewise wore off. The rain alternated between steady, and torrential, and she was soaked through every layer of clothing before she passed the Oasis. If not for the cool puddles, which were practically everywhere, her feet, no doubt, would be throbbing from the long, barefoot trek.

Oddly enough, she did not cry. Still mostly in shock, the act of putting one foot in front of the other kept her fully occupied.

Left foot. Right foot. Left foot. Over and over again. And rain. Always the rain.

Thus, it was almost a surprise when she finally arrived back at the farm. That it was fully dark by this point was largely to blame. Passing the mailbox with its dents and fixed post, she marched to the house. More than anything, she was tired and cold. Hungry too. In the back of her mind, she scolded herself for not grabbing the dinner plate when she had the chance. Now she just wanted to crawl into bed.

Peeling off her wet clothes, she dropped them in an unceremonious heap on the floor, not bothering to even hang them up. Etta spared a full minute to wring out her hair, letting the water likewise fall to the floor before crawling into bed naked. At last, there was nothing left to distract her, aside from the sound of rain pounding the roof. With the lack of anything else to do, she finally closed her eyes and started to cry.

Daylight. For the second time that summer, the sun had gotten up without her. It remained such a vanishingly rare event, that she had never bothered with putting up a curtain. The sunlight shone straight through the window, and drove her to bury her face. It had not been a restful night. The drinking and lack of food only added to the general malaise.

The second thing she was aware of was that she was not alone. Remaining otherwise still, she slowly pulled the blanket down below her eyes. Squinting against the bright of the sun, it took her a moment to recognize Mildred standing in the doorway. That was odd. As her eyes adjusted, she recognized the older woman's stern expression, which quickly pulled her sluggish thoughts into focus. Compelled by anxiety, she fell back on habits. How late was it if Mildred had come to check on her? None of her chores had been started.

"My goodness. What time is it?" she croaked, pushing the covers aside and sitting up on the bed. It had been without thinking, and she was immediately grateful that she had slipped into a dry shift before going to the outhouse last night.

"Etta..." Mildred started.

"I have to tend to the chickens. And everything else. It's a grocery day too. I… I have to get going." She realized that she was rambling, and she felt her throat constricting as the events of the previous night came back to her.

"Etta..."

This time Etta looked, and saw more clearly. No, it was not sternness. Mildred was grim. And there was something more.

Has she been crying?

Etta had only seen Mildred cry on a handful of occasions. Very specific occasions – all of which had been funerals.

"Mildred," she said, fighting down a lump in her throat. "What's happened?" A sense of dread took hold as she awaited the reply.

It took an eternity for Mildred to form words. Finally meeting Etta's eyes, she said, barely above a whisper, "Robert is dead."

It had been Daniel who brought the news. He was in shock as much as the rest of them and his expression was vacant. Details were limited and obscured by rampant speculation. As Daniel had it straight from the firemen who were there, Etta trusted the bones of the account.

All agreed that there had been an explosion in one of the ammunition magazines at the Naval Storage Depot, a few towns over. Lightning, of all things, was the most likely culprit, although blame was ascribed to everything from Communists, Anarchists, and even agents of the Weimar Republic, depending on who was asked.

The artillery shells were huge things, nearly the size of a man. Many had exploded, and others were scattered throughout the region. People had died. More had to be evacuated. The Bott's lake fire company, among others, had been called to assist those leaving their homes amid the confusion.

Robert McCormick and Carl Dickerson had gone into a house that was compromised by a fallen shell. Miraculously, the thing had not exploded, but the sheer weight of it had weakened the structure, and it collapsed with the two men inside.

Thankfully, no one else on the ladder company had been injured. This struck Etta as strange. Knowing what her cousin was like, especially around the likes of Carl, a nagging suspicion took root in her mind.

Pastor James had been in touch with the clergy in nearby Dover, which was hosting many of those displaced from the blast. The way he handled the whole affair did nothing to improve Etta's opinion of him. He had additional information, but refused to discuss it outside of Sunday mass, which would double as the funeral service for Robert and Carl.

Moreover, he had insisted on a joint funeral. To Etta, cramming everyone into the church for a combined service was beyond distasteful. Disrespectful even. That she suspected it was due to the McCormicks being Irish-Catholic only deepened her animus for Pastor James.

It was rumored that the caskets would be closed for the service due to the injuries both men had sustained when the house collapsed. Etta hoped that this was merely salacious gossip and tried not to dwell on it. It was bad enough that yet another family member had been taken so young, and Etta had barely slept. At night, when she had finally run out of tears for Robert, and her mind was about to settle, she was troubled for a second time thinking about Art.

Getting in touch with Papa had been a challenge, but he returned as quickly as he was able. It was the first time he had been home since the wedding. Having him close helped Etta a great deal, and not just for practical matters, of which there were many. It might have been the most time they were together all summer and his presence was comforting.

For two days, she spent the majority of her time with the Saunders. On top of the preparations for the funeral itself, nearly everyone affected still lived on a working farm. Animals, after all, do not give much care for matters of bereavement. While Papa tended to her usual duties at the Wozniaks' farm, Etta helped the Saunders in whatever way she could.

The Saunders' cozy home was once again host to a large group of friends and family. For the first day, Helen was inundated with mourners and their condolences. Those who knew that Robert and Etta were cousins sought her out as well and she was soon overwhelmed. When it became too much, she buried herself in dirty dishes and laundry. She and Helen had barely seen each other since the wedding and spoke little that first day. Instead, they shared tears and provided each other with a shoulder to cry on rather than words.

The second day was comparatively lighter, but Etta decided to keep out of the house as much as possible. Collecting as many articles of laundry as she could find – a few of which were already clean – she retreated outside.

Some time later, Susie joined her, escorted by Max. Her expression was neutral and Etta suspected that she was troubled but did not fully comprehend the gravity of the situation. It took some time for her to resume asking her usual questions. Even then, it was with less fervor than normal.

"Why is everyone so sad?"

Etta paused in her scrubbing, and sighed. She was exhausted, mourned, and now mildly discomforted that she had to be the one to explain the facts of life to Susie.

"Because Robert died."

"Right... but when's he coming back?"

Despite all going on, Etta was struck by the sheer absurdity of it. "Susie, you know what 'dead' means..."

"Sure. Like when we take a chicken for dinner."

"Yes. Exactly. So, why-?"

"But the chicken always comes back... like what happens with the eggs."

"It's not the *same* chicken."

Susie thought on that, but remained unconvinced. Max had nothing to add to the discussion, and soon left. Susie followed and the two of them disappeared among the corn stalks, taller than she was.

With a sigh, Etta resumed scrubbing, though intentionally going slower than she might have. Work had always provided a sufficient distraction before, and now she needed it more than ever. So intently was she focused on the soapy water and washboard that she was surprised when Mildred appeared next to her.

"You don't have to do that right now, Etta." She was almost apologetic.

Etta shrugged. "Really, I don't mind."

Mildred sighed. "Yeah. It helps to keep busy, doesn't it?"

Then, to Etta's astonishment, Mildred withdrew a cigarette and struck a match on the well pump. Etta's surprise must have shown, because Mildred suddenly appeared uncomfortable.

"Haven't had one of these in a while," she explained. "I quit around the time I got pregnant with Susie. More like Lena *made* me quit. She thought they were bad for me." Mildred flashed a wan smile at Etta. "God, you look so much like her. She was a wise woman even if she was a troubled one. I'm beside myself over Robert. I can't even imagine what Lena must have gone through. Four of her own children... I remember thinking how strange it was that she wouldn't talk about it, even months later." Mildred sighed. "I'd like to think that Robert's with her now. Maybe his own mother too. We never did find out what happened to Alicja.

"I mean, to *lose* a child is bad enough, but to *leave* her sons, even grown... Lena was so much like her in that regard. The way she treated you after-" She stopped abruptly, and looked embarrassed. Letting out a long, smoky, breath, she muttered, "You just can't account for bad luck."

Etta was unsure of how to respond, and said nothing. After a moment, she started to hang the wet clothes from the line, and Mildred continued to puff away in silence. With about half the length remaining, she extinguished her smoke and approached Etta.

Her eyes were glistening but also intense. Since hearing the news about Robert, Mildred had generally appeared so. Only now, there was something more. When she pulled Etta into a tight embrace, she assumed it was for bereavement.

"You take care of yourself," Mildred said. "I hope you know you always have a place here." Then, she looked at Etta in a way that was familiar, but not in mourning. It reminded her of the strange look she had received at the wedding. Etta watched Mildred walk back to the house, wondering about several things.

It was quiet again, save for a hot breeze whispering through the corn stalks. The laundry was finished, but Etta remained outside as the water dripped off and splashed to the dirt. If she could not keep busy, at least she would stay where it was peaceful. Sitting and watching the distant hills, she thought about recent events. It was hard to believe that only the other day she had been dancing with Art. She tried not to think about him, but he kept popping into her thoughts.

Of course, the alternative was thinking about Robert. At least the last words they exchanged had been pleasant ones. That was more than she could say for her mother. As Etta was considering the full implications of what Mildred had said, someone flopped down on the bench beside her.

"Hey, Chicken Farmer."

Helen's voice was tired. After nearly two full days of receiving condolences, it was the first time they had been together, just the two of them. Neither spoke. Instead, Etta put her arm around Helen and pulled her close. The only sound was the chirping of sparrows as they flitted above the stalks of corn. It was a while before Helen said anything more.

"The *day* after our honeymoon. I mean, the first day..."

"I know," replied Etta, her voice cracking.

Together, they sobbed quietly for a minute or so. Etta, of all people, knew that sometimes it just had to come out.

Eventually, Helen dried her eyes and sat up. "I'm glad that you were still here. Don't know what I would have done if you had already gone."

Etta grimaced. In truth, she had done much thinking about her plans to leave town since the wedding. The house had started to feel less like hers and Jakob's and more like hers and Art's. At least, it had been until their falling out. Helen knew about none of this, owing to how little they had spoken. Already distressed, it was the last thing Etta wanted to talk about.

"So much for making our last summer count," she said instead. She withdrew her arm from Helen's shoulders and tucked her knees to her chest. "I had no idea your mom smoked."

Helen wrinkled her nose, clearly not expecting that. "She usually doesn't. I don't think she's had one in at least two years."

Etta's mouth flattened to a line. "That was probably my mom's funeral, right?"

Helen looked to her and grimaced. "I suppose it was. You've been through a few of these, haven't you?"

"It's not something you get used to. It helps to keep busy."

Helen looked up. Her eyes dry for the first time since she joined Etta. "Is that the real reason why you work so much?" After a day and a half of receiving condolences, she seemed to crave for a change in subject.

"That's part of it," Etta replied without elaborating.

Helen started to gnaw at her bottom lip. A thought was forming. "I think you're making a mistake by leaving."

Frowning, Etta turned toward her. She had not expected this. "You never said anything before."

"It's just..." Helen hesitated. "Have you thought this through?"

That's funny, coming from you.

Rebuking herself, she pushed the thought away. That had not been kind, especially not now. The last few days had frayed her nerves more than usual. Even though Etta had started to reconsider her plans, she had not quite come around.

Instead, she replied, "We don't have to talk about this right now."

Helen pressed on. "Etta, I just lost my husband. I don't want to lose my best friend too. I mean, Art seems pretty well off, but-"

"I won't be going anywhere with him," Etta said abruptly. Thinking about Art had merely been troubling, but hearing his name spoken made her blood boil.

Helen was confused now. "Did something happen with you two?"

Etta found it remarkable that Helen could not help but gossip, even at a time like this. That was just who she was. They were both busybodies, but in different ways. Under other circumstances, Etta might have wanted to let it all out and tell Helen everything, but not just now. It was wrong, she thought, to taint her sorrow with angry feelings.

"We're no longer together," she replied.

Helen waited a long time for Etta to continue, but nothing more was offered. She might have been about to press for details, but at the last moment, Helen's expression changed. As though she had been struck with sudden inspiration.

"Why don't you come and live in the cottage with me?"

Etta shot her a sidelong glance. Feeling vulnerable from mourning, and generally sensitive to being pushed, the suggestion put her on guard. She shook her head as calmly as she could manage, but her friend doubled down. Up until now, Etta had assumed that Mildred would try the hardest to prevent her from leaving town. Apparently, it would be Helen.

"I think it would be good for both of us. You wouldn't have to work as hard as you do at the farm. Neither of us have to go it alone."

You need someone to do your chores for you, is that it?

Her eyes narrowed. In a sudden flash of anger, she wanted to tell Helen that it was time to grow up. To take some responsibility for her own life and to stop relying on others. Especially her. Etta bit her tongue, trying above all else to remain civil. Up until then, she had been undecided and would have preferred to think on it in her own time. Helen's pushing had forced her to confront the issue, and she reflexively decided on the opposite.

"I'm leaving town," Etta replied. "Like I said."

Helen was dismayed. "You're making a mistake," she repeated. "What if something like the thing with your hands happens again? My mom was saying..." She trailed off.

Etta let out an annoyed breath. "So, Mildred knows." It was not a question.

Not denying it, Helen looked away with what Etta assumed was guilt.

"You promised you were going to tell her by now," Helen said.

Somehow, she had managed to deflect blame, yet again.

"And you promised that you wouldn't," Etta retorted. Her blood pressure was rising, but she managed to keep her voice down with effort.

Helen, on the other hand, looked offended. "How *dare* you? *I* didn't. I *promised* you I wouldn't." She paused. "It was Robert if you must know. He had too much to drink one night and blurted it out." She looked away and started crying again. Though, whether it was in grief or anger was not clear.

"He…?" Etta started to say, but her anger vanished and she was soon at a loss for words. Beneath her dark feelings, she realized now that she just wanted to grieve, but it was too late to go back.

"Yes. It bothered him," Helen spat. Then, she hesitated, as if unsure whether or not to continue, but ultimately did so. "You wouldn't be the first woman to leave him."

Helen might as well have slapped her. If Etta had been at a loss for words before, now she was stunned into silence. Dismayed, all she could do was look at Helen who refused to meet her eyes. Helen sobbed quietly until she eventually sighed.

"I'm pregnant and mourning, dammit. I don't want to talk anymore. If you want to be on your own so badly, I won't stop you."

Without another word, Helen rose to her feet and returned to the house. Etta remained where she was. Despite her attempts to dismiss Helen's words, they gnawed at her conscience.

Motion at the edge of the cornrows drew her attention. Etta looked up to find Susie looking at her. It was actually something of a relief. Etta realized that she too had been crying, and hoped that Susie would come sit with her and ask questions again. Instead, the young girl simply turned around and disappeared back into the corn.

Etta was alone again.

At church the next day, Mildred sat between Etta and Helen. The two had not spoken since the previous day. At first, Etta thought that Helen simply needed some time, and that they would make amends as they usually did. But this was different. Helen made sure that they were never alone and never had an opportunity to talk. By the time they arrived at the funeral service, Etta was numb. Resigned even.

From the front pew, she stared blankly at the two caskets in front of her. Standing before them, Pastor James droned on with empty platitudes, praising the life of the departed with words that could apply to practically anyone. The eulogy was so generic that Etta was not sure whether the words were intended for Robert or Carl.

While Mildred cried quietly next to Etta, sniffling and letting escape only the occasional sob, Helen was more open about her emotions. It was frustrating. Desperately, she wanted to apologize and make things right. Once again, the two of them were feuding at the worst time.

On Etta's other side was Papa. His presence was both steady and comforting. His usual sullen appearance had been replaced by a stoic acceptance. Like her, Jakob was no stranger to funerals.

The joint service had brought in a lot of faces that she did not recognize, which made her uncomfortable. She was never one for crowds, especially a strange one. Etta decided they were probably relations of Carl, which only served as reminder that Pastor James could not be bothered to perform two separate services.

An open Bible sat in her lap, but she stared straight ahead, not looking at it. As they were the nearest kin, they sat in the front pew, closest to the departed. Distractedly, Etta noticed a scuffmark on one of the coffins, as if it had been bumped into a doorway during transit. Once discovered, she found it impossible to ignore.

Gradually, Etta was less numb and more annoyed with every passing minute. At first, it had been directed at Helen then at herself. Now, it was Pastor James, whom she held personally responsible for the scuffmark. Etta realized that she was grinding her teeth and made an effort to stop.

Even that was fleeting and she was surprised to find her dark feelings had turned to Robert. The same question came up again and again: why? He was going to be a father. He had only just become a husband.

Etta was only half-listening to James' milquetoast eulogy, but gave her full attention when he began to provide details of what had happened to Robert.

"And no one could doubt their bravery. Even after ensuring that the family had been safely removed from their damaged home. Carl and Robert, heedless of the danger to themselves, returned inside to check for others."

What? Why on Earth would they do that?

If the family was already outside, could they not have just said that the house was empty? Etta was suddenly reminded of her initial suspicion from when she first heard the news. The question of "Why?" came up again.

Etta began to mentally piece together a series of events, and it seemed she might have an answer, albeit, an unflattering one. Robert, never particularly blessed with an abundance of caution, combined with Carl, made for a dangerous recipe. "Why" indeed. Quickly losing her inhibition of thinking poorly of the deceased, the insidious thought grew. Soon, it was practically undeniable that Robert had somehow brought this on himself.

At the very least, he had allowed Carl to egg him into going back inside the house, when no one else from the ladder company had done so.

You wanted to see the bomb, didn't you?

Etta shook her head, in a token attempt to banish the troubling conjecture. Stubbornly, it persisted and she was grinding her teeth again.

Next to her, Mildred let out another sob, pulling Etta back into the church. Helen was nodding along, leaning against her mother's shoulder and crying. It was then that Etta caught a few more of Pastor James' words.

"...and even though Robert was taken in the summer of his life, we can take some small comfort that he lived a full one."

"That's so true," Helen whispered, either to herself or her mother. James continued on, but Etta had fallen back into her own, poisonous thoughts.

A full life? He had barely started it. His child would never know him. Etta could stand it no longer. The insincere priest. Her friend, who could be so stubborn at times, but just nodded along with this injustice. Her late cousin, who could not be bothered – even once – to exhibit the slightest bit of caution. And Art... damn that liar most of all.

The sound of a book slamming pulled her attention back to the church. It was loud and made worse by the acoustics of the room. The echo reverberated for several seconds, and the disruption had been such, that even Pastor James stumbled. Blinking, he looked up for just a moment before carrying on with the eulogy.

Who's the rude clod?

Looking around for the culprit, it was with slow and agonizing realization that Etta noticed every eye in the church squarely focused on her. Mildred's and Helen's chief among them.

Slowly, Etta turned her attention to her lap where the now closed Bible remained.

Slumping lower in the pew, she made her best attempt to melt into it. Suddenly, the anger was gone. What replaced it was utter embarrassment, but that too faded. All the wicked thoughts, which had served as a buffer until now had been entirely stripped away, leaving her with an all-consuming grief, which she realized had been underpinning it all. Everything that she had lost in the past week was finally laid bare. Art. Robert. And now Helen. Giving in at last, she too began to sob.

A repast followed in the yard between the church and the cemetery. Etta followed along with everyone else, all fight gone for the moment. She let herself be led by Papa who put a comforting arm over her shoulder after her outburst. Both physically and emotionally exhausted, she wanted nothing more than to curl up and fall asleep. However, there were still respects to be paid.

Etta had not yet spoken to Daniel except from when he first told them about what had happened. Doing so now, Etta noticed a rift that she had never been aware of before. Robert had always been the one to carry the conversation. A fact that was now inescapably clear. Etta offered her condolences, but it was soon clear that she and Daniel did not have much else to say to each other. Feeling uncomfortable on top of everything else, she walked away, thinking that she and Papa might then return home.

Instead, they met with old friends from around town, and the next hour was mostly a blur. Several times, Etta's eyes drifted towards the cemetery, where her late family rested. The thought of going over was oddly comforting in that moment, but she remained with the living. Eventually, Etta and Papa were pulled into separate circles and she realized that they would not be leaving anytime soon.

Excusing herself, she made her way over to a catered table that the Ladder Company had set up. If she could not sleep, at least she would eat. After scooping food onto a plate, she sighed despondently. By rights, she should have been famished, but for once Etta had no appetite.

Staring at the plate, she noticed someone approach. Even before he spoke, she suspected who it was.

“Hi,” Art said simply and without inflection.

Etta remained still, not looking at him. She tried to summon even a shred of the anger she had felt earlier, but simply could not muster the energy. Sighing, she dropped the serving spoon back into the bowl and turned around. Since they last spoke, she had given some thought about what she would say to him if they met again. Granted, with everything else going on, it was not much. Now that he was here, she could not remember any of it, and once more she felt the urge to sleep.

“Go away, Art,” she said tiredly and turned to leave.

“If I could just explain-”

“No, you cannot,” she replied brusquely, but still quietly enough to avoid making a scene. That is, another one. She took one step away from Art, before an appalling thought occurred to her.

“Wait. Did you come to the funeral just because you knew I'd be here?” Finding the anger she had been seeking a moment ago, her eyes were wild with disgust. “Of all the-”

“No. That's not it at all,” he shot back, incredulous that she could even consider such a possibility. “Since you asked, I'm here for Daniel.”

Etta was mildly stunned into silence. “Daniel?” she repeated, genuinely confused. “I didn't realize you were friends.”

“As a matter of fact, yes. We quiet, younger brothers need to stick together after all.”

This caught Etta off guard and she hesitated. Likewise, Art remained quiet. They faced each other in silence, neither of them sure what else to say. Several of the funeral attendees suddenly left in a hurry. Distractedly, she recognized a few of the firemen.

“How is Helen doing?” Art asked.

“What do you care?” Etta replied. She had intended for it to be scathing, but she ended up sounding only tired.

“Well,” Art shrugged. “She's your friend... and a widow now.”

“We're not speaking at the moment,” Etta replied.

“Again?”

“Yes, 'again!'” Etta growled.

This time, she delivered the desired level of venom, but its effect on Art was lackluster. Instead of recoiling in terror, he looked at her over the rim of his glasses in an expression that conveyed more annoyance than anything else. His lack of reaction only made her more angry.

"I'm just trying to talk with you," he replied with maddening calm.

"No," she replied through gritted teeth. "You're trying to make this all better. You feel guilty about lying to me, but some things you just can't fix." Etta forced herself to stop as she realized her voice was rising. Looking around, she was relieved to find that no one was looking at them. The incident with the Bible would be difficult to top, but she did not care to try.

I want to go home.

"I'm not going to marry Dorothy," Art whispered, as if trying to help offset her raised voice from before. Under different circumstances, that might have almost convinced her. It had been a wonderful couple of months. Up until the other night anyhow.

Maybe if she was not at yet another funeral. Maybe if she and Helen were not fighting. Maybe.

Faced with so many things in her life, utterly beyond her control, Art became the only available target for her frustration. Yet, there was still an annoying desire to mend that bridge. It occurred to Etta that she was withholding forgiveness from Art in a similar way that Helen was doing so from her. With stubborn determination, she pushed the notion aside, and decided that her mind was made up.

"That's between you and her then." Etta looked him square in the face when she spoke, then turned to walk away. "Goodbye Art."

"I'll be in town for a while, if you change your mind."

"Good for you. I won't."

Art got that bewildered look on his face like when he was trying to figure out a problem. A look she had once found endearing. It only annoyed her now, and she kept walking.

"Do you mean you won't be in town or you won't change your mind?" he asked blithely.

Etta made no response other than to stride toward the street with purpose.

Despite her state of mental exhaustion, the walk home was comforting. It occurred to her that she had taken the plate from the repast and started picking without thinking about it. Surprisingly, the knot in her stomach gradually loosened. As she walked and cleared her mind, Etta's thoughts drifted back to leaving town.

Despite what she had most recently told Helen, her determination had wavered, but not about sharing a roof. She may have lacked certainty in some matters, but she had no doubts about the realities of a domestic arrangement with her friend. Though, Helen had been absolutely right about one thing: Jakob would not keep the house. His home was Newark now.

Since finding the jalopy, Etta had intended to leave town herself, but in her plans a Wozniak would always keep their old house. Despite the ghosts and memories and general dilapidation, it was still the place she had shared with her family. The very thought of a bunch of strangers moving into it left her distraught.

Sirens wailed in the distance, temporarily pulling her from her thoughts. Shaking her head, Etta was conflicted. The farm was simply too much work, even with Art's help. But what about the house itself? It needed a tremendous amount of work, to be sure. But perhaps without the chickens and rest of her usual chores it might be manageable.

The land had not been used for anything besides weeds for years. Perhaps she could sell or lease it. Why bother farming at all? Touching the bag at her side, she felt the bulge of the nest egg. It must be close to the amount she and her father owed the town. If not, surely it would be after she sold the excess property. If she kept working for the Van Dycks, the whole thing just might work.

Etta thought of her pantomimes in the car, and her time spent at the Beckett's old place. Maybe leaving town was not really the answer after all. It occurred to her that what she needed, and what she had actually been working for all this time, was just a place of her own. Somewhere she could do as she pleased, drive her own car, and turn on the radio whenever she damn well wanted.

The thought actually brightened her mood for the first time in a couple days. It felt like she might be able to regain some semblance of control over the things in her life. She thought about Helen again. They would never be able to peacefully live in the same house, but she was still Etta's best friend, and she wanted to be somewhere close.

Distractedly, she noticed that the sound of sirens was only getting louder.

Lizzie Hunley was another reason to stay. It had been so good to make a new friend, especially one who understood the things she could not discuss with Helen. And they actually had a profitable little farm. Maybe Etta could work there... after she bought her own car. Although, she might have to avoid Art for some time while he worked on their truck.

Or did she? Maybe she had been too harsh with him. After all, she had been angry at the time, and had not asked him about the particulars of his engagement. It was easy to forget what a shy fellow he was around most other people. And that Dorothy girl seemed the pushy type. Maybe that whole thing had been genuinely out of his control.

I should talk with him at least...

The droning wail of sirens had intensified to the point it could not be ignored. Recognizing them now, she recalled the haste with which the firemen had left the repast. With dread, it also occurred to Etta that this road led directly to the farms. Her pace quickened with the sudden realization.

The Saunders home.

In their haste to get to church, had they left the oven burning? It was something that they had done a thousand times before, but this time, it must have gotten out of hand.

Etta started to run. Slipping out of one shoe by accident and soon discarding the other one, she left them where they fell. Likewise, she dropped the church plate that she had fully intended to return just a moment before.

Smoke was visible now; a thick, gray column towered above the trees. Her bare feet pounded the dirt road. She stumbled and grunted in surprise when she struck a partially exposed rock. Recovering, she kept going.

Etta soon passed the Beckett's old house, and approached the final bend. Truth told, she had no idea what she intended to do once she got there without shoes or so much as a bucket to douse the flames. Still she ran. She had to see it.

Maybe she could rescue a few of the Saunders things. Something that the firemen did not think to grab.

Of all the days...

Breathing heavily, she kept up the grueling pace. As she drew closer, the sirens became louder. She braced herself, fully expecting to find the Saunders' home engulfed in flame.

Rounding the curve, her pace slowed as she tried to comprehend the sight before her. To say she was surprised did not cover it by half. While still some distance away, it was unmistakable. Sitting where it always had, completely unscathed, was the Saunders' home.

It was neither burned nor disturbed in any way. Etta should have been relieved, and for the briefest moment she was. But the dirt road was still host to both the town's pumper and ladder trucks. A score of firemen went about their business. So focused was she on the anticipated loss of the Saunders' home, that it had never occurred to her what was happening at her own.

With mounting dread, Etta pivoted toward her house. She noted with numb understanding that the pumper truck had knocked over the mailbox in its haste to get up the driveway. Finally, her gaze reached the house itself, confirming what she had already come to anticipate.

As she looked, the fire company continued to spray water but most of the flames had already been doused. The damage was done. Etta could not remember walking up the drive. Nor did she respond when one of the firemen pushed her back, behind the relative safety of the pumper truck. In later hindsight, she would realize she had been in shock. Her nerves blasted beyond their limit after so many blows.

Expression blank, she was utterly incapable of mustering up a reaction of any kind. Etta simply stared at the smoking, charred remains of what had once been her family's home.

Chapter 28
Art

Art sought out Daniel, who was, in fact, the reason he attended in the first place. He was clearly glad for a reprieve from the constant flow of mourners. Like Art, Daniel was a quiet type, and it was understandable that the multitude of faces, while trying to convey sympathy, only added to his stress.

For all appearances he remained quiet, taking the loss of his brother in stoic acceptance. Little that he knew him, Art could tell from the look in his eyes that it was just that: an appearance. Thus, he was surprised when Daniel brought up a completely unrelated subject.

"How's your eye?" he asked suddenly.

Art hesitated to respond, but eventually figured that Daniel was desperate to focus on something else, if only for a short time.

"Fine now. A little tender if I poke it, but doesn't really bother me any more."

Daniel nodded. "You don't really look like a fella that gets in too many dust ups. Y'know. With the glasses and all."

Art shrugged. "Got into more than a couple with my brothers over the years..." He trailed off upon realizing that he had said the word "brother."

Daniel sighed. "Yeah. Robert and I had our fair share growing up. We get along well enough now – er – y'know what I mean. Everyone always liked him. I only ever tagged along, but he never tried to ditch me. After Ma left, he always made sure the two of us stuck together. Robert was a good one.

"Thought I might see her today. Is that strange? My dad too, but truth told, I'm not sure I could pick him out of a crowd. Robert talked about him a lot. I think that's why he wanted a family of his own so much. Even when we were little he'd talk about his future kids. 'Course, once he finally was about to have one, this whole mess had to happen."

Daniel shook his head, and worked his jaw for a moment. "I want to be there for Helen and the baby - a kid shouldn't have to grow up without a father. Thing is... I just don't think I can be a fireman anymore. Not now."

When it was clear that he was finished speaking, Art spoke up.

"How are you with tools?"

Before another gaggle of mourners descended on them, Art invited Daniel to come by the shop when he was ready. There was plenty of work to go around. Having paid his respects, Art left the funeral, but was not ready to go back to the cottage. Things had remained tense all week.

Choosing the route with more shade, even though it took longer, he began to walk. He needed time to think, or rather to come to terms with the inevitable. Etta had been both clear and consistent that things between them were over. The grand total of his failures with women had ticked up to three. He had debated whether to even approach her at the funeral. Only a few days had passed since their unfortunate parting. Initially, he intended to wait longer, but upon seeing her, could not help himself.

He had actually attempted to follow through on his decision to end the engagement. The day after his date with Etta, he had gone to breakfast to confront his parents. Having disappeared without explanation the day before, both of them lashed out with a ferocity that he had not expected. Rather than endure it, he turned and walked out of the house mid-tirade. No doubt, he would pay for that little defiance.

Art tried not to dwell on his own troubles. He had, after all, just attended a funeral. Things could always be worse. As he walked, his thoughts were a sullen tangle of a thousand different threads. A few hours of cutting and shaping metal seemed just the ticket to clear his mind. He found comfort in one of his father's unofficial mottoes: busy hands are happy hands.

Maybe he would go see Etta later that afternoon, after things had a chance to settle.

Finally arriving at the shop, he was surprised to find that Gregory was not there. For a moment, Art thought maybe his days were mixed up in the chaos of the past week. It was plausible. Was Gregory visiting his daughter? Trying to remember, Art took a moment to change out of his suit and into the coveralls he kept at the shop. No, it was definitely a workday. After all, Gregory's truck was still parked out front.

Art briefly considered doing some work alone, despite his mentor's strict prohibition on such things. He stopped, deciding not to antagonize the last person in his life with whom he was on good terms. Besides, now sure that it was a workday, the absence was troubling. Art started a more thorough search, beginning with the entire shop. No evidence that Gregory had even entered. Next he checked the stock shed, the loft, and even the outhouse.

Nothing.

Finally, he thought to check the house itself, which he had never been inside before. Art knocked on the door out of habit, and waited a full minute with no answer. He was about to turn away, but thought to try the knob at the last moment.

It was unlocked.

Entering the foyer, he called out. “Hello?”

The house was surprising in its contrast to the shop. Art would have expected to find half-completed mechanisms and random junk piled everywhere. Indeed, from the marks on the wall and floor, it looked to have been so until recently. Now, it was pristine. Aside from the occasional cobweb and a little dust, it was strangely normal. When Art received no answer, he ventured further within, feeling like an intruder despite his growing relationship with Gregory.

In passing, he noticed a few pictures on the wall. Most of them featured a much younger Gregory with a woman and a young girl. Except for one. It stood out as the only one not covered with dust. This was a portrait of a woman and a different young child, presumably, mother and daughter. At first glance, she was the spitting image of the woman in the family portraits, whom Art concluded was Gregory's late wife. Looking more closely, her eyes were just like Gregory's. This was clearly the daughter he often visited.

The sound of creaking floorboards above his head pulled Art's attention to the ceiling.

Was Gregory just getting out of bed? Without knowing specifically what, he sensed that something was wrong. Art walked quickly to the bottom of the stairs, but did not ascend.

“Gregory? You alright?” he called upstairs.

No answer. Frozen with indecision, he waited another moment.

“I'm coming up.”

Art climbed. A quiet, low moan, escaped from one of the bedrooms. His pace quickened. Even though it was clear that something had happened, he still felt compelled to knock on the door. A wall of unpleasant odors assaulted him as he entered the bedroom. Gregory was curled up on the floor, tangled in his bed sheets.

On first glance, he might have simply have fallen out of the bed. Then, Art began to notice things. Gregory's face was sweaty and ashen, utterly devoid of normal color. His breathing was raspy and labored, and the general miasma present in the room refined itself as both sour and foul.

With no small effort, Gregory opened his eyes. Seeing Art, he made an attempt to raise his hand, but only succeeded in flexing it at the wrist. Art stood immobilized with uncertainty.

Unable to think of anything else to do, he asked, “What happened?”

Without answering, Gregory dropped his hand, and sank further to the floor. The only movement was the slow rise and fall of his chest. After another moment of stunned inaction, Art finally snapped out of his stupor.

“I- I'll go get help,” he said.

Though it was clear that Gregory could not hear him, he sprinted downstairs. Art nearly tripped in his haste, and began searching the house for a phone. Not entirely surprised to discover that Gregory did not own one, his next thought was the neighbor.

The next closest house was nearly a quarter of a mile away. Breathing heavy from the run, he pounded on the door for a full minute before he realized that no one was home. Frustrated, he ran back to check on Gregory. It was a hot July day and, wearing his work coveralls, his eyes were stinging with sweat by the time he arrived back upstairs.

Gregory had regained enough of his faculties to look up at Art again.

“Don't... leave...” Gregory managed before losing consciousness again. Sensing that he was quickly losing time, Art considered trying to simply carry him to the truck. He almost did, but without knowing what was wrong with Gregory, he did not want to risk making it worse. Far better, he thought to drag him, but that left the problem of the stairs. Still breathing heavily, he stopped to think.

From the workshop, he retrieved a long, shallow tray. Carefully, he pulled Gregory onto it, using the blankets as grips. Moving Gregory from where he had fallen revealed a pool of unspeakable filth that nearly caused Art to retch. Gagging, but focused on the task at hand, he pulled some extra pillows and blankets from the closet to give Gregory some padding. The older man remained unconscious but his chest at least was moving.

"I don't know if you can hear me, but I'm going to move you. It's not going to be comfortable but hang in there."

Inch by inch, he dragged the makeshift litter out of the room and let it down the stairs. A bead of sweat streaked down his glasses and his muscles were aching from the exertion. He dared not let go. An eternity later, he had Gregory on the front porch. Sweating buckets, he ran to the truck and backed it closer to the porch.

As luck would have it, the porch was just about on a level with the bed of the truck, but the stairs only allowed him to get so close. Bridging the gap with some wooden boards, he pulled Gregory into the back. In his current state, he nearly lost his grip, but recovered before Gregory could fall off.

After making a few adjustments to the padding on the improvised gurney, Art secured it to the inside wall of the box truck.

"Wha's go non?" Gregory asked, barely over a whisper. His teeth were clenched and he only spoke out of one side of his mouth.

"We're going to the hospital," Art replied as he worked. "This is going to get bumpy. I'm sorry."

Gregory's eyes had closed again, and Art was not sure that he had heard. Hoping to give reassurance, he put his hand on Gregory's shoulder and they were soon underway.

The ride to the hospital was nearly ten miles, and Art felt every turn and bump. Each time the truck bounced or shuddered, he winced and looked through the window to the enclosed truck bed. Gregory lay still, except for where he was jostled by the motion of the vehicle. For the whole duration of the trip, Art could not be sure if the man was awake or even still alive.

Little that he knew of the area beyond Bott's Lake, Art had actually passed the hospital in nearby Dover during his trip to buy parts for Etta's radio. He lost precious minutes attempting to retrace his steps from a month earlier. In the day's only good fortune, temporary signs had been erected as a guide for those affected by the recent depot explosion. Art just hoped that it was not too late.

As the building came into view, he was forced to stop a hundred or so yards away. The streets were congested, not just with injured, but also many of those displaced by the explosion and family members coming to search for them. With no clear way forward, Art stopped the truck and ran around to check on Gregory. His eyes were closed, but he was still breathing.

"We made it, but I can't get to the front door. I'm gonna go and find some help." Art thought he might have heard a grunt in reply, but could not be sure.

Hours later, Art was pacing the waiting area when a middle-aged nurse approached him.

"Excuse me," she said. "Did you bring in Gregory Robbins?"

Looking up, Art was taken aback by her smile, which stood in jarring contrast to the rest of her appearance. Her cap sat at an angle as though it had almost been knocked off her dark hair more than once. Her apron was smeared in various places with fresh stains that Art decided he would rather not think about. In her eyes, he saw the trudging, exhausted visage of someone who was clearly having a worse day than him.

And yet she smiled. He found it oddly reassuring despite the knowledge that it must have been forced.

Art nodded in response. Gregory was awake and asking for him. As he made his way to the ward, he passed clear evidence that the hospital was still dealing with the effects of the recent explosion. Thankfully, Gregory's bed was in a quieter area. Most of the patients here were sleeping, and did not notice as Art poked his head through the privacy curtains, searching for his mentor. At last, he found Gregory in a bed near the corner. His eyes were closed, but opened upon Art's approach.

Recognizing him, the older man attempted to smile. It was plain that something was wrong. Half of Gregory's face remained slack in an unnatural grimace. The sight distressed Art on a deep, visceral level but he tried not to let it show. Thinking of the nurse and the simple power of a happy face, he forced himself to smile back.

"Hey, Old Man. How ya feeling?"

Gregory tried to speak, but the slack side of his mouth refused to cooperate and Art found it impossible to understand him. Gregory quickly grew frustrated, and stopped talking after letting out an annoyed groan. Looking around, Art found a pen and pressed it into Gregory's good hand. A discarded newspaper was in the waste bin. Tearing out a mostly blank section, he set it on a book in front of his mentor.

The old man's handwriting suffered from the same ailment that had taken his speech, but it was readable after a few tries.

Stroke. How get here?

Art breathed a quiet sigh of relief, thankful that they were communicating at last. “I found you in your bedroom. Brought you here. Do you remember anything?”

Gregory was still for a long moment, and struggled to think. The faraway, unseeing expression reappeared on his face, and Art wondered just how long this had been brewing. After a few seconds, he started writing again.

Bouncing truck. Lousy driver.

The good side of his face curled up in a smile again and Art actually chuckled. Mostly at the sheer absurdity, but it was good to see Gregory's humor was still in there.

“I blame the truck's owner myself. Seems like someone failed to maintain it.” Art's smile faded as Gregory continued writing.

This bad. Get Kevin McHenry.

Art was unsettled by the word “bad.”

“Okay. I can do that. Who is he?”

Gregory did not answer directly. With some struggle, he managed to get four more words onto the paper.

Address at house. Desk.

Gregory's hand slipped on the last word, streaking the pen across the paper. Even writing was proving to be difficult, and Art decided to let Gregory rest and figure out the rest by himself.

“That's fine. I'll get him over here. Just sit tight.”

Gregory jerked his head in what might have been a nod, and closed his eyes.

It took most the rest of the afternoon for Art to make his way back to Gregory's house and find anything with Kevin McHenry's name on it. While the house itself was clean and orderly, the study and desk were another matter. To Art’s eyes, it was like the shop used to be, before he learned Gregory's system. That felt like a lifetime ago.

After an interminable search, Art finally located an address for Kevin McHenry. Unfortunately, there was no phone number, but even if there was, Art had no idea where to even find one at this moment. Jumping back in the truck, he headed out. The office was in Netcong, which Art had at least a passing familiarity with, having been to the train station twice.

He arrived at a corner building with a sign saying “Law Offices” prominently featured in front, and not a moment too soon. Art caught Kevin just as he was preparing to leave for the day. After he explained the situation, Kevin collected a few last-minute items from inside his office.

“Bring an extra pen and paper,” Art quickly added before Kevin closed up.

When the two of them arrived at Gregory's bed, Art thought that his mentor might be showing signs of improvement. Or maybe that was only wishful thinking.

“I brought Kevin,” Art said.

Gregory's eyes fluttered open and Art motioned for Kevin to offer the pen and paper. Gregory wrote two words.

Go home.

Art blinked, not entirely sure of what he was reading. “Me?”

Yes.

“We usually conduct these sort of things in private,” Kevin said. “Or near enough to it.” He regarded the curtains on either side of the bed and motioned for Art to leave.

Somewhat taken aback, Art stood up, unsure of what to do with himself. As he turned to go, Kevin stopped him. Gregory had written something else.

Good working with you.

Gregory looked him straight in the eye while favoring him with another half-smile. Art nodded and returned it, hoping he appeared more at ease than he felt.

“I'll come visit you tomorrow.” And then he left.

Remembering that the front door of Gregory's house was still open, he felt obliged to go back to close it. Briefly, he considered the mess in the upstairs bedroom, but decided that was a problem for tomorrow. Art resolved to make everything right again before Gregory returned home, but for now he was utterly exhausted. He felt an irrational pang of guilt at continuing to borrow the truck, but he meant to go back to the hospital the following morning, and did not want to waste time by walking all the way back to the shop.

It was late evening by the time Art arrived back at the cottage. Dinner was long over, but most of the family remained seated at the table in the back yard. Hungry and exhausted, Art was briefly tempted to join the others if only to get something to eat. Ultimately, he decided against it. The sweat he worked up earlier had dried, leaving him feeling grimy, and for a variety of reasons he was not keen to be anyone's company just now.

Standing at the entrance to the kitchen, footsteps approached from behind. Remaining still, he hoped that whoever it was would simply pass without remark.

"You missed Dorothy again," said a voice, which Art immediately recognized as Ralph's. "Franklin gave Father an earful over it. He's sure sore at you."

Art said nothing. Somewhere in the cold, rational part of his mind, he knew this deliberate goading by Ralph should elicit more of a reaction, but in his state of utter exhaustion, he was surprisingly indifferent to it.

Sensing that his jabs were not landing, Ralph pressed on. "Maybe he'll give you the paddle for old time's sake, eh?"

Ralph's words were just beginning to slur together, evidence that he had been in his cups. The Kennedys must have left some time ago, if the wine had come out of hiding. Art finally turned around, and regarded his brother with an even stare. Mistakenly, Ralph interpreted this as success in getting under his skin. He stared back, apparently emboldened. The corner of his mouth twisted up in a sneer, and his eyes danced mockingly.

Art knew the look well, as he had been seeing it all his life. Junior may have tormented Art with his own brand of grief from time to time, but by and large, he had generally fallen below his oldest brother's notice. Ralph had always been the one to make Art his personal punching bag.

"Not to worry though, I made sure your intended didn't get lonely."

Art narrowed his eyes.

"Oh, yes," Ralph continued. "Had a nice conversation, the two of us. She loaned me another book. Batted her eyes at me..."

Art suppressed the urge to wince as spittle flecked from Ralph's mouth. At the same time, he recalled his brother's odd behavior since Dorothy arrived in town. Much of it was starting to make sense. This knowledge might have presented him with a neat solution a few weeks or even days ago.

In fact, Art wondered why Ralph had not acted on it sooner, as it was just the sort of thing the jackass would do. Perhaps Art was not the only one among his brothers who would hesitate to defy their parents. It was all so preposterous and he nearly laughed. Tired as he was, it came out like a sigh. Ralph pressed on, now thinking that he was getting somewhere.

"Then, you can run off with your little blue-collared husband all you want. Tell me: is he a gentle lover?"

Art's response, which might have bordered on civil, died on his tongue. Up until now, his exhaustion had overruled all other emotions, but bringing Gregory into it, who was laid up in a hospital bed at this very moment, cut too deep. It must have showed too. Ralph's sneer erupted into a wide, taunting grin at this apparent victory.

Eyes unblinking, Art leaned in a bare inch. He spoke evenly and clearly. "Ralph. Fuck off."

Without waiting for a response, he turned to walk away, but was stopped before he could take even a single step. The collar of his coveralls went tight, suddenly caught in Ralph's vice-like grip. Yanking it, he pulled Art close.

"What'd you say to me?" he growled. Ralph's breath was hot and stank of wine.

For the briefest, fleeting moment, Art was about to apologize and beg forgiveness. It was a reflexive thought, born out of decades of conditioning. A bare handful of times in his life, he had dared to directly challenge his brother, and it always ended the same. Ralph would hold him immobile until he cried for mercy, and only then let him off with a couple of parting jabs. Lest there be any doubt as to who was boss.

However, on this particular day, Art found he had absolutely run out of cares, and had no patience for Ralph's nonsense. When Art said nothing, Ralph shook him in his grip. Oddly, it reminded him of his fight with Walter. He had never intended for punches to be thrown in that case.

In truth, he had been frightened. His history with fighting was about as successful as his record with women. That was to say, poor. In both situations, he was usually left defeated and hurt.

Strangely, thinking of the fight reminded him of Etta.

If only she could have let me explain...

Ralph, growing impatient, gave his brother another shake.

"What. Did. You say?" he demanded again.

Instead of eliciting the desired fear, Ralph's prodding and attempts to bully him into submission only served to annoy Art. Annoyance, which soon gave way to anger. Only with his usual, cool and sober judgment sufficiently clouded, did Art make a questionable decision.

He turned around in his brother's grip so they were facing each other. Mistakenly, Ralph thought Art's squirming was an attempt to escape and made to pull him closer. Clearly, Ralph was unprepared and particularly surprised when Art reached out with both hands to grip the front of his shirt. Once they were looking eye to eye, Art recognized something in his brother's expression that he could never remember seeing before.

Not fear exactly, but doubt at the very least.

His muscles tensed as he pressed close to Ralph. In a sudden reversal, Art felt his brother attempt to push him back to arm's length. It was too late. Their faces almost touching, Art repeated himself, clenching his teeth, and biting off the words with as much venom and hatred as he could muster.

"Fuck. Off."

It was hard to say who threw the first punch, and the next few seconds were a blur. Art lost all sense of time or even where they were. There were only fists, and elbows, and Ralph's face filling his vision. They fell to the floor, grappling on the rug. Each tried to gain room to throw a punch before the other could do so. Art's coveralls ripped where Ralph had been holding them, which temporarily threw them off balance.

Not thinking anymore, Art delivered a jab to Ralph's gut. Over a decade of retribution went into that strike, but it only served to make his brother mad. Ralph quickly recovered and delivered a punch of his own. The air was driven from Art's lungs. He grabbed Ralph's tie and pulled his face into a small table, knocking it over. With it, fell a lamp that landed on his head.

Rolling away, Ralph grabbed Art by the lapels, picked him up and slammed him into the floor. For a second, Art saw stars. In a distracted way, he was thankful that they were still on the carpet. With Ralph straddling him, Art threw another wild hook to his brother's ribs. As he moved to protect that side, Art knocked him over, and scurried out from beneath.

Oddly, there was not much in the way of pain. That would, of course, come later. There was no telling how long the fight went on for, but to Art's surprise, everything was suddenly cold. And wet.

Nearly as one, they broke off their scuffle and rolled away from each other. Art remained laying on his back, and Ralph likewise stopped to catch his breath. Looking up, he saw, what was probably the entire family looking down at them. Albeit, things were blurry since his glasses had fallen off during the scuffle, but it was fairly simple to ascertain their various reactions.

Luciana stood in front of the lot, holding an empty but dripping pot. The look on her face was a mix of shock, disbelief, and above all, anger. George was surprised as well, but oddly enough, also concealed a smirk. Senses temporarily dulled, Art was distantly aware that his mother had asked a question. Actually, it was more that she demanded an answer. He did not quite hear it as his ears were ringing from when his head hit the floor.

When neither Art nor Ralph made a response, she repeated herself, and his blood ran cold when he recognized that she was speaking Italian. Only then did his thoughts finally coalesce into some order.

"He started it," Ralph said between heaving breaths. His nose was bleeding, though he had not yet noticed. Slowly, he rose to his feet. "I simply asked little Arty about his day. Don't know what set him off."

Art regarded his brother, still unsteady in his attempts to rise.

In for a penny. In for a pound.

He gave Ralph a solid shove, knocking him back to the floor. Ralph had not been expecting the dirty pull, but recovered quickly, and rounded on Art with murder in his eyes. The fight might have resumed then, but Ralph immediately stopped at the sound of their father's voice.

George was no longer smirking. "ENOUGH!" he bellowed.

It had been a while since George had cause to raise his voice, but the effect was immediate. Ralph and Art both froze in place, as their father towered above them. "I'll not have you behaving like damned savages in my house, especially not around the children. The two of you stand up and shake hands. Now!"

Grudgingly, they rose to their feet, and complied, glaring at each other the whole time, but wary of their father, who was doubtlessly still capable of throttling the two of them together. Art momentarily gave up the search for his glasses, but was close enough to Ralph for his features to be clear. With both of them physically spent from the fight, they were past using fists, but a simmering animosity remained. As they shook hands, Ralph could apparently not resist a parting shot.

"Sorry for hitting you, Little Sister," he said, upper lip now covered in blood.

"Nice nose," Art replied.

Ralph touched his other hands to his face, and finally realized he was bleeding. His eyes went wide and the muscles in his neck bulged as he squeezed Art's hand.

"I said that's enough, damn you!" George roared.

Art and Ralph separated, for good this time, but the damage had already been done. Art thought he had seen his father livid once or twice before. It was nothing compared to this. His face was a shade of red that was truly terrifying. George stepped closer, just inches from their faces and glared at each in turn. His sheer height and bulk was never more apparent. Finally showing some sense, neither of them met his eyes.

"Pack your things," he said in a tone that allowed no room for debate. "Neither of you are spending the night here."

"What?" Ralph asked, taken aback.

"You damn well heard me, boy." At that, he turned around and walked away. "Come back tomorrow if you can be civil."

"Where am I supposed to go?" demanded Ralph.

"Not my concern," George called as he left the room. The rest of the room, likewise, filed out in short order, now that the show was over. Art remained silent. The white-hot anger had gone away. With fresh bruises layered over his old ones, they promised a painful morning ahead.

Ralph stormed upstairs, ostensibly, to collect his things, but Art suspected that he had some final, petty mischief planned as well.

He was beyond caring. As exhaustion settled in, he rubbed his face. After a long moment of quiet, he noticed that only he and his mother remained. She stared at him, balled fists resting on her hips. Without his glasses, she was blurry, even at this distance, but her stern look of disapproval was obvious. That actually hurt more than all his fresh aches.

Looking around, he spotted his glasses and frowned as he returned them to his face. They were bent again, but lacking the energy to fix them, he let them hang at an odd angle. Art and Luciana stared at each other, and her look weighed on him. Somehow, it was worse now that he could see more clearly. Averting his gaze to the floor, the silence lingered.

With sullen resignation, he eventually asked, "Aren't you going to say something?"

Luciana cocked her head, her frown deepening. "And what would you like me to say? I'll be honest, I'm at my wits' end with you. You're gone for four years, then we finally get the family together for a nice holiday, and you disappear again – I don't know where. You're out all night and show up with unexplained bruises. I find you a nice girl, and you barely give her the time of day. And now you get into a fight with your own brother. I'm looking at a stranger right now."

She stared, silent again, and let him stew. It had been a while since she had successfully evoked such intense guilt, but it turned out she still had the knack for it. Eventually, Art cleared his throat.

"I don't suppose it would help if I said I'm having a bad week?"

Her scowl remained, but now it was offset to the slightest degree by curiosity.

“It probably couldn't hurt. Is there something you want to talk about?”

Art thought about Gregory and the events of the day. He thought about his falling out with Etta. A defeated malaise came over him, as he realized that there was nothing to be done for either of them. In fact, thinking about it in that moment, feeling slightly dizzy and with nothing else to lose, Art realized that there was only one problem that he currently had any semblance of control over.

“I'm not going to marry Dorothy,” he said, and the words surprised even him.

His mother stared without saying anything for a long moment.

“I beg your pardon?” she asked, brow furrowed.

“I meant to say something sooner. Sorry.” Art shrugged and winced with the motion. Ralph had landed a couple good hits on his shoulder. Or maybe it had been his neck? There were scarce few places that did not hurt just then.

“We've already sent out invitations. And Gertrude reserved a mass.”

“Dorothy is nice enough, I suppose,” Art replied, “but we really don't seem to match.” He probed one of his front teeth with his tongue, hoping that the loose feeling was his imagination.

Luciana went to fold her arms across her chest, but remembered she was still holding the pot and resorted to returning her fists to her hips. Her expression of disbelief and annoyance remained unchanged.

“And how on Earth would you know? You've barely spent any time with her.”

“I think I know enough.”

Luciana scoffed, and her expression darkened. “Aren't you just your father's son?”

Art was rendered speechless.

Where did that come from?

“Typical Adams man, who knows every damned thing, and has it all figured out. And I suppose I'll just have to smile along with whatever flapper *putana* you bring home, who does nothing but talk behind my back and hide my grandchildren from me?”

This was the most worked up that Art had ever seen his mother, and he suspected that at least some of it was not directed at him. Art forgot about his aches and exhaustion for a moment and wondered about Luciana's reaction. She caught herself mid-diatribe and returned her composure as quickly as if she were replacing a mask. Her flared nostrils gave the only evidence to the underlying disquiet.

When it was clear she would say nothing else, Art ventured a thought.

"Is there something *you* want to talk about?"

The mask slipped once more, but only just. "No," she said too quickly. "You heard your father. Find somewhere else to sleep." With that, she turned on her heel and stormed off.

Sighing, Art walked outside. Unsure of what to do next, he stood at the base of the porch steps and considered his next move. A soft *whump* caught his attention as he noticed a bunched up shirt fall to the ground. Frowning, he looked up. The window of the room he shared with Ralph was open. As he stared, a pair of pants flew out and landed next to the shirt, which he now recognized as his.

What an ass...

Looking at Gregory's truck, it occurred to him that there was only one real option for a place to spend the night.

Arriving at the workshop a few minutes later, he parked the truck, and lay back. Art only intended to rest his eyes, but quickly fell into a deep, dreamless sleep.

He was awakened by harsh sunlight reaching into the truck's cab. Art had sprawled out across the bench seat during the night, and was now feeling the full consequences of the previous day. His faced throbbed, his back ached, and his neck was all out of sorts from resting at an odd angle during the night. Still, he supposed it was better than being hung over.

More than anything, his bladder was full beyond discomfort.

After tending to the necessary, he walked over to the well pump and splashed water on his face. After an initial sting, it fell to the ground tinged with red. With his senses gradually returning, his next thought was of Gregory. However poorly his own night had been, Art suspected that his mentor had a worse one. Getting back into the truck, he headed straight for the hospital.

Making his way to the same ward he had been twice already, Art wondered if perhaps he had been hit on the head worse than he thought. Gregory was nowhere to be found. He checked every bed, and got a few angry responses for his trouble. The old man was not there. Next he considered that he had simply gone to the wrong ward, but that was quickly debunked. In a moment of optimism, he thought that Gregory might have been released.

Looking around, he found a nurse reading a chart. Glancing up, but only half-paying attention, she smiled pleasantly.

"Oh, hello again. I hope you didn't spend the night here," she said.

It took him a moment to recognize her as the same one he had met the day before. Her clothing was fresh and clean, with none of the stains she had accumulated on the previous day. The difference between seeing her at the end of her shift yesterday and now at the beginning of her shift was staggering.

"Ah, no," he said. "I just haven't had a chance to clean up."

Looking at him more fully, she frowned suddenly. "Good God, have you been looked at?" she asked, voice full of professional concern as she started to evaluate him on the spot.

He was suddenly self-conscious about his appearance. Looking down, he noticed for the first time that there was a considerable amount of blood on the front of his coveralls, and he could only imagine the discolored mess that his face was.

"Long story. I'm fine," he lied. "I brought in Gregory Robbins. Was he moved?"

The nurse flipped through her clipboard. After she stopped, and read through a page, her frown deepened. Lowering the chart, she bit her lower lip.

"I'm sorry to be the one to tell you this..."

She continued speaking, though it was not necessary. Understanding came over Art, and the rest of her words faded away. If he was being honest, he had known it before coming here, but there had been some shred of hope that he was wrong. Perhaps he would be surprised by some miraculous recovery. As the nurse continued, the cold, hard truth of it was impossible to deny. There would be no implausible, however pleasant turn of events.

Gregory was dead.

Chapter 29
Etta

Etta knelt down at the usual spot, flowers in hand. With her thoughts troubled as they were, she did not speak for a long moment. Automatically, she pulled up a few errant weeds that had grown between the headstones and made a note to speak with the groundskeeper. Sighing, she realized there was little point.

"I know I wasn't supposed to visit for another month, but this is kind of an unusual occasion," she said to Edward's gravestone. Looking at the others, she laid a single flower at each one. "Hope you don't mind the daisies. They were all I could find on short notice."

Etta sighed, trying to focus her thoughts, but constantly fought the urge to glance over her shoulder. This had been an impromptu visit, and Papa was waiting back at the truck. It was not her preference to talk to the family with anyone else around; even Papa. However, events had forced her hand.

"This may be my last visit for a while," she began. "You might have already seen, but we lost the house."

Etta cringed as she imagined the heap of steaming and blackened timbers. For two days, it haunted her and intruded upon whatever small peace she found amid the other unpleasant business.

The less she thought about it, the better, but she had to wonder if the kerosene lantern had been the culprit. The same lantern she hung from the kitchen ceiling each morning. For years, it had done its job without incident, but in recent months, she had noticed the hook was just a bit looser than she remembered. It had seemed a small enough thing. After all, everything in the house was in similar disrepair. As a precaution, she never left the lantern on the hook for long and always extinguished it before leaving the house. Except for the day of the funeral.

Despite Papa's reassurances that he too had forgotten, she could not completely dispel the guilty notion that she bore the most blame. Etta was never one to let others carry a burden that was rightfully hers. Their home had become her responsibility, and she managed to destroy it.

Looking to the headstones and feeling their silent judgment, Etta continued.

"The barn was spared, so there's that I suppose. And the ladies were far enough away not to be hurt, but everything inside was lost. The radio. Your old things. Gone. Aunt Mildred gave me a couple extra sets of clothes or else I'd have nothing but what I was wearing at the funeral.

"Irene... I don't know what happened to Howler. I looked around and called for her, but she never turned up. I'm sorry." Etta felt foolish at the last, then added. "Maybe she's finally back with you.

"Papa took it surprisingly well. To be honest, I think he's been ready to move on for a while. Now he has an excuse. He sold everything in the barn to Owen Hunley. We were going to just gift the chickens to the Saunders, but they insisted on paying for them.

"Papa said he's not going to bother with the taxes. The town can have the land and what's left of the house. Strangely, the police wanted to talk with him. They even asked – none too subtle – if he had set the fire himself. The very idea! Not that it was insured or anything.

"And... that's it. We're leaving today." She paused. "I'm not sure how I feel about it. Of course, I *thought* I wanted to leave for a while now, but I started to reconsider. I certainly didn't want this… I would have rather had another family move in than see the place burn down. And I wish I wasn't leaving things with Helen the way they were. Papa and I spent the last two nights at the Saunders' house. Helen didn't say much... to me at least. I know she's missing Robert something terrible. I tried to apologize for what happened at the funeral, but I think it was too soon. If she asked me to live in the cottage with her now, I might have said 'yes.'"

Etta glanced towards the far side of the cemetery, where two fresh plots had recently been laid.

"Hope Robert found the rest of you okay. I'm not sure how the whole thing works."

Etta stopped talking, and spared another glance towards Papa and the truck. He was looking elsewhere, but too obviously. She had a sudden pang of self-consciousness.

What am I doing?

For the first time since making these visits, Etta saw herself as a foolish woman talking to some rocks on the ground. It was potent but also fleeting.

No. They're family, dammit. She shook her head and carried on.

"Anyway. I suppose I'm saying goodbye this time."

Etta leaned back, sitting on her feet and distractedly picking at the folds of her dress. Brushing them flat, she thought of Art then. For a moment, she considered going out to try and find him, even though she was not sure where to look. Etta wanted to say goodbye but also give him a piece of her mind. She had hoped that he might come find her at the Saunders, even though she had specifically told him to leave her alone. With no ready outlet, her anger intensified.

After years of scraping by and working her hands to the bone, and enduring one loss after another, she had been teased with a glimpse of something better: a life to live as she pleased. With Art, she might even have found someone to share it with her rather than push her to his own end. Only, it had fallen apart – all of it. And now she had nothing. Just a long car ride to some other town.

Staring at her mother's headstone, her thoughts turned darker still. She imagined what Lena might have said.

Leaving town at long last, it accused. *You finally got what you wanted, didn't you?*

It was true, she supposed; a grotesque parody of the dream she had harbored for so long.

"I could have sworn that I shut that lamp off," Etta said, under her breath. All the while, she looked at Lena's grave marker, as though trying to convince it.

And all you had to do was burn the house down.

"I... I always turned it off before."

Tell it to the ashes. And the cat. Killed her the same way you killed your sister.

"I didn't get Irene killed."

Who was driving?

Etta clenched her teeth and truly wicked thoughts, long suppressed, bubbled to the surface. Thoughts she refused to accept for two years had festered into the same venom she had unfairly loosed on Helen a few months earlier. Only now, Etta directed it at herself.

Strangely, Mildred's words came back to her, slicing through Etta's black thoughts.

You can't account for bad luck.

Etta’s blood started to cool. Mildred was no liar. For that matter, neither was Helen.

It wasn’t your fault.

“The out-of-towner hit me,” Etta said, her voice low.

It’s what drove your mother to the long walks.

The deaths of the other Wozniaks could be attributed to simple misfortune. Even Irene. Only Lena's death, far as Etta was concerned, could have easily been prevented.

“It wasn’t my fault,” she repeated, more coolly this time. “But you always thought it was.” Indulging the bitter memories, Etta felt the anger swell up once more. Something had changed in Lena after the death of Irene. More so than with any of the others. With Irene, she could put the blame on someone, even if it was misplaced.

It was never directly accused, but Etta could feel it. It was in furtive glances. In cold shoulders. The way Lena's smile would fade as soon as Etta entered the room. For a time, Etta thought she could win back her mother's approval by taking more responsibilities around the house. When it seemed like that might actually work, Lena started to leave the house for hours at a time.

“You just had to go for the walks, didn't you?” Etta continued. “Couldn’t bring yourself to run off like your sister, but you carried a grudge just as well as her. Why didn’t you just talk to me? I could have told you it was an accident, but you didn't want to hear it. You couldn’t accept the fact that we’re just an unlucky bunch.”

Etta’s eyes narrowed as she worked herself into a veritable froth. “And I’ll bet you told Papa I shouldn't ever drive again. Didn’t you?”

Etta had never said that out loud before. At first, she felt guilty for it. Thinking ill of the dead was not something she was comfortable with, even now. Once she started, it was impossible to stop. The venom had returned. And this time, there was no stopping the deluge.

“You didn't have to die, damn you! You knew that road was dangerous.”

Worked up as she was, Etta surprised even herself by spitting.

Oh, God. What have I done?

Etta set her lips into a hard line, as if trying to undo the desecration before her. Looking around to make sure Papa had not seen, she quickly wiped it away, but the stone remained wet and discolored.

“Sorry,” she muttered. “I didn't really mean that.”

Etta lingered until she calmed down, and sighed with finality. “I'll come see you next time I'm in town,” she muttered.

The gravestones, of course, made no reply, but as she walked away, Etta could not help but feel as though they radiated disapproval.

The drive to Newark took well over two hours. They were delayed, navigating the cluttered streets of Morristown, which had become another temporary home to many of those displaced by the recent explosion. Seeing the effects of the event that took Robert's life briefly reminded Etta of him, which in turn made her think of Helen and everyone else. Not for the first time, it occurred to her that she might never see any of them again.

Leaving Morristown behind, Etta considered that she had never been this far from home before. Everything was new. Eventually, the troubles of her old life were less sharp and she watched the passing scenery with hungry eyes. Papa had said little to her for most of the journey, and vice versa. At first, this had bothered her, but less so as they put more distance between themselves and Bott's Lake. A genuine excitement grew in her for what lay ahead.

A pattern emerged as they followed the same road and approached each new town. The trees and pastures on either side would gradually transition to small buildings, and then disappear entirely as they passed through each town's main avenue. Then, the woods and farmland would return and the pattern continued. Time passed. Here and there, she caught a name that she recognized from her map, which currently sat safely in her bag. She had made a point to retrieve it from the jalopy before leaving town.

In the time after the funeral, Etta had been second-guessing her decision to go with Papa. For a short while, she disappeared from the Saunders' house. Perhaps one last visit to the car would help settle her thoughts, and steel her resolve for the journey ahead. It had been what first inspired her to leave town, and always provided hope that a fresh start would yield better days.

To her surprise, the red paint, and beat-up seats only filled her with regret that she was leaving it behind. On top of that, this had recently become a favorite spot for her to go with Art. They had shared more than a few kisses in it. Thinking about him still made her angry, but less so than before. She had doubts after the funeral, but the loss of the house was a sign in much the same way as the car itself had once been. Before she could become immobilized with indecision, Etta grabbed the map and left.

At the time, she thought of it as a memento from her old life. Maybe it would serve to finally push her to New York. The City was much closer to Newark than the lake was. With each new town behind them, Etta's head continued to clear. Eventually, the green space shrank until it disappeared entirely. The buildings grew closer together. And taller. Soon, that was all there was.

They had reached Newark.

Etta had long considered the Oasis beach during high summer to be a crowded place. At its worst, it could not compare to what she was seeing now on practically every street corner. People were everywhere.

Etta noticed a sign for Broad Street just before they pulled onto an avenue that lived up to the name. The wide, paved road was utterly teeming with activity. Papa pulled the truck into a line of cars, but the roadway was equally populated with trolleys, people on foot, and even a horse-drawn carriage, which seemed out of place even to Etta. A brick building caught her eye, easily taller than anything she had ever seen before. She stared until it was out of sight.

The sound of Papa chuckling brought her back to the truck, and she realized that she was partially lifted off her seat in her attempt to see everything. Almost bashfully, she sat back down.

"It's something, isn't it?" he asked. "Perhaps not so grand as New York, but still nice. Just don't stare at the buildings or they'll mark you for an out-of-towner."

During the entirety of their journey, the fact that she would in fact be a stranger somewhere had not occurred to her. Out-of-towners were always *other* people. How could *she* be one? Now, she recognized it for an inescapable truth. Aside from Papa, Etta did not know anyone for thirty miles. She grew anxious at the thought, but quickly returned her attention to the sights around her, drinking them in.

They passed a well-manicured, grassy area that caught her eye.

"Is that someone's garden?" she asked.

"No. That's a city park. There are a few of them around. I haven't had the chance to spend much time there."

Etta thought about how long they had been in the car, and how frequently Papa had been making this trip.

"And you've been driving out here all summer?" she asked.

Jakob nodded. "It does not usually take this long. That business in Morristown slowed us down," he replied. "Though, some days were better than others."

"I suppose I can't blame you for spending so much time away from home."

Papa's shoulders slumped, and Etta realized that her tone sounded just a shade judgmental.

"I only meant that this is a long ride. I can see why you wouldn't want to do it too much."

Papa waved it off. "Do not worry. I understand. The farm was much work, and there used to be more of us." He paused. "I suppose I also thought that your boyfriend was helping you."

Etta bit her lower lip in thought. Aside from when the two of them met at the wedding, Etta thought of Art and her father in two separate worlds. The implication that he was aware of her and Art being alone in the house briefly made her uncomfortable. Oddly, he gave no sign that anything was amiss.

Papa continued, "I'm curious. What did you tell him about moving? Did he take it well?"

"As a matter of fact, I didn't tell him anything," she said with the smallest pang of regret.

In hindsight, she wished that she had at least tried to look around the cottage neighborhood for him. Or even walked to Gregory's. It was too late now. Reminded of him again, she realized that she was less mad than before.

Papa remained silent, waiting for her to continue.

"We... had a falling out," she said by way of explanation.

Papa grunted in response. "He seemed a pleasant young man when I met him. Maybe a bit bookish."

Among other things. Not all of them bad, Etta thought.

"So, what happened?" Jakob asked.

Etta opened her mouth, about to tell him the entire story, but held back.

Instead, she replied, "He had other commitments."

This shortened explanation omitted a great many details. Right away, she meant to elaborate, but stopped. Thinking of Art now caused regret that she did not make more of an effort to find him before leaving town. It seeded doubt. Wordlessly, Etta's attention returned to the world beyond her window.

When it was clear that she did not mean to continue, Jakob let the matter go. They eventually pulled off Broad Street, passing a small cluster of shops and restaurants. A narrow lane was lined with, what she assumed were houses and decorative trees. The buildings were so close together, there was barely enough room for one person to walk between them.

"Do you live here?" she asked.

Papa looked out the window where she was pointing. Giving her a wan smile, he shook his head. "No. At least not yet. We live closer to the factory. There is much work at the moment. Maybe once things calm down we think about a nice place."

From his use of the word "we," Etta was reminded that she might be here for a long time. She pushed the thought away, returning her attention back to the new sights, letting other concerns fall by the wayside. A few minutes and several turns later, they left the compressed, yet upscale neighborhood, and their surroundings quickly deteriorated.

The clean and immaculate stucco buildings began to show cracks, and gradually disappeared entirely until they were replaced with plain, red brick. The handsome, well-manicured gardens went away, leaving only the occasional empty dirt lot. Soon, they arrived on a street between two rows of plain buildings with little in the way of distinguishing features. Trash littered the street and various unfamiliar people sat on their front stoops, watching as they passed. Etta began to feel anxious, and willed Papa to hurry up and pass through this area.

To her frustration, it was taking far longer than she would have liked. With mounting dread, she realized that they were not passing through, but in fact, slowing down. As Papa stopped the truck entirely, a sudden, sinking feeling took hold in Etta's gut.

"We're home."

Papa had offered to carry the suitcase Etta had borrowed from the Saunders, but she insisted on doing it herself. It was small enough. Even so, she briefly reconsidered when she learned the apartment was on the fourth level. To her initial relief, Papa guided them to a metal grate off to the side of the entrance. It was an elevator. She knew of them of course, but had never actually seen one, let alone ridden one. Unfortunately, a sign next to the grate read, "Out of Order," which came as no surprise to Papa.

He opened a small cubby door, which Etta quickly determined was a mailbox. "To the stairs then," he said, after retrieving what was inside.

The stairs were narrow, and the two of them were obliged to climb single-file. So close were the two walls that, had anyone been coming in the opposite direction, there would be no avoiding brushing shoulders at the very least. Accustomed as she was to walking for most of the day, it said much that Etta felt winded by the time they reached the fourth floor. Arriving at one of many identical doors, Papa retrieved the keys from the chain on his belt.

Turning to Etta, he said, "Never leave the apartment without the key. The door will lock behind you. And remember to engage the second lock as well. This is not the farm."

Etta noted that he was more stern than usual about those instructions and she glanced around the hallway with some suspicion.

Once inside the apartment, her first thought was why did the foyer have a table? It was quickly followed by the realization that what she was now seeing consisted of everything except for the bedroom. In a space obviously not intended for two people to occupy at once, she and Papa had to shuffle around each other in order for him to lock the door. As he did so, Etta took in her surroundings.

The main area of the apartment consisted of a combined kitchen and living area. On her left was a sink, enough counter space for maybe a single cutting board, and a small electric stove. A table with two chairs sat across from it, with only enough room for someone to stand at the sink if the chair was pulled in. Directly across from the entrance was a small seating area and the only window that she could see.

Approaching, Etta peered outside. The apartment was on the opposite side of the building from where they had entered, so instead of a view of the street, she peered into an alley and the back of another brick building. A soft thud brought her attention to the ceiling. Out of habit, her first thought was that a raccoon had gotten into the attic. Of course, she soon realized that there were living areas above her.

A fleeting, yet potent sense of claustrophobia came over her, and she needed to sit down. After Papa finished locking the door, he turned to her, but remained in the kitchen. Small as the apartment was, he barely had to raise his voice.

"Is that comfortable?" he asked, indicating the couch. "If it's too lumpy, we can get you a cot to sleep on."

Etta looked down at what was, apparently, going to be her bed. Her blood suddenly ran cold, as the reality of her new situation finally sank in.

"It's not very private," she muttered.

Papa spread his hands apologetically. "No. Things happened very quickly. I would offer you the bedroom, but..." he trailed off, and grew uncomfortable.

“But what?” Etta asked, genuinely confused by his reaction.

For a long moment, he stared at the floor, searching for the right words. As he did so, Etta's eyes wandered the room, and she began to notice things. An article of clothing here. A hairbrush there.

They were interrupted by the sound of a key unlocking the door. Papa moved to open it. His face was a strange mixture of relief but also apprehension. The door opened partway before he stopped it and spoke to whoever was outside. From across the room, Etta could not hear what was being said or who it was, but she did not have to wait long.

Papa glanced over his shoulder and stepped to one side as he chewed his lip. Standing in the doorway was a woman, probably in her mid-fifties. She wore a friendly, if unsure smile and raised a hand in greeting as she stepped into the apartment. Her brown hair was heavily streaked with gray and tied back beneath a round hat. Despite the warm weather, she wore a business jacket over her long skirt. To Etta, she gave the impression of someone familiar with long workdays.

In the confines of the apartment, Jakob and this new woman were pressed close together in order to shut the door, and it occurred to Etta that neither of them seemed the least bit uncomfortable. A growing suspicion formed in her mind.

“Etta,” began her father. “Meet Eloise.”

“Hello,” Eloise nodded. “It's so nice to meet you finally. Your father has told me so much about you. He never said how pretty you are.”

“Nice to meet you as well,” Etta replied automatically, still trying to make sense of everything. “Papa didn't tell me anything about you.”

Eloise frowned for a moment, looking at Papa. “Jake?” she said in a tone that was clearly a request for an explanation.

Papa looked increasingly uncomfortable. “Things happened quickly... with the house and all,” he stammered.

“Yes,” Eloise said to Etta. “I'm so sorry about your home.”

Etta shrugged, unable to ignore the feeling that she was missing a vital piece of information here. Both women turned to Papa, who wilted under their combined scrutiny.

He let out a breath and turned to Etta. “Eloise owns the factory where I've been doing the bookwork,” he said, by way of explanation.

Eloise continued to stare at him, silently urging him to continue.

Placing a nervous but affectionate arm around her, he turned back to Etta. “This is our place,” he said at last.

Etta said nothing, having already come to suspect what he had just confirmed, but looked away. Eloise likewise grew uncomfortable.

"We should all sit down for supper," Papa said, removing his arm from Eloise. He took a step towards the door before anyone could voice objection. "Should I get something from Anthony's? How about meatballs tonight? You like the thin pasta, yes?"

Papa continued speaking until the door was closed behind him and he was safe from further questions. The sound of his brisk footsteps quickly faded, leaving Etta and Eloise alone together. They regarded each other in silence for a long moment.

"I hope you don't mind sleeping on the couch," Eloise started. "We can get something else if it's uncomfortable."

"Papa already mentioned. It's fine," Etta replied, sighing. Briefly, she wondered where a cot would even fit in this place.

Eloise started to fidget as the silence dragged on. It was apparent that this woman had just finished a long day of work, and the last thing she had been expecting was to play host to a stranger. The thought of being a burden to someone, even in a small way, put Etta ill at ease.

"So... 'Jake'?"

For all her life, no one had referred to her father by anything except "Jakob" or "Papa." The shortened nickname seemed wrong somehow. Eloise chewed the inside of her cheek, unsure of Etta's tone, but eventually smiled.

"Yes, for a couple of months now. It's been quite a summer. I'm sorry. He made it seem like you knew."

"We haven't spoken much lately. Don't hold it against him." Etta considered the many things she had kept from her father. This seemed like fair turnabout. "You own the factory?"

Eloise nodded, clearly happy to change the subject. "Calling it a factory makes it sound grander than it is. There's only the seven people that work there. Well, eight now with your father. But, yes it's been mine these last five years or so. It was my late husband's, but he was never right again after the winter of eighteen. Spanish Flu, you know. I started off helping him here and there, and then one day he was gone. I've been struggling to keep it going ever since."

Etta nodded. "Our farm was something like that as well."

"Yes. Your father told me about the rest of your family. I can't even imagine what that must have been like."

Etta remained silent. She was never any good at small talk, and her mind was preoccupied by countless other things just now. Being reminded of her late family made her think of all the others she had left behind and did not help her nerves.

"Do you like music?" Eloise asked suddenly.

The question caught Etta by surprise, and all she could do was nod. Smiling more genuinely now, Eloise walked over to a small cabinet next to the couch. Inside was a radio that was smaller than any Etta had seen before. The station was already precisely dialed in, and Cliff Edward's voice filled the apartment. The sound was much crisper than Etta was used to and she began to relax. Eloise joined her on the couch; the only place to sit other than the kitchen.

At first, Etta was annoyed – this was her bed after all – even if it was the older woman's couch. She kept a respectful a distance between them – or at least as much as was possible in the small confines. This arrangement would take some getting-used-to. Deciding that Eloise was making an effort, Etta let it go, and simply tried to be good company. The music helped a great deal.

The small talk came in fits and starts at first, then more easily. She learned that Eloise had a grown daughter, and she was, in fact, a recent grandmother. She in turn, listened attentively as Etta explained some of the things that were troubling her: Robert, Helen, but not Art. Not yet anyway. Still, it felt good to get at least a few things off her chest.

Papa returned some time later with a bag of food, and they all sat down to eat. As there were only two chairs, Papa offered to sit on the overturned garbage can. The mood improved as their bellies were filled, but increasingly, it became difficult to find common ground. The conversation shifted between gossip about things at the factory, which excluded Etta, and news from Bott's Lake, which excluded Eloise. Papa did his best to balance the two worlds, but it was a difficult task at best.

Things did not improve as the days wore on. As Eloise grew more comfortable with having Etta around, she began to reveal previously concealed habits. Despite her neat, put-together appearance at work, at home she proved to be quite messy. In the small apartment, this soon became intolerable for Etta. The errant hairbrush she had glimpsed upon her initial arrival turned out to be just that – a glimpse.

While ostensibly keeping a closet for the sole purpose of storing clothes, Eloise tended to deposit garments wherever happened to be convenient at the moment. Most intolerable were the articles strewn over the couch – Etta's de facto bed. This was likely a habit picked up after a number of years of living alone. Clean. Dirty. It did not seem to particularly matter. Dishes also tended to accumulate near the sink. As it turned out, Eloise rarely cooked, and it was commonplace for a dish to meet with a little more than a quick rinse before being deemed fit to return to duty. Etta was appalled, but kept such thoughts to herself. She was, despite all attempts to make her feel otherwise, a guest.

For a time, it was manageable. The music especially, made things feel just a bit homier. After years of near constant work, Etta spent her first morning in the apartment just lounging near the open window and listening to the radio. With Papa and Eloise out working at the factory, Etta found that the apartment was merely cramped instead of oppressive.

This was the most leisure time she had ever had. For a while, it was pleasant. She could actually sit, and listen to the radio with nothing else to distract her. She even closed her eyes and nodded off a few times, making up for, what might have been months of lost sleep. By the time Jakob and Eloise returned home, she felt positively rejuvenated and most of her old troubles were gone from her mind.

The next day started out much the same way. Etta turned on the radio, but soon noticed that many of the songs were repeats. This was not much of an issue at first, but it was not long before she began searching for another station. Finding a radio play, this held her interest for a while longer, but increasingly her eyes went to the clock, and she marked the time until Eloise and Papa returned.

By the third or maybe fourth morning, Etta turned on the radio again, but was too restless to sit. In fact, she was pacing the floor by noon. It took her some time to comprehend the underlying cause of it, mostly because the feeling was altogether unfamiliar. Simply put, she was bored.

At one point, she considered joining Eloise and Papa at the factory for something to do, but never asked. Doing so would have put the three of them in inescapable proximity for nearly every hour of every day. Instead, Etta kept busy with tidying up the area that currently served as her "bedroom."

She explored the various cabinets and drawers of the apartment, searching for a place to keep her belongings other than the suitcase. This actually took a surprising amount of time considering the smallness. Most of it was spent rearranging Eloise's things in order make room for herself.

By the time Papa and Eloise returned home, Etta was halfway through cleaning the kitchen. This continued for much of the first week, with Etta occupying her waking hours with cleaning and organizing. Once or twice, she considered going outside on her own. Perhaps she could find her way back to one of the parks she had admired on the initial drive. Papa left his key with a reminder to lock the door behind her. However, with each attempt, she never made it farther than the sidewalk.

The neighborhood featured a multitude of unfamiliar people sitting outside, or otherwise milling around with nothing to do but look. Their stares made her uncomfortable. Even walking with Papa to get dinner from Anthony's left her more than a little self-conscious. Each time, she would return to the apartment, and tried to find some new way to keep busy.

By the second week, Etta thought to fill her time with reading, but there was little material in the apartment. Eloise had no books, and the few magazines that were present could not hold her interest. While initially hesitant to do so, Etta eventually brought out the map from the jalopy, and spread it out on the floor in front of the couch.

Marking Newark, she found Bott's lake and recalled the long drive with her father. Then, she looked at New York, and marveled at how close it now was. Once or twice, she thought about asking Papa to make a day trip so she could see the sights, but somehow, the idea did not hold the appeal it once had. Thus far, her experience of a city was leaving her under whelmed. In addition, seeing the word "Home" over Bott's Lake, written by Art's hand did much to sour her mood.

What did he know anyway?

Eventually, the map too failed to hold her attention.

Doing something – anything – helped her to ignore the things beyond the room's narrow walls. Thus far, she had confined herself to the shared living area, but there was only so much that could be done. While Eloise never confronted her openly, it became clear that she did not care for Etta's meddling. Indirectly, she complained about suddenly being unable to find things.

Weeks passed in this way, and resulted in a number of quiet standoffs. The apartment shrank even smaller.

Then, Etta had her mishap.

Garbage accumulated quickly. The bin was so small it needed to be dropped in the chute down the hall at least once per day. At first, this was preferable to building a fire once each week, as would have been done on the farm, but the exercise soon grew tedious. On this particular morning, Etta had already exhausted the short list of chores that could be done without entering the room that Papa and Eloise shared. With a grudging respect for Eloise's last refuge, she stayed out of there as much as possible.

Unfortunately, it meant that Etta lacked for distractions much earlier than usual. Mostly out of boredom, she decided to empty the bin, which was only halfway full. Going into the hallway, she let the door close behind her, as she always did, and walked to the garbage chute. Returning to the apartment door, she only realized her mistake as she went to reach for the key, but found her pocket empty.

Panicked, she dropped the bin and searched the rest of her dress, even though she now recalled setting the brass key down on the counter. Sighing, she stared at the door for a full minute, willing it to open of its own accord. Flipping over the now-empty bin to use as a stool, she thought through her options. For lack of things to do, she was acutely aware of the time. It was barely three in the afternoon. Papa and Eloise would be gone for at least another four hours.

Etta contemplated her predicament, and considered simply remaining where she was. Going outside among the neighborhood, especially by herself was not appealing. Several doors down, she heard muffled voices in the midst of an argument. In the opposite direction, a baby was crying. Sighing, Etta jiggled the doorknob once more and decided that she could not simply sit on this garbage bin for the rest of the afternoon.

At least I'm wearing shoes, she thought as she made her way down to the street. On the way, Etta checked the few doors that she passed through to make sure that they would not also lock behind her.

Emerging onto the sidewalk, Etta started walking. Her knowledge of the neighborhood was extremely limited. Once or twice, she and Papa had gone for a Sunday walk, but he had always guided them home. More often, she accompanied him to retrieve dinner from the Italian restaurant around the corner. Since it was the only route she knew with any confidence, she headed there. Drawing closer, the smell of food wafted out to the street, and her mouth began to water.

Thinking of her empty pockets, she decided to continue walking since the enticing aroma would only serve to remind her that she could not have it. A number of restaurant patrons were gathered outside. Some were eating. Others were only passing the time. It was not an uncommon sight. In fact, she recognized a few regulars from when she came here with Papa. Thus, she was not paying particular mind as she passed by.

A sound caught her attention. Etta knew what a wolf whistle was, but had previously only heard it done in jest. Usually from Robert or one of the other boys when the girls changed clothes at the swimming pond. It was harmless fun among close friends. Hearing it now, in this unfamiliar place, it chilled her. By reflex, she looked in the direction of the sound and found one of the lounging patrons looking back at her. A wide grin was on his face. He was slightly older than her, with dark, greasy hair, and a pencil mustache. Under other circumstances, he might have been mildly off-putting, but combined with the salacious look he was currently making, she found him bordering on disgusting.

"Looking good," he called.

Without meaning to, Etta had slowed down as she made eye contact. As she did so, she noticed that several of the other patrons were also now looking at her. Etta's face heated red and she returned her eyes to the sidewalk, plodding on. She increased her pace to a brisk walk, but did not run.

The interaction left her uncomfortable. Even the out-of-towners back at the lake were not so rude.

This was beyond the route with which she was familiar. Fruitlessly, she looked around hoping to find a familiar landmark. As she walked, the sound of footsteps approached from behind. Resisting the urge to turn around, she saw out the corner of her eye, someone matching stride beside her. Of course, it was the greasy, mustached man from the restaurant.

"Good day for a walk?" he asked.

Etta said nothing, and remained looking ahead. Undeterred, he pressed on.

"What's your name?"

Again, she made no response, and in her distraction, she quickly found herself in a completely unfamiliar area.

"Not much of a talker, eh? That's alright."

Etta sighed. "Please go away," she said, but it did not have the desired effect.

In response, the greasy man merely laughed. "Hey now. Don't be like that." He pointed back down the street. "Come on, I've got a table at Anthony's, and I know the guy. Could get us a bottle of wine. The good stuff. Not the swill he sells to the others."

"Go. Away," Etta repeated, more forcefully this time, and the man seemed to get the message.

"Alright. Hell with you then," he replied nonchalantly, and walked off.

What is it with jerks and mustaches?

Returning her attention to navigating the road, she took a few turns that led back in the general direction of the apartment. Along the way, she passed more restaurants that were occupied similarly to Anthony's. While no one else made any unsolicited remarks, she still passed each one with trepidation. In one instance, she went so far as to move off the sidewalk and into the street to avoid a crowd.

For her trouble, she was nearly hit by a car.

Eventually, she found her way back to the apartment. The garbage bin was right where she left it. Sighing, she sat down hard, and leaned her elbows on her knees. A long hour passed, which she spent adjusting her position. The underside of the bin was not quite large enough to sit on, and she found that she could only rest one half of her bottom at a time.

When she was not distracted by muffled voices, and trying to find a comfortable position she let her mind wander. There was plenty of time to think. At one point, she let out a mirthless laugh, recalling when she had once said that anywhere with a flushing toilet would be an improvement.

I should have been more specific.

When Eloise and Papa eventually returned, they were more than surprised to find Etta perched on top of the garbage can in front of the door. They had arrived later than usual, but Etta was in surprisingly good spirits.

She had reached a decision.

Chapter 30
Art

I can't believe I'm at another one of these already, Art thought sullenly.

Wearing the same black suit he had worn to Robert's funeral, his ensemble featured the recent addition of a couple new aches and bruises. There was no hiding the black eye, but frankly, over the past month, he had one more often than not. The low light of the mortuary at least helped to conceal it. To his surprise, the crowd was substantial. Considering how little Gregory got out, Art honestly thought that he did not know many people.

Not immediately recognizing any of them, and feeling just the slightest bit self-conscious about his face, Art figured he would quickly pay his respects and leave. As he waited in line, he overheard bits and pieces of several conversations going on around him.

From one, he listened to a man who had been with Gregory in the Navy. Another remarked on a piece of machinery that Gregory had once fixed free of charge, as a favor. At first, it was comforting to hear about the different lives the man had been a part of. Slowly, it became apparent that he had known Gregory the least out of everyone here and Art felt even more out of place.

Continuing to wait, he lost himself in his own thoughts. A tap on his shoulder eventually pulled him back to the present. Turning around, he recognized Gregory's lawyer, Kevin McHenry whom he had brought to the hospital a few days earlier.

"Arthur?" Kevin asked uncertainly.

Art supposed they had only met the one time and his face was not all bruised up then. He nodded.

"Please remain after the service. There are a few formalities I need for you to address."

So much for paying my respects and leaving, he thought. *Probably something with the hospital bill or some such.*

He sighed, not knowing how that had become his responsibility, but resigned himself to it. Art said nothing, but nodded. Kevin left him to his thoughts, of which there were many.

As the coffin grew closer, it occurred to him that he had never actually seen a dead person before. Let alone someone that he actually knew. Robert's casket had been closed, which incidentally, had been his first funeral. As the line conveyed him closer and closer to his late mentor, he felt a mild pang of dread. Had he not been distracted with all the other problems demanding his attention and a myriad of aches and pains, it might have bothered him more. At last, it was his turn and Art knelt down. Looking at Gregory, the growing anxiety promptly disappeared.

It doesn't even look like him, he thought. Instead of anxiety, he felt guilt. As though he should be feeling something more. Gregory's face was waxen, and devoid of color. It could have been a statue of the man. For a long moment, he felt he should say something, but his mind had gone blank. All the while, he was dimly aware of the line of mourners still behind him. Everyone ahead of him had taken only a minute or so at most to pay their respects, and Art grew more agitated the longer he remained.

Upon realizing that he had nowhere else to go, he actually calmed down. After all, here was one of the last people in his life with whom he had been on good terms.

"Sorry you went out the way you did," he whispered. "That was a bum deal."

Upon saying it, he felt foolish for a number of reasons. In the intervening days, he was troubled over the ride to the hospital and how bumpy it had been. As if grabbing another pillow for the makeshift gurney would have made a difference. Then, it occurred to him that a confession might be in order.

"I've been sleeping at the house. Hope you don't mind. I went back to clean the place up and stayed. Couldn't go back to my parents just yet. I only went inside the shop to tidy up... I'm not working by myself. Figured that would bother you more." Art sighed. "Thanks for giving me a chance."

Standing up, Art remained lost in his thoughts. He might have left but suddenly remembered Kevin's request. Instead, he wandered the parlor aimlessly until Lizzie and Owen Hunley found him.

"I'm very sorry for your loss," Owen said reverently, and reached out with his one hand. Art shook it, remembering to use his left without hesitation this time. Lizzie gave him a hug and said the same. Of course, he mourned the loss of his mentor, and the uncertainty of what lay ahead preyed on his thoughts. But self-doubt overruled his other troubles at just that moment.

My loss? Who am I?

Listening to everyone else who clearly knew Gregory much better than he did only exacerbated the feeling that he did not belong here. They had worked together for just a few months, but even so, Art had come to feel less like an outsider among the Bott's Lake residents. Especially when he was with Etta. Up until a recently, he fully intended to remain here. The double-blow of losing Gregory followed so closely by Etta's departure had made him reconsider.

Lizzie looked around. "Where is Etta?" she asked.

Art had wondered that himself. The days since Robert's funeral had been tumultuous, to say the least. Still, he managed to carve out a moment to drive past the Wozniak's farm, despite Etta's firm demand that he leave her alone. The charred ruins of the house were obvious from the road.

Through Daniel, he learned that Etta and her father had left town not long after Gregory died. Art probably missed her by mere hours. The Saunders said they were in Newark, but knew nothing more specific. Currently on the outs with his family and with his mentor now gone, Etta's leaving without a word stung Art even more deeply.

Instead, he said to Lizzie, "We're no longer together."

"Oh," she replied quietly. "That's a shame." Looking at him with, what might have been sympathy, both Lizzie and her father remained.

"Art," Owen hesitated. "This may not be the best time, but there is the matter of the truck. You were doing the work with Gregory, and…" he trailed off meaningfully.

This was something else that Art was aware of in an abstract sort of way, but had not fully considered before. Gregory left a great many things unfinished, but most of those had been in place prior to Art's arrival. The Hunleys, on the other hand, made a tangible investment of real money and equipment. And they only did so because of Art's doing.

It was natural that they would expect him to make good on his end of the deal.

Owen continued, “It’s just that we need that truck, one way or another. If what we planned isn’t going to work out-”

“Daddy,” Lizzie interjected quietly. “Maybe later?”

Glancing at his daughter, he nodded. “Of course. Later.” It was plain that he was still concerned.

Then, Art was surprised to find his mouth working, possibly of its own accord. “The truck will be delivered as promised.” After he had said the words, he almost tried to take them back.

What am I saying? I can’t do that.

Perhaps as a safeguard to ensure that he could not back out, Art was suddenly unable to speak at all. Instead, he only nodded to underscore his promise. Owen’s relief was evident and Art felt vindicated.

“I appreciate that,” Owen responded. “We should still talk. Come by the farm whenever you have time.”

Art, still not quite trusting himself to speak, drew himself up and nodded again. Taking his silence as marking the end of the conversation, the Hunleys turned to move on. Before leaving, Lizzie surprised Art with another hug, leaving him to wonder about more than a few things.

Alone with his thoughts again, Art realized that he meant what he said. How he would actually go about fulfilling it was another matter entirely, but there would be time to work it out later. At least he had a direction. Just now, additional mourners confronted him. The word was out: Gregory’s apprentice was here.

Art knew them by their broken equipment more than by name. Many, he had met before, but he was never great with names. They all had something that Gregory was fixing and each of them, though sympathetic to the reality of the man's passing, wanted to know what was going to become of their property. Art reassured each of them the same as he had with the Hunleys. Each time, he meant it. Soon, the nagging voice in the back of his mind gave up, and for the first time that evening Art was at ease.

Eventually, he had spoken with everyone who had an interest, and was alone again. He was doubly relieved since his jaw was growing sore from prolonged talking. With things now quiet, he started to think through the practical considerations of what he had committed himself to. Art once again recalled that he was a visitor in this town, with nothing to his name. He could squat at Gregory's house and borrow his tools for a short while, but eventually the electrical bill would come due or the town would claim it. It was nothing resembling a long-term solution.

That was tomorrow's problem. He had given his word and would find a way to deliver. Still, the sheer volume of work he had just accepted was staggering. Simply put, he knew it was more than he could handle alone. Even working with Daniel, the two of them would be hard-pressed to accomplish everything. As he was left considering his options, or rather the lack thereof, his thoughts were interrupted yet again. It was Kevin, who, wordlessly, beckoned Art to follow. He did so, but quickly withdrew back into his own mind, contemplating the very real possibility of failure. Unable come up with an immediate solution, he grew frustrated.

It was not until Kevin closed the door behind him that Art realized he had arrived in a small office at the back of the mortuary. Besides the lawyer, there was a woman about Art's age with a young child. Opposite from them was a short, older woman.

The three of them regarded Art with disinterest as Kevin moved behind the desk. They might have wondered who he was, but were too distracted to inquire. They were familiar in a way that Art could not quite place. He assumed they had met before and that his usual poor memory for names was to blame. At a gesture from Kevin, Art sat down in the only other available seat.

The young child waved at him while attempting to hide behind her mother. Art did his best to appear at ease and waved back before turning his attention to Kevin. Clearing his throat, the gray-haired lawyer began.

"I will now read Gregory's Last Will and Testament." Kevin raised a pair of thick reading glasses to his face. Even so, he was obliged to hold the paper closely in order to read it.

"'To my sister, Kathryn. I would leave you a swift,' ahem, 'kick in the ass, because you deserve it.'"

The young mother yelped a short laugh, caught by surprise amidst the otherwise somber mood. The woman, who must have been Kathryn, frowned at Kevin.

"I am just reading it as it is written," Kevin shrugged by way of apology. "'But my,' excuse me again, 'Damn grandmother of a lawyer tells me I can't do that. So, instead, I'm leaving you the clock from Mother's house. I know you always wanted it, and truth be told, I should have given it back to you sooner.'"

Kathryn looked at Kevin expectantly, and her frown deepened when he turned to the young mother.

"'To my daughter, Cassandra. I leave my entire estate with the exception of my mother's clock. This is to include the land and outbuildings at the property on Mill Road. To me, it will always be your home, and I think you and Mary would be happy there.'"

Cassandra nodded acknowledgment, but also sighed quietly. As if this was the culmination of an on-going debate with her father, which he finally had won. The room was quiet as Kevin paused in his reading.

"Are we going to live with Grandpa?" asked the little girl, whom Art assumed was Mary. Her voice was respectfully quiet, as if she understood that this was a somber time, but not the full implications of it.

Her mother, Cassandra, scrunched up her face, as if trying to come up with an explanation that she would understand, but was unable to do so.

"There was a pension as well," Kathryn said during the pause. "And a trust account. Is that mentioned?"

Up to now, Art had mostly been staring at the floor, but looked up at Kathryn, wondering at her apparent concern. The contrast between her state of mind and Cassandra's was striking.

"Yes." Kevin replied, in the same formal, even tone. "Both of those items are included under Gregory's estate."

Kathryn grew agitated. "Now, as to that house, Gregory inherited that from our parents." She spoke to Cassandra. "You should know you have no real claim to it."

"Please, not now..." Cassandra said quietly.

Kathryn's eyes narrowed and she opened her mouth to speak but Kevin interjected.

"There is another portion which was recently amended, and witnessed by myself. It may help clear up any remaining uncertainties."

Kathryn stopped herself, and nodded for Kevin to continue.

"'To Arthur Adams, I leave all my tools, material, and equipment. If it is inside the workshop, and not bolted to the ground, it is yours.'"

Silence fell over them as Kevin allowed the information to sink in. To put it mildly, the three bereaved were surprised. The lawyer looked at each in turn, and confirmed that they had understood. Satisfied, he nodded.

"Gregory goes on to elaborate, 'Cassandra, please give him all the time he needs to move things out. Art, don't' – again, I'm just reading what's here – 'don't screw around and make her wait.' That is the relevant information. As the executor of his Will, I will make all the necessary, legal arrangements."

Art was speechless, and everyone waited another long moment to see if Kevin would say anything else. As he continued to sit mutely with his hands folded on the table, it became clear that Kevin was truly finished.

Did I hear that right?

Kathryn turned in her seat, and looked at Art. She did not even bother to hide her confusion and derision. At last she broke the spell of silence.

"Who is this now?" she asked, apparently of Kevin, but her eyes were focused directly at Art.

"Art?" asked Cassandra. Her tone was considerably less harsh than her aunt's.

Turning at the sound of his name, he nodded.

She continued, addressing both Art and Kathryn. "I know that name. You've been helping Daddy in the shop this summer, right? Yeah, he talked about you. Said you were probably the only other man he'd met with gears for brains as much as him. And a... tall fella."

Cassandra stumbled, as if she had been on the verge of almost saying something inappropriate for this setting. Art could only imagine what description Gregory might have provided. Knowing him, it was probably colorful. His suspicion was confirmed when Cassandra nearly smiled at the recollection, but stopped herself. Art could sympathize. Thinking about Gregory's sense of humor only underscored the empty place he had left.

Kathryn, on the other hand, maintained her scowl with determination.

"So, this 'tall fella' shows up, and just all of a sudden finds himself in the Will? And then Gregory dies?"

"Aunt Kate, please," implored Cassandra.

"I'm sorry, but does no one else find that a little strange?" She was not even looking at Art now, perhaps to show that he was too lowly for her notice. He might have been something she had stepped in and was now trying to scrape off. The name "Kathryn" meant nothing to him, but something clicked in Art's mind when Cassandra had called her "Aunt Kate." The older woman was about to press on when Art spoke up.

"'Kate?'" he repeated, looking directly at her. "Gregory mentioned you too." Art's expression was hard. His most recent assortment of bruises made it painful to move around too much. Yes. Gregory had mentioned his sister once or twice. None of it was flattering.

Kate was put off by Art's interjection, but soon recovered.

"I should think so. I'm his sister, after all. Who the hell are you?"

"Aunt Kate." Cassandra's tone was louder and more insistent this time. "This is the man that brought Daddy to the hospital."

Kate focused her gaze on the younger woman and scoffed. She was getting worked up now, and whatever restraint she had before soon fell apart.

"Put him there I'll bet. And you and I need to have a talk about that house-"

"You're 'Cheapskate Kate,'" Art replied evenly, remembering now. It was painful to emote, and the result was a much sterner expression than he might normally have made.

It had the desired effect. Kate went silent.

"I couldn't think of it before." He nodded to himself, but continued to stare her down. "From what I've heard, you would have checked his pockets for loose change before you took him to a doctor. Certainly make a habit of arguing at funerals, don't you?"

She sputtered, clearly put off balance by her unflattering nickname.

"And who the hell are you? You're a nobody. You have no business in this family." Some of her confidence returned as she went on the attack. "I'll tell you what you're going to do. You'll keep Gregory's tools, but you're going to pay me for them."

His heart beat just a little faster at the threat of confrontation. Then, to his surprise, he responded with a single word.

"No."

Kate was becoming livid. "It's the right thing to do," she pressed.

"I'll tell you what I'm going to do. Gregory was a good man and people depended on him. He made promises, and he would have wanted someone to honor them. *That's* the right thing to do."

"I..." she turned to Kevin. "Surely there's something that can be done here."

The lawyer had maintained a quiet, stoic visage throughout the exchange. Hands folded, and eyes half-lidded, he responded. "My duty is to read and execute Gregory's Last Will as written and witnessed," he intoned formally.

Grumbling, Kate rose from her seat, and glared at Art. Once, such a look might have caused him to buckle. To give her what she wanted and avoid a fight at whatever cost. But this time, he was at a loss. Having been in two fistfights in the span of a month, he was simply unable to get worked up. He held her gaze, but otherwise did not move. After all, it hurt to move.

Sensing that she would get no other response, Kate stormed out of the room, slamming the door behind her. Mary jumped with the noise and buried her face against her mother's side. Cassandra rubbed her daughter's back in a comforting way, but otherwise did not react to the outburst. As if she were accustomed to this kind of behavior from her aunt.

Indeed, Cassandra was more annoyed than anything else. When it was clear that there were no more questions, Kevin excused himself, promising to be in touch with further details. Art and Cassandra remained where they were, and said nothing.

“No. See what you did there?” Art said. “You've got the cord across your body. Never do that.”

Daniel nodded acknowledgment and made the correction before resuming his work. A fountain of sparks erupted from where he held the grinding tool up to the work piece and Art stepped back. This was their fifth day in the shop together, and Art had gotten comfortable enough not to hover over his trainee's shoulder. In truth, he could not be more pleased with Daniel's progress. There had been a few hiccups, mostly in the form of bad habits that needed to be corrected, but otherwise they had been doing well.

The downside was that they were getting precious little accomplished in the way of actual work. While all of Gregory's – now Art's – customers had been understanding of the inevitable delay, they had been less forthcoming with providing additional payment, and every day that Art failed to deliver was money out of his own pocket. This cost was unfortunate, but absolutely necessary, as he was compelled to uphold Gregory's attention to safety.

The down payment for the refrigerator truck project, which he and Daniel had come to refer to as the “Cow Cooler” carried them for the moment, but it was limited. A fact that Art was well aware of. Finding the right balance of training Daniel and doing work that paid was an on-going struggle.

Confident that Daniel was safe for the moment, Art's eyes wandered the shop. Movement at the main door caught his attention, and he looked over to find Cassandra standing outside. She waved and smiled pleasantly, but Art suspected that she was not making a social visit. Eyeing Daniel one last time, Art left him. Outside, he and Cassandra exchanged pleasantries.

"How is your move going?"

"Well enough," she replied, looking up to the house. "Thank you again for your help with everything."

It had been a busy week. For good measure, he had given the upstairs bedroom another scrub, as it still smelled faintly sour. Then, between making Gregory's old house livable again and carrying most of the boxes with Cassandra and Mary's things, he had lost two days of work. Days he did not have to spare. He felt a certain sympathy for her as Gregory's daughter, but also had another, mildly self-interested motive; he hoped the gesture would elicit some goodwill on her part. The longer she let him stay in the shop, the better. At this point, a move on top of everything else would cost precious time.

"My pleasure," Art replied. "How is Mary adjusting?"

Cassandra brightened at the mention of her daughter. "Very well, thank you. Right now, she's exploring every room in the house and 'testing' all the doors." Her smiled faltered a moment. "She's nervous around unfamiliar people..." Cassandra's voice trailed off and she remained silent.

Art grimaced. He had anticipated this scenario, but hoped it might not come up for a few more days yet. "Are Daniel and me 'unfamiliar people'?"

Cassandra's mouth formed a thin line, as if she was hesitant to bring up the subject. "I know this isn't a good time, and thank you for being so understanding, but when are you leaving?"

Art bit his lip and looked to his feet. "Honestly, I was hoping we could stay for another month. Maybe more."

From her expression, this was clearly not the answer she was looking for.

"That long? I was thinking maybe a week at most."

"I'm not sure we could even get packed in a week." An idea occurred to him. "What about this? You and Mary could stay at the apartment a few days a week so we won't bother her?"

Before he even finished, Cassandra was shaking her head.

"She's already picked out a bedroom. And even if she hadn't, I returned the keys to my landlord. We have nowhere else to go." The hesitation she had been showing a moment ago was disappearing fast, and she conjured a stubborn look that was clearly inherited from her late father. "I don't mean to be a nag, but it is my barn."

Art frowned. "Yes, that's true. And the deal was that you had to give me time to move out."

"But you're not moving out. You're working. I'm pretty sure Daddy would agree that this constitutes 'screwing around.'"

For the briefest moment, Cassandra had an uncanny resemblance to her father. Art might have laughed if he weren't so frustrated.

"You're right, it is your barn. What if we rented it from you?"

Art had hoped it would not come to this, and held his breath on her answer. He was acutely aware of his current finances, which were limited to say the least. Cassandra considered this, but only grudgingly. Her eyes drifted across the yard, which was still strewn with random items and Gregory's half-finished projects. It was with some reluctance that she shook her head.

"Listen, this house was always cluttered with junk. I love my father, but it's why I moved away in the first place. I want this stuff gone."

Art sighed when it was clear that she would not be convinced otherwise. His thoughts turned to everything in the shop and the amount of time it would take to move. It was daunting, and made worse by the knowledge that he could not afford to go that long without working. There was another solution, but before now, it had been too unpleasant to consider. Seeing Cassandra with her hands firmly planted on her hips, and an implacable expression on her face, Art knew he had no other choice.

In the end, they agreed that if Art and Daniel stopped working in the shop by the end of the week, they could use it for storage for a couple of months. They would move out as time allowed, and only when Mary was not home. To further sweeten the deal, Art offered to clear out the yard, and paid her for Gregory's old truck. Ownership had not been specified in the Will, and she had no particular use for it, but it seemed the fair thing to do. After they shook in agreement, Cassandra left, and Art turned his thoughts to two things.

The first was where his fledgling company would move to, and the second was what he would say to his father.

Chapter 31
Etta

"Are you sure you want me to drop you off here?" Papa asked, stepping down from the truck. "There's nothing left but ashes."

To say nothing of ghosts and memories, Etta thought.

Papa had parked the truck in its customary spot, next to where the house once stood. A few scattered timbers, blackened and charred sat among the ashes, soggy from the rain. The empty chicken coop and barn stood off by themselves, having been spared the ravaging effects of the fire. There remained a few random articles scattered around the property that had remained un-burnt. A bucket here. A shovel there. Etta stood motionless, surveying it all.

"I could drive you to the Saunders' house." Papa continued.

"No," Etta replied after a moment. "I'd like to look around once more before I go see Helen."

Papa stepped beside her, taking a final look for himself. They were both silent. Nothing intruded on the moment but the wind and the crow of a distant rooster. Then, to Etta's surprise, Papa let out a single chuckle. Confused, she looked at him, unable to imagine what could have provoked such a reaction.

Smiling, Jakob pointed at something across the empty field, near the rock wall. "There used to be a large oak tree over there. Do you remember?"

Etta glanced to the spot before nodding. "Actually yes. There was a tire swing, wasn't there?"

Papa nodded, still able to see it in his mind.

"That's right. John asked for it. For an entire summer he played on that swing with every spare moment. Even when it got cooler, he loved it." Papa sighed then, and his smile faltered. "When he was sick, I felt awful cutting that tree down to keep the house warm. He was older by then – more interested in girls than childhood games. Still, I remember being afraid to tell him. In the end, I suppose it made no difference."

Etta looked at him. His eyes were glistening now, but a smile remained on his face.

"And I'll never forget this," Jakob continued. "Mama and I were having an argument, so I left to work on something in the barn. Some time later, I see her walking across the yard towards me. And her face was strange. I was thinking, 'Why does she smile? We are fighting.' That's when she tells me she was pregnant with you."

Jakob was quiet again as he composed himself. "When we left the old country, Mama and I wanted to find a place that could be our own. To put down roots. To have a family. For a long time, we had that." He raised his hands toward the old farm before dropping them to his side. "This was our dream. But... it was not meant to last." Papa turned to face Etta. "This was a good home. Many good memories were made here. But the memories are all that are left."

Jakob bit his lip. When he spoke again, it was delicately and with care.

"I loved your Mama very much, but she left us long before she was taken. In this house, she might have eaten food and slept in our bed, but she lived in her memories. Edward. John. Florence. Irene, I think was hardest for her."

Papa faltered on his next words.

"I've never spoken of this before, but sometimes I think she may have wanted to join them. She kept going on the walks. At first, I thought it was just - *zaloba* - grieving, and I left her alone. I caught her at the cemetery several times... just staring at the headstones. Her Visits, she called them." He trailed off, quiet for a long moment.

Etta swallowed hard, fighting the knot that had suddenly been tied in her stomach. She had, of course, known about Lena's walks, but not about any visits to the cemetery. The implications were troubling.

Papa continued, "Etta, I will say to you what I should have said to Mama: life is for the living. I hope you find what it is that you need."

Etta's vision had started to blur. It was not until she blinked, and hot tears streamed down her cheek that she realized she was crying. She let Papa pull her into a hug, and put her own arms around him. They remained that way for a while. Whether it was a few minutes or an hour she could not say.

Before they parted, he said quietly, "I will not come back here. But you are my daughter and you will always be welcome in my home. Wherever that may be."

Not trusting herself to speak, Etta nodded against his shoulder. It was a long time before they finally separated. Looking her in the eye, Papa nodded one last time.

"Be seeing you," he said. Then he climbed back into the truck.

He did not say 'goodbye.'

As he drove away, she wondered when they would meet again. If ever. Etta stood in the driveway, back turned to the ruins of her old life as she watched Papa's truck bounce down the dirt road.

Several more minutes passed before she took her gaze away from the copse of trees where it disappeared. Slowly, she turned her attention to the rolling fields and the distant hills. A train crawled along the bottom of the valley, and a tractor pulled up the first summer harvest. It was a strange feeling. This view she had seen nearly every day of her life, and from a certain perspective, things carried on as they always had. The simple act of turning around would reveal the truth, in cold, rigid clarity.

Her old life was gone for good.

In the literal sense, Papa had been right; there was nothing left here. The chickens had since been moved to their new home. The barn was cleared out, and everything of value sold. The deed had been given to the town, and Papa considered his debt of back-taxes fulfilled. All that was left was for someone new to move in and begin their own life.

Someone else. This time, Etta did say goodbye.

She began walking. In truth, she had only asked Papa to drop her off here because it was a shorter walk to where she really intended to go. Upon deciding to leave Newark, Etta was once again confronted by the modesty of her nest egg.

Despite her reluctance to do so, Walter's ill-gotten offering was something she could no longer afford to do without. The necessity of it notwithstanding, she still did not want Papa to know about it. Additionally, she thought she might resume squatting at the Beckett's old place. Not for long. Just until she got back on her feet.

Arriving a few minutes later, Etta approached the front door without a second thought. The hesitation from her initial forays into the abandoned property were behind her now. Likewise, she saw no reason to sneak in through the back. With her hand mere inches from the doorknob, Etta turned still. A sound that had no business in her adopted home reached her ears.

A child was laughing.

As Etta slowly pulled her hand back, she continued to listen. Somewhere inside, an adult voice, muffled through the closed door, responded and there was another round of laughter. Etta stood there as the realization set in. Of course someone had moved in. It had been foolish to think otherwise, and yet she had held onto that hope, thin as it was.

As she prepared to step back from the door, the sound of irregular footsteps caught her attention. A young, grinning girl, who could not have been more than three years old came running around the side of the house, but abruptly stopped when she noticed Etta.

Each regarded the other. Despite the separation in age, they exchanged the same surprised, yet mildly affronted look of finding a stranger in their home. Another woman, about Etta's own age, who she assumed to be the girl's mother, interrupted the moment.

"Oh," she said, clearly started by Etta's presence. "Can I help you?"

Etta bit her lip, not wanting to admit her true purpose, but also fumbled for an alternative explanation.

"I'm... sorry. I used to know the people that lived here."

The little girl regarded Etta with righteous suspicion, but her mother was satisfied by the explanation.

"Wish I could tell you more about them, but we just moved in a few days ago. Still getting settled." She paused. "Were they here recently? We found a couple odd pieces of furniture left inside. Like someone was trying to make do with very little."

That's closer to the truth than anything else, thought Etta.

Putting on a polite smile, Etta nodded to the other woman. "That's alright. I'm sure they'll end up where they're meant to be." Her eyes were suddenly drawn to movement, around the woman's feet, and the little girl bent down to pet, what Etta assumed was, their cat.

She did a double take, thinking that the resemblance was uncanny. The woman glanced down as well, before speaking again.

"You don't happen to know if the old owners had a cat, do you? This one has been hanging around." Etta looked again, afraid to believe it at first. After all, it was not a particularly uncommon pattern, but could it possibly be the same cat? Recognition slowly dawned on her, and there was no mistaking that feline look of utter contempt.

Well, look at you.

Normally grumpy and aloof, Howler rubbed against the other woman affectionately and even seemed to tolerate the young girl as she pulled her into a hug. Etta sighed.

Stupid cat...

"I honestly can't say that I recognize her," Etta said,. shaking her head. A growing sense of finality came over her along with resignation. The money in the jar was never really hers anyway. Neither was this house. Still, it hurt for practical reasons, and was yet another mark on the ever-growing list of things she had lost.

All that tempered the feeling was the knowledge that this family would make a life here, and even her sister's damn cat was doing fine. In that moment, Papa's recent words came back to her: life is for the living. Etta shifted her weight, preparing to leave, but stopped at the last second.

"I've been told that the previous owners had a habit of stashing things around the house. Be sure to check inside anything before you throw it away." She left before the woman could ask any follow-up questions.

By the time she arrived at her next stop, Etta was nervous. With no small amount of trepidation, she looked at the door in front of her and seriously considered leaving without a word. After forcing her hand to the knob, Etta was about to let herself in, as she had done countless times before, but hesitated. Somehow, it did not feel right this time. Instead, she knocked.

Mildred answered the door a moment later, regarding Etta with a tired smile. Without saying a word, they embraced, and Etta thought it was as much for Mildred's benefit as her own.

"Thought that might have been the last we saw of you," Mildred said after they separated. "Helen will be glad to see you."

"Will she?" Etta asked, her voice heavy.

"You both acted unfortunately, but sisters forgive."

Etta found Helen in the new cottage on the far side of the potato field. It was the first time Etta had seen it up close. From the outside, it was small but cozy. Just enough room for a pair of newlyweds and their baby.

Etta sighed. Robert and Helen would have made a nice life here.

Next to the cottage were a small chicken pen and coop. Peter and Michael must have built it since she left for Newark. That man was always working. It was just large enough for the dozen or so hens pecking around the yard. Etta recognized her former ladies.

Out of habit, she noted that they were properly watered and well fed. No one was missing feathers. Helen had been taking good care of them. Doubly surprising was the appearance of smoke rising from the cottage stovepipe. Helen was cooking? Etta could scarcely believe it. But lo and behold, there she was, just inside the kitchen window. Helen looked up as Etta approached, her expression unreadable.

They regarded each other in silence. After a long moment, Helen disappeared from view only to emerge from the front door. Right away, something was different about Etta's old friend, though she could not quite articulate what it was. Something in the way she carried herself. "Mature" seemed too strong of a word, but neither would Etta expect this version of Helen to hide out in the barn, leaving others to clean up dinner.

Neither of them spoke, and the only sound was the soft clucking of the hens. Unable to think of anything else, Etta nodded toward the birds.

"I hope they're being good for you."

"They're giving me a dozen eggs a day," Helen shrugged. "I never realized just how much work they were. Beatrice is my best egg layer, but Gladys is right behind her."

Etta winced.

You named them?

That would be a rude awakening at the first culling.

"You never told me how loud they were," Helen accused, but the corner of her lip curled up just enough to be noticed.

"You get used to it," Etta replied, relaxing a shade.

A silence crept into the space following her words, threatening to engulf them both before Helen spoke up.

"You want to come inside?"

Etta nodded and followed Helen into the cottage. She looked around, taking it all in. It had the fresh, resin smell of newly cut pine, mingled with the aroma of melted, slightly burned butter from whatever Helen had been cooking. The walls were made of wood panels instead of plaster and covered with practical shelves. A number of Helen's baskets already hung from the ceiling, making use of the limited space.

Peter and Michael might have built it, but it was clear that Mildred had influenced the design. The home was built around the kitchen, with the stove as the centerpiece. The sleeping area was a loft above the kitchen, which would capture warmth during the winter months.

"What do you think?" Helen asked, catching Etta's appraising look.

"It feels like a home," Etta replied. While no bigger than the Newark apartment the abundance of windows made it feel larger. Helen nodded and smiled affectionately, but she retained a guarded appearance. At the stove, she gave the contents of the sizzling pan a stir, before removing it from the heat and turning back to Etta.

Attempting to fold her arms, but unable to find a suitable location between her ample bust and her now-conspicuous belly, Helen settled for resting her hands on her hips.

Etta looked her over, and asked, "How are you feeling?"

"There are good days and bad days. Today is a little of both." She smiled tiredly. "I tell you, I never thought I'd like eggs as much as I do now. Or cooking for that matter."

Etta smiled back. It felt good. "I noticed that. Really taking after your mother, aren't you?"

Helen scoffed. "Not that bad... yet." This elicited a chuckle from the both of them. Not as strong as the hearty laughter they used to share, but it was a start. "I thought about moving back into the house, but she wouldn't let me. I'm glad she didn't to be honest. It's weird, but I'm starting to like doing things for myself."

Helen said nothing more, but looked at Etta meaningfully. Etta slowly nodded and likewise remained quiet. After a moment, Helen's smile faded and she was serious once more.

"Are you back for good now?" she asked.

"I'm not sure," Etta replied. "Newark was something of a mixed bag, but – you know... the house."

Helen grunted in reply. "Sorry to hear that. About Newark I mean. But it's good to see you."

There it was again. The silence had followed them into the room, once again settling between them. To Etta's surprise, Helen was again the first to address it.

"Listen, I'm sorry. For trying to keep you here. I was being selfish. It didn't occur to me until days later that we didn't even say goodbye. I can't even imagine what you were going through."

Etta shook her head. "I was the one being selfish. You lost your husband after a matter of days. And I should have trusted you to keep your promise."

"I do miss Robert something awful," Helen replied "Probably always will. It helps having my family so close. But I don't know what I would do if we lost our home."

Etta paused. She heard something that she never thought to come from Helen. This woman, having so recently lost the father of her unborn child actually felt sorry for her.

Pity. From a widow.

Where once, such emotional charity might have gotten Etta's hackles up, now it only laid bare the full extent of her predicament. It was both sobering and mildly depressing. Thankfully, Helen continued before Etta could wallow for too long.

"My offer still stands. If you want, you can stay here with Daniel and me. It's small, but Daddy built it for three."

Etta blinked. "You and Daniel?"

Helen looked confused before realization came to her. "Right, you wouldn't know. Um... Daniel has been staying here. Mostly just in case there's something with the baby, but he's also been helping me with errands."

Despite everything, Etta could not help but grin with amusement. "Really? My *other* cousin?"

Helen responded with an exaggerated pout and they both laughed again. "Oh, your wicked mind. It's nothing like that. He's not staying in the *loft* with me."

Then, more seriously, "Robert was his brother. I think he feels protective over the baby. He'll be here for dinner if you want to say 'hello.' Actually, he should be home soon. Daniel said they're closing the shop early today. Art's having a business dinner or something at the Hatakawana."

Etta frowned at the mention of Art. The summer was growing late and she assumed he had left town by now.

"Art? What shop?"

"I suppose a lot has happened since you left."

She briefly explained about Gregory's passing, and how Art took over for him. It had been a recent topic of concern among the farmers. Many of them were skeptical at first, but Art and Daniel were proving to be reliable.

She hesitated before continuing. "You may want to talk with him."

Etta sighed, falling back into a simmering anger more comfortably than she would have cared to admit. "I'm not sure there's anything that needs to be said. I won't tolerate a liar."

Helen stared, once again surprising Etta with a look that would have been right at home on Mildred, but was strange on her daughter. Awkward even. It was as if she was trying it on for the first time, and had not quite gotten it to fit just yet. With practice, it was clear that she would get there eventually.

"You do what you want, Chicken Farmer," she said calmly and with a degree of maturity. Yes, "mature" was the right word this time. "But take it from a recent widow, there might come a day you wish you had done things differently while you had the chance."

The Saunders had, of course, invited her to stay for dinner, but with everything on her mind, Etta was not sure she would make for good company. Despite lacking for any better options, the feeling that she would somehow be imposing was hard to shake. Without any particular direction in mind, she slowly began walking, if for no other reason than to clear her head and consider what to do next. The walk, in fact, did much to improve her mood. The familiar valley, ripening crops, and bird songs soon put her at ease. Even without a house, this place still felt like home.

In hindsight, leaving Newark had been brash. Her plan had consisted of little more than returning to the Beckett's old house. With that option lost to her, Etta was confronted by an uncomfortable reality. Not for the first time, she thought about her old routine: chores, chickens, and church. Used to be, she loathed backbreaking labor from sunup to sundown, but now she reasoned that at least it meant a roof over her head.

As she continued to walk, she considered what Helen had said. Maybe Art did deserve another chance. After all, things had been going well. Right up until they were not, that is. It was tempting to try and blame him for every misfortune that had recently transpired. Not unlike her mother had once done. The ill feelings Etta had mustered up soon fizzled with the realization.

Distracted as she was, Etta was surprised to find herself at the head of the trail that led up to the jalopy. A smile came, unbidden. Old habits. Climbing up the usual hill, the trail had become moderately overgrown since her last visit. Etta was forced to tread carefully and hold up the hem of her skirt as the passing underbrush tried to snag her.

Eventually, she reached the clearing at the summit, and walked passed the large rocks to get to the old car. To her relief, it sat there, just as it was supposed to be. With everything else in her life completely turned upside down, this final touchstone, this anchor actually remained. Even the sheet tucked into the front seat had been left undisturbed, albeit soiled from constantly being outdoors.

Brushing the seat as best she could, Etta sank into it and let out a contented sigh. Late afternoon brought the sun ever closer to the horizon. The view was slightly obstructed, as everything was now full and green, but still the third best in town. A light breeze whistled through the trees, gently swaying the branches; the only sound besides her own breathing. It was the most quiet she had found in the past month, and easily the best thing she had ever heard.

Maybe I'll just live in this car, she thought flippantly.

On the other hand, she did not have an abundance of options. Things were better with Helen, but not quite to the point where she felt comfortable staying for a night. Invited or no, playing third wheel to Papa and Eloise left Etta wary of repeating the experience.

Aunt Mildred, of course, had offered to take her in. Etta strongly considered it, but ultimately declined. After all, she knew what it was like to be under Mildred's wing. While it was a safe and comfortable place, it was also a restrictive one. If nothing else, Etta knew she could not tolerate being someone's guest for long.

Her thoughts drifted to the mention of Art's dinner plans. It seemed a lifetime ago that the two of them had their own business lunch with the Hunleys. Smiling fondly, she recalled the strange turn of events. From finding Art asleep in her family's barn and fixing her mailbox to running a business in her home town.

Out of habit, she reached for the console box, only to recall that the map was in her bag. Briefly, she considered unfolding it, like she often did, but decided against it. She knew the route by memory, and had since traversed most of it. Maybe she had not made it all the way to New York, but somehow, she no longer felt as though she needed to. The fantasy of leaving everything in her old life to go somewhere new had lost just a bit of its luster. Instead, Etta returned the map to its rightful place.

Oddly enough, her thoughts turned to Bridget and Edgar Beckett. For how much time she had spent in their abandoned home, she had not given much thought to the people themselves. Etta wondered about their journey to the dairy farm. At the time, she had been almost envious. Now, she simply hoped that Bridget's experience had been better than hers.

At least she didn't have to do it alone, Etta thought.

A long while passed before she stepped out of the car. By then, the sun had dropped close to the horizon, just kissing the top of the distant tree line. Feet on the ground, Etta rested her hand on the burgundy paint as she let the image burn into her memory for safe-keeping.

Until next time.

Giving the jalopy an affectionate parting look, she started down the hill.

Chapter 32
Art

Progress on the Cow Cooler slowed drastically while Art and Daniel packed up the old shop. Only after getting into it did the sheer volume of work involved become apparent. In desperation, he agreed to bring on one of Daniel's friends. It drained his dwindling funds even faster, but saved time, which he had even less of. The extra help proved absolutely vital, as Cassandra started asking almost daily if he was ready to leave yet.

Speaking with the Hunleys, they were tolerant of the delay, which was a huge relief. Despite the challenges, Art made some progress on the truck. Though mostly superficial, it was enough to quell the worst of Owen's misgivings.

That was the upside, but it was little comfort. While Daniel was finally able to work on his own and even began training his friend, Art wrestled with his new responsibilities as manager. The very idea that he now had two fellas answering to him – and expecting payment – was something of an odd situation. This was in addition to all the other tasks that had previously been dealt with by Gregory. The first time Art saw the bill for electricity to run all the machines, he had stared, mouth literally agape.

Then, there were all the favors that Gregory had relied upon to keep things going: extra scrap materials from a junk yard the next town over, salvageable parts from an old Navy friend, and so forth. Many of these disappeared with the old man's passing, and Art found himself in a bind, forced to do something he found truly distasteful.

He went to his father for a loan.

George, who had once tried to prohibit Art from even working at the shop, was surprisingly agreeable to loaning money in support of it. Only after they began discussing the specific terms did Art understand the full implications. With this loan, his father would retain partial ownership of the new business, and any hopes for complete independence were gone.

The first of many compromises was the name change: Robbins Repair became Adams Engineering. Art had hoped to keep Gregory's name, both to honor his mentor as well as remind everyone who had started it. Unfortunately, that simply was not negotiable. George had been adamant for two major reasons: one practical, and one vain. The “A” in Adams would put the company on the first page of most business listings, which Art conceded had some merit. Secondly, the old man wanted to plant the family name at a new place on the map.

Luciana, while generally content to remain out of George's business dealings, decided to involve herself in this particular discussion. Or rather, she jumped in at the end when conditions were being discussed. Her expectations were both clear and firm: Art was to resume his courtship with Dorothy. George was ambivalent on the matter, but nonetheless waited on Art’s answer.

“Ma, we talked about this,” he replied, making an effort to keep his voice even, despite his frustration.

It had taken a fistfight with Ralph in order for Art to work up the nerve to break off the engagement in the first place. Hoping to cut the argument short, he said nothing but assumed a firm expression. Unfortunately, Luciana was not to be lightly denied. Having since regained her own composure, she remained adamant, but also realized that she could not quite force the issue. Instead, she relied on guilt.

“Arturo,” she said slowly, “It would mean a great deal to me, if you would give this girl a real chance. Sit down with her and talk – really talk. Don’t just nod through the conversation. You may find you have more in common than you think. If she’s still not for you, then so be it. I won’t ever bring it up again.”

Involuntarily, Art slumped in his chair and nodded his acceptance. By the time he realized she had succeeded in getting him to reverse his earlier decision, Luciana had already left the room and he could not argue further. Art shook his head in astonishment.

Witness to all of it, George chuckled and shook his head. “That’s some trick she does, isn’t it?”

A thought occurred to Art. “Were you really going to withhold the loan over that?”

“No. But, ‘Happy wife, happy life,’ son.”

Art's frown deepened as it occurred to him that he might have pushed back more.

"Aw, don't be so glum. So, you have to go on a date with a pretty redhead. There are worse things."

"I don't want to marry that girl."

George shrugged his shoulders, as if this were a trivial issue. "So don't. For your mother, I think it will be enough for you to give her an honest chance. Actually, I'm rather envious of you. Not for this," he clarified. "For the new business, I mean. It's an exciting time. Plus, you're going to get to do some actual hands-on work."

"What are you talking about?" Art was confused. "You've never wanted me to do hands-on work."

"I didn't want you breaking your back for little pay and some schlub who didn't respect you. There's a good reason I'm not laying bricks anymore. Working on your own business is different. You'll be your own man. And then there's your family to consider. Whether it's with Dorothy or someone else, you'll start your own soon enough. Wait 'til you see out how expensive they are.

"That's why we left the New England house. Sure, I liked fixing things, but it just wasn't going to do for us to stay there. The house was small and the prospects were slim. Still, some good years there. The country air especially. Kind of like it is here. I can see why you decided to stay." George grinned and was almost wistful as he continued, "Can't say I wouldn't be tempted to do the same."

This was a side of his father Art had never seen before. For years, he thought the two of them had practically nothing in common, but for the first time, the old man made just a little bit of sense.

With the summer coming to an end, Art's parents and Thomas' family left the cottage and returned home. Only Ralph remained in town, explaining that he could do with a few more weeks on the lake before going back to the city. George and Luciana had some concerns over this, recalling the knockdown, drag-out fight from just a few weeks earlier, but Ralph waived them off.

"Water under the bridge, and all that."

Realizing he now had no place to stay, Art took a room at the Hatakawana: the same hotel as Ralph and Dorothy. While he never actually asked, he briefly considered asking Ralph if they could share. It said much for the leanness of his finances that he even considered it. Art was currently mindful of each and every penny to his name. Despite the loan, his recent purchase of a property in town had made a significant dent.

Still, he assured himself that the hotel room was only temporary. Once he finished moving the tools and equipment to the new shop, he would find a cot and sleep there. For once, he had a solution for tomorrow's problem if not the day after that.

To his surprise, Art did not feel any of his usual trepidation when he went to call on Dorothy. He was prepared to give her an honest chance as his mother had asked, but did not expect anything more. Thus, they did not travel far. The Lenape Valley restaurant was only next door to the hotel. As it was, it had been a challenge to convince Dorothy to go anywhere without chaperone. She had only acquiesced on the premise that it was a busy public place.

Mostly, they were among other couples, engaged in their own intimate conversations. None of which carried beyond the privacy of each table, which were small – barely large enough to hold two full size dinner plates. According to Dorothy, it was usually busier, but some hubbub was going on further up the lake and pulling in a big crowd.

At least it was well lit and there were enough people that no one could accuse the two of them of being alone. However, their seats were close together, owing to the smallness of the table; a fact that Dorothy was inclined to fuss over.

"This is hardly appropriate. Meeting like this," she said for the third or maybe fourth time. "I really should see if Irving can join us."

Art sighed, glancing around the restaurant. Already, he was tired. It had been a long day and an even longer month.

"Surely," Art began, "Even Franklin would agree that the chances of me ravaging you in the privacy of a busy restaurant are minimal."

Dorothy scoffed. "You clearly don't know my father. Or me for that matter." Folding her arms across her chest, she looked away and made clear her annoyance. Having abandoned her usual beret for the evening, an errant lock of her wiry red hair fell down her face, alongside her nose. Dorothy did not even bother to push it aside, lest she compromise her surly posture.

Making an effort to tread lightly, Art considered his words with care. He sighed, but more at himself as he noticed for the first time what had probably been plain all along. Beneath the distracting veneer of her quirks, Dorothy was hurt.

As Luciana had so thoroughly reminded him, he had neglected this young woman for most of the summer. That he had been put into this situation without being consulted had once seemed a valid excuse, but no longer. The more he thought on it, the more he recognized it as childish and wrong. Even though his presence here tonight had been coerced to an extent, he had still made the decision on his own.

With this in mind, his frustration with Dorothy relented.

"You're right," he started, letting the words hang for a moment. "I don't know you. You don't know me either. And yet, we're supposed to be married in a few months."

Her annoyed expression was replaced by indignation.

"There was no shortage of opportunities to get to know each other this summer. But you always had other things to do."

He was about to protest, but realized that he had no rebuttal. "I'll grant you, I have been spending a lot of time away from my family lately for a number of reasons. My mother surprised me with this whole thing, and I wasn't prepared for it. I hope you don't take my behavior as a personal slight."

Dorothy considered this, but moved on before it could compromise her moral high ground.

"It's no matter. I took the opportunity to spend some much needed time with my sisters, especially Emmie." Perhaps forgetting that she meant to convey annoyance, her inclination for verbal gushing soon took over. "I must say, I don't understand some of her tastes, but then I suppose she doesn't understand mine either. Still, we accommodate each other.

"Why, just yesterday, she came with me on a nature walk before she left town. Though, I daresay she owed me after I went to that dreadful speakeasy. Oh, they *claim* the bottles are just for show, but you won't fool me. It was the night of that awful storm. Do you remember?"

Art blinked, barely keeping up. Knowing how this apparent invitation to reply usually played out, he spoke more boldly than usual.

"Oh, I remember, but-" He emphasized the last word, just as Dorothy was ready to overrun him as she usually did. "In all fairness, the Wigwam isn't a speakeasy."

"The Wig- how did you know that's where I was?"

In his boldness, he had forgotten that he was not supposed to be there on the night in question.

"Um... someone must've mentioned it. Maybe one of my brothers."

"All the same. The music was not to my tastes."

"What kind of kind of music is to your taste?"

"To be honest, none."

"Then, I suppose dancing is out of the question?"

"I don't see the point," she replied, shaking her head.

Art suppressed a groan. As he expected, this was not going well. Determined to make an effort, and keep an open mind, he pushed on.

"You know, a first dance for the married couple is customary at a wedding."

She made a dismissive sound. "Surely, even you can see that I don't think much of custom. Mother has insisted that we shop for a dress. Thus far I've entertained her, but in all honesty I probably won't wear anything."

Art stared, raising a single eyebrow. It was an innocent comment, born of Dorothy's lack of social awareness. Still, it struck him as humorous, and he could not resist the urge to point it out.

"Nothing, eh?"

Dorothy frowned, before understanding dawned on her. When it did, her freckles practically disappeared into the redness of her cheeks. "Don't be fresh, Arthur."

As his attempt at levity fell flat, Art sighed. It had taken him most of the summer to determine acceptable boundaries with Etta, and now he was starting again from square one.

Then, Dorothy continued in a much quieter voice, "Save it for the honeymoon."

Art blinked. Such was his earlier dismay that he was not sure he had heard her correctly. Watching her face, he remained doubtful until a mischievous grin curled up the corners of her mouth. His befuddlement only amused her further and she parted her lips, revealing smooth, white teeth.

That was unexpected. Too surprised to speak, Art stared. As his surprise faded, he grinned as well.

"Better watch that kind of talk," he teased.

"Why? Does it make you nervous?" Her words were a challenge, but her tone was more playful than he had previously heard from her.

"Maybe. Your father has tried his hardest to glare me to death if we so much as bump elbows."

"Oh, don't mind that. He's harmless. These days, anyhow."

Without particularly thinking about it, he asked, “Speaking of the honeymoon. Where did you want to go?” The question surprised him, as he was supposedly only doing this to humor his mother.

Dorothy’s expression grew thoughtful as she considered this.

“Actually, I’m quite flexible on that matter. Assuming you can go so long without working.”

While it was a rebuke, Art noted that it was less barbed than it might once have been.

“In that case, maybe we should stay in a tent, away from everything.” He said it almost flippantly, recalling her earlier reaction to the idea of remaining in town.

“Shall we?” she asked. “I could do with a week or so of camping.”

“Really?” Art was genuinely taken aback, but she nodded.

“I want to live in the city, but I do appreciate nature. This town has some wonderful walking trails.” Her smile faded by an almost imperceptible degree. “It would have been nice if we could have enjoyed some of them together.”

I probably deserve that.

“Which trail did you go on? I’m familiar with a few of the ones around town. Was it off the north end of the lake?”

“No, it was off the back of the hotel here,” she nodded in the general direction. “But I know the one you’re referring-”

“Good evening,” interrupted the waiter. He was a younger man, and Art thought he might have recognized him from one of the parties at the Kovaks' barn, but couldn't be sure.

“Can I get you something to drink?” Then, in a lower voice, he added, “We have some good Italian wine if you two are interested.” He grinned pleasantly.

Art was about to accept the offer, but stopped short when he saw the look of utter disdain on Dorothy's face. As though the waiter had just offered them two glasses of water, fresh from the toilet. Her eyes narrowed dangerously as they bore into him. Such was the intensity of her visage that his professional smile wilted.

“Perhaps this is news to you,” she said, biting off each word, “But the sale of alcohol is illegal.”

The waiter glanced around to make sure no one was listening, then cleared his throat and scrambled for a reply.

“I ah...”

As Dorothy wound up for another verbal onslaught, Art interjected.

“Maybe a couple of fountain sodas if you have them.”

Thankful for the out, the waiter nodded and beat a hasty retreat. Dorothy, ready with a lecture, was clearly annoyed that she now had no one to lay into. She settled for glaring at Art, who stared back dispassionately.

Well, it was nice for a whole minute.

When it was clear she was not going to get a reaction from him, she refocused her surly expression to some distant, unseen point.

"You really don't like alcohol, do you?" he asked finally.

It was more something to say than an actual observation. Dorothy stiffened. As if their earlier banter had damaged her carefully crafted veneer and she was trying to restore it.

"It's a vile drink that promotes looseness in women, vulgarity in men, and breaks families."

Don't forget rotness of gut, and crackedness of heads.

"I'm sure those are extreme cases. It seems harmless enough for the most part."

"And should we ignore the extreme cases?" Dorothy demanded, shooting him a look.

It was loud enough that Art reflexively glanced over his shoulder to check if any of the other patrons were looking at them. Dorothy caught herself, and took a calming breath. Art remained quiet, sensing this was a tender subject.

"This is something of a family secret," she continued after a pause. "But I suppose we're going to be family soon, so you have a right to know.

"My father used to be fond of the drink. Quite fond. Mother says it started during the Spanish Flu. He had a dreadful time, trying to keep his business going and it calmed his nerves. As it turned out, his nerves needed quite a bit of calming. Even after the whole thing passed, he kept drinking. He often came home at night, stumbling and incoherent. That's when he came home at all. Waking up to find that he had not returned wasn't uncommon. Once, he was gone for an entire week. Occasionally, Mother would try to talk to him about it, but he always reacted poorly.

"You understand. She was concerned for her daughters. Just imagine the effect of such behavior on young girls. I tell you now; he never struck her, or any of us. Not once. Be assured, Mother would not have stood for that. But... it was frightening.

"Then, the Prohibition came. It was like a signal from the Divine. He didn't stop immediately, of course, but that was when things started to get better. He has not had a drink for nearly eight years now. It hasn't been easy. As I grew older and knew what to look for, I could see his struggle. But never once did he fall off the wagon. Perhaps some of that was my mother's standing promise that if he ever did, she would take my sisters and me and leave.

"For all of my father's faults, you cannot say that he does not possess both devotion to his family, and an ironclad will... at least now he does."

Shrugging, she concluded, "So, to answer your question. No, we do not care for alcohol."

For once, Dorothy had nothing more to say.

That explains much, thought Art.

Both remained silent even as the waiter returned. Wordlessly, he set the pair of sodas on the table and retreated again. Dorothy attempted to conjure another glare, but her heart was no longer in it. Still, Art resolved to leave the poor fellow a generous tip for his trouble.

"Do you want to get married?" he asked suddenly.

"Is this a proposal?" she asked, brow furrowed. "We're already betrothed." Noticing the errant ginger lock for the first time, Dorothy blew a puff of air to try and shoo it away but found little success.

"I know we are, but do you want to be?" Art tried to clarify. "I guess I just don't understand how a New England college girl gets into an arranged marriage."

She stiffened at what might have sounded like a rebuke, but her expression quickly turned thoughtful.

"Because I want to be," she replied simply. "How else am I to filter out the riffraff of suitors while also tending to my studies? Luciana swore you were a young man of temperance and good character, and I trust my mother's judgment. It's seen our family through some difficult times. Why wouldn't I let her help me to select a husband?"

"I suppose... but is that all you want?"

"All?" she repeated, cracking a bemused grin. "You make it seem like a thing of such little consequence. I'd say it's just about the most important thing anyone could do. Why, what is the point of marriage, if not to raise children? And what are children, if not the very continuation of this wonderful accident we call life?"

"I think I follow you," Art replied, and noted with surprise that Dorothy made no attempt to talk over him this time. "Though, you have to admit that's not a very romantic take."

"Depends on your definition of 'romantic' I suppose. It's funny, you use that word but have you given any thought to the root of it?

‘Romantic.’ As in 'Rome.' You know, they considered the family unit to be the very bricks on which civilizations are built.

“I’ll grant that you could claim it isn’t 'fun.' Certainly, my sister would agree with you. I love Emmie, but she enjoys the flapper lifestyle a bit too much in my opinion. I’d say that fun is a matter of perspective. You spent an awful lot of time at that workshop this summer. Why is that?”

“Well, that was a job.”

“But why that job? If you only wanted employment, you could have stayed with your father, making sales. Why would you choose to dirty your hands?”

“I like to see a thing take shape.”

Dorothy slowly nodded, as though he had made her point for her. She very much reminded him of a schoolteacher just then.

“And so do I. Though I daresay the scope of my interest is rather larger that yours. I want to see a whole life take shape. Maybe even a few of them. And I want to build a life together. So, how about it, Mr. Adams? What do you want?”

Finished, Dorothy looked at him with an expression that he was unaccustomed to seeing on her. In fact, Art had witnessed it exactly one other time that summer as she watched the grandchildren play at the cottage. At first, he had interpreted it as simple, professional interest, but seeing it a second time, he realized that he had it wrong. Not interest, but longing. Perhaps not for him specifically, but here was someone who knew what she wanted out of life.

She remained silent, awaiting Art's reply. Eventually, he returned her half-smile, feeling even more ashamed of his earlier behavior. Beneath her quirks, she was a thoughtful, complicated sort, and Art could sympathize with poor first impressions. A moment passed as he reflected on what she had said; the choice of words resonated with him.

Build a life together.

She continued to stare, not letting him off without an answer. The lock of her wiry red hair remained, but she made no further move to correct it. Without particularly thinking about it, Art reached out. Tucking the rebellious strands behind her ear, his palm gently brushed the side of her face. Only after he sat back, did it occur to him that this was the first time they had physically touched aside from their hands. Dorothy’s freckles practically disappeared as her face blushed a furious shade of red.

“That's forward of you...”

“To answer your question,” Art replied. “I think I want the same.”

He almost shook his head, bewildered by the strange turn of events. Despite surprising him with the whole thing, Luciana must have seen the potential here. Art had to concede that he was beginning to see it as well.

While he was not quite ready to marry Dorothy, he saw how they could get there in time. For once, Art did not feel anxious or helpless about the whole thing. As one with an unfortunate habit of neglecting the future, he thought Dorothy’s vision for her own was something worthwhile. Whatever circumstances had brought them together he saw how this could work out.

You have a very practical way about you, Arturo.

Unbidden, Etta’s word came back to him, a bitter reminder of what might have been. But she was gone from his life now, like Sarah before her. And unlike Sarah, Etta had left by her own choice. Reluctantly, Art looked back to Dorothy and pushed other thoughts aside. They were not fair to anyone.

Chapter 33
Etta

It was a loud night on the lake. The August Pageant was typically the high-water mark for the town. After which, most everyone would return to wherever they had come from, and the farmers and Townies could resume their simmering feud in peace. Etta had only been to the pageant once, and found the crowds off-putting. Now, compared to her brief experience in an actual city, it was a downright mellow affair.

Walking through the Oasis beach area, she passed a multitude of out-of-towners in various stages of sobriety. Where a few months ago she might have avoided the area or at least sought a comfortable distance from the crowds, now it just felt like home.

The sun was below the horizon, and night soon descended. A few stragglers remained in the water, not quite ready to end the day. In no particular rush, Etta followed the waterfront as it gently curved towards the Hatakawana Inn. Out of a multitude of thoughts swirling through her mind, the most prominent was of the last time she had come this way. It was the night Robert died; the night of her last date with Art.

What am I going to say?

All told, it had been nearly a month since they had even seen each other. As she walked, and as the sky continued to darken, her thoughts turned to what Helen had said, about doing things differently. She also reflected on what she and Art had said to each other at their last meeting. Whatever complaints she had, they seemed less important now.

Assuming he is, in fact, no longer engaged, she reminded herself.

It was full dark by the time she reached Route Six, where the crowd was growing thick. The pageant would culminate on the west end of the lake, and most revelers were now heading in that direction. It was enough to warrant a police officer on the scene to direct traffic. Without particularly thinking about it, she looked up as she passed and made eye contact with the officer.

Both did a double take. Each recognized the other in the glow of car headlights. If not for the crowd carrying her along, Etta might have stopped mid-stride. Officer Hoffman frowned. After what had only been a second or so, but felt longer, he returned his attention to directing the cars and pedestrians. With his attention off of her, Etta hastened her pace until she was down the road and safely out of sight. Only after she put nearly a hundred steps between herself and Walter's uncle did she dare let out a sigh of relief. Reminded of one of her worst experiences of the summer, she soon found herself with another.

The Hatakawana sat at the top of its hill overlooking the lake's southern shore. As Etta made the short but steep ascent, her hands tingled with the memory of her disastrous experience as a hotel laundress. It seemed a lifetime ago. The top of the hill was much quieter than the throng making its way to the pageant. The noise from the waterfront crowd became distant and muffled. A few stragglers milled around the hotel, but would likely join the festivities soon. One lone figure hung back, keeping to himself on the far side of the hotel porch. Though it was dark, Etta quickly recognized Heber Wells.

Her temper flared up at the sight of him. Here was the man who had cost her the use of her hands for a solid week. The feeling was short-lived, however. His faults were ineptitude and disregard, not malice. Otherwise, he had, in fact, been quite courteous to her. Though, at this moment he was extremely agitated by something.

Alone, he paced the front porch of the hotel, moving in and out of the cones of lamplight. Stopping in the shadow again, he took a drag from his cigarette. The cherry glow wobbled midair in the dark, as if the hand that held it was trembling.

Etta passed him by and left him to whatever troubled his mind. The restaurant sat adjacent to the hotel, and she hoped that Art's dinner meeting might still be going on. Her heart started to beat faster as she approached the windows. Unconsciously, she tucked back her hair, fussed with her dress, and adjusted the strap on her black bag. It was more nervous energy than an earnest attempt at grooming. Art had, after all, seen her in work clothes more often than not. Still, a month was a long time. In her anticipation, she could hardly remember what had driven them apart in the first place.

Harshly, she was reminded.

Right away, Etta recognized Dorothy, the chatty redhead who had suffered a torn dress. Her mood was clearly much improved from when she and Etta first met. Indeed, she was genuinely enjoying herself and laughing with someone seated across from her. Dread grew as Etta turned her attention to Dorothy's companion.

Even before she saw him, she knew it was Art. Like his date, he was having a good time, though it was difficult to tell as his back was turned to the window. But there was no mistaking that hair.

Etta did not know for how long she stood there, or when she started to move. But soon she was walking. With nothing guiding her, save a desire to be away from people, she wandered. Not particularly thinking about it, she arrived at the new construction site and sat down heavily on a stack of wood. Head turned down, Etta wiped at her face as she felt drops fall into her lap.

What did I really expect? she sulked.

Had she been fooling herself? Had Art really intended to break off his engagement or was it Etta's leaving that pushed them back together? It was the uncertainty that bothered her more than anything. Was this yet another misfortune that could have easily been prevented?

"If you're feeling guilty, let me just say, 'you should be.'"

Etta's breath caught, as if she had been walking on ice that suddenly spider webbed and cracked beneath her feet. Her despair fled as she recognized this voice. What took its place was dread, equal in intensity.

Eyes wide, Etta slowly raised her head. Standing across the clearing, next to a dormant piece of construction equipment was Walter.

They locked eyes, and Etta knew she should run. She wanted to, but panic kept her rooted to the pile of lumber. Unsteady on his feet, Walter stepped away from the machine and took another swig from what he was holding. Even in the minimal light, she recognized one of the Brandelson's mason jars. Despite his inebriation, the look he gave her was steady and angry. Etta said nothing, but Walter carried on, regardless.

"You got me kicked out of the band, y'know. Runnin' your mouth the way you did."

Confusion briefly overcame Etta's fear, as she had no idea what he was talking about. "What?"

Walter reacted to the sound of her voice with fury, and took an angry step in her direction.

"You ratted me out, is 'what!' Next time we played CasinO, I thought I'd help myself to the safe again and that mustached bastard was waiting for me. Made a big stink over it with Rick. Only person that could've told him about it was you."

In a blur, Walter hurled the nearly empty glass towards Etta. It smashed to pieces on the stack of wood, close enough that she could feel cold droplets splash against her arm. With a yelp, she jumped to her feet. Whether he had missed on purpose or by accident, she did not know. Etta tried to step backward, but her feet were already up against the wood. Walter moved towards her.

"Wait-" She raised her hand, as if to block him.

Why don't I run?

To her surprise, Walter chuckled and stopped before he reached her.

"Gotta say. I'm surprised to see you back here. Figured you might've left town with that four-eyed bastard. Since you don't have a house, I mean."

The urge to run subsided, and she was held in place by curiosity and uncertainty.

"How... how did you know about that?"

A wicked grin spread on Walter's face.

"Did it burn quick? My cousins make some pretty potent stuff."

"Wha-?"

"I mean I'd be lying if I said I was torn up over it, but in all fairness, it was kind of an accident. I only meant to break a window. Guess I could've used a rock instead of a twenty dollar jar o' hooch. Never thought it would just go up like that."

Understanding came over her as she pictured Walter standing in front of her house. A jar of moonshine in his hand and a lantern burning in the kitchen.

"But hey, I s'pose we're even now. More or less." He spread his hands in faux apology.

Etta thought of the flames as she approached the house. How the wood hissed and cracked as the fire company sprayed it with water. Despair turned to anger as she thought about all the things that had been inside: the only picture of the family, Mama's wedding dress, Irene's favorite book. All gone.

Because of him.

Before she realized what she was doing, Etta closed the gap between them. Her hand flew. Not a slap either, but a closed fist thrown with all the hatred and anger she could muster. Walter's head snapped around with the impact, but it was her second attempt at a punch and only the first time she had successfully connected. Her wrist collapsed under the impact, and the bones of Walter's face were hard against her strong yet thin fingers.

Etta recoiled instantly, the pain quenching the momentary rage she had just indulged. Bent over, cradling her wrist, she grunted in pain and let an uncharacteristic expletive escape her mouth.

It occurred to her, as she massaged the pain from her stinging hand that Walter's feet had not moved. Slowly, he turned his head around to face her again. Her best punch had done little more than make him angry.

No. Not angry. Murderous.

"You. Bitch."

Walter lunged, but he was slow and unsteady on his feet. In a distant part of Etta's mind, she was thankful that the Brandelsons did, in fact, make strong stuff. Walter was close, but his sloppiness gave her just enough room to stay clear. Finally, she listened to the voice that had been telling her to run.

In her haste, she forgot about the stack of lumber and tripped over it in her scramble to get away. Rolling on the ground, she became entangled in something as Walter's footsteps approached. Urged along by sheer panic, she wiggled free but it cost precious seconds. Walter managed to stay close behind, despite his drunken state.

Need to get somewhere with people.

The hotel was nearby, but the few guests that had been milling around just moments before had disappeared. Walter was on her heels, and she had little doubt of the beating that would ensue if he caught her. What she did doubt was whether he would stop before he killed her.

Etta ran, driven by a pure, instinctual drive for survival. A scarce few steps separated her from Walter. Any stumble or awkward landing on her part and he would be on her. Etta needed to put something between them. Something to buy time until she could reach people. Unable to think, she went for what was familiar.

Despite her previous vow to never set foot in the Hatakawana Inn again, she headed for it with speed and determination. Reaching the hotel's back door, she wrenched it open and dashed inside. Spinning around, Etta managed to get it closed just as Walter slammed into it from the outside. The door stayed shut, but Etta was rocked as Walter pounded it with a ferocity that terrified her.

Catching her breath, Etta looked around, finding no one to call for help. She knew this part of the hotel. None of the guest rooms were back here. There was only the door to the basement.

The pounding stopped and she felt the doorknob turn in her slippery grip. Using both hands, she tried, desperately, to hold it in place, but only succeeded in slowing the progress. In a matter of seconds, Walter would overpower her. Etta's only hope, she figured, was to get to the basement. There were plenty of places to hide, or otherwise lose him down there. At the very least, maybe the stairs would slow him down in his drunken state. With no time to consider, it was her least bad option.

The basement door was across the hallway. She would have to abandon her fight with Walter and release the doorknob in order to reach it. Knowing she would have to act quickly, Etta took a deep breath and let go. Dashing across the hall, she grabbed for the basement door.

Her heart sank when it refused to open.

The knob turned in her hand, but the door itself was stuck in the frame. Behind her, Walter burst in. In his anger, he charged and there was no time to react before he barreled into her.

The basement door gave way, and Etta’s feet lifted off the ground.

One of the last things she remembered, before falling into the darkness of the stairwell was the overpowering stench of Vaseline. Close as a lover’s embrace, the two of them fell. Time seemed to stop as they careened through empty space. When the first impact came, strangely, it did not hurt. It was more like her previous landing on the armful of bed sheets. Only this time it was a man that broke her fall.

Walter grunted as she landed on him. Hard. Unlike her first experience, they continued to roll. There was a second jarring impact. This time, she actually hit the stairs, albeit, not as badly as Walter. He grunted again, but not as loudly. Or perhaps Etta was just stunned.

Over and over. Falling. Crashing. Falling. Rolling. Lights flashed behind Etta’s eyes with each impact. Her arms and back took the most punishment.

At last, the world stopped moving. Etta had managed to avoid hitting her head directly, but her mind was sluggish from the buffeting. She came close once or twice, but never actually lost consciousness. Eventually, Etta recovered enough to realize that she was lying on top of Walter, and remembered that she was supposed to be fleeing him.

Moving as quickly as she could manage, which was still a slow crawl, Etta got away. Propping up on her elbows on the cold basement floor she winced, becoming aware of the numerous scrapes and bruises she had acquired in her tumble. No bones were broken, as far as she could tell.

Walter did not move. This was her opportunity to get away. Etta tried to force herself back up to her feet, but her back screamed out in protest and her wrist flared with pain as she put weight on it. Shifting to her good hand and knees, she took a deep breath. Before she could try again, it occurred to her that Walter was still. Very still.

Where Etta's chest was heaving as she caught her breath, Walter made no movement at all.

Still cautious, Etta crawled to him, dragging her one leg to limit the tugging sensation along her back. All of her new aches protested, but she pushed through, driven by a newfound urgency.

Looking up close, even in the dim light of the basement, there was no mistaking his glassy-eyed vacant expression. Etta willed him to blink. To breathe. To lunge and attack her. Something. But there was no denying it, and no amount of willpower or prayer could change it.

Walter was dead, and she was in trouble.

Chapter 34

Art

Whatever event was happening down at the lake had grown boisterous. Walking the grounds outside the hotel, he listened to the distant sounds of merrymaking. His eyes remained fixed on the ground in front of him. It was getting late, but he was too restless to sleep. Instead, he had gone out for air and to reflect on his first real date with Dorothy.

It had gone well enough, he supposed. Maybe lacked a certain spark, but it was a vast improvement from their typical encounter. Having parted on good terms for once, the two of them made tentative plans to meet for breakfast the following morning. In another deviation from their standard dynamic, Art intended to follow through on it. He reasoned that they should make up for lost time since the summer was drawing to a close and things with the business were only going to get busier.

“You're not going to vanish on me again, are you Mr. Adams?” Dorothy asked.

Mostly in jest, he had replied, “Room one one seven. Feel free to check on me.”

Before going upstairs, she waved and favored him with a genuine smile. Had he not met Etta, Art and Dorothy might have gotten along much earlier.

Etta. He smiled wanly at the thought of her. Much as he tried, he could not quite move on. A month passed since they had last spoken and he still thought about her every day. If he were not actively working on something to distract himself, she would intrude on his thoughts.

Walking around town was worse. Every blonde he saw reminded him of her, and anyone that bore a passing resemblance gave him a fleeting hope that it might be her. Of course, it never was, and he would be left with a fresh ache in his heart. Art considered himself a creature of reason and cold logic. It was one his favorite things about machines; they would never break his heart. But in matters of love, he remained stubbornly irrational. Even if he was destined to be with Dorothy, he just wanted the chance to talk with Etta one more time.

As his thoughts wandered, he glanced up at the sound of someone leaving out the back door of the hotel.

Ugh, I'm doing it again, he thought.

The blonde girl bore a particularly striking resemblance to Etta. Returning to his thoughts, he shook his head. This was only the second time he had to get over someone, and it was rough. Not so much with Rebecca, but he had thought about Sarah for months. He did not want to carry a torch for Etta forever. Besides, it was not being fair to Dorothy.

The blonde girl approached, but Art assumed she meant to walk past. Instead, he was surprised to find her blocking his path. He finally looked up, giving her more than a cursory glance.

She really looks like Etta.

"Hi Art," she said.

He was almost too stunned to notice the tremble in her voice. Her mouth was a flat line, and she stared at him intently.

"Etta? What...?" All remaining powers of speech took their leave. Barely trusting his eyes, he could do nothing but stare.

"I- I need your help." Etta's sanity was holding on by the thinnest of strings.

Getting over the initial shock of seeing her, Art started to notice things. Her hair was a mess, and it looked like her clothing had been ripped in a few places.

"Have you been in a fight?" he asked.

In the dim light, Art noticed the haunted look in her eyes, and evidence that she had only recently calmed down from a veritable panic. Etta took a shuddering, deep breath.

Slowly, she repeated, "I need your help."

"So, just walk me through this one more time," Art said.

He wondered if lunacy was a tangible force that could only be transferred but not created or destroyed. Just as Etta regained most of her composure, Art fidgeted and began pacing the basement of the hotel. Walter's body lay on the ground behind a row of washing machines. Oddly, in a now distant, rational enclave of his mind, he thought about the fact that this was only the second dead person he had ever seen.

"He attacked me," she continued, her voice rising. "We fell down the stairs. What more do you need to know?" Reaching the last word, she sounded, of all things, annoyed.

"But... how did he roll behind the washing machines?"

The angles were all wrong and it made no sense. Granted, it was a trivial detail to latch onto, but this sort of nitpicking grounded him.

"Well..." Etta hesitated, her newfound composure cracking. "I was afraid someone might find him so I dragged him there. I tried pulling him up the stairs, but he was too heavy. That's when I came to find you."

This was another detail that did not add up. "But how did you know I was here?"

"Helen told me you were at the restaurant. What does it matter?"

Etta was becoming agitated again, as she attempted to focus Art on the issue before them. Oddly enough, seeing her put off balance helped him to calm down. He wondered what Dorothy might say about the implications of that. Art put his hands up in a disarming gesture.

"I just want to understand so we know what we're going to tell the police."

The color drained from Etta's face. "We are not telling the police." Her calm tone was obviously forced, yet adamant.

Art looked at her, not understanding. "How can we not tell the police?" he demanded.

"Walter's uncle is a cop," Etta explained. And he already has it out for me. He'd never believe this was an accident."

Art scrambled for solutions. "Fine. So, we just leave. Someone will find him eventually and we were never here."

Etta shook her head. "His uncle saw me tonight. He'll just know." She paused a moment in apparent calculation. "And there's no shortage of people that saw the two of you fight."

It took a second for the full implication of her words to sink in. Up until now, he had mostly been panicked in a general way and on Etta's behalf. Now, the idea of him somehow being directly involved added a more specific element to the cocktail of disquieting emotions.

"No. You are not dragging me into this."

Etta said nothing, but stared at him.

What if I just leave? Grab the truck and start driving.

Immediately, he dismissed the idea. Whatever else had occurred between them, Art did not have it in him to abandon Etta to her fate. Sighing, he nodded.

"Alright, what do we do?"

Etta breathed a sigh of relief. “We need to get him out of here,” she replied. “There are miles of forest to hide him.”

“Alright,” Art replied. “I've got the truck, just outside.”

Etta nodded, and moved to grab Walter's feet.

“Wait,” Art stopped her. “We can't just carry him out like this. We need a sheet or something.” He looked around.

“There's extra linens down here,” Etta said.

Walking to the only other door in the basement, she tried the handle twice before admitting it was locked. She stared at it, confused.

“This wasn't locked the last time I was here.”

“Never mind,” Art replied. “We'll take the sheets from my room.”

That would create different problems, but they were manageable by comparison. They went up the stairs quickly, but turned cautious as they entered the hallway. Peaking around the door, Art made sure that it was empty before they emerged from the stairwell. Etta followed closely behind as they approached room 117. It occurred to Art that the two of them were doing their best to appear suspicious.

Entering the room, he began to pull the blankets and sheets off the mattress. Etta likewise collected the spare linens from the closet. As they worked, he saw her in full light for the first time that evening. Her tumble down the stairs had been rougher than he originally thought. Already, she was beginning to bruise in multiple places, including her face.

I know that feeling, he thought sympathetically. *She still looks good.*

In the relative calm of his room, he had a chance to entertain some thoughts that had been forced out of his mind up until now. A question nagged at him.

“Why were you here tonight?” he asked.

Etta paused, and grew uncomfortable as if she were searching for a response that was not embarrassing but failed to do so.

“I...” Then, in a flash, she covered it by going on the attack. “Are we really going to talk about this right now?”

She had a point, but despite everything going on, Art could not help but think, *That was telling.*

A knock at the door caught their attention and they turned to the sound as one. Holding their breath, both exchanged a startled look of disbelief and anxiety.

In a voice softer than a whisper, Etta asked, “Who's that?”

Mildly panicked, Art shrugged his shoulders and shook his head. Then, desperately searching the room, his eyes landed on the closet.

Without a word, he gently grabbed Etta by the arm and pointed to it.

Get inside.

Etta frowned and shook her head. *Too small.*

Exasperated, Art looked from her to the door as it knocked again. *No time to argue.*

Sighing, Etta pushed aside the hanging articles and squeezed between them enough to close the louvered closet. Art went to the hallway door, and after glancing back one last time, opened it.

A young redhead was standing just beyond. Upon seeing Art, she lowered her hand as if she had been preparing to knock for a third time.

"Dorothy. Hi." Art realized he was breathing heavier than he should be, and made an effort to calm down. She had a strange look about her, which Art did not recognize at first.

Is she being shy?

An interminable moment passed with neither of them saying anything. Dorothy spent much of it looking at her feet, as if she had forgotten what she had come here for. All the while, Art was keenly aware of both the dead body fifteen feet below and the blonde girl standing behind him. It took an agonizing moment for Dorothy to find words.

"Hello Arthur."

Growing more anxious, Art tried to help things along. "What – ah – what brings you to... my room?"

"I just- I wanted to say that I had a lovely time at dinner tonight."

Of all the times...

"Yeah," he recovered, clearing his throat and sounding more casual. "Me too. Sorry it took all summer for us to talk."

"Yes. You've been busy. I understand. And that can be an admirable trait for a husband. But so is making time for your family. I just wanted to say that it meant a lot to m-" she stopped suddenly, frowning at something behind him.

Shit. Did she see Etta?

Art turned, and remembered the bed sheets heaped in a pile on the mattress.

"Did the maid not come by today?" Dorothy asked.

The situation was beginning to fray Art's nerves, and he was unable to think. Only react.

"Yeah. Don't know what happened there. Only did half the job."

"It's getting late. I can help you put it back together." She took a step into Art's room, and he moved to block her.

"No!" he said more loudly than he meant to.

Dorothy pulled up short, startled by the uncharacteristic outburst.

"I'm going to leave it. Y'know, I thought I saw a bedbug anyway."

"A bedbug?" Dorothy recoiled and wrinkled up her nose. "I didn't think this establishment had vermin. I'll go to the front desk for you. Tell them to have it dealt with."

"Wait. Ah. Let's go to your room."

She stared at him blankly before she blushed again with understanding.

Oh, what did I just say?

"Well, now..." she managed at last.

Art clammed up and took several slow breaths, lest he drop another gaff. To his surprise, she considered his apparent proposition.

"Emmie left yesterday. I do have the room to myself." She hesitated, before looking at him in a way he had never seen before. "It's not strictly proper, but I suppose allowances could be made for an emergency. If you promise to be honorable."

"Why don't you go up first? I'll just... put a few things away and come up in a few minutes."

Dorothy bit her lower lip, but her gaze otherwise betrayed no other reaction. "How scandalous." She made an impressed noise before a mischievous grin spread across her face. "I must say, Arthur, this is a side of you I was completely unaware of." Dorothy quickly glanced up and down the hallway before leaning in and – to Art's complete surprise – actually kissed him on the cheek. Grinning, she turned and headed down the hallway, with a noticeable bounce to her step.

Art watched her walk away, mouth agape. It was yet another stark reminder that his understanding of women was completely and utterly lacking. A muffled voice from behind intruded on his thoughts.

"Is blabbermouth gone yet?" Etta asked from inside the closet.

Quickly, Art closed the door, and cleared his throat. "All clear," he replied.

Etta wasted no time in letting herself out, and pointedly looked away.

"I'm not really going to her room," Art insisted.

"I don't care," Etta shot back, eyes darting back and forth. Her nostrils flared as she let out a heavy breath, and added, "Do we not have more pressing concerns right now?"

"Right."

Figuring more was better, each of them gathered as many sheets and blankets as they could carry. Art checked the hallway once again, before they headed out. Walking cautiously but quickly, they made their way towards the basement stairs. With each step, Art looked around, paranoid that someone might step out of any one of the different rooms and discover them. Once again, he was aware of just how out of place and suspicious they were. They had almost reached the basement door when Art heard footsteps descending from the second level.

In a panic, he looked around for somewhere, anywhere, to duck into, but there was no time. He stopped so quickly, that Etta bumped into him.

Ralph emerged from the stairwell and Art froze. At first Ralph only glanced at him with disinterest, but did a double take upon recognizing his younger brother.

"Art?" Ralph looked from Art to the bundle he was carrying. "What are you...?" Then, his eyes turn to Etta and he frowned with confusion. "Who's this?"

Not again. Art groaned, more annoyed than anxious.

"Ralph. Just keep walking."

"Wait, are you fooling around on Dorothy?" His eyes settled on the bed sheets.

Art narrowed his eyes in disbelief for a brief moment. "What? No." Then, thinking about it, "Why do you care?"

"I can't believe you. Dorothy Kennedy is such a catch, and you're going behind her back?"

"Are you actually moralizing on me? Ralph, this is not a good time."

"I've got a mind to go to her right now, you know. Mother and Father too. They're going to-"

"Ralph, will you kindly just piss off?" Art spoke through clenched teeth, and in the silence that followed, he was immediately afraid he had pushed too far again.

The last fight with his brother had started nearly the same way. For a second, it looked as though another was about to ensue. Ralph tensed up, and glared at Art. Then, just as quickly, he narrowed his eyes and actually smiled.

"Oh. Sure, thing, Little Brother. Sure thing." The last two words were drawn out, in an almost singsong tone. Ralph took a single step backwards before turning on his heel and returning up the stairs. All the while, he did his best impression of the cat that had just cornered the canary. As the sound of Ralph's footsteps faded, Art glanced at Etta, who appeared just as confused.

No time to worry about that now.

"Go slowly on the stairs," Etta whispered. "Trust me."

Art nodded and reckoned there was wisdom to that. He could not see much beyond the pile of linens he was holding. Arms laden, they carefully made their way down to the basement. Ironically, he almost tripped upon reaching the basement floor.

His foot snagged on something, knocking him off balance. Etta bumped into him and he dropped the sheets. They landed, much to his confusion and surprise, on another pile of sheets.

“Was this here before?” he asked, almost to himself.

Moving beside him, Etta's face scrunched up as she sniffed the air. Art noticed it too. Something astringent and familiar, but out of context, he was unable to immediately place it. Out of the corner of his eye, he noticed that she had turned her head to look at something, and followed her gaze. The previously locked door stood open, and shadows moved within. In a flash, Etta dropped her own bundle, and grabbed Art by the arm.

“Someone's here!” she hissed.

Etta pulled him behind the only thing in the basement that was large enough to hide behind: the laundry machines. Except she had forgotten about the corpse already there and stopped short. Art carried forward and his face collided into the back of her head. This both knocked her to the ground, and caused Art to cup his nose in both hands. Etta landed on Walter's body, and barely suppressed a shriek before scrambling off of him. Art grunted in pain.

“...hear somethin'?” It was one of the voices from the other room.

Eyes wide, Etta motioned for Art to get down. He flattened himself against the floor, trying to get as much of his body behind the laundry machines as possible. Etta did likewise, with each of them careful not to touch Walter who lay between them. They exchanged a look as two men emerged from the far room.

“Hey, cuz, that you?” called one.

“Naw, he's on lookout. Ain't no one down here,” replied the other.

“Tellin' you I heard something.”

The voices were familiar to Art, but he could not place them. They stopped just in front of the row of laundry machines and dropped another bundle of sheets onto the pile with a soft *whump*. Daring to peak through the frame of the laundry machine, Art caught the barest glimpse of the one's face before hiding again. He knew it immediately. The last time he had seen it was at the Kovaks' barn party just before they were chased off.

“Supposin' you did hear somethin'. Is it gonna matter?”

Jeff Brandelson sighed. “I reckon not.”

Art and Etta exchanged another confused look.

What does that mean?

For a second, Etta looked as though she was about to ask the same thing, but caught herself. Walter remained stubbornly ambivalent on the matter.

Tim and Jeff started up the stairwell. The last thing Art could hear, before their voices faded beyond comprehension was, “Damn, waste of fine product.” Their footfalls grew muffled as they reached the top of the stairs, leaving him to puzzle their meaning. Finally daring to speak, Art kept his voice at a whisper.

“What was that all ab-” he was cut off by the sound of glass shattering, immediately followed by the flash of a small fire. Somewhere in the back of his mind, Art made the connection: product... moonshine.

Etta yelped and sprang to her feet in a flash; an instinctual response to get away from the fire. Stunned, Art did likewise. Things happened so quickly, both of them were in shock, and could do nothing but stare. In a matter of seconds, the pile of sheets was engulfed and quickly spread to the base of the stairs and adjacent shelves.

“We have to go,” Etta cried.

Art nodded, but it still took him a moment to comprehend the true depth of the trouble they were in. The stairs were effectively blocked.

“What do we do with him?” he motioned to Walter.

Etta looked around in a panic. “I don't think he's our problem anymore.”

“We need a window or something. Is there one down here?” Even as he asked, he moved away from the fire and toward the wall, searching frantically.

“No windows. It's pitch dark in the middle of the day.”

Art did not ask how she knew that, but took her at her word. Even so, he followed the wall, hoping for a solution to present itself. Smoke quickly filled the basement, and Art had to crouch to keep his eyes from stinging. The fire intensified and had already spread up the stairs to the level of the ceiling. Smoke was quickly filling the basement. As they failed to discover another means of escape, Art started to feel real fear. Reaching a corner of two walls, with still no solution, he turned around to face Etta.

“Is there another staircase? An elevator? Anything?”

She was about to shake her head, but stopped. “Of course! There's a dumbwaiter in the pantry behind the linens room.” Turning in place, she dashed to the previously locked room, which the Brandelsons had left wide open.

Art followed. Inside, they were met by another locked door. Frantically, Etta desperately tried to turn the knob to no avail.

"No! Nononono!"

"Stand back!" Art called. He took a running start and kicked his foot into the pantry door with all his might. It stood firm.

Trying again, he met with the same result. He sputtered and coughed as the smoke found them. Forced to stop, Art noticed the hinges were on the wrong side of the door. There would be no kicking it down.

"What about this?" Etta asked.

Art turned to her, and pulled back as she shoved a brick in his face. Automatically, he grabbed it, and felt the weight in his hands.

"That might work."

In truth, he suspected it was too light to be effective, but they had no other options. He crouched down where the air was cleaner and set to work. At first, the doorknob resisted his attempts to knock it loose. Thankfully, and to Art's relief, it proved to have its limits. Little by little, it gave way with each strike. His hand soon began to ache and his shoulder was burning with exertion. Just as he thought to take a rest, Etta started to cough.

With the heedless energy of a desperate man, he swung the brick with all he had. The doorknob finally snapped off. It took precious seconds to clear out the guts of the mechanism and jimmy the door open. A rush of fresh air burst forth as he ushered Etta into the pantry.

Thankfully, the dumbwaiter was there, but their escape route presented them with two new problems. First, a strong draft, pulled from upstairs kept the now broken door from staying closed. Art was obliged to hold it shut to keep the pantry from filling with smoke. Meanwhile, Etta opened the dumbwaiter and discovered the second problem.

"There's a shelf," she cried with dismay. "We won't fit."

Art looked, but from where he was standing, could not see much. Releasing the door, the draft pushed it open, and smoke began to enter the room. Examining the box, it was clear that there was not enough room even without the shelf. A thought occurred to Art, and he pushed down. Under his full weight, he created just enough of a gap to see where the rope attached. He nodded to himself.

"I have an idea. But I need something to cut with."

"There might be an extra set of knives down here."

Etta left and rifled through a couple boxes. Meanwhile, Art looked up to see smoke gathering around the single light bulb that hung from the ceiling.

"Will this work?" she asked, holding out a serrated bread knife.

"It's gonna have to," Art replied. He pushed back down, straining with the effort. "Reach in and cut the rope."

Etta nodded, but hesitated as she regarded the small opening between the dumbwaiter box and the surrounding frame.

"Whatever you do," she said. "Don't let go."

Art's muscles, already strained from earlier, were already cramping up, but he nodded all the same. "Try to work quick."

Reaching in up to her shoulder, Etta began to saw on the dumbwaiter rope. All the while, the room steadily filled with smoke. Soon, orange light flickered and danced across the wall as the flames grew closer. Back and forth, Etta moved.

The layer of smoke along the ceiling pressed toward them. Had they not been breathing the fresh air from the dumbwaiter shaft, they would have been in real trouble. As it was, Art's eyes were stinging, and in his distraction, his grip slipped. The dumbwaiter only moved a quarter of an inch, and he caught it in time, but the sensation of Etta's arm being pinched caused her to yelp.

"Sorry," he said.

She let out a shuddering breath and resumed cutting. Finally, the rope snapped and the lift gave way. They fell backwards, landing in a tangled heap on the basement floor. Art pushed the dumbwaiter box off of them, and regarded their now clear route to the next floor.

"Inside! Go!" he cried with urgency.

Etta crawled through the opening and not a moment too soon. In the next room, a portion of the staircase collapsed, sending up a shower of embers and sparks.

"Etta! Hurry!" he called. From the pantry, he could see her feet still on the floor of the dumbwaiter shaft. "Why aren't you climbing?"

"There's a foothold, but it's too high for me to reach."

Art squeezed in beside her, kneeling in the confined space. Telling her to step on his cupped hands, they were pressed together in a way that might have made them blush under different circumstances. After a moment of contorting themselves in the darkness, Etta managed to get a foot on Art's shoulder and he pushed her up.

"Got it, she called."

The pressure on his shoulder released as she found the foothold, and he followed close behind. Inch by inch, they climbed up the exposed frame until they reached the kitchen. Of course, there was no handle, as the dumbwaiter was not designed to be opened from this side. Between the two of them, they managed to pry it open.

Falling out onto the kitchen floor, they both took several gasping breathes of mercifully clear air. Etta was on her feet first, and pulled Art up with her.

“Come on. Almost there.”

Grabbing the handle of the door, Etta cried out. “Agh! Hot!”

Looking again, smoke was creeping past the jamb and into the kitchen. The hallway beyond must have already been burning. Their efforts with the dumbwaiter had cost precious minutes, giving the fire time to spread.

“Oh, God, are we trapped again?”

“Not quite.” Etta pointed to a set of windows behind him, above the stove.

They were wide, short, and high above the floor where, already a wispy, meandering layer of white smoke had gathered. Right away, Art understood her intent, and they made their way over. Art was about to climb up on the stove to reach the window, when Etta shot a hand across his chest.

“What?” he demanded.

Carefully this time, she tested the stove, and Art immediately realized that it was still hot. “Oh, of course it is.” he said through clenched teeth.

Looking around, Etta spotted a large wooden cutting board. It was large enough to cover the entire stovetop, but they both needed to lift it. The trickle of smoke squeezing past the hallway door had grown steadier, and the layer of smoke had reached the windows.

Dropping the board on top of the hot stove, they climbed up, careful not to touch the metal. With their heads now well within the ever-thickening smoke, Art's eyes stung. He snatched up a meat-tenderizing mallet from its hook on the wall and began smashing out the glass.

A coughing fit start started to take hold of Etta, just as clean – almost sweet – night air rushed inside. It provided them with only temporary relief from the now pervasive smoke. Across the kitchen, the hallway door was charred black along the edges, and smoke gushed through in earnest. Art knocked at several jagged pieces of glass still stuck in the window frame, but time was growing short and a few little daggers stubbornly remained.

"It's going to be a tight squeeze," Etta grimaced, looking at the window.

Even standing on the stove, the bottom edge of the window was on a level with her chest with not much of anything solid on their side to stand on.

"I'd be more worried about the drop," Art replied.

Etta looked at him, hesitating. "I meant, for you."

Art looked from her to the window and recognized that his size might present an issue. The thought had not occurred to him up until now.

A loud cracking and popping sound came from behind them. Turning toward the noise, they saw the door to the kitchen now completely charred black. It was burning in multiple places. Hungry flames licked the bottom edge as they probed into the kitchen.

"Nothing to do for it," Art said. "You first."

Etta opened her mouth, about to say something, but stopped. Instead she just nodded. Putting one hand on the window frame, and one foot on Art's knee, she pulled herself through. Art leaned out, lowering her as far as he could. She cried out as she released his hand and crashed into the bushes below. Disentangling herself, she rose up holding a hand to her side and groaning.

Looking around, Art saw no one else was on this side of the hotel. Somewhere close but unseen, he heard voices raised in alarm. Across the short clearing, the trees glowed with reflected orange light. For the first time, Art had a sense of the scale of the fire and could only marvel at how quickly it had spread. With his head sticking out the window and smoke wafting over his shoulders, he was momentarily oblivious to the mortal peril surrounding him. A distant, ever-curious place in his mind wondered – for the briefest of moments – why he did not hear any sirens.

"Come on!" Etta called to him.

Still distracted, Art glanced over his shoulder to witness the door fully engulfed in flames. The layer of smoke had reached the floor and even with the window smashed out, he had difficulty taking a full breath. A crash from the hallway, immediately outside the door caused it to burst inward. An inferno lay beyond. Satisfied, the logical portion of Art's mind withdrew entirely, and gave way to pure, animalistic survival.

Shoving his head and one arm through the window, Art was caught for the first time around his chest. Feet scrambling for purchase, they found a shelf, and he pushed hard against it. His torso slipped through, and snagged for a second time on his belt buckle.

Pressing his foot against the shelf eventually caused it to give way. Taken by surprise, he slipped back into the kitchen up to his chest. Pulling with his hands and feet scrambling, Art regained his progress. Avoiding the belt buckle this time, he slipped through another few inches as a red-hot line traced across his back. He grunted in pain and scolded himself for not doing a better job of clearing the glass. All the while, smoke billowed past him as if he were emerging from a chimney.

Nearly out, but for his legs, an involuntary fit of coughing made it difficult to balance long enough to swing up his foot. Etta moved beneath him, arms outstretched to help steady him.

After another agonizing moment, he finally slipped one leg free of the window, and felt himself fall. It was only about seven or eight feet to the ground, but landing on his side was rough, bush or no. Art coughed and tried to catch his breath as he untangled himself. Another crash, larger than any before it, sent a shower of burning embers out the open window. Shielding his head with an arm, Art glanced up to see the second floor windows glowing bright orange.

"Let's go," Etta coughed. "Need to get away."

Art took a step before he realized he could not see. "My glasses!" he cried.

Etta pulled on his arm. "Forget them! C'mon!"

Art tore his arm free and fell to the ground, searching with his hands. "Just a second."

In his scramble, he noticed the heat. The second floor was quickly being consumed. A falling piece of window glass shattered on the ground, just next to his outstretched hand. He flinched involuntarily before resuming the search.

"I've got them!" she shouted.

Art looked up, little good that it did him. He could just make out the blurry outline of Etta holding something in her hand. Art took them, and with shaking hands, tried to return them to his face. This was made challenging as Etta forcibly pushed him from behind and away from the building. By the time he returned the glasses to his face, they had reached the safety of the tree line. Exhausted, coughing, and sporting more than a few scrapes and cuts, the two of them collapsed to the ground.

Feeling the heat on his back, even at this distance, Art looked over his shoulder to see what remained of the Hatakawana completely in flames.

Fire belched out of every window, including the one he had been stuck in barely a minute ago. Etta propped herself into a sitting position, and watched. Her face was a mix of awe and disbelief. Slowly, Art rose to sit next to her. To their left, and a safe distance away, the other hotel patrons and a few passing gawkers had assembled. Many of them wore bedclothes, and stood among a menagerie of random articles and pieces of luggage saved from the fire.

Etta rested against his side and put her head on his shoulder. Now that the imminent danger had passed, he had a moment to appreciate the closeness. The combination of relief and physical contact was euphoric.

"Art," she started. "I want to-"

He was seized in a sudden panic. "Oh, my God! Ralph. Dorothy."

Standing up in a flash, his eyes scanned the crowd. In the course of their escape, he had completely forgotten about them. Involuntarily, he took several steps in the direction of the crowd, but stopped when he wandered too close to the heat of the building fire.

Why did I tell her to go back to her room? Why did Ralph go back upstairs?

There was little love lost between Art and his brother, and his feelings for Dorothy were lukewarm at best. However, he did not want either of them to meet an untimely end. In the case of Ralph, it was more in the sense that he did not want to have to be the one to tell their mother.

Eyes sweeping back and forth, he looked from the gathered crowd to the burning hotel. Fearing the worst, his gaze settled on something that was, at first, incomprehensible. Despite all that had transpired in the past hour, what Art saw now truly surprised him. Quickly, he removed his glasses and wiped them off on his shirt, using one of the two remaining clean spots. Returning them to his face, he looked again.

It was Dorothy. Her red hair blended into the general orange glow of everything surrounding her, but it was her. Her wiry locks stood up in disarray, and both her face and clothing were smudged with soot. What was more, she was also embracing the tall man next to her.

Brow furrowed, Art looked again. They separated when the tall man winced in pain. His shirtsleeve was burned away up to the elbow and he extended his arm gingerly, trying not to touch anything. Dorothy looked at it with concern and it was then that Art recognized his brother. For all of Ralph's faults, no one could accuse him of not being one tough bastard.

Then, suddenly their lips pressed together. Heedless of both the public display and the destruction around them, they kissed. A surprised, mirthless laugh escaped Art's mouth before he turned away. They were safe. That was good enough. Despite everything going on, it occurred to him that his engagement to Dorothy Kennedy had just ended.

And just when I started to like her.

It was for the best, of course. Etta had come back to him. With a start, he realized that he had left without even checking her for injuries. Her fall from the window had been at least as rough as his own.

Finally, sirens wailed in the distance. Art returned to the spot where he had left Etta, but she was nowhere to be found. He searched. Perhaps this was the wrong place and he had gotten turned around. Some time later, the crowd had parted for the fire company to get close enough to spray what remained of the inn. By then, Art gave up the search and was forced to admit that, once again, Etta was gone.

Chapter 35
Etta

Some events from that night were etched into her mind with jagged clarity. Even months later, she had broken out into a cold sweat after only smelling a whiff of Vaseline. Likewise, her escape with Art from the hotel was clear in her memory. Things grew murky after that. Etta vaguely remembered Art leaving in a hurry, and she was both angry and hurt. At the time, she had been about to say something. What, she could no longer recall.

Shaken, and not quite in her right mind, Etta fled. Things were chaotic around the hotel, and she was mostly able to avoid the throng of onlookers that had gathered to watch the flames.

Briefly, she considered going to the Saunders' house. They would take her in, but they would also ask questions. Reeking of smoke the way she was, it would eventually come out that she had been at the hotel when it burned. With all the best intentions, they would ask her why, and she had little confidence of her ability to keep the rest of the events secret.

Remembering that she no longer had a house in this town, she stumbled to the nearest familiar landmark. The church and cemetery were not far from the hotel. Upon reaching the small plot – the only part of Bott’s Lake that any Wozniak could now claim – she curled up on the cold ground, and fell into a dreamless sleep.

In the calm of the following morning, she realized that the bag she always carried was missing. At first, she assumed it had been lost over the course of her and Art's escape, but then remembered her initial confrontation with Walter. Panicked that she had left some telltale evidence, she returned to what remained of the hotel. The hilltop was nothing but a steaming pile of burnt timbers and ash.

Walking past the ruins to the construction site, she found her bag where it had fallen near the woodpile. At the same time, it occurred to her that since their first meeting, Walter had never been separated from his trumpet. Even at the barn party and his fight with Art, he came back for the case. However, she could not recall seeing it the previous night.

After a short search, she found it tucked behind the track of a construction vehicle. With hesitation, she opened it, feeling uncomfortable at the intrusion even though its owner was gone. Eyes wide, she regarded the contents: a dinged up trumpet that was showing its mileage and most of the money Walter had stolen from CasinO.

The temptation to ditch the trumpet and abscond with the cash was nearly overwhelming. Nearly. In the end, Etta left most of it on Mr. Mustache's doorstep in a nondescript brown bag. She reckoned that even though he was a petulant, mean little man, he had not deserved what he got. However, the Fireman Widows' Fund also received a large, anonymous donation, some of which Etta hoped would find its way to Helen.

The trumpet, she dropped off the dock behind CasinO. As before, it bobbed in the water before eventually slipping beneath the surface and out of sight. This time, no one would be jumping in after it.

That left only the money she had come by honestly: her nest egg. At last, she would use it for its intended purpose. Once, it had seemed like a vast sum, but practically it was just enough to pay for a clean set of clothes and a train ticket to Denville.

It had been with no small amount of trepidation that Etta made her way to the dress boutique. After all, the wedding had been months ago. Would she even remember Etta? To her relief, Helen's Aunt Amelia lit up with recognition as Etta walked into the store. Indeed, Amelia was pleased that she was accepting the offered job. Etta felt likewise. At long last, her fortunes were turning around.

Coming into town with absolutely nothing, the prospect of a roof over her head and a steady job had been a huge relief. Amelia employed three other girls including Helen's cousin, Megan. It had been a tremendous boon to have even one familiar and friendly face in this new town.

All of them lived in a small house, just a short walk from the store. The living situation had more than a few quirks that took some getting used to. After living practically by herself for so long, sharing a cramped space with three other girls was jarring. While Amelia had her own private suite, Etta shared a single bathroom with the other three girls. It was the worst aspects of the Newark apartment with none of the leisure time. At least it had an indoor toilet.

Ethel and Joan, were about the same age as Megan, making Etta the oldest by five or six years. Instead of granting her seniority, it only served to alienate her. Ethel in particular saw her as an intruder. This difference in age was laid bare when the younger girls would sneak out three or four nights per week. Returning just before dawn and laughing too loudly, they typically smelled of alcohol and tobacco. Somehow, they never managed to wake Amelia, but Etta was not so fortunate.

The work itself was less physically demanding than what she was used to, but they were at it all day long, six days a week. On Etta's first full shift, her leg cramped up from pumping the treadle on the sewing machine. At first, she assumed the work would be much the same as when she made dresses as a hobby.

In a way it was, but with much less creative leeway than she would have liked. Amelia's preferences were the only ones given consideration. Etta's days fell into a new sort of drudgery as she added the same five or six details in various combinations to nearly finished dresses.

Amelia, used to dealing with younger girls, spoke authoritatively and bordered on condescension. This served to keep Ethel and the others in line, but Etta was accustomed to living by her own rules and soon chafed under the older woman's heavy hand. She had all the controlling tendencies of her sister, Mildred, but with none of the motherly warmth. In addition, the working room was without windows. Etta barely saw the sun during the week.

Had that been the whole of it, Etta might have buckled. But despite the quirks and the rules, things were not intolerable. She and Megan developed a close friendship, and she even made an acquaintance with Joan. On Sundays, they all attended morning mass together, and Amelia let them have an hour to themselves in the afternoon before it was time to prepare dinner. To her credit, Amelia never let them go hungry. Dinner was always a big event and the food was plenty. On Christmas, she had treated them to an entire ham out of her own pocket.

Even so, she almost quit a few times. After all, she was not entirely without options. The Saunders would take her in. Even Papa and Eloise would make room if she asked. Still, Etta never considered these to be real alternatives. She was determined to make her own way, and also keen to avoid going back to the Lake.

Even months later, Walter's death remained foremost in her mind. Perhaps for far longer than it rightfully should have. She had feared that the events of that night would somehow come back to haunt her. Eventually, when such concerns never materialized, Etta began to relax. It was at that point that she finally realized that she had fallen into another rut. She had traded ghosts and memories for a few girls she did not particularly get along with, and a domineering older woman.

To make matters worse, Amelia did not provide the room and board free of charge. Etta handed back a significant portion of her meager earnings in order to pay for her shared accommodations and food. This made saving difficult. Gradually, she came to realize that she might be stuck here for a long time.

In her scant personal time, Etta wrote letters to the most important people from her old life. Mostly Helen and Mildred, but occasionally to Papa. From his fast scribbling and short sentences, he was just as busy as she was.

Helen had given birth to a healthy baby girl in December of the previous year. While happy for her old friend, Etta was troubled by deep regret; she should have been there. Her feelings for Amelia only continued to sour when the older woman refused Etta's suggestion that the three of them – Megan, Amelia and herself – go to visit the new baby. Helen was the woman’s niece after all.

Amelia's only response had been, “And what? Leave Joan to mind the boutique?”

In her correspondence with Helen, Etta had learned that Art's engagement with Dorothy was officially broken off. All of a sudden, a knot was released that was conspicuous now, only in its absence. It was mentioned only in passing, and despite her burning curiosity, Etta refused to ask any follow-up questions. That was beyond her new world. The warts of this life were easier to accept if she simply ignored the possibilities beyond it. She used to look at maps, and fantasize about the places on them. The disappointment of her trip to Newark had served to temper such longings.

In time, she grew to appreciate the company of the other girls. Even Ethel had tenuously warmed to her, with her silence feeling more deferential than it had previously been. Still, there remained an “in” group, and Etta was not part of it. Thus, when the chance came up for her to get away, she jumped at it hungrily.

It had been nearly six months since Etta’s arrival when one of the Singers jammed up. With Amelia fully involved in several other tasks,

Etta had been charged with getting it fixed. As it happened, she knew just the repairman for it.

It had taken some doing in order to actually get in touch with Art. His last known mailing address had burned to the ground and Amelia's business listings were somewhat dated. Etta had used a phone maybe twice before in her life, and on top of that the Lake did not have its own switchboard. She had to go through each of the neighboring towns before reaching someone with the connecting line for Adams Engineering. At last, she got through.

It was the first time she had heard his voice in nearly half a year. Though it sounded tinny through the phone, she recognized it immediately and it was wonderful. For several seconds, Etta forgot what she had been about to say.

"Ah, hello?" he called.

Etta snapped out of her stupor. "Hi Art... it's Etta."

It was Art's turn to go quiet. Even through the phone, Etta could hear his smile when he finally spoke, and pictured it clear in her mind.

"Damn Etta, it's good to hear from you." He paused again. "It's ah... been a while."

"Yes, it has. How's the Lake?"

"Only recently thawed. I still like this place, but the winters are rougher than I'm used to."

"I'll bet they are. Were the Fichners busy?"

"Couldn't say. They won't talk to me. The Old Sarge seems to think my family is trying to put him out of business."

Etta chuckled. "Well, aren't you?"

"Sure, just go and take his side, then."

Even with the distortion, his playful tone was apparent, and Etta grinned all the while. A disapproving glare from Amelia cut through the levity. Etta was still on the clock, after all. As her boss's priorities became more apparent, Etta liked her less with each passing day. When she remained quiet, Art continued.

"So, Daniel mentioned you were in Denville. Is that where you're calling from?"

Clearing her throat, Etta replied, "Yes." Her smile was gone now.

Art continued, "I almost forgot. Have you come back to see the baby yet?"

"No. Ah..." Etta stumbled as Amelia stared without relent. "Listen, the reason I called... would you be able to fix something?"

The next day, Art showed up to look at the Singer. He wore clean coveralls instead of his old suit, but carried himself in a way that made them look good. He kept his hair short and neat these days, and the sight of him in rolled up sleeves still gave her shivers. Upon seeing her, Art lit up. Even behind his glasses, his eyes twinkled.

"Here's a sight for sore eyes," he said.

"And you," she replied. "Certainly look the part of a working man, don't you? Your poor father must be beside himself."

This elicited a toothy grin from him and a glower from Amelia.

"Etta, if you wouldn't mind, show him the gummed up Singer."

Reluctantly, Etta did as she asked. Art must have noticed her sudden change in mood, but said nothing. She wanted to explain so many things just then. Perhaps she could get him to stick around until after dinner, and sneak out. Or maybe late enough for Amelia to fall asleep. The other girls were due to go out tonight and Etta might join them for a change.

Alas, it was not meant to be. Once Amelia was satisfied that Art understood the issue she pressed him for an estimate to fix it. Instead of answering right away, Art gave Etta a look of indeterminate meaning. His calculating and appraising look shifted between her and the room they were in. Even without his saying anything, Etta suspected what he was thinking.

You ended up working in a room without windows.

Etta's shoulders slumped, but Art spoke before her mood could sink too far.

"I can fix it," he said to Amelia. "But I'll need to bring it to my shop. Might take a week or two."

Amelia did not like that answer, but neither did she challenge him on it. Before Etta could say anything else, Amelia dismissed her and she watched as Art carted the sewing machine away. Their eyes met one last time before he disappeared from view. Much was left unspoken.

That night she started to write a letter. She had not thought to ask for his new address, but figured Helen could get it to him. Even so, she only made it as far as "Dear Art," before she seized with indecision. Etta had no idea where to even begin.

Thanks for helping with that guy in the hotel. Sorry I almost got you killed for it. I passed up on a small fortune and I've questioned myself every day since then.

Etta sat in her cramped bed each night, staring at the two words and the otherwise blank piece of paper. This would go on until she fell asleep, pen still in hand. After a week, she gave up on the letter and once again lost herself in the comforting drudgery of the routine.

It was two weeks after the Singer had gone to Art's shop that Amelia burst into the back room unannounced. Cutting Megan off mid-sentence, she ignored the blatant violation of her talking-of-the-clock policy and motioned for Etta to follow her.

Am I in trouble?

Amelia wore a deep scowl, which by itself was not unusual, but she was clearly annoyed by something specific.

"I need you to go out of town," she said without preamble. "That repairman you recommended is finished with the Singer, but he wants someone to test it before he delivers it. He asked for you. Specifically." Amelia said the last part in accusation.

Etta had to suppress a grin, but quickly nodded when it was clear that her boss was finished speaking. Leaving Etta standing, the older woman walked around her desk and opened a small lockbox from somewhere out of sight.

"I'm giving you some cash to cover the train ticket, but as far as I'm concerned, you're off the clock until you get back."

Etta frowned. Losing half a day's wages would sting. Reflexively, she was about to protest, but Amelia spoke before she could.

"Don't dawdle."

It was the closest she had been to Bott's Lake in half a year, and springtime had come again. The trees were just starting to bud, and a new Season would begin soon. With it, Etta knew the out-of-towners would return as they always did, though she supposed that she was technically one of them these days. Etta breathed deep. Already, it was like she had returned home, even though she had not yet left the Netcong train station. The hills and trees out in the distance were the same ones she had always known.

Etta drank in the view. A freshly tilled field out in the distance caught her eye. She had seldom seen the valley from this perspective. Somewhere in the back of her mind, she thought about all the work that had to be done before summer. Despite Amelia's instructions to not dawdle, Etta could not overlook the fact that this was the most time she had spent outdoors in months.

"Aren't you looking spiffy?"

Etta stopped, recognizing the voice immediately. She had been so busy admiring the scenery that she was completely oblivious to anything else around her. Looking over, Art stood next to a freshly painted truck. The words "Adams Engineering" were prominently displayed on the side. His smile was warm and familiar.

It took her a moment to acknowledge what he was referring to, and the reason she had nearly missed the train. Amelia had insisted on a change of clothes. If Etta was going to represent the boutique, then, by God, she was not going out looking like a seamstress. At the time, she had been in a hurry to get out the door, but now she was glad for the older woman's insistence. Standing just a little taller, Etta tilted her head up in an affected pose and raised her eyebrows at him.

He rolled his eyes, but also grinned.

"Meanwhile," she replied, "You look fully prepared to climb under that truck and start fooling with something mechanical."

Still smiling, he nodded. "That I am, and often do."

As she approached, he started to reach out to her, but stopped. Etta frowned, since she had been about to do the same, but was now unsure. They remained an arm's length apart and regarded each other. He soon recovered, but still made no move.

After all this time, he's still nervous? It was odd, but Etta supposed that six months was a long time.

"So, ah..." he trailed off. "I've got something for you."

She scoffed, good-naturedly. "Of course. That's why I'm here."

"Oh, right," Art replied, as if he had genuinely forgotten. "Besides that."

Etta cocked her head. "A surprise? What's the occasion?"

Sensing that he had her attention now, Art made a show of shrugging his shoulders.

"Just something that made me think of you."

"Lead on then." The two of them climbed in the truck and started bouncing down Route Six towards Bott's Lake proper. Etta's attention switched between the rolling hills and fresh greenery in the distance and the man sitting next to her.

"How's Denville?" Art asked. "Seemed like a nice enough town."

Etta bit her lip. "Not sure I could say, seeing as how I've hardly been outside the sewing room."

"That's a shame. You like the work at least?"

Etta shrugged. "It's fine I suppose."

In truth, she probably could have complained about it for hours. But thinking about her life under Amelia reminded her that this sojourn was only temporary. Soon she would return to her nitpicking boss and gossiping coworkers. Looking out the window again, she realized that no matter where she happened to be living, this was her home. And she meant to enjoy her time here, fleeting though it may be.

"How are my chickens? Have you seen Helen at all?"

"The ladies are doing well. Every time I see her, Helen remarks on just how loud they are."

That drew a smile from Etta. "And the baby?"

"Daniel says they're both holding up alright. Little Irene is a hungry one. Has Helen up at all hours of the night."

Etta blinked, unsure whether she had heard right. "Who?" she asked.

"Irene. That's what she named the baby."

Etta had thought it strange that Helen never mentioned her daughter by name. At the time, she assumed it was a simple oversight. Hearing her sister's name carried on in a new life caught her by surprise and her face heated up. Before tears could spring forth, Etta quickly changed the subject.

"Are those two... together?" Helen had not mentioned Daniel either, and now Etta had to wonder.

Art made a non-committal gesture. "Yes and no. From how Daniel tells it, he just wants to be there for baby Irene since his brother can't be. She's family after all. Then again, he does spend a lot of time with Helen... who really knows?"

Etta nodded, but the comment about being there for family caused her to quietly scold herself. She had not thought about Daniel in months, and decided to make a point of visiting her last, living cousin while she was in town. The cemetery too. She had never gone so long without a visit, and she had quite an apology to make.

Etta stopped, remembering that this was to be a short trip. There would not be enough time for all these things. Growing frustrated, Art's next question surprised her.

“Are you – ah – seeing anyone these days?” he asked and she glimpsed just a bit of his old shyness.

Reminded of better times, she grinned. Had it really been a year since they met?

“Sadly, I don't have a mailbox for anyone to break or a barn for them to sleep in. So, the pickings have been slim.” A teasing grin played across her face.

Art’s face scrunched up in thought before he nodded with understanding. “Hm. Y'know, I've done a more proper job of it since then. You'd never know anything had happened.”

Now Etta was the one confused. “Why bother? Papa and I moved out last summer.”

Art opened his mouth, but stopped before he could explain. Instead, he simply nodded in unenthusiastic agreement. Etta narrowed her eyes, sensing the evasion, but let it go.

“I heard things didn't work out with Dorothy,” she said.

Art's smile returned, and this time it was genuine. “No, things didn’t. I suppose you left before that whole business came out. That night, Ralph went to tell Dorothy that I was with some 'blonde floozy'. In the middle of breaking the news, they smelled smoke and had their own dramatic escape. All told, Dorothy came out of the experience feeling... passionate. One Adams got her affection. The other got her ire. I’ll let you sort out who was who.”

“Blabbermouth didn’t exactly shower you with kisses, did she?”

“To say the least… Ralph had this smug look for a solid week, as if he had somehow gotten the best of me. I still don't get it, but they were both quite taken with each other. Dorothy found him charming and Ralph was utterly enamored with a woman 'whose spirit is as fiery as her hair.' His exact words.”

“Your brother is quite the poet.” Etta rolled her eyes but grinned.

“To his credit, he’s been reading more and drinking less. They were married at a quiet ceremony. Kept the original date at the church and everything, just with a change in groom. I barely see them these days, but she spends a lot of time with my mother. They’re all practically neighbors now.”

Curiosity got the better of Etta, and without particularly thinking about it she asked, “So... the night of the fire...” She trailed off, not sure how to put it.

Art nodded. “As far as anyone knows there was, thankfully, no loss of life. Folks were hurt, and a lot of belongings were lost, but no one was missing. Except of course for the Brandelsons who skipped town.”

At a wordless gesture from Etta, he continued. “It turns out that the owner of the Hatakawana was behind on his taxes. But one day he noticed that his insurance policy was rather generous in its coverage of fire damage. So, after consulting with a pair of infamous moonshiners and noted dabblers in arson, he comes up with a solution.”

Etta listened in stunned silence, thinking back on memories long suppressed.

“Where'd you hear all this?”

“It's been all anyone around here has been talking about. Apparently, Heber broke down and revealed all after the plan went awry. The Brandelsons were supposed to start the fire in the middle of the day when the hotel would be empty. Of course they didn't. All else aside, Heber never wanted anyone to get hurt.”

Etta could only shake her head in astonishment.

“Not all bad though,” Art continued. “I'm sure Ralph and Dorothy will be telling that story to their children for years.”

Etta was relieved. The potential consequences of the hotel fire had bothered her for months. At long last, she was well and truly off the hook.

Spirits high, she admired the scenery as Art continued to drive. Familiar landmarks passed her window. The Van Dyck's butcher shop. Dominic's grocery store.

The cemetery.

The road leading to the old farm would be coming up soon. Briefly, she thought about asking Art to drive past it for old time’s sake. Just as quickly, she dismissed the idea. At first, she did not want to admit just how badly she longed for it, but then he turned onto the road without her asking.

With mounting suspicion, she asked, “Where are we going?”

“To get your sewing machine. It's at the workshop,” he replied smoothly.

Etta knew just about every detail about this part of town, but she could not picture any vacant lots that might host a repair shop. As they rounded the last bend before the old farm, she looked up the hill, hoping to catch a glimpse. To her surprise, she caught more than that.

It was the farm, but where she had been expecting a heap of charred timbers and a lonely barn falling to neglect, the place was bustling.

There was not one, but two barns now. A new farmhouse – albeit a small one – was in mid-construction. Etta's breath caught at the sight of it. Her first impulse was horror and even offense at the idea of all these strangers walking around her old home. As Art pulled the truck up the old driveway, she noted the new mailbox. His cryptic remark from earlier now made sense.

"Welcome home," he said, almost bashfully.

Clearly, he was unsure how she would take this news. In truth, she was not sure herself.

Strangers in my home, was her first thought. Mentally, she picked at it like a piece of corn stuck in her teeth. The truck stopped, and Etta noticed one of the young men as he passed.

"Is that Larry Summers?" she asked.

Art nodded, looking somewhat relieved. "Sure is. His cousin, Harold is around here somewhere too. He's very particular about that, by the way. I made the mistake of calling him 'Harry' once. But then-"

"-then they would be Harry 'n Larry," she finished.

Grinning with recognition, her anxiety started to fade. The Summers were good people. Stepping from the truck, Etta nearly stumbled in the ridiculous shoes that Amelia had forced on her. A farm was no place for heels. Looking around, she recognized more familiar faces. Each one of them greeted her as she and Art made their way to the old red barn.

"Did you hire the entire town?" she asked with a smirk.

"Not yet, but we've got another two coming on soon." He jerked his head towards a small, half-constructed structure where her house used to be. "Gonna have them finish building the kit house before we start them on a project. Knock-on-wood, none of them have had any accidents. All farm boys and they know how to respect machines."

Etta looked to the old red barn just as Daniel emerged. Usually reserved and quiet, he brightened upon seeing her.

"Hey, Etta! It's been a while!" he called. With a big hug, he greeted her like his brother might have done once upon a time.

Surprised, Etta could only return the hug before Daniel continued.

"Are you in town long? You should come by and see Helen."

Etta bit her lip. The thought, of course, had occurred to her, but she knew that any visit to the Saunders would turn into a huge affair, and she had to get back to Denville.

Instead of declining, she replied, "I will try."

Still beaming, Daniel turned to Art and said something about getting supplies before slapping him on the shoulder and walking away. Etta watched him go, barely recognizing this confident man with purpose.

"Wow," she said before turning back to Art. "You sure did a number on him."

Art shrugged. "He just needed a chance is all."

Both fell silent as they regarded each other. The only sounds were distant, muffled conversation and the sound of progress from within the barn. Too many things still remained unspoken. Etta thought about everything she had wanted to write, but still could not find the words.

To her relief, Art took a breath, and began to speak.

"Listen, I want to-"

"Hello there!" A new voice interrupted him.

Lizzie Hunley approached from the driveway. Another familiar face.

"Hi, Lizzie. Fancy seeing you," Etta greeted warmly.

Where Etta's first reaction had been to smile and wave, Lizzie actually frowned. In fact, Etta might have described her initial expression as bordering on hostile. Quickly, she recovered and favored Etta with a courteous, if not a warm smile. It did not extend to her eyes.

"Yeah, good to see you," Lizzie replied. Her eyes flitted between Etta and Art, making Etta oddly uncomfortable, but not entirely sure why. This was an old friend, after all.

Lizzie's smile became more genuine as she turned towards Art.

"Hi, Liz," he said, mirroring Etta's discomfort. "I wasn't expecting you until tomorrow. The Cow Cooler needs about three hours' more work."

Etta frowned. *Liz?*

"Oh, I know. I just wanted to bring this over while it was still fresh." She held out a parcel. "Carrot cake from last night. You said you liked it."

"I sure did. Thank you much." Art bit his lip as Lizzie stuck out her chin, looking pleased.

A lump formed in Etta's throat.

Art smiled, but was clearly uncomfortable. "I'm going to enjoy this," he said, holding up the cake. "And I'll see you tomorrow?"

Lizzie's smile faltered but she quickly recovered.

"Of course," she replied. "I have to get back to the farm anyway. But yeah, tomorrow." Turning to leave, she flashed Art a warm smile. It was rather telling that she said nothing to Etta.

Art cleared his throat.

"We're just friends," he said once Lizzie was safely out of hearing.

"It's no business of mine," Etta said evenly. Her voice was brittle and she glanced down at the gift he was holding. "I just had no idea you two were... sharing cake."

Art shuffled his feet and squirmed as he searched for a spot to set the plate down. Etta reckoned it was the first time a dessert was incriminating evidence. Sighing, he set it down and put up his hands.

"Look. It's not-"

"Where's the sewing machine?" she interrupted. Her voice was annoyed and tired, even to her own ears. At the same time, she grew increasingly uncomfortable in the ridiculous and gaudy dress.

I don't want to be here anymore.

"If this is a business relationship, then let's get to business. Let me check that it's working, and then let me get out of here."

Art was about to say something, but quickly shut his mouth. For a second, Etta felt a grim satisfaction. It was immediately tempered by the keen awareness that she would soon be back in Amelia's realm where she would once again be powerless.

In a strange way, it hurt that this place was getting along just fine without her. So be it then. This was her old life. Her old routine. For so long, she had wanted to get away from it. Away from working all the time, and constantly feeling tired.

Is the new routine really any different?

She shook her head to cast the nagging doubt aside. Then, to twist the knife, Art smirked. Etta's eyes went wide, and she fought the urge to scream at him.

How dare you!

His ability to read people was improving, because he quickly bit his lip and tucked any hint of amusement safely out of sight.

"As you like," he replied.

Etta followed him to the red barn, which was barely recognizable. Art had reorganized almost everything and removed all the farm equipment. Where before it had been pitchforks and chicken feed, now it was workbenches, cabinets and tools everywhere. Two more local boys worked within. The first, she recognized from church, but could not think of his name just now. And one other.

Bradley Heckel of all people. Etta cringed, awaiting the inevitable, sad, puppy dog eyes. To her surprise, he was busy with whatever task Art had set him to, and glanced up only briefly. He paused and gave her only a disinterested but pleasant nod before returning to his work.

That's all?

She was *almost* let down. No matter how bad things got, there was absolutely no way, on God's Green Earth, that she would miss the clumsy affections of Bradley Heckel.

Art directed her to a tarp that covered something bulky. Distracted as she was, Etta could not help but notice that it was similar to the canvas Art had been sleeping beneath the day they met. Briefly, she wondered if it was the same one, but dismissed the thought. It made her nostalgic and doubt the course she had already decided on.

Art uncovered the sewing machine and invited her to inspect it. At first, Etta gave it only a cursory glance, then a more thorough one. Slipping one foot out of a shoe, she pumped the treadle trying to find some defect or flaw. Despite her simmering frustration, she raised her eyebrows in appreciation. The motion was smooth and Etta sighed.

Art was good at fixing things. She had to give him that.

"It's working really well," she admitted.

"I'm glad it's satisfactory." Art was reserved, but pleased at the compliment. Still, his eyes hinted at a subdued excitement. As if he knew a secret that she did not. Though curious, she pushed it from her mind.

And that's that.

"When can you have it back to the boutique?" she asked.

Art shrugged. "Today if you like."

That would please Amelia. Etta nodded, feeling her spirits rise by just a small amount. If she would be doing this job for a while, at least she would do it well.

"You want to help me tie it down?" Art asked.

She frowned, hoping to simply be on her way, and let everyone get on with their lives without her.

"I'm really not dressed for it."

The annoyance in her voice was genuine, but Art carried on, oblivious as he led the way out of the barn.

"Oh – ah – I just want you to make sure that we tie it down properly. Don't want to break it by mistake."

Now she was simply confused.

You fixed it, but you don't know how to tie it to the truck?

Shrugging, she supposed it was not the first time he exhibited an utter lack of common sense for a simple thing.

"I just need to get some rope from the other barn," he continued. "Come with me."

Lacking anything else to do, Etta followed him to a part of the property that she had mostly ignored during her time here. Where once there was brush and tall grass, it had since been cleared away and a small barn raised in its place. Art repeatedly looked over his shoulder, checking that she was still following him.

Standing in front of the doors to the new barn, he paused.

“Close your eyes,” he said.

“What? Why?” Etta frowned.

Art struggled and failed to suppress his grin, and looked at her expectantly. He held one hand to the barn door as if it were hostage to her compliance. Etta shook her head and rolled her eyes, but closed them just the same.

She motioned with her hands, as if to say, “There. Satisfied?”

Curiosity replaced annoyance at the sound of the door sliding open. She actually had to resist the urge to peek. Finished, Art took her by the hand, and led her within.

“Can I open them yet?” She had intended to sound impatient, but it came out as anticipation.

“Soon,” he said.

They took a few more steps.

“Now, it's a work-in-progress,” Art continued. “So please bear with me.” He positioned her. “Okay. Now.”

Etta opened her eyes... and nearly fainted. The lump in her throat returned with a vengeance, and she did not know whether to laugh, cry, or punch him. If the familiar places around town had been like seeing a bunch of old friends, this was being reunited with a sibling, long thought to be lost.

Inside the new barn was the jalopy.

She stared hardly believing it. The burgundy paint. The torn canvas roof. Even her blanket remained covering the front seat. Approaching, she held out her hand, and ran it along the length of the body. It was solid. The metal was cold and smooth beneath her fingers. Even then, she almost doubted her own, lying eyes. She pictured its former home among the rocks as it silently watched the world go by. Her thoughts were muddled to the point where she could hardly form words.

“I have a confession to make,” Art said. “The Singer was fixed in about six hours. The last two weeks I spent getting this down from the overlook. Thought I could do it in one.” He shrugged.

Etta remained silent. Eventually she managed to condense her swirling thoughts into a single question.

“How?” she asked.

Art approached from where she had left him, and the grin on his face intensified.

“I guess you like it then,” he said instead of answering right away.

Standing at her side, Art put his own hand on the car. With an affectionate look, it was clear he was recalling a job well done. “It was quite the accomplishment, if I do say so myself.”

“Are you going to fix it?” she asked.

Art nodded as though it was good as done. “I mean, it's going to take a while, and it won't be easy. But then, if it's worth having then it's worth the work.” Art looked at her meaningfully.

She nodded, but remained staring at the old car.

A peace came over her.

Much as Etta wanted to linger, the afternoon was growing late. Amelia and the girls would be closing up in a few hours. There was still another visit to make. And an apology to go with it.

Epilogue

The air was brisk and made more so by the steady breeze. Chilly as spring often was, there was not a cloud in sight today. Etta took a deep breath and let the sun warm her. While there were all the signs that it would be an early summer, it was not quite there yet.

Adjusting her skirt, she knelt down in her usual spot. Reaching out, she pushed aside the leaves that had remained from the previous autumn. Frowning, she resolved to have a talk with the church groundskeeper. Clearing her throat, Etta felt just a bit awkward, but mostly guilty.

"Hello, everyone. It's been... a while. And I'm sorry for that." After a pause, she muttered to herself. "God, where do I even begin? I don't mean to neglect anyone. It's just-"

Someone bumped into her, and Etta stopped abruptly.

Looking over, she came face to face with a young girl, whose familiar brown eyes were on a level with her own. Her curly, dark hair was all in disarray, and she regarded Etta with intense defiance.

Sighing, Etta frowned. "And where is your hat, young lady?"

The little girl shrugged. "Don't like it."

Shaking her head in resignation, Etta reached out to in a futile attempt to smooth her daughter's hair.

"I told you: the brush or the hat, but you have to pick one."

"Don't like the brush either. And Daddy doesn't brush his hair."

"No, I don't," called a new voice. "But you don't want to look like me, do you, Thelma?"

She already does, Etta thought as her two men approached.

While their daughter had inherited the Adams' messy curls and Daddy's large thoughtful eyes, their son was all Wozniak. The blonde-haired boy squirmed in Art's grip. Since learning how to walk, baby

Gabriel would only tolerate being held for a few minutes at a time. Like his mother, he was a complete busybody. And also like his mother, he was prone to stumbling. Though, in his case, it was more literal.

Art placed their son on the grass and let him take a few cautious steps.

"Let's give Mama a few minutes, okay?" Reluctantly, Thelma accepted, but maintained her pout with determination.

"No brush," she insisted.

Art rolled his eyes, bemused. "Alright. Deal."

Gabriel, meanwhile, refused to take his father's hand. After all, he had been walking for a few months now. He was practically an expert.

Etta watched them walk away before turning back to her late family.

"Not to make excuses, but I've been busy. I guess a lot of things have changed. You'd barely recognize the farm now. We rebuilt the old house, with a few improvements. It's cozy with the four of us, but I like it. The view from the front porch is still great. Helen and the rest of the Saunders are right down the street, but Sunday dinners take up two full tables now.

"Little Irene is getting old enough to start asking about her father... I don't envy Helen that conversation, but Daniel has a surprising way with words. I'm happy to say that her second wedding went a lot more smoothly than the first.

"Speaking of weddings, Papa and Eloise tied the knot. Truth told, I didn't even know about it until they came to visit Thelma. The last time I had seen him was when Art and me got married. Lately, Papa and I have tried to be better about keeping in touch. We write letters almost every week now.

"I suppose I forgot to mention that as well: Art and me. My goodness, has it really been five years? I really must try to be better about visiting. I ended up going back to Amelia's boutique for my dress, but on the condition that Megan was the one to make it for me. I wouldn't trust it to anyone else. She'll be running that place before long.

"I got to see New York finally. Art and I spent a week there for our honeymoon. I think, in the end, it's a nice place to visit, but I'm living where I'm supposed to be.

"The business has been giving us both plenty of work, which is more than a lot of folks can say these days. Turns out people are much more keen to try to repair their things rather than buy new when money gets tight. The refrigerated truck was a hit. George has sent a few orders for them.

"Art remains a wiz at all things mechanical, but not so much with people. So, he handles the shop, and I handle the customers. Mostly folks from around town, but we've been expanding recently. Strangers don't bother me as much as they used to. If you asked, I couldn't quite put my finger on when that happened. One day, I greeted a new client without even thinking about it.

"It hasn't been perfect. Art picked up an unfortunate hobby of fixing old machines and keeping them at the house for much too long. Though in fairness, he never complains when I hog the blankets at night.

"When I think back to how things used to be, working the farm by myself, it makes me shudder. Not for the work itself – the days are busy as they've ever been, but in a different way. Now, at least, it feels like there's a purpose to it all – if that makes sense. I think about how hard I tried to get away. To leave the farm for anyplace else. I came so close too, but I realized that it's not so much where you are, but who's there with you."

Etta took a long, slow breath, and was at last finished saying her piece. With a final look at each headstone, she lingered on the one marked "Lena" for longest. Her mother had flaws, yes. Perhaps she had been unfair, but Lena had also endured more loss than Etta could imagine. Where once she been conflicted, even angry toward her mother, these days she could only feel sympathy.

"I still miss you all. See you next April."

Etta returned to the car, finding the rest of her family there. Art was in the passenger seat as Gabriel attempted to climb into the back. Thelma had claimed the spot behind the steering wheel, and regarded her mother with suspicion. While still prepared to defy Etta at any mention of a hairbrush, she also had the sheepish, cautious look of someone about to ask a favor.

"Can I drive?" Thelma asked without preamble. "Daddy said it was okay."

Etta raised an eyebrow in response. "Did he now?" she looked at Art with mock accusation.

"You little fibber," he replied playfully. "You forgot about the part where you have to reach the gas pedal."

Thelma put on a thoughtful expression, as if she had not considered this part. Then, sliding down the seat, she placed both feet on the floor, apparently meeting the strict letter of this criterion. Her head was well below the dashboard as she looked up at her mother expectantly.

"You also have to see over the steering wheel." Etta added.

Thelma's pout returned.

"Here. Sit on Mama's lap. You can help me drive."

The jalopy had remained a side project for the better part of a year, but Art was adamant about getting it finished as a wedding present. His restoration had been meticulous, and his attention to detail was apparent everywhere. Even if it was not a surprise, to Etta, there could hardly be a better gift. Although, their radio, which was hardly ever turned off, was a very close second place.

Leaving the church cemetery behind them, the car bounced and kicked up road dust. Etta let Thelma honk the horn as they passed Franke Van Dyck sweeping the front steps of the butcher shop. Behind was a boxy structure that was clearly a recent addition. Art gave a prideful look as they passed. It had taken a few years, but he had made that sale after all.

They followed the road through the Oasis and around to the far side of the lake. Eventually, they pulled off the road and entered the forest on what was little more than a pair of worn ruts. Winding through the trees, they finally emerged into a wide, grassy meadow. The jalopy turned towards the large oak in the middle of the field.

They had discovered this spot purely by accident, during another one of the family's Sunday drives. Having lived here all her life, it amazed Etta that her town still had secrets to be discovered. They had made this trek a handful of times already, and carefully avoided one or two spots where the jalopy could get bogged down in the mud.

The McCormicks were already at the tree. Helen sat on a blanket, beside a small pile of rushes as she worked them into a new basket. After so many years of practice, she was getting quite good at them and they were popular with the out-of-towners.

Spotting the car, Irene haphazardly dropped the armful of rushes she was collecting and ran over to greet them. At six years old, she had recently been forced to relinquish the title of "Little" to baby Robert, the newest McCormick, and Helen and Daniel's first.

Likewise, Thelma hopped off Etta's lap before the car fully stopped, to her mother's chagrin. Etta sent a halfhearted rebuke, but did not expect that she had been heard. Thelma and Irene were already laughing and shouting at each other. Inseparable friends, just like their mothers.

With the car now safely stopped, Art set down Baby Gabriel who toddled after the older girls.

Helen paused from weaving her basket long enough to wave at the new arrivals. Next to her, little Robert teetered in place as he attempted to grip one of the rushes in a tiny fist. Steadied by his mother, the baby was about to make a fuss, but contented himself to chew on the stick instead. Before Helen could protest, Daniel approached from behind and surprised her with a kiss on the neck. Gently, he took the stick from Robert and scooped him up in the air. Nothing quite settled him like being high above the ground. They would have to keep an eye on that one.

Etta stood in front of the jalopy, watching the scene before her and drinking it all in. Art did likewise, taking his usual spot beside her. The sun warmed them. His arm crossed her shoulders as she leaned into him, fitting snugly against his side.

"Good day for a picnic," he said.

She nodded agreement, feeling content, and glanced up at the cloudless sky. "I think it's safe to say we're finally though with the snow."

"Seems to be," he agreed. "We should make that trip to the ocean this year. After it gets a little warmer, but before the summer gets away from us. Gonna be busy once we break ground on that addition."

Etta nodded, placing a hand over her belly.

"And not a moment too soon. The house is cozy enough as it is. It'll be downright crowded next year."

Giving her shoulder a gentle squeeze, Art managed to convey much without speaking. There was no need to say it out loud, since she was thinking the same thing. As Art had once said, if it was worth having, it was worth the work. And it had been a lot of work, but that was nothing new for Etta. What made all the difference was who was with her.

As she and Art pulled apart and started towards the blanket, Etta marveled, as she had done with increasing frequency of late.

Look at what we've made together.

Meanwhile, Back at the Lake...

This was a work of fiction, and the persons depicted within are a product of my imagination. Events and places with real-life counterparts are portrayed fictitiously.

An explosion did occur at the Dover Naval Depot – what is now Picatinny Arsenal, NJ – where unexploded ordnance remains a concern as of 2021. However, it took place in July of 1926, and not 1928 as depicted in the story. Many were displaced by this event, temporarily housed at the Armory in Morristown, NJ during the cleanup effort for the affected region.

The explosion was the unfortunate result of a lightning strike. 22 service members lost their lives when several ammunition storage magazine detonated. In all, it is estimated that hundreds of thousands of pounds of explosives were involved. The event might have been even worse, but the day shift at the on-site manufacturing plant ended shortly before the storm rolled in. This is considered to be the largest explosion to ever occur in the state.

The Hatakawana Inn was a hotel at a lakeside resort town, which burned down in 1928 – as did many contemporary structures. The depiction of its unscrupulous owner is a complete fabrication and arson was not suspected as the cause. Put simply, it was a common issue in a time when electrical safety was in its infancy, wooden structures were the norm, and municipal fire departments were under-equipped.

Chickens are loud. Roosters crow long before sunrise. I don't know why.

The Dutch word *zakkenwasser* is a disparaging term that literally translates to "ball washer." In case you were wondering.

Made in the USA
Monee, IL
16 August 2022